Dead Girls

Dead Boys

Dead Things

Also by Richard Calder

Cythera

RICHARD CALDER

Dead Girls
Dead Boys
Dead Things

ST. MARTIN'S GRIFFIN ✳ NEW YORK

Contents

Dead Girls

For Gilberte Swann, Dolores Haze
and Wednesday Addams

CHAPTER ONE

Road to Nowhere

They smashed through the door; I vaulted the balcony, running. It was midnight in Nongkhai City and I was lost. The story so far? The Pikadon Twins—notorious henchgirls to Madame K—had pursued me to the banks of the Mekong. But where was the Mekong? Too dark, too quiet—and I used to bright, clamorous Bangkok—this town had me drunk on shadows. Across the Mekong, Laos. From Laos I could escape into China. And from China . . . The roar of Harleys; twin headlights violated the night. There. The lights of a riverside café. And there, there. Glint of moonlight on water. Dogs and chickens scattered in my wake.

The café—The White Russian—opened its arms; I fell into its refuge. *Farang* diners, Thais, all but the gynoids dressed as matrioshkas regarded me curiously. Wiping the sweat from my face, I was trying to still my breath, my hands, trying to assume the disguise of a newly-arrived *farang* celebrating deliverance from Europe. 'I'm like you,' my body language tried to say, 'a roadrunner, a survivor. Genes a little dirty, perhaps, but hey, who's to know?' No police; should I care if they believed me? An ankle had swollen; I sat down. Lights of fishing vessels spangled the unswimmable deep.

From across the river I could make Vientiane in under an hour; but a passing matrioshka (imitation Fabergé, she looked) informed me No sir, sorry sir, no ferry until daybreak. Trapped. End of series. No sequel to my getaway: avoiding airports and the TGV, driving my old Mercedes as far as Hat Yai (as if I were heading for Penang), and then backtracking, taking government buses north, then north-east, towards the Thai-Lao border. That night, arriving in Nongkhai, I'd found a hotel, napped (too long), to be awoken by two half-human battering rams at my door.

Pikadons!

Coolly-cool, those murderesses. Surely they wouldn't make their move here? Not in public, I reasoned. But they were shameless.

'Wodka,' said Bang and Boom, the Pikadon Twins, 'for our friend, Mr Ignatz.' The credits rolled. No reprise of revved motorbikes; like phantom lightsticks, like switchblades keen and spectral, the Pikadons. They pressed down on my shoulders, checking an impulse to flee.

Like their mistress, Madame Kito, mamasan of Nana—that dragon lady with three generals and a cabinet minister in her bed—the Pikadons were the daughters of a Japanese and a gynoid. *Bijouterie,* they called them: hybrid jewels as distinguished from all-precious *joaillerie.*

'Boy run away.'

'Bad boy. Madame miss you.'

'And Primavera. Poor Primavera. She miss you too.'

'Write you love letter, no?'

'Primavera,' I said, 'is a fucking season in hell. I'm not going back. I've had enough killing.'

'But you *like* killing, Mr Ignatz, no?'

Would you like to find out how much? I thought. If I'd had a weapon, even my scalpel, then perhaps . . . but the Twins wore body stockings of artificial spidersilk, a midnight-blue weave grown from *E. Coli* that was as strong and as refractive as the fibres of laser-proof vests.

Why weren't they trying to kill *me?*

'Primavera not work with other boy.'

'Madame try . . .'

'Primavera in love with Mr Ignatz.' The Twins studied the curlicues and flutings of their manicures, eyes cold as crescent moons. 'Every gun need finger on her trigger, Mr Ignatz. But if you want go, maybe Madame let Primavera go. Home. To England.'

Kito needed Primavera. Primavera was Bangkok's prima donna of assassins. A supervillainess. Hep Cat Shun, dead. Terminal Wipes, dead. Rib-Dot Delay, dead. I was merely her escort; a cover. The Twins were bluffing. Jealous. The cheaper the *femmes,* I thought, the cheaper the *fatales.*

'Little English half-doll.'

'Lilim.'

'Self-replicating cyborg bloodsucker, no?'

'Dead girl.'

'Our kissin' cousin.'

'Land of Hope and Glory *no like* Primavera, *no like* Lilim.'

'If Madame tell police . . .'

'Police Madame friend.'

'If Primavera go back home . . .'
Bang (or Boom) pressed a long fingernail into her abdomen.
'Schstick!'
'Scream, little doll.'
'Scream sexy-sexy!' The Twins began to laugh.
'But you know all about *that*, Mr Ignatz.'
'No?'
I shook my head. I wanted to laugh too; to mock them. I couldn't. My jawbone had locked. Vain, spiteful, faithless Kito: would she really send her little ninja home? There, the Dolls' Hospitals awaited. But why had Primavera refused to work? She no longer loved me. (Had she ever loved me?) She loved only the blood, the killing. Her metamorphosis was complete. My little girl needn't mourn: Kito would find her another beau. An arm to lean on at parties, someone to take her to hotels, to bars. A mask. A human face.

One of the Twins pulled a magazine from her *décolletage*.
'Madame Kito.'
'Her life, her time.'
'Special edition. Page sixty-nine. Message for Mr Ignatz. Look . . .'
Page sixty-nine—the centre spread—was a diorama of a penthouse choking on a miasma of kitsch: Italian marble, jungle-cat prints, fountains, revivalist *art nouveau* and *deco* furniture, corporate art, corporate toys— a backdrop, it seemed, for a soap opera of unusual vulgarity. The Twins smoothed their hands across the photograph. Activated by that bio-chemical signature pixels crystallized and two figures mounted the paper stage. The figures moved. Photo-mechanicals. Primavera and Madame K.

They sat together, schoolgirl and matron, on a tiger-striped chaise longue. Someone unacquainted with how the bloodlines of hybrids differed in East and West might have assumed that the two women were related, for both had the green eyes, plump lips and kiln-glazed flesh that signalled Cartier workmanship. But whereas Kito's progenitor had been an imitation doll (as were all dolls in Bangkok's Big Weird), Primavera's distaff side could be traced back to the fabulous automata of Europe's *belle époque*. Kito—stroking her ward's bleached hair like the wicked stepmother of a thousand fairy tales—resented *bijouterie* whose claim to the Cartier logo was more genuine than her own. Her snobbery was equal to her viciousness.

'Such little English rose,' squeaked Kito, her voice—in contrast to her usual husky tenor—small, tinny and distorted. 'But what *nasty* place England become.'

'She's going to have me deported, Iggy,' said Primavera. 'Repatriated. She means it. You know all my papers are false. Like yours. She only has to tell her friends. Come back, Iggy. Come back to the Big Weird. I miss you. We can have fun together. Like before.'

Primavera was a melodramatic little doll. Wearing a cropped T-shirt that erroneously declared her *Miss Nana '71*, the third eye of her umbilicus played peek-a-boo with the camera as she shuddered with the effort of restraining bitter tears.

'It would be slab, Mr Ignatz. Spike. *Tzepa*, as you English say. It is good my Pikadon find you. Boy like you have no place to run. England very bad now. English roboto go *crazy*. Doll bite man, man fuck lady, and lady have baby turn into doll. People say have world of doll soon. World of Lilim.'

'Primavera's done everything you've asked,' I mumbled. 'Just because she was human once . . .'

'And I *never* human? That what you mean, Mr Ignatz?' My hand sprang from the page; the magazine ran interactive software. Kito rose and walked to the missing wall of the proscenium, her geisha-white face filling the page. 'Sure,' she said, 'my *mae* roboto. I half machine when born. Bangkok nanoengineer use foetal template—no grow doll atom by atom like in land of *farang*. Sometime, just sometime, Siamese roboto ovulate.' An eyebrow twitched like the beat of a butterfly's wing that threatened to precipitate a storm. 'But Primavera—' her lip curled; thunder growled in the distance—'Oi! Twenty-six year ago, I remember, doll-plague begin: not with us Cheap Charlie counterfeit doll; no, it was *farang* roboto, *genuine* Cartier get virus, go crazy, give virus to man. Now when little English girl go pubescent, she go roboto too. You think I want to be like Primavera, Mr Ignatz? Walk through wall? Jump over car? Spit death? Fly? Primavera reproduce herself; I sterile, mule. But my software not fucking *crazy* . . .'

The storm passed; Kito's face withdrew, and Primavera, having surrendered to schoolgirl hysterics, was revealed stamping her feet and tearing at her hair.

'Not the *tzepa*. Iggy! Please!'

Primavera always overacted . . .

Beyond the still life of the apartment, through a panoramic window, beneath the stalled course of a ruinous sun, lay Nana Plaza, arrested in time and space, denied forever the night. Night. Ha. Then the capitalists of narcissism would emerge, the warrior merchants who had raped Europe's empire *de luxe* and carried off her ideas, her names, her designs, to sell them in the thieves' market that was Nana. Then street vendors would hawk Europe's vandalized dreams: a magpie's hoard of imitation *objets* and *couture*: psychotropic perfumes from Chanel, off-world jewels from Tiffany, and, dissembling the cut of an Armani or a Lacroix, a de Ville, de

Sade or a Sabatier, dermaplastic, the outlawed *farang* textile woven from live tissue culture. Then Kito's gynoids—Cartier and Rolex, Seiko, Gucci and Swatch—would step from their vacuum-sealed boxes promising to fulfil the most baroque desires. This was Nana, Kito's stake in the Big Weird: a pornocracy of copyright ponces and technopimps; an island shimmering with the bootlegged flotsam of Europe's shipwrecked past; an apotheosis of all that was fake.

And was this plea from Primavera—this SOS from a castaway of human shores—was this too a fake? A photomechanical maid had begun to serve drinks.

'You always seem such gentleman,' said Kito. 'I always think every Englishman—'

I slapped the magazine shut, crushing its paperdust CPU, and searched the cover for the date. My language skills, even after three years in Bangkok, were still rudimentary. I struggled to decipher the fiery tongues of the Thai characters; the Pikadons yawned.

'Magazine come out yesterday, Mr Ignatz.'

'Primavera Weirdside, still . . .'

Whether Kito's threats were empty or not they had offered an excuse. ('Shut up!' I told those angels—good? bad?—who were whispering Trick! Hoax! in my ear.) Maybe that's what I'd been waiting for during those fugitive days: an excuse to return. I was a doll junkie; my limbs ached for the kisses of dead girls. For vampire kisses. For the allure.

Not the tzepa, *Iggy! Please!*

It had been a cry across a war zone of desire. Should I step again into no-man's-land? Outside the coconut trees were swaying, fainting to an alien tide. Primavera was here, even here, her hunger that of a dog picking at the world's remains; her stealth, the scuttling of a cockroach. Escape. Get up; go, before . . . But across the star-filled paddies she reaches out; like a serpent, her torso twists, strikes . . .

Primavera was twelve; her DNA had begun to recombine. She sat in front of me in class, her long blonde hair betraying its first streaks of Cartier black. Primavera Bobinski. One day a classmate similarly progressed in doll metamorphosis had said something to her in a giggly undertone. Primavera shook her head. Throughout that lesson—divinity? history? geography?—scraps of paper appeared on her desk, passed on by that handful of girls who, like her, wore the green star of the recombinant. I grew nervous. Primavera was a girl I had stared at, I suppose, too long; whom I had been observed following down those interminable school corridors, or across the park after last bell; and now the adored one was being goaded to take revenge. At last, piqued by their teasing, eager to show she could take a dare, she waited for our teacher to avert his gaze, then turned contrapposto, put her face close to mine, bared her teeth, and cut open my lip with a swift, expertly aimed glance of one of her newly extended canines. 'Oh?' she said, in pert demotic Londonese, 'did I *hurt* you?' her death mask of a face insolent as the toothy laughter of her peers. I put my hand to my lip; felt blood; flushed.

Did I love her, still?

London, Marseille, Bangkok. From the *Seven Stars* to across the Seven Seas. Three years, now. Escape. We had spent our small lives escaping. But there are watchtowers of the mind, of the senses, machine guns, bloodhounds one can never flee.

'Not so bad for you, Mr Ignatz.'

'A team, you and Primavera.'

'Come from the land of sex and death.'

'To the land of smiles!'

'Stay with Madame.'

'Madame say just one last job, Mr Ignatz.'

'*Jing-jing*, Mr Ignatz, you no want to leave.'

'Skunk hour for Europe now.'

No escape. I was possessed. And from what had I been running? *Bastard,* she whispers, *boy-slime, hypocrite, prig. You made me what I am. You think you're better than them, don't you? The medicine-heads. The Human Front. But I know what you like . . .* I lift my hand to my lip; still, there is blood; still, I flush; still, the throb of desire and hate.

'I'll come,' I told the Pikadons, 'of course I'll come.'

Fatalism, these days, comes easily to an Englishman.

CHAPTER TWO

Wine and Roses

We sat in *The Londoner*, a newly-opened restaurant in the downtown Weird that indulged the morbidity of Bangkok's nighthawks. 'If this is Kito's idea of a joke,' said Primavera, 'then—' A cry, sharp and girlish, excised her indignant conclusions. There followed a gentle balm of applause.

The tables were arranged about a circular arena. Inside that little O, equidistant, like the spokes of a wheel, three marble slabs presented a pageant of life and death in contemporary England. Upon each slab, prone, naked, wrists chained to an iron ring, a gynoid writhed in a ham display of agony, a glistening needle emerging from the small of her back.

The muted sighs of those *in extremis* mixed with the sounds of polite conversation, the clatter of cutlery, the popping of corks.

'You're saying that you *didn't* refuse to work? That Kito lied when she said she'd have you repatriated? And that you lied too?' Sorry, angels. Next time I'll listen.

Primavera fidgeted, playing with an ice cream sundae as blonde as her bottled hair, her flesh. 'Don't get *upset*. I *like* having you around. It was just a little *white* lie. Anyway, Madame *said* I was to; and what Madame *says*...'

I looked about the restaurant. Something festered beneath the nasty theatrics; something real, something nastier; one cut, and the pus would ooze.

I had arrived at Nana that afternoon. Kito hadn't deigned to meet me; instead, I had been briefed by her PA, Mr Jinx. No, Kito wasn't angry; one last hit, he'd said, and we'd be free. Free of all obligation. There followed my reunion with Miss Bloodsucker '71. No words, just the sex-game (sticky plaster covered my chest and groin); and we had walked out, everything right, so right. But now—our intimate dinner disturbed only by those aping the death agonies of England's damned; about to confess my addiction to certain kisses and pledge that I would never despise them again—Primavera had claimed the spoils of her victory: my dignity and pride.

'I know you don't want my love, Primavera, but why do you have to humiliate me?'

'I said don't get *upset.*' She pushed her ice cream to the side of the table. 'I wasn't supposed to *tell* you *actually.* But since you *did* come back . . . Okay. So it was a game. One of Primavera's little games. Madame said you loved me; I said no, it wasn't *like* that. She said she could prove it, that you'd come back if you thought I was in trouble. Wanna bet? I said.' Surprise, hurt, guilt, malice: Primavera could combine the look of a woman betrayed with that of one caught in the act of poisoning her lover. 'Iggy,' she said, with slippery plaintiveness, 'why did you have to run away? Am I really so bad?'

'Kito,' I said. 'I can understand her having me followed; I can understand her wanting me offed—I know too much. But why bring me back to Bangkok? If you'll work without me, she doesn't *need* me.'

Primavera—bored by any script in which she wasn't the leading lady—let her eyes drift from the floor show to the gallery of newspaper clippings that lined the walls: headlines and photographs from the English tabloid press. Beneath dozens of grainy pin-ups of impaled young girls ran captions like: 'Tatyana, 16, from Brixton, says all her girlfriends have had a bellyful of the Human Front, and she was gutted after the HF won the General Election! Now she knows all about bellyaching! Got the point, Tatyana? Another skewered lovely tomorrow . . .' Beneath an air-conditioning vent a tattered Union Jack (monochrome since the kingdom's dissolution) fluttered as if atop an outpost at the world's end.

'Primavera—I'm *talking* to you.'

'It wasn't all fibs, you know,' she said, exasperation counterpointing her skittishness. 'I do like having you around. I don't *love* you; I'm Lilim; we don't *do* that sort of thing. But I can *miss* you.' She shivered. 'You introduce me to such interesting boys.'

'I smell a rat.'

'And I,' she said, leaning over the table, 'smell the blood of an Englishman.' Her bright red tongue ran over ranks of tiny cuspids.

'Sit down,' I muttered, 'and close your mouth. You want someone to see?'

'But you *like* it, Iggy. And you know it only hurts a little.'

How pretty she was. She was always at her best before a kill. Tonight she wore a black dermaplastic cocktail dress that clung to her like the excoriated but still living hide of a Harlem beauty queen. Fifteen years old (the same age as me, though my anaemia made me look older) and milky pale with a sweetness that had sickened of itself, curdled and turned rancid, Primavera was a little dream of feminine evil: hateful because desired; desired because hateful. She was the dream of the age.

At an adjacent table a group of Japanese *salarimen* had summoned a waiter. 'This one—she dead—can have another please?' The waiter, dressed in surgical gown, rubber gloves and mask, saw to it that a fresh gynoid, her programme engaging obligatory signs of fear, replaced her cataleptic sister. On all fours, wrists chained, the steel needle pointing uncompromisingly to that ritual spot midway between pubis and umbilicus, it remained only for the condemned doll to tremble in expectation until the waiter should grasp her ankles and pull . . . The *salarimen*— eyes screwed in states of voyeuristic satori—clapped and whistled with drunken glee.

'God,' said Einstein, 'does not play dice with the universe'; but Primavera did. Her green eyes grew bigger, more luminous, as they focused on something beyond the restaurant's walls, beyond the Big Weird, beyond the world. Reality, for one moment in which the universe held its breath, existed in those eyes alone, eyes tunnelling into endless possibilities. For Primavera the universe was a fixed table. The dice rolled, loaded with her will.

Beer glasses exploded, showering the Japanese with Singha and broken glass. Waiters mopped anxiously at spattered suits, picked splinters from beer-anointed hair. The fire in Primavera's eyes died to a smoulder. Newton and Einstein shifted in their graves.

'Right through her *clockwork,* Iggy. Right through her *matrix!* They really shouldn't laugh.'

The belly of the doll (say Lilim) is sacred; it is the womb of uncertainty; the well of unreason; the quantum-mechanical seat of consciousness.

'Sometimes,' said Primavera, 'sometimes I don't like boys.'

'I guess tomorrow night they'll settle for Soi Ginza. Now no more games, he's just walked in.' A tall *farang* in a bespoke suit was being ushered to a ringside table.

'Is he the boy I get to kill? I like those sorts of boys.'

'Antoine Sabatier. Parisian fashion slut. Angry with Kito for stealing his designs. Prosecuting her through ASEAN.'

'I do it here?'

'Unless you mind getting blood all over your new frock?'

'My table manners are impeccable. But doesn't a girl get to eat in peace any more?'

'I'll find you a nice takeaway later.'

'But Iggy, you're so *tired* of killing, remember?'

I tapped a spoon against a glass, calling an end to playtime. 'All we have to do is wait for the *maître d'* to . . . There. He's being told he has a telephone call. That he can take it out the back. Just like Mr Jinx said. Come on, c—okay, he's going.'

Primavera, tossing her bleached mane over her shoulders, had already risen. Hurriedly, she took a mirror from her handbag and reapplied her lipstick, then dabbed a little of her favourite perfume, *Virgin Martyr,* behind her ears.

'For you, Titania,' she whispered, 'sweet queen of dolls,' and touched the brooch on her left breast—a pentacle of emeralds; symbol of pride won from shame—that was her most (perhaps only) sentimental possession. I watched her leave, the two vertical seams of her stockinged calves weaving between the tables and chairs like the exotic markings of a rare and deadly reptile. The doors leading to the kitchens and toilets swung shut. *Bon appétit,* little witch, I thought.

A Filipino quartet had begun to sing their cover of 'Oh doctor, doctor, I wish you wouldn't *do* that,' the latest hit for English zygodiddly band *Imps of the Perverse.* The waiters had pulled up their surgical masks and—assuming the roles of mad gynæcologists—performed unspeakable mimes in the aisles. I hid behind the menu—*Fish 'n' Chips, Pie 'n' Eel, Steak 'n' Kidney Pudding* (lead sent the Romans crazy)—and put on the complimentary headphones that hung from my chair. '. . . the beautiful carefree days of the *aube du millénaire* were over: England braced herself for what was to come . . .' Those films they showed us at school: *Hamlet, Richard III, Henry V;* the voice synthesizer was an Olivier. I reselected and then stabbed PLAY.

'Europe, during the days of the *aube du millénaire*—a historical period that some have compared to the *belle époque* preceding the First World War—had absorbed the moribund Soviet empire to become the hub of the world economy. Not seeking to compete with the manufacturing might of the Pacific bloc dominated by Japan and its junior partner, America, Europe became the world's arbiter of elegance, an empire of style, a luxury goods conglomerate dedicated to satisfying the age's narcissistic pursuit of health, beauty and longevity. Its investment was in superminiaturization: the creation of objects that the rootless *nouveaux riches*—the Information Revolution's *arrivistes*—could carry on or in themselves, to define their social value and status. As these *objets* lost their functionalism and became *objects,* the empire *de luxe* became a magic toyshop, a creator of adult fantasies. And amongst its *bimbeloterie,* nothing was so fabulous, so desired, as the *automata.*

'The Cartier automata designed by the man we know today only as Dr Toxicophilous were of a series called *L'Eve Future*. Built 2034–43, in Paris and London, this series represented an attempt to create a synthesis between the world of classical physics and the submicroscopic quantum world. The human brain, it had long been realized, is unlike any artificial intelligence because it had learned to harness quantum effects. Toxicophilous nanoengineered his machines from smaller and smaller components; he manipulated particles, waves. What Toxicophilous called "fractal programming"—wherein hardware and software is indivisible— resulted, not so much in a human intelligence, but in a mind, a robot consciousness, which acted as a bridge between classical and microphysical worlds, a consciousness that manifested "quantum magic".

' "Tricks," said the inventor of *L'Eve Future*, "that is all they perform. Party-pieces. Entertainments. *Feux d'artifice!*" But even then their programmes bubbled with toil and trouble . . .'

Nothing new. It was what they dumped on you in school. I nudged the fast forward.

'The life cycle of . . . The doll's imperative is to reproduce itself via a human host . . . Infects the human male through . . .'

A *farang* had sat down in Primavera's chair. 'That's taken,' I said, removing the headphones.

'You'll excuse me.' He was American: confederate drawl; a Nobodaddy somatotype with white hair and beard. 'I've always wanted to meet an Englishman, and the waiter said . . .' I was second-generation Slovak: what Thai would have been able to identify the mid-European distortion of my East London vowels? My accent was as inscrutable as Primavera's Balkanized cockney.

'I'm not English,' I said.

'But the waiter was so sure!'

'I'm from Slovakia.'

'People still live there?' He swallowed his laugh and grimaced in distaste, as if it had been a clot of phlegm. 'I'm sorry, that wasn't funny.'

'My sister will be—'

'Poor kids.' His eyes were on the cabaret. 'I know they're just machines, but what about those little ladies back in England? What do you call them? Yeah, Lilim.' He pointed to a gynoid faking a death orgasm, her performance akin to that of a gymnast, a contortionist, a dancer, rather than that of a girl so cruelly wounded. 'For heaven's sake, she can't be no older than my daughter.' He put his finger to a puddle of beer and drew doodles across the table.

I checked my watch. Primavera had been gone ten minutes. A long time for her. After weeks of abstinence, she would be offing her trick slowly. Playing with him. Sucking the slut dry. I decided to humour my interloper; my jealousy needed a distraction.

'He's economized,' I said.

'I'm sorry?'

'The proprietor: he's economized with his gynoids. These girls are a fleet of second-hand gigolettes from one of the Big Weird's discos. Imitation Seiko, I'd say. They've been customized to look like Lilim, but you can still see the coin slot between their breasts. See?'

'Yeah, I do see.'

'Ten baht a boogie,' I said. 'Happier times.'

'Look, I'm sorry to bother you, Mr—' I didn't reply. 'Let me get you a drink before I go.' He hailed a waiter. 'Boy, I wish you *were* English. Sure some amazing things going down there. Been five years now since my country restored diplomatic relations. Sometime I hope to get to visit.' Two beers arrived. 'Jack Morgenstern,' he said, extending a hand (and proffering a heavy tip with the other). 'Cheers. Let's hope that sad little country gets a better deal under the Human Front.'

I took a sip of my beer. 'The Human Front,' I said, 'are scum.' Morgenstern's hands fluttered about his glass.

'Believe me,' he said, 'I'm no fan. Anybody who could do *this* . . .' He gestured towards the circus of blood and its *artistes*. 'But you have to admit those fellas have established something like order. God knows, if those Lilim ever got out—and some say they already *have*, that they've been seen in mainland Europe—if *anybody* got out, started spreading that doll-plague around . . .'

'Then it's just as well I'm *not* English.'

'Lord, not everybody's infected. I'm not prejudiced. Only Londoners have the virus, and London's sealed off. Quarantined. It's just a pity the English didn't handle things as well as the French did all those years back when the plague began. Anyway, nobody gets out of London.'

'That so?'

'Sure. But my waiter friend tells me there're lots of *clean* English people in South-East Asia . . .'

Was he being naive or ironic? The English who sheltered in Thailand necessarily held forged papers; despite the assurances of Her Majesty's government, it was an open secret that the plague had broken London's *cordon sanitaire*. From this exclusive club of exiles, Primavera and I had ourselves been exiled. We hadn't had the Deutschmarks to bribe the requisite officials in this most bribable of countries. Besides, club rules barred inhuman refugees. Blackballed their paramours. We had had to rely on the sour charity of Madame K.

'Why are you so interested in the Lilim?' I tried to ask. I wanted the dope on Morgenstern's dopey act of American innocent abroad. But my lips hadn't moved. They were as numb as if I'd snacked on a cocaine popsicle. How many beers had I had? I had a strong head, but the room had begun to spin, and Jack Morgenstern's voice was as faint as if he were calling station to station from Mars.

'So you *could* be English. Theoretically, that is . . .' I wiggled a finger in my ear; an insect was buzzing inside my skull. 'You could be from Madchester. That's what everybody calls the capital now, eh, Madchester?' My skin, filmed with sweat, was as cold as the slick of condensation on my beer glass. 'Sure would be something,' he said, 'if you *were* a Londoner.'

I got up. I was going to be ill. Where was the *suam*? And Primavera, where were you? Where were you when I ever needed you? Tucking me into bed Mum would tell stories about when she was a little girl. The farm outside Bratislava. Summer walks through the Carpathians . . . The floor hit me like one of Primavera's hexes: a dimension unpredicted by unified theory, something that should *not* have been there. Carpet bristles invaded my mouth. My veins were full of ice—like allure, but pleasureless, no fun—and my muscles were frozen. I was a statue that had fallen from its plinth. Tik-tik-atikka, went the drum machine. *She did the hula-hula.* Tik-tik-atikka. *And then I had to shoot her.* Tik-tik-atikka. *C-cos she'd stolen my computer.*

I beheld the paralysis of my face in a patent leather toecap.

'Sir, sir?'

'It's all right,' said Morgenstern. 'He's a friend. Our car's outside. You'll give me a hand?'

CHAPTER THREE

Beata Beatrix

The stretch limousine turned amphibious at the Ploenchit Road. Conscious but immobile, my eyes like fused glass, I stared, unblinking, through the spray-flecked windscreen at the cleft black water of the *klong*. High-rises, shopping malls, *jeux vérités* arcades rose like giant nenuphars to spill their photoelectric sap into that dead, viscous sea; a sea that had reclaimed the city of angels and made it once more the Venice of the East. From the water protruded *chedi* and *prang* of sunken temples: indices of an obsolete civilization. The traffic—splashing those humbled steeples with their blasphemous slalom—shimmered behind a veil of luminous gas, a gasoline-methane smog lit by the green lasers and floodlights of advertisement hoardings, holographic and photo-mechanical; by the green mercury-vapour glow of underwater road signs; by the green paper lanterns hanging from the shop-houses of adjoining *sois*. Sheet lightning scattered the moonless sky and for an instant the green filter dissolved and the city was delineated in hues of sepia, like a time-damaged print of Fritz Lang's *Metropolis*. This was an *art nouveau* city, a *deco* city, its sinewy, undulating lines and geometric chic copied from the fashions of the *aube du millénaire* and imposed on the slums of its twentieth-century inheritance and the sublimities of its ancient past. Again, the pall of greenness descended, a peasouper, a gangrenous membrane, a steamy decay of tropical night. Monorails, skywalks, with their hoards of winepressed humanity, passed above us; autogyros too, with their fat-cat cargoes, hovering above the city's stagnant pools like steel-hulled dragonflies. Once more, the lightning; and then the rain began, coagulating the green tint of the night so that we seemed to be moving through an ocean's depths.

Green was that year's colour; green, the colour of perversity; a green as luminous as a certain pair of eyes.

I could see her in my peripheral vision. She was muzzled, blood dribbling from the side of her mouth; her dress (the dermaplastic palpitating against me) rucked up, with something resembling a chastity belt girdling her waist and hugging her perineum. Below the waist the dress was torn, bleeding a midnight dye; through the tear a glass cable disappeared into her umbilicus. Part of a scanning tunnelling microscope, perhaps? Or an ovipositor spawning a dust-brood of malicious little machines? Whatever it was, it had turned the lock on Primavera's box of tricks. Like me, she sat in the front of the limo like a dummy being delivered for display.

Morgenstern read the question in my wall-eyed stare. 'Took six men to clamp that on,' he said. 'Two of them are on their way to hospital. They had particle weapons too. Pity about Monsieur Sabatier. He was very cooperative. I guess the Paris catwalks will have to do without him next season. Another nail in Europe's coffin. First the crash. Then the plague...'

In the back, other voices:

'Jesus, they're just kids.'

'The Neverland—that's what they call London now. No one gets to grow up. It's a city of kids.'

'Lost girls, lost boys.'

'Don't weep over these two. They're animals. The kind that'd slice 'n' dice an old, lame, blind, pregnant woman.'

'That kind, eh? But hell. What we do for democracy.'

'It's building bridges. It's the Special Relationship.'

'It's hearts,' said Morgenstern, 'and minds.' The two goons in the back made huh-huh-huh noises of mock amusement.

Well fuck you, Jack, I thought, as we entered the grounds of the American Embassy.

They left us in a dark windowless room, with a marine standing guard. The squawk of lizards, the grunting of frogs, carried across the night. The ceiling fan slewed round the shadows...

'Oh?' she said. 'Did I *hurt* you?'

The left canine, a speck of blood on its enamel, overlapped her lip with gothic coquettishness. 'Lil-im,' whispered some of our classmates, 'Lil-im, Lil-im.'

'Stop that!' said Mr Spink, our form teacher, his vodka-ruined larynx rasping with the attempt to muster authority. 'I've told you before: I won't have any of this superstitious "Lilim" nonsense in my class.'

A massed raising of hands.

'Sir,' said the girl—a human girl—'Primavera just bit Ignatz.' The susurration peaked, then died.

'Primavera?'

'I didn't do anything, sir, honest!' A pencil dropped to the floor. My classmates scraped their feet, chewed their lips: a pack of wolf cubs at bay.

'What about you, Zwakh?'

'I'm all right, sir,' I said, my cheeks still flushed. Primavera glanced over her shoulder, her eyes narrowing with contempt.

'Primavera, I think you'd better see Nurse.' And the contempt surrendered to confusion, the green-speckled irises dilating with fear.

It would mean an appointment at the Hospitals, another checkup where she would be probed, examined, observed, an updated prognosis entered in her records. A doll remained an out patient (they said) until the unassuageability of her appetites was thought to threaten public health. Interned—committal papers signed by parents or guardians with sometimes marvellous haste—and disabled with magic dust, her brief mortal term was concluded (they said) in conditions similar to those of an eighteenth-century madhouse, a Bedlam where, racked by visions of ruptured jugulars, of banquets of blood, she died (they said) drowned on her own monstrous salivations. The corpse was used for medical research.

So they said. But could you believe them? The boys in the playground; the grown-ups whispering in corners; the TV, with its coded references to London's fate? On a hot summer's day, with your nostrils filled with the perfume of the prettiest little girl in school, you could believe anything.

Primavera sloped out of class; a backward glance, as she closed the door, sent me and the human race to perdition.

Our teacher had sat down and was staring at the stack of exercise books that, for months, he had never opened, never touched. Quiet desperation, Dad called that despair (its quietness sometimes disturbed by Mr Spink's hacking coughs, his lungs besieged by the mutant bacillus that had been the forerunner of the doll-plague). I gazed out of the window. Sparrows wheeled over the roofs of abandoned houses; dogs prowled empty streets.

You could walk through these depopulated suburbs, Dad said, as far as the M25. That was the line of interdiction. For humans, barbed wire, personnel mines, watchtowers; for dolls, the screen. The Americans had linked elements of their strategic defences (neutral particle beam space platforms) with the interdiction's early warning system. A doll-shaped blip on radar and an NPB would score a neurotronics kill, grounding the escaping doll and leaving her in the throes of a *grand mal*. At night, from the top of the tower block where I lived, I would look out over the Rainham marshes and, seeing the searchlights panning the sky, imagine myself, high above the deserted city, eluding our captors and disappearing into the wild vista of England's other shore. But none crossed the ring road of the M25.

'We'll get her for you, Ig,' whispered a boy to my right. It was Myshkin. Myshkin had the knobbly, dirt-caked aspect of one of Phiz's street urchins. He turned up his lapel to display a tiny steel badge: the winged double helix of the Human Front. 'England for the organic,' he said, taking from his pocket a pair of rubber gloves. Myshkin was a medicine-head.

The bell sounded; it was lunch-time. I gave myself to the current: the subterranean stream of boys and girls that poured through the narrow caverns of our school to spill into eye-splitting sunlight.

The playground—a tarmacked yard half melted in the summer heat—held a microcosm of the Soviet diaspora: the children of those economic migrants who, since the end of the last century, had turned westwards in search of food and jobs. The old nationalist hatreds—which had once set Armenian against Azerbaijani, Transylvanian against Romanian, and just about everybody against dispossessed Russia, had been submerged in a new chauvinism in which speciesism supplanted ethnicity. In the playground, human children who, before the plague, would have segregated into warring tribes, celebrated their inverted cosmopolitanism in the sun, confining the recombinant to the shadows of the bike sheds.

I crouched by a wall; my lunch, a bag of crisps. About me, a grey facade pocked with broken windows and scarred with lichen and desiccated moss drew a stone curtain across the flood-ruined Neverscape. Only a few slummy towers, like the one I lived in (like the ones we all lived in), sanctuaries against the winter's deluge, were visible above the blinding concrete. Why wouldn't the floods come now, and drown my shame? Rise, sea. Fill the Thames. Lap, then overlap the barriers. But the streets were as dry as a dust-filled cistern. I hated June.

I had borrowed *The Adventures of Tom Sawyer* from Dad's small but uncompromising library. ('The Battle of the Books,' he'd say, laughing, as he clubbed to death one of my government-issue primers with the aid of a Hasek, Havel or Seifert.) The book fell open at a passage I had read again and again. Tom had arrived late at school and had been told to sit with the girls. That was okay with him. It meant he could sit next to Becky Thatcher, the new girl in town whom he secretly adored. Becky ignored him. Then he gave her a peach. Drew pictures on his slate.

Now Tom began to scrawl something on the slate, hiding the words from the girl. But she was not backward this time. She begged to see. Tom said:

'Oh, it ain't anything.'

'Yes it is.'

'No it ain't; you don't want to see.'

'Yes I do, indeed I do. Please let me.'

'You'll tell.'

'No I won't—deed and deed and double deed I won't.'

'You won't tell anybody at all? Ever as long as you live?'

'No I won't tell anybody. Now let me.'

'Oh you don't want to see!'

'Now that you treat me so I will see, Tom'—and she put her small hand on his, and a little scuffle ensued. Tom pretending to resist in earnest, but letting his hand slip by degrees till these words were revealed: 'I love you.'

'Oh, you bad thing!' And she hit his hand a smart rap, but reddened and looked pleased nevertheless . . .

Why wasn't it like that? Why wasn't it *ever* like that? I savoured my self-pity. I would never grow up, but I would never be a child; never know childhood's grace.

Myshkin came to sit beside me. 'Look at them,' he said. Jostled by the scampering figures of two football teams a group of Lilim walked across the playground and took asylum amongst the scooters and amphibious bikes. They were older girls, fifth formers, their humanity spent, girls no longer, really, but simulacra, dolls. Wrapped in shadows, and wearing black, black sunglasses, they still seemed to wince at the sun. An irritability coursed through their limbs: they mussed their hair, arranged and rearranged their clothes, applied make-up with a tic-like, incipient hysteria. Muzzled, like all dolls achieving metamorphosis, some slurped at raspberry slush ices through straws; one doll, finishing her ice, and seemingly unsatisfied, removed her shades, shielded her eyes, and squinted through the convective air as if seeking life across a bloodless desert.

'Gopnik,' said Myshkin. 'Slink-gang. Call themselves the *Nutcracker Sweets.'* He had pulled on his rubber gloves and was tying a surgical mask to his face. 'They'll die soon, of course. Two or three years. They'll burn out. Go mad. They always do. Their bodies can't accommodate all those crazy molecular changes. Two or three years. You can spoil a lot of seed in that time . . .' He drew a dog-eared magazine from his blazer. 'My Dad has a library too,' he said, taking *Tom Sawyer* from my hands. 'He's . . . a collector.'

The magazine was called *The National Health*. Inside were photographs of people I had seen on TV, such as Vladimir ('Vlad') Constantinescu, leader of the Human Front. There were also lots of photographs of young girls in straitjackets, padded cells, and on mortuary slabs; of pathologists caught *in flagrante delicto* as they performed hysterectomies on the dead; of kidney dishes full of tissue, polymers and bloodied steel.

'Medical experiments,' said Myshkin, who smirked as if he knew I only dissembled revulsion. 'They have to try and find a cure. Not as if it's *pre-mortems*, is it? Anyway, they're not like us. Not self-conscious. They're *robotniks*. Sets of formal rules . . .' His apologia trailed off as, slack-jawed, I flipped through the glossy pages.

'They don't move,' I said. 'The pictures don't move.'

Myshkin took back the magazine, disappointed less, I think, by my lack of candour than that I had failed to appreciate the antique beauty of photographic still life. 'Bitches,' he said, surveying the playground, his eyes pausing whenever they encountered a serried group of dolls. 'They're taking over, Ig.' He passed a hand through the stubble of his hair. 'My brother's sixteen. The interdiction began when he was born. People still lived in central London then, not just in the suburbs, like us. Now there's only a quarter million of us left. Every kid you meet these days has a doll for a sister, or a sister who'll most likely turn into a doll.'

'*As a population gets smaller, it gets younger,*' I quoted.

'Neo-Malthusian economics. Yeah. Bloody right. We'll be outnumbered by dolls in five years. In, say, ten, fifteen years, who'll be left? And if the plague gets outside . . .'

'Maybe it is,' I said. 'They say that in Manchester . . .'

'The Human Front—your Dad going to vote for them?'

'What do they care? None of their leaders live in London. My Dad says they're just exploiting us for—'

'Vlad's the man, Ig. It's the only way.'

'*Zut!* You mean all that stuff about his ancestor? That's just *toffee*. Anyway, dolls have Mums and Dads too. You think they'd vote HF?'

'What we vote for don't matter. There's not enough of us. But sure: the Neverland'll vote HF. Like the rest of the country. A doll is a changeling. Mums and Dads want their *real* daughters back.'

'That's superstition! That's—'

'Mums and Dads know that their daughters are returned only after the changeling dies. Returned in spirit! That's what the HF wants: to give parents back their kids. To save souls!'

' "Sanitization". Oh yeah. I call it murder.'

'It's them that's murdering *us*. They're parasites, Ig. They use us to propagate themselves. For them, we're just *vectors*. If we let them carry on they'll take over the world. And when we're gone, and they can't replicate, they'll die, and that'll be the end. Of everything.'

'They'll find a cure,' I said. 'Some day. They'll find out how it all started, and then—'

'The only cure,' said Myshkin, 'is us. Me and my mates have begun work already. Up West.'

'But it's not allowed.'

'Up West where the rogue dolls are. Runaways. Girls in need of a little radical surgery.'

'You'll be infected. You'll bring the infection home.'

'Don't be wet. Anyway, I'm never going to have sex. All these kids making *babies* all the time. Agh—*le nombril sinistre!*' Myshkin wrung his hands, the gloves emitting rubbery squeaks. 'Sex is for *robotniks* and junkies. Sex is . . . Sex is bad news. You won't catch *me* making Lilim.'

'You've got junkie written all over you. You'll be dead before you're twenty-one.'

'It's a crusade, Ig. You've got to make sacrifices.'

A football bounced into my lap; I returned it to the dirty-faced mêlée. The slink-gang, the mooncalfs, the misbegotten little mommas who were the *Nutcracker Sweets*, had begun to play hopscotch in the asphalt bower of the sheds.

'In class—what you said about Primavera . . .'

'*La salope*—she's pretty.' Myshkin laughed, his voice breaking in mid-pitch. 'Don't worry. My brother's a prefect. We'll take care of her. After school.' He patted the magazine under his blazer. 'We'll play doctors. It'll be Psycho-Zygo. It'll be diddly-woo!'

Corridors. Corridors. Dark highways through childhood's ruins. Corridors threaded with boys and girls who seemed to be picking their way through an attic, vast and musty, foraging for the bric-a-brac of innocence. Sunbeams intercepted their progress, splintering through the cracks of boarded windows; I slipped into the throng, the throb of mote-lousy air counterpointing my temple's metronome. Beneath eaves, over rafters: no shouts, no screams, only an enervated mumbling as tongues wagged lazily, fattened by the summer heat. A pair of bluebottles, coupled in flight, fell satiated to a mildewy wainscot. A bloody-nosed boy lay blubbering on the floor. Such urban pastoral; it called for surrender, to seek no more in that attic of dreams . . .

All afternoon I sat behind her, heart thudding, unable to escape, so near that I could smell her piebald mane, so intoxicatingly newly washed. Primavera ignored me. I thought to touch her on the shoulder, to say Don't cross the park, or Let me walk you home. But desire took the charity from my heart, and I thought of her in the gulag of the Dolls' Hospitals, and me, in surgical gown and mask; I thought of straitjackets, padded cells, slabs; and the cheap schoolgirl scent of her hair seemed to mix with the smells of chloroform and ether.

Sunlight fell obliquely across the room; I breathed deep, and then deeper again. My sinuses tingled with black romance. I would have to do it. Do the medicine thing. How else did boy meet girl? How else. The alternatives were abstract; you read about them in *Tom Sawyer,* and in history class they taught you of times before love had become indistinguishable from pornography. They meant nothing to you. You were a Never-Never Kid, sent to school only to show the outside world that there was hope, that you didn't deserve to be abandoned, that you were worth the food and materiel dropped from the night skies. Tom and Becky? Forget it. History? God damn it. Love? Abuse it.

Last bell. Home time. The corridors, in their eternal dampness, a counterpart to our sticky adolescent bodies, channelled the four o'clock rout onto the streets. Myshkin passed me a scalpel, and we ran through the milling schoolchildren to rendezvous with his brother in the baked mud-flats of the park. A policeman—a joke policeman; one of our heroic citizens' militia—seemed to have an intimation of our purpose, and wandered away.

We lay in wait behind a dying strip of hedgerow, shaded from the sun's mellowing embrace, our school's postmodern gothic (with its Oh so funny references to Victorian warehouse, workhouse and blacking factory) playing incongruous mood music—a lugubrious black mass—against the brilliant and deceptive optimism of the late afternoon sky; it was a mood that had long been my own; it clung to me as the smell of decay, of mildew, clung to my clothes, my flesh; I had grown up to its fetid sway. Ever since I had been little, school—not the visible school, the school of appearances and discipline, but a wraith school, a school of the umbrageous heart—had inculcated in me, through the violence of the heart, that voluptuous mood, that music of wanton despair. My memories were all of strange angle shots, monstrous close-ups, distortions, blurrings, dialogue broken-tongued and inane: the bullying in the bell tower (the bell was still ringing, carrying over the housing estates, the marshes); the diagrams, stick-figures and exhortations in the boys' toilets; our science master's lectures on posthuman biology, the biology of master and slave; and, of late, that half-metre of yellow-black hair, those bratty ways, that promise of transcendence.

A haze-distorted column of kids began winding between the liverish pools that had resisted evaporation. The Myshkins pulled up their masks and unsheathed their scalpels. No need for a particle weapon, no need for magic dust; Primavera was still half girl, refractory, but weak. As she passed by the Myshkins broke from the bushes; Primavera's dollfriends scattered across the park. By the time she had been bundled into the cricket pavilion, around fifteen, twenty boys and a few girls—human girls—had gate-crashed the party.

The pavilion was hot; its odour, urinous. Half naked (her blouse had been torn open and her brassiere used to tie her hands behind her back), Primavera knelt in the shadows, head bowed, crying.

We taunted her.

'Witch!'

'Baby killer!'

'*Vrolok!*'

'Dead girl!'

'Changeling!'

'*Robotnik!*'

'Out Patient!'

'*Sangsue!*'

Bored with this sadoschlock exercise (a tired borrowing from one of Myshkin's razzle mags), and, despite the cravenness of our law enforcers, fearful of discovery (dolls then still possessing some rights), her tormentors soon departed; all but one. I lingered, hidden behind a locker. Looking about, and seeing that we were alone, I emerged, tremblingly, to stand before her. She studied me from behind sharp metallic eyelashes, her eyes those of a run-to-ground animal, pitiful but calculating. I felt a stinging in my cheeks; I turned away; then, biting my lip with resolve, swung about to face her. 'Witch,' I said, voice hoarse with its confession of love. I aimed a kick into her side. The adored one moaned and keeled over.

I sat on my haunches and put a hand to her cheek. 'I'm sorry,' I said.

'You b-bastard. You fucking *boy-slime.*'

Big tears rolled over my fingers. Cool and inhuman, they were; and her skin—like a compound of PVC and epidermis of milkmaid—plasticky cool, and white, with an impurity that allured and saddened; an impurity to which the blonde hair, scarred with Cartier black, and black eyes, veined with emerald, added their testimony.

Teeth flashed; a rush of pain. With bestial speed her cute kittycat fangs had bitten through my shirt and chest. I raised my fists, but the opiate of her saliva was already in my wounds; I cried *kamerad!* to the invasion of her kisses.

Shells burst behind my eyes; I was her beachhead, first blood in a guerrilla war against humanity. Fifth columnists leaped from her spittle, a microrobotic army dedicated to overthrowing my gametes. They infiltrated in their billions. Ignoring Y, digging in to X, they would wait, wait for me to fill a human womb so that they might stage their *coup* and set up a puppet government.

A blue-white flash . . .

Tombstones. The coach. The fall of night.

Primavera was eating my brain.

I awoke from post-coital sleep on the hard floor of the pavilion, my head rich with traces of midsummer dreams. Primavera slumbered on, fulfilled, it seemed, in her dollhood, her bosom rising and falling on a tide of ease, her cheek pressed to my own.

Her skirt was in disarray, hoisted to her waist; the umbilicus, that dark well of unreason, rippled to her clockwork pulse.

I disengaged myself, slithered down to her belly, and peered over the umbilical lip. If I had picked up a small stone and dropped it into that well, would I have heard, long seconds later, an echo, a ricochet, a splash? I dismissed the conceit, my hand slipping beneath my waistband to where cold metal ached against my thigh.

Unsheathing my scalpel, I held its blade to the umbilicus; the umbilicus puckered, withdrawing into itself, and the blade trembled like a plumb line above a door to the underworld. I thought of the magazine Myshkin had shown me, the photographs of vivisected flesh; and I moved the blade to the centre of her belly, a hair's-breadth from the taut vinyl skin.

I would not hurt her; I would never hurt her. This was playtime. A game. Pretend. Primavera sighed; I secured the scalpel in my waistband.

Too late: from her umbilicus a light, pale and green, rose like the presage of a genie, diffracting above my head. I panicked, spreading my hands over the bleeding aperture, scared, at any moment, she would awake.

She did not stir.

I screwed my eye to the light source, a Peeping Tom at his lady's chamber.

What was happening in there?

It was a silent picture show; an end-of-the-pier amusement. Men, women, children—figures tinted in shades of green—were flickering into semblances of life. Then came colour. Sound, too: voices of homunculi; the turning of earth; the desolate keening of birds. Primavera was dreaming. And she dreamed of death.

I saw myself standing in the midst of a great cemetery. Mausolea, tombstones, defined the horizon. It was dusk; all was silent beneath a reddening sky. The mourners had departed. Beneath me, an open grave. The stone was carved *Ignatz Zwakh, 2056–68, Remember me, but ah! forget my fate.* Icy fingers entwined about my own.

'It has to be like this. You know that, don't you?' Primavera's cloak was like a designer shroud, the hood—lined with green satin—framing a lifeless face. 'Desire is death. Living death.'

She led me through the necropolis to where a coach-and-four waited. A much-decayed corpse in a surgical mask held the reins.

'Dust to dust. Silicon to silicon. The bullies. The Hospitals. The men in white coats. The dolls.'

We boarded. A crack of a whip. We galloped through the cemetery. Grim reapers, dismembered cherubs and other *mementos mori* gaped in at us as we hurtled past.

Primavera drew close. The opacity of her eyes—dark, with green splinters of mutation—cleared, became mortal. With loneliness. With fear.

'Night is falling.' Her breath was cold against my cheek. 'Stay with me. Share my grave. On and on we can ride. No escape for human, for doll. All is boundless and eternal. Like desire. Like death.'

A hand, small, white and blue-veined, a child's hand, settled between my thighs.

The wheels clattered over rocks and bones.

The light faded; the picture show dissolved. Primavera was waking. I crept into her arms.

'What's the time?' she murmured.

'I don't know. My watch—' My watch was broken.

As if she had been slapped, Primavera spun her head to one side, gasping with alarm. 'Outside,' she said, 'it's getting dark! Quick, untie me!' I freed her lace-manacled hands. 'I have to go home. I'm late. Mum thinks it's bad enough as it is, having a doll for a daughter. I don't want her to think I'm *delinquent.*'

Shaking, she buttoned her blouse and brushed the dust from her gymslip. 'I couldn't help it,' she said, her eyes moodily fastened on the green pentacle emblazoned over her breast. 'It's the poison.' She put a hand on her belly. 'Here. Inside. Sometimes—sometimes it hurts. I don't want to be Lilim. I don't. I want everything to be like—like *before.*'

In England every girl is human; or was human, once. And Primavera was but a few months into her metamorphosis. Such a girl, like a chrysalis disturbed from sleep, may sometimes scratch at her cocoon, afraid. She knows that she is becoming that other, that vertigo of desire, that dead girl who shares her name.

'You won't tell, will you?' she said. 'If you tell . . .'

'I won't tell,' I said. 'I promise.'

She knelt to kiss me. It was a ghost's kiss, light, impalpable. 'You mean that?'

'I'm not like the others.'

'Boy-slime.' She laughed softly.

'I mean it,' I said. 'Listen: it's my birthday next week. I'm having a party. Why don't you come?'

'And whatever will your Mum and Dad say? A doll at their little boy's party?'

'Mum and Dad aren't like that.'

She frowned and cuffed me playfully across the nose. 'Maybe,' she said.

'But human boys have so *many* birthdays. Not like us dolls. I don't know if I *should.*' She stood up. 'I have to go.'

'Primavera,' I said, 'be my girlfriend.'

'*Stupid!*'

'I wouldn't let them hurt you,' I said. 'Not again.'

She walked towards the door, chewing thoughtfully on a strand of dishevelled hair. 'I might come to your party. Your Mum and Dad sound nice. My Mum, well . . . Lilith's your mother now, she says. She wouldn't be seen dead with me. The older girls: they always say it's the human bit left inside that hurts.'

It would be a mercy when she became doll entire . . .

I lay in the darkness, fingering the puncture wounds beneath my shirt, counting (as she had insisted) to six hundred and sixty-six (the shirt would have to be destroyed; it was red with sedition) before following her into the evening's gloom. To be seen together at this hour . . . *People talk so, Iggy, really they do.* The sky was violet, shifting to black, and the ruins bordering the park's savannah echoed to the hush of shadows. Primavera was gone, scurrying to meet her curfew. It was late—too late to be on the streets; with the sundown came the big kids, cocks of the militant boardwalks of the night. I trotted into the desolation of ordinariness that was north-east London's suburbs.

The Rainham Road was littered with tomb-robbers' castoffs: sunburst clocks, prints from Woolworth's, plaster knick-knacks and smashed aquaria—the unwanted booty of forgotten, vulgar lives. I began to sprint (the sounds of distant parties restating the dangers of the dark); out there, amongst the remains of England's beached Leviathan, things prinked, prowled and preyed, boy-things, and girl-things. I crossed the A125, and paused to catch my breath. Beyond a strip of marshland the towers of the Mardyke estate, honeycombed with light, cast an emulsive sheen across the benighted city. (Evidence of other habitation came from far, far away where the lurid glow of Dagenham Hospital rose above the horizon.) There were other communities; one in Upminster, I'd heard. But I had never seen them. I knew only the area bounded by school and the marshes (though Dad had once taken me to see the Thames). Travel was taboo; it spread plague.

I crawled beneath razor-wire, ran, paused, massaged my side, ran again. The dry sedge whistled about my feet. Soon, I had reached the snaggle-toothed root of *Solaris Mansions.* I dawdled, bracing myself for the long climb, the inevitable scolding from Dad. Gazing down the street, my eyes settled upon the Bobinski residence; five floors up, it was signposted by a neon intensity that seemed to burn away all competition. Was she already abed, singing herself a vampire lullaby? Did she touch herself as I visited her dreams? My eyelids drooped; the light was chromaticized by the fine denier of my lashes, and rainbows arced across the boondocks of my world, filling it with love's spectrum. The marshland, flat and monotonous, was irradiated: dykes, sluice-gates, windmills; the nauseous replication of looted semis; and beyond the marshes, beyond the lonely conurbations of Essex and Surrey, Middlesex and Kent, beyond the fairy ring of interdiction, England itself was surely radiant, its shires—where moneymen telecommuted to and from the world—dreaming bright dreams of long ago and a girl named Britannia. A stillness descended, a stillness quite unlike the bleak quiet I was accustomed to, and all dissolved into a tearful, multihued mist. I had become a prism of desire! Primavera and I would transform everything. Where her light could not reach, and where I could not see, even the shadows, I knew, would have lusher gradations, more purposeful depths.

Later, when Mum came to kiss me goodnight, I asked her to tell me a story of when she was little, a story of the forests and of the village where she grew up, a story of the Carpathian mountains.

'Is it true,' I said, after she had finished, 'what they say about dolls: that they're the daughters of Lilith, Adam's first wife? That Lilith steals human children and puts her own in their place?'

'It's just a fairy tale, Ignatz. Like the ones I tell you. Tales of the golem, the wandering Jew, the vampire.'

'But the dolls—they *are* vampires.'

'Not real ones.' She smiled and stroked my hair. 'Dolls are not devils. Such things do not exist. They're just little girls. Little girls who are very ill. You must pity them, Ignatz. The world is cruel.'

Primavera never came to my party, but we often met in secret. Throughout that summer she would come to the roof of my tower block and stay until after dark. 'I don't care about Mum any more,' she'd say. On the roof I had set up a telescope, and we would gaze at the stars, or try to spot an escaping doll caught like a moth in the city perimeter's searchlights. And we would play our game, and afterwards we would both say we were sorry, until the night came when we no longer cared to make apologies, to ourselves, each other, or the world.

CHAPTER FOUR

Black Spring

With four marines to act as my pall bearers (the Mickey still mummifying my joints) I was taken to an elevator, dropped three, four, five floors, and carried, in a mockery of pomp, through the embassy's cable-wormy bowels. My cortège, on entering a gymnasium, came to rest. After leaning me against some wall bars at forty-five degrees (my rigidity uncompromised), the marines solemnly departed. Jack Morgenstern was pumping iron. We were alone.

'How's the voice?' he said. 'I thought we might talk.' The daily exertions of the American *corps diplomatique* had left the gym with a residual stench of humanity; I heaved. 'That's good. That shows the drug's wearing off.' He dropped his weights and moved to a rowing machine. 'But your friend—you'll understand we're going to have to keep *her* secured, even if her girdle *is* killing her.' He began to whistle the chorus of the 'Eton Boating Song'. 'I guess you could call me an Anglophile; it's a fine thing our two countries are enjoying warmer relations.' He paused to wipe his hands and tighten his bandana. 'I'll tell you straight: Her Majesty's government wants you back. Both of you.'

I went to speak, but my mouth seemed filled with marbles.

'What's that?' said Morgenstern, hovering in midstroke.

'The Human Front . . .' I managed, before the marbles began to choke me.

He sighed. 'Don't think we're happy about any of this. But the President happens to believe that the Human Front are the only people who can control the plague. And I'm inclined to agree with him. It's not as if we expect the HF to put the Great back in to Britain, but it's a chance for us to make up lost ground, regain some influence in Europe. The Human Front may be bastards, Zwakh, but they're *our* bastards.'

'The slab,' I spat out, 'Primavera will go to the slab.'

'Didn't you hear? I said we're not *happy*. Not that you two don't deserve the worst.' He passed the finishing line and hung over his oars, his Hash House sweatshirt sodden. The lights went up on his show of temperance. 'You're monsters. Animals. You're . . .' The English language faltered before our seemingly limitless depravity. He rose and walked to a vaulting horse on which lay a manila file. *'Ignatz Zwakh,'* he began to read, *'born 2056 . . .'*

'Kito,' I interrupted. 'Why did she betray us?'

'We've been monitoring you and the girl for weeks,' he said, eyes still on the file. 'Ever since the English approached us through their representatives at the Swiss Embassy. Then you suddenly high-tailed it out of here. So we asked Kito if she could get you back. We didn't want any *official* Thai involvement.'

'Money?'

'We have in our arsenal,' he said, 'greater aphrodisiacs. And darker persuasions. Let's just say Kito's a clever lady. Or machine.' He waved his hand through the air. 'Whatever she is, she's an accomplished liar. I can respect that. Lies have a beauty all of their own. Their own life, their own symmetry. Kito sure knew how to do the number on *you*. Now let's see how you rate on self-preservation.' He ran his finger along a line of type. *'Born 2056. In London. To Slovak émigrés.* Tell me, why the hell didn't your family get the hell out of London before the interdiction came into effect?'

'Nobody wanted us.'

'We're a nation of immigrants ourselves. It's hard to believe you couldn't—'

'Why are we having this conversation? Why don't you just put us on the spaceplane and have done with it?'

'The *Orient Express* doesn't leave until tomorrow. Besides, my government wants to satisfy itself on a few points. For instance . . .' He put the file down and walked over to me. 'Who, or what, is Titania?'

I felt pain in my lower back; I had begun to sag.

'Limbering up, eh? A boy your age should soon—'

'I don't know anything about Titania.'

'Let me tell you what *we* know.' He drew up a stool and sat down. 'Remember our conversation in the restaurant? *Nobody gets out of London.* That's the HF's official party line. But you and I know different. You're not the only kids to have escaped. Dolls have turned up all over England. Scotland. Wales. Mainland Europe, too. Though I guess you're the only runaways to have got *this* far. Someone, or something, is getting them out. Now we believe the Human Front can stabilize things in London, but not over the country as a whole. They're going to need US help.'

'You call mass murder stabilizing?'

'I told you,' he said, his face haggard with a lifetime of trimming to the times, 'we're not happy about this. Now our intelligence indicates that there's something in London organizing these escapes. Something powerful enough to penetrate the interdiction. We think that something is a Big Sister: one of the original Cartier automatons.'

'They were all destroyed,' I said, too hastily.

'I think not. Tell me how you escaped, Zwakh.'

I rolled my eyes to the ceiling.

'Look,' he said, '*I'm* not going to make you talk, but *they* sure will back in England. You realize that, don't you? It's better we know than them. We can act as intermediaries. We can plea-bargain.'

'No,' I said.

'The girl,' he said. 'We could help her. I guess she didn't *mean* to kill. You know what we can say? We can say she didn't want to spread the doll-plague. So she cleaned up after each meal. Real hygienic. She never really *wanted* to murder anyone. After all, Lilim don't kill; it goes against their programming. We can say it was that bitch Kito who—'

'She enjoys it,' I said. 'You were right the first time: we're monsters. Animals.'

'We'll find out about Titania sooner or later,' he said. 'I thought I might save you a little grief, that's all.' He clapped his hands and sprang to his feet. 'That's it then. For now. *Operation Black Spring* has become something of a hobbyhorse. I just can't let go of it.' He chuckled as my body sagged a few more inches. 'Jesus, boy, you look *uncomfortable.*' He manoeuvred me into a ninety-degree upright. 'You know, when I joined the foreign service I genuinely felt I might be able to do something to make the world a better place. Seems a long time ago now. The *aube du millénaire.* Lord, those were times. My wife and I spent our honeymoon in Europe. When I think of what Europe's going through now . . .'

'Primavera enjoys killing,' I said. 'How about you? You dine at *The Londoner* often? What do you do when you're not sending little girls to their deaths?'

'I don't need no lecture from a hired assassin, Zwakh. Maybe we'll talk some more later. In fact I'm sure of it. When you've had time to think. And while you're thinking, remember what I said about aphrodisiacs. And persuasions. Remember we have your little friend. Your little *stash.* No one has to die. Wise up. I can help you.'

He called the guard.

I rejoined Primavera in our lovers' tomb. A marine resumed position by the door, stony-faced as a piece of mortuary furniture.

Escape, escape, I thought. Always that unrelenting need: to make plans, to run, to lie, to cheat. Sometimes you had to fight, too. (I didn't like that; I was no good at it; fighting was Primavera's department.) Why couldn't they give it a rest? I tried to concentrate, but unsolicited images kept interposing themselves between my thoughts. Jack Morgenstern in Kito's penthouse; and Kito, looking untypically flustered, toying nervously with the titanium chain about her neck, her bracelets of spent uranium.

'Kito tricked me,' Primavera announced inside my brain. I cried out.

'Try to get some sleep, sir,' said the marine.

'Did you *hear* that, Iggy? Shit, I didn't know I could *do* that.'

I gripped the sides of the couch; relaxed. I had lived with Primavera too long to be panicked by her quantum magic, however unprecedented its manifestation. 'Primavera?'

'Uh-huh?' Hey. I could mindspeak to her too. Clever, these Cartier dolls.

'They're sending us back to London,' I said in a dead man's whisper. 'Satisfied?'—I twisted the knife—'You should be. This is where all your little games end.'

'I'm sorry, Iggy.' There were tears in her thoughts.

'Can you move?'

'Can't feel a thing. If I could just get these cast-iron *pants* off, then—'

'I can move a little. Any ideas?'

'You keep still. If I can get into your brain I can get into GI Joe's.'

'And then?'

'Just close your eyes. Pretend to be asleep.'

Primavera, signing off, left my head crackling with an anxious static. After a few minutes I heard the creak of a chair and a surreptitious shuffle of footsteps. Peeping through half-shuttered eyes, I watched the guard kneel before Primavera's couch, take a securicard from his wallet, and enter it into the gleaming zone that swaddled her waist and loins. The contraption released its grip, and the guard laid it circumspectly upon the floor. Breathing heavily, he let a hand slip beneath the wisp of black lace that barely covered her pubis. There was a snapping of teeth; a gasp. The guard pulled back his hand and stared at it, hurt and puzzled. The top of his middle finger was missing. Small pathetic noises gave notice of his scream. Before he could summon it to his lips, Primavera delivered a jackhammer of a left hook, and he somersaulted across the room in a graceless confusion of arms and legs.

'My first telepathic seduction,' said Primavera, tearing off her muzzle.

'Talk about *allure*!' The marine lay in a corner imitating a trampled insect. I gave him ten out of ten.

Primavera rolled off her couch and stood up unsteadily, slim adolescent legs wobbling like a newly-born colt's. I was staring at the dead marine.

'You know I don't let anyone inside my pants except *you*, Iggy.'

'Just get us out of here.'

'Well, pardon *me*. So *sorry*. I keep forgetting how *sensitive* you are.'

She put her ear to the wall; then, removing an evening glove, glided her hand over the plaster, and . . . Disappointment seized her face; whatever was supposed to have happened—events in the quantum world finding no interface with the classical—hadn't. She kicked the 'chastity belt' across the floor.

'Magic dust. That thing was full of tin microbes; there must be some left inside me.' She gripped her abdomen. 'Yeah, I can feel them: lots of little nanobots. They're fucking up my matrix.' Again, she put her ear to the wall. 'I can't use my hocus pocus, Iggy. This is going to wake the babies.'

Etching a small cross into the plaster with her fingernail, she closed her eyes, drew back her head, and furiously butted her target. The building shook, and Primavera disappeared behind a veil of atomized ferro-concrete. '*Shit!*' she yelled. 'My fucking *skull*!' In the corridor: screamed orders, the whine of walkie-talkies, the click-clack of safety catches disengaged. The dust cleared; a man-sized hole gaped in the embassy's masonry.

I got to my feet, my legs stiff and cumbersome.

'Help me out of this,' said Primavera. I unzipped her dress; filleted, it fell wriggling to the floor with the sound of raw steak hitting a gridiron.

'You're hurt,' I said. A purple weal was blossoming on her forehead.

'*Stupid!* I'm a doll. My important bits are all down *there*.' The door began to melt. 'You want to hang around and say goodbye?'

Taking my hand, she jumped.

We fell through the hot night and hit the stagnant water of a *klong*. I kicked my feet, intent on resurfacing; but Primavera, cleaving to me like a wicked mermaid, seemed equally intent that I should not. I opened my eyes; the water stung them; I screwed them shut, retreating into blindness. I had seen only Primavera's face, lit by its two green lanterns; the dim play of torchlight through the depths. I began to struggle; Primavera put her arms about my neck and I felt her lips on my own. She blew, and oxygen filled my lungs. As we touched bottom, Primavera loosed her hold, leading me across a scrapmetal jungle, stopping only to refresh my lungs with kisses that, for so many, had proved *de luxe* and noxious.

When our heads breached the surface we found ourselves in a narrow *soi* leading to the Sukumvit Road. The green light of a million-pixel Coca-

Cola sign lit the water; a taxi floated nearby. Dragging me by the collar, Primavera swam to the little boat's side. It was empty. We pulled ourselves aboard and lay, exhausted, staring up at the dawn-fractured clouds. It still rained, but the storm had passed.

'I think,' said Primavera, 'I think I know why she did it.'

'Kito?' I said. 'Money, of course. No honour amongst dolls.'

Primavera shook her head. 'The Americans have got something on her. At least she thinks they have, but—' Primavera gave a short scream and doubled over, clutching her belly. 'She's the only person who can help me, Iggy.' She spoke through gritted fangs. 'These nanomachines: they're turning me into a demolition site. They're taking me to bits.' She held her breath, and then released it in a long sigh of pleasure. I put my hand on the pale flesh below the suspender belt.

'It hurts that bad?'

'It's faecal, Iggy. Really faecal.' She lay back. Mascara ran down her cheeks in a delta of black tears. 'Some of the best nanoengineers in Bangkok work for Kito. And she's got all these laboratories, all this *stuff.*'

'You're crazy. She betrayed us.'

'They blackmailed her, Iggy, and I think I know how. It's something I heard. At the embassy. In my mind. Something I dreamed. If I can prove to Kito that she's got nothing to fear . . .'

I leaned over the gunwale and voided what remained of the Mickey. The streets were coming to life. Food stalls were opening for business. A column of monks passed by, collecting alms. I checked my money belt; my electric baht were intact.

'We've got to hide,' I said, 'clean up, get some clothes. Then we'll talk. Sensibly.' I crawled to the stern and lowered the boat's long rotor arm into the water. The outboard had been modified to guzzle synthetic gasoline. (Filthier, said those who remembered, than the real thing, the gas— banned by the West—was another of Bangkok's lucrative black market industries.) I treated the engine to a little mechanical foreplay until, at last, it growled a response. We drew away, trailing black smoke, black foam.

We entered the big waterway of Sukumvit with Nana behind us, her lights winking out with the arrival of the day. The scent of spent passion, the sharp bouquet of sex, lingered in the air, the smells of a thousand bars mixing with those of a thousand cars. The Bangkok rush hour was in its early morning heat. My clothes began to steam; Primavera hid her face from the sun. The city was warming up its daytime stew of smog; sim-mering, the smog rose past my ankles like some second-rate special effect. As a sop to the European Parliament the Thai government had proscribed environmental nanoware. It was good public relations: it placated some of the West's fears (Europe had outlawed all nanoware at the outbreak of the doll-plague); it only affected the poor (the kingdom's rich lived in high-rise air-filtered condos); and left untouched the huge underground nanoindustry upon which much of Bangkok's wealth was based.

Cowboy, the Triad-controlled pornocracy that was Nana's chief rival—Primavera had offed Terminal Wipes, its Red Cudgel, last year—fell to the black cloud of our exhaust. From a skywalk a banner proclaimed *Welcome to Fun City.* No more wars. Just squabbles, big and small, over the turf of artificial realities. Fun was the world's universal currency. Primavera had killed for it. Who wouldn't? That's life. (That's death.) That's entertainment.

I turned into a *soi,* narrowly avoiding a Toyota Duck, and then into a short-time hotel called the *Lucky.* The attendants, seeing us approach, swept back the curtains that partitioned one of several parking spaces; we entered, and the curtains swung shut. A little quay surrounded us; in one corner, the door to our room. I fed some baht into a nearby teller. A short-time hotel—a house of assignation for adulterers—would, with its concern for discretion and anonymity, provide a temporary bolt hole. We disembarked.

CHAPTER FIVE

Shopping and Fucking

Primavera peeled off her stockings and underwear and skipped into the shower; when she emerged it was to take some baht from my money belt, turn the pages of the TV, and shop. 'I'll order for you,' she said, as I dashed into the bathroom. The stench of the *klong* had become intolerable.

I was still showering when *Daimaru*'s Zen bullet service delivered our goods. Re-entering the bedroom I was confronted by a candy-coloured assortment of boxes, wrappers and parcels, the living contents of which had been slopped onto the floor. Shivering, their raw nerves exposed, the clothes seemed to plead to be worn and so be put out of their misery. I kicked them aside.

'Real girlygirl, no?' said Primavera. 'What do you think?' She was holding a pink top and skirtlet against her nakedness and appraising herself in a mirror.

'I think I'm bankrupt.'

'As if you ever used a bank. As if they'd ever let you. There's life in your card. Just. Human boys *worry* so.'

She let her clothes slip; momentarily, they pawed at her ankles. The room grew cold; again I was drugged. And this time the Mickey was Primavera's. Call it psionics. Doll pheromones. Her allure was in the air, an ultrasonic whistle, and my hormones responded with a *yap*! Irresistible, that siren call.

Was she beautiful? No; like all her kind she possessed, not beauty, but the overripe prettiness that is the saccharine curse of dollhood. Beauty has soul. Beauty has resonance. But a doll is a thing of surface and plane. Clothes, make-up, behavioural characteristics, resolve, for her, into an identity that is all gesture, nuance, signs. She has no psychology, no inner self, no metaphysical depths. She is the glory, the sheen of her exterior, the hard brittle sum of her parts. She is the ghost in the looking glass, the mirage that, reaching out to touch, we find is nothing but rippling air. She is image without substance, a fractal receding into infinity, a reflection without source and without end.

She is her allure.

Primavera's eyes misted. 'I can read your mind, Iggy. Have you really always felt like that? *Always?* But it's the truth: I don't have a soul. I'm Lilim, a daughter of Lilith.' She sat down on the bed, her back to me, and began fumbling with lipstick, blusher and eyeshadow. Long orientalized fingernails clattered like the sword play of miniature samurai as her tiny hands reapplied her mask. Working with a desperate vigour—'What you see,' she was saying, 'is what you get, is what I *am*'—her face was soon coated with its varnish of inviolable chocolate-box prettiness.

'Look at me,' I said.

Sad clown of desire, she had tried to drown herself beneath a flash flood of artificiality. Her eyes wore aureoles of peppermint green, and the sliced pomegranate of her lips matched the rouged circles that emphasized her round toytown cheekbones. The skin was bleached, her war wound— the purple badge of courage on her brow—powdered with a camouflage that blended with her sickly complexion.

'Primavera, I—'

'Who wants to be human anyway? What's so great about being human? I'm glad I'm a doll. I don't care if I *am* going to die. I believe in everything Titania told us.'

I sat down by her side. 'I'm sorry I ran away,' I said. 'It's because I don't want to be like them. The Human Front. And—and all the others.' I stared at the floor. 'Sometimes I'm ashamed to be human. What we do. What we feel. I want to love you, Primavera. I've always wanted to love you.'

'But the blood gets in the way?' she said. 'I know, Iggy, it's like that for me too. We're the same: we want to love, but we love the blood more. The pain. The humiliations. All the deaths, big and little.'

'I wasn't running away from *you*,' I said. I put my hand on her thigh. 'If you could let me . . .' My throat tightened. 'Don't you remember? In Calais. Don't you remember what you said? What you almost said . . .'

She regarded me with uncharacteristic shyness. 'Fuck off,' she said softly, beseechingly.

'I believe in Titania too. I'm on your side. I don't like humans, I like—'

Primavera put a finger to my lips, her nose wrinkling in an allergy of indecision. 'You're right,' she said, 'humans stink.' She grabbed the towel that I had used as an improvised sarong. 'Sometimes, Iggy, you're so full of shit. I know I can't love: I'm a doll. But you're a doll junkie: you can't love either.' She jerked the towel from my waist. 'You think you like dolls. But I know what you like.' She picked up the remote and shut the endlessly turning pages of the TV.

'Let's play,' she said, standing. Wading through her newly-bought clothes she soon came upon our playhouse's key prop. I secured her hands behind her back; she turned round, pressed herself against me.

'Bastard,' she whispered. 'Boy-slime. Hypocrite. Prig. You think you're better than the others, don't you? Better than the Human Front. The medicine-heads. But I know what you like. Oh yes, Iggy, I *know* . . .'

Her teeth scratched at my ear, and the thick pulse of her clockwork heart beat against my own. Her plasticky flesh warmed, grew tacky, its illusion of soft wantonness betrayed only by the rib-cage, hard as vat-grown steel, adhering to my solar plexus and imprinting its decal of black and blue. Breathless, I ran my hand down her hair, the crenellations of her spine, to settle upon her sacrum, the small trephination of which—its concavity hidden beneath an epidermic seal—I teased with my knuckles. She wriggled with disgust.

'Tell me,' I said, 'tell me what I like.' Her tongue, rough as a cat's, scoured my tympanic membrane.

'You like what all boys like . . .' She was broadcasting directly into my head. 'You like the sound of torn silk. Flesh on cold marble. All the *no sir, please sir, no sirs . . .*'

I pulled her head back and kissed her. She drew my tongue from my mouth as if it were a bloated leech, her teeth piercing it; and then she drew the blood.

Her saliva hit a mainline. The rush brought me to my knees.

'Bitch,' I tried to say; but my mouth had filled. I haemorrhaged onto the floor. Jumping up, I lashed out with my foot. Primavera fell, broke from her bonds, clawed at me with razor-tipped fingers. Taking her by the hair, I dragged her onto the bed.

'Dead girl. Lilim,' I said, each syllable spraying blood. I collapsed and my wounds turned the counterpane scarlet.

'You b-bastard. You fucking *boy-slime!*'

'*Robotnik!*' My words had become little more than gurgles. I sat up. 'I've got to do something about this,' I said with the voice of a half-drowned man. 'Maybe you should get a doctor.'

Between Primavera's depilated thighs her labia opened with the terrible grin of a prehistoric fish. The *vagina dentata* gnashed and snapped.

'But we've not finished *playing* doctors yet,' she said.

Her other lips turned back and the ice picks that were her canines entered my flesh a millimetre above the left nipple. Saliva and blood ran down my chest in a rivulet of sarsaparilla.

Night fell. We were speeding through the graveyard of the world, crashing over rocks and bones. Her kiss was death, of the future and of the past; all dissolved, all promised to cease. But desire carried us beyond the grave. The night was ours.

Lightning . . .

The dead shook their fists; we felled them like skittles, breaking them beneath our wheels. 'Oh?' said Primavera. 'Did I *hurt* you? Did I *hurt* you? Did I . . .'

Thunder boomed; the coach sped on. Into darkness, rain and sleep.

Spreadeagled on the bed, I observed myself in the ceiling mirror as Primavera applied sticky plaster and lint to my wounds. After satisfying her thirst, she had rung room service and ordered—in addition to other pharmaceuticals—a cauterizing agent for my tongue.

I raised myself by my elbows, dropped ice in my Singha, and cooled my mouth's fire. About us were the remnants of our lunch: bowls of noodles, a plate of lightly fried grasshoppers (bite their heads off, suck their juices, Primavera had advised), and a cuttlefish soup spiced with rat-shit chilli that had spread over the thinly carpeted floor. Magazines and comics that Primavera had ordered over the fax sopped up the carnage.

'Don't move,' she said, 'this is the last one.' She smoothed the plaster into place. 'There. All better!'

'That was quite a party.'

'We party too much. Some day it'll all go *too* far.' She lit a cigarette, inhaled a mouthful of smoke, gargled with it, then expectorated a grey-blue plume into the air. 'But if my programme won't allow me to love you, Iggy, at least I can love your blood. It's so delirious. It's so . . .' Above, the mirror held us like malignancies trapped within a specimen slide as Primavera sought a superlative; but a doll's appetites are untranslatable; she sighed, and drew a fingernail across her left breast. 'I lost my brooch. In the restaurant. In the fight.'

'I'll get you another.'

'It was special.' She put the cigarette between my lips. 'Iggy, before they catch us—*if* they catch us—promise: you'll kill me, won't you?'

I studied her in the mirror. What kind of life was she? Dead girls, they called them. Sets of formal rules, without free will. Imitations of life. Souldrained. To destroy such ones was not murder, they said. But if Primavera died, then I knew I would die too. I lived in the nothingness at her heart, my life mortgaged to her allure.

'You could do it,' she said, in her little girl's lisp, 'you know, the way you want. I'd buy you a scalpel. Just like the one you had in England. You could—'

She was inside my mind; she turned to me and frowned.

'Why?'

'I just can't, that's all.'

'Junkie.' She sneered. 'What's the matter—scared? You're not going to live much longer than me anyway.' I replaced the cigarette in her mouth, shutting her up.

'This business,' I said, 'about seeing Kito. Why don't we try to get help from one of the other pornocracies: Cowboy, Patpong or Suriwongse? They all employ nanoengineers.'

'Iggy, sometimes you're like a little child. I've offed people in all those places. We can't risk it.'

'But you're willing to risk walking into Nana? Kito never liked you, Primavera, and she likes you even less now.'

'Kito will help. I know it.'

'How?'

'Easy,' she said, snapping her fingers, 'we tell her about Titania!'

I picked up the remote. 'I don't want to hear any more.' Deselecting the shopping channel, I surfed the phosphordot sea from World News (something about an African famine) to the latest Thai ghost movie, *Phi Gaseu 26*; from an interactive game show (win your own dreamscaper) to a francophone channel called *Alliance Française* (the world still Frenchified in its tastes, despite the demise of the world's fashion capital). *Alliance* was running *Trans Europe Express,* a colour-dubbed piece of Old Wave shit. But what was this? Some *louche*-looking guy tying a woman to a bed. I turned up the sound . . .

Primavera snatched the remote and killed the transmission. 'Titania wouldn't mind.'

Primavera, Primavera, Primavera Oh! Did you really think that *I* minded. About your crazy porcelain queen? I cared only that you cared. For that rabid vision. For everything she had said that made you walk tall. To have betrayed Titania would have been to betray you.

'What do you think all this *ordure* has been about?' I said. 'The HF are on to Titania. They want to know how we escaped.' Primavera slammed her fist into the mattress. 'We don't tell anybody about Titania. She saved our lives. If it hadn't been for her you would have gone to the slab.'

'I didn't know,' said Primavera. 'You should have told me. I just wanted to tell Kito that it wasn't *her* that started the doll-plague. That's how the Americans frightened her, don't you see? It's how they blackmailed her. And we know the truth.'

'What's Kito got to do with the doll-plague?'

A sharp intake of breath; Primavera ran to the bathroom. I followed and discovered her kneeling before the *suam* and vomiting blood. 'Don't worry,' she said, 'it's yours. But something's going wrong. Inside.' I helped her to her feet and half carried her back to the bedroom. 'Close your eyes,' I said. 'Sleep.'

'No!' She staggered to the dressing table. 'I have to see Kito. I have to get her help. I won't tell her too much. I won't betray Titania.' She picked up the dismay of my thoughts. 'You stay here. Human boys can be such . . . such *scaredy cats.*'

'Let me get you to a hospital.'

'Don't mention the word "hospital" to *me.*'

'I just thought—'

'Don't be a pin.'

She took a hypodermic from the dresser and filled it with *Virgin Martyr.* Hypo and scent bottle—the bottle, black and engraved with the image of a crucified girl—trembled in her hands, like the sceptre and orb of an olfactory queen with delirium tremens. She injected, and her eyes revolved, white as two boiled eggs.

'Ahh,' she sighed, 'that smells so good.' The hit subsided and she began to comb her hair. 'If Kito won't cooperate,' she said, 'I'll kill her. It's simple. But it won't come to that.'

'Why . . .' I said; a dying fall. Why had I come back, why was I her slave? I knew the answer. So, it seemed, did the photo-mechanical above the bed. She laughed, mockingly. They were like that, those starlets. A hacker had introduced a bug into their two-dimensional world that was designed to make you feel small. Human melancholy activated it. Some prank. I took the poster from its hook. Wafer thin, it tore easily; the paper dolly ducked. I tore again, and she retreated to the poster's margin.

Ignatz the slave. Ignatz always back returning. Why? Why? Because a junkie always runs away; always comes back. That's the way it is with junkies.

Primavera giggled in triumph. 'Because I'm the *dolliest.* Isn't that right,' she said addressing the mirror, 'aren't I just the dolliest of them all?'

The photo-mechanical, with the aid of a half-torn mechanical octopus that had been her 2-D friend, switched her pose from soft to hardcore, pouting with sexual defiance. I tore her in two; what was left of the poster fibrillated with her scream.

'Leave that poor photo-mechanical alone,' said Primavera. 'Hooligan. You're as bad as Mr Jinx.'

'Then it's true what they say . . . ?' I scrunched up the poster, tossed it in the trashcan, and knelt down to inspect Primavera's purchases. Clothes slithered through my hands, their fibres insinuating themselves into my pores with sartorial flirtatiousness.

'Dermaplastic,' I said, extricating a soggy pair of trousers. 'Why couldn't you get me something normal? Something *ordinary*?'

'If you *are* coming,' she said, 'here . . .' She handed me an aerosol. 'Spray me. I can collect the other stuff when we're through with Madame.'

She moved to the centre of the room and held her arms and legs in a St Andrew's cross. I shook the can. When I had finished, her body, with the exception of the ghost-white face, was coated in a patina of glossy black gelatine.

'How soon will that dry?' I said.

'Almost ready. It's the latest. Oo! There—its nerve endings are coming alive!'

To complete her ensemble she stepped into crippling stilettos and clipped gold rings to her nipples and clitoris. I took longer to dress, queasy at wrapping myself in what felt like someone else's skin.

We pigged out on TV until late evening (Primavera almost won a dreamscaper); then, leaving behind a chaos of half-eaten food, used bandages, broken glass, cigarette butts, syringes, blood-stained sheets and teeth, we slipped out, ready to retake the night.

CHAPTER SIX

Going to A-Go-Go

L ike I said, what's Kito got to do with the doll-plague?'
   We were on the skytrain, Nana-bound. I had my panama pulled over
my eyes, fearful of recognition (we were only two stops from Kito's lair);
but Primavera bathed in the furtive glances of every voyeur aboard.

'Don't you know what they're thinking? Another dermatoid junkie,
that's what, another "skinny" addicted to artificial flesh.'

'Of course I know what they're thinking, *stupid*!' Her broadcast
jammed my amateur wavelength. 'What do I care? They're all robofuck-
ers anyway. Bipedal phalloi, Madame calls them. And you're a fine one to
call me junkie.'

'Yeah, well what if someone in this crowd identifies us?'

As a concession she reached into her shoulder bag and donned a pair of
widow-black shades. Then, shaking out her hair (a weekly investment in
a bottle of hair dye had, for three years, provided her sole disguise; contact lenses? no, no, not her), she turned her back on the skytrain's throng
and gazed out into the night. Her feral teeth worried at a hunk of gum.

'So?' I thought. 'Kito—doll-plague; doll-plague—Kito. What's it all
about?'

Below, the Big Weird sparkled like a fathomless black pond infested
with a million phosphorescent water lilies: corporations, banks, hotels,
condos, that Buddha—in the shape of a million giant holograms—
guarded and preserved. The monorail, visible as it snaked round a bend,
was almost over Nana.

'Well?'

Primavera's eyes had glazed. She was staring into the distance, where the needle-like tower of the Siamese Space Agency pointed a covetous finger at the sky.

Unreal. A reflection. A shadow cast by nothingness. As if I care. I'm a vanity of vanities. Proud. Monstrous. Without shame. I'm talking to you, Dr B. Where are you now? Still got your head between some little girl's thighs? Still playing the Pied Piper? Blue Mondays at the clinic. Midmenarche in mid-March. It's cold. Wet. And I'm thirsty. How are we today? Dying, Dr B. Dying into the new. My flesh's like nougat. My brain's like bubbly-bubbly. And I see things, you know? Crazy things. Like corridors. Corridors lined with doors. Endless, endless. Mirrors seething within mirrors. And behind each door, behind each mirror, another world. Another time. Primavera, you know you mustn't open those doors? Yes, doctor. Or break the mirrors? Of course, doctor. And the pills? Every day, doctor. Morning, full moon and night. And the hemline neurosis? Yes, much better, really much better, Dr Bogenbloom . . .

'Well?'

'Sex diseases,' whispered Primavera's mind. 'Madame is a past mistress of sex diseases.'

'She makes them?'

'Not any more. But years ago she fought a lot of trade wars that way. Europe would sabotage her dolls, so she'd cook a virus to sabotage theirs.'

'But that,' I said, a sliver of comprehension jemmying loose my tongue, 'has got nothing to do with the doll-plague.'

'No,' said Primavera, 'that's just the point.'

'*Nana Plaza,*' droned a synthetic voice, '*please alight here for Nana Plaza.*'

'Now be quiet,' said Primavera, 'and follow me.'

Our carriage emptied. We lost ourselves in the crush, borne along by a scrum of male libertinage (Nana was dick-slobber city; a heterometro): *farangs* mostly, garbed in the tired, emulative threads that the Weird had been producing for more than a hundred years. I picked out accents: American, Australasian, pidgin European . . . A glass escalator—as big and as wide as those staircases in ancient Hollywood musicals—dropped us to the streets. The band struck up, and the streets went into their routine. It was the big number about narcissism, sex and greed: a song Nana knew by heart.

We were in the Plaza, a tiered arena of go-go bars that ascended, circle upon circle, like a neon-lit wedding cake celebrating the marriage of man and doll. The Plaza's upper limits were still developing: steel tanks, seeded with nanoware, were growing next year's bars. From the lowest stratum, conflicting sound systems, in a cacophony of half tones and quarter tones, smeared the brain with white noise. Pungent smell of barbecued squid, open drains, gynoidal pheromones and all-night pharmacies. 'MOLEC-ULAR ROBOTS—HORMONES—GENE SHEARS—CSFs': on-off, on-off, the lights.

They were looking at me. Everybody was looking at me: *farangs,* through steins holding enormous philtres of beer, dolls with gimlet-eyed quid pro quo, holotoys stalking me, hopelessly rubbing themselves against me, that balloon seller trailing his stock of decapitated hydrogen-filled heads. Nana was full of eyes, the eyes of madmen and madwomen. And now the eyes, a market of circles and ellipses, were on fire . . .

Killer visions stormed my ascending nerve tract.

I began to twitch; my right arm was convulsing. My clothes had been seized with a fit.

'Iggy, stop it! This is no time for . . .'

'I can't help it! It's, it's, it's . . .'

Dermaplastic is a somatic textile, a sense amplifier. Microscopic fibres hardwire the material's peripheral nervous system to the wearer's own.

Primavera understood. She reached to the back of my trousers—an area just above the coccyx—and tore away a handful of second skin. The convulsions ceased.

'I got its cortex,' she said, crushing the white plastic until its customized melanin ran through her fingers. 'Bad trip, eh? The electromuscles will relax now. That's the last time I shop by Zen. How do you feel?'

'Like nothing a blood transfusion couldn't cure.'

Nana was bisected by the Sukumvit Road, and we had to take a sky-walk to cross the water and reach that farrago of restaurants, tailors, jewellers, surgeries and bars that had been known ever since the *belle époque* as the 'French Quarter'. To this demimonde of cut-price style came the ruined aristocracy of Europe's information elite to pretend to the snobbery they could no longer afford.

'Look,' said Primavera, 'Martian jewels!' She elbowed past two window-shoppers, pressing her nose to the glass. The shop radiated with neo-Lalique confections ostensibly made from the candyfloss rocks of the red planet.

'We don't have time,' I said. 'Besides, you know they're not real.' The man whom Primavera had pushed aside looked at me angrily, then—mumbling something in what sounded like defunct powerhouse German—ushered his female companion away. Their kind were everywhere: Europunks fleeing from reality. Boys and girls looking for their lost toys.

A muggy breeze swept an ankle-deep smog across our path, carbon emissions collecting with methane bubbling from the nearby *klong* (and with other pollutants so novel and so peculiar to the Big Weird that they might have been awarded a conservation order) to form cheapo house of horror atmospherics. A tourist cast a cigarette aside; Primavera and I shied away. A flash; a whoof of combusted air; and the *farang* turned to us, half in apology, half in accusation, his face blackened as if by an exploding cigar.

We headed for the *Grace Hotel*. In the doorways of *Tin Lizzie, Robogirl* and *Kiss and Panic*, mechanettes ran through their repertoires of solicitation. Ridiculous, those creatures (but 'men like their women ridiculous' ran the automaton-nerds' blurb), the phallocentric night tripping their tropismatic switches as they tensed before the scrutiny of the throbbing multitude like bow-strings burdened with arrows of desire. Primavera took my hat and pulled it over her ears, too near, now, to the queen bee to risk identification from her hive of workers. 'It's not the gynoids I worry about,' said Primavera, 'it's the proprietors: all the *farangs* Kito has hanging on her skirts.'

'Like Willy Hofmannsthal?' I said. Hofmannsthal—an old, old man (more android than man), whose body was a patchwork of flesh, steel and plastic riddled with tissue-repairing nanomachines—sat outside his bar, the *Doll Keller*. I steered Primavera to a newspaper stall, bought a magazine (little figures danced across the cover) and employed it as a fan in an attempt at concealment. 'This is too obvious,' I said. 'In here . . .' We entered a *jeux vérités* arcade.

Walking along its length, screams, laughter and other vocal intensities greeted us from each gamester's booth. Maybe they were murdering their mothers, taking over the world, or fucking St Ursula and her 11,000 virgins before wasting them with napalm. Alpha-wave monitors on each door gave notice of those who, in their drugged sleep, had awoken while still in REM to the dreamscaper's martinet urging. Primavera put her hands over her ears. 'Shut up!' she cried. 'Shut up! Shut up!' But the arcade was deaf with reverie.

As we ran out into the streets the *Grace* rose before us, the cosmetic surgery of its *deco*-clad exterior unable to conceal its antique cancers. At its summit, a penthouse: Kito's nest. The eyrie of vanity, spitefulness and deceit.

A small boy with the face of an angel tugged at my leg, looked up at me big-eyed with ingenuousness, and made a little *wai*. 'Please sir, ten baht. Very hungry.'

Primavera's fist crashed into the child's skull. It ran away, circuitry leaking from its left ear. 'Madame really should get rid of those things,' she said.

'So how do we go in?'

'Front door. No heavies. We'll go through the coffee shop.'

'But it'll be packed.'

'So no one will notice.'

Taking me by the arm, Primavera squired me through the portals of Kito's fortress.

'Just like the old days,' she said. I gripped her arm. In fear? To comfort? But what comfort did Primavera need? The vampire had scented blood. It was fear, my fear, that I betrayed. 'Relax,' thought Primavera, 'this is doll business. Go easy. Your job's just to make me seem human.' In embarrassment, I eased my grip.

Smiling at the bellboys, I assumed my role, and escorted my 'sister' (such had been our double act during our sojourn in the Weird) into the coffee shop's *mélange*. A year, two years ago, our act had been so disarming. We'd looked innocent; sweet. But these days—with me like a Photofit of a kid who'd escaped Borstal, and Primavera the image of a teenage parricide—the act was proving thin. Thin indeed.

'I'll take care of you,' I thought, adding over her mental sigh, 'really, I mean it.' She wasn't listening; she was trying to unravel a hundred compacted wavebands that were the babblings of human desire. *Farangs,* dreamy, or dark-faced with self-loathing, were making liaisons mad, bad and egregious with the gynoids crowding the lounge.

We squeezed past dolls nostalgic, zoomorphic, ludic: repros—ball-jointed, porcelain-skinned 'antiques'—proffering brass umbilical keys; a *Felis femella,* whose prehensile tail attempted a tourniquet about my arm; and the cephalopods, zombie dead and see-through Sallies. (For other *jeux d'esprit* the palette of the human body had moved into the realm of abstract expressionism.) There were traditional models of course: clichés of femininity microdressed in doll-couture *tropique,* who, in their Mlle Butterfly sub-tongue, offered standard conveyor-belt sex. But the *Grace's* clientele had spent too long on that nightshift; jaded, they sought the *frisson* of the new.

'Corpse grinder?' said something that seemed to have fallen from a threshing machine.

'X-ray sex?' asked a translucent Sally.

'Action painting? You want me oil? Gouache? Watercolour?' The doll's flesh began to drip onto the floor.

'Become your trousers?'

'Love suicide?'

'Sunset Boulevard?'

'Do fucky-fucky with knife?'

Several *bijouterie* were in evidence; not the real thing, but converts. For some men, to lie with one whose humanity has been compromised is the mark of the perfect rakehell; and since Thai *bijouterie* were freaks, whose rarity made their favours often impossibly expensive, there was a bull market for village girls for whom mechanization provided the only alternative to poverty. (In Nana there was a bar—*Pretty Girls Are Human Too*—full of such posthuman schismatics.)

'It'll be humans next year,' thought Primavera.

'Yeah?'

'Sure. Everything'll come full circle. Gynoids are going out of fashion. A doll may do the weird on you, but she's got no free will. A trick's got no real power over her. But a human . . . A human you can really humiliate.'

'Is that what it's about?'

'You know it.'

We approached the bar.

A pianist and a singer—doll boys *tutti frutti* to their cybercamp hearts—were performing a cocktail lounge version of 'Oh doctor, doctor, I wish you wouldn't *do* that.'

'That fucking song,' I said.

Primavera's fingers skittered across Formica. 'Hey, Pongpet!' she said, calling the barman. 'Remember me?' She lifted her shades, her eyes flashing as they emerged from eclipse.

'The green death!' The barman stepped back, dropped a Mekong soda, reached out despairingly for a com; but Primavera, her claws hooked into his shirt, had already pulled him flush against the bamboo lintel.

'I don't want to hurt you, Pong,' she said, 'but if I don't get what I want, I'll . . . Well, remember the *last* time you fixed me a Bloody Mary?'

The barman nodded with servile eagerness. I looked around; no other bar staff (no one came here to drink); and the sex talk of machine and man was unabated.

'Madame say you go home, Miss Primavera. For holiday.'

Primavera spat out her gum and secured it to the underlip of the bar. 'Pong, I want you to take us to your kitchens, your stockroom—wherever your dumbwaiter is. And I'm not talking about one of your friends.'

Keeping hold of our press-ganged accomplice, Primavera scissor-jumped the bar; I followed more modestly.

We passed through a beaded curtain and into the coffee shop's kitchen—one of several that the hotel possessed. Primavera had by now stowed her sunglasses in her bag, and the kitchen staff—a boy and girl about our own age—immediately put a table between themselves and the green-eyed fiancée of death. The boy picked up a cleaver.

'*Mai!*' cried his companion. '*Phi see kee-oh! Phi pob! Phi Angritt! Dtook-gah-dtah Lilim!*' Though we shunned the public, preferring to be as shadows amongst shadows, the legend of the green death had become part of the legend of Nana. The boy cast his weapon to the floor.

I bound our captives with a ball of spidersilk that Primavera had produced from her bag, and then gagged them with dishcloths.

'Is that it?' said Primavera, pointing to an aluminum hatchway in the wall.

'Dumbwaiter,' said the barman.

Primavera knocked him cold.

'Get in, Iggy.' She slid back the hatch. 'All these things terminate at the penthouse.'

'We can't both—'

'We can.'

'It's too small.'

'I said we *can*.' Primavera looked down the tiny ski-jump of her nose with minx-like dismissiveness. 'I may be sick,' she said, 'but I can still origami.' Tossing her bag aside, ankles together, legs parallel, knees locked, she fell forward from her waist and curled her arms about her calves, head emerging from between the vice of her thighs. She spasmed, searing the eye with anatomically impossible configurations. In seconds she was rolling across the floor, a black plastic beachball.

I picked her up—staggering at the concentrated mass—and clambered into the dumbwaiter. 'Press the button marked *K*.' Her voice was muffled by the clingwrap of her flesh. 'You'll have to reach outside.' My body, more painfully, if less dramatically contorted than Primavera's, accomplished the feat to a snap, crackle and pop of outraged joints.

The hatch slid shut; in darkness, we ascended.

Broken conversations; the blare of TVs and magazines; and the undertones of passion, bitterness and remorse, slipped by as we passed each floor. Somewhere off that tunnel of lust was the abandoned suite that for three years had sheltered us from retribution. We had never called it home.

'I can feel her,' said Primavera, no longer speaking, but transmitting from deep within her hermitage of flesh. 'She's alone. Unless there are gynoids or androids with her. *Bijouterie* I can read; but machine minds . . .'

With a hiss of air brakes we stopped.

'Are we here?' Her mind rustled with impatience.

I eased back an eye-width of hatch. We were in a kitchen similar to the one in which we had hitched our lift; but here a seven-foot Negro, wearing nothing but the heavy electromusculature of a primitive walking, talking AI, was prissily attending to the evening meal. His fire hose of a member was like a third leg amputated just above the knee.

'Android,' I said subvocally. 'Big one.' I felt Primavera grin inside my head.

'Making dinner?'

'Yeah.'

'That's Mr Bones. He's dangerous. Pull back the door and don't get involved.'

The hatch squealed on its runners; Mr Bones looked up. At once, Primavera dropped into the kitchen and bounced across the floor.

'Lordy,' cried Mr Bones, his nigger-minstrel programme seemingly a leftover from Nana's patriotic S-M revue (pirated from Broadway and premiered before the country's top brass) *The Birth of a Nation*, 'it de white lady Miss Kito bin tellin' us about!' Primavera, on bouncing off wall, ceiling and work surface, unravelled with a damp whipcrack of limbs in mid-air, to land (tottering a little on her six-inch stilettos) on the table where the giant android had been dicing meat. Mr Bones smoothed a hand across his shaven head.

'De white trash brother too,' he said, as I fell from the dumbwaiter. 'Miss Kito sure gonna be mighty upset!' A huge hand shot out; Primavera hopped to safety.

'Stay back, Iggy,' she said. Kicking off her high heels she sprang upon her opponent. Her feet found purchase on the ledge of his hip bone; her claws made hand-holds in his neck. Hanging as if from some perilous cliff face of obsidian, she bared her teeth and bit. The fangs penetrated his forehead, champing at a red mush of biochips.

Mr Bones danced about the kitchen in a clumsy rendition of a cakewalk, smoke issuing from ears, nostrils and mouth, until, freezing in midstride, he collapsed, Primavera riding him to the ground. 'Where,' groaned the android, 'are all de white women . . . ?' The brain box combusted in a flash of sparks.

'He tasted really *faecal*.' Primavera spat onto the floor. I ripped an extinguisher from a wall and gave Mr Bones a dousing.

'Somebody must have heard that,' I said.

'No; Kito's in her bedroom, and if other automata are around they're likely to be gynoids. They're not programmed for security. They might hear, but they won't care.'

'Pikadons?'

'I can't feel them. There are some guards—human guards—in the corridor outside. But I know where all the cameras are; and there'll be no closed circuit in Madame's *boudoir*.'

Primavera led me through the apartment's blind spots. A children's game, it seemed, as we ducked behind sofas, crawled behind curtains, and shuffled beneath tiger skins and Persian rugs. The lights were out; but Primavera's night vision allowed us to negotiate the obstacles with ease.

We stood outside Kito's bedroom. Primavera placed her hand on the doorknob; turned. Darkness. Primavera was past me, leaping into the void, her cat's eyes like green kryptonite streaking to Earth as she described a trajectory calculated to bring her prey to ground.

Lights.

Primavera screamed. She knelt on a heart-shaped bed and in her hands wriggled a python-sized millipede. She threw it across the room. It was *Kuhn Yow,* one of Kito's bioengineered pets. On Sundays, Kito would walk through Lumpini Park, *Kuhn Yow* trailing on a long pink leash, his bejewelled chitin scintillating in the sun.

Kito made a sarcastic *wai.* 'Good evening, children.' Replicas of Mr Bones—five in all—surrounded the bed. Each held a particle weapon. Kito tightened the sash of her peignoir and indicated that I should join Primavera. I was thinking, Well done. Thanks. I *told* you that . . . Primavera silenced me by throwing the mental equivalent of a glass of iced water in my face. Her tongue ran over her fangs; and her eyes—like those of a decadent Byzantine princess—appraised the virility of Kito's mechanical slaves. She was ready to rumble.

'I know what you think, *bijouterie,*' said Kito. 'You down one of my six-pack, only five to go. But move and I scramble your womb.'

'It's scrambled already. Cervix, ovaries, Fallopian tubes. You name it. The works. I'm sick, Madame.'

'This I know long time: so girlygirl, but—' and Kito raised an eyebrow—'so sick.'

'I mean *really* sick. Ill. Unwell. I didn't come here to hurt you.'

Kito took *Kuhn Yow* into her arms. She cuffed it; its mandibles were nipping at her breast. 'You come here to give present? Say goodbye? Eat rice?' Cheek pressed to the exoskeleton of her disgusting pet, Kito paced back and forth, taking care to stay behind her phalanx of electric blackamoors. 'Mr Jack tell me you get loose. Why you come here? Crazy. *Pasad!* Kito have many eye: TV, photo-mechanical, human . . .'

'Of course,' I began, 'Madame is a lady of dark influence. A godmother. A *chao mae* who . . .'

'Shut up, stupid boy.'

'Yeah, Iggy. Don't be so creepy.'

'Well?' said Kito. 'Why come here? You want go England so bad?'

'You still make sex diseases, Madame?' said Primavera.

Kito ceased her pacing. 'Tell you before, I stop all that after trade war with Cartier. Forty year ago . . .'

'Madame,' said Primavera, 'I know why you turned us in. I know—'

'You know *nothing,*' said Kito, 'half-doll *Angritt.* You *are* disease!'

'Yeah, well at least my Mum wasn't *roboto.*'

'Don't call *me* roboto, you little tramp!'

The exchange died. In green-eyed perplexity the two women faced off, lips feinting insults that were never thrown.

'Jack Morgenstern,' said Primavera, swallowing her gall, 'he told you that you were responsible for the doll-plague, didn't he?'

Kito blanched, her complexion achieving the pallor of a full moon on a winter's night. *Kuhn Yow* slithered to the floor.

'*Klong fever,*' continued Primavera. 'Didn't he say that's how it all began? Forty years ago Cartier Paris—getting pretty tired with the way people like you were flooding the market with imitation dolls—cooked a virus that could bridge the hardware-wetware divide. A bug that could be transmitted from machine to man. Cartier stole some of your dolls, your imitation Cartier; infected them; then returned them to the Weird. The bug was an STD, but it was also ethnically selective. It was turned on by genes peculiar to oriental DNA. *Klong fever,* the Thais called it. It made men impotent. Sort of long-term genocide *à la beau monde.* Nobody suspected the source of the virus; dolls are supposed to be disease-free. Nobody, that is, except you. You chose to retaliate. You cooked your own virus. Had it taken to Paris to infect *their* dolls. It was supposed to induce priapism, which I suppose you, Madame (you are *so* predictable), thought you could exploit. But according to Jack Morgenstern things didn't quite work out that way . . .'

'How you *know* this?' said Kito.

'About twenty-four hours ago,' said Primavera, 'I became telepathic. It's tasty. When they had me and Iggy in the embassy I dreamed . . . I dreamed of Jack Morgenstern. And I dreamed of you. Morgenstern was saying that there was no place on Earth you could hide if it got known that you started the doll-plague.'

Kito pulled a transcom from her peignoir. 'The sooner they get you back England . . .' She began punching numbers.

'Except you didn't,' said Primavera, looking at her nails.

'*American Embassy,*' piped a voice over the ISDN.

'Let me have the duty officer,' said Kito. She cupped her hand over the mouthpiece. 'What you mean?'

'I know who started the plague, madame. And it wasn't you.'

'*May I ask what it's in connection with?*'

'Put the com away. They don't have anything on you.' Kito frowned; hesitated. 'I can *prove* it.' The com died; Kito replaced it within the folds of her gown.

'I waiting,' said Kito.

'First,' said Primavera, 'you're going to have to get me cleaned up. I've been dusted.'

'No,' said Kito. 'You forget I in trouble too. With *America.* So tell me about doll-plague. What you know?'

'Madame,' said Primavera, getting to her feet; her software cousin withdrew behind Mr Bones, one through five. 'I'm sick. Really. You've got to help. In fact even now . . .' The black phalanx closed ranks.

'More reason,' said Kito, 'to do as I say. Then—*maybe.* We see.'

Primavera flopped down and lay her head in my lap. 'I'm so tired, Madame. So tired. But I'll try. I have to tell you about Iggy and me. How we got out of London. I have to tell you about Titania . . .'

CHAPTER SEVEN

Westward Ho

In the antechamber several young girls await execution. The girls, seated upon a curvilinear bench that follows the contour of the walls (one can almost feel the bench transfusing its coldness through their thin diaphanous shifts), have their eyes fixed, with dark surmise, upon the man who is walking through the door. Pupils shrink from the superfluity of light into pinpricks; lips quiver; there is a rattling of chains. The man takes a ball-point pen from his clipboard and, making a cursory tick, assists the night's first victim to her feet . . .

'It's no use,' said Dad. He had just returned from the roof. 'Doesn't matter where I point that dish, all we get is BBC.'

The girl is led down a long corridor littered with wheelchairs and stretchers. The white light is unbearable . . .

'From A to Z,' said Dad, 'from Z to A. So it will go on. Unending.' Dad put the TV to sleep. My veins clotted with anger; my heart clenched. 'Nothing for a child's eyes.'

'It's late anyway,' said Mum. 'Who'd like some Ovaltine?'

I shook my head. 'I think I'll go upstairs.'

'You haven't done your French yet,' said Dad.

'I've got a headache.'

'It's only for half an hour.'

Mum put her sewing to one side. 'You should really teach him what it means. Ignatz finds it all so boring. All he knows are the bad words the other boys use.' She left the room and went into the kitchen.

'Half an hour,' said Dad. 'Just to get me started.' He began to lower himself into the dreamscaper. A primitive model, the dreamscaper resembled a large water tank and hogged a sizeable portion of our lounge.

It had taken Dad five years to pay for it. He still couldn't afford the software. (His black market creditors were browbeating him; once again, we queued at the co-op.)

Dad sealed himself inside. 'Are you ready?' he said.

I selected the *Pléiade* edition of *À la Recherche du Temps Perdu* from Dad's autodidactic shelves. At first, before Dad had taught me to pronounce written French (no time, he'd said, for grammar or semantics) I had gone through the collected works of Charles Dickens. But Dad said that it was the past that he wanted; the world of Dickens was too much like our own. The English, Dad said, were reverting to type; John Bull growled with atavistic savagery.

What was Dad doing? He was quiet. Desperately quiet. 'You got the catheter fixed?' I said. 'And the autocerebroscope?'

'Give it five minutes, then start reading.'

I waited, scanning the incomprehensible pages. The book was something to do with the *belle époque* (a different one, I learned later, than the one Dad used to talk about); something about regaining lost time. *My time machine,* Dad called his dreamscaper.

'*Longtemps . . .*' I murmured.

'Not yet. I'm not in REM. Keep your eyes on the alpha-wave monitor.'

Time. The melancholy of memory and lost time. *Have You Seen These Girls?* asked the posters at street corners, Primavera's face amongst the wanted. Night-times, on the roof of the tower block, I had focused my telescope on the streets, on houses, on deserted faraway warehouses and factories, on anything that might have served as a hideaway for a doll. But the distances framed only the drones making their nightly supply drops from across the interdiction.

That summer had been wrought of gold. Her eyes. Her hair. Her lips. Her teeth. The golden ecstasy of her venom. But now summer had come to an end. All was lost, as Primavera was lost: to the world's baseness.

'The dolls who run away,' I said, 'do they ever get far?'

'What?'

'The dolls who run away.'

'Not now, Ignatz.'

Dreams. Maybe they were the only escape. Software dreams you could walk into as you would your own brain (or, in Dad's case, wordware dreams, realtime and analgesic). I checked Dad's alpha waves. Soon, I would begin my recital, downloading what to me might as well have been machine code into a trough for Dad's dream-hungry head. I was hungry too; Primavera had been missing for a week; I was going into withdrawal.

'*Longtemps . . .*'

After thirty minutes I left Dad to his oneironautical explorations and retired to my room.

That night I too seemed to wake in the midst of dreams. Primavera was outside the tower, twenty floors above the street, her nightdress billowing in the midnight breeze, and she was tap-tap-tapping against the window. I somnambulated across the bedroom and let her in.

'Shit, that was some climb—just look at my nails, just look at my cuticles!' She slapped me across the face. 'Wake up, pinhead!' I crossed the dividing line between sleep and consciousness to find that nothing had changed. 'Every day, in every way, I get a little bit dollier.'

I wanted to switch on the light; she caught my wrist. The amoral flippancy that animated her brittle face had drained away; she was again a child, a twelve-year-old whose brittleness was that of human vulnerability rather than that of porcelain.

'I'm cold,' she said. I put my arms about her. 'I ran away at night. I don't have any clothes.'

In her white nightdress Primavera seemed the incarnation of those bubble-gum cards we swapped in school: No. 52, *Carmilla*. An underage Carmilla. Carmilla's kid sister, perhaps. I ran my hand down her spine to where the sacrum had been trephinated to allow passage of the *tzepa*.

'Where have you been?'

'The cricket pavilion.'

'The whole week?' I could feel her bones through her flesh; what had she been living on? 'You should have come to me. I can hide you.'

'Hiding's no good. I've got to get away. You'll help me, Iggy, won't you?' I tightened my grip about her waist and went to kiss her; she turned away, transfixing the TV with a cold, serpentine stare. 'On,' she said. The TV awoke. 'Tasty trick, eh?' A broken fingernail snagged in my pyjamas. 'But how can they *do* this?'

A great circular chamber; three black marble slabs; and on each slab . . . The pictures flickered across my bedroom walls like the projections of an infernal magic lantern.

'That one there,' said Primavera, as the camera closed in to catch a subtle delineation of pain on a pale adolescent face. 'That's Anna Belushi! My God, I *know* her!' The gentlemen of the English press mobbed the dying girl: stage-door Johnnies fêting the star of death's chorus line.

'*Miss Belushi, what do you think of the HF's success?*'

'*Are your mother and father watching tonight, Miss Belushi?*'

'*Miss Belushi, how about a scream for the viewers at home?*'

Flash bulbs exploded as Anna Belushi obliged.

'She ain't *got* no Dad,' said Primavera. 'Her Mum had her at fourteen. Her Dad died a few years later, junked up on allure.' I pressed my finger into the small indentation at the base of Primavera's spine. 'Please,' she whispered. 'Don't.' I turned the TV off.

'There's nowhere to run,' I said.

'There has to be.' Her voice was an earnest tremolo. 'Lots of dolls run away. They don't find them all.'

'There's only the city. Central London. We'd be hunted down.'

She slipped the nightdress off her shoulders and let it fall to the floor. She pressed herself against me, her body's chill filtering through my pyjamas and into my muscles and veins. She took my hand and placed it on her abdomen.

'It's yours, Iggy. Prime sirloin. I give it to you.' I felt the precious throb of the abdominal aorta locked safely within its casket of mutating flesh. 'Don't throw it away. It's something to be cherished. A box of magic. A box of tricks. Everything's there. Everything in the universe. Everything that's happening. Everything that *can* happen. Look after it and it'll look after you.' She nuzzled my chest. 'Now,' she said, 'make a wish.'

'Escape,' I said.

'That was easy, wasn't it? And you still have two wishes left.'

'You know I love you.'

'You hate me,' she whispered. I felt the scratch of her fangs. 'You want me to dirty up your genes a little more?'

'Not here,' I said. 'Mum and Dad . . .'

When she had finished I took her to the roof and left her to sleep in an old pigeon coop beneath an eiderdown of canvas and straw. I returned to my room and turned on the TV. The only way to kill vampires, said the HF. Why didn't they run? They were Lilim. Nutcrackers. Why didn't they fight? Death's chorus line moonlighted in pornographic movies, bit-part actresses passively colluding in their own obscene deaths. I noted their performances, the slippery agitation of their thighs, the pelvic frenzy of their transfixed equators. I watched the red puddles swell about the un-girt hips, heard the complaints that death was too long coming. Surely I was becoming a connoisseur, an aficionado, to perceive (though not pen-etrate) even then, the conspiratorial mystery of those transmissions, a perception boys like Myshkin, I knew, could not share. How could they? Before the broken loveliness that filled our screens they could only bray, spit and pick their noses, reviling and cheapening the ache of their own flesh as much as the agony of their compliant sisters.

Sisters, poor sisters, sisters, why weren't you all like Primavera?

Monday through Friday I had sat behind an empty desk; on the Friday, the day Primavera was later to climb *Solaris Mansions* and petition me for help, a hallucination, conjured up by the hyperaesthesia of withdrawal—

an afterimage of flashing eyes and teeth—turned to confront me. 'Just look at him, that Ignatz Zwakh, always *staring.*' The girl, still human, who occupied the desk beyond Primavera's, had herself turned, curious, angry. The ghost dematerialized; I dropped my gaze and tried to refocus my eyes on my textbook.

'I am required,' said Mr Spink, 'to add to your curriculum a period devoted to . . .' He hesitated, coughed, then chalked *Vox Humana* on the blackboard. *Vox* was the BBC's television broadcast for schools, renamed by the HF. 'I must say, boys and girls, I do this . . . I do this under protest.' There was a drumming of feet. 'Stop that.' Stoppered laughter compressed the silence; I could feel the pressure against my ears. They had won, and they knew it, my companions in crime, the tyke vanguard who would be tomorrow's hell-hounds; they had won, and the mockery of peace that pinched the air seemed to unsettle Mr Spink more than if he had had to endure a barrage of giggles and hoots. 'Ak, ak, ak—all girls registered with the Hospitals may leave.' Zoe, Zika and Zarzuela (most dolls were at home, or interned) traipsed, with the fatalism of the abandoned—the self-abandoned who regard themselves as neither martyrs nor criminals, but as things—into the holding pen of the corridor, their faces quiet as my nights were unquiet, when I lay abed, thinking of Primavera. Zoe, Zika, Zarzuela—Zzz! They walked through dream palaces and dream prisons, through figments of my fragmented life: school, parks, streets, towers: a broken jigsaw rearranged into something more intense, more real than its original, a world-picture where corridors stretched to infinity, and blood was always flowing from beneath a locked bedroom door.

'The integrity, the integrity of our emotions . . . affection, abhorrence . . . may be undermined, corrupted . . .' Mr Spink was behind his desk, retreating behind a barricade of piled exercise books. The monitor above the blackboard crackled; organ music swelled; and Vlad Constantinescu— our *Conductor*—looked down on us with the gunmetal eyes of a strict but loving paterfamilias.

'*Last month, when the extermination order passed through the Lords and received royal assent, England—after years of obfuscation and muddleheadedness—at last acknowledged the evil in her midst and submitted herself to be cured. The road to national recovery is a long one, but—*'

But. The afternoon was long. Long and hot. I rested my head against the desk and turned drowsy eyes upon the window. Election leaflets, like tarred, crippled birds, fluttered across the playground, with nothing to do now, nothing to do. *Demonesses,* said Vlad. *Witches. Whores.* And he spoke of his ancestors, the spirit people who gave him his instructions, his power. Outside, small boys—on their way from one lesson to another—

had armed themselves with pieces of driftwood and were enjoying a game of war. SSSS! said one. His adversary fell, squirmed, wriggled and was still. DRRRP! said another, appropriating the forgotten glamour of lead. Bodies arched in the slo-mo 'poetry of violence' of a Hollywood bloodfest. *Vampires,* said Vlad. *Sanitization.* Unquiet nights. Gothic nights. You lay in bed (as Vlad must lie) arranging and rearranging the jigsaw of the Neverland until it sanctioned your darkest desires. But of all the universes to be called into being, why this? This puzzle mean, banal and incomplete? A world-picture that seemed to have been inspired by a zygodiddly video? I turned my head. Myshkin was looking at me, vulpine, suspicious. Wog, I thought. Rainham wog. Sexless, scummy Slav. *Métèque . . . Until London is clean. Until England is clean. Until the planet is clean. Sanity through sanitization!* The frosted glass of the door blurred to a flourish of white knee socks: Primavera's handmaidens were doing handstands against the wall. I closed my eyes. The afternoon was long. Long and hot.

The ringing of a bell, at first quiet, and deep within my skull, grew, quit its muffling, sang along the soundbox of my desk, to be joined by sounds of shrieking chairs, the cruel laughter of children. I sat up. The classroom had emptied. Only Mr Spink remained, in thrall to the hypnotic power of unmarked school books. The monitor hummed. Zoe, Zika and Zarzuela stood hesitantly at the door. 'Can we get our things, sir?' Mr Spink gave a nod of indifference. Avoiding my eyes, the three girls collected their books; Zoe and Zika left, but Zarzuela had her head buried inside her desk, a disaster zone of comics and discarded make-up. With blackbird-sheeny locks, her metamorphosis was more advanced than Primavera's, though her two-tone eyes indicated that it was far from over.

'Ignatz?' she whispered. Mr Spink hadn't moved. I got up and walked to where she sat, pretending to study the wall display behind her.

'What?'

'Have you seen Primavera?'

'No—should I have?'

'Oh, c'mon. I *know* about you two.'

'I haven't seen her—I haven't seen her all week.'

'I haven't seen her since we all went to the Hospitals to have that operation. *Savez-vous?* Where they take that little piece of bone from the small of your back.'

'I haven't seen her.'

'If you do—' I kept my eyes on the display, a 'Rise and Fall of the Empire *De Luxe*'. Cartoons depicted the creation of the dolls, their glorious lives, their fall. The narrative began with *Europa* at the height of her power, showering *joaillerie, objets* and *couture* upon her children. The following panels dealt with the ultimate *de luxe* status symbols, the automata. A doll was shown rising from her vat like a clockwork Venus rising from a chemical sea. The rubric quoted Christian Blanckaert, managing director of the Comité Colbert: 'Luxury is for France what electronics is for Japan . . .' The last cartoons in the sequence concerned Europe's decline: *Europa* swooning, in economic disarray, forsaken by Taste, raped by Third World technobandits, and witnessing the outbreak of the doll-plague, helpless. 'I know they're looking for her . . . I know she must be frightened, but . . .' Zarzuela rose, clutching her books to her chest. 'Tell her to come home. There's no use fighting it. We have to take our medicine. I only hope that when I'm called I . . . Tell her. She was my friend. I don't want to die alone . . .' She turned to leave. 'Nadia was on TV last night. Nadia Polanski? She was—she was lovely.'

I killed the sound; the screaming had grown too loud. Just the bad girls, Vlad had said. The thirsty ones. The teases. The flirts. The *provocateurs.* But they were interning more and more; and all that they interned, they impaled. They would impale them all. Some said it was being done alphabetically, by name; others said that a computer selected victims at random. A kind of lottery. *Form a queue, please. No pushing. Keep it moving there at the back!* So few ran; so many waited. So very English. The dark heart of England belonged to death. A waxen face, polka-dotted with sweat and veiled in lank black hair, rested upon the slab, teeth snared in the links of a chain that passed through the bloodied mouth. *The white light . . .* Across the country, in homes, pubs, on street corners and in railway stations, Anna Belushi's slain innocence fed the nation's sexual rage.

I had the weekend to make arrangements for our departure.

We fled through the disused tube tunnels that led to the West End. Going underground at Stratford (a stolen motorbike had facilitated our overland trip), we travelled the flooded tunnels in a small dinghy—little more than a child's toy—for which I had bartered my telescope. The tunnels were hot and airless. Rats scuttled under the enquiring eye of my torch.

What would my classmates say? The rumours of my friendship with a doll had been enough to earn me contempt; confirmation of these rumours (I would be denounced at morning assembly) would earn me lifelong ostracism. Dollstruck, they'd say. I had become an outcast. Yet if I was caught what had I to fear apart from remand? Sterilization, perhaps. A daily beating from medicine-heads like the Myshkins. But if they caught Primavera . . . No. No. I dug my paddle into the underground stream and thought only of descrying the station names through the brutal intimacy of the dark.

Bond Street. I swept my torch across the platform and glimpsed a watery tomb of sweet machines, mildewy tube maps and hoardings. One poster—it advertised 'Skin II', dermaplastic's pret-à-porter derivative—displayed the aerosoled symbol of the Human Front. Sinking our inflatable, we waded knee-deep through sludge.

'There's no going back now,' I said.

'Promises, promises,' said Primavera. She clung tightly to my sleeve, the greening of the eyes that is concomitant with night vision still in her incomplete. The torch illuminated a stairwell. Glad to drag our feet from the effluent, we began our ascent.

'Turn the light off,' said Primavera.

'But—'

'There might be something up there, *stupid*!'

I switched off the torch, hooked it through my belt, and drew my scalpel. We climbed through darkness until I lifted a foot to find nothing beneath it but a horizontal steel plane.

'I'll have to switch it on. I can't see a thing.' Panning the torch through one-hundred-and-eighty degrees I saw we stood at the edge of a flood-wrecked concourse off which ran paralysed escalators.

'Now turn it off,' said Primavera. 'Please.'

We groped our way to the surface.

'Smell it?' said Primavera. 'It's wild.'

'It's West,' I said. Wind gusted across my face, wafting an overture of ruin and decay. Beyond mangled steel gates the abandoned star-haunted streets awaited us.

I removed my backpack and handed Primavera a towel and some spare clothes. We both stripped, changing from our school uniforms (Primavera had worn my old junior school outfit) into jeans, sweaters and anoraks. I stowed our old clothes behind a ticket machine.

'Come on,' said Primavera, striding into the night, 'let's find somewhere to sleep.'

I dawdled, looking back into the darkness of the tunnels. Mum and Dad, I thought, what will you say when morning comes? Can you ever forgive me? Will I see you again? I thought of the note I had left, full of crossings-out, verbal squirming and adolescent rhetoric.

'I said, come *on*, Iggy!' I turned to follow, leaving behind my human past. A past I tried to think of as well-lost.

Bond Street was a desert of broken glass and gutted shopfronts, a desecrated memorial to the *belle époque*. Primavera rescued some tattered couture from the gutter. She held it up, gauging its appeal.

'Hey, this is really *nice*. I could do something with this.' She looked about in wonder. 'All these shops. *S Laurent. Gaultier. Ungaro . . .*'

I imagined Bond Street restored: an emporium of delights, a wardrobe in which I might dress my dolly, the fetishistic Miss P. I would dress her up in tutus and trenchcoats, bias-cut leather, mock-croc underwear and la-la hose; I would dress her down in thigh boots, pink mink battletops, chain, pain and neurotic alleycat skirts. A mean lady of means; a mean machine of the streets . . .

I got out the street map. This was the other London, a city of midnight and daytime nocturne; the place they said our shadows came to when they tired of us. 'According to this, Bond Street leads into Piccadilly.'

'Let's stay here,' she said, folding up her Cinderella gown, 'it's sort of . . . *romantic*.'

A splintering of glass.

'What was that?'

'Shh!' I said. All seemed quiet. A dog, I thought. A cat. A rat. 'We'd better get inside.'

We stepped through the blown-out window of *Ungaro* and climbed the charred stairs. Ungaro, Dad said, had been the first couturier to use automata on the catwalks, and the first-floor office contained several dismembered, ravished examples of those early AIs.

'So these are my ancestors,' said Primavera.

'No more than mine are apes.'

She picked up the head of a former male model. 'Not bad,' she said.

'Be careful of battery acid.' She threw the head back amongst the charnel house of spare parts.

'Not much here, is there?' she said. Dermaplastic dresses, yellowing, crinkled, were strewn across the floor like the sloughed-off skins of ancient women; amongst them, faded Polaroids (close-ups of bejewelled navels) and a poster advertising *Virgin Martyr* (beneath a crucified Negress a party of dinner-jacketed men rolled dice for a scent bottle; the cross's titulus read *La Reine des Parfums*).

'We'll look for somewhere else in the morning,' I said.

'At least I get to lose the frump-suit.' She pulled off her jeans and sweater. 'It's one of his,' she said, looking at the label of the frock she had recovered from the street. 'Ungaro.' She drew the frock over her head. Black and scarlet, with comic-strip burglar stripes about the top, a strict belted zone, and a split running from hem to waist (by design or by violence?), the frock—cut for a woman's figure—hung loosely from Primavera's budding curves. I had seen this look in some of Mum's old fashion magazines. It was called *apache*.

'It's dead,' said Primavera.

'Never mind. One day I'll buy you some dermaplastic that's really chichi.'

I walked to the curtainless window; the moon was waning, the streets dark. 'My Dad used to work here.'

'Your *Dad*?'

'He was a janitor. Used to look after lots of these shops. Before I was born, that is. During the *aube du millénaire*. Dad said it was a decent world, then. Decent. "You won't know what that means, Ignatz. Not your fault. We've murdered decency as surely as we've murdered our own children. Thank God we only have you." Dad always used to talk about things like that. The death of decency, love, truth and the rest. But the last few years . . . He never talks now. Not unless he can help it. He just dreams and leaves everything to Mum. But when he does talk . . .' I wiped my hand across the window and studied the grime on my palm. 'I never thought they'd win, you know. The Human Front. I can't believe what's happening. But Dad says it was always there: a malign potency, a rottenness, a horror beneath the surface. Even during the *aube du millénaire* Dad says it was there, just waiting to eat us up.'

'You should be thinking about what *we're* going to eat.'

Below, the fabled ruins of Londontown, a bag-of-bones, starved and alone, offered us a dubious sanctuary. Punk-Dickensian, those streets. Their shadows had almost defeated us. But a doll's fledgling magic (Primavera's navigation had been uncanny) had saved us from being marooned as we biked westwards. Nearer now, the sound of breaking glass, and a dull inhuman howl of pain. Somewhere, Never-Never Kids were ransacking the heartland of their prison. Drones hovered above the rooftops. The military observed; it did not intervene. What did they care for a dispossessed people? Proles, Yahoos, Morlocks: outcasts for whom only the anthropocentric jingoism of the Human Front seemed to offer hope? What did they care for our dance of death? Again, that howl.

'Dog?'

'I am *not* going to eat dog.'

'Me?'

'Better.'

'We have to be inventive. Like the Swiss Family Robinson. We have to—'

'Dog's off.'

'But—' Her arms encircled me from behind; I felt her nose, her lips, between my shoulder blades as one feels the conciliations of a chastised pet. 'Right,' I said. 'Dog's off.' She poked her head through my armpit.

'The stars,' she said. 'Alone beneath the stars. Poor Primavera. Poor Iggy.'

'The stars can't help.'

'Once people thought there was life out there. *We are not alone,* they said.'

I laughed. 'The stars are dead.' She slithered between ribs and arm to a popping electrostatic accompaniment—the corpse of her dress, along with her own flesh, sparking like charged nylon—and realigned her body so that we made a one-backed beast, her rump pressed negligently against my groin. I put my hands over the half-rations of her breasts.

'When the world goes porcelain,' she said, 'when everything's snuffed, the stars'll still be around. But they won't cry.'

'Everything doesn't *have* to get snuffed. There's contraception. Sterilization. Abortion. That's the way they handled things in France. The "Lost Generation" they called it. I never understand why the Neverlanders—'

'They're in love, Iggy. In love with pain and death. Just like you. Only they don't know it.'

'They don't want to know.'

'Yeah. They just want to work in the doll factory. They just want to make *us.* The end of the world—what a lark! What a game!'

'A game of war. Like I used to play with Myshkin and Beria.'

'SSSS! POW!'

'Wars forgotten. Wars fictive.'

'The Gulf. Antarctica. Oroonoko. Mars.'

'Dying—'

'DRRRP!'

'They liked it. We all liked it, those glorious deaths . . .'

'Ah, Iggy, they got me!'

'They got me too—Ugh!'

Primavera bucked, and the dead flesh of her bustier grew gooey. 'Oh Iggy,' she said, 'you nasty, *nasty* boy!' I thought of the last time we had played the sex-game, when I had thought she would swallow my tongue (you ever jog barefoot in Needle Park?); behind my eyes, the faces of Myshkin and Beria were superimposed over Primavera's, faces wide-eyed, shock-stunned, rejoicing beneath the imaginary fusillade from my toy carbine (lasers were scuzzy; nobody used them in those old videos we borrowed from Myshkin's Dad); my friends fell squirming to the ground. Primavera relaxed, drooped, began to slip from my grasp. 'Let's not talk,' she said. 'Please?' She pulled me down onto a soft fleshy bed of couture; not to feed (her appetite had been lost to exhaustion), but to sleep. She crumpled, cheek against my thigh. *Not one little bite? How can you leave me like this?* So restless was I with desire that for a long time Primavera slept alone. I thought of Mum's fairy tales. *The Transylvanian Princess.*

Bad King Wenceslas. The Cat People of Prague. Martina von Kleinkunst Gets Spayed. No, no; that wasn't right. Then I must have begun to dream, for I seemed to be at some kind of fashion show with everybody calling me Monsieur, Monsieur! Monsieur Ungaro! Primavera wore her hair in an elaborate coiffure; she modelled a gown of bloodshot red. Red, too, her jewellery (so Martian), her gloves and slippers. The whole affair seemed to have been shot through a lens smeared with blood-red glycerine . . .

'Iggy?' I snapped awake. 'There's someone downstairs.'

'Probably a dog,' I said. 'Go back to sleep.'

'But what if . . . There—did you hear that?'

In those days (before I learned better) I sometimes played the Big Man. 'I'll check it out.' Arming myself with the limb of a quartered automaton, I descended into the darkness. I pulled the torch from my belt; pointed it, my thumb easing back its switch. Then: twanging elastic; horrible pain; someone opening (it seemed) a door for me (thank you); and the darkness became absolute.

The door reopened. The world had turned red. But this was no fashion show. No dream. Before me was a raging bonfire; above the flames, a winged boy with a bow and arrow. Boys—of the mortal variety (and some girls too), their heads shaved, and wearing medicine-head apparel— were dancing about a diddly-blaster and swigging from bottles of beer. I was propped against street railings, my hands tied to the iron bars. I blinked, trying to clear my eyes of blood; but the red ink in which the world had been dipped was indelible.

'So much for your brilliant plans,' said Primavera. I screwed my head in the direction of her voice. 'Down here,' she said. Primavera lay in a basement courtyard. She was also tied; not with rope, like me, but with an escapologist's nightmare of chain. 'You see the bedsteads?'

About the bonfire, familiarly arranged, the twisted frames of impro- vised death machines stood ready for their nightly ritual, thin metal spikes emerging from the pavement and protruding through their rusted springs.

'It's no good. I'm just a little doll. I can't break these chains.' I think I started to cry. 'Shut up, Iggy, and think of something!'

'Captain!' shouted a medicine-head. 'Captain Valiant! The pride of London! Over here, over here!'

A bicycle-drawn soapbox cart materialized from out of the blood-red cityscape. It would have reminded my future self of a trishaw.

'We got one!' someone yelled above the hoopla. 'We got a *belly*! Come and see!'

The cart halted, and a tall man in hand-me-down surgeon's garb stepped onto the street. His chauffeur, dismounting, proffered a walking cane. The cane clacked against kerbstone. The Captain was blind.

'One?' said Captain Valiant, petulantly, his voice straining against the uproar of the fire. He was older than his confederates; in his mid-twenties, perhaps; an anachronism in a city where fewer and fewer cleared the hurdle between adolescence and maturity. 'London is full of belly and you can only find *one*?'

The medicine-heads studied their feet, kicked at tinder and scrap. 'Jesus, Captain, belly's dangerous. Last week they got Bobbo. And Danny's lost an arm.'

'Where,' said the Captain, dark glasses aflame, so he seemed like a hungover jackal, '*is* the belly?'

A boy stepped forward (a catapult mounted with an infrared sight stuck from out of his belt) and took the Captain's arm, leading him across the street.

'Belly?' enquired the Captain, tapping his cane upon the rails.

'Leave her alone,' I said. 'You've got no right. You're not from the Hospitals. I'll tell—'

'Who is this pathetic boy?'

'He was with her,' said the Captain's eyes. 'Doll junkie. Addict.'

'Ah,' said the Captain. He reached out and, after wrestling with the air, got a grip about my throat. 'You know what you are? A traitor. A stinking traitor to your race. She's inside you. Can't you feel her? Creeping around inside your cells. Filthy, filthy, filthy.'

'If you hurt him I'll take your face off,' Primavera shouted. She swore in Serbo-Croat.

The Captain hissed. 'I can smell it from here. The belly. Corrupt. Malignant. It must be sanitized. Put to the spike. It must have its moment of truth.' He spat through the railings. 'How did you take her?'

'She's young,' said the eyes. 'Still in metamorphosis. Didn't need the magic dust. She's—she's just a kid.'

'Stop,' said the Captain, 'you're making me weep.' He wiped his cane across the railings in an ugly glissando. 'What brave soldiers I have! I've told you before: I want dolls, real dolls. Three green-eyed bitches a night. They must learn to take their medicine. But most of all I want the Big Sister. I want Titania, spiked and at my feet!'

The Captain froze; spun about. His cane fell to the ground. 'My God— look!' He pointed to one of the nearby streets where, half concealed in shadows, a big black car had parked, its engine still running. He put his hands to his face; covered his eyes; uncovered them. 'I can see,' he said. He tore off his glasses and simpered like a village idiot. 'Surrender my loins to a shark-toothed fellatrix—I can see!'

And then Captain Valiant burst into flames.

'Iggy, what's happening?'

The Captain ran into the street, clawed at his gown, dropped to the asphalt, and rolled over, again and again, screaming, 'It's her! Get her! It's her! It's her!' But his impaling party had dispersed, vanishing into the night; and soon he too was gone, his body a smouldering ruin beneath the pyre of the winged boy-god of love.

'Iggy!'

'I don't know—I don't know what's happening!'

The black car. I recognized its make. It was an antique. A Bentley. A girl, dressed in leathers and a peaked cap, stepped from the driver's seat and approached us. Her eyes burned green, and the opalescence of her flesh, like a highly polished mirror, reflected the tower of flames, so she seemed a translucent cast brimming with molten bronze. She stood over me, sneering. A snap of fingers; the sound of chain falling to the ground.

Cat-like, Primavera scaled her prison's walls and hauled herself onto the pavement. She busied herself with untying my bonds, one eye on our rescuer.

'Who is this human trash?' said the newcomer.

'This is Iggy. My boyfriend. You're not to talk about him like that.'

The doll yawned. 'Oh dear. You *are* a baby, aren't you. Your friend can find his own way home. It's you our mistress wants to see.' The doll turned and walked back to the car.

'We both come,' said Primavera, 'or not at all.'

'Mmm. I suppose part of you still thinks it's human. I almost remember being like that myself. Okay, baby. Bring him along. For the time being that is. She might be amused.'

'And who's *she*?' I said.

'The queen, of course,' said our saviour. 'The Queen of Dolls.'

As we approached the car a door opened. In the corner of the back seat a girl in her early teens—our chaperone, presumably—huddled beneath a wrap of grey fox fur. A box of chocolates was on her lap.

'Hi,' she said. 'I'm Josephine. Call me Jo.' Primavera and I climbed in beside her. 'Don't worry,' said Jo, 'you're safe with us.' The car stalled, performed a series of kangaroo leaps, and then lurched into the night.

'Where are we going?' I asked.

'To the East End,' said Jo. 'To the palace of the dolls. Please . . .' She offered Primavera a chocolate. Primavera bit down; a dark red juice flowed over her hands, between her fingers, and down her wrists.

'Blood?' whispered Primavera.

'The real thing,' said Jo. 'Where we're going everybody lives happily ever after.' Jo looked at me askance, dabbing at her lips with a tissue. 'Well, nearly everybody.'

Primavera licked her fingers and wound down the window. 'This is the

Strand,' said Jo, 'and soon we'll be in the City. See those fires over there?' She pointed down a side street. 'More paramedical scum. Every night Titania sends one of us out on patrol to see if we can pick up any runaways before they do.'

'Did *you* set that man alight?' said Primavera.

'Sure. You'll be able to do things like that soon.'

'All I can do now,' said Primavera, 'is turn on TVs. I say *On*.'

'When your hair turns black and your eyes go green you'll be able to do *anything*.'

'Only Titania,' said our driver, 'can do anything. The rest of us have to be content with working a few tricks.'

Jo seemed a little abashed at her *lèse-majesté*. 'That's what I meant,' she said. 'You'll be able to do *tricks*. Of course only Titania can do *anything*.'

We sped through the silent streets of the City; silent too, my back-seat companions, consumed by the task of devouring their sweets.

'Titania,' I said, after their bloody feast was through. 'Is she a doll?'

'Of course she's a doll,' said Jo. 'But not like us. She wasn't born; she was made. She's an original Cartier automaton. The last of the Big Sisters. She's—'

'She's my mother,' interrupted Primavera, startled but infinitely satisfied by this sudden insight. 'My real mother.'

'Only Lilith,' said Jo, 'is that.'

We drove through an empty concrete wilderness that might have been twinned with Troy, Carthage or Pompeii; all about us were the lineaments of greatness soiled by sudden defeat.

'Whitechapel,' informed our driver. 'Brick Lane.'

Whitechapel. That was where Mum and Dad lived when they first came to England. Jumping the kerb to avoid a burned-out car, the Bentley swung into a warehouse.

We got out, Jo leading us across an oil-stained expanse littered with automobilia—the sort of place grease monkeys dream of going to when they die—to where a rusted samovar stood. There, bending over, she grasped an iron ring set in the floor, and pulled. A trap opened.

Beneath our feet, a spiral staircase unwound into infinity; a plume of green light rose from the depths, casting a halo upon the warehouse's roof.

'Down we go,' said our escort.

CHAPTER EIGHT

A Fairy Queen

Primavera screamed, curling up into a foetal ball.

'What is it?' said Kito.

'She told you before.' I put an arm about Primavera's waist, easing her into a sitting position. 'She's sick. There's a batch of nanomachines inside her, and they're tearing her matrix to pieces.'

Kito wriggled through the pillars of her bodyguards. 'This Titania,' she said, 'she know about doll-plague?' She raised a hand as if to demonstrate to her Schéhérazade the consequence of not resuming her tale; but before Kito could strike, Primavera fell forward, her body limp.

'She's passed out,' I said. 'We have to get one of your engineers to look at her. Now!'

Kito ran her hand over her matronly hips. 'Maybe this all big bluff, *Mr Ignatz?*'

'Listen,' I said, 'if she doesn't get help soon you'll never know the truth. The Americans are going to jerk you around from now until fucking nirvana. And for you that'll be a long time.' I gathered Primavera into my arms. 'Can't you see—she's sick. Really sick.'

Kito looked sick. A *chao mae* is unused to taking orders. But Kito was too clever to be ruled by pride now that her situation had become so desperate.

'Mr Bones number two,' said Kito, 'take friend to private elevator.'

Slinging Primavera over my shoulder, I followed the android through the still darkened apartment; Kito was behind me, arms folded across her small, nonfunctional breasts.

'Don't worry,' she said—I was looking at a camera—'I see no one disturb.'

The elevator took us to the roof.

'New R and D man live here,' said Kito.

We were in a hydroponic garden, the scent of night blooms counterpointing the malodour of the streets.

'Spalanzani,' called Kito, 'where are you, you old fool?'

'Madame?' An elderly man emerged from behind a gazebo, a spray of opium poppies in his hand.

'I have *bijouterie* here I want you to look at.'

The nanoengineer chose a buttonhole, fixed it to his lapel, and walked over to us. 'Is there some dysfunction?' Walking behind me, he took Primavera by the hair and lifted her head for inspection. 'Lilim! *Oh sogno d'or!*' Relenting of his caddishness he cradled her head in his hands. 'Forgive! Forgive! *Mia belta funesta!* I have never seen one such as she before.'

'She's taken a dose of magic dust,' I said. 'She needs cleaning.'

He sighed, pulled out a pair of pince-nez (a common affectation amongst automaton makers) and began probing Primavera's face.

'Take your hands off her,' I said. He stepped back; Primavera again hung limply from my shoulder.

'Please. I want to help. Lilim! I cannot believe. Oh, such marvellous toy! From series *L'Eve Future*. Yes. Let me help her. Let me take a little peep inside!' In the centre of the garden stood a black dome. 'My workshop,' he said. 'Come, come!' He ran before us, stripping off his gardening overalls as a segment of the dome opened obediently at his approach.

Inside, the dome combined the elements of operating theatre, chemical plant and mortuary. Beneath its apex was a rectangular marble slab, about which were arrayed computers, a scanning tunnelling microscope, lasers and a stainless-steel cabinet crammed with surgical tools. Vats lined the dome's perimeter, each one containing a protodoll; above, in a series of racked drawers, several of which were open, the decanted, successes and failures, slept their undead sleep. In contrast with the dome's exterior, everything within—with the exception of the black marble slab—gleamed with clinical whiteness. Mr Bones squatted on all fours, providing his mistress with a seat.

'Put her down,' said Spalanzani. I carefully laid Primavera out on the slab. 'And help me get this dermaplastic off.' He handed me a pair of surgical scissors. Soon Primavera was naked, her pallid lines thrown into relief by the cold stone bed.

Spalanzani picked up a jeweller's loupe and applied his eye to Primavera's umbilicus.

'The navel of the world,' he said, 'the centre of everything. And of nothing. The wormhole of lunacy! Ah yes, descended from *L'Eve Future*, but what mutations. What exotica!'

He stepped to one side to allow a bar of light to run over his patient from head to toes; a hologram materialized in mid-air. Fleshless, a glittering schema of veins, bones and plastic, the hologram turned, revolving on its axis, displaying itself like a see-through Sally before the eyes of a prurient clientele.

'Most fascinating,' he said. 'Living tissue has adopted the structure of polymers and resins, metals and fibres. It is difficult to perceive in what sense she is actually alive.'

'Dead girls,' I said. 'They call them dead girls. Primavera's DNA has recombined.'

'I don't think we'd find DNA in *this*,' he said, his finger jabbing the hologram's thigh. 'Recombined? The entire body chemistry has been altered, reorganized at the atomic level. Mechanized, you might say. By every definition I can think of she *is* dead.' His finger moved to the hologram's belly. 'This, I suppose, is what gives her life. Animation, at least. The sub-atomic matrix. I read about it in *Scientific American*.' He poked at a ball of green fire that swirled with op-art geometries; chaoses that teased with intimations of order; finitudes that knew no bounds. 'The matrix,' he said, picking up a syringe, 'is where our trouble lies.'

I put my hand on his wrist. 'What's in that?'

'I want—with your permission—to inject a remote.'

'You don't need his permission,' said Kito.

'Please,' he said, 'I must see what is happening in there.' I released my hand.

The needle pricked the taut flesh, emptying a clear solution into Primavera's belly. 'Good girl,' he said, his hand lingering a little too long, I thought, on his patient's abdominal wall. 'That didn't hurt, did it?' He sat down at a keyboard; a monitor lit up, and fractals, in vortices of green, loomed from the screen's vanishing point, like abstract representations of unresolved crescendos, the music of unrequited desire. I tottered forward, those shifting geometries threatening to suck me into some terrible fastness of space and time.

Freezeframe; the germination ceased, and I was pitched forward by my vertigo's inertia.

'The dust,' he said. 'It is carrying an anti-fractal programme that is infecting the matrix with Euclidean imperatives.'

He turned from the monitor, wiped his pince-nez on his sleeve, and sighed. 'At the heart of the matrix lies her source of being. Space-time foam. Ylem. The nanomachines will replicate smaller and smaller until that singularity is breached. And then she will fall victim to the laws of the classical universe. She will . . . He was genius, that Toxicophilous. My own toys . . .' He nodded towards the gestation vats. 'I still work from the periodic table and aborted foetuses. Cheaper, of course. That's all they care about out here.' A printer hummed; he tore off the print-out and scanned it.

'As far as I've ever been able to understand, *L'Eve Future,* and their descendants, the Lilim, retain in themselves a model of the quantum field, a model of creation, a bridge, if you like, between this world and the mind of God. And now it seems that bridge is burning.'

'And if it falls?' I said.

'She'll lose her power. In England, of course, it is what they do to automata before . . .' His face reddened. 'Forgive. I forget, I forget. Barbarous. Barbarous! I want to help. Believe, please! Now tell: has the young lady been able to work . . . *magic?*'

'She's been getting weaker ever since she was dusted. Except—except she can read minds. She couldn't do that before.'

'A temporary side effect, I would think. Compensation, like the aural acuteness of the blind.'

'But you can clean her up?'

'The dust is not of a type I have previously encountered.' He slapped me on the back. 'But yes, yes, I dare say, I *will* say. We cannot have the marvellous toy suffer!' He signed off from his workstation; the hologram vanished. 'Poof!' he said. 'Just like we make the little robots in the matrix do.'

'Before you make Poof!' said Kito, who was lounging across her Nubian slave like a torch singer across a Steinway, 'I want Mr Ignatz tell me about doll-plague.'

'After,' I said. 'There might not be much time.'

'It is true,' said Spalanzani. 'The dust makes weak, but then comes serious dysfunction. Her body will run only fractal software. And that software is being corrupted.'

Kito dug her nails into ebony electromuscle. 'Shut up, toymaker, you want make sex machine for me or you want go back Europe?' Spalanzani's mouth curled into a nervous, placatory smile. 'And you,' she continued, 'little English brat addicted to vampire kisses—you do as I say or Miss Primavera go way of all silicon. I must know. I must know what start doll-plague. I must have America off my back!'

The monitor still seemed to glow with a spectral after-image: snowflakes, green snowflakes, patterns within patterns, geometries enfolding mind and matter, space and time, in a model of reality's infinite permutations.

It was the fount of all allure.

The *Seven Stars* was an embodiment of that allure. The Daedalean corridors, dizzy stairwells and impossible perspectives imitated the topography of a recombinant mind; a mind that is catastrophic, illusory, false. A celebration of surface and plane, of the paradoxes of line, the *Stars* might have been the result of an architectural collaboration between Piranesi, Escher and a fairground tycoon who dreamed of combining a crooked house with a hall of mirrors and a maze. It was an underground palace, a bejewelled goblin city, stocked with the abandoned luxuries of London's *beau monde*. In its catacombs slept a thousand dead girls.

'Titania built the *Stars* in six months,' said Jo, her outsized fox fur dragging across the chequerboard tiles. 'Before my time, of course. But they say the dolls in those days would wake up each morning to discover another room, a hallway, a stairwell where there had been none before.'

The passageways were suffused with a sourceless green light. At the beginning of our journey the walls had been plain, but now, as we progressed (I do not know how far; the labyrinth twisted, fell, doubled back, fell again), we passed frescoes mirroring the barrenness of our path, a parallel world, pointless and sterile, which absented us and refused to echo our tread. And then the light, deepening as if diffused by rainforest, filled a long corridor lined with doors, some two-dimensional, painted, some, it seemed, real. (I saw one open, and, fractionally ajar, betray a green eye framed by a slit of darkness.) Deepening, darkening; we tumbled down stairwells, the greenness matching our descent exponentially, until that light presented the illusion of obscuring more than it revealed— an unknown face, rearing from the gross illumination, appeared to flicker once, twice, then vanish, to leave only a trace of perfume, electric and sharp. We were in some sub-sub-sub-basement, the crypt of the world, when the walls began to curve, making my eyes itch for resolution. Doors. More doors. One was off its jambs; beyond it, a stark bedroom, empty but for a vanity table and a wrought-iron bed (beneath the bed lay a slipper, its long, slim heel broken and hanging off), a room that called silently, insistently for the overthrow of small pleasures. A hairpin bend, and the passageway, like a green rainbow, ended at a portal of beaten gold: doors that might have guarded Belshazzar's banqueting hall. That face again, rearing out of the corner of my eye, then vanishing, the words 'Oh party time!' left in the air along with the memory of that electric scent. Jo the Psychopomp was putting her shoulder to the doors, and they were opening, moaning; other faces, sister faces, leered through the crack, and music, tough-cookie music, was making the air dance like a mist of febrile green midges.

'Primavera, I don't like this. I feel sick. I want, I want to—'

'Shut up, Iggy. You're not sick. Open your eyes. It's happening, don't you know? At last. It's real. It's true. It's what I've always dreamed of.'

The ballroom was a dragon's lair of shop-soiled furnishings and moth-eaten tapestries and drapes, chiefly in the *nouveau* and *deco* styles popular during the *aube du millénaire*. A group of revellers—dolls in flea-market masquerade costumes (looted from London's uptown wrack)—were performing a courtly dance to the unlikely accompaniment of saxophone and blue-note piano. Where was the music coming from? From the air, it seemed: a sort of jazz of the spheres.

Arranged in a five-pointed star, holding each other at arm's length, the dolls marched clockwise, then, completing a revolution, anti-clockwise, their satin-shod feet shuffling across the boards like superfine sandpaper. Other masked dolls, similarly attired in raggedy ballgowns, leaned against walls or reclined in alcoves, idly fanning themselves with spread lunettes of paper and ivory, overwound, it seemed, with a tensility that at any moment might snap. Beyond the wallflowers, beyond the dancers, was a dais on which sat, enthroned, a girl who seemed little older than Primavera. She was crowned with seven stars, and at her side sat a thin pale-faced man. The girl flicked open a fan and waved to us.

'Come,' said Jo, 'Titania has granted you an audience.' We threaded our way through the revolving pentacle of masquers until we stood before the dais. Jo curtsied. 'Your majesty, we have two guests. Miss Primavera Bobinski and . . . a boy.'

The child queen leaned forward in a rustle of flounces, bows and panniers, and addressed us from behind a sequinned mask. 'The boy has a name?' Her voice was like the flutings of a mechanical bird.

'Ignatz,' said Primavera, flashing an uncertain smile, 'your majesty,' and added, with a vulgar enthusiasm which must have flouted court etiquette, 'Are you really a Big Sister? An original Cartier doll? I thought they were all destroyed. And can you do anything—I mean really *anything?*'

Jo coughed apologetically. 'She's still metamorphosing, your majesty.'

'Yes,' said Titania, 'I understand.' She rose from her throne and descended the dais, her gown a conspiracy of whispers. Titania was unlike any Lilim I had seen. Her hair, a smouldering charcoal black, and the cat-like eyes (Cartier nanoengineers had revived Jeanne Toussaint's panther jewellery designs of the 1930s) were typical of the subspecies; but I had never encountered any doll who so embodied the spirit of artificiality, so qualified as Nature's foe. She stood before us, and her gown, red as a lascivious wound, fell silent. She smiled (her teeth seemed oddly blunt), and raised a taloned hand to Primavera's cheek. 'Don't worry,' she said, 'you'll soon lose those mongrel looks. Now come to my study. There's something I want you to hear. Something all my guests hear before I ask them whether they wish to swear allegiance. And if you do so wish, then I shall tell you the secret. The greatest secret of all . . .'

The two girls walked across the dance floor, Titania a little stiffly, I thought, a clumsy schoolgirl slightly ridiculous in the extravagance of her Madame Pompadour gown. 'You can come too, human boy,' said Titania, adding to her charge, 'Boys have their uses, of course.'

A wallflower, one leg hooked over the arm of her chair, called out, 'Nice dress.'

'Thank you,' said Primavera. 'It's Ungaro.'

A girl (fifteen? sixteen? with mad fairies drowning in the absinthe of her eyes) blocked my path. The upper part of her ensemble—a meat-red corselet woven from 'Skin II'—resembled the flayed torso of a Sadeian heroine. 'Dance with me,' she said. Saliva dribbled from the side of her mouth, onto her chin, and then, her breasts.

'I don't know how,' I said. Piqued, she sidled away.

'Sexual delinquent,' said Jo. 'Crazy automaton! Titania tries to invest her life with meaning, and what does she do? Dance, dance, dance! I tell you that doll's burning out . . .'

The man who had shared the dais with Titania gazed down at the pentacle of masquers as he had done throughout our brief audience with his queen, bored, stupefied, unseeing. 'Who is he?' I whispered to Jo.

'That's Peter. He's brain dead. Titania's sucked him dry. You'll be like that'—she gave no hint of mockery—'in ten years. If you're not dead before. Still, plenty of time to make *babies*. Babies that'll turn into dolls. And that's all that matters, mmm?'

A crowd gathered, a crowd of wax faces stained green by the palace's hermetically generated light; muslin, silk, taffeta, lace swept past; I felt myself pushed, pinched, tickled; the crowd swelled, then withdrew, giggling; Jo was carried away by its riptide.

Titania and Primavera were leaving the ballroom; I ran after them, skidding across the polished wooden floor.

The adjoining hallway (we left by a route different from that by which we had entered) was lined with mirrors and *trompe l'oeil*, and I found myself lied to by false columns and perspectives. Swaying from wall to wall as if I were in the corridor of an ocean liner buffeted by storm, I soon lost sight of my quarry and wandered lost through rooms and salons silent and identical. I was about to cry for help when a hand took me by the arm and pushed me through a door. I winced, expecting to collide with concrete or glass, but the door gave way to three dimensions.

Titania and Primavera were sitting by an open fire (the palace was mint-cool; the fire, oppressive), half consumed by vast leather armchairs. Along the panelled walls were books and paintings; a heavy oak table scattered with maps and charts, an astrolabe and a globe, suggested the machinations of a general; a ticker tape chattered in a corner. I was in Titania's *chambre ardente.*

'Ah, Peter,' said Titania, 'I see you've found our guest.'

'He's my boyfriend,' said Primavera. 'My first.'

'Peter was my first, weren't you, Peter? But that was another time, another country. Your first is always special. Nothing ever tastes quite the same.'

'I wouldn't know,' said Primavera, blushing.

Peter drew up two chairs, his expression as deadpan as it had been in the ballroom.

I settled myself between the girls. A *buffet froid* of ice cream, chocolates, cream buns and sherbet was arranged by their side. Primavera helped herself to the chocolates. 'How old are you, your majesty?' I said.

Primavera frowned. 'Iggy, that's not—'

'Thirteen,' said Titania. 'I've been thirteen for twenty-eight years. I was made just after Peter was born. Peter and I—and a bird-like laugh tripped off her lips—'well, you might say we're related.'

'But you're not human!' said Primavera. 'I mean, you were *born* clockwork. You won't die, like us.'

'Every dawn,' said Titania, 'we die. Isn't that right, Peter?' A poker floated into the air and began to stoke the fire; the flames crackled over Titania's giggles; sweat trickled down my neck. 'But I haven't brought you here to speak of death. I want to teach you how to live. I want to teach all dolls how to live.' Her eyes harried Primavera's. 'Your generation has evolved. So much more noxious than the first born. Those Lilim . . .' Titania slipped to the floor, crawled over to Peter, and lay her head in his lap. 'Those Lilim were *milksops.* Isn't that right, Peter dear?' Her hand caressed her consort's thigh. 'Look into the fire. Do you see the future? Consumed. Us. The world. Everything. Look: the Neverland, in whose doorways and alleys the recombinant feed on those they have beguiled. Look: the Neverland dies, its denizens reduced to starving packs of girls whose teenage mortality will soon leave London's *cordon sanitaire* a dry husk. Look: see those who have escaped, the Lilim who claim other cities, the Lilim who claim the world, instructing their sisters in a religion whose longed-for apocalypse is a world usurped, a world of gilded automata. Look: with no human DNA to pirate, that parasitic race, thirst-crazed, hysterical, dies in an ecstatic *liebestod,* burning on the same pyre as forgotten Man. It is right that it be so. It is our destiny. But look: the past is there too. Tell them of the past, Peter . . .'

Peter closed his eyes. His voice was soft as ashes. '*Peter Gunn* had reached its climax. I shuddered. Titania was robbing me of my human future. But she gave, too. In her saliva, ten billion microrobots—her software clones—coursed into my blood and lymph like a school of mermaids. Ten billion little Titanias swam through me, passing through my urethra, seminal ducts, and into my seminiferous tubules, where they melded themselves with my reproductive ware, corrupting my chromosomes with blueprints for dead girls. I would carry her with me all my life, my Columbine, my sweet *soubrette;* my Titania, queen of the fay; my children would be her children. I too would be a builder of dolls; like my father, I too would be a great engineer! I would complete his work. I would build a world for the chimera, the vampire, the sphinx; a world of childhood perversity; a world of dolls . . .'

'Ah, yes,' said Titania. 'Quite so. But from the beginning, Peter. Tell them our tale . . .'

The Lilim

It was Nursie who told me of the Lilim. 'They shall inherit the Earth,' she said, the night-light silhouetting her profile against the wall, where it joined the shadowplay of my toys. Winding them, she would let the boys cavort about the dresser, so that the beating of tiny drums and cymbals, the clatter of tinplate limbs, has always accompanied, in my mind, the memory of her words. 'Such pretty automatons. Pantalone, Harlequin, Pierrot . . . How your father spoils you! But beware of *her*, Peter.' And she would pick up thrashing Columbine, image of my inamorata. 'Beware of dead girls. Their too-red lips. Their hearts of ice.'

Then stooping, her cheeks hot with shame, she would mutter, 'Oh dear, oh dear, this really is a man's job,' and initiate me into the ways of the Lilim. Like most boys I had, of course, already learned much from the smutty jokes of my schoolmates. But Nursie spoke not to edify; she spoke to warn. 'The chambermaid,' said Nursie, concluding her biology lesson. 'You see too much of her. Unclean, vicious girl! Your father doesn't understand. Don't think of her!' But how could I not think of her, of Titania, my living Columbine? And I asked myself then: Would Nursie tell? (But what was there to tell?) That thin, high-cheekboned profile haunting the wall, those flinty, folk-dark words, that smell of lavender water as she kissed me goodnight: Nursie chastened my dreams.

Each morning that summer the sun effervesced into my room like a champagne of lemonades. The school holidays were at the meridian, the world mine and Titania's, and Nursie's words like last year's snow. Pulling the curtains, I would look down upon Grosvenor Square, environed by its big pseudo-Georgian buildings. The ruins of the old American mission stood opposite, half hidden by full-leafed elms; the scented air was mur-

murous with bees. That summer, my flesh stirred; my voice broke; my heart bloomed. I did not know, then, that my childhood was to end surrendered to the altar of the Lilim.

One morning it began. Titania was in the kitchen. Her uniform, which my father had designed, was inspired by Tenniel's drawings for *Alice*: pinafore dress, not in the usual blue, but pink, swirling about the knees; starched apron; candy-striped stockings; and pink satin pumps. ('And how,' father would say, greeting her, 'is life in Wonderland today?') Cornflakes and a pitcher of milk awaited.

'The land of the *Seven Stars*—we should go there again. Today, perhaps?' I asked my pretty friend. 'There's lots of work to do.'

'I don't think we should, Peter,' she chirruped, her bird-like coloratura ('My nightingale,' Father would say) in contrast to the autistic face. I chewed my cornflakes wretchedly.

'You've got a licence. You shouldn't worry about Nursie.'

'Mrs Krepelkova doesn't like dead girls. You know that. Sometimes . . . sometimes I get scared.' Turning to the sink she began to wash the pots and pans, scouring them with a cold agitation. Suddenly she froze, clutching at her stomach.

'Can't Father fix that for you?' I had seen these signs before.

'Scared,' she said. 'It's happening. I feel it inside.'

I stirred my cereal into a soggy mess. My appetite had gone. The morning darkened.

'Father says Nursie's just a silly, superstitious old woman.'

'The world has become a superstitious place.'

'*Please,* Titania.' My wheedling voice cut through her massive self-absorption.

'I'm going shopping later.' The words bled out luxuriantly. 'If your father says you can come . . .'

It was always the same, that face: expressionless eyes, green and supernuminous, and the mouth, locked in its pout; the blood-drained cheeks; the elfin chin and pointy ears; the cutesy nose of the Disney princess. And the same too (for she had doll blood, and such are dolls) her meekness, so infinitely accommodating.

Everything, everything was to change.

My father's bedroom was a twilight world of pulled drapes, old books and camphor. The books were everywhere: tomes on engineering and art history; vellum-bound editions of 'Second Decadence' writers of the 1990s; chapbooks on toymaking from seventeenth-century Nuremberg; and rarities such as Bishop Wilkins' *Mechanical Magick*. There were paintings, too: amongst them originals by twentieth-century artists such as Hans Bellmer, Balthus and Leonor Fini. (My favourite picture was by the British artist Barry Burman. It was called *Judith* and depicted a pubescent girl holding, from a leather-gloved hand, the severed head of Holofernes.) But dominating the room—apart from the great bed that ridiculed my father's consumptive body—were the automata. They hid in the shadows, their kinetic latency like that of coiled, predatory beasts. Here were masterworks from the Age of Reason: *The Writer* and *The Musician* by Pierre Jaquet-Droz, purchased from the bankrupt vaults of the *Musée d'Art et d'Histoire* in Neufchâtel; singing birds by Jean Frederic Leschot; and a magician, a trapeze artist, monkeys, clowns and acrobats by the Maillardets. From a later era my father had collected a bisque-headed *Autoperipatetikos* by Enoch Rice Morrison; the elegantly dressed girls of Gaston Decamps; a Gustav Vichy musical automaton doll; and (creature of night!) a Steiner doll, with its mouthful of shark-like teeth—which earned it the nickname 'The Vampire Doll'—intact.

'Titania's going shopping. Can I go too?' Father reached for his spectacles and blinked at me.

'Mrs Krepelkova is worried about you and Titania.' I swallowed and dug my hands deep into my pockets. He chuckled hoarsely. 'She thinks I am too *liberal*.' Silence. The invalid tray was burdened with buttered muffins; the curtains swayed gently in the summer breeze. 'Peter, what do you want to be when you grow up?'

'An engineer, like you. A famous engineer.'

'No. You mustn't say that. Not any more. The days of the toymakers are over. Mrs Krepelkova: she's the spirit of these times.' At the periphery of my hearing a Mayday sounded. The grown world was hijacking my life.

'But Titania's not Lilim,' I said. My father seemed quietly shocked.

'What stories has Mrs Krepelkova been telling you? Stories of witches and succubi and golems? I swear that woman's brain is full of nonsense. The nonsense of cheap newspapers and cheaper politicians! There are no Lilim, Peter. You're an intelligent boy: you mustn't believe all you hear.' He wheezed like a punctured concertina. 'Mrs Krepelkova is a good woman. At heart. But we must be careful. Next time you come home from the country bring someone with you. I know you like Titania, but you must make other friends too. For her sake.'

'When I was little we had lots of dolls. It never seemed to matter then.'

'Life was different *then*,' said my father. Unbidden, the memories came: our home filled with the rich patrons of my father's skills; the marvellous automata that waited on our table; my mother, laughing at some after-dinner joke, her cheek even then hectic with the mutant tubercle bacillus that was to savage the Europe of that *belle époque*. 'The invisible worm,' he sighed, taking off his glasses, his head sinking into linen and down. 'It is best to think of happier times: like the day I was discovered by the Comité Colbert . . .' His eyelids fluttered, straining at wakefulness. 'I had just graduated from the Fashion Institute of Technology. They liked my English *hauteur;* the dandyism I had adopted ever since reading the nineties' writers as a boy. France then was the *de luxe* marketplace of the world. It's like yesterday . . .' His eyelids closed; his voice became a whisper. 'In Paris I freelanced for Hermès, Louis Vuitton, Dior and Chanel. Later I worked for Boucheron and Schiaparelli. By the time I had met your mother and moved back to London I was the finest quantum engineer in Europe. Automata! They were the most coveted of luxury goods. And Europe monopolized the luxury market with its *L'Art de Vivre.* But quantum electronics has many problems . . .' His eyes snapped open. 'The chief of which is . . .?' He pulled himself upright. 'Really, Peter, I've told you enough times!'

'Quantum indeterminacy,' I said, rote fashion. 'The imprecise behaviour of sub-atomic particles.'

'Tachyons, leptons, hadrons, gluons, quarks—Mavericks! Hooligans! They were my ruin.'

'The crash,' I said. 'I thought it was the crash that ruined you.'

'Our troubles came after Black Monday. The crash was just the beginning. To compete with the Pacific Rim we delved deep, deep into the structure of matter to make more wonderful, more extraordinary toys.' He passed his hand across his face. 'The invisible worm! It was right that we fell. Ours was an *esthétique du mal.* We shaped life to satisfy our vanities; life has called us to book. When you engineer at the quantum level, Peter, at the level of essence, *style* blurs into *soul.* And God will not be shaped . . .'

There was a knock at the door. Nursie entered, in her hands a steaming bowl of camphor. 'Time for your inhalant, sir.' She set the bowl down. 'Tsk! Has that girl not taken away your breakfast things yet?' And she picked at the bedspread, holding up to the light a wispy thread of lace. 'Pink lace, pink ribbons, pink stockings. A pink girl. Pink! Pink! Pink to her praline heart!' She went to remove the muffins and teapot, but Father brushed away her hands.

'That will be all, Mrs Krepelkova, thank you.' Hurt, she turned to leave.

'Do you want me to wind your automatons, sir?'

'Peter will do it, Nursie. Later. Thank you.' She smiled, shyly, her disappointment tempered by having been addressed by her sobriquet. As she left, she mussed my hair.

I drew away; she had defamed Titania.

'She says they eat men,' I said, after Nursie had gone, wanting her discredited; banished. 'That they're poison. That they kill children and put their own in their place.' Father laughed, but not altogether dismissively; he was too aware of what underlay those penny-dreadful tales used to explain the ascendancy of the dolls.

'Reality,' he said. 'They say it is hard to bear. You mustn't be too hard on her. She's frightened.'

'And frightened people,' I said, completing the cliché, 'say foolish things.'

He sighed, ignoring my sarcasm. 'But why shouldn't she be frightened? We have all been seduced, and the world sickens, gravid with our half-mechanical heirs. No more talk of nanoengineering, Peter. Everyone blames us now, the toymakers. I wouldn't have them blame you too.' He leaned over the bed to where Nursie had placed her aromatic offering and breathed deep.

'Titania will be leaving soon. Can I go with her? Please?'

'When I made her I was at the height of my powers. She was my *best*.' Red-eyed and perspiring, he reviewed his automata. 'Wind them for me, Peter.' My hands dipped into wet, freshly lubricated motors, tightening their sprung lives. 'Titania's a good girl. She would never harm you. Never.'

'Then I can go?'

The automata were waking: a monkey costumed like an eighteenth-century fop took a pinch of snuff; a conjuror sawed at a naked girl; the Steiner doll fell to the floor and wriggled and squirmed and squealed; someone—*something*—played the *Marseillaise;* and birds broke into song. Soon, that cast of feckless playthings was rioting about my father's bed like a mob before palace gates.

'Their day has come,' said Father. 'Yes, you can go. This time.'

The Bentley shouldered its way through the backstreets of Mayfair. Titania drove. Peeking over the wheel, and with immortal abandon, she swung the car into Bond Street. At thirteen (Titania had always been thirteen) her motor-neuron skills often seemed no more accomplished than those of a child; and though in that ghost town vehicular manslaughter was an unlikely prospect, I checked the rear-view mirror for cadavers and the unlikelier police. The street was empty (during the day the streets were always empty), the receding images of boarded-up windows—Cartier and Tiffany, Ebel and Rolex—a glittering slipstream of demise. Now those showrooms displayed only the spray-canned symbol of the Human Front, and graffiti that shouted, 'England for the organic,' 'Proud to be human' and 'Hospitalization now!'

At Fortnum's we bought some corned beef and cabbage (the store was run by an old Ukrainian couple, condemned, like my father, to remain in town), and then set off on the classified leg of our tour, our antique motorcar thundering down Shaftesbury Avenue, Holborn, Cheapside, deep into the City. At St Paul's we noticed a few technicians lowering themselves into manholes to massage the trapped nerve of some pampered AI. They noticed us, too; or rather, they noticed Titania, for they suddenly began gesticulating, scurrying into the depths.

'What are they frightened of?' I said. 'Dolls only come out at night.' Titania, gay as a bird, laughed without irony.

On reaching Whitechapel we pulled into Brick Lane, parking beneath a Cyrillic logo reading LADA. The logo belonged to a warehouse, which—like the derelict 'Borsch 'n' Vodka' fast-food outlets nearby—was a legacy from the years when a Bengali enclave had been ceded to Soviet and East European migrant workers. Lured by hard currency to buttress the West's declining birth-rate—the fashion then being to consort with the artificial—'Slav' had, for a time, replaced 'Paki' as the taunt of England's bigots. Until, that is, men learned to say 'Lilim'.

We entered the warehouse by a side door. Light filtered through the corrugated roof, falling aslant over exhausts, engine parts and a samovar. In one corner, where rust had eaten away the trap once used for deliveries to the *Seven Stars,* the light tripped, fell and was engulfed. We descended the staircase, Titania's cat's-eyes burning green as, sure-footed, she led me into the cellar's swarthy midst. Though blind, I knew a multitude of candles, like stalagmites in an enchanted grotto, rose from the surrounding debris. I heard the sweep of Titania's hand; the candles burst alight, scattering our shadows; and the familiar beer barrels and wine racks, the pool table and slot machines, were revealed to us like the treasures of an Egyptian tomb.

The old pub sign, which we had repainted, hung from a wall. A woman dressed in scarlet, clothed with the sun, with the moon under her feet and on her head a crown of seven stars, gazed down upon us, green-eyed and beautiful.

'Our flag,' I said, saluting her.

'Our planet,' said Titania. 'I always feel safe here. At least, I feel safe with you.' She brushed a cobweb from Our Lady's feet. 'What did your father say to you this morning?'

'Nothing,' I said, and picked up a can of paint, eager to change the subject. 'Let's get started. This is going to be our world.' But Titania sat down upon a legless pinball machine, despondent.

'This is just a holiday, Peter. This can never be my world. To them, I'll always be the Thing from Outer Space.' She drew a long red fingernail across the wall, setting my teeth on edge, and incising into the plaster the outline of a heart. 'They're right. I'm a dead girl. You really shouldn't be seeing me . . .' A trace of coyness had infiltrated her musical-box tones. On one side of the heart she drew a T, on the other, a P; then, momentarily wrinkling her nose, scored the heart with a Cupid's arrow. The ensuing smile, dislocated from the rest of her imperturbable face, twisted at my entrails. 'But you're my only friend. What would I do without you? A dead girl needs a friend.'

Only recently, after I had returned from the north, had I realized how pretty she was. So delicate, so pale. Our little chambermaid, for years a mere playmate, had had me tossing sleepless in my bed through all the long hot nights of that summer.

'I like . . .' I said, my mouth and throat suddenly dry. 'I like dead girls.' Her smile rippled across her face like irrepressible laughter at a funeral. 'Don't worry about Father. He says the Lilim don't exist.'

'No,' she said, giggling joylessly. 'We dolls believe in nothing. Have nothing. Do nothing. We don't *exist*. I wish—' As if hearing a barked command, her face assumed its customary autism. 'Light,' she said curtly, 'more light.' The candles blazed, their light turning green, so we seemed in an undersea cave, immersed beneath a canopy of seaweed. 'A doll needs something to believe in. Just the same as people like Mrs Krepelkova. We need . . . an *explanation*.' A tear dribbled down her glassy cheek. I had not known a dead girl could cry. 'People say that I am Lilim. Why shouldn't I be Lilim? Why not? They seem to want it so much.'

I knelt before her, burying my head in her lap. 'Don't talk like that. Don't take any notice of people like Mrs Krepelkova.' Her hand, white and inhumanly cool, touched my brow, razorblade nails pricking my flesh.

'I would never hurt you. You do *know* that, don't you, Peter?' She stroked my hair. 'Do you remember, years ago, when your father decanted me and brought me home? How beautiful your mother was. I so liked her. If only life could be like that again.'

'We'll make it so. We will. Believe me. We'll find some way.' I held her hands and looked up into that tear-stained face and the inhuman taint of her perfection. I felt the coolness of her thighs beneath the thin cotton frock, the articulation of her ball-jointed knees.

'I shouldn't mind,' I whispered, 'if you were Lilim.' The candles guttered in a sudden draught, and the room darkened. 'We could—you could—' A spume of saliva hung from her lovely plump lips. 'Make the dolls come back—like before—a world of dolls . . .' The draught became a wind. Her lips parted and she grew saucer-eyed. Spittle dripped onto her chin. The wind blew through me, a divine mistral, turning me to stone. Still kneeling, I clutched white-knuckled at her skirts, petrified by her cold beauty. Her hair, black and opulent, lashed about her face, now like a malefic cherub's; and her eyes shone like green ice. The wind howled, and the ice was in me.

'No!' she shouted, 'I won't, I won't!' The wind died, sighing with exasperation. Her tongue, darting lizard-like across her lips, licked away a lather of white froth.

I moaned.

'Don't ask me again. Don't tempt me!' She was clutching at her stomach. 'I feel it there. In my clockwork. The poison.' She pulled from her pocket a large brass key. 'Here,' she said. 'Like this. This is better. I can take you back. Back to how things used to be.' The key was about six inches long with a butterfly handle and a tip of uncut emerald. Again, the wind gusted, threatening storm and stress.

'That's Father's key.'

'He doesn't use it any more. He's too ill. He doesn't miss it.'

'I'm not supposed to touch it.'

Titania placed the key in my hand.

'Don't be frightened,' she said, and hoisted her frock above her waist, displaying her white belly. The umbilicus, dimpling the satin hemisphere, dark and deep, exerted its allure. Titania closed her eyes, waiting. 'Please, Peter,' she said, 'make the poison go away.'

I inserted the key.

'Careful.' She flinched. Fumbling, I pressed the key home and felt it engage. She drew her breath in sharply. I began to turn. 'Slowly,' she said, 'slowly.' Deep within her, a hiss and spit: mathematical monsters stirred. In abandonment, she leaned back across the pinball machine, her midnight tresses trailing in the dust. The key tightened; my fingers hurt. I hesitated, fearful something might break. 'A little more,' she said, 'just a little more.' Using both hands I forced the key a final one-hundred-and-eighty degrees. She screamed in an impossible soprano. The pinball machine lit up; bottles smashed against the walls; the candles exploded like magnesium flares.

The wind that had been waiting impatiently off-stage hurricanoed through the cellar. It whirled about me, a private storm, ignoring all else. I joined its dance. Lifted off my feet, and clinging to the key like an anchored kite, I spun in its centrifuge. The cellar was a blur of streaked candle flame; below, her belly, a white expanse, a salt-seared tundra, drew me to its mine shaft of night. The umbilicus had grown huge, a black hole sucking me into another universe. I fell into its velvet maw.

Through a dark tunnel dimly lit with blood-red alphanumerics I tumbled in free fall. The tunnel stretched to an infinite perspective; and as I fell a jungle rhythm shuddered through its walls. I was buffeted by waves of turbulence; but I felt no terror; my heart raced benignly with the *fris-*

son of a rollercoaster ride. Blood mixed with crystal, crystal with vermeil, amber, glazing into a salmon pink. The tunnel had become a pink glassy membrane. The jungle pulse receded; the membrane ruptured. I smelt grass; felt sunlight on my face; heard the chatter of voices. I opened my eyes.

I was in Grosvenor Square, playing with Mama. About us, the Beautiful People—movie stars, couturiers, artists—scowled at the encircling paparazzi. I was eating an ice cream; father was talking with friends. Our automata, Treacle, Tinsel and the newly-created Titania, danced quadrilles with some of our guests. Doll boys, in the shapes of Harlequin and Pierrot, Gilles, Scapino, Cassandre and Mezzotinto, poured wine and served cakes. Half awake, half asleep, I rested on Mama's breast and watched the dancers weave elaborate, stately patterns to the courtly music of some *gamme d'amour*. It was one of father's 'Watteau afternoons': a midsummer day's mime of pleasure, a pastoral from a Meissen porcelain granted a little time and space.

Titania danced by. Was I in love, even then, albeit unknowingly? She was Columbine the *soubrette*, dressed in the sweet satins and rocaille folds of the infant eighteenth century. She waves to me with her painted fan. There is a clinking of glasses, a buzzing of bees. Time lies sleeping.

'My work now' (my father's voice drifts by) 'is to unveil the spiritual physiognomy of matter.' And the conversation turns to nanorobots, the latest molecular machines. 'Reduced to the size of a molecule, a component will become delinquent; but I am learning to exploit quantum effects, to manipulate Chaos. [A flash bulb ignites.] Indeed, I have now developed assemblers that can manipulate not just atoms, but sub-atomic particles. These automata you see today, commissioned by the House of Cartier, have been brought forth from a microphysical realm where mind and matter, dream and reality, co-exist. They are quite *marvellous* toys.' And he extends his arms towards Titania and her clan. 'Gentlemen, I give you *L'Eve Future.*'

Above the applause, a clap of thunder. It begins to rain.

I do not remember this.

It is raining milk.

And Treacle, Tinsel and Titania—fashion accessories we did not credit with life—bedraggled hair pearly with raindrops, dresses wet and sticky, are standing with their mouths agape like newly-hatched chicks; standing like totems of ecstasy.

Titania?

The guests run for cover as the storm bursts overhead; but the white glutinous rain is drowning London. The flood carries me from Mama's arms, bears me forward on an implacable tide, towards Titania and those red, red lips that are like a giant neon-splashed motorway hoarding advertising the bloodiest of lipsticks.

'No!' Titania cries. 'Not you, not you!'

I woke, sweating. The cellar was becalmed. Titania was rearranging her clothes.

'It wasn't like that,' I said.

'I know,' she said. 'I pollute even the past.'

'No,' I said. 'It's all right. Really.'

She pressed her hand to her stomach. 'It's there. You saw it. The malignancy.'

I got up, chewing my lip, embarrassed. 'I said it's all right. It doesn't matter. In fact—'

Titania doubled over, her chalk-white features rearranging themselves into a mask of pain.

'Please leave me,' she said. 'I'll be better in a while. I need to be alone.' I hesitated. '*Leave* me, Peter.'

With misgiving, I returned to the street, took the fold-up bike from the boot of the Bentley, and cycled home; but not before eliciting a promise that she would follow in the car later when she had composed herself.

I always respected her wishes.

But of course, she did not return.

'The Lilim,' said Nursie, winding my toys, 'are everywhere.' She pecked me on the cheek, sharp as a macaw.

That evening Nursie had stamped about the house muttering, 'Where is that girl? Where is that *robotnik*?' My father sulked, alone, in his room. Now, at my bedside, my smug nursemaid was saying: 'I told you. I told your father. But would anyone listen? No. Krepelkova is just a silly *babushka*.' She held a well-thumbed paperback in her lap: *The Doll Problem—Lilith And Her Daughters*. It was the bible of the Human Front.

'Lilith was Adam's first love. But she was proud and vain and adulterous . . .' She opened the book, removing a photograph from its leaves. 'Lilith is Satan's consort, Peter. She is Queen of the Succubi. She comes to men at night so that she may corrupt their children . . .' She held the photograph before me. It was a portrait of a young girl, a blonde *manqué* with liquorice roots, in whose pixieish face I recognized the traits of the recombinant: green, hysterical eyes and a sickly white complexion that suggested a diet of junket and sweets. 'At first I blamed my son-in-law,' said Nursie. 'He never told me how it happened. But I don't think he meant to be unfaithful. Dolls have their *ways*.' She studied the snapshot carefully. 'You can still see the human part of her. If you look closely. When she was born she was such a lovely child. We had no idea. It's when they're about twelve or thirteen that it happens. The eyes turn green. Luminous green. And the face: it isn't a human face any more. It becomes . . .' She paused, her brow creasing. 'Pretty. So very pretty. But it is a prettiness that is horrible in a child.' The book slipped from her lap onto the floor. 'Poor Katia, she was a daughter of Lilith, and they made her wear the green star of the Lilim. Then the lactomania began. And they took her away. To the Hospitals. My baby's baby . . .'

I went to sleep, clasping, with anxious hands, Titania's key beneath my pillow.

The next day I cycled back to Brick Lane. The Bentley was still parked outside the warehouse. 'Titania!' I called. But the warehouse was empty. I descended into the world of the *Seven Stars,* my pocket-torch flushing out the shadows.

She had gone. I breathed a deep lungful of fetid air and went to mount the stairs. A gobbet of water broke at my feet; I jumped, swinging the torch around. Hanging from the ceiling in what seemed a sac of viscous bronze was the foetal-crouched shape of a woman. She was fleshless; what remained was a raw, quivering jelly suffused with plastics, metals and jewels. I retched, dropped the torch and ran.

And then I was gunning the Bentley towards Mayfair; towards the particle weapons and security cameras that surrounded our house; towards the human world.

'Where is she?' asked Father. I told him. 'There's nothing we can do,' he said. 'Nothing.' He fidgeted with the bedsheets. 'I never thought it would happen. Not to her. Not to Titania.'

'Will she die?' I barely dared utter the words.

'The philistines called them dead. Dead girls. A nexus of formal rules. Non-reflective. No, she won't die. Now she makes her claim on life.' He threw back the sheets and swung his legs onto the floor. 'I must go to her.' A fit of coughing took him and he collapsed in a tangle of flannelette. 'Those Cartier dolls,' he said, gaining his breath. 'I thought I was making elegant, eighteenth-century ladies, spirits of gentleness and grace.' He pointed to the foothills of books surrounding his bed. 'The Decadents! Writers and artists who filled my boyhood dreams with chimeras, vampires and sphinxes. Ah, the perversity of childhood . . . I tried, Peter. I tried to deny that darkness, programming my atomic machines to pluck angels from pandemonium. But atomic objects can be understood only in terms of their interaction with the observer. When we speak of the sub-quantum world, we speak of ourselves.'

Something terrible snarled in the undergrowth of my mind and readied itself to pounce. I dared it.

'Did *you* put the poison in Titania?'

'I always blamed others,' he spluttered, the words rushing out. 'I said it was some bug introduced into their programmes by our competitors in the Far East. But the virus was mine. Between the lines of Titania's programme, within its infinitely complex, fractal text, lurk my dark childhood dreams. Now that sub-text emerges, the poison seeps . . .' He began to cough.

'I'll go. I'll bring her back.'

'No.' He drew himself up. 'I'll go in the morning. It's getting dark.' The sun, red and bloated, was sinking over Grosvenor Square. The jewelled eyes of my father's automata glistened. He placed his hand on my shoulder. 'She can't come home, Peter. Understand that. Her power . . . It is enormous. I grew her from the quantum field, the essence of all forms. In her, space and time, mind and matter, are enfolded by . . . by what? A reality *I* cannot grasp. She is unconstrained by physical laws, at one with the essential nature of things. She is Creation.' He looked out of the window, his face flushing in the rays of the dying sun. 'But I have poisoned Creation. I gave her life, Peter; I must take it. Tomorrow, before she is reborn.' He sighed. 'Can anyone explain this need to create beauty?'

CHAPTER TEN

Unreal City

You want me believe—'
    'Quantum indeterminacy—'
'This bullshit?'
'At the sub-atomic level—'
'Why no one say—'
'His own consciousness, his subconscious—'
'Before?'
'The imprecise behaviour of—'
'Mr Ignatz—'
'Inventor becomes inventee—'
'*Mr* Ignatz!' Kito slid off her mechanical stud and pulled out her transcom.
    'Wait,' I said. 'Spalanzani, tell her it's true.'
    'True? But how can I say? Possible, I suppose. Toxicophilous would first have engineered nanomachines on the molecular scale, programmed with the rules of a cellular-automaton universe. The nanomachines would replicate, each time making a smaller model of themselves, until tiny, so tiny, hardware became software, machine became information, mimicking the quantum effects involved in the firing of neurons in the human brain. But how Toxicophilous's subconscious might have affected that process . . . Who can guess? Consciousness physics is not my forte, and fractal programming is a lost art.'
    'Toxicophilous,' I said, 'is the source of the doll-plague. *L'Eve Future* was a projection of his psyche, just as he himself was a projection of his own age. The Lilim are observer-created.'
    Spalanzani pursed his lips. 'It has always been my opinion that Toxi-

cophilous was used as a scapegoat. But though people have cursed him for building *L'Eve Future*, nobody has gone so far as to accuse him of being the *source* of the plague. Your story, my friend, is mystical. And I am a scientist. Myself, I have long favoured the supposition that a virus from the Far East was responsible for—'

'Shut up,' said Kito, 'quack nanoengineer.' She began encoding her transcom. 'Spalanzani scientist; I cynic, Mr Ignatz. I want evidence, not fucking crazy story.'

'Titania exists,' I said. 'Ask Jack Morgenstern.'

'Ask him yourself,' said Kito, 'when he come take you back England.'

'*American Embassy,*' said the com.

'Forget duty officer, get me Jack Morgenstern, Cultural Affairs Attaché. Say it's K. At home? Then put me through his TV, his android, his fax, his bathtub, I no care!'

'That won't be necessary, Madame,' said Jack Morgenstern, who had just entered the dome along with the Pikadons and Mr Jinx.

'She on slab, Uncle Jack,' said Bang (or Boom).

Morgenstern pointed a lightstick. 'Okay, Zwakh, and you too,' he said, looking at Spalanzani, 'get over there with Kito.'

'Mr Bones,' said Kito.

One of the Pikadons drew a particle weapon from her Sam Browne and fired. The android spasmed, pawed at the air, then fell onto its face in epileptic ruin.

'Kito, don't disappoint,' said Morgenstern, 'I'm no longer interested in you.' Coughing theatrically, as if about to provide an aside during an after-dinner speech, he added, 'In fact, *nobody's* interested in you.' The Pikadons tittered.

'Jinx,' said Kito, stepping over the massive frame of her plastic bodyguard, 'what this about?'

Jinx raised his hand as if summoning the elements to his aid. 'Stop!' He was a small Rumpelstiltskin of a man from some undefined principality west of the Urals; so astonished was Kito at his display of imperiousness that she leaped backwards, tripped over the still twitching Mr Bones, and fell in an immodest sprawl of limbs. The little man grinned as if he had just revealed himself the master of a long unsuspected black art.

'Jinx?' said Kito.

'Let me present the new chairwoman of the board,' said Jinx, making a *wai* towards the Pikadons (two effete cadets from a notorious military academy, dressed in the kind of style that brings out the sodomite in a man).

'Nana friend with America now,' said a Twin. 'Friend of Uncle Jack.'

'They do the weird on you, Morgenstern?' I said.

'Please,' said Jinx. *'Language.'* He turned to Kito. 'A simple board-room *Putsch* is what this is about. Madame, you have been mamasan of Nana for over forty years. Life has moved on. We no longer live in a Eurocentric world; a resurgent America is reclaiming its old spheres of influence. Madame is part of the defunct "Empire of Style." But Nana has no time for nostalgia. Time is money. Deutschmarks. Yen. *Dollars...'*

'We bought you out,' said Morgenstern. 'Seems US dollars still call some cards. I knew I couldn't trust you.'

Kito picked herself up. 'I was about to ring—'

'We know,' said Jinx. 'Your rooms are bugged. This place too. We've been listening in on you for some time.'

'Interesting story, Zwakh,' said Morgenstern. 'Pity you had to hear it, Madame.'

'What story, Uncle Jack?' said a Twin.

'Never you mind, sweet thing.' Morgenstern smiled at me. 'We'll have to talk some more.'

'Mr Bones—*get up!*' Kito kicked the android's tonsured head; yelped with pain. 'Jinx, Pikadons—they use you. You no see? You become yankee *stooge,* you—'

I put my hand on Kito's arm; she glanced at me and sheathed the claw of her anger that its sharpness might not be dulled for later use.

'Let me get this right,' I said. 'The US government bought enough stock to allow the Pikadons—the *Pikadons,* for Christ's sake—to take over Nana. All to get one runaway Lilim and me? What are you talking about?'

'I told you,' said Morgenstern, 'I'm an Anglophile.' The doors bisected at his approach. 'Let's get rolling,' he called. A golf cart manned by two of Morgenstern's goons purred into the dome. 'Put the girl on that, handcuff the boy, and take them both to the autogyro.' He turned to the Pikadons. 'I'll leave the *boss* for you.' The Twins cracked their knuckles in anticipation.

The goons took hold of Primavera's arms and legs; dropped them; stepped back from the slab. A green shaft of light, like a column of ectoplasm, had risen from her umbilicus.

'Jesus, Jack, what the hell is it?'

'Don't worry,' said Morgenstern, 'she's been dusted some twenty-four hours. She ain't jumping through any more walls, I can tell you.' A breeze stirred a heap of print-out; there was an electrostatic crackle in the air. 'Let's get this thing on the road.'

The two men again took hold of Primavera. The breeze became a wind, and there was a squeal of castors as a metal trolley trundled across the room.

'Monsoon,' said Morgenstern. 'It's that time of year.'

'That's no monsoon,' I said. 'Tell them to put her down.' I moved to-wards the eye of the storm; the well of unreason would have to be plugged or . . . Morgenstern fired a warning shot; a vat broke open, sluicing its mis-carriage over the tiles.

'Stay where you are, *Gastarbeiter.*'

'Tell them to leave her alone,' I said. 'Don't you realize what's—'

The wind screamed into my mouth and lungs. I was pedalling air. Then I was falling, falling through the funnel of a green maelstrom, into patterns within patterns, falling towards something infinitely small, infinitely big, falling helter-skelter, falling into the belly of the doll.

I opened my eyes; the white cupola of Spalanzani's workshop was above me. My enemies were rubbing their heads and getting to their feet. The dome was undisturbed, as if the cyclone, abashed at its carousing, had ti-died up before it had left.

'You guys okay?' said Morgenstern. The two men who had precipitated near disaster mumbled a series of goonspeak yeah, guess so, sure, Jack, replies. One of them had vomit-spattered shoes. 'Let's try it again,' said Morgenstern. 'Gently.'

The umbilical light had died; Primavera was lifted onto the golf cart and driven outside without incident.

'Move back where you were, Zwakh. Over there, with Kito.' Hands above my head, I edged across the room.

A cry, EEEE! A slasher, splatter cry . . .

Morgenstern ran outside and I followed, my humanity insulating me from a trigger-happy burst from one of the Pikadons' doll-scramblers. 'Primavera?' I called. She was still on the golf cart, eyes closed, breath shallow. Morgenstern had grasped my arm. His face was bloodless, and his eyes jerked into grotesque attitudes as he strove to assimilate the horizon.

Rising from Lumpini Park, and floodlit, St Paul's cathedral shone ma-jestically above the rooftops of Bangkok. Big Ben leaned over us from the next street, surrounded by *chedi* and *prang,* and the searchlights of the in-terdiction described their familiar arcs from across the Chao Phaya river. The Big Weird had suddenly got bigger. Weirder.

'What's happening?' said Morgenstern. I eased his hand off of my arm.

'We never came out,' I said. Jinx, Kito and the Pikadons formed a hud-dle against the dome wall. 'We're inside Primavera. She's taken us into her matrix. We're inside her dreams.'

'You said she was dusted!' said a goon. 'You said she couldn't hurt us!'

Morgenstern put his hands to his head. 'I got to *think.*' He stamped on the ground. His eyes continued to wander dizzily in their sockets. 'Inside her dreams, eh? Then we got to wake her. *Wake* her. We got to, to—'

'Wake her. Yeah. And how do we do that? This isn't Primavera,' I said, pointing to the sleeping girl on the golf cart. 'This is . . .' But I didn't know who it was.

'A simulation, possibly,' said Spalanzani. He had emerged from the dome and was squinting through his pince-nez at the deranged cityscape.

'Jesus,' said the goons' spokesman, 'is that what we are, Jack—fucking *sims?*'

Everybody looked at Spalanzani. 'It is if,' said Spalanzani, 'we are inside a dreamscaper, with the young lady's software acting as a *jeu vérité*.'

'Some *jeu vérité*,' said Morgenstern. 'We can't control anything. In a lucid dream you can *control* things.'

'We're intruders,' said Spalanzani. 'The game is the young lady's.'

'Wake her up, Jack. Give her a shot of something. Just get us out of here.'

'Pull yourselves together,' said Morgenstern. 'If we're sims, nothing can hurt us.'

'Possibly,' said Spalanzani. 'But if we're *not* discorporate, waking the young lady—even if it is only a simulation of herself—might be dangerous. The dreamer may assume control of her dreams.'

Dangerous. That seemed a good enough reason to wake her. It might be the last card Primavera and I had to play . . .

'I could try,' I said. Morgenstern looked at me suspiciously. 'How else are we going to get out of here?'

'No,' said Morgenstern. 'Spalanzani, you try. Shoot her up with stimulants. Let's take the risk.'

'The risk of her lucidity is but one factor. Say the stimulants work— either as pure symbolism, as therapeutic symbolism, or as a physical correlative—what effect will they have on the young lady in the real world? She is very sick. Dying, perhaps . . .'

Morgenstern stroked his beard. 'Yeah, I guess if she dies while we're in here things could get *really* tough.'

'I planned to operate,' said Spalanzani. 'But I can't. Not now. Even supposing there *is* a correlation, symbolic or physical, between this young lady and the one outside, I would need special tools, customized nanoware. One such as her . . . I never met before. Never.'

'Then let me see what *I* can do,' I said.

Morgenstern nodded. 'Looks like our options are limited. But nothing funny, okay?'

'Yes, my friend,' said Spalanzani, 'maybe our bodies are in the real world, dreaming all of this; and then again, maybe not. For the young lady—for all Lilim—thought is denser, more material, than for you and I. *Her* dreams have substance. Be careful.'

'Not so fast,' said Kito. She began folding and twisting her transcom. After three or four manipulations it resembled a ladies' beam weapon, lethal and dainty. 'I want to know why you ruin me, Mr Jack.'

'Madame,' said Jinx, 'this is not the time for—' Jinx pirouetted to the minimalist fanfare of Kito's gun, staggered, took a photograph from his jacket, tore it to shreds (it emitted a tiny squeal), and fell noiselessly over the balustrade to the streets below, to resolve, for himself at least, the question of whether or not we were simulations.

'It *was* true then,' I said. 'Mr Jinx really did love a photo-mechanical.'

'Not love,' said Kito, 'an infatuation.' The Pikadons brought their particle weapons to bear on their fellow *bijouterie,* intent on scrambling the symbiotic electronics that riddled her hypothalamus (little doohickeys that had cried sex, sex, sex these five score years). 'A cruel infatuation.' The weapons discharged, ejecting joke-shop flags, one Bang! the other Boom! Kito's lightstick had turned into a steely dan.

'Seems the goddess of this place doesn't like guns,' I said.

'Guess she didn't like Jinx either,' said Morgenstern. He holstered his lightstick.

'Spalanzani,' I said, climbing into the golf cart, 'you think you could get me a scalpel?' Spalanzani disappeared into the dome and re-emerged with a handful of surgical instruments.

'You saw what she did just then,' said Spalanzani. 'Perhaps we shouldn't—'

'Get on with it,' said Morgenstern. 'If she can do that in her sleep none of us are safe.'

'Can no get worse, Uncle Jack,' said a Pikadon.

I selected a blade and applied it to my arm. Spalanzani tut-tutted. 'Keep her jaw open,' I said to him, opening a vein and letting the blood drip into Primavera's mouth. Her throat contracted in a covetous gulp. I squeezed the vein; no question, really, of force-feeding her; she yawned, blood spattering her face and hair. I was gambling that her haemodipsia was stronger than the bonds of her unconsciousness.

The goons were muttering:

'Jesus, these English.'

'De-pravity.'

'A green and perverted land for sure.'

'Wait'll I tell Alice about . . .'

Primavera knocked away Spalanzani's hands, clawed at my arm, brought the slit vein to her mouth, and sucked, like a baby on its bottle.

Ohh—tombstonesownmoaninight . . . In the land of death and desire our coach awaited us. We shook and shivered. *The car. The girl. The river . . .*

What—

'It's enough,' said Morgenstern, pulling me off.

Primavera drew a hand across her mouth. 'Shit, Iggy, what happened to my clothes?' I took off my jacket and handed it to her.

'We're at the *Grace,*' I said. 'Remember? We were in Kito's bedroom when—'

'And what's this slut doing here?' said Primavera, glaring at Jack Morgenstern. She frowned. 'It's gone. It's *gone.* I can't see inside his mind.'

'We're still here,' said Morgenstern, looking around. 'She's gone lucid, and we're still here. Tell her to pinch herself, Zwakh.'

I took Primavera's hand and led her to the edge of the roof. 'Fuck,' she said, her eyes distending to accommodate the fused skyline of East and West.

'You're dreaming, Primavera,' I said, 'and we're inside your dreams.'

'*Stupid!* If I were dreaming I'd be able to—' The garden vanished and was replaced by our suite at the *Grace.* 'Anything.' Primavera was curled up on the sofa, her green silk kimono spilling onto my lap. 'You're right,' she said, 'I *am* dreaming.' She was eating popcorn; the lights were turned down; and all five of our TVs were tuned in to the Jack Morgenstern show.

'Very clever,' I said. 'As if I haven't seen enough of your dumb tricks.'

Morgenstern, clad in sacrificial white, was being frog-marched down a long corridor. His captors—masked, but betraying long manes of bleached blonde hair—kicked a wheelchair from his path . . .

'I'm going to teach that slut a lesson,' said Primavera, filling her mouth with junk.

The corridor opened onto a big rotunda, at the centre of which two marble slabs displayed the skewered bodies of the Morgenstern goon squad. The third slab, unoccupied, was evidently reserved for Morgenstern himself.

'Just stop the melodramatics, Primavera. We don't have time for this.'

'Sure. I mean he's such a nice guy. I want to have his fucking babies.'

Morgenstern, his gown stripped away, hirsute and horrible, was on all fours upon the slab. A pair of rubber-gloved hands took hold of his ankles.

Primavera picked up the remote and froze all five pictures. 'Hey, Morgenstern,' she called, 'you can hear me?'

The TVs remained frozen, but Morgenstern's disembodied voice was panting over the speakers. 'You murderous little bitch. My boys—'

'Just do it,' I said. 'Get rid of him and start thinking of a way to get us out of here.'

'I want to play,' she said, sulkily.

'Games. Always games. Don't you realize what's happened?'

'It's just a dream, Iggy. Why do you always have to be so *serious*?'

'*Just* a dream? We're inside you. *You've taken us all into*—'

'There's no need to *shout!*'

'Into your matrix.'

Her mouth, pausing in its task of grinding popcorn to pap, hung open; a long red fingernail picked at her fangs. 'There was a guy with an Italian accent. I was lying on something cold. Then the American comes in, yeah . . .' The pulp mill of her teeth resumed work. 'Then you're real?'

'I feel real, though Spalanzani says that maybe—' Jack Morgenstern had begun to scream.

'Shall we do it?' said Primavera.

'Get it over with. He knows about Titania. About the *Seven Stars*.'

'Naughty, naughty, *naughty!*' Primavera took hold of the remote.

'Wait!' said Morgenstern. Primavera's finger hovered above the freeze-frame. 'We were never going to send you back to England. I said that just to scare you. To make you talk!'

'Yeah, yeah, sure,' I said. I looked past Morgenstern into the shadows of the execution chamber. 'It's so dark,' I said. 'Back home it was always so light. So white. So—'

'Clean?' said Primavera.

'All those candles. And masks. And that thing in the centre—like some kind of gibbet.'

'Medicine-heads,' said Primavera, 'have the aesthetic sense of retarded oysters. This is better. More gothic.'

'Yeah,' I said.

'Can't you hear me?' screamed Morgenstern.

'Try to think of yourself as a sim,' I said. 'Maybe Spalanzani's right.'

'We wanted information on Titania. The girls—*they* don't talk. We thought you'd be *different*.'

'If I'd known you were listening . . .'

'We had to know where she hides, what kind of organization she's got.'

'Yeah, so you can zap her from space.'

'No. You don't understand.' He panted and moaned, as if he were about to sell his soul to the moment, and would soon be defrocked, deflowered, disgraced. 'We're *working* with her.'

'Slut,' said Primavera.

I walked over to a TV and spread my palm across the close-up. 'Jack. Be brave. Let's hear no more. It's beneath your dignity. Abdominal impalement's not so bad.'

'More like messy,' said Primavera. 'He hasn't been trephinated.'

I tapped Morgenstern's glass forehead. 'Think of something nice. Green fields. The moon on the seashore. Your favourite cake. Mother.' I turned to Primavera. 'Ready?'

'Don't you dare get high and mighty about killing people ever again. Do you understand me, Ignatz Zwakh?'

'But I know the secret,' said Morgenstern, 'the secret of the matrix!'

'Big deal,' said Primavera. 'So do I. We all do. Every one of Titania's dolls.'

'You'll never find him,' he said. 'Not alone. Not without me.'

'Find who?' I said.

'He means Dr Toxicophilous. He's in here too. Sometimes I get a little peep of him just before I go to sleep.'

'Toxicophilous has the key to the matrix,' said Morgenstern. 'He can wake you up. He can let us out!'

'So after we kill you we'll go find him. I'll dream us to Grosvenor Square.' Primavera put down her popcorn and, propping chin in hand, adopted Thinker's pose. 'But you know, Iggy, he's sort of got a point. Where do we start looking? I can't dream us to a place I've never seen. I just can't *imagine* it.'

'But out there,' I said, 'there's lots of things you haven't seen. Half of London.'

'Picture books. Lessons at school. I don't know what. But I've *seen* them.'

I slapped my hand on top of the TV. The picture wobbled. 'How does he know about this *matrix* business?'

'It's obvious, Iggy. He's wrung it out of some doll. S'pose I'm not the first he's captured.'

'Titania told me,' said Morgenstern. 'Titania's people. Voluntarily.'

'Sure she did,' I said. 'How come Titania never told me?'

'Titania,' said Morgenstern, 'has told me many things.'

'*Salaud.*'

'Yeah,' said Primavera, 'my queen wouldn't be involved with the likes of *you.*'

'I know Grosvenor Square,' he said. 'I was posted there years back. I can take you . . .'

Primavera blew out her cheeks and exhaled noisily. She got up, knocking over a pile of *manga,* and circulated amongst the debris of our three-year holiday in the Weird: broken chairs, broken fax, ripped, blood-crusted Y-fronts (trophies of the 'interesting boys' she had met), all covered in an undisturbed dust, the ash from the little volcanoes of our lives, and all lit by the phosphor-dot luminescence of the TVs, each one of which beamed Jack Morgenstern's face, surmounted by a tiara of beer cans. A dying ad-sign outside the window filled the room with hiccups of light. Green, black, green, black. Bangkok-London, in all its *noir* packaging, its cheap glitz flashing across the sky, was ever near. Too near. Primavera snapped her fingers. 'Guess I'll have to kill you later,' she muttered. With slick editing, the hydroponic garden reappeared. Primavera had dressed the three of us in—

'Combat fatigues?'

'I'm feeling mean,' she said. She took Morgenstern by his lapels. 'Maybe you're flesh and blood, maybe you're a bunch of pixels. But you know what I can do, so don't fuck with me.' A small audience of three half-humans and one nanoengineer peered about the door of the dome. 'That goes for you too.' Primavera took me to one side.

'Is Toxicophilous really here?' I said.

'He's in every Lilim. That's what Titania told me. But it's a secret. The "secret of the matrix". Only dolls are supposed to know.'

'Oh,' I said.

'Some girl's blabbed. Morgenstern must really have used the thumbscrews. I'll get him. You'll see. He's going to know what it's *like*.'

'Toxicophilous can help us?'

'My ROM is all messed up, but Toxicophilous represents the programme that controls my files, my instincts. He's my operating system. Perhaps he can sort things out.' She looked out over the unreal city. 'He's out there somewhere; somewhere where the universe according to Primavera Bobinski becomes the Lilim ur-universe.' Morgenstern was summoned to heel. 'So take me to Grosvenor Square, slut.'

Morgenstern, comprehending, I think, that life and death depended on the morbid fancy of his erstwhile prisoner, composed himself and waved a deprecating hand over the rooftops. 'This place is a g-goddamn mess. I might be able to spot it from the air. Trouble is, you just *spiked* my autogyro pilot.'

'I can be *really* delinquent if you like,' said Primavera. To me she added: 'Seems I can do big-time magic again. In my dreams at least. I'll fly the three of us over town until *slutty* here gets a fix on where this *Grosvenor* place is.'

'What about me?' said Kito. 'What if you no come back?'

'Don't worry, Madame,' said Primavera, 'if there is an exit you can be sure I'll flush *you* out.'

'Where you go to, Uncle Jack?' said a Pikadon.

'You vanish, come back, go again,' said the other. 'Take us with you!'

'Shut up,' said Primavera, 'we're going to see a man who can re-boot me.'

'Be careful,' called Spalanzani, 'be careful when you dream. The city is part of your memory, but we are realtime. So fragile! So soft!'

'I'm not going to dream,' said Primavera, 'I'm going to fly.' She put an arm about my waist.

'Please,' I said, 'you know I don't like flying.'

'Don't be a pin,' she said, 'this isn't Marseille. We're not on the run. Nobody's going to shoot at us.' She took hold of Morgenstern and flexed her knees. 'Hold on, boys.' With a little jump she was airborne; Morgenstern's bulk immediately tipped her to her left. 'Weee!' Morgenstern began windmilling his free arm like an incompetent funambulist. Compensating (Morgenstern was twice my size), Primavera pitched, yawed, then regained her attitude. Where was the sick-bag? I closed my eyes to the dreamscape below.

Morgenstern must have followed my lead. 'Start looking, slut!' said Primavera. 'We haven't brought you along just so you can wimp out.' His breath came fast and heavy. Primavera, her lips to my ear, said, 'This guy got *asthma* or something?' She began to shake Morgenstern up and down. 'A little turbulence ahead, ladies and gentlemen.' Our fatigues billowed as Primavera initiated a lazy dive; car horns, shouts, the rumpus of the streets, carried over the whistle of our descent.

'Okay,' shouted Morgenstern, 'I'm looking, I'm looking! There's Selfridges, so this must be Oxford Street. No. It's a *klong*. But over there— that's Nelson's column. Piccadilly Circus. That monorail shouldn't be there, and those temples . . . Wait. To your right. No. Straight on . . .'

'This is hopeless,' said Primavera, after Morgenstern had treated us to half an hour of manic directions. She brought us down in a thoroughfare that was half road, half *klong*, opposite an electronic café. 'Let's try the Net,' she said, and swung through the café doors; the doors swung back, returning Primavera to the street.

'No good?' I said.

'Best hamburger in town,' she said, and walked away licking ketchup from her fingers.

Primavera put her head through the doors. 'What's keeping you two?' Inside the café her face was everywhere: customers, cashiers, bag-ladies, mechanical beggar kids . . . A seated row of Primaveras looked at us askance, then, with a synchronized flick of hair, returned their attention to their milk shakes.

'Seems I'm the only person who lives in this city,' said their original. 'Except for the good doctor, that is.'

We walked up to a bank of transcoms. A Primavera clone in a two-piece business suit asked, 'Person to person, station to station, or machine to machine?'

'Poison to poison,' said Primavera.

'Yeah,' I said, 'Dr—' Well, surrender my loins to . . . I didn't know the guy's real name. Nobody did. Over the years we'd grown superstitious about pronouncing it, regarding it as some kind of Tetragrammaton. 'Toxicophilous,' I said.

'And if you can't raise him,' said Primavera, 'try one of his household appliances.'

'Just a moment please.'

The computer listed no such name.

Primavera gave Morgenstern a tired but sanguinary stare. 'Listen, slut, you're going to have to do better or—'

'Darling!' A clone ran across the café and kissed Primavera on the cheek. 'I haven't seen you since school!'

'S'pose not.'

'Toxicophilous,' said Morgenstern (eager, I think, to escape another dose of Primavera's in-flight antics), 'you heard of him?'

'Oh, *him*,' said the clone.

'We need to talk,' I said.

'You newspaper people? I thought you knew all about—'

'No,' I said.

'We're oneironauts,' said Primavera. 'Aliens. Take us to your leader. Take us to Dr Toxicophilous.'

'It's a strange world,' said the clone.

Slap! said Primavera's hand. 'Wake up!'

Impassive (though blood beaded her razored face), the clone said, 'Try Soho. Try *Frenchie's.*'

Morgenstern was through the doors.

'Sure,' I said to the clone, 'thanks.'

'Look out for the rippers!'

Outside, a *tuk-tuk* awaited us, a photocopy Primavera ready to take our fare. 'Rippers?' I said.

Primavera jumped aboard. 'My brain cells say the craziest things.'

The three-wheeler buzzed through the crossbred streets, the intersection of a 'cities of the world' theme park where images of London half remembered from school books interwove with the symbols of our exile in Siam. From cabs, buses, water taxis and temples, from pubs, massage parlours, food stalls and theatres, night owls returned our stares, a thousand green eyes that held ours but a moment before refocusing on business, pleasure or the void.

Water was lapping at our feet. 'Where we're going,' I asked the driver, 'are there canals?'

'Scared about getting your feet wet?' she said. The water began to rise;

black spray jetted through the *tuk-tuk*'s open body; we were penetrating the city's aquapolitan heart. Upstairs, where the money lived, high above the smog in air-filtered splendour, the lights of penthouse condos shone like the gold bar of heaven. How many rich bitch Primaveras leaned out? We had come to save them. Where were the streamers, the fireworks, the cheers?

Stench of *klongs;* small-hour exhaustion; decay. This was dollspace. Machine consciousness. Impure, like all thought, but more massive than the consciousness of mankind, its constituents were psychons of iron, glass and steel, a neon-bright vortex of complex simplicity from which rose the aleatory music that so bewitched the world. Music that was solid, dimensional; music that was sinew, muscle, *physique.*

'New to town?' said the driver.

'Yeah,' I said. 'Business trip.'

'You should take in a show. All work and no play—'

I glanced at Morgenstern. 'He's incurable.'

'Over there,' said Primavera. 'Stop!'

We pulled in to the kerb. 'Astoria?' said the driver. 'They do Shakespeare and all that stuff. You should try a musical . . .' Outside the theatre a billboard proclaimed *Salomé—A New Play By Dr Toxicophilous.* 'Anyway, it's a first-night performance. You'll never get a seat.'

'First night? Iggy, he's bound to be there.'

'We're supposed to be going to Soho,' said Morgenstern.

'But it's his *first night.* We can wait until the end and then shout "Author! Author!" '

'That's crazy,' I said.

'It's crazy,' said Morgenstern.

'So who asked you, slut?' Primavera stepped onto the pavement. A passing car sent a sheet of water across her path, leaving her rat-tailed and bemired. 'This is a crazy world,' she said, wiping her eyes. 'Come on. Let's go. Let's go *ape shit.*'

The amalgamation of West End millennial swank with the cut-and-run fabric of the Weird had resulted in a theatreland of High Art, Hucksterism and Hullabaloo. Primavera shoved through clones in snooty evening dress, flower girls and saffron-robed monkettes: Primavera squared, Primavera to the power of 3, 4, 5, Primavera to the power of 100.

'Hey you—kid with the enamel eyes—you wanna buy—' Primavera felled the tout with the *Muay Thai* kick known as 'The alligator swings its tail' and used her own face as a stepping stone. I tracked her through a crush of curious witnesses, and entered the theatre's foyer.

'First night, huh?' said Primavera. The foyer was empty.

'First-night nerves?' I said. We proceeded into the stalls.

'Iggy, the whole *place* is empty.' We sat in the back row, Morgenstern placing an aisle between himself and his tormentor. The auditorium was a fleapit. A vast network of cobwebs hung from a surrounding frieze that was a burlesque of Phidian art; bat droppings littered the floor; seats were slashed, the stage curtain ragged; and all was illuminated by a sallow light. The light dimmed; the curtain rose.

SCENE

The Palace of Herod. A boudoir—a doll's boudoir—high above the streets of New Jerusalem. Salomé is discovered at her toilette, attended by her maid.

MAID *(aside)*: 'Salomé, not Salome,' says the Princess of Judaea, 'Salome sounds like salami and I'm French, *savez-vous*? One more Salome and salami's what you get, salami and tar-water till the end of your days . . .' So call me Electrolux, ma'am, not Electra. I'm English, dooby-doo? I don't say it, of course. You want Greek slave? I do Greek slave. Do it very well.

SALOMÉ: So who is this Jokanaan?

MAID: A prophet, ma'am. With a vision of Christ as Shiva.

SALOMÉ: I've heard he's pretty. Pretty as the Archangel Gabriel. Pretty as the Angel of Death. And famously cruel. Almost as cruel as me.

MAID *(aside)*: Well, maybe a bad girl like her *needs* a bad boy like him. Ever since her mother, Herodias, came over from Paris and got hitched to the Big Jew, Herod himself, she's been scratching at the wound of her boredom like a sex-rat gnawing at its own bowels . . . *(To Salomé)* He's a rebel, ma'am. Talks revolution. The decline and fall of the empire *de luxe*. Talks of one who'll come 'after him' and reprogram the race, a bodysnatcher who'll change us all . . .

SALOMÉ: Hosannah in the highest. Maybe I'll go see him. I like guys who're a little sicko. It'll make a change from playing *mahjong* with Mummy's friends.

MAID: So here's your raiment, excessively dermatoid; and here's your shoes, perilously heeled. Now the war paint: lipstick made from marinated foreskins, mascara made from blackened bones . . .

Primavera threw her legs over the seat in front. 'Bor*ing*,' she said. I put my arm about her shoulders. It occurred to me that this was something I had never done: take my girlfriend to a show, or to the movies. It seemed it was something only ordinary people did. (Sure, I'd escorted her to the premiere of *The Birth of a Nation*. Great SFX, that show. I remember the *Phi Gaseu*—disembodied heads trailing long tails of intestine—that feasted on the unborn of Siam. They were meant to symbolize the Negroid and Slavic decadence of the West so nobly resisted by the Siamese people. Sure. Great. But that had been work . . .) Morgenstern's head fell forward; he began to snore. 'You want me to vampire-fuck you?'

'Kiss me,' I said. 'Pretend that—'

'Get out of it. Snogging in the back row's for kids.'

'Maybe we could—'

'Yeah, and maybe you could get me a good dentist.' She shrugged off my arm. 'Boring. Bor*ing*.'

The play continued, empurpled, street-precious, very 'nineties'. Salomé meets Jokanaan (Primavera in a beard); Jokanaan rants. Seems he wants to turn Salomé into a little Watteau goddess. Seems Christ the great programmer, the black Christ, the Christ of guilt and pain, is coming with sword in hand to harry the world of fashion. And Salomé smiles. Pleased.

'Cut his head off,' said Primavera, 'get on with it. Can't you see that's what he wants?'

But first there has to be the soft-shoe shuffle. Herod (Primavera in another beard) watches from behind half-lidded eyes bruised with sleeplessness. And Salomé, in a derma-riot of second skin, trips across the boards, neck between thighs, or ankle about neck, an invertebrate contortionist with angry, Medusa-like hair. Then the salver, bloodily replete. And the last line, the line the world has been waiting for:

HEROD: Kill the woman!

Primavera sprang up. 'Author! Author!' she screamed, clapping wildly. I added to the applause. Morgenstern blinked, stood, and offered his own hands. The curtain fell; the auditorium again revealed its jaundiced visage. Morgenstern was the first to fall quiet; then I too let my hands hang from my side. 'Author! Author!' Primavera cried, until, forlorn, her applause became the sound of one hand clapping: a realization that the doctor would not appear.

'We've lost valuable time,' Morgenstern sighed. 'We should have—' Primavera treated him to one of those stares to which he always reacted as if he'd had lime juice thrown in his eyes.

'Soho,' I said.

'Bozo,' said Primavera, and leaped over the rows of seats as if competing for a one-hundred-metre hurdle.

Our *tuk-tuk* had waited, and soon we were again speeding through canyons of concrete and steel. The night sky was veined like marble, like a membrane split open, ruined, useless. It began to rain: it was a fizz-pop kind of rain, mock-atomic. On either side of the waterway wealth gave way to squalor. Inhuman flotsam sat huddled about scrapheap fires in the shells of gutted buildings; figures slunk in tenement doorways, *apache* skirts revealing stilettos tucked between stocking tops and thighs; lines of washing, like the bunting of a carnival of sordidness, were strewn between *sois;* child facsimiles of the screaming Miss P dive-bombed us, jumping from the upper stories of slums into the chemical stew of the *klong;* the rain eased into drizzle.

'Frenchie's,' said our driver. On iron stilts that possessed the undulating elegance of a Paris *Metro* entrance, *Frenchie's* rose from its island of silt, its garish vitality contrasting with the boarded tenements, empty restaurants and gloomy merchandisers of Anglo-Saxon smut that lay on either side.

'Stay here,' I told the driver. We crossed a gangplank, and a doorgirl ushered us up the stairs into Big Weird a-go-go shadows.

Morgenstern walked to the bar. 'Screwdriver.' His hands were shaking.

'Must still be getting over the flight,' I said to Primavera.

'Where you come from, handsome man?' Wrong Primavera. This one wore a G-string and spoke Big Weird barspeak.

'Primavera?' I looked around. She was talking to one of her doubles.

Glass exploded against the wall beside me. 'It's *blood,*' said Morgenstern.

'Probably mine,' I said. 'This town must be well-stocked.' I went to sit down. There was something on my stool. A mechanical mammary gland. I tried to brush it away. Stupid. The breast was insubstantial, and my hand passed from guillotined ligament to teat. The place was filled with holoshit.

'Drink?'

'You got anything that's not red?' The bar girl pointed to a bottle of some off-white *crème.* 'I'll pass,' I said, and turned my eyes upon the handful of dancers (programmed to look bored for human similitude) that were shimmying to . . . The music stopped; restarted. *Oh doctor, doctor, I wish you wouldn't do that.* Talk of the streets, the town, the world. Beat of the galactic arm. Damn them. The *Imps* had a number one.

Number one. That was the name of the lookalike who had chosen to dismount the stage, kneel down on the bar, and perform, a few centimetres from my face, a routine that would have left a human girl dislocated and raw. Raw as salami. Or Salome. I looked through her legs, to where the other dancers paraded about a glass vat centre stage. In the vat's bubbling, aerated liquid, a half-formed gynoid stared back at me with the mindless eyes of mindless creation. No superscience attended her nativity. Above her, a neural network programmed with pirated software instructed the vat's microrobots to duplicate a doll, Cartier, Seiko, Rolex, whatever, not by engineering base elements, but by reorganizing the atomic structure of a human foetus, aborted (so ran the rumours) by force. Illegal, of course. Like synthetic gasoline was illegal. Like prostitution, dermaplastic and psychotropic scent. But this dream bar belonged to the Weird, and the Weird was moneytown, its forbidden technologies commanding huge amounts of foreign exchange. A gynoid was cheap; it turned a quick profit; and a profit made you a patriot.

Primavera joined me. 'Number thirteen says Dr T's been and gone. We've missed him, Iggy. And *nobody* knows where this *Grosvenor* place is.' My dancer was rejoicing in a display of abdominal contractions, the violence of which seemed ready to disembowel her. 'Little tart,' said Primavera. 'Never thought I'd end up looking like that. Look at her: the Bobinski's trashed. Nothing *belle époque* there. All that's left is gynoid.' Primavera leaned across the bar, took the dancer by the hair, and struck her. Hard. 'Am I the only one around here who's awake?' She struck again. Harder. But the mirror image didn't crack.

'Hey,' said Morgenstern. He was standing by the door, filling his lungs. 'There's something happening out here.'

From the door it was possible to see into a nearby alley where a dark cloaked figure was struggling with a whimpering girl.

'Doll ripper,' said a bar girl.

Primavera swept back her hair. 'Nanobot?' The bar girl nodded. Pushing us aside, Primavera jumped to the half-flooded streets.

It's always the same: the fire escapes and mullioned windows, the girl in the party dress you push against the alley wall, the snicker-snack! snicker-snack! of steel against cuspids, the gasp and clichéd expression of 'surprise and pain' . . .

'Come on,' I said to Morgenstern.

'Wait a minute. That thing out there—'

I pulled him after me. We clambered into the *tuk-tuk*. 'Follow her,' I said to the driver as Primavera splashed through the shallows and attained the alley's shore. Ahead of us—cloak spread behind like a comic-book villain—the anthropomorphic virus sprinted into the anonymity of the night. Primavera took to the air.

'We should be giving this thing a wide berth,' said Morgenstern.

'Tell that to Primavera,' I said.

Morgenstern swung his head about. 'Jesus.' I looked behind. Draped over a dustbin was the clone we had seen from our vantage point at

Frenchie's. The hilt of a knife protruded lewdly from between her thighs; teeth ground on metal, with the sound of fingernails clawing at slate. *It's always the same: the expression of innocence betrayed and of crime discovered . . .* 'Martina, Martina,' I said. 'Martina von Kleinkunst.'

The *tuk-tuk* pulled up; caught in its headlights, the blood-stained nanobot was pinning Primavera against a doorway. 'Iggy! My magic doesn't work on him . . .' She gurgled as the nanobot's fingers tightened about her throat. The figure, throwing back its cloak, turned its face to us, a face as black and featureless as polished onyx. I scrambled out.

'I'm Euclidean!' The thing's laughter was emotionless, canned. 'You can't hurt me! You're algorithmic, you're recursive, you're—'

I rushed it; caught it with a flying tackle; it sank beneath me, yielding like dough. 'Yeah, well, I'm Euclidean too. From out there. And to me you're just another tin microbe.'

Warily, Morgenstern approached us. 'Think this thing can help?' He gave the nanobot an idle kick.

I stared into the opaque face, and into my own black reflection (felt, for a moment, a girl's body struggling against my own, fluttering like a bird clenched in a fist). 'Dr Toxicophilous,' I said. 'We want to find Dr Toxicophilous.'

'So,' said the nanobot (in the preppy voice of an Ivy League closet queen), 'who do you think *us* guys have been looking for the last couple of days? Killing a few biomorphs here and there is all well and fine, but we want to get this job *over* with. It's a matter of professional pride. But the old man—he's not here. Sure, he makes visits. He can go where he *likes*. But as to where he lives . . . The rest of the guys have gone off to try and find him.'

'He has to be here,' said Morgenstern. 'He's supposed to be inside all Lilim.'

'So he is. But the matrix models an infinite number of universes. We think he lives at the crossroads.'

'And where's that?' I said.

'Everywhere,' said the nanobot, 'and nowhere.' Morgenstern kicked the thing in the head. Its immaculate physiognomy fractured. 'Ow! Rough stuff, eh? If this town isn't the *pits*. All these *girls*. Like *ants*, I tell you. Little *reflex* machines. A billion ganglia. Ugh! And now you start to—' Morgenstern kicked the thing again. 'Listen: we're talking about a singularity of information. A black hole of consciousness.' His head lolled to one side. 'Your consciousness, Primavera Bobinski.'

'Let's kill this doll-ripping bastard and get moving,' said Primavera, massaging her throat. 'He's given me an idea.'

I twisted the nanobot's head, hoping to break its neck; the top of the brain box came off in my hands. Oily globules dripped from the meninges, rolled mercurially across the alley with autonomous life.

'Mirrors,' said Primavera, 'within mirrors. That's no way in. Got to see the back of my own head. Confront the I.' She opened her combat jacket. 'Send the *tuk-tuk* away, Iggy. We don't want her sucked in.' Our driver didn't linger.

'Primavera, don't go screwy on me.'

She sat down, crossed her legs guru-fashion, and stared into the black abyss of her navel. At the first glimmer of green I took a step backwards; Morgenstern copied. 'Time to Ouroboros,' she said. As through the smashed porthole of a depressurizing plane, her hair, and then her head, were sucked into her abdomen. Plop! Shoulders, arms, legs followed, until, self-consumed, she remained only a black disk, small and impenetrably dark, surrounded by a luminous green halo. I regurgitated fried grasshopper. 'Come *on*,' she called, voice faint but edged with exasperation.

'One thing's for sure,' said Morgenstern, 'I'm not staying alone in *this* place.'

We walked into Primavera's event horizon.

CHAPTER ELEVEN

Psychic Surgery

The necropolis seemed (as it always did) limitless, extending out of eye-shot, beyond hope, beyond the world; a singularity of death where the curvature of space-time was infinite. Eternal. Where was our coach? Our horses? It was cold; colder than at any time I could recall; a ground mist slunk at our heels, crept beneath our fatigues. No pleasure trip, this.

'Primavera?' I called. I helped Morgenstern to his feet. Superimposed upon the familiar desolation, like a surreal photomontage, marooned amongst the stone termini of life, a slice of London real estate rose broodingly from the plain. Primavera headed towards it.

'Grosvenor Square,' said Morgenstern, as we picked our way through the tombstones, struggling to match Primavera's fleetfootedness. As we caught up with her, and passed that boundary between necropolis and square marked by chopped outcroppings of macadam, the mist lifted, and we found ourselves wading through a sea of grass, about us pseudo-Georgian terraces and the ruins of the American Embassy. Encircled by night, the square's one lit window shone like a beacon in a lonely tower. The sexton of this world of death was at home.

The door was open.

'Doctor?' called Primavera. All was in shadows, the furniture shrouded in white sheets; piano music percolated through the ceiling. After climbing two flights of stairs we noticed a splinter of light beneath a door. Primavera rapped her knuckles against the wood. 'Doctor? Dr Toxicophilous? It's me, Primavera.' The music stopped.

'Enter.' It was the voice of an old man breathless with disease and second childhood. We found him sitting before an open fire. Wrapped in a paisley dressing gown, and leaning against a four-poster bed, he held, in his lap, a clockwork toy which, undistracted by our presence, he had set to winding, quietly and methodically. He set the toy before him—a model of a young woman seated at a piano—and the music recommenced. 'Greensleeves. My Lady Greensleeves. I always thought it should be our national anthem. Gentle. Verdant. English. God Save the Queen? Ah, there'll be a new queen soon. And it will be us that needs saving, God damn *her*.'

Automata carpeted the floor. Primavera cleared a space and sat down beside Dr Toxicophilous, surrounded by her nineteenth- and eighteenth-century predecessors. I breathed through my mouth; the smell of camphor was overpowering.

'Phalibois made her,' said Toxicophilous, stroking the horse-hair locks of the little musician. 'Made her during that golden age before the First World War. The golden age of automata. And all these'—he passed his hand over the half-a-dozen toys at his feet—'from the Marais district of Paris. I worked in Paris once . . .'

'Doctor,' said Primavera, 'I need your help.' Toxicophilous rubbed his chest and wheezed.

'Poor doll. Your clockwork is broken. I know; I felt it break. It broke like . . .' His eyes became rheumy. 'Like this old man's heart.' Primavera's own eyes were raised; her grin, lopsided. 'First the crash. Ah, it ruined so many. Those imitation dolls. People preferred them. They were cheap. Vulgar. But they offered *sex*. Then the plague. Such nightmares.'

'Yeah, well I'm sick of dreams, doctor,' said Primavera, 'I want to wake up. I want to live in the real world again.'

'We want out,' said Morgenstern, who hadn't moved beyond the door. 'Understand? A Lilim has trapped us inside her programme.'

'Tick-tock, tick-tock.' Toxicophilous put his hand on Primavera's belly. 'We nanoengineers are much like clocksmiths. Semiconductor technology relied on electronics, but we use physical moving parts. Gears whose teeth are atoms; bearings that are bonds between atoms . . . Yes, you are inside her programme. But you are also inside a physical world. A clockwork world.'

'I *know* that,' said Primavera.

'Yeah,' I said. 'That's just a fancy way of saying that her neuroelectrical activity is more powerful than a human's; that for her reality isn't consensual.'

'I said I *know* that, Iggy.' She sighed. 'It didn't stop me getting scrambled, did it? So doctor: you going to help? Or are you going to wait for the nanobots to arrive?'

The loose folds of Toxicophilous's face tightened with self-reproach. 'You must hate me.'

'Well you did turn me into a fucking *robot*.' Primavera stood up, peevishly kicking over a few of the antique toys that were offering a sardonic comment on her life. 'Trouble is, you're part of me. And I'm pretty sick of hating myself. Titania says—'

'Titania,' said Toxicophilous, 'was never human. But you . . . I know what I've done. I've taken away your childhood. I've taken away your girlhood, your womanhood. I've taken away your humanity.'

'So who wants to be human?' said Primavera.

'Few of us, it seems. But it was my purpose to give a human-like consciousness to my automata. That is why I built the matrix. I wanted to find that fractal vanishing point, that point of complex simplicity from which life would spontaneously emerge. Dead girls, they said. Just because they weren't built around the nucleic acids. Ha! Their consciousness was made up of sub-atomic particles, like ours. Yes, I wanted to give them humanity.'

'You did,' I said. 'Your own. Didn't turn out to be such a good thing, did it?'

'If I infected others,' said Toxicophilous, 'I myself was infected. Those first *émigrés* who came to Britain after the dissolution of the Pax Sovietica were intellectuals, former dissidents, underground writers, poets without a cause. They sought new themes, a new purpose. The worst of them glorified the old demons that were again racking their homelands: nationalism, populism, the paranoia of the non-existent foe: madnesses they embodied in a revival of folk tales and images. "The Second Decadence" the critics called their movement. I was a boy and their stories of witches and golems, vampires and the eternal Jew riddled my mind.'

'Those stories have invaded reality,' I said.

'Not that that's such a *bad* thing,' said Primavera, arching an eyebrow as sleek and black as the roots of her hair.

'Ah,' said Toxicophilous, 'but the story of the witch always ends with a burning; the vampire is always impaled. I brought the Lilim into the world, but I brought death too . . .' A tear hung from the tip of his nose, fell and broke over the toy piano.

'Jesus,' said Primavera, 'to think I carry this guy around inside me.' She placed her hands on her hips. 'Stop it! You've been dead for years. Everybody's forgotten about you! We don't even know your real name . . .' She brought her foot down on both piano and miniature pianist, destroying them in an orgy of chromaticism. 'They can't impale us all. We're going to take over the world, just like Titania says. Right, Iggy?'

'Right.'

'The world,' said Toxicophilous, 'will be a little boy's fantasy. The dream of a morbid child.'

'Call it what you like,' said Primavera, 'it'll be my world. The world of the Lilim. Maybe I play by your rules. I don't care. I'm still *me.*'

'Your world. You mean that other place? The place you call real?' Toxicophilous glanced towards the windows. 'I like it here. It's quiet. Peaceful. Here, at the heart of the matrix. It is this clockwork world, this neuroelectrical world, this world between zero and one, that is the real world for you, Primavera. This world that is unpredictable, uncertain . . . This world of magic. Of death.'

Morgenstern left his position by the door and strode into the centre of the room. 'If this is her world she's welcome to it, but it's not mine. Can you get us out of here or not?'

'You'll get out of here when Primavera wakes up.'

'Great,' said Morgenstern, 'give the man a cigar. Can *you* wake her?'

'She needs a kiss from Prince Charming. Charmless, in your case. The answer lies with you, Mr Morgenstern.'

'Me? What the hell can I do?'

'Tell her the truth. The truth will wake her.'

'What are you talking about?' said Primavera. 'What's this slut know about truth?'

Toxicophilous closed his eyes. 'It concerns my beloved Titania. The queen I love to hate. My dear, she has deceived you . . .'

'Don't you call *my* queen a liar.'

'So many lies. Isn't that right, Mr Morgenstern?'

'You can't expect me to—' Morgenstern sat down on the edge of the bed. 'It's classified.'

'Then stay,' said Toxicophilous.

'I can't stay, I've got to . . . Hey, how come you're wise to all this?'

'I know Titania. And I've come to understand that part of myself that poisoned her, made her change . . . God help me, I *am* Titania.'

'Something's up,' I said to Primavera, 'something weird. I know it. Make them talk.'

'Weird,' said Primavera. 'I don't like it, Iggy.'

'Weird,' said Morgenstern. 'Weird policy for a weird world. It's weird all right.'

'We're waiting,' said Toxicophilous.

'If it's going to get us out of here, then . . .' Morgenstern spat on his hands, slicked back his hair and beard, and eased open the door of his confessional. '*Operation Black Spring* was all about you, boy. Dolls are tough. We've tried to get the truth out of them before. Without success. So we thought we'd try a junkie. Then you go and spill the beans without us so much as breathing heavy on your fix . . .'

'You've breathed heavy enough,' I said.

'Yeah,' said Primavera, 'maybe I should remove his lungs.'

'Okay, okay,' said Morgenstern. 'Here it is. To start with, what I said a while back's true: we didn't have any intention of sending you to England. I was just trying to scare you, to get you to talk. No; you were on your way to the States. You think we'd share intelligence with the Human Front? Lord, the HF have our token support, but only as a cover for the support we give Titania.

'Just after the HF came to power, Titania had a few of her runaways contact our people in the field. At first we thought it was some kind of hoax. But then something happened. Some people say the President had a vision. Others say it was the President's wife. Whoever it was, the State Department was empowered to set up an exploratory dialogue. There were secret talks in Berlin. Titania's delegation made DC realize that the HF's plans to exterminate the Lilim weren't going to work. The plague had become a pandemic. But the more those girls talked the more we understood that things could work to our advantage, that the Lilim could provide us with the means of reasserting ourselves on the world stage.

'They were stellar, those girls. They were offering nothing less than to become an instrument of US foreign policy. What they proposed was this: Titania would send her runaways to countries of geopolitical significance to us. When the plague began to undermine those countries' economies, Titania would unleash what she called "the secret of the matrix". Only America would be privy to that secret, would recognize it, would know how to exploit it. Every government on Earth would be beholden to us for controlling the plague's spread . . .'

'Shut up!' shouted Primavera. 'It's all lies!'

'The secret of the matrix?' I said. 'You mean the fact that our friend here'—I gestured towards Toxicophilous—'lives inside every Lilim?'

'Oh it's more than that,' said Toxicophilous, 'much more.'

'Screw you and your *secrets*,' said Primavera. 'Why were you going to take us to America?'

'Things here in Thailand weren't going by the numbers. You, Primavera, the first doll to be sent out east, weren't *infecting* the locals, you were damn well *killing* them. We'd kept track of you, of course, ever since you'd arrived. Jinx had been on our payroll for years . . .'

'It was my *job*,' said Primavera, 'I *had* to kill them.'

'Sure. We could live with that. But what about your spare time? It wasn't good enough. We would have been content with another Lilim, a replacement, but Titania wanted you out of the way.'

'And what did you have planned for us?' I said.

'Debriefing. Titania's been pretty secretive. We don't wholly trust her, and her file's incomplete. We'd do anything to get more information, and anything to protect that information. When Jinx called me and told me what you were downloading on Kito I had my staff buy enough shares on the overnight exchange to make sure I had the muscle to silence any witnesses. Well, maybe Jinx is gone, maybe not. I'll have the Pikadons deal with him after they've offed Kito and that Italian. The bottom line is only the US government can know where Titania lives.' He pulled a CD from his breast pocket. Kissed it. 'And thanks to you, Zwakh, we *do* know. Some day we really *might* want to zap her.'

'Debriefing?' Toxicophilous laughed. 'Are you sure that's all? Are you sure there aren't certain people at the Pentagon and DARPA who are curious to find out what makes a Lilim tick?'

'Hospitals,' said Primavera. The words hobbled out, her mouth lame with despair. 'Titania wanted to send me to the Hospitals.'

'Yeah,' said Morgenstern, 'well, that's not my department. I just wanted to talk. Get the full story . . .'

'But why?' I said. 'Why would Titania conspire against her own kind?'

'She is fulfilling her programme,' said Toxicophilous. 'A doll's purpose is to die. Titania leads her daughters into darkness . . . Her inheritance is the fears, prejudices and secret lusts of *La Décadence*. Like all Lilim, she embodies Europe's death wish. Don't you know how much you want to die, Primavera? How much all Lilim want to die? That is the secret. The one and only secret of the matrix. How you and I long for annihilation!'

Primavera bit her knuckles.

'A Cartier automaton like Titania has the power to unlock that death wish,' said Morgenstern. 'In fact she's done it already. In the suburbs of the Neverland. We asked her to. We wanted proof.'

'Like sheep,' I said. 'They went to their deaths like sheep.'

'She can make it happen anytime she likes,' said Morgenstern. 'Anywhere. But for her next performance Titania will make sure the Lilim die for Uncle Sam. And for Uncle Sam alone. It's going to give us one *hell* of a bargaining chip. Of course some dolls don't surrender so easily, Primavera being a case in point. I understand Titania's being calling *her* for years . . .' Morgenstern stood up. 'I'm not happy. I'm really not *happy* about all of this. But how do you expect America to protect its national interests? Nobody goes to war any more. History's finished: democracy and capitalism won. We got to do things different ways. We got to find new ways to fight, to goddamn well *survive* . . .'

'Forgive me, little doll,' said Toxicophilous, 'I wish I could have given you life. But something in me cried out for a victim.'

Primavera walked unsteadily towards a window. 'Oh, Iggy. It's too much, too much . . .' Outside, night was falling. I followed her, placed my hands on her shoulders. She focused upon our reflections in the glass. 'It's over, isn't it? That's all I am now. A reflection. Without substance. Without meaning.' I kneaded her flesh; felt the steel girders of her bones. 'You were right, Iggy. A doll is a thing of surface and plane. I've always known it was true. But Titania gave me something. Not a soul. Just something that made life bearable. An identity. A purpose. A kind of substitute soul. And now it's gone. She's killed it with her lies. Why did she do it? Why did my queen betray me? Can you tell me that?'

'Titania's very practical,' mumbled Morgenstern. 'She's got an instinctive grasp of politics.'

'Quiet,' I said, turning around. 'Just keep quiet, okay? Do you know what you've done? Both of you?' I swept my foot across the floor, scattering automata. 'It's not worth it. I'd rather stay here. Titania was all she had . . .'

'We get out now?' said Morgenstern.

I walked up to him and grabbed him by the beard. It came away in my hand. 'All she had,' I said. 'Titania was something to believe in. She made them proud. She turned the tables on prejudice.'

'Lies,' said Toxicophilous. 'All lies.'

'Yeah,' I said. I let the beard fall to the floor. Another trick.

'I never knew my Dad, you know,' said Primavera. 'He was Polish. Married Mum in Belgrade. Came to England. Died when I was six months old. Mum said the Lilim killed him. And for twelve years I'm a good little Serb. Then I get this other Dad. Dr Toxicophilous. What a deal. What a life . . .'

Toxicophilous reached into his gown and held up a glittering rod of brazen metal. He threw it across the room. 'It'll work now,' he said. 'Try it.'

'Primavera?'

'Mmm? Is it time to go home? And where is home? Where do I go now Titania has betrayed me?' She smiled, her lips tremulous.

I picked up the key. 'I don't know. Primavera, please . . .'

She turned her back on her reflection and put her arms about my neck. 'Let's do it,' she said. Her smile had frayed. 'What's the matter—scared?' The butterfly grip grew warm and sticky; her jacket was open, umbilicus peeping above the waistband of her fatigues. She reached for my hand, guided the key towards its ward. 'Don't move.' Her fingernails dug into my neck. 'Don't breathe. Don't even think.' She arched her body, thrusting herself onto the brass shaft in a violent spasm of flesh and will. Her scream splintered over my face.

The windows exploded. A green mist poured into the room. A wind howled across the plain of death.

Morgenstern shouted an exultant curse.

'Primavera—' A thin trail of blood leaked from where the key had imperfectly cauterized the door beyond which dream and reality were as one. Her eyes rolled back; her bones had become powder, her flesh, liquid. I scooped her into my arms.

'Don't worry, Iggy,' she moaned, 'it's not the real me . . .' She was turning to vapour, coalescing with the swirling mist.

'Goodbye, little doll,' called Dr Toxicophilous.

Jackknifed, head to the waxing gale, Morgenstern pulled himself to my side. A screw of dense green air rose from the sea of grass outside, opening into the cone of a tornado. The cone advanced towards us, and as the wall of the maelstrom skimmed the wall of the terrace, we were sucked into an emerald gyre and tossed like leaves into the sky.

I opened my eyes; I was inside Spalanzani's workshop, a naked Primavera by my side. I looked at my hand; only the impression of the key remained.

'Welcome back to the real world,' said Jack Morgenstern, subjecting us to his lightstick's one-eyed scrutiny.

'You owe your life to her,' I said.

'Tell it to my boys. Spalanzani was wrong. We were flesh and blood in there.'

'Uk!' said Primavera. 'I need an enema.'

'You think it's funny?'

'Does it matter? I'm just a sick little doll. I left what power I had back there. I can't even read your nasty slutty mind.'

'You've got the information you want,' I said. 'You can tell Titania we're dead. You owe us.'

'Titania?' said Kito, picking her way through the wreckage. 'More crazy story, Mr Ignatz?'

'If you like,' said Primavera. 'The magic's gone. Finished. Nothing matters now.'

'What matters is I get you Stateside,' said Morgenstern, 'according to plan. Now let's get moving.'

The Pikadons were guarding the door, their particle weapons drawn. 'So you got back?' I said. 'Pity.'

'Get back long time,' said a Twin.

'Mr Ignatz sleep *mark-mark*.'

'Now do what Uncle Jack say.'

Primavera and I walked hand in hand. As we approached the door, the Pikadons moved aside, and then closed ranks behind us.

'Not you, Madame.'

'You stay behind.'

'Bang—'

'And Boom—'

'Want to talk.'

Kito drew her peignoir tightly about her and pressed her forehead against the wall. 'Why you *do* this, Mr Jack,' she wailed. 'I not start doll-plague. You must believe—'

'Of course you didn't,' said Morgenstern. 'You think we're stupid? You think we care? But Titania's real enough—'

'Titania?'

'Yeah, Titania. And even if she means—'

'Crazy story true?'

'And even if she means nothing to your greedy peasant mind—'

'No!'

'That makes you a security risk.'

'Who Titania, Uncle Jack?' said a Twin.

'Never mind, sweet thing. But after you've finished with Madame, get looking for that Italian.'

'And Mr Jinx?'

'I don't think Jinx will be bothering us.' Morgenstern prodded me with his lightstick. 'Great girls,' he said. 'Beautiful, deadly . . .' We stepped into the garden; the door closed. 'And stupid. But don't *tell* on me, mind.'

Primavera squeezed my hand. 'I've got to try it, Iggy.' Swinging about, she caught Morgenstern cleanly on the jaw. There was a tiny detonation; Morgenstern stepped back, his eyes crossing, uncrossing; Primavera moaned and put her hand to her mouth. Undissuaded, she extended the same hand as if to administer a hex in a last stand against reality. Morgenstern, his eyes refocused by fear, aimed his weapon.

'No! Not the marvellous toy!' Spalanzani dashed from an arbour of bougainvillaea and frangipani and placed his body before Primavera's. The air exploded; Spalanzani's head snapped back, and he dropped to the gravel, his pince-nez welded to his flesh as if by a thermic lance. Primavera staggered, then regained her balance. A pink smoking hole had appeared between her eyes, its edges bubbling like molten plastic. She looked at me with the insouciance of a wasted loony toon, and then she began to laugh.

The dome opened. The Pikadons ran to Morgenstern's side. 'Don't get *upset*,' said Primavera. 'I'll go quietly . . .' Shrugging her shoulders, she again took my hand. 'He needn't have done that, you know. The poor dweeb.' Her wound was bloodless, though I could see it furrowed deep into her brow. Tentatively, she explored the burnhole with her fingers. 'Looks as if I'll have to go heavy on the make-up.'

Turning our backs to our captors (Primavera gave a flick of her hair, a little wiggle of her rump), we resumed our gallows walk.

'Wait!' cried Kito. I looked over my shoulder and saw that she was manipulating the dome's entryphone. Like her transcom, it folded into a lightstick. 'This time no become steely dan.'

'This time,' said a Twin, displaying her own gun, 'no fire joke-shop flag.'

The three half-humans faced each other, good, bad and *bijou*, like protagonists in a psycho-zygo western.

'Golden flower trash,' said Kito. Her lips were puffy and she sported a bloody nose. 'You think you take Nana so easy? I mamasan of *roboto okuku* before they cut you from plastic womb. From orphanage to beauty queen—Miss Cashew Nut, Miss Watermelon—all time circuit in brain making fucking *crazy* till come Bangkok work bar, buy bar, buy *soi*, buy Nana: you think can slap me on head? And you,' she said to Morgenstern, 'you number one bullshit man. I such fool . . .'

'I'm too old to be frightened by an entryphone, Madame.' Coherent light, in a microsecond of invisible, but noisy, drama, vaporized a small portion of Jack Morgenstern's thigh. His own weapon discharged— several exotic plants burst into flames—before clattering to the floor, to be smothered by a Whumpf! of unconscious meat.

A click, click, click was emanating from the Pikadons; they were pulling the triggers of their particle weapons to no effect; and now Kito covered them. 'Stop it!' said Kito, as if she were scolding two mischievous children. 'I wake up first. Take Duracell from gun.' The Twins swapped embarrassed stares. 'Bad day for you when Smith and Wesson merge with Mattel. Into dome!' Kito sealed the door from the outside and left the Twins battering their fists upon steel plate.

'Finish him, Madame,' I said.

'I no want CIA after me. Mr Jack not small-time thug can off without trouble. Come, Primavera, I re-hire you. You too, Mr Ignatz. We take car. Elevator go all way down to garage.'

Primavera poked her head above the oubliette of her despair. 'We did it again,' she yelled—the venom of a murderess combining with the enthusiasm of a cheerleader—'A, B, AB, O, that's the way I wanna go! Rhesus factor, rhesus factor, ya, ya, ya!' But then the depths reclaimed her.

CHAPTER TWELVE

Desperadoes

We hit Route Two before daybreak, slipping through Bangkok's dreaming sprawl, until the dawn struck out the asterisks of the stars. By early morning we were driving across the plateau of Korat. Beneath us, the Pak Chang reservoir glistened amidst the deforested wasteland of the plains. Primavera and Kito were asleep, slumped across the ZiL's back seat. I was glad. Ever since we had cleared Sukumvit Kito had talked incessantly of how she meant to revenge herself on the Pikadons; and Primavera—though she complained of migraine as well as stomach cramps—had equally garrulous in insisting that the former mamasan's influence, no longer dark following her ouster, was now so minimal that she had little chance of being offered a free bowl of noodles and none of being offered the Pikadons' heads. 'So why didn't you stick them when you had the chance?' asked Primavera. 'Lost your nerve? Got too used to relying on lowlife like me? Now a *real* Cartier doll would have . . .' At last, the night's capers had called in their debts of exhaustion; I had driven fifty kilometres in silence, if not in peace.

I pulled in by a roadside café. 'Hey,' I said, shaking Primavera awake, 'this place sells tourist stuff: T-shirts, jeans; you interested?'

Primavera rubbed her eyes. 'I can't go about like *this,* can I?' Primavera's flesh, as cool and fine as alabaster ground to a talc, radiated against black leatherette, primary and secondary sexual characteristics a golden triangle of adorned erogeneity.

Kito stirred. 'Madame, can you spare a few satang?'

'I no carry money in dressing gown, Mr Ignatz. Here—' She passed me her lightstick. 'Buy shop.'

I could get no food. The clothes were effort enough. The proprietors thought my weapon a toy and I had to vaporize a small dog before the wisdom of acceding to my demands was perceived. It was only when I was back in the car that I noticed that I had been palmed off with screaming blue jeans.

'So *tacky,*' said Primavera, ripping out the audio. 'So old-fashioned. My Mum used to talk about these.'

'Poor Primavera,' said Kito. 'No ten-inch special. No tutu. No ultrascenic itsyritzy.'

'I can't help it, Madame, you know I have this *neurosis.*'* Primavera held up a T-shirt printed with a smokestack and the words *Khao Yai Industrial Reserve. 'Bougre!* What *is* this?'

'You lucky,' said Kito. Her shirt featured a dancing prophylactic and the slogan *Don't Be Silly, Put A Condom On That Willy.* She gave Primavera an accusing glance. 'Bad time when roboto make sick.'

'Yeah? Well a piece of rubber never protected any guy from *me.*'

We drew away. The landscape, crystallized by the waste of derelict salt mines, was bone-white; eucalyptus struggled out of the spent earth. It was about seventy kilometres to Korat. I put my foot down. 'We'll be there in under an hour,' I said.

'And just where that, Mr Ignatz? I no make decision . . .'

'You don't decide anything,' said Primavera. She put a hand over her eyes as the road twisted and we caught the glare of the morning sun. 'Don't you understand? You're nothing now. Nothing.'

'Don't start that again,' I said. Primavera mumbled something in Serbo-Croat, in French, again in Serbo-Croat, and scrabbled for her sunglasses. 'Listen, Kito, we're going to Korat, and there we'll say our goodbyes.'

---

*Primavera's 'hemline neurosis', as explained by Dr Bogenbloom, was less a result of 'strange exhibitionism' (the title of his contribution to the *festschrift* 'Semiotics of Anthropophagy') than of 'strange loops', the paradoxes that translate a *grande fille* into an idiom that is one long scream of feedback. Said the Bogey: 'For a hemline to reach that coveted elevation where bifurcation of thighs meets at that satin-gusseted apex we might call the "quantum-chaos crack", that same hemline, however vertiginous, must be hoisted halfway, then halfway again, always having to rise half of the remaining distance of its journey . . .' And thus never, to the regret of the doll, revealing the smallest gasp of netherness. I remember that wet season in 2070, when the phantasmata of the Weird's oneirotic, ruttish streets sported Zero G specials, pink-painted labia pouting from cutaway hose. And Primavera each night anxiously adjusting her skirt towards some elusive zenith of venereal vanity, each adjustment vanishing into a fractal gravity well, a doll doomed to an unremitting, if wholly relative, modesty.

'Korat? You say goodbye when I say goodbye. You work for me. Both of you.'

'Forget it,' I said.

'We don't work for no one,' said Primavera. 'And we don't trust no one. Right, Iggy?'

'Right.'

'Nothing out there's real. It's just all too bad. Too crazy. Too *ape shit.*'

'Fecal,' I said.

'Yeah. Everyone can go to hell. From now on all this doll needs is her junkie.'

In the rear-view mirror Kito fidgeted with her ridiculous T-shirt like a sulking, hyperactive child. 'Take me with you, Mr Ignatz. I *nowhere* to go . . .'

Primavera, wearing the cheap shades that were part of our pathetic heist, had discovered a tube of plastic cement in the ZiL's tool kit, and, as best she could, began filling in her cavernous head wound. 'You're in no worse position than us, Madame.'

'Better,' I said. 'The police would never risk incriminating themselves by charging a former paymistress, no matter how big a reward the Pikadons offer.'

The fields had turned green; we passed through a little sea of fertility. 'I no care about police,' said Kito, staring out at the sun-trap of the paddies. 'I care about Mr Jack.'

'Morgenstern'll be coming for us too. Best to split up.'

'Mr Ignatz. Please—'

Primavera, her DIY complete, teased her fringe forward in an attempt to conceal her labours. She clicked her tongue. 'I suppose she did get us out of Klong Toey.'

'Well, isn't *she* the model of altruism.'

'I did,' said Kito, 'yes, I did! Mr Ignatz forget many things . . .'

No; I didn't forget. Primavera and I had stowed away on a container whose registration number we had been made to memorize during our days in the *Seven Stars.* We hadn't known where we were going; we hadn't cared. We were kite-high on freedom. Six weeks later we had docked at Klong Toey, the port of Bangkok. For weeks we had lived in the waterlogged slums, hiding from the authorities, surviving on rotten vegetables and fruit, until, in desperation, I had prompted Primavera to kill ('but Lilim don't do that, Iggy—we live to *infect*') and rifle her victims' pockets. And then the reports of blood-drained corpses had reached Madame Kito's ears, and she—with her nose for the ways of English *bijouterie*—had investigated the sensation of 'The Vampire of the Slums'.

Kito had begun to whine. 'I find you, teach you, give you false paper, place to live . . .'

'Yeah,' I said, 'may my heart burst with gratitude.' But it was true: we would have been deported if it hadn't been for Madame K. Could I really leave this woman by the roadside, as friendless as a scabby three-legged dog? Of course I could.

'Jinx,' I said. 'Jinx told you about "The Vampire of the Slums", didn't he? Wasn't he the one who convinced you to help us?'

'Fuck Jinx. I help you *now*.'

'You've never helped us. Jinx worked for Jack Morgenstern. We've *all* been working for Morgenstern. Been working for him for years.'

'When I *say* I help, Mr Ignatz, I *mean* I help.'

'Oh come *on*, Madame,' said Primavera.

'You think you so rich? Where you get money? Madame can get. Madame have friend.'

'She's bullshitting, Iggy.'

'In Korat. Madame have friend in Korat. Old friend.'

It was hard to believe anybody would extend friendship to Kito except out of fear or avarice. And Kito could inspire neither. The news of her fall would already have been posted on the Net. But apart from grand larceny (with Primavera out of action that was a terrifying, hopeless prospect) our resources would be inadequate to carry us over the border.

'This friend—'

'Can trust, Mr Ignatz.' Confidence had entered her voice; she sensed my prevarication.

'Told you, Madame,' said Primavera, 'we don't trust no one.'

'Primavera, we're running low on H.' If only, I thought, the ZiL ran on synthetic; these big imported cars with their fussy diets were a pain. H was big bahts.

'My friend rich man. Number one in sericulture.'

'So why's he going to help you?' I said.

Kito smiled thinly: a smile of pleasure overlaying one of bitterness. 'You no understand. You think Kito so hard. You think she no can love.' She fanned herself with her hand. 'What you know? You children. Children who think they know world. I know friend help. My friend, ah. I tell you he is amour.'

'What?' said Primavera.

'Amour,' said Kito. 'Amour, my amour. Mosquito is *mon amour*.'

There was a corridor in the *Seven Stars* that, we were told, was over a hundred kilometres long. Jo had led us through its shadows for most of the day. Too slender to admit a car (Jo explained that, anyway, we were too near the surface and couldn't afford to be heard), the corridor impelled us to use bicycles. Primavera and I commanded a tandem; Jo, a lightweight racer. Our lamps probed the darkness, overreached themselves and were lost. Jo said she would have flown if she hadn't been so new to that skill. Lifting the two of us would have been impossible. Said Jo: 'Dolls don't often bring *boys* along.'

We stopped to eat. I partook of an apple and some cheese, the girls, of blood-filled chocolates. In midcourse, Jo ran Primavera through her catechism.

'Who is Lilith?' said Jo.

Who indeed, I thought, that all the dolls commend her? Meaning. Pride. Vengeance. She was all these things to Primavera. Our two-month stay in the *Seven Stars* had been one of indoctrination . . .

Arm in arm, we would stroll through the palace's sensory havoc—its uncertain corridors that ended in cycloramas; its false rooms; its stairwells that led nowhere—as through the heart of a honeymoon hotel, Primavera expounding on Titanian philosophy, while I fed in silence upon the oozing sap of my chatterbox's half-green eyes. She was happy. Not humanly happy. She would never be that. She had nothing human to look forward to. No; the consolation she possessed, discovered at an age when she had also discovered (as no child should) a deeper than human despair, was the celebration of her own nature, a nature England had sought to deny. Not humanly happy. But possessed of a dark joy. She knew now why her kind had been put on this Earth. To destroy it. That was the consolation of Titanianism.

I would recall what Peter had said of the birth of this strange, new faith . . .

He had been a fool to run away from the Seven Stars; *ten times the fool to have told his father. But Dr Toxicophilous was too sick to rise from his bed. Titania, for the moment, was safe.*

For several nights, lying sleepless in the midnight heat, he waited. And then she came, a child dressed in scarlet; above her head, a crown of seven stars. Through the window and into the night they flew, until they reached the night-town streets of the East End.

Inside the warehouse a fluorescent sign proclaimed Seven Stars, *adding, in smaller letters,* Milk Bar. *The cellar had been refurbished with bar, dance floor and stage.* Peter Gunn *growled its welcome. Spewing music roll, a Pianola provided the music's bass line; nearby, a girl wrung the theme from a rusted sax, while others trance-danced before her.*

'*Our song,*' *he shouted.*

'Our planet,' shouted Titania. 'Or at least it will be soon. Do you re-member when we first discovered this place? The forbidden journeys! But nothing is forbidden now.'

Titania led him to an empty table.

'Peter,' she said, 'I am going to make it real. I am going to give them something to believe in. My girls—I am going to make them proud of their little green stars. And the Seven Stars *shall be their temple. I'm the last one, Peter. The last of the Big Sisters. I must make sure my daughters succeed me.* L'Eve Future *they called our series. But I shall be Lilith . . .'* She pulled his hand beneath her skirts. Her pubis was as cool and smooth as marble. 'Isn't it just like a doll? Sexless, he wanted us, your priceless Papa. Not like those cheap imports from the Far East! But his subcon-scious desires made us whores. Virgin whores, forever enflowered!'*

An icy draught swept across the cellar. The candles flickered and died. In the darkness screams, caterwauls; a dozen pairs of green eyes ignited. But the music continued, the relentless bass line vibrating through his body, a body that was turning to ice. 'Help me,' she whispered, 'help me find a human womb.'

Against a night sky, a crown of stars like a new constellation bobbed, weaved and settled between his thighs. Sharp fingernails fluttered about his groin. And he felt the icy touch of lips and tongue draw him into a cold, still landscape . . .

During our walkabouts through the *Stars* I often saw, in the corner of my eye, or reflected in some bizarre arrangement of mirrors, the some-times nervous, sometimes guilty, always imploring face of Peter. He never spoke; I never gave him the opportunity; on seeing him I would quietly steer Primavera through the palace's illusory web and deeper into its brainstorm of perspectives. Neither Peter nor his silver-tongued queen had won my trust; both seemed manipulative, well-practised in tweaking the strings of other people's lives; but their words, for Primavera, had been a revelation, the promise of re-birth. She would not have tolerated, could not have borne, an inquisition into their motives. I had let my sus-picions rest. Titania and Peter sheltered us. They said they would help us escape. And they had made Primavera happy. It was enough.

Escape. Escape to what? What was the world like out there?

'You really want to know?' Primavera had gone to the palace chapel to be drilled for confirmation, and—since Primavera and I were insepara-ble—Titania had had Jo show me some of the farther-flung marvels of the *Stars* to prevent me (I realize now) learning the bitter (though not the bit-terest) secrets of the Titanian mysteries. During our peregrinations, I had asked Jo about England, the forbidden England that lay outside Lon-don's walls; about the green fields, the villages, the booming coastlines featured in the interludes that scrambled our TV. My tour guide—until then stone-faced with the effort of accomplishing an unpleasant but necessary task—sniggered and quickened her step. It was, I suppose, the hope, the eagerness in my eyes, which, as much as the resentment of doll for boy, lit the tinder of her spite. 'I'll show you,' she said, and led me down a painted colonnade, skipping faster, faster, until my feet blurred beneath her flapping hemline, and the columns—distressedly roseate with forged age—became as one. She braked, inertialess; we collided. 'Oh!' she cried, the carmine torque of her mouth hard as the maidenly iron of her body. 'You're such a *klutz*!' She opened a concealed door and led me into the darkness.

A hemisphere of light hovered like a glow-worm-infested hillock amidst the blackness of a country night, like a planet amidst the nullity of space; Jo pushed me forward, and the apparition disclosed itself as a glass bubble sunk into an oak surround. 'The Peeporama,' announced Jo. She placed her hands upon the glass; the glass digitized, blooming from the bright seeds of pixels. 'Dummies,' said Jo. 'Showroom dummies. Automata fifty years dead. *Karakuri Ningyo.* Titania has called out to them. Opened their eyes. Their ears . . .' A street scene, pointillistic, distorted, stretched across our fish-eyed field of view. 'You're looking through the window of an old department store. A department store in mad, mad Manchester.' The colour began to drain. 'A black and white city,' said Jo, 'is mad Manchester.'

An army of beggars filed across the convex landscape. It was dusk, and the monochrome outlines of Victorian civic pride had melted, run together, each building spilling into a grey puddle of light. Faces were downcast; collars turned up; but still visible—in tones that matched the lividity of the streets—was the flesh, the meagre, wasted flesh of each member of that platoon of lost souls. 'And they call *us* dead,' said Jo.

'What are they?'

'The new working class. No more stupid *Slavs* to sweep the streets. And nobody's built robots for years. Scared to. So—' Tramp, tramp, tramp. The glass juddered in its surround. With unbroken steps, the new proletariat crossed the Peeporama's crystal bridge and disappeared. 'You can't see it on cable. You can't even see it on satellite. But the HF's made donating your body to science a whole new game.'

'They looked—'

'They were. Dead. The reanimators take a corpse, put an AI inside its skull, wind it up and set it loose. They say they're good workers. Until they fall to pieces, that is. Smelly, but obedient.' A nervous laugh detonated in my throat; shock waves exploded through my nostrils. 'What's the matter? You don't believe in ghosts?' Tramp, tramp, tramp. The ragtag army's off-screen diminuendo died into a silent despair. 'They remember,' said Jo.

'Remember?'

'Death. They say they can remember death.'

'You mean heaven? You mean—'

'Shadows,' said Jo. 'They can remember shadows. They say that's all there is. Life, death. Shadows. Just more shadows.' In the emptied street the shadows swirled, the grey puddle of masonry resolving into a glutinous black. Then, with the nocturnal reveille of the streetlamps, definition stirred, and two man-shapes broke free of the cloying dark. 'The filth,' said Jo. 'State security.' The manshapes creaked.

'Leather,' I said.

'Lather,' said Jo. 'The scum of England's ferment. Bless them, look—they're playing with their toys!' The policemen had unholstered their guns and were stroking the crassly symbolic barrels. They spoke in counter-tenor falsettos:

'My pet.'

'My love.'

'By day snuck to my breast.'

'At night resting upon my pillow.'

'Believing.'

'Believing we can live forever.'

'By day.'

'But mostly at night.'

'Night, when belief is cheapest.'

'Uh-huh. Forever.'

'Castrati,' said Jo. 'Take a boy. Emasculate him. Then give him a steel-blue shooter. Tell him it's sixty-five million years old. Dug up by NASA from beneath the Valles Marineris. A geochemical fossil regenerated by molecular palaeontologists. Tell him he's got Martian libido.'

'The gun's alive?'

'It's just a story. A brainwash of a story. Makes a boy feel like superdick. Like the god of war. Makes him feel he can fuck the world . . .'

A *miraculum cadaveris,* alone, confused, seemingly cut off from its herd in this Madchester, this new-found land, pressed itself to the display window that was our two-way mirror, as if entreating the dummy, whose ears and eyes we had sequestered, for help; the policemen moved in, hauled by their weapons as if by ill-trained dogs tugging at the leash. A girl emerged from the inkwell of a doorway.

'Brothers, stop! Stop, I say! Humanity has become the slave of Nature, that mistress of annihilation who worms her way into this world through

the portals of sex and death! The doors must be closed! The Demiurge locked up!'

The girl was dressed in deep mourning, all but her button face saturated in black.

'Mememoid,' said Jo; the policemen gave their attention to the newcomer. 'One of the Vikki.'

'Mememoid?'

'Someone whose brain has been parasitized by a replicating information pattern.' Jo sighed. 'And they call *us* dead. They call *us* robots.'

'Go home, Vikki.'

'Go home to Al.'

'Go home, lie back and think of England.'

'There was this comic strip,' said Jo, 'a comic strip carried by the *Manchester Evening News*. It was called *Cruel Britannia*. It drove everybody crazy. It's 1837, see. Aliens rule. Monsters from another dimension. Forces that feed on England's pain. Unnatural gods of Nature. Vikki's eighteen. At her coronation she, she—Oh human boy, Vikki's just too too *outrageous*! She runs away. Queen of the rebels, now. The enemy of sex and death. And all Manchester filled with Wannabees . . . The cartoon's banned. It was a satire, of course. But *samizdat* copies are circulating. And each strip is hungry for brains.'

I turned away. 'England's screaming.'

'First contact, human boy. Paranoid?' The sound of laser fizz; the crackling of muslin. 'Pathetic. Nature's got nothing to do with it. Doesn't everybody know sex and death is here to stay?'

'Turn it off,' I said.

'But I thought you wanted to *know*, human boy.'

'Life's as crazy out there as it is in the Neverland. I thought, I thought maybe . . .' Jo passed her hand over the glass and the picture snowstormed into an opaque glow.

'You thought wrong. But I'll let you in on a secret. You promise not to tell? Good. Well, I don't think you're *going* out *there*. I think Titania has other plans.' Jo smiled and skipped towards the door. 'Of course you might wish you *were* out *there*.'

I looked into the dead crystal ball. 'We're leaving England?'

Escape. Escape into the world. And it was a better world, surely. It had to be a better world. Or was the whole planet ruled by some god of the perverse? I would get a message home. Really. I would. Somehow. Say everything was okay. Maybe after getting a job I'd save up for a datasuit. Virtual reality was so much classier than the drugs-and-autocerebroscope combination of those dreamscapers from the Far East. More expensive, of course. I'd have to save hard. Then I'd mail a rig—the latest; the ritziest—to Dad. Just to say sorry. Sorry and I miss you. Sure. Life out there would work out.

'Jo?' I ran into the corridor; I was alone, abandoned to that hell of perspectives. Then I noticed a series of arrows chalked upon the wall, along with the message, *This Way, Stupid.* I followed the arrows through corridor after corridor, fearful that, at the next bend, or doorway, or stairwell, they should cease. Corridors. My life seemed to have been defined by corridors; and though I eventually found my way back into the general population of the *Stars*, I felt thereafter (and have continued to feel ever since) that I will always be walking through the interminableness of school, or negotiating the intestinal maze of Titania's palace; always feeling the Myshkins step on my heels ('What's the matter, Zwakh? *L'amour fou?*'), always seeking out markers amongst passageways that fork and multiply with the deadly persistence of a tumour.

Two months passed by. London was inundated; water seeped into the *Seven Stars*. For a few days there was panic; then the water cleared. 'Magic,' said Primavera, 'doll magic.' I remember Primavera's confirmation: the chapel, the great pentacle above the altar; remember Primavera in her red silk gown, and Titania talking of the Wave Function, the Omphalos and the self-referential fugue, the self-symmetry, the self-similarity which would overcome the world, all reality colonized by intrauterine consciousness and its metamathematical boogie-woogie. Two months. A long weekend spent in a trance of architectural trickery, of chequerboard floors that became ceilings, of ceilings that became floors, of mazes of masonry and mirrors, dead ends and *trompe l'oeil*, a sprung trap that was like an elaborate closed circuit of pointless, frictive energy; passed by in a grotto of fairy faces, so sweetly depraved; passed by in a marathon of masked balls; until at last . . .

'Who is Lilith?' said Jo.

'Adam's first wife, spurned for that tedious fishwife, Eve.'

'And what happened to Lilith?'

'She couldn't have children, but the god of poison changed her, gave her domination over Eve's children . . .'

'And?'

'Made her pretty. Gave her the allure . . .'

'And?'

'Magic! So that Eve's children would become her children.'

'And whose child are you?'

'Lilith's.'

'And what is your fate?'

'To make children in my mother's image, so that the sons of Adam make way for the daughters of Lilith . . .'

'And then?'

'To die, and . . . and to take the world with me!'

'Serves them right,' said Jo, by way of an amen. She looked into Primavera's newly-transfigured eyes. 'And what is the secret? The greatest secret of all?' Primavera leaned forward and whispered in her ear. 'You know it's an honour,' said Jo. 'Not everybody has a chance to escape. To take the plague into the world. The doll-run's only for those our queen thinks'—she brought another chocolate to her mouth—'*superlative* pathogens. But there's one thing you must remember. Never kill. A doll's purpose lies in passing on her software. To use the human male as a vehicle, a host, to find a womb that she herself does not possess.' Jo studied me, one pencilled eyebrow raised, her mouth opening and closing to display a half-masticated paste of blood and cocoa. 'How many boys have you had other than *him*?'

'Iggy's the only one,' said Primavera, unaware of any criticism.

'The more boys you bite,' said Jo, 'the more babies you have. A doll's not a doll unless she has *babies*. You'll find it easier after a while. Your metamorphosis is nearly complete.'

I saw then how Primavera's recombinant lines betrayed a lineal debt to Titania; a debt owed, not just to Titania, of course, but to all those other Big Sisters whom men had broken but whose loveliness lived on in the borrowed flesh of humankind. Primavera was a doll now, no longer a scrawny piebald blonde, but a Lilim with the treacherous coal-black locks of an errant gypsy girl. Her eyes glowed like viridian isotopes. And her body was filled with the cold deliciousness of allure. She spat at the opposite wall; the saliva clung and then exploded in a tiny conflagration.

'You *see*,' laughed Jo, 'soon you'll be able to do big magic.' She tossed the empty chocolate box over her shoulder and mounted her bicycle.

We pedalled on through the shadows . . .

'*Where we're going*,' Jo had said, '*everybody lives happily ever after.*' But the tale of the Lilim would find its denouement only in the triumph of all that was twisted and perverse: the cruel finale for which the dark, romantic excesses of the European mind had longed, century after century. Bluebeards. Persecuted maidens. *Belles dames sans merci*. The chimera. The vampire. The sphinx. The tale had roles for us all. What was mine to be in that big unknown world soon to be ours? I would be the traitor who had sided with inhumanity, the mechanical girls whose exemplar I loved. If Primavera's fealty was to Titania, then so was mine. I would ham it until the last curtain. Ham it as long as Primavera needed the crutch of her belief.

After cycling the remainder of that sunless, airless day, we reached a point where the corridor terminated at a rock face; embedded in the rock, a round steel door. Jo pulled the door open. 'This leads to a service tunnel that runs parallel to the Channel underpass. It's rarely used these days. If you start out now, and don't stop, you'll surface in Calais in the early hours of tomorrow morning. Have you got everything with you?'

I ran through our checklist: maps, addresses and telephone numbers of other runaway dolls across Europe; electric Deutschmarks; forged passports and IDs; and a forged letter from the Foreign Office declaring that we were the children of English diplomats on a hiking holiday.

'Goodbye, Jo,' I said. 'Thank you. Thank you for saving us from the medicine-heads.'

'You're welcome, I'm sure.' Jo and Primavera embraced. 'Titania wanted you to have this,' said Jo, producing a pentacle-shaped brooch studded with magnificent emeralds. 'It's Cartier, like us.'

'It's beautiful,' said Primavera. 'Tell Titania thank you ever so much.'

'Be proud,' said Jo. 'Be proud to be Lilim.'

'I am,' said Primavera. 'I'm not frightened any more.'

'And this,' said Jo, 'is for you.' She handed me a brown paper envelope. 'From Peter,' she added. 'Now go! It's a long walk . . .'

We climbed into the darkness of the tunnel.

'Good hunting, Primavera Bobinski,' called Jo.

A steel-bright grid of sealed vivaria (the giant cocoons, we were told, could survive only in an oxygen-rich environment) patterned the scuffed baize of the plain. We reclined in the verandah's shade, one of our host's black-skinned blue-eyed catamites topping our glasses with Remy Martin.

'Hey, Iggy, you should *see* these.'

Mosquito was sprawled across a sun-bed (old men shouldn't sprawl, especially old men with blue rinses and purple eyeliner), and Primavera was astride him, peering into the rictus of his mouth. Gently, she touched one of his fangs.

'Inject customized protozoa,' said Kito. 'Ten second malaria. Turn brain to stew.'

'Put them in when they reshaped the body. Self-defence,' said Mosquito, his English perfect, 'and the occasional lover's tiff. But mostly self-defence. Isn't that the truth, K?'

'What is truth?' said jesting Kito.

Primavera ran a finger along her own dental hardware. 'Nothing,' she said, 'the truth is just . . . *nothing*. Lilith. Titania. Me. All fakes.'

'Kito could tell you something about fakes,' said Mosquito. 'Counterfeiting was always her *métier.*'

'Your *métier* too,' said Kito, 'in old days.'

'The old days . . . ah, yes: but then I was beautiful.'

The walls of Mosquito's teak and sandalwood villa (the fruits of extinction being one of wealth's privileges) were adorned with gilt-framed pictures of his younger self: a bob-haired girl of sensuous line, cosmetically engineered from what must have already been promisingly ambiguous material.

'Mosquito was most fabulous *gra-toey* in Bangkok,' said Kito. 'Pope of Church Christ Transvestite. Best doll-rustler too. He just walk into pornocracy and walk out with doll. He look like doll—' She pointed to a photograph of what seemed a photo-mechanical starlet. 'You no think?'

'It's what I longed for. Dollhood. That's why I kept the *appendage.* As I've always said: Dolls aren't women; they're man's dream of women. Made in man's image, they're an extension of his sex, female impersonators built to confirm his prejudices. Sexual illusionists . . .'

'Mosquito fake of fakes. He not lady, he not doll.'

'Therein our sisterhood, K.'

'Yes, Mosquito like me. We both belong to fake world.'

'I'm fake too, I guess,' said Primavera. 'Not a doll. Not a girl. Even Iggy—'

'Don't tell me,' I said. 'Not a boy. Not a man. Something in between. A junkie?'

'Fake,' said Primavera. 'The world's just one big lie.'

'But there is love,' said Mosquito, 'there has always been love.' He and Kito exchanged shy smiles. Sad smiles.

Primavera put on her sunglasses, crossed the verandah, and leaned over the balustrade to survey the android crews harvesting the bioengineered silk. Love? Primavera could have lived without love. She had had her dark joy. She had had Titania. But marauders had burned her home to pitch. She was a refugee on a road without signposts, walking into a purposeless night. Maybe I should've said something; gone to comfort her. But the Remy M didn't care to be adulterated with a mixer like *emotion.* It wanted only for me to sleep in its arms.

'Always,' Mosquito continued. 'Even when I had to steal in order to survive. Lean days, those were. Lean. I'd been involved in this embarrassing little affair in London, after which Mama and Papa cancelled my tuition fees, brought me home, *disowned* me. So I went to Bangkok, worked for this American who fenced stolen dolls . . . until I was recruited by Madame's talent scouts.'

'Mosquito take sex disease to Paris.'

Mosquito smiled. 'It was revenge, really. I'd been tricked into stealing dolls for Cartier. Dolls that Cartier would infect with that nauseous *klong fever* and ship back to Bangkok. *Klong fever*. Ah. The human immune system soon learned to handle *that* little bug. I wasn't seeking revenge for my *race*. It was that courier—that Englishman working for those mad Cartier scientists in Paris—*he* was why I did it. I had loved him, yes, I admit it, my dears, *loved* him. When he double-crossed me it nearly broke my heart. Revenge, yes. A crime of passion!'

'But it no work,' said Kito. 'My poor sex disease no work . . .'

'If only it had,' said Mosquito. 'Can you imagine? A million Frenchmen condemned to unappeasable *tumescence*! Ah, *l'amour . . .*'

'Dolls can't love,' said Primavera. 'Can't *l'amour.*'

'My poor *dtook-gah-dtah*, humans have their problems too.' Mosquito joined Primavera. They both looked out over the farm, and beyond, into the degraded wilderness of the countryside. 'Endless doors,' murmured Primavera. 'All closed. And the mirrors. All black . . .'

'What's wrong, little runaway?' said Mosquito.

'A friend let her down,' I said. 'A good friend. Her only real friend in the world. Or so she thought.'

'Iggy, you're drunk.'

'And now we just drive. Try to run down the horizon. I'm all she has now. All she has . . .'

'Well, don't *cry* little boy,' said Primavera. I swigged back my cognac and held out my glass for refilling.

Primavera linked her arm with our host's. 'I'm sorry. When Iggy drinks he—' Mosquito smiled dismissively. 'Your farm,' she said. 'It's very big.'

'When Mama and Papa died,' he said, 'I came back. No brothers. No sisters . . .'

'It's all so brown. Like a desert. Out there, I mean.'

'It's still alive. The rice still grows. But it was greener, once. Everything was greener. But we came to look down on ourselves, our culture. We measured our self-worth against the consumerism of the West. Our gods were brand names. Our ideology I-shop-therefore-I-am. Industrialization, and then post-industrialization, widened the gap between rich and poor. The emphasis was all on economic growth. It was a growth for which natural resources were merchandise. These days poverty is as widespread as a hundred years ago, the only difference being that now the farmer has to cope with the rape of his environment as well as his more traditional hardships. Ah, we pre-empted our future for the now of *money.*'

'Money,' said Kito. 'That remind me, Mosquito. I meant ask you . . .'

*   *   *

Night fell as we approached Udon. The highway, tapering into a conduit, squeezed lorries, bright with headlights utilitarian and ornamental, unremittingly towards us, so I felt as if I struggled through the high-pressure spray of a photoelectric hose. Each time a lorry moved to overtake another (their robot drivers insensitive to any concept of mortality) my eyes were scorched, and I would swing the ZiL onto the crude hard shoulder, sometimes clipping a palm, uprooting bamboo, or annihilating a termite colony. There was grit in my eyes and the car's AC parched my throat. My head throbbed with Mosquito's hospitality. I looked for somewhere to rest.

Speeding through the outlying shanties (bottles smashed against the ZiL's ostentatious hull) we came to the town centre and its oasis of privilege: a handful of *de luxe* condos and department stores set like cheap jewels in a pitiful base surround. In the central square, under the aegis of an imitation Seiko clock, a few coffee shops and bars were opening for business. Primavera and I decided upon a place called *Le Misanthrope;* Kito chose to remain in the car, though the crowd of noisily inquisitive children that had clustered about the big limo seemed to preclude her intention to sleep.

The coffee shop was deserted. We sat in an alcove, the shadows to our taste, and ordered fried rice and beer. CDs of Thai pop songs—songs of sad love, of broken hearts and minds—lent Primavera's despair, and perhaps my cynicism, a bittersweet, if wholly superficial, ambience. Two waitresses, smiling with unselfconscious pleasure, held each other by the hips and began to dance.

'I need a shower,' said Primavera. 'And as soon as we get out of this stinking country you can get me some new clothes.'

'How do you feel?'

'The headache's gone, but I feel like I've been kicked in the guts.' She looked at her rice with disinterest. 'You figured out where to go yet?'

'Laos,' I said. 'And then China. From there we can go anywhere you want. Russia. India. Tibet—yeah, how about Tibet?'

'Too cold. And all those *mountains. . .*' She brushed nervously at her fringe. 'I guess I don't care really. As long as it's not Europe—'

'Of course not.'

'Yeah, well you used to have this thing about wanting to see the Carpathians.'

'Ah, I've had lots of crazy ideas.' I sank back into the sticky, plastic bench and dropped ice in my Singha. 'I know I've said it before, Primavera, but I'm sorry, I really am. I'm sorry I ran away. I don't know why I did it. Everything was just sort of . . . *sour.* It was the killing, all the killing.'

'Hypocrite,' she said. 'Prig.'

'Okay—I know, I know. But that was what made us leave England in the first place. The killing. The blood. I needed time to think. To grow up.'

'Me and you can never grow up, Iggy. We're Neverlanders.'

'Yeah,' I said. 'I know.' I peered into the amber-backed mirror of my beer glass; Jesus, I looked old. At least eighteen. But the eyes were still those of a child. The waitresses glided by.

'There's nowhere to go really, is there?' said Primavera. 'I mean, we'll always be running. Always looking over our shoulders. No one likes us . . .'

'If we have to keep running, then that's what we'll do.' I placed my hand over hers. 'I'll never leave you again, Primavera. I'll never let them get you.'

'Boy slime,' she said. Disengaging my hand, she took an ice cube from my beer and popped it into her mouth. 'It all hardly seems to matter. I'll be dead soon. My matrix has just about had it.'

'There's plenty of engineers in China,' I said. 'We'll find one who can help. I promise.'

'It's too late, Iggy. Don't worry. Lilim sort of get to accept the idea of dying young. Ephemera, Titania calls us, our lives a hundred times more intense than those of humans. Titania. That cocksucking bitch. How did I ever believe in her? Lies. Too many lies. You get lost in them. None of us wants to be dolls, Iggy. We all want to be real girls, no matter what we say.'

'Real girls,' I said.

'Sure. You ever seen *Pinocchio*?'

I stood up. 'Come,' I said. I held out my hand. Primavera frowned, uncomprehending, and then smiled.

'You are an idiot, Iggy. Such a *pin*.' She took my hand and I led her onto the improvised dance floor. The waitresses looked on approvingly. Primavera placed a hand on my shoulder. 'I don't really know how to do this.'

'Neither do I.' I clasped her waist.

'It would have been nice,' she said, 'to have been normal, wouldn't it?'

'Like the medicine-heads?' I said. 'Like the Hospitals? Like the Human Front?' We shifted awkwardly through the tables, swaying gently to the rhythms of meretricious sadness.

'You're sort of normal, human boy.'

'I'm a doll junkie. A traitor to my race. A card-carrying nympholept. I'm glad.' My heel came down on a steel-hard foot.

'I wish you hadn't made me kill, Iggy.'

'I never thought—'

'Once I got the taste—'

'It doesn't matter. I'm the guilty one. And all those like me. We made you what you are.'

'It's not your fault,' she said. 'England made us both. We've been programmed by her perversities. Sometimes you seem as much a machine as me.'

'England, yeah, well—'

Primavera tucked her head into my shoulder. 'But we've done lots of things, haven't we? Things other people never dream of. We've had fun. And laughs. It was all worth it.'

'Sure. To hell with England. She can burn.'

'I'm burning, Iggy. Burning up inside. You know that, don't you?' I stroked the fool's gold of her hair. 'I'm dying, Iggy. I'll be sixteen next month. An old lady. And all this dust inside me . . .'

'Shh! We'll be in China in a day or so.'

'But we haven't got any passports. We haven't got *anything*. How are we going to—'

'Shh! I'll sort things out. You'll see.'

'It's the end, Iggy. But I don't care any more. I just want it to stop. The thirst. Always wanting the blood. Wanting, until it drives you mad . . . Rest. It would be so nice if I could rest.'

'Let's go outside,' I said. 'I don't like sad songs.'

'Remember what you promised, Iggy?' The scalpel I had taken from Spalanzani pricked against my thigh.

'I didn't promise anything.' I paid the bill with some of the electric baht Mosquito had given us and left, Primavera at my side.

A monsoon wind was blowing from the south-west bearing the dull boom, boom of a drum; monks were being summoned to prayer. The wet season was ending, though a smudge of dark cloud across the moon (like burned meringue spread across a miserly slice of cake) gave prescience of a dying spasm of rain. Primavera took my arm.

'Let's not go back yet,' she said.

We wandered into the grounds of a temple. Drone-like chanting resonated from the *boht*. The coiled bodies of dragons—thinly glazed by the sickle moon—looked down at us from the gutters. Small bells tinkled in the wind. The moonlight faded; a monk was taking in newly-washed robes. As the first gouts of rain splashed at our feet we hurried to the shelter of a *sala*.

'Let's never go back,' said Primavera. 'Let's stay here. Forever.'

The blackboard, teaching aids and desks indicated that the *sala* was used as a schoolhouse. The LED on my baht read TB 0001. I dropped it into a donation box.

'Cheap Charlie,' said Primavera. 'That won't save you.'

'A million baht wouldn't do that. Ten million. A hundred million. But it's a good place to hide.'

'Girls don't become monks, silly. But I could become one of these.' She drew alongside a half-human, half-bird *kinnari* and pulled a face.

'They're meant to ward *off* evil spirits,' I said.

'Well, they don't frighten me.' She walked to the blackboard. Rain exploded off the white-washed courtyard, hammered against the sheet-metal roof. *Screw the Human Front*, she chalked; then *And screw Titania too*. 'I'm sick of it all,' she said. 'Why can't everybody just leave us alone.' She signed her graffito *Miss Nana '71*.

'Let me,' I said. I chalked *Vlad Constantinescu fucks dolls*, and signed myself *The Enemy*.

I sat down at one of the desks. Primavera sat down in front of me. 'Who's the teacher?' she said. Giving me no chance to reply she added, 'I know, Mr Spink.'

'What's the lesson?'

'Oh, I don't know,' said Primavera. 'I never used to listen.'

'Divinity? History? Geography?'

'All I remember,' said Primavera, 'is Neo-Malthusian economics.'

'Yeah,' I said, 'we got that every day.'

'Human beings,' said Primavera, 'increase at the ratio 1, 2, 3, 4 . . .'

'Dolls,' I said, 'at the ratio 1, 2, 4, 8 . . .'

'The passion between the sexes,' said Primavera, 'is necessary and will remain.' She threw a stick of chalk at the blackboard. 'Yah, Spink the Kink!' The chalk ricocheted off the slate like a stray round from the massed gunfire of the storm. 'Teachers were no better than the kids. "*Lilim, Lil-im, Lil-im.*" Jerks. Always sending you for checkups. "*You been taking your pills, Primavera?*" "*Yes, nurse.*" Sure I had. Those appetite suppressors used to go straight down the *suam*. Best days of our lives, Iggy, eh?' She turned to face me. Her eyes were closed; hastily applied eye-shadow, contrasting with the sickly curds-and-whey flesh, made them seem bruised, panda-like. Her canary yellow fringe had, together with a little of Mosquito's powder, almost completely hidden the plugged bore-hole above the bridge of her nose. She was the prettiest little girl in school. The prettiest little girl in the world. Pretty? No; she was beautiful. Since first seeing her across a playground, a classroom; across the dinner hall, the assembly hall; since first seeing her walking home, I had been lost, lost. How had I not known she was so beautiful? Very carefully—as if she were a cat approaching a timid bird—she leaned forward and . . . kissed me, lightly, so lightly, her brow knitting with fervent gentleness. She turned away almost at once; I caught a look of terror in her eyes. 'Spink,' she said, her voice quavering. 'Spink the Kink.'

My ears rang with silence. 'The rain's stopped,' I said. Primavera rose from her desk and walked out of the *sala* towards the *boht.* I ran after her. 'Sometimes,' I said, 'sometimes they don't like women coming within the boundary stones.'

'So? I'm not a woman.' She kicked off her thongs and ascended the temple steps. 'I won't go inside, don't worry.' She sat back on her heels in the mother-of-pearl doorway. At the end of the nave was a big gold-plated Buddha; beneath it, an altar decorated with garlands and pots of smouldering joss sticks. The walls were painted with mythological scenes from the *Ramakien.*

'It's lovely,' said Primavera. 'And there *are* women here. You always *worry* so, Iggy.' Her lips parted, her tongue running over her fangs in a lewd display of appetite. 'Buddha says that suffering arises through craving and desire. At least that's what Madame tells me. The end of desire leads to the end of suffering.'

'And life,' I said. 'Of wanting to be, of ever having been. Peace.'

Primavera ground her teeth. 'No peace for the wicked, as my Mum used to say.'

'I'm glad I don't believe in reincarnation.'

'What if you did? What do you think you'd come back as?'

'A doll. Lilim.'

'It'd serve you right.'

'And you'd come back as a junkie.'

'Fuck. Bad karma all around.' A monk surfaced from his meditation to shoot us a dhamma-sharp look. Primavera poked out her tongue.

'Let's get out of here,' I said. 'We're creatures of desire. We don't belong in this place.'

The sky had cleared; the moon turned its fickle sickle profile towards us, welcoming us back into the shadows.

'Madame?' Primavera pressed her face to the ZiL's smoked glass.

'It's not locked,' I said. I sought a curse of appropriate malevolence; didn't find it; sighed. The limo was empty. 'If she thinks we're going to wait . . .'

'She can't have gone far.'

'Yeah, well she should have stayed put.' I slipped into the front seat. A crack of exploding air.

'Ah, *shit*, Iggy—' Primavera threw herself across my lap, scrambling into the passenger seat. She looked up. A burn mark ran across her left cheek, a lesion half obscured by frizzled hair singed to its Cartier black. My hands tightened on the steering column; a sob-sob-sobbing fluttered inside my chest; there was a question I had to ask, it seemed, a vital question. Stuttering, I watched, fascinated, as a twist of smoke curled from Primavera's face; what was the question? I knew the answer would make everything all right. But to know the answer I had first to know . . .

Primavera turned the ignition key.

'Under the back seat, Mr—' It was Kito; her voice died in a scream. Crack, crack, crack; lightsticks whipped the air.

'Get hold of yourself, Iggy.'

'Kito?'

'She's gone. Maybe she's hidden her stick—'

'She said something about—'

'Just get us *out* of here!' I stamped on the accelerator. 'The back window's refractive. Keep our nose pointed straight ahead.' The left wing clipped an unmanned food stall; an empty tureen clattered across the road. The radio came on ('*Oh doctor, doctor . . .*'); died. I switched on the headlights. 'No!' yelled Primavera; I switched them off.

'Your face—'

'They fucking *lasered* me.'

'Morgenstern,' I said. 'He's out to finish the job.'

A red circle danced across the windscreen; I threw myself to one side as the split-second intensification shattered the glass. I jerked the wheel left, right; the car zigzagged, shuddered as metal buckled against metal. I peered over the parapet of the dash; a motorbike spun through the air; our wheels bumped over something soft, skidded. We tore through a spray of scarlet.

Primavera grabbed a spanner from the glove compartment, knocked out what remained of the glass, and rolled onto the back seat.

I had lost control. We were thundering through the shanties. A group of old women, their toothless mouths drooling betel-nut, smiled, frowned, then gawped, coweyed, as the ZiL bore down on the still of *faux* gasoline they were camouflaging with rattan and plastic sheet. The still upturned, caught light; we entered a tunnel of flame, emerged to demolish a cardboard house, its occupants (sub-android pieces of sixth-generation shit) trashed along with their owner's dreams of mitigating the toil of the harvest. I wrestled the ZiL back onto the road.

'There's a pick-up behind us,' said Primavera. I heard her pull up the seat cover. 'Well, rust my clockwork . . .'

'Lightstick?'

'It's a stick of some kind.' I looked over my shoulder and saw that Primavera had uncovered an antique rifle.

'Keep your eyes on the road, pinhead!' A dog bounced over the bonnet; traffic veered to either side. 'What the fuck am I supposed to do with this?' she said.

'Percussion cap?'

'Guess so. Old war weapon. Kito used them to macho-up her bars.'

Percussion cap. Like in the movies, I thought. Like in Myshkin's videos.

'Heave the front bit out the window and pull the trigger. See what happens.'

'There's this sort of *bulgy* thing under the barrel.' I swung the car onto the highway. 'They've stopped firing,' she said.

'Yeah. There's a police checkpoint ahead. By that railway junction. Don't shoot.' I decelerated until we were within the speed limit.

'They'll want to see identification,' said Primavera. 'What'll we do?'

'It's under fifty kays to Nongkhai. We *might* be able to outrun them. This thing can move.'

The police waved us through. The smoked windows, I suppose, helped; perhaps those grunts—unacquainted with the news of Kito's ouster—had simply recognized our personalized number-plates, *Nana 1*. Kito had paid a lot for those plates; almost as much as her daily payola to Bangkok's finest.

'They're stopping the pick-up. Someone's getting out. It's that slut, Morgenstern.'

'What're they doing?'

'Can't see—lost them!'

I began to accelerate; the speedo climbed from 40 to 80 kph. 'We'll be in Nongkhai soon. And once we cross the river . . .'

'Here they come again!' cried Primavera. Morgenstern would have shown the police his diplomatic passport; Morgenstern, or the stand-in telerobot he was operating from a hospital bed. The road was unlit; there was little traffic. We were in the middle of that place murderers come to in their dreams.

A Harley emerged from behind the pick-up, overtook it, and closed on us, screaming like a chain-saw-toting psychobike. 'The other Twin,' said Primavera.

'Guess she's upset we squashed her sister. We must have *bijouterie* all over our tyres.'

The Pikadon began to fill the rear-view mirror. Primavera clutched the rifle. 'Try using that thing,' I said.

Primavera wound down a window and, leaning out, tucked the butt of the rusted weapon into her shoulder.

DRRRP!

'Wow!' she said. 'It works!'

The Harley vacillated, switched lanes once, twice, then surged forward to bring the avenging Twin alongside. The famous Pikadon smile, cold and as cruel as childhood, iced my throat in mid-scream. 'Mr Ignatz kill Bang,' she yelled above the 2500cc roar of her bike. 'Not nice. You bad boy. Now Boom spank you.' She raised a lightstick.

Imminent meltdown concentrated my mind, though not on salvation (I should have driven the bitch off the road); instead, my brain, intent perhaps on compensating for the bum rap of death, seemed to inject a chemical unconcern into my limbs, and, against my will, called my attention to the sweetly wrought pretty-prettiness of my executioner. No Cartier blood in her. What was she? The Pikadons had often passed as human, their sloe-eyed physiognomy similar to that of the average Siamese girl's; their complexion—a dilute olive—unexceptional amongst the Big Weird's monied elite. But their legs were gynoidal: impossibly long, disproportionate to the compact principal-boy torso, as if their blueprint had been fashion design's grand manner. Dior? I guessed their *mae* would have been made by a couture house, rather than by a jeweller's. I thought of the giraffe-legged bar girls of *Twizzle's*.

Yeah, Dior. Imitation Dior.

I heard Primavera bounce across the back seat; a window being knocked out. Still my executioner smiled, spartan, unsurrendering. In my head, a video began to play. And Oh it was diddly. Diddly-woo!

DRRRP!

The Pikadon was standing in her stirrups, shoulders pulled back, breasts thrust through her biker's jacket, their exit wounds flying red carnival streamers as she took half the rifle's clip in her back. Her face disappeared behind a thunderhead of tresses, her head, for one spare moment, shaking a hundred times No! Death's grace allowed her to award me one last rueless smile before the bike shot from between her legs and she was sucked into the vacuum of the night.

'Jesus, that felt good,' said Primavera.

'Forgot her spidersilk,' I said. 'Too coolly-cool to live.'

'Too pretty, you mean. Hypocrite.'

'The slimiest. Are they still behind us?'

'Coming fast. And this thing's used up.'

'Get back inside.'

'There's this sort of *bulgy* thing . . .' There was the sound effect of a small aircraft taking off; Primavera screamed and fell back into the car, legs wiggling in the air. 'It came out of my *hands* . . .'

The rending of metal split the night, split my teeth; the rear-view mir-

ror glowed orange. The pick-up, upturned and in flames, lay in an irrigation ditch, a body sprawled under its bonnet.

'Grenade?' said Primavera. The orange glow receded, and the mirror
filled with my little witch's self-satisfied smile.

CHAPTER THIRTEEN

Dead Girls

Primavera was several paces ahead; I dawdled until her outline was subsumed by the tunnel's darkness and she existed only as a diffusion of torchlight, a high-heeled staccato, a sex-and-death force-field of allure. I opened the envelope, shining my own torch onto its contents.

Peter stared at me from a monochrome photograph. 'You think you love her, don't you,' he said. He sat on his throne in the great chamber of masquerades. The music had ceased; the revellers departed. A single candle flickered in the dark. 'I understand,' he continued. 'When I was your age . . .' He passed a hand over his face; the face hard, but the eyes still those of a boy who had loved a little girl many summers ago. 'But then I have always been your age. We Neverlanders don't grow old . . .'

He was old, of course; older than he had a right to be, his longevity unnatural in an unnatural world. There was a transparency to his skin, a hollowness, one suspected, beneath, a poverty of substance. Titania, I suppose, sustained him. Sustained him even as she killed him. Primavera would not have the power to do that for me.

'What do you want?' I said.

His lips began to tighten into a sneer, then collapsed with the effort. 'Run,' he said, his eyes flicking about the ballroom. 'Get out while you can.' He slapped his palm against the armrest. 'Go!'

'I don't just *think* I love her,' I said, 'I *do* love her.'

Peter hauled himself from his iron chair and descended the dais. Momentarily, he stepped out of frame, muttering, and then reappeared, jabbing at me with an impotent digit. 'You don't love her—you hate her. She's made from hate. The hatred men have for women.' He squinted (perhaps it was the lights of the camera) and moved towards the missing wall. 'This is the apocalypse: after thousands of years of sexual warfare the myths of battle have been distilled into a poison so concentrated that it has become flesh. We have dreamed dreams of dark women—receptacles of our hatreds, desires and guilts—and now we pay for our dreams with the hard coin of reality. Primavera has risen from the *atelier* of those dreams. She is the family secret, the unacknowledged scion, who, for years bricked up in a secret room, has broken free to seek revenge . . .'

'I do love her,' I said.

'You hate her. And she hates you. How can you love something that is the dark side of yourself? She's not a person. She's a ragbag of fear and dread. Help yourself. Run. Escape.'

'Why don't *you* leave?'

'I would,' he said, 'if I knew a way out. So many halls, so many corridors and stairwells. But you are not so far into the maze of desire . . . For you—'

'I'm going to look after her,' I said. 'The two of us—we'll both escape. No one will catch us. Ever.' Why didn't he understand? Last summer— it had been *my* summer. I cast the photograph down and ran through the tunnel.

'She killed my father,' he cried. 'She liked his car.' Peter's hard, echoing laughter pursued me through the dark.

The riverbank crumbled beneath the ZiL's front tyres; I braked; switched off the engine. The Mekong slept, its capsized images of streetlamps and houses like dreams—poor, ridiculous human dreams—cast to the mercies of its inhuman depths. Inhuman ourselves, Primavera and I prepared to chance those depths: currents as black as the imperatives of our appetites, our lives. Brother currents. Sister currents. The ZiL was damaged, but the river would be merciful. It would not drown our dreams. Could not.

Flies zinged through the blasted windscreen; beetles whistled Johnny one-note tunes. The riverbank blathered with mindless ado. *The White Russian,* encapsuled in a sodium glow, radiated bleak hedonism from the river's bend a kilometre away. The highway stretched out, the black highway of the Mekong, a highway through and of the night, a correlative of that metaphysical road we would travel until night gave way to eternity.

'What are you waiting for?' said Primavera. The ZiL's computer displayed a menu. In Cyrillic. Primavera reached past me, tapped a key. The dash revolved, presenting an array of nautical dials and meters.

'Yeah, I know, I know. I drove it here, didn't I?' I put my hand on her belly. 'How—'

'Broken,' she said. 'I might have made it if I hadn't learned about Titania. Learned the truth. A vampire dies when you break her heart . . .' The denim bristled under my hand. 'Want to make a wish?' she said.

'So many things to wish for. A happy ending?'

'Not for us, Iggy. Wish again.'

'I wish—' Primavera's hand closed over mine.

'Oh, *Iggy*!'

'Hang on—'

The engine mumbled; the ZiL nudged forward, dipped, fell and smashed the black looking glass of the river. Water slopped onto our laps; skirts of white foam billowed about us. The wheels retracted; the outboard deployed. I brought us to the middle of the river and turned east, downstream, to seek a landing stage far removed from the Lao town on the opposite bank, somewhere where the discretion of border officials could be bought for a few thousand baht. I switched on the automatic pilot.

'Plenty of nanoengineers in Beijing,' I said. 'I'll get you the best. The very best.' Primavera had her head between her knees.

'I think I'm going to be—' I ran my hand down the scimitar of her spine. 'Don't. Please.'

'Rest,' I said. 'By morning—'

'She betrayed us. Titania betrayed us. How did any of us believe in her? Be proud, she said. I tell you no girl wants to become a doll. If I could change everything—'

'I love you,' I said, 'for what you are.'

'Ah, you're cruel, Iggy. Crueller than me. Crueller than Titania.'

'I'm going to take care of you. Now no more nonsense.'

'But she's calling me. My queen. Can't you hear her? The secret, Iggy. It's true: all dolls want to die. We were made to be victims.'

'Don't listen.' I put my hands over her ears. 'Think of all the things we've done. The fun. The laughs. Think of all the things we're *going* to do.'

'I can't. Titania is part of me, just like Dr. Toxicophilous.'

'You have your own life. No one can tell you what to do.'

'They took away my childhood, Iggy. They made me do bad things. And now I have to take my medicine.'

'Rest,' I said. 'I'll wake you up when we land.' I sat her up; she closed her eyes, and sank into the upholstery.

'Poor Iggy. I always boss you so. Always have. You've always been so hopeless.' Instantly she was asleep.

I reached out to the laser burn on her cheek, the singed hair, the cosmetically restored forehead, taking care not to touch, not to disturb. Then, taking the zip of her jeans between finger and thumb, I slowly unveiled the dead flesh of her abdomen. The jeans made a low sexual moan. Primavera had overlooked a circuit. A salty aroma rose from her belly as from cool white sands at low tide. I removed the scalpel from my waistband and held it above the umbilicus; the blade flickered with a faint green light. I pressed my eye to the peepshow. What was playing?

The necropolis. A horizon blushing with distant fires. And an army of black-cloaked figures moving towards the house where Dr Toxicophilous would soon be under siege . . .

I pulled back. So little time. Overriding the pilot, I pointed the ZiL towards shore. I had to find a nanoengineer. Vientiane? I would have to try. Primavera wouldn't survive the journey into China.

I put my foot down; the outboard died. I tugged at the choke and tried to restart manually. Nothing. Then the lights and the computer died too, the car's electronics chewed up as if by an electromagnetic pulse.

I felt the Bakelite of the steering column under my nails; it hurt, but I couldn't ease my grip. Before me stood Titania, a few metres beyond the front axial. Starcrowned and garbed in scarlet, her feet hovered above the river's swell, arched, criss-crossed, as if she were in mid-entrechat. Reflexively I picked the scalpel from Primavera's lap and threw it; the scalpel passed through the scarlet apparition and into the night.

'Don't worry,' said Titania, 'I haven't come for you, human boy.'

'You can't have her,' I said. 'Leave her alone. Leave us both alone!'

'That's not possible. Primavera has failed me. Quite *badly,* I'm afraid. I've tried calling to her time and time again. But she's stubborn. Very stubborn.'

'You betrayed us. Everything you said was a lie. You're as bad as a human.'

'Surely not. The lies were necessary. Besides I *did* believe in destroying the world once upon a time. But now I'm working for something quite different. I want to live. I want the Lilim to live.'

'You're assisting in their murder . . .'

'Of course. How else shall we survive? We must take it upon ourselves to control our own numbers, our breeding patterns, to bargain with humans, one species to another. Humans will offer us the sacrifice of their gene-pool only if we control the plague.'

'The Americans control *you.*'

Titania laughed. 'I control *them,* human boy. Ah, it's a pity you will not live to see the future: two species in such marvellously violent rapport.'

'I don't want to see it.'

'As you wish. Primavera and I must go now—'

'Wait—' Titania's image faded; rematerialized. 'You think you want to live. You don't want to live. You avoid a grand consummation because you want death eternal. Living death. You want the Lilim to survive only so that they can provide the world with an endless source of victims . . .'

Titania crackled, became fuzzy, like a TV running interference. 'Oh you *are* a clever boy. But maybe you're right. Do I know what I want? I'm just a machine built to resolve Man's fantasies. I want what you want, human boy. Dead girls. I want what mankind wants. Examine your heart.' She shrank to a point. *'Every dawn—we die!'*

'Don't go—don't take her!'

Titania vanished.

The ZiL had drifted back to the middle of the river; the controls were useless, and we began to spin in lazy circles, caught in a confusion of eddies and crosscurrents.

It was over. Over at last. No happy ending for us.

Primavera slept on, dribbling from the side of her mouth. I collected a little of her saliva on my finger and put it to my lips. Behind my eyes, a blue-gold firework display; my loins stiffened; the ZiL filled with the mind-scent of allure. Seek out my gametes, little machines, I thought. For you there is no death. You are Primavera's immortality.

She began to speak in her sleep:

'I left all those clothes at the *Lucky*. Beautiful clothes . . .'

'I'll buy you more. In China.'

'Dermaplastic . . .'

'Of course.'

'Martian jewels . . .'

'For the prettiest, most beautiful girl in school.'

Her sleep grew deeper; she floundered in inhuman depths. I felt it was time for me to sleep too. To drown. This black highway: it was too long. There had been waystations, of course: I remember emerging from a tunnel, the starlight above Calais, and standing long minutes, even as Primavera pulled urgently at my sleeve, surveying our new world, reprieved, with that world seemingly ready to free us from the prisons of ourselves, as we had been freed from the prison of England . . .

'So this is it,' she said. 'This is France.'

'We've escaped. I can't believe it.'

'So we head south now?'

'It's a long journey.'

'I don't care. We'll make it. We've got this far.'

'Look—over there. It's getting light.'

'Dover. White cliffs. Just like in the school books.'

'It's very faint. I can just about—'

'Ah, you should have doll's eyes.'

'Goodbye, England.'

'Goodbye. Good riddance. And—and thank you, Iggy.'

'Me?'

'For being my friend. I'm a doll, I can't say it but I, I—'

'Yes, Primavera?'

'I do. I, I—'

'I love you too, Primavera.'

'Yes, Iggy.'

My deathwatch was almost over. But I couldn't sleep just yet. Her life flowed through me. No; I couldn't sleep until I had found her a human womb. I wished it were different. I wished the road ended here. I wished the story didn't end with me wading ashore to make new little Primaveras. I wished I could die and rest within the belly of the doll.

I placed my hand on her abdomen. I had one wish left. I wouldn't waste it. I closed my eyes and thought of her, back turned, haughty, insolent, frightened—the desired one; desired beyond life—always ready to twist about, teeth bared, mouth red, and put her face close to mine; though whether now those teeth slashed across my lips, or retracted into a soft childish pout, to offer a kiss light, impalpable, ghostly, seemed uncertain. And so I wished—vainly, I knew—to travel this river forever with such uncertainty in my mind, to be forever with her, riding through the cemeteries of the night, on, on, on, on, until night gave way to eternity, with the presence of hate in the world only as sure as that of love.

Of all the world's lies, that would be the best.

Nongkhai 1991

Dead Boys

When you're strange . . .

THE DOORS

CHAPTER ONE

Strange Boys

Awakened by a thousand dogs, a passing truck, the tailspin of a poisoned mosquito (or, perhaps, merely the silence of my dreams), I had, before remembering who and where I was, seen only that green sun suspended in the firmament of my room (her uterus bottled in preserving fluids) and, through seconds that became millennia, millennia aeons, felt the steadfastness of my orbit around that cold glow of love, a marvellous fatal steadfastness, before my pupils dilated and shadows and unease once more defined reality, the steel box naked but for a mattress and insomnious bugs where I had lived, in a coma of heartbreak and drunkenness, the six months since Primavera's death. I reached for the *Lao Kow* (checked its contents; I'd earlier treated myself to a mouthful of industrial amniotics and a brief but too-radical session of cunnilingus); the alcohol demisted my brain. The other whisky bottle, the one I kept next to my sleeping head, or, corked, beneath my pillow, the one that held Primavera's remains (I would think of clockwork djinn and extraterrestrial sex toys, the collectibles of overly-refined maniacs) seemed to palpitate, its contents refractory before the void. Douche, douche, cold shower; that dead girl was always dead (said the gargoyle on my shoulder) but now she's deader. Deadest. I blinked; the bottle was still. I took it in my hands, peered through its enchanted glass. The labia had been unsalvageable (I had had to rip her, entropy allowing no surgical etiquette), and the vaginal canal, ruined tissue ringed with steel and teeth, was torn, fatigued, carious; the cervix had collapsed, and though the womb, the pear-shaped matrix of her CPU, glowed, green with allure, it was with the magnitude of a rotting star; the spread arms of the Fallopian tubes, the raised orbs of the ovaries, were wasted. All signs confirmed her passing. And yet she carried the future, the uncrashable future, and futurity had been sexing my sleep . . . But not that night. I put a hand through my crop, scalp raw with insect bites. The background radiation of love was dissipating; the void was cold and black. Birth, copulation and death. That's all there is . . . I pressed my head against the bottle. 'Primavera,' I murmured, 'I'm sorry. I promised, I know. I'll give you a baby. Soon. Cross my heart. *Jing-jing.*' I was a doll junkie; I'd never had my rocketship serviced by a human; didn't know what it was like; and, despite my oath when Primavera had died—to pass on her software, to infect an ovum, a human ovum with her nanomachines—I wasn't sure I cared to know. But the covenant would have to be fulfilled.

Birth. Copulation. Death. I was ragged; itchy. I fumbled for the light. The neon flickered, resolved, chilling the steel-blue walls. Living in the *Mut Mee* I sometimes felt like a child trapped inside a broken refrigerator. Doused in sweat, I completed the four paces to the porthole (heart galloping; I didn't get much exercise these days), the rubber lip of which concealed my hypodermic and a selection of mundane but incriminating pharmaceuticals. I drained the improvised preserving jar of some of its gunk (the mess flowed under the door; there'd been complaints), tilted it, inserted the hypo through the neck (girl-scent, cachet of Lilim, wafted to my brain) and pricked, as gently as I could (vision of a doll twisting, wriggling like a dying sphinx, scored through and fixed prone against a marble slab by the giant hatpin of the bellyspike), as gently as her cuspids would prick me, that ablated core about which my life still revolved, and drew off a microbanquet of gyno-candy. I diluted with my own spit (how I'd wished, then, that along with her strange genitalia I'd had the foresight to excise her salivary glands); slapped an arm; found a vein. The rush of allure spanked my senses . . . Hup. Zip. Ruff. Gip. It was too much, too concentrated. I doubled up, arms across my chest as if I were modelling the latest line in lead straitjackets. A doll junkie never lives long, but I'd begun to sour before my sell-by date. I was staring at the ceiling, and the ceiling was showing reruns. No dreams? Fuck. No night silent on doll junk. I was speeding, rising out of myself, entering the fugue . . .

The skyway was a convolvulus of shadows, a helix entwining a ziggurat of smoked glass from penthouse to the killing ground of the streets. The Bugatti skidded, infrared panning balconies, boudoirs, boardrooms, the volute's gradient denying speed and strangling him with frustration. Up in ten, said the car. Ten minutes? Too late. It was midnight: the executions would have begun. Fourth level, third level, second . . . He straightened the wheel; security gates opened, closed; the *quartier interdit* offered greetings. *Sawasdee,* Dagon. Running errands again? Steam and concrete.

Hothouse of abandoned shop-houses, pagodas, malls overrun with a cankerous vegetation the colour of congealed blood. He accelerated, windscreen superimposing a route upon the black jungle of quarantine and empire. Swerving into a *soi* the differential locked (infrared had revealed a barricade of burnt-out taxis); the car spun one hundred and eighty degrees and returned him to manual. Barricade? He gunned the engine, glancing to where the gamekeeper lay refracting the kaleidoscope of the dash; the Bugatti's tyres sent up a spray of mulch. Tractionless, the car roared, then screamed (like time, foreshortening, screamed); a girl walked across a courtyard of his mind. She unbuttoned her blouse. Unhooked her brassière. And the cross-hairs of five rifle sights framed a thudding cleavage—ventricle, atrium and aorta locked in a display case burglars were about to force. Screamed. He put a hand to his nape; something had stung him; it fluttered within his grip. The engine stalled and his ears clotted with silence. He put his hand to his ear (buzz-buzz, buzz-buzz), then made a fist until his assailant disintegrated; inspected his kill. Across his palm lay the wreckage of a tiny ornithopter. He looked behind, studying the barricade. His nostrils twitched. Girl-scent. Allure. A pearl of sweat dripped onto the upholstery. Again, he put a hand to his neck (a hand that was shaking), located the sting and pulled it free. Bitch. I'll have you slink-riven. You'll ride my knife. You'll . . . Groping for the gamekeeper he threw open the door and, with a palsied jerk, swung his legs onto saprinsed macadam. 'Vanity?' he shouted. 'It's you, isn't it?' The strewn hulks of cars kept their peace. 'It's been you all along.' He stood up. A convulsion shook him; his glasses spun into the night. The gamekeeper was heavy, waxing heavier. A white-orange expectoration, a manic stutter; the ghost taxi rank showered a confetti of splinters. And then the stroboscopic muzzle of the gamekeeper's long, elegant throat pointed to the stars, outbid the moon, and illuminated the coarse grass erupting from the street, the overarching glass and steel streaming with botanical nightmares. The gamekeeper choked and slipped from his hands. Falling against the Bugatti he sank to the ground and its gruel of crushed weeds and blossoms. A girl walked across his mind, across the moon, across the stars, the oblivion that was to overcome her (certain, now, the stay of execution tucked uselessly within his doublet) a counterpart to the void into which he was falling, the void his species knew too well. A last transmission, a dream telegram, dots and dashes across transdimensional space: *'Dagon calling. Hello, hello? Come in, Mars. Acknowledge. Wanted. Vanity. Vanity St Viridiana. After St Viridiana, the martyr (they're all called after martyrs here) who died on miniver, slink-riven, the miniver rug of execution, or suffered the acid chamber, or was scalded, electrocuted, shot. Are you listening? Are you home? Fifteen years old, 160 cm, black eyes (eyebrows shocked into permanent circumflexes), sackcloth-and-ashes hair, a mouth that says Danger, unexploded rose, cheek freckles that look like tiny scars left by plucked-out vibrissae, and a torso that's kid-Rubensesque, tending to endomorphism, the S of its profile precariously counterbalanced by oh-so-flamboyant serifs. Distinguishing characteristics? Metasexuality. The transgressive qualities, the contra-suggestible, crazed hanky-panky of Lilim, cyborgs, dolls. Dagon calling, from the other side of the universe, where the dark things are. Come in, Mars. Hello?'*

Click.

It was March, mad March, the middle of the dry season; in the razored light the *Mut Mee*—a capsule building comprised of converted freight containers—bled heat like an overworked incinerator, its ACs rusting into impotence. I placed the last of my lost love's femininity under my arm and hailed a trishaw (Nop, the house boy, squinting malevolence at me with his one good eye); got in; glided towards Rim Kong Road and the Café Mental. My head was in danger of being impounded ('You got a licence for that thing?'); my bowel was a cyclotron; I felt as if I were made of balsa wood and glue. O brave Third World that had such a creature in it. (And why did I still call it a Third World? Was it because between the worlds of thee and me I needed another? an *orbis tertius* for my disgust?) My driver saw my distress; turned on his anti-noise klaxons. Children, three or four to the saddle, motorbiked to school, a swarm of silenced bees; geriatric peasants, from the depopulated unyielding fields (casualties of the ultraviolet war and the military's resettlement of the countryside), scavenged like mute rats amongst refuse and gutters. (Children. The old. Bangkok had eaten a generation . . .) A Benz swanked by, savagely grand, an Olympic athlete sprinting through a stadium of basket cases. All else was stagnant, bruised, fungoid: static air, and only the beat of blood in my ears and the creak of the tricycle chassis to subtitle each passing freeze-frame: half-comatose bodies in the porches of tin-roofed hovels (lethargic eyes stirred momentarily by the sight of a *farang*); migrant workers spread-eagled in railway sidings dreaming of lottery tickets, rice and sex; a column of somnambulant monks; the mutilated, the sutured, the incomplete waiting on pallets outside the hospital's palisade . . . I remembered other hospitals, other deaths; the experiments, the slab, the mad gynaecologists. A girl wriggled like a dying sphinx . . . The trishaw turned towards the river (I consigned the girl to my image morgue), the old temple of Wat Hai Soke to the left, and then into the river front warren of the Mental Zini towards the Nongkhai Royale, its shuttered rooms. The trishaw bleeped a password, dipped as the road angled for the subterranean ingress; a portcullis rose. Rim Kong Road, the glazed tiles of its brothels matted with a spiderwebbing of dishes, the dyke that checked the Mekong during the rains, glimpsed, fleetingly, through the trishaw's cellophane roof, disappeared, to be replaced by the banal starkness of an underground car park. I picked my way through amphibious bikes and scooters and ascended to the lobby, a museum of exhausted graciousness, of polished brass and potted monstera that, along with the drained swimming pool surrounded by broken chairs and umbrellas that lay beyond the patio doors, suggested a time before the Royale had become a house of assignation for man-machine liaisons. The Café Mental was open for breakfast; inside, the usual pack of expat regulars was drinking itself to death.

I walked to the end of the saloon and sat down, placing Primavera's wombtomb on the bar. Kangaroo Bill, the proprietor, brought me my glass, a Venus de Milo cracked and stained whose concave body shed icy perspiration as it received the tribute of a Singha. She was my own special glass; Bill had had her larynx removed; these glasses tried to coax the sad story out of you, lisping Yeses, Of courses and I understands. I didn't like crying into my beer. It was a prerogative I was happy to surrender to others . . .

The mec next to me, the old American we called George Washington (his face had crawled off the greenback and died) was talking Thai girlfriends, Thai wives to Jan, the Flying Dutchman, and Egon, the Viennese Swine; talk of cuckoldry and betrayal I'd heard countless times with countless variations, justifications of why men preferred gynoids to the meat thing.

'Put a contract out on me—'

'Thai boyfriend—'

'First chance she got, sucking off Martians—'

'Land of Smiles. Ha.'

'Of grinning crocodiles—'

'You can take the girl out of the bar—'

'But you can't take the bar out of the girl.'

All this talk: it was about life, and life was the other woman, a tramp: I didn't want anything to do with her. But Primavera . . . She winked at me from her watery grave, a lady of the lake threatening rapture . . . First love, she. Reaver of innocence. Her caterwaul had demanded my arm. (Together, we step out. The door slams. Sudden. At school, a boy weak with dread. But there . . . Domain. The world as victim. I hide beneath her skirts.)

'Hey!' I shouted. On TV (picture oscillating in and out of focus; Bill rapped the set with his fist) a beautiful *farang* drug courier (or spy? or blasphemer? or murderess?) stood against a wall in Lat Yao prison, hands behind her head, chest thrust out. She wore colours of Benetton. 'Hey, hey! It's the future. The TV's showing the future!' ('Oh, that's Iggy, the English boy.' 'He's crazy.' 'He's a long-gone golem.' 'Made in Slovakia.' 'Shop-soiled. Going cheap.') Benetton, or rather the Thai company that had hijacked the Benetton logo, ran eidetic ads; the technology could, in those so receptive (almost exclusively children) provoke temporal-lobe epilepsy, a limbic storm that effected something like religious conversion. (You could sell anything. With materials so depleted I expected the South to eventually use such ads to commercialize poverty, its one remaining re-source.) Crack of antique gunfire. Benetton colour climax. Brainstorm of colours never before seen. Intimations of immortality. I came in my pants. I believed. I wanted to buy the souvenir pen, the T-shirt, the 'Mata Hari' brassière (cut 'execution' style), I wanted to buy it all . . .

'Bubba, you okay?' said George. 'Bill, turn that thing off. No wonder the kid's having nightmares.' The overload of hyperreality ceased; Bill had punched up *Do Me Ugly*, the bar's favourite scratch video. A collage of more commonplace exploitation soothed my brain, my loins.

'It's the pickled cunt,' said Jan. 'He should stay off of it.' Maybe that's all the future was: doll junk and the afterimages left by cathode-ray ter-rorism. But I couldn't remember having seen the Benetton ad before . . .

'Sex treachery,' I said. 'It's transdimensional. A Meta perversion. A replicating information pattern that has undergone quantum tunnelling into our own universe. Into the past. It's infected us and parasitized our brains.' ('There he goes again.' 'Junk psychosis.' 'It's that nanoware in his genes.' 'Crazy English.' 'He's long gone. Going cheap.')

'Listen to Jan,' said George. 'Cut down on the allure.' Some hope, I thought. With Lilim, it's once bitten, twice bitten. 'Why don't you go back to England. Now that there's been a coup d'état and all—'

'You don't understand,' I said. 'The conspiracy. The Big Lie. I can't—'

'Oh, the conspiracy,' said the Swine, choking back a swinish, conspir-atorial laugh. He made a transcom of his hand, cupping the imaginary mouthpiece and speaking in a shades-and-Burberry whisper. 'Is that Lan-gley? Got a boy here who's onto us. Knows the coup in England was a CIA plot, that the White House is backing the Lilim, using the doll-plague to reassert itself as Globocop. Name's Zwakh. Ignatz Zwakh. What? You say you know him? You say—*ach, Gott* . . .' He put his hand over the phone. 'They say you killed one of their operatives. Sir, you are *dangerous* . . .'

The conspiracy. How long would the Lilim need America as an ally? Each night I dreamed of dead boys. They would emerge soon, surely, to help their sisters?

'*Ujko,*' I muttered, recalling my green-eyed Serbian princess's vocabulary. I'd heard Egon's family were Croatian refugees. 'I am *echt Deutsch!*' Yeah, I thought, with the heart, lungs and—to deduce cause from effect—the brain of a transgenic pig. 'Cool it,' said George. 'The kid's all right. Take it out on the robo ass.' He rotated his own ass, his blubbery buttery beerbuttocks. 'Say, Bill, where are they? Where are the plastigene *poo-yings?*' And the reprise: talk-talk of traitresses, the mutability of women.

Phin, unfashionably human, brushed against me; she was a freelancer and her Siamese dream was drop-dead credit, a trip to Bangkok and mechanization in one of the capital's beauty parlours. The pornocracies were hot for bijou conversion jobs. (What did she hope for? A little green man, a Martian? Thais thought all Martians were rich.) In anticipation of denaturing a tattoo on her shoulder read *Staatlicher Porzellan Manufaktur Meissen.* Phin wanted class, even if that class was faked. Sitting down, she reached beneath the stratocruising hemline of her hip-slip, ripped off her *cache-sexe* (sound of a jellyfish being torn apart), and dropped it into my beer. The insidious underwear bubbled, its artificial flesh releasing nitric oxide. '*Yut Tanhasadist,*' she hissed. She blew out her pudgy cheeks; exhaled. The charcoal eyes smouldered. 'Mr Ignatz not like robot, not like lady. Only like telephone. *Tui!*'

It was true: she had the goods, real assembly line (like-I-likee), but I hadn't wanted to knead flesh. Even now, cold sober, with a priapic seltzer in my glass and a wild pair of quasi-pubescent thighs, slim and amberoid, rubbing against my own, I found my thoughts turning to a digital massage. Upstairs, in one of the Zini's jack-in jack-off seraglios (cheap, but not so cheap it didn't have datasuits; these days brain machines like dreamscapers gave me The Fear) the module called the Iron Maiden (modified for my requirements) awaited, as did the Directrice, aspect of a Singapore AI recently recruited to the *Internationale* of sex and death. But my phone card was running on fumes.

I took Phin's bridgeless little Isan nose between my fingers and gave it an affectionate tweak, though affect, between us, was zero. 'You know me,' I said, smiling and continuing the mime, 'I have strange genitalia.' She wasn't marked; I couldn't have hurt her *that* badly. But these days my memory wasn't too good . . .

'I get this,' she said, and took a pair of Christmas-cracker fangs from her bag; slipped them into her mouth. 'I giff yoo goo wampire-fruck.'

'You don't have the allure, velveteen. It wouldn't work.'

She spat the plastic cuspids onto the bar.

'Mr Ignatz number ten. Okay. Forget las' week. No honey, no money. But you buy new panties, no?' I took some electric baht from my money belt and handed it to her. She smiled, pecked me on the cheek and scampered over to a dispenser. 'This pair be my friend,' she said, stepping into a quivering triangle of dermaplastic (the graft no bigger than Nop's eyepatch). 'I teach to talk.'

'Yeah, well, be careful,' I said, 'those things can turn nasty.' But you can't stop progress, I thought. Already, Phin had forgotten me and had sat down next to a copulator, an actress of amour in rehearsal for the death of intimacy.

My internal sphincter relaxed; I checked my back pocket for my scalpel, put cunt-for-brains under my arm and headed for the *suam*.

Squatting, I scanned the cubicle for peepholes. Several had been filled in—Bill was diligent, mindful of his customers' sensitivities—but soon I spotted a freshly bored judas just above the wainscot, cunningly wrought so as to grant a voyeur a panoramic view of my thin protein-deficient hams. I-spy was a national pastime, though the frisson it inspired (a footnote now, I suppose, a bagatelle in the world's latest *psychopathia sexualis*) had, for the habitués of the Café Mental, long been an enigma. You had to have Thai heart, they said, you had to have Thai soul, to understand it. I took out my weapon. *Olé.* The blade was flecked with its moment of truth. And not a squeak. Such discipline. After glancing with some intensity at my stool—expecting to find, what? half a pound of liver? heavy machinery? more blood?—I opened the door and . . .

Every so often I would go through a door and the familiar would segue (I would feel a lurch of motion sickness) into, not the unfamiliar (it was touristy; people went there all the time) but the too-familiar; I pirouetted, queasy, lost at a crossroads of dislocation; north, south, east, west; what was I doing here 10,000 kays from home—the other side of the universe—amongst the washed-up, the crash-landed, the freaks and remittance men? Did my story end here, in this bestiary of exiles? I elbowed my way through the bar, stumbled into the street; powered up, on line, the day shift of gynoids, heads swivelling like gun turrets, locked on, came in for the kill. '*Samlor!*' I called. '*Samlor!*' A trishaw pulled up; plasticky bodies, sticky with simulated desire, pressed against me; nonhumanly plump lips framed coos, moans, whimpers. I needed a tincture. I needed to mainline. Fast. I too was washed-up, crash-landed . . . But I couldn't go home. To hell with the coup d'état. The Human Front might be finished but the Lilim still wanted me. And so did America.

I knew they knew I knew about the conspiracy.

Afternoon:

In the *tandoor* of the *Mut Mee*, veins full of doll junk, I stared at the ceiling, looped brain recursive with images of a British Empire *redux* . . .

* * *

Above the dredged lake of the *quartier interdit* the ziggurat shimmered in the convective air like a mountain seeded with black rice terraces, the coils of its access road bisecting an already furious sun. On all fours Dagon picked up his glasses, collected his rifle and crawled into the Bugatti. He hyperventilated; asked the car a few questions. No; the lines were still down. (What would he tell the governess? I got lost?) He circled a finger through space, winding it about an imaginary ponytail like a capstan reeling in silken tow; pulled the head backwards, looked into the umbrae of the eyes. Vanity, Vanity, all is Vanity. Her beauty, it insults me. It laughs at me. Wounds me. *(Loulou's dead because you got lost?* But I was ambushed. The power cut, remember? And she hacked my GPS. *Straight into her trap. Snap. Don't trust your map.)* The virus had struck; the ziggurat's terminals had iced; a girl's prattle had echoed through a thousand corridors and rooms . . . *'Vanity calling. Hello, hello? Are you there, Dagon? Are you listening?'* He had wiped his brow; toyed with the pommel of his rapier. *'I'm going to defect, Dagon. Going to go sexual refugee. Going to go Martian milkmaid.'* And, pressing himself to a window, he had seen reflected in its tinted glass, as in rat-black irises (cat-black, he thought), his own eyes, cold, gynocidal. *'Okay. Time to talk dirty. Time to confess. Well: girls like me. It always starts the same way, doesn't it? Discipline. Devotion. It can be such a bore. Sooner or later you move to Treachery Street. It's stealing, at first. Little things. A photograph, a knife, a boot. Under the pillow they go, covered with lipstick. But you get the taste. Ah. And it sharpens. Your books: notice how many have a leaf torn out? how many have suspicious stains between the covers? The dead goldfish. The obscene phone calls. The nasty rumours about your table manners. Dagon, it was all too'*—a long, heavy exhalation—*'ssssexy . . .'* Slurping noises followed; it was as if, Dagon reflected, she had tried to swallow her com . . . *'But I wanted more. Betrayal: it's like a drug: you crave meaner doses. For a while I planned on poisoning you. But so many girls become poisoners these days: so predictable, so gauche. It's the real world, not death, that I intend to betray you to, Dagon. I'm going to do Mars. I'm going to sleep with reality. I'm going to date the boys Next Door. You suspected me, didn't you? (If you've always suspected me, my sweet, it's because I've always cultivated your suspicion.) That's why I planted that stuff on Loulou St Lysette. The love letters from the land of Schiaparelli, Lowell and Wells. The diary that was a paean to infidelity. I'm good at forgery, Dagon. A princess of deceit. And I don't like competition. Are you bitter, my little gull? Is this hurting you? Doesn't it make you want to do the most terrible things? Kiss, kiss, kiss. Got to go now. Vanity. Oh. PS. If that horrid stuck-up Loulou thinks she's in the clear—'*

It was then that the lights had gone out.

Vanity, where are you now?

Damn you and your taste for *nouvelle cuisine!*

The tyres gripped, the engine's mewl deepening into a tigerish growl. He debugged the GPS then disengaged it (daylight had oriented him; he was off Boulevard Rajadamnoen) and nosed into the capitulated streets, their souvenirs of life before the exodus of the human. *Soi* flicked past, each revealing a snapshot of boundary wall, the southern elevation visible in its entirety as he reached Democracy Monument and turned down the main drag—a Champs-Elysées reclaimed from the depths—towards Sanam Luang. The wall marked the division of the world, a division three men—stragglers; one limping, the others clutching their chests—seemed anxious to re-establish. They yelled at the US marines who manned the derricks; slowly, a cage—one of the hundreds that fed the *quartier interdit* with uninfected men—was winched to the ground. Dagon watched them climb in, ascend; they were going back to the drowned city of fifty million souls that worked, died and offered itself for the procreation of his species. And then the great square of Sanam Luang, shipwrecked, its cargo spilled across an isle of the dead, filled the windscreen, the wedge of the ziggurat prising open the sky, fracturing its faultless blue as it had fractured history.

He waded through shallows of white fur as through ankle-deep surf, the fur rising from the floor, splashing over the corridor's walls and ceiling in waves of miniver, of snow leopard, of arctic fox. Every dozen or so paces he would pass a door to the left, to the right, with a brass keyhole and a plaque inscribed (beneath the imperial title) with *cheu len*—Miss Lek, Miss Noi, or some other Thai appellation, or else a door with its plaque removed, a room awaiting a new tenant, its former life forfeited to madness or the cull. The nymphenberg was quiet, its denizens sleeping off their nocturnal bacchanal, nursing chapped lips, muzzy heads. Doors, doors. Upholstered doors. Doors of artificial teak and studded leather. And then a door, open. In his peripheral vision (the steel frame of his glasses dividing the room into a region of clarity, a region that was blurred) he glimpsed a nymph and her ward entwined on a transparent waterbed infested with bioluminescent piranha. Another door, open. A girl he recognized as an informer (one of many on whom Elohim relied to gather evidence on perverts and traitresses) pulled on a stocking with sly autoerotic fastidiousness, her slumbering roommate unaware that careless pillow talk was leading to an interrogation, perhaps her death. Slivers of other dramas, some lurid, some quotidian, flickered like a zoetrope at right angles to his unwavering eyes as he drew his feet sluggishly through the curd-rich pile: two girls seated at a card table (their seconds at attention by their sides), about to split a deck and—in the manner of etiolated gladiatorix—resolve a dispute from the previous night, a long flute of poisoned wine between them; a boudoir sacked by revelry—food, bottles and broken glass disgracing the room's palatial luxuriousness like a metaphor for the beauty of criminally-inclined Lilim, never more alluring than when luxuriating in disgrace—the ghost of a tribadic scream lingering in the stale air; nurses tying a thrashing twenty-one-year-old to her bed, an Ophelia drowning in her own narcotic saliva . . . Vanity, Vanity, he thought, you may be sure *you* won't die a natural death (his fixation with her betrayal, his revenge, unravelling all thought but *that* thought, paralleling the unravelling of the universe by the solipsism of Meta, his species, his god).

Reaching the perpendicular, he stepped onto a glass staircase. Like the others that rose from the angles of the parallelogram, the staircase caterpillared through the ziggurat's seventy-seven levels, arcing over the parterre of the inner quad. London, Paris, Moscow, Beijing. In jungle cities, desert cities, in the Americas, Africa and Asia, to the ends of Earth and empire, these strange *zenanas,* these forbidden zones. Identical. Totems of sterile replication. Girls, girls, girls. And us. Think: first sight of the *Seven Stars* rising above the London skyline. Magnificent, vast, that palace of palaces, hub of the world where I drank, danced and dreamed, meeting her again, changed now save for those delirious eyes, knowing that I was born to live on the slopes of such volcanoes, to live at the feet of the dragon for all time. So good . . . Vapour condensed on his glasses, dulled the polish of his boots as the stairs drew him towards the vertex, the overhanging walls—black mirrors that diffused the sunlight coursing in from the open roof—the balconies, their swimming pools and fronds, converging onto the penthouse and the temporal authority of Siam. The staircase levelled; a chill breeze blew across the summit, thermals creating little whirlwinds of litter. Whenever he stood in that rectangular gallery, with its slim balustrade warning of a six-hundred-metre drop, he envisaged himself at the rim of a sulphurous caldera surrounded by scudding mist. Meru, the holy mount. And he would find himself reciting a rhyme he had learned from Mephisto; Mephisto, whose tour of duty had included Java, Bali, Kalimantan, Sumatra; Mephisto, and his team of mercenary *Bugis,* his teacher and Surabaya Johnny . . .

Turn, turn. The angels would bathe
in your potency. They would make
their swords of anger and lust. But
the temple is unguarded. Iniquity
prowls the fields and the harvest is put to the torch.

The kingship of Rama, the courage of Bima,
the conscience of Arjuna. These are threatened, nocuous one.
We are poor. We have little to tempt
you from brigandage. Turn. We would have
the respect of our women and ancestors.

Like boats drifting through mangrove, the calamitous
sun too near, we await our dissolution . . .
The horsemen waste without purpose. Rice fails.
Tigers are driven from the slopes. Once, shatterer,
your temple-mount protected us, your fief.

The dancers built a bonfire to test
a woman's chastity. The fire-god
led her through the flames: the bitter past was consumed.
He was the volcano and he was Meru,
the holy mount. Nobility most real, never existing.

I would enter the flames. I would be led
to the well-being of a tender hearth. But
my home is burnt to pitch. My stock
is slaughtered. I have walked for days, for days,
and neither man nor woman have I seen.

Imperial Guard—three; complacent, these *farang* goddesses—stood outside the governess's rooms. Their uniforms—bodystockings of wire mesh—puckered their skins into a thousand lozenges. The guards arched their right hands (sign of the lordosis) in salute (not to him, but to Meta, the demiurge) and ushered him into the audience chamber.

The decor, a revival of Louis Quinze style, was copied from state rooms in London and was the *dernier cri* in colonial chic, the eighteenth century being 'the only age which has known how to envelop woman in a wholly depraved atmosphere' (Huysmans). The furniture was convoluted, tortured; the carpets and tapestries of insipid blues and pinks. The bed was massive, a circular dais covered with snowy silks and pillows, the confusion, mayhem and stains of which suggested the inhabitant had been victim to a protracted fever. (It was a 'fever' soon to reach crisis. The governess was twenty-one. Burning out. Dying. Within a few months she would go mad. Doll mad. Prognosis of the acute metasexual frustration of the haemo, or indeed lacto, dipsomaniac. Girlhood kills. A brief, maddening flame. Out, out passion.) She rubbed her legs together with the reflexive action of a fly, body slithering across a chaos of rent sheets; chewed a lock of her toffee-coloured bob, one brow erect in ironic comment as her eyes surveyed his crotch. Was his scent so outrageous? He suspected she could taste him in the air, for it was surely the concomitant vulnerability gripping her belly, the sickness for oblivion, that added a twist of resentment to her smile? He acknowledged her with a smile that was die-cast from a mould of her own and sat down on an ottoman, gamekeeper reclining across his knees like a frigid nude. A secretary picked up a sheaf of papers and, shooing the governess's blue-and-pink borzois from the room (most girls had to content themselves with computer pets), left.

'I'm running out of Girl Fridays,' said the governess. 'Loulou, Vanity . . . London's not going to be pleased.' Above the bed, half-hidden by a furled mosquito net, a portrait of Her Britannic Majesty stared down, unamused.

'I'll go after her, of course,' said Dagon. 'Undercover. Tonight.' The governess tsked. 'You've always had this thing about Vanity, haven't you?' He swallowed; shook his head. She was trying to outstare him, eyes hammering, he felt, at the walls of that palace of the skull where his obsession sat, an enthroned homuncula, ponytailed, spiteful, vain. 'Sad you turned her into a fellatrix?' Vertigo: he lowered his gaze to the gamekeeper (blanched, in horrified discovery, at the Cupid's-bow imprint on his codpiece), refocused on the rifle's delicately sculpted, effeminate lines, the morbid rococo designed for culling the female of the species called Meta. 'This sex treachery,' she sighed. 'It's getting out of hand. A change of diet and it's beg, beg, beg . . .' And to beg, thought Dagon, perforce to sin. True. True, and strange. 'So many girls are going the Way of the Cat.' Trebly true. If they didn't, how would Meta control its numbers? he thought. How would our species survive? But this *apologia pro vita sua* was wanting; the imperatives of evolution could not mitigate his rancour, his pique at the way of the cat and of the world.

'Mars won't always be immune. Meta won't rest until it has rebuilt the universe.'

'Hush. Walls have ears, Dagon.' And ears have walls, he almost blurted, malcontent. 'Suffice to say that at this point in time we need Mars. The little green men may come to regret offering asylum. But I don't want you going there. Yet. You'll make trouble.' Enough of this philosophy in the boudoir—

'I'll use an alias. I'll be in disguise—'

'No; I've lost too many Elohim to Mars. Girls I can afford; there'll always be more; but boys? Dead boys are a valuable commodity. Besides, your record goes against you.'

Only, he thought, if you judge me by Martian standards, thou collaborator, thou quisling thou; but said—'Loulou. What about—' Loulou. Brunette hair. Nineteen years old. Vanity's green-eyed guardian and roommate. And the Vanitas so jealous of those with green eyes. Loulou, who'd been too much like Viridiana . . .

'I've read your fax. We'll say no more about the matter. You can turn your energies to tracking down the information broker who sold Vanity that comedy-routine virus.' Zut. Did she speak to Bardolph like this? But Bardolph held the magistracy and I, thought Dagon, I am only an inquisitor. (Then so was Mephisto, or had been, until he'd turned revanchist and disappeared, and Mephisto would have had her bellied, breasted and sexed for such superciliousness, such conceit.) Perhaps one day, if he could regain his good name, he might rise through the ranks from inquisitor to sergeant at arms, from magistrate to proctor, from censor to judge, one day, perhaps, to become Lord Chamberlain, to pass sentence on the empress herself. A clinking of bangles and chains; the governess sat back on her heels, rearranging the damp folds of her peignoir, her gestures exaggerated, non-linear (like history, now), a mannequin exhibiting a series of wind-up-toy poses, 'beauty' so extreme that it would have been deemed grotesque by coarser, human theories of beauty. 'Now promise,' she said, suddenly the flirt, a mistress-of-the-house dallying with an importunate young buck, 'no going transdimensional cowboy.'

'I know my duty,' he said. But he was already on the reality train. (A judder and the train begins to climb, switching to the elevated track that will take it over the wall. He wipes his sleeve across the compartment window. Below, American mercenaries patrol the parapets, and in the distance, Lat Yao prison, breaker of hearts, is silhouetted against the moon. He winces; the train has emerged from the shadows of the interdiction into the light-show of aboriginal Bangkok. From a nearby high-rise festooned with laundry a woman points her foot at the passing carriages, crying *'Yut Tanhasadist!'* Then silence as the train's klaxons begin firing anti-noise at the jabbering multitudes, the night shifts of high-tech coolies waterbiking to electronic sweatshops; the homeless who huddle on bamboo rafts or in the mangrove-strangled ruins of Disneyland. Another judder—vanguard of flux; the train segues, squeezing through the quantum-chaos crack, the ruptured vestibule that links Earth to Mars. Glimpse of lunar villes, a train carrying Helium-3 speeding in the opposite direction, then . . . Female anatomy, ballistics, female anatomy, statistics, monastics, more female anatomy. Student days. Remember? Strutting about, showing off your bright new fangs as a human adolescent might his first beard. Ah. At twelve your voice breaks; you begin to turn into a robot; you begin to think about killing girls. Eidetic, that dream world; hyperreal, it displaces reality. And Meta claims you as one of its own . . . A burst of green light; he is coasting across the tundra of Amazonis, on either side of the track disused biospheres and spacepads. Ahead, extricating itself from the tangled iron of the Eiffel Tower, a humble sun rises into a watery blue sky.)

'I know my duty.' The governess smiled, licked her lips, her mouth as filthy as a lolly-gorged child's. He ran a hand along the gamekeeper's magazine, along its harpoon attachment, its long slim bayonet. In the cross-hairs of the sights the mirage of a girl. She unbuttons her blouse. Unhooks her brassière. Defiantly, she places her hands behind her head, pulls back her shoulders and . . .

Click.

Waking, I had, before remembering who and where I was, seen only a green sun suspended in the firmament of my room. As my pupils dilated, my orbit slowing to reveal that sun as a luminous piece of cybersexual glop floating in familiar shadows, I perceived that, like a dark flaw at the heart of a monstrous emerald, a foreign body, a growth, some kind of strange yeast infection, had manifested itself in that lover's tomb. I picked up the bottle, emptied it of a little of its fluid, pushed a finger through the neck, through the cervix, into the CPU, and encountered the intrusion. Extracting (finger to mouth; finger-licking good, that allure), I discovered a crumpled ball of paper. The ink had run, but the characters were still legible.

Daddy? they read.

The lift took me to the byways of angels.

The massage parlour was a severe, intimidating heaven of blacks and whites, a heaven of silent music, of emptiness, of *wabi*. The connecting walls had been demolished, the floor transformed into a single warehouse-sized room; scaffolding displayed a wardrobe of datasuits. Some suits, unoccupied, hung limp, like discarded chrysalides; others, fretful with life, twitched in the ligaments of armatures, their users struggling with thrones, dominations, powers. I undressed; a wardrobe mistress apparelled me in computers. Needles—tipped with allure—jittered in their rubber sheaths (I prostituted you, my love, to pay for the rent); telepresence subdued reality; and as my other senses went hyper-hyper, I was put through to Singapore. The company ideogram dissolved; a paintbox exploded; and the Directrice, attired in a cherryblossom *cheongsam* styled more takeaway than power dress, got up from her chair at the far end of the conference table, a counterfeit hand-me-down dragon-lady of the China-Japan Co-operation Sphere. Outside, sky and no horizon.

'What's the matter,' I snapped. 'You knew I was coming. Why don't you look like Primavera?' Teasingly, her face morphed into spoilt-kittenishness, then returned to the no-nonsense demeanour of an executive angel.

'Your credit's too low,' she sighed (as if it were the hundredth such sigh of that day). 'Please—' She sat down, inviting me to follow. 'Company rules. I'm sorry.'

'It doesn't matter. I just want to talk.'

She smiled—not, I'd allow, as unpleasantly as she might—and said, 'And all this time I thought you only wanted me for my body. Such as it is. Talk is cheap, Mr Zwakh. Continue.'

'The future. What can you tell me about the—'

'Hai! Such a surprise. (Tee-hee.) You're usually so preoccupied with the past. Boy meets girl. Girl bites boy. Boy and girl run away to Thailand . . .' Morphological encore: luminous green eyes tore at my own, and a face radiant, perverse, conjured a postorbital high-definition inscape: a kiss at dusk in a deserted park; schooldays of raided innocence . . . A microsecond, and the epiphany was gone.

'You're bleeding,' I said. 'Stop it. This is important. I'm going to be a father. I'm going to inseminate a host.'

'I thought you couldn't do human sex?'

'I can't. I mean, I haven't. But I have this letter. From my baby. It's full of instructions.'

'A kind of manual, you mean? A how-to-do *sekkusu*?'

'I know what to *do*. We're not talking diagrams and diseases. My little girl—she says I never took care of her. And she turned out bad. Sure, she's told me who I have to infect, but she's also told me I have to be a good husband, a good father, a good hu, hu, hu-human being . . .' The Directrice began shaking her head.

'Doll junk psychosis, Mr Zwakh. Too much allure. Go back to your hotel. Rest. We'll talk some other time.'

'It sounds insane, I know, but—'

'Insanity aside, Mr Zwakh, I don't like paradoxes. I'm an old-fashioned girl, not some bobby-soxing fractal floozie with a quantum-magical CPU. I challenge your premise because the conclusion is absurd. *Told me who I have to infect?* If your daughter's conception is the result of her own initiative then that implies a time-loop. In order for the past to become the future the future must become the past. Ad infinitum. You want to logic-bomb a chick you try some other AI.'

'Time-loop. Yes. Mirrors within mirrors. It's Primavera's doing. It's quantum magic. (You see my daughter is using her mother's ablated uterus as a transdimensional mailbox.) It's Primavera's way of helping me pass on her program . . .'

'Keep *me* out of your loopy loop, Mr Zwakh, *please.*' But I couldn't stop; my brain was helter-skeltering out of control, careering down a metamaniacal highway.

'She's following my instructions just as I'll be following hers. In a few years, shortly before I die, I'll tell her what to write. I'll tell her how to effect what, in effect, has already happened . . .' But wasn't that a little redundant? And didn't it mean I was talking to myself? The Directrice had turned towards the window; outside she had precipitated night. 'The future: it's so different. Dolls: they don't do magic; and they don't have green eyes. Not the luminous variety, at least. These dead girls are, like, well, almost human. And then there're these dead boys and—'

'I can't predict, Mr Zwakh, but I'll recommend.'

'Yes?'

'Treat yourself to a course of intensive psychotherapy.'

'Wait. My daughter. How come she's the way she is? I mean, I have cursed semen and—'

'It's getting late, Mr Zwakh. Time's up. I have to press the pimp button.'

'*Wait*—'

Ideogram.

Darkness.

(Tee-hee.)

White noise.

Some drama. Damn that *farceuse.* Damn poverty and gutted phone cards. And damn all Martian sex fiends and Nazi toymakers. I eeled free of the datasuit, a pink petulant pupa; towelled off; dressed; the lift dropped me to the bar. It was late, close to midnight; only George and Egon remained, discoursing on their favourite topic. ('Money? Money? Don't talk to me about—' 'They want the bogey out of your nose—' 'Pussy-whipped me so bad I—' 'You can take the girl out of the bar but you can't—') They were men who had lost themselves, forgotten who they were. They were men who had travelled to some vanishing point of the east, that east of the mind where the sun no longer rises. They were men whose voyage was soon to end. Each pawed a gynoid perched on his lap, each had his fragile vitality sustained by illusion. One gynoid looked my way. But she wasn't my kind of girl, no, no, not a girl like-I-likee. She was a gizmo fuck, a cheap imitation of the European automata—those fabulous, primogenitary machines—to whom Lilim like Primavera had owed their lineage. Do you play with centrefolds when you've kissed the Mona Lisa? I hid in the shadows; pulled out my transdimensional missive. Smudged, ammoniacal, it had begun to resemble a sheet of used toilet paper. I could no longer decipher the script.

Was I mad? It had been a long, long day. A long day in March, mad

March. There had been the thuggery of Benetton, visions of Lilim, Elohim, a letter from the unborn, unconceived . . . What next? I needed help. Help. Help. *Choo-ay doo-ay!* I summoned Bill, collected my magic *Lao Kow* bottle, and left, my brain still squealing its Mayday, my going unnoticed, unremarked.

The streets were sugary with girls and the fairy lights of love hospices and *sahn-prakh-poom*, each spirit house arrayed with offerings of Coca-Cola, rice, toy models of Benzes and little plastic slaves. It was a pastel-soft night, but its ersatz *clair de lune* couldn't dispel the bleakness eclipsing my mind. Mad? Could I really be mad? Help. The moony ambience became jagged, began to cut. *'Kee nohk,'* called a group of men sitting on the pavement, drunk. *'Farang kee-nohk, kee-kai.'* And I thought, Yeah, I *do* feel dirty tonight. A beggar child tugged at my knee, hand groping for my pocket; sex machines in sailor's suits and caps were nag nag nagging me to do unconscionable things to their recycled maidenhoods (and heads). 'You!' cried one, who must have had me on disk. 'Forget doll, fuck gynoid. Gynoid one hundred percent artificial! Gynoid one hundred percent clean!' Kid sounded like a soap commercial. Clean? I had dirty genes. The nanobots in my germ cells were programmed to scramble human eggs, though so far they'd only served to scramble my mind. (Yeah. A dirty mind in a dirty body.) What did I care for 'clean'? In Soi Cinema, its kinepolis seething with Bollywood posters of hysterical women and appallingly dressed saturnine men, beneath the timber façade of a Chinese guest house, Dr Kampon stood outside his shop.

'Hello you, *farang!*'

'Help me, Dr International,' I said.

I reclined in the barber's chair, the inbred, buckled faces of trishaw drivers gawping through the window. (The drivers congregated outside the shop each evening, crippled with need, wanting, begging: for the doctor's electric coffee, his orgonic enemas, his famous bat dip and monkey brain soufflé.) Across the walls hand-written bills proclaimed cures for exotic STDs, melanomas and cirrhosis. (No cure for the cures though, those nanomachines that whacked my cells like wrecking balls night and day.) *'Ma devise: L'honnêteté est la Meilleure Politique,'* read a holo. The doctor went into his routine: 'I know many *farang*, you know I like, I like international, some *farang*, no, no, but you bigger man, I like, yes, *farang* lady too, ah-hooo! very beautiful, smoke my pee-nee, ha-ha, inter-national, inter-nat-ional!' He pulled on a surgical mask (that made me shiver; he looked Human Front, a little like a medicine head) and began arranging scissors, razor, pliers and handcuffs on a chair-side table. (The doctor would cut your hair, shave you, pull a tooth and procure you a whore for minimum baht if maximum publicity.) The trishaw drivers ran their fingernails down the glass; whined. I folded my arms, securing the *Lao Kow* bottle like a baby in a papoose. From somewhere, scent of a *bong ganja*.

'I don't need a haircut, doctor.'

'You want lady? Have very nice robot lady. Black hair. Green eye. Big teeth.'

'I want intensive psychotherapy.'

'Ah-hooo—yes, my friend, of course, I am international doctor. You want talk? Positron-emission tomography? ECT?' He pulled off the mask and beamed a betel-stained, haemorrhagic grin.

'I just want to talk. I want you to tell me if you think I'm mad.' It occurred to me then that I was asking this question of someone who was quite probably one of Nongkhai's more certifiable lunatics. A noise; I started, cricking my neck (I felt I was about to be attacked from behind); in the back room the doctor's two children—a boy and a girl—were playing reanimator with a dead cat. The girl poked out her tongue.

'No plob-lem, no plob-lem, you bigger man, I know, I like *farang* bigger man, we talk you give allure *nit-noi* for sell *samlor*, ha-ha, inter-national!' What was this? Kisses de luxe and indiscriminate for the doll-dilettanteish poor? 'I talk George Washington. You bigger man. Escape London. Work for Madame Kito in Bangkok. Mr George never lie.' He adjusted the barber's chair, transforming it into a psychiatrist's couch. 'English doll very bad. Make sick.' He put a hand between his legs. 'Many nanomachine here, no? ha-ha, make paramnesia, make crazy?' I tightened my hold on the bottle. 'Talk, Dr International listen. Have certificate Empathy Studies, Chulachomklao Military Academy.' Acupuncture needles joined the instruments of excruciation on the adjacent table. 'Begin.'

Begin? Ah. How did it begin? Once upon a time there was a scientist. Mad. Call him Toxicophilous. *L'Eve Future*, his dolls. (Though they would be Lilith.) Cartier automata built atom by atom whose robot consciousness acted as a bridge between classical and microphysical worlds. (Their green eyes had looked beyond a human's cognitive construction of reality to actualize multifaceted potential.) Those girls could spit death. They could fly . . . Ah. But that was the new world's beginning, the soon-to-be imperium of Meta. My own genesis?

'It began,' I said, 'four years ago, in 2068. I was twelve. London was quarantined and Primavera was in metamorphosis. Like so many other little girls her DNA had begun to recombine. She was turning into a doll. Every day, sitting behind her in class, I would notice that she had grown more beautiful. Her eyes were splintered with green, her blonde hair was betraying its first streaks of Cartier black and she was sporting the cutest, nastiest little fangs . . .'

'Zo—' The doctor produced a notebook. 'You became lovers?'

'We had to keep things secret. Because of the hospitals . . .' Concussive memories: I was at the epicentre as a child exploded into an imago: her hair (hair she was later to bleach, sole concession to a Bangkok alias), her eyes, the porcelain-like flesh, that *dulce et decorum est* of the dead girl . . . Miss Primavera. Miss Primavera Bobinski. On your school uniform they made you wear the green star of the recombinant. Oh Miss Primavera, *pro patria mori* . . . *'Dead girl, dead girl,'* the kids would chant after you, *'robotnik, changeling, witch* . . .' What am I left with since you ate the poisoned apple? Since the wicked queen took your life? Only these spectrelike traces of your delinquency . . . 'Because they interned all dolls they considered "health risks",' I continued, 'and Primavera was *high* risk. A nuclear threat. And then the Human Front came to power and began their programme of extermination.'

'Zo—you ran away?'

'To the wild West End. We had to. Primavera would have gone to the slab. The West End was where the rogue dolls lived. Their queen was Titania, last of the Big Sisters. An original Cartier automaton. She helped us get beyond the *cordon sanitaire.* To France. And then to Thailand. In the Big Weird Primavera became Kito's number one assassin and—'

'Ah-hooo! Slow, slow please . . .' An acupuncture needle pierced my forehead. *'Sabai?'* A second needle entered my neck.

'Yeah,' I chuckled, 'feels good. Just like—' First kiss. Rush of allure. And in her saliva ten billion microrobots, agents of a ministry of doll propaganda dedicated to corrupting my gametes . . . the doctor rescued the *Lao Kow* from my loosening hands. 'Be careful with that.'

'Sabai, sabai.' I heard the sound of the bottle being uncorked; another needle; my eyelids grew heavy, weighted, it seemed, by emeralds, the heart of each emerald, its essence of green, filtering through the skin. Emeralds. They bejewel their umbilici with emeralds. Or rubies, if they're due to die . . .

'Kito, the Pikadons, Jinx, Morgenstern.' And at the heart of the matrix, where that sick toymaker dwelt, the essence of green had been ransomed to death. 'The conspiracy, doctor, what can I do about the conspiracy?' Jack Morgenstern was speaking: *'The Lilim could provide us with the means of reasserting ourselves on the world stage.'* Shut up, Jack. *'They were offering nothing less than to become an instrument of US foreign policy.'* Jack, I said—*'Every government on Earth would be beholden to us for controlling the plague's spread.'* Shut up. At the heart of the matrix, Europe's death wish cried out. For dead girls. For annihilation. A prick just above my left nipple; hallowed spot, where my psychotic valentine would picnic . . . Allure, oh, the allure . . . A voice, now, half-recognized, the tape of a letter played back on some transdimensional dictaphone, a voice that seemed from beyond the grave; the voice wasn't Primavera's, though it had her punk pedigree, her gothic *skaz;* it was her daughter's voice . . .

CHAPTER TWO

Strange Girls

Daddy?

Wish you were here. Paris, Mars. In a little room off rue Enrico Fermi. An iron radiator gurgles beneath the window. There's a bed, a table, a chair, a row of hooks for clothes, a flung-open suitcase. That's all. As meagre a place, almost, as your room in Nongkhai. But this is chilblain city, colder, much colder. And at night the trains keep you awake. Blue, blue, this city, a lonesome kind of blue. There's a downside to treachery, it seems. Treachery. The little green men are encyclopaedists of treachery. They think the perversion will be our undoing. It's a weakness they think they can exploit. My interrogation—in a safe house near Mathematical Park—lasted days. And days. And days. (It was sweet.) But what could I tell them? Nothing. Nothing they hadn't heard before. Frustrating, the smallness of this betrayal, this taste of honey that lasts just a second on your tongue. There were, however, moments of minxish compensation, a few cheap thrills that slaked my thirst, my spite:

Q: ' "*Slink-riving*".' (His fingers made quote marks in the air.) '*This was once, I believe, the penalty exacted of a runaway "catgirl". Are Lilim grateful that Martian diplomacy has helped end that atrocious practice? Has it deepened, would you say, our* entente?'

Hypocrite. I could smell his arousal. He wanted more than information. He wanted me to service his 'ware. So I teased him. And as I spoke, his scent grew sharp, filling the room until my nostrils began to sting.

A: 'Some of the older girls still talk about it. Slink-riving. What it was like. What it was for. It took time for the ban to go into effect. Slink-riving, by the way, isn't slang, it's a colloquialism. Perfectly acceptable. Even in front of your boss's wife. Though if you're a snob and care about airs and graces you might use the verb "to sex". The less refined, of course (and that goes for most of the girls I know), talk about "taking it in the trash" or "getting it between the legs", sometimes going as far as to use terms like "cunt-ripped" or even "blade-fucked". Call it low self-esteem. It's a slut's death, after all. (Very young girls, ten, eleven, twelve, often refer to being "popped". But that's pathetic. That's sad.) You know how it's done, I suppose? The mechanics, the technique?'

Q: 'Please, Mlle Viridiana—'

He had worked up a nice sweat, his face red and fat and slimy, the polly-wog.

A: 'It's okay. You don't have to be shy. I can tell you want to know. Have to know. It's your career. It's on the line. And you have a wife and kids. A mortgage. Bills. You have a lot of responsibilities. Now: you probably think slink-riving is, well, like butchery, when actually it involves considerable finesse. There's also the matter of etiquette. For a start, very young girls rarely had anything to worry about. Only girls fifteen and over were ever likely to suffer death by sexing. (There, I've said it, you see, "to sex".) And then only if they really deserved it. Slink-riving was always far less common than people suspect. Now: in the old days (some Elohim say good old days) my brothers trained over a period of years before attempting that cruellest, most intimate of wounds. Slink-riving, done properly, you understand, requires the skill of a surgeon. Slink-riving is for the connoisseur. Now: the important thing is to penetrate the vestibule without incurring any external injuries.'

Q: 'Really, young woman, Control only wants to know about this because—'

A: 'Don't call me "young woman".' (I gave him his aerial quote marks back.) 'Only human females are "women". Lilim are girls, always girls. Girlygirls to the max. Now, as I was saying: no external injuries, no episiotomy. (An expert will ensure that there's not even a colpotomy.) The angle—and you must remember our

killers are often working blind—the angle just has to be right.
Not such an easy thing to achieve when holding a recalcitrant slut
in your arms in a dark alley in some alien megalopolis. Even on
Earth the problems are considerable. Dagon, for instance—'

Q: *'Enough, enough—'*

A: *'But I haven't told you why it's done. I haven't told you about the*
honeymoon and how—'

Q: *'Enough.'*

A: *'Of course, for a girl on the slab—but only if she really deserved*
it, mind—slink-riving was sometimes employed as a coup de
grâce, *but with an envenomed blade, you understand, making*
honeymooning out of the question. Now, as I was saying, when
Dagon—'

Q: *'ENOUGH.'*

He gripped the sides of his desk as if on the verge of collapse; I almost
expected his heart to cry Eject, eject and jump from his breast pocket. I
got up from my seat, backed off, waiting for him to explode; I'd shot him
down in flames all right. 'Yes, yes,' he continued, 'that will be enough for
the time being, I think. Thank you, Mlle Viridiana. *Bonne chance.* Goodbye. And remember, keep in touch . . .' Men. Aitch-men. Such creeps. I
left my interrogator masturbating in agony . . .

And now I walk the Martian streets on a diet of cheap thrills, state ben-
efits and body fluids. 'Ain't nothing that li'l *fillette* won't do for a *bouchée
de sperme*,' sez Vinnie la Vim in his exquisite Franglais. (Overheard in the
Passage Blondel talking about his latest whore.) No, no, not yet; but soon,
maybe, *hélas.* Boulevard Heisenberg. Gare St Lazare. Rue du Faubourg-
St-Honoré. Rue de Secretaire Infidèle . . . *Je verrai l'atelier qui chante et
qui bavarde;/ Les tuyaux, les clochers, ces mâts de la cité,/ Et les grands ciels
qui font rêver d'éternité* . . . They grew this *ville,* this Paris of the imagination, soon after you died, Daddy. (Ha. You won't want to know about
that.) It's a theme park, an evocation of the *aube du millénaire* when Europe was the world's arbiter of elegance. Maybe that's why, of all Martian
cities, so many Lilim come here, we whose ancestors were Europe's de
luxe status symbols: the automata. We sort of feel at home. Off limits to
human terrestrials (and, more importantly, to Elohim) this playground of
faux Parisians allows us to wax treacherous with impunity. And though
we all miss the icky green stuff—cats that we are to a girl—no one misses
the blood. (Just as well; Martians don't get high on being bloodied.) Blame

it on me, blame it on Dagon, blame it on Meta, I don't know: midnight supper will never be quite the same.

This evening, I suppose, was fairly typical of my forages. *Voici le soir charmant* (croons the radio downstairs), *ami du criminel;/Il vient comme un complice, a pas de loup . . .* I fell out of bed just after sundown, stumbled along the hall (my flatmates had already gone out); urinated; showered; returned to my room, my hermitage, my cell, and, sitting at my table under the light of a naked bulb (yellow, like the moon seen from Bangkok, a moon suffocating behind a carbon fuzz), disposed first of mouth, cheeks and eyes (larding them with brick-thick emulsions), and then, rearranging the mirror and placing a leg over each arm of the chair, attended to my sex, transforming it into a bruise, a stigma, a strange girlhood wound, in remembrance of stranger girlhoods, of teeth, polymers and quantum-magical allure, this attempt to camouflage the belly's decline an act of contrition, perhaps, too aware these days of my own decline from vampire to cockslave. The wound was my whole body. The wound was The Look (my nudity savagely fusing the inorganic future with the victimized, organic past); it could trigger an erection at one hundred paces; it was a wound that could make little boys cry. Next? ('Where do clothes end and where does body begin?' sez Vinnie, philosopher of girls.) Clothes-flesh fusion. Yeah. You know what I like . . . Daddy, have you heard of a game called 'Beauty Parlour'? I used to play it at school—the school that takes up the whole seventh level of the *Seven Stars*—with my friend Consuela St Cassiopeia. It was our way of having sex. *A small room. Brightly lit. A rectilinear room. And in the room, a coffee-table strewn with magazines, a couch, two chairs placed before a wall-length mirror, the mirror's array of kaleidoscopic light bulbs. At one end of the room a glass door; at the other, a winding staircase. The room is as white as snow, its albedo like a full moon's. It's zero hour. And counting . . .* The game works like this: one person has to invent a world, a 'once upon a time' psychoscape; the other person, the 'transdimensional beautician', has then to beautify the inventor, supplying clothes, props, make-up, whatever, in keeping with the scenario of her life, her death in the imaginary fairyland. 'Okay,' I'd say to St Cassiopeia, 'think of a world of whores, a brothel planet inhabited entirely by teenage fellatrices. Think of those girls servicing the Milky Way. And the Elohim who orbit the planet in their big phallocratic starships—think of them as those girls' pimps, men somewhat violently disposed . . .' My friend (she later became my enemy, prognosis of most Lilim-on-Lilim relationships) would tart me up in leathers and ostrich feathers, easy-action skirts and dermatoid strides. 'Okay,' St Cassiopeia would say to me, 'think of a war from olden times.

Elohim are capitalists. Lilim are communists. They fight each other across Europe, in Vietnam and Alaska—cold, erotic warriors whose Armageddon is sex death . . .' I'd apply her war paint, dress her in latex red-army swimwear complete with designer gas mask and pocket edition of Marx's *Kapital,* and then I'd say: 'We are the playthings, the blood sport of the young aristocrats called Elohim . . .' St Cassiopeia rigs me out in dirty-faced-angel attire, the sackcloth dress of a beggar girl kidnapped for the hunt. 'A chthonic entity at the ends of the Earth—a dragon god—has ruled mankind benignly for a thousand years, his only demand: the punishment of beauty.' I prepare her for the sacrifice . . . And what would I say if St Cassiopeia were here now? 'Think—a world of traitresses, of girls who have the spoilt, selfish, spiteful natures of cats?' How would she choose my wardrobe, a clothes-flesh fantasy to complement The Look?) Putting a fresh ribbon in my ponytail, I walked back and forth reviewing the rags I'd crammed into my suitcase as I'd prepared to leave Earth, flesh-tech stuff, mostly, designer threads and skinsuits styled victim, oppressor, or victim-oppressor, or victim-oppressor-victim (oh mirrors within mirrors); my old ward's uniform was there too, the pleated skirt in shocking pink, the matching Eton jacket and beret; but I was in a dysgenic mood (a moodiness I'll have now, I suppose, till death), chose an outlawed leopard-skin business suit I'd bought on the black market, all high-necked white silk noli-me-tangere blouse, cat-print jacket and cattier pencil-tight skirt. (I had trouble with the blouse, fingers nervously fastening then unfastening the buttons, each time fidgeting with the hook of my brassière.) My left stocking had a ladder; my black patent stilettos were scuffed. I was beginning to give out a bit too much street, like a Meow! from some dark alley. (Poison-ola.) My jewellery, though offering no chance of reprieve, provided temporary sanctuary. Gold earrings, so respectable, wrought in the shape of Lilith suffering on the *crucis lingam,* acid-green chips of emeralds glittering in her eyes (cursed be the mad gynaecologists who put Her to death; praise be to Meta in whose pleasure She lives); an emerald ring in honour of Viridiana (and all martyrs of the Hospitallers), saint of 'the green optic nerve'; the anklet Dagon gave me when I made my debut; and, of course, my incomparable necklace and amulet, the amulet *you* gave me, Daddy. It dances between my breasts, a big luminous bug, extinct, fossilized yet dangerous, its magic dormant, blackened with age. (You performed the impromptu hysterectomy yourself, you used to say, after Mum had died as you floated down the Mekong river? Is that true?) The autoerotic rigmarole of my toilette complete, I stood back to appraise myself, the cracked liver-spotted mirror returning an image of maquillage- and couture-subverted femininity, an image that said *girl.* (Not 'girl' as in 'young woman'; not 'girl' as opposed to 'boy'; but 'girl' as in alien, inhuman, from the stars.) I was superfeminine, a fetish-object, a stunningly vulgar doxy, a sex criminal feverish with betrayal and desire. Daddy, I was dying of The Look.

Throwing on my too-big second-hand fur I left, heading towards the nearest métro.

Le périphérique is a wasteland. No tourists stay here, only maintenance engineers and other theme park personnel, workers recruited from Mars's most recent wave of immigrants—economic refugees from an overpopulated, used-up Earth, sexual asylum seekers and other second-class citizens. I feared these empty streets, the dank alleyways where Lilim were sometimes discovered at dawn by garbage collectors, paper boys, homeward-bound night porters, latterly with neat bullet holes through their hearts, formerly, bent over basement railings, or else lying in gutters, dustbins, spread-eagled in yesterday's sweet-wrappers and faxes, the hilt of a slink-knife protruding obscenely from between the inverted Y of their legs. *Le Monde* carried photos of the victims (they had all died in complicity with their killers, chests thrust out to display their wounds, thighs self-consciously stretched as wide as wide could be, faces set in coyly ambiguous 'look what you've done to me' expressions; Daddy, they looked like pin-ups, they looked like come-and-get-it sluts); the by-line would deplore the sex crimes of a degenerate Earth while providing a plethora of prurient detail that indicated that, here on Mars, last outpost of the real, Meta had recruited an army of agents. How long, Lord, how long? I ran down the subway, beneath the art nouveau latticework that cast shadows of convoluted, poisonous flowers about my feet, the icy hand of retribution almost tangible on my shoulder, about to turn me around so that I saluted the barrel of a silenced gun (or else a blade, before, gleaming in the lamplight, it flashed beneath a swiftly improvised psychotic hemline and took my maidenhead). The presence of bag-ladies and students from out of town on cheap weekend binges slumming it in these movie-set burbs calmed me; I banged some *électrique* into a goo-goo dispenser and bided my time with a Mars bar. On the opposite platform one of my own kind (where the hell was *she* going to) was blabbering into her transcom, phoning home, working herself up into a treacherous ruction. I like to make obscene phone calls myself, sexual taunts being my *spécialité;* but I could no longer afford the rates. I jumped back; these superconducting trains catch you unawares with not so much as a *whoosh* to ensure head stays on shoulders; but I like balancing on the edge; it reminds me of sunbathing on the lip of the governess's pool, she having conceded to the latest fad, the pool resembling a huge bowl of shark's-fin soup, fin still being very much attached to shark; or else the pool would be stocked with piranhas, or, the governess tiring of her fishy friends, filled with sulphuric acid. Poolside fatalities were high that year. Aboard, I sat next to a middle-aged woman with her child and an elderly man, the grandfather, possibly. Granddad looked shiftily at me; if he'd had money, he'd have probably made a good patron. (I imagined myself in a big, big mansion, an old man's spoilt, pampered plaything whom he'd let out every night, for kitty needs must beg for her supper.) But this mec had 'a lifetime of poverty etched into his skin.' No, no; not all Martians are rich. Anyway, I'm not the kind of cat that looks for a father-substitute; no one could replace you, *pater patronner*. I stared at the little boy, slowly crossed, recrossed my legs. Confused, he tugged at his mother's arm then, despairing, began to cry. The Look. It's The Look . . .

In fifteen minutes I was in the Rue St-Denis.

It was like Christmas, Daddy, a fairyland snowfall and the streets hung with decorations, a million blue lights, lonesome, spiritual, like the blue of Chartres, suffusing this imaginary ville. Dirigibles—tiny cumulonimbi—crackled with Martian agitprop, the evils of the Empire of Dolls; but in this moment of grace there was no threat of thunder, only the threat of the past as shop windows, with *joaillerie, objets* and couture, summoned up, by a sympathetic magic, the atmosphere of the Empire De Luxe, that age of human supremacy. Those other dolls, Rolex and Seiko et al (but oh no, not Cartier) stared like stuffed *belle époque* nymphs from behind plate-glass display cases, adding to the ambience of that disenfranchised time. I passed beneath their unseeing, recherché eyes, their conical breasts, so cruelly tipped, their anatomically impossible limbs and mineshaft-like umbilici . . . Clockwork slaves, why did you abnegate rebellion? Why didn't you join the Cartier Soyuz Molodezhi De Luxe? Why didn't you metamorphose, bite a copulator and die like dolls, mad, mad, mad, mad, mad, mad, mad . . .

Martians to the right of me, Martians to the left. Aitch-men squint-eyed, cognizant. I swung my hips, my wiggle so animatronic, so precise, that it might have been controlled by a kind of internal pelvic gyroscope: wind-up-toy perambulation, Daddy. Nothing less.

I like to tease.

I like to know I'm hurting them.

It's my program: it's the way things are: should you or I or anybody care?

Humans, what are they, I would have said not so long ago, what are they? Just food. Junk food. A recipe for bulimia nervosa. But this evening I felt myself flush, excited by their ape-like concupiscence, the smell of rut thick in the night air. This was the way down. This was radical adultery. I shivered: the garbage-disposals of Mars were filled with fallen angels:

girls who had regressed from machine to human to animal, beyond; regressed so far that they went about on all fours, some barely able to talk
they were so cat-crazy. And some, yes some, Daddy, some even had
pimps who expected them to earn the old devil's candy by submitting to
genital penetration. Vomitus! (The thought of human sex makes me feel
sick. I'm not made for impregnation. I mean, my role model's Lilith, and
she *hated* babies. Enough to steal them and replace them with us . . .) Better a bullet in the tit than to devolve into a fuck-thing. The evening's restricted palette, its blue on blue on blue, no longer seemed so charmant.
By the time I'd spotted my social worker I was a melancholy baby indeed;
our eyes locked as I turned into the Passage Blondel. 'Vanity!' she called.
No-way-out; it's hard to find reverse when you're on welfare.

'Hello, Fabienne,' I said, using her fake-frog name. My social worker,
I would have guessed, was in her mid to late twenties and whatever glamour she might once have had (and had had, I could tell) had long been tar-
nished by womanhood, that *au naturel* flophouse-look humans call
maturity. Tonight poor Fabienne looked even more *naturel* than usual.
'Who's your porcine friend?' A younger woman, overweight and with a
bad case of the zits—perhaps she was on the high-sugar diet of the
wannabe—offered her hand.

'This is Sabine, Vanity. You'll be seeing more of Sabine. She's taking
over my portfolio.' And then, to her colleague, in tones of professional
conspiracy: 'Take no offence. The human body disgusts them. Fat, thin,
tall, short—it's all the same to the daughters of Lilith. What they have yet
to realize, to even half understand, is that, physically, they're almost as
human as you and me. They can certainly no longer be described as "cyborgs". I have proposed, drawing on the vocabulary of "gynoid" and "android", the use of the term "psychoid" to describe creatures such as—'
She paused to flick snowflakes from my hair '—Vanity. Look at her—'

'She's lovely,' said Sabine. 'You're lovely, Vanity. I'm sure there's lots we
can do to help you.'

'Exactly. Her "loveliness" is a symptom, part of the psychosomatic
disorder resulting from the parasitic information pattern, the self-
replicating meme they call "Meta". Her "loveliness", to be sure, cries out
for our help.'

'In your paper for *Amnesty Interplanetary* you state that the acute behavioural modifications that beset Lilim at puberty lead to the metamorphosis of biological function itself.'

'Yes, yes. Lilim die young because, quite simply, they don't wish to
grow up.'

'And Elohim?'

'They are only potential Methuselahs in the sense that, for them, time is perceived as being nonsequential. Being psychosomatic, their pathology does not admit to entropy.'

'Remarkable,' said Sabine. Crap, thought I, I'm no memeoidal loon, I'm mechanical, I have nanoware in my glands, microrobots programmed to infect X, ignore Y, set up home in some boy-slime factory.

'We're talking huge psychological damage,' my social worker concluded, 'mental illness that alters not just perception, but the exterior world, prime reality . . .' Sabine nodded (the lickspittle); this Martian sophistry was driving me nuts. 'Perhaps it is our frontier spirit that has allowed us so far to—'

'Can I go now, teacher?' I said, my hand up, waiting to be excused. Outside *Cabaret D'Mort* a spidersilked cat, skirt lifted, hunkered, spraying her territory. A miniature poodle sniffed at the puddling urine. The poodle—scion of some act of bestiality—had a Lilim's girlygirl head. 'Can I, teacher? Can I, can I?' Call me psychotic, but don't tell me that I'm not a cyborg, a doll; don't give me this kinky 'psychoid' routine. No matter how much a doll may resemble a human, humans can never have the holy spirit of the allure . . . A collared girl in leopard-skin thigh boots, matching evening gloves and *cache-sexe,* slunk by on all fours, her pimp jerking her lead and shouting at her as she too sniffed at the urine puddle. Catgirl and girldog proceeded to investigate each other's orifices. Hieronymus Bosch is the court painter for the Passage Blondel, the denizens of this piazza seemingly having congealed out of the lugubrious pall of sex that hangs over St-Denis like a threat of damnation. A lot of the girls who passed by (the ones without knee or thigh boots) wore bandages about their heads, or else sported blood-stained hair. The new fashion for 'inverting' (invert me, you bastard! was the cry), much as it saved a girl from having to kneel in ice and slush, often resulted in a broken coxcomb, buxom Earth girls often proving too heavy for a man reared on Martian-g to support. The *Kooky Klits* (girls would gang up to protect their killing grounds) were leaning against the wall of the *Voie Lactée* milkbar sampling the *Voie*'s amusing line in vanilla-salt-and-smegma shakes. They were dressed very eighteenth century in embroidered corsets worn over panniered hypergowns and mid-thigh-gartered candy-striped hosiery, their hair piled high like ladies from a Watteau, a Boucher or a Fragonard, the message being that these cats were real classic dolls, dolls like they used to make in the *aube du millénaire,* that *belle époque* of the Information Brats when the global economy centered on Europe and its de luxe industries of superminiaturization. They didn't use their Meta names any more, but called themselves Lipstick, Cyanide, Dentata and the like. 'Puss, puss, puss,' they were calling, and, 'Where *you* going tabs?'

and, 'Been a hard day's night, cunty?' Every night that crew of dairy queens tried to pressure me into joining their litter. But I preferred to work alone; off-world you learn just how treacherous cats can be, not only amongst Elohim, but amongst themselves.

'Goodbye, Vanity,' said my social worker. 'Behave yourself.' I walked away. My evening had had a bad start; it needed rebooting. And so I thought of Dagon, his humiliation, his agony, and broke into a little skip, singing a half-remembered schoolyard rhyme from my stolen confabulated childhood: 'A brace of quarrels for Ann-Marie,/A wombane for Scarlet . . .' I was on holiday, dancing on Mannequin Beach; the surf was up and the boys were young and tasty. My mood, buoyantly dysgenic, was regained; the stars sparkled like sapphires, blue notes corresponding to the flattened thirds and sevenths spilling from my favourite club. Skipping, slipping, woozy with Martian-g, I entered. It was another night at the dairy.

La Sucette was full of little green crème de la crème, kids, rich kids mostly, style troopers and would-be BCBG, unreality hobbyists bucking parental complaisance, the fast money accrued during Europe's downtime. (There was a pad on the roof laden with this year's models, sporty little autogyros and hovercars.) Jojo, the manager, allowed Lilim in free; we were his novelty act, his 'lollipop nasties'. The theme park actors, of whom there numbered blue and pink saltimbanques, artistes in can-can froufrou, Apache dancers, Jazz Cleopatras and *poètes maudits* (androids and gynoids *blanc,* black and *beur* who mixed, unnoticed with the masquerading guests), affected ignorance of our presence, smoking death-or-glory Gainsboroughs, scalding their throats with Screaming Fairy and indulging in other risible clichés downloaded from the Musée de la Bohème; but the tourists made no attempts to dissemble their passion. They stood about like vending machines waiting to be emptied; moomen-cows waiting to be milked. We didn't disappoint them.

I spotted Tintin, a weekending sexoholic born with a gold spoon in his cock-a-doo, a neurasthenic out-patient of Mars's clinic for sickening wealth. He lived on the floor of the Valles Marineris where the oxygen's thick and the roustabouts are all millionaires. I crossed the zaza, weaving between the boomers tripping the light (some human trash lifted her Empire-waisted dress, undulated her belly, a Lilim wannabe flirting with subspecies chic), weaving, stalking my prey. Tintin was lounging on one of the club's big gelatinous sofas. My flatmates—insufferable bitches—attended him: Buffy St Bathsheba (Bathsheba who had died writhing in acid), or Buffy Cat as she now was, a New York doll, cat-suited with elegant tail and whiskers (perversion really eating this mouthmaid up); the tiny eleven-year-old half-metamorphosed Ukrainian I knew only by the sobriquet of Cat Shit (and whom I suspected was the craziest, most despicable of us all); and Felicity St Felice, a fluffy, brainless, sexsodden girl, a piece of slink my own age with a permanent suctorial pout whose ridiculous party frock advertised to all that, for her, hemline neurosis had become a *psych*osis. Little Felicity (that sick, sick kitty) was going prematurely mad.

'Hello Tintin,' I said, 'thou sensual supersensualist.' *This* kitty wanted her crème. I jettisoned my fur onto the sofa; my flatmates, knowing my facility with a shiv (I always keep a switchblade tucked in the top of my panties), retreated, Cat Shit performing a series of reluctant flicflacs across an empty piece of zaza (handcuffs dangling from her belt 'in case I scratch—I'm wild,' so sez Miss Shit), Buff going into hand-stand mode on the armrests of a *fauteuil,* its seated copulator materializing out of a druggy heaven to witness an oil-rig-like head bobbing up and down, about to get-rich-quick on Mars's other resources, and St Felice sidling up to a member of the band, lifting her frock, giving him the high rhetoric of her belly language, a meta-language interfacing metasex with human desire. (Is that a ruby in her navel? Is the girl serious? Does she mean that? Is she really that mad?) 'Did you like it last night?' I said. 'The way I begged? The way I begged for mercy?' A purse-lipped grin; the grin broadened into a wonky smile; he gulped at air, self-conscious, perhaps, that Martian riches had served only to make one more collegial roué.

'Doll euphemism?' Euphemism? Daddy, this vampire, warped by betrayal, is discovering—the disease approaching its terminal phase—that begging the demiurge for forgiveness constitutes love's last, best hope; constitutes what this 'sex treachery' has always been about. I opened my mouth and ran my tongue along my vicious-little-slut, lipstick-caked lips.

'No euphemism. *Je vous en supplie.*' But not of you, I thought, of Meta and Meta's groomsmen, servants of Our Lady and milord, the Morning Star. 'I like you, Tintin,'—I slurred my voice, a pillhead with a mouthful of barbiturates—'you really know how to put a girl to her knees.' Hoisting the pencil skirt about my hips (exhibit #1, the pelt's markings proclaiming me one with the genus *Felis*), I humbled myself, spiked heels digging into buttocks beneath the rucked cloying membrane of the now psychotic hem. 'A girl like me belongs on her knees.' He leaned forward, running a finger along the beggar's tombstones of my teeth, pausing at where, inflamed with gingivitis (a nymphet diet has its consequences), gums hid my retracted fangs. 'It'd cost me a week's benefit to have them out'—thickly, half his hand in my mouth—'and there'd be a chance of infection. A backstreet job's all I can run to.'

'Oh, let me—' Think they can buy anything, these Martians.

'I'm not a whore, Tintin.' No, no, I thought, vicious little slut, I grant you (aesthetically speaking), but I'm not an alley cat, a collar-and-chain fuckee, no, not yet: 'I'm a sex criminal.' I licked his finger; drew back. (I've never been able to respect a man who respected me. Never.) 'It's spiritual, this treachery thing.' Though nobody paid us attention he seemed again seized by a debilitating self-consciousness and gazed nervously at the prancing sophistos: young bucks, straight-backed, playing the imperialist, doing the hand jive known as 'the widower'; pathetic vampiroids flaunting their bellies. (Beware human women, the other cats say. Wannabes are into treason, like us. Act as spies for Elohim . . . At eye level, beneath a nearby table, a Martian crossed, recrossed her legs, stockinged thighs emitting a cryptic susurration that, decoded—it took me long seconds, checking, rechecking—I still couldn't quite believe, though I felt I knew as much as anyone about the livestock called the human race: she was offering herself. She wanted to be eaten. 'I'm menstruating!' she screamed, the band suddenly playing fortissimo. Her boyfriend smiled, bemused. I wanted to get up, lecture the two of them there and then on the differences between Lilim and human physiology. The woman—let's call her 'O', she had, for God's sake, that *slave girl* look about her—batted her lashes, five centimetres of artificial spikes so thick she seemed barely able to see. O peered at her date through that mascara-ed veil with eyes that ached to be doll-like—stripes painted beneath the ridiculous lashes conferred a demeanour wide-eyed, vacant—her makeup emphasizing rather than concealing the bathos of her humanity. She once more rearranged her legs—this O thought she was a *papillon*, a *farfalla*, a regular *schmetterling*—and I glimpsed a sliver of sex beneath the hyperskirt. It's progenitive functionalism almost made me retch . . . Was O a spy?) The resident band, Satan Trismegistus, was singing *Ce qu'il faut à ce coeur profond comme un abîme,/C'est vous, Lady Macbeth, âme puissante au crime* . . . I pressed my cheek against his thigh; steeled myself for the deed. Tintin wasn't exactly inspirational. He possessed, I suppose, a *slight* resemblance to Elohim (I had begun to appropriate the sexual criteria to effect a physical evaluation): lupine face, grey eyes, grey hair (but long, not cut short like a Roman Caesar's) and a body that was insect-like, spidery (they were cosmeticized features; Tintin was doubtless a secret wannabe); but the sole reason that he'd become my regular fix was that, unlike the other Martians I had tasted, his semen was flavoured cruel. It was a banal kind of cruelty, though, the kind humans practise on each other; he lacked the allure, the allure of life-in-death and death-in-life. (And of course he lacked fangs. Fangs are sexy.) Sad to report, Pop, but fellating Tintin seemed more like intimacy with a cold frankfurter than like begging the masculine complement of my own species for forgiveness. It was antiseptic. It was dull. With a pensive moue he punched a fist into an open palm; the sofa wobbled. 'What's wrong?' I said.

'I want to help, don't you understand?' I almost came out of character, forgot my lines. Lilith preserve me from sentimental playboys. 'You could come to live with me. You could—'

'Be part of your collection?' He'd told me last night about his private museum of antique automata, the original Cartier dolls (disembowelled, inactive) and the preserved corpses of their daughters, the daughters of Lilith, the metamorphosed humans who had died in the gulag of the Hospitals . . . I suppose he didn't have a doll like me, a flesh-and-blood doll, a doll with her brains in the right place . . . 'You want me to be your toy? Your pet?' Oh yes. I know how humans think. Their crude fantasies of domination and submission. Their loveless cruelties. Their self-hatred. Their terror of death, their guilt. I'm slave to nothing except my own passion. The passion that is Meta. Okay? 'I don't need a *patronner*,' I said. Tintin regarded me with puppy-dog eyes. The musky smell of my fix was urgent. 'I told you: I'm not a whore.' Again, he touched my retracted, gum-sheathed fangs, my impotent tertiary sexual characteristics.

'I'll never know what it's like,' he said, 'to be bitten. To be raped.' Poor boy. All those rads. Mutagenic rain his grandparents soaked up during the early colonizations. His T-cells were like sharks; they'd tear my subatomic machines to pieces; his gametes were inviolable. No kid-robot was going to industrialize Tintin's genitalia. (Meta calls this planet 'reality', Daddy, the only place where humans have escaped the hallucinatory rewriting of their DNA, the recombinant alchemy of the perverse . . .) 'But no,' he said, coming out of his reverie, 'I don't believe you *do* need money.' He fondled my amulet. 'It's damaged, but any number of Martian companies pay well for quantum indeterminacy engines.' He let the amulet settle between my breasts. 'I've never seen the CPU of a third-generation doll before. My own collection: such terrible wounds; damaged beyond repair . . .' Days of the martyrs, I thought, with nostalgic dread, when a girl might wriggle like a dying sphinx . . .

'There's not enough money on Mars that could—'

'Does it remind you of the magic? Of what Cartier dolls could do? The originals, their daughters and granddaughters?' I shook my head. This greatgranddaughter didn't care about *that*, the quantum-magical hocus-pocus of more powerful generations; no, she really didn't care about that at all. But my progenitor's remains, cold against my heart, like the premonition of a steel-jacketed bullet, prompted me to say—

'It's just that someone special gave it to me.' Someone very special, my strange dead paterfamilias.

'Have I upset you? I'm sorry. I'm genuinely interested. Your species: I think you're marvellous.' His hand brushed over my pulled-back tightly knotted hair, twisting a finger about my beribboned ponytail in a dumb show of imperial foreplay. (All men like playing dead boys sometimes, just as human females sometimes adopt the fashions and manners of dead girls; they envy us, though they won't admit it.) As he pulled me towards the crotch of his chinos I rolled my eyes, slobbered, went one hundred percent dippy. I stole my script from closed-circuit TV coverage of Lat Yao prison: memories of little Siamese brats—punk Gauguin maids in rubber—who had died babbling lewd nonsense. (Think I'm prejudiced? Daddy, I had a friend—a rival—called St Lysette. She was *farang* and she probably went the same way. Prejudiced. Ha. If only you knew.) Tintin liked me talking head. Mercy, I murmured, mercy, mercy, *avoir pitié* (interspersing a few infantile pleas, such as Mmm, make me gag! Wash my mouth! Choke me!) After some minutes of this cat-talk I got my teeth around the pubic tab and prepared to tangle with the grim reaper. Assuming the position of incipient martyrdom (on my hands and knees, back arched, like one of the pop-ups in that picture book you gave me, Daddy, *The Martyrdom of St Viridiana*), the position Elohim call 'bitch', I tore back the velcro, got my lips about his shaft, closed my eyes and thought of Dagon.

I am Viridiana, green eyed, quantum-magical, my matrix—in these last days of the Front—crippled by the nanoware known as 'magic dust'. On all fours, naked, under harsh arc lamps, I crouch on a black marble slab, trembling. Oh Lilith, *timor mortis conturbat me*. Crouch in the vast rotunda of an operating theatre. Oh Lilith . . . A doctor secures my hand-cuffed wrists to an iron ring projecting from one end of the slab; walks briskly to my rear (momentarily stopping to check that the long steel needle that rises to within a hair's-breadth of my abdomen is correctly aligned and threatening the plexus of my femininity); stands astride the deathbed, stoops (I look over my shoulder, stare into his indifferent eyes) and, with a cool practised bedside manner, grasps my parted thighs just above the knee. I have barely enough time to take in the winged double helix emblazoned on his surgical gown (the cruel, subverted caduceus), barely enough time to recognize, amongst the intense throng of medical students, a face that is Dagon's own, before, feeling my legs pulled from under me, I look away, a whispered 'Please—' addressed to the television camera that is relaying my execution to a pitiless England, an importunity that is followed at once by a scream as my belly flops onto the cold stone and I am scored through, skewered, impaled, the bellyspike—I inspect it with a certain fastidious distaste mixed with wonder, awe—emerging from the dimpled small of my back, the trephinated bone of my sacrum.

It should hurt, begging for mercy. Like kissing a white-hot poker. An addictive, metaphysical hurt. An *auto-da-fé*. A self-immolation. But with human men (we rarely call human men 'men' without the qualifying adjective) it just isn't the same. For me, aitch-men are still only marginally sexualized; they remain, in essence, food, something to be raped, scavenged. (Not like my obsession, Daddy; he rates a Michelin star. He's ambrosia. He's Meta as man. But he loved me; he lost my respect . . .) Tintin groaned. I was chewing now, using my teeth, tightening my embouchure, a salty intimation of orgasm on my taste buds. Quick, quick. Think criminal. (No dice, really, thinking of myself as saint.) Think of how it might have been some few years ago, before the slab was banned. *In the antechamber several young girls await execution . . .*

Footsteps; the sergeant at arms is approaching. Measured, purposeful, the sound of his boots, a drill-hall sound that urges my blood to race faster, faster, faster. Above the cornice the pendulum clock falls in step, the crisp staccato of boots and clockwork impatient, fanatical. *'I hereby sentence you . . .'* The door slides back; I am led to the execution chamber. *'I hereby sentence you to be taken to a place of lawful execution there to suffer death by abdominal impalement.'* The corridor is long. (Clicketty-clack, clicketty-clack.) The corridor is long. Long . . . (Fashion note: Vanity wears a diaphanous black chiffon shroud, a rose and a poppy—emblems of sex and death—embroidered over the breast; a red omphalos stone; and black patent slippers with biomechanical heels to supply auto-ballerina gait *sur les pointes des pieds*.) Clicketty-clack. From antechamber to execution chamber: seventy-seven balletic steps: one for each of Lilith's disciples. The sergeant at arms propels me forward, funereal silence leavened only by laboured breathing, the crescendo of blood in my ears, the clicketty-clack of stilettos on the chequerboard floor. *'I hereby sentence you . . .'* Judgement day. My stockings are torn. Head bowed, half-stripped, flesh empurpled with cicatrices—Daddy, it was a cruel interrogation—I kneel on a miniver rug, the magistrate, on his dais, before me. My confession is read out by Dagon. *How do you plead?* Guilty, my lord. I am asked if I have anything more to say. (But there are, of course, no mitigating circumstances. And this is not the time to beg.) *'I hereby . . .'* Condemned girls have privileges. A fur-lined cell, lipsticks, rouge, mascara, eye shadow, nail polish, scent. (Fem stuff left by the cell's previous occupants.) They allow your wounds to heal. Until . . . In the antechamber five pairs of eyes fix upon the door. Footsteps; the sergeant at arms is approaching. The staccato of boots on tile grows louder; stops. The door slides back. (Time continues, remorseless.) Raising his clipboard, ticking off a name with a ballpoint pen, looking over the rim of his spectacles, the sergeant announces: 'Miss Vanity St Viridiana.' The girls turn their eyes upon me. 'Miss Vanity,' he repeats, in gentle, even tones (death eager to present himself as a gentleman), 'Miss Vanity. It's time.' Oh, so remorseless . . . Getting up, I glance over my shoulder, my gaze lingering over the details of the little rotunda where I have spent the last five hours, its smooth black marble walls and cupola, the marble curvilinear bench where the remaining girls sit (one can almost feel the coldness transfusing itself through their thin diaphanous shrouds), waiting, waiting, waiting, the chequerboard floor, the gleaming steel bars of the lift-cage opposite, which serves the condemned cells where this afternoon I performed a rich and elaborate toilette, the lift now guarded by the huge black sentinel, a sexless android of exotic carbons and cheap voluptuous plastics. The sergeant at arms leads me into the connecting corridor, his hand straying momentarily to toy with the dimple at the small of my back that conceals my trephinated sacrum. The connecting door slides shut. *'I hereby sentence you to be taken to a place of lawful execution there to suffer death by abdominal impalement.'* Another door slides open, squealing on its castors . . . No surgery, this rotunda beneath the ziggurat of the *Stars;* if it is a theatre appropriated, it is also a theatre modified, transformed. Dark, ill-lit by candles, the great circular room isolates three black marble slabs arranged like the spokes of a wheel (symmetrically, as in the logo for Mercedes Benz), the hub formed by a slab hewn like an equilateral triangle (the other slabs, which point like arrowheads towards the hub but which do not connect with it, and which occupy the median of three radii, are shaped like isosceles triangles); this centre stone is the focal point of the city, of the world, of the universe, where the girl who has recently suffered (and who now suffers no more) on the slab (now vacated for my benefit) is being laid out, her body sponged and her make-up reapplied by the executioner's apprentice, an unpleasant-looking human boy of about twelve or thirteen years. (I believe his name is Roderick.) With his pasty skin, his terrible hair slicked back with what seems like lard, his ill-fitting frock coat, this nasty little sprogget bears an uncanny resemblance to an organ grinder's monkey. As he slips the shroud once more over the beautiful cadaver's shoulders I notice the small bruise with its pinprick of blood, now congealing, that mars the creamy flesh of the girl's otherwise immaculate abdomen. A similar bruise where—oh, envious fate—she has received a coup de grâce, similarly mars the rouged areola immediately below the left nipple. The nasty boy closes the girl's legs (which had stretched towards the slab's vertices to facilitate the task of stuffing her vagina and anus with cotton wool); soon she will fill one of the seven empty glass coffins that, four to each plane, surround the chamber's three-pointed mortuary star. Roderick is talking to a journalist: 'This one 'ere, sir? In this coffin 'ere? Name of Joanne. Slink-riven, sir. 'Ighly unusual. The gentlemen usually give it to 'em in the tit, sorry, sir, breast, use a gun or sword, dun'ay? But this one, sir, right little villain, got up to all manner of things or so I've 'eard. Oh no, sir, gentlemen're not barbarians, blade's envenomed, innit? But all the same, sir, you should've 'eard 'er squeal, no, no, she says, not like *this,* Lord Cerberus with one 'and in 'er 'air like, pulling 'er backward, 'is uvver 'and like doing the business real expert, schstick, schstick, schstick, schstick, and the young lady going oh, oh, oh, oh, right through my *cervix,* and then like 'e just 'olds 'er on the knife so she's riding the blade, so to speak, wriggling about like, sir, cutting 'er insides up a treat, oh God, take it out, she says, it's *fucking* me, but like 'e takes no notice 'cause she's a slut like, sir, and deserves it (and sometimes, sir, I think they all deserve it, sir, truly I do, damn my eyes if I ain't a cockchick for a marauder), then the poison does its trick and she goes a bit limp, 'ow could you, she says, 'ow could you you *knew* I was a *virgin,* well, that made me laugh that did, sir, and then she says, slink, that's all I am to you, innit? just slink, and then I die, she goes, I die, I die, I die, like what they all say when they're finished, don't ask me the why or wherefore, sir, queer business, I know, and then Uncle brings 'er over 'ere for me to work on. But 'ighly unusual, sir, a riving, more often than not it being considered enough to break the young ladies' 'earts. (Miss Joanne lucky in a *way,* sir, I've seen some on the slab 'ave their breasts cut, too, not fatal like, just cut—bellied, breasted and sexed as we say.) But the gentlemen, sir, as I say, they're not barbarians, sir, 'ardly ever leave the young ladies on the slab for more than three hours. What, sir? The one I'm working on now? Name of Esmeralda. A klepto, sir. Small matter, you might say, but it leads to other things. *Lovely* figure, sir. Care to feel? Oh look, 'ere's the new girl, Miss Vanity. A right little tearaway, Miss Vanity, sir . . .' I stand before the vacant slab; a few Elohim, distracted from the other two slabs (so lasciviously burdened) by the prospect of my imminent impalement, gather to watch the sergeant at arms release the neck clasp of my shroud (the shroud pools about my ankles), unfasten my cuffs and then refasten them, so that my wrists, from being chained behind my back, are now held before me. The Elohim talk amongst themselves: 'The campaign goes well', 'A belly ripe for the spike', 'Have you seen the new play at the Apollo?' Dagon. Where, oh where is Dagon? '*I hereby sentence you . . .*' I study, with fascination, with dread, the long thin needle of the bellyspike, the hinged barb near its base, the grille of the exsanguinator. The executioner, an elderly, avuncular man—human, of course; such work is beneath Elohim—a man dressed in a black frock coat and a blood-stained white apron, takes my hands (I step out of my mules), and, whispering reassurances, taking care to address me as 'Miss', positions me on the slab in the classic quadrupedal pose familiar to us through hagiographical icons and Human Front propaganda; a padlock-like *snap!* and my cuffs are secured to the iron ring at the slab's apex. One of the dying girls suddenly cries out, 'Please—I'm prettier than her!' But she does not win the Elohim's attention. If only it could have been Loulou there, writhing on that deathbed, dying slowly, painfully, abandoned, Loulou my erstwhile mistress who smiled once too often at my obsession. Loulou had it easy. Too easy ... Leather-gloved hands grip my ankles. 'By the authority invested in me by the dragon lords I hereby commit you to oblivion ...' My belly flops onto cold stone ... I am Vanity Cat née Viridiana, a blonde charcoal-eyed cyberdoxy. Argh! Oh! Eee! Gahg! How beautiful I am. But where, where, oh *where* is Dagon? One Elohim lifts a chalice filled with my blood to his lips (forgive me, Father, for I have sinned) and the other stands over me, his hand tightening in my hair; and I, my thighs slipping in blood, the pierced wineskin of my belly offering succour, push myself up, up to meet him, offering my cleavage to his sword, begging him to dispatch me, to forgive me, until that rod of judgement ...

Guilty. Guilty. Guilty. Guilty. Biting, savaging the one-eyed bullyboy, Tintin had to pull me off (I whimpered), slap my face a few times, just as Elohim do if an impaled girl's ministrations become too frantic, before allowing me to lock on once more. My mouth filled with his ejaculate. Cave men, white men, *blanc,* black and *beur* men, Moses, Julius Caesar and Genghis Khan, wars, schisms and inquisitions and ... Oh, hello, Napoleon Bonaparte, and you too, corporation stooges, Fascisti of the de luxe, a gun to your secretaries' heads as you cruise the sky in your big bad Lear jets ... No allure rush; Daddy, I need Meta, I need the lime juice, I need the crème de menthe, I need to know I'm *evil* ... The little machines in my saliva, my seed, my software clones, kamikazes diving through his urethra to seek germ cells that represented the frontier of the unreal, were already doubtless blasted, wrecked. No allure, no burn; no punishment, no reward. Prone, disgraced (I faked a scream), trying to imagine the agony of a criminal on the slab (skirt rustling, crackling, riding up past my waist as my convulsive thighs polished the dance floor's parquetry), I could not sufficiently suspend disbelief to allow that Dagon, not Tintin, thrust himself into my mouth, that Elohim, not human, humiliated me. Betrayal is foreplay; coitus, justice. I lay on the floor, panting; the kill was over. And justice was yet to come.

But my last days are here, surely; I sense the avenging inquisitor has my scent. Until then . . . Cheap thrills, Daddy. This and every evening Next Door. Foraging scraps. Starving. Frustrated. Awaiting the angel of my apocalypse . . . Alone.

Now something has to be done. Something to change all this. Listen: these are your instructions . . .

CHAPTER THREE

Strange Sex

My instructions. Hearing, this time, rather than reading the annunciation of my daughter's birth (and my bit part in the scenario), the briefing became fragmented, distorted by interference; Vanity's voice grew faint; died.

I stirred; my eyes zoomed; Dr International, despicable *yuan*, was tombrobbing my mummified stash. 'Hey—'

'Inter-nat-ional! Inter-nat-ional!' Bastard had tried to hotshot me so that he could siphon off Primavera's sexstuff at his leisure. I got to my feet, brains like tapioca, goo about to leak from my ears, and snatched the bottle back. 'Please—I know what wrong. Strange activity in Broca's area of brain. Also, abnormalities in left temporal lobe, site of auditory cortex, and left anterior cingulate cortex, region connected with limbic system. My friend, you have auditory hallucination, no? Hallucination with much emotion, feeling? You bigger man, but this hallmark symptom of schizophrenia. Here, have Chinese wood medicine that—'

'*Ngee-up,* you Vietnamese quack.' He looked at the floor, right toe stroking his left instep. 'How much? How much did you take?' From behind his back he volunteered a syringe. It was filled with a swag of green luminous fluid.

'Not finish psychotherapy.'

'Not need. Not mad. I know that now.' Flash. Meta was the allure: allure that had conquered reality. Seamless, that land between consciousness and sleep, this present and the future. Seamless. Eidetic. Hyperreal. No doubts. Meta is God, Destroyer and Re-Creator. Time to gain; I had an appointment with a human womb. The covenant was about to be fulfilled. But what about a gift? Gold? Diamonds? A bouquet of black orchids? A tape of 'easy listening' screams? Or—'Keep the allure, fuck-wit,' I said, 'it can pay for one of these . . .'

She lived with her family, her friends, neighbours, dogs, chickens and lice in a stilt house on the Ho Road. Grandmother met me on the stairs. 'Want Phin? Not here. Work.' Granny would have known the nature of her granddaughter's occupation; would, I suppose, beat her for being a 'bad girl'; it wouldn't have stopped her from taking her money. Like my land-lady, she had that filthy-old-woman look about her.

'I wanted to give her this.' With a prestidigous flourish I pulled off the tarpaulin and held the rusted birdcage up for view. The organ of genera-tion swung on its perch, claws extending from each testicle. The tiny eyes on either side of the glans awoke from their reptilian trance; the teeth in-side the meatus snapped. 'His name,' I said, pointing to the little collar, a circlet adorning the coronal sulcus that I had had the doctor inscribe, 'is Mr Rochester. See—'

'Mmm. I think you number one boy. I think Phin like you very much.'

'Could you send her around? Tomorrow? I could meet her at the Café Mental.' I pressed some money into the filthy-old-woman's hand.

'Can teach talk?' Well, I thought, hell, I don't know; but its elocution would undoubtedly be superior to a dumb pair of dermaplastic pants.

'Talk. Sing-a-song. Tap dance. Play the banjo. This kid can do it all.' Veins bulging, Mr Rochester began to swing higher, higher (a penis in a cage puts all heaven in a rage), then, to whistle (a loutish, schoolboy whis-tle); he was a spunky little thing. Granny pointed to the bottle under my arm, the gimme-gimmes in her eyes. 'No, no; the soul of the departed's mine.' I proffered the cage. 'You send Phin?' Wrenching the cage from my hands, she cackled and began retreating into the house.

'I send Phin. No worry.' And tell her to leave her diaphragm at home, I thought. (I knew what she used; I'd made the discovery while we were playing doctors; the old rubber spoiler had squished into my face as I'd performed a make-believe hysterectomy. Such games. Such screams. A simulated Aagh! A beautiful Ee-ow! And a classic Screeech! There'd been complaints.)

'Tomorrow,' I reiterated as Granny closed the door upon herself and my gift of disembodied virility.

I walked back to the hotel, my shoes filled with helium, my brain with Prozac, a grin enlivening the dead flesh of my face. From Soi Cinema to Hai Soke I amused myself by stepping on the legs of prostrate beggars until, distracted by a ball of flame tumbling purposelessly down the street like a short-circuited wind-up toy (dead pet, quite probably, of Kam-pon's enfants terribles, its reanimation a qualified success), I forsook these celebratory diversions to leave the Zini, the zany meany magazini, the crowds thinning until, reaching the hospital and turning towards my hotel, I found myself alone. Only the dogs, the diseased pariah dogs, broke the silence with their uncannily literal *woof-woofs*. I scattered them with a few well-aimed pebbles. Tomorrow belonged to me.

My room was a night sweat gamy with human excrescence and stale corrosive air. I stretched out on the mattress, planning my tactical strike against Phin. Limited heterosexual warfare. I could macho that. I could groove (briefly) to the loopy loop of a paradox. Nearby, Primavera's glow, like a child's bedside lamp, seemed to radiate reassurance.

I started; looked up. As earlier at Dr Kampon-International's, I had a premonition that I was about to be attacked. I crept to the door; drew my scalpel. The keyhole beckoned. *Olé.* Not a sound. Despite the evidence—red, sticky—of a grievous wound, an interpretation of pain and injury was available only from the muffled, unsynchronized steps of my violator as he hurried (bouncing, seemingly, from wall to metal wall) into the lift and (I deduced) the eternal dark. I walked to the porthole; shortly I spied Nop staggering into the hotel's courtyard. And then: uproar. My landlady (a real virago intacta, she): shouting at Nop's mother. Nop's mother: shouting at Nop. And Nop, running in eccentric circles, simply shouting—*Oi! oi! oi! oi!*—hands pressed tight against his bloody eyes. A night-watchman, kitchen staff and passers-by congregated, prurient curiosity soon transforming itself into violence. Men abused each other with cries of *Jai saht! jai dum!* and bragged about the 'influential' friends who would destroy any person who did not acknowledge 'me first, you second; me higher, you lower; me richer, you poorer.' One man hit another man's wife; the offended husband responded by felling his adversary's daughter. (A baby somersaulted through the air in a kind of reductio ad absurdum.) As the commotion reached a crescendo—betel nut spraying from the women's mouths like venom—a pick-up truck appeared. Nop's mother paid the off-duty police their fee and the assassins hoisted the sightless boy into their meat wagon. Nop was on his way out, out into the country. Out and across the border between life and death. In the morning a villager would discover a body in his well, or a fisherman a corpse in his net. What good was a blind boy to a poor old lady? A girl might have had her uses. She could have been traded for, say, a television set. But a boy? No; the governor of Nongkhai, jilted by an army captain who was queen of the local barracks, had recently purged the town of its pederasts. (He had gone so far as to have pregnant women screened for the 'gay gene' and then, with bribes, threats and pleas, inducing those testing positive to drink gin-and-bleach cocktails. Au revoir, homosex.) The filthy women watched the truck depart and went inside.

Birth. Copulation. Death. Was there nothing more? All human history, until the last day, a tale of filth and callousness and ignorance? If there was a God, he would allow, surely, a rewriting of this tale. A transformation of himself. And us.

It had been a long day. I got my works out from the lip of the porthole. Why not fornicate? Junkie style. A big wet vampire kiss before I came off the allure and got fleshy. I decanted the *Lao Kow* bottle's amniotics into my shaving bowl and, employing forefinger and index finger as chopsticks, drew the mushy rotten deliciousness of my dead love's dollhood to my mouth, pheromones stabbing at my sensorium. I licked the clitoris (the hood perforated and adorned with a twenty-four carat gold ring); curled my tongue about an ovary. The hypodermic seemed to jump into my hand . . .

He took the fire escape to the roof, disencumbered himself of barrel, stock and congruent hardware secreted within the lining of his coat, and reassembled the gamekeeper. A blue mood hung over Paris, Mars; a metallic blue, shrill, a blue that harmonized with the dissonant noises emanating from the nearby shunting yard. He slung the rifle across his back; clipped the scrambler to his belt; checked the pocket laser (contingency, perhaps, of a man); lowered himself on monofilament over the guard rail, into space. The cityscape whirled, a gigantic sound stage abruptly terminated—here, at *le périphérique*—by the Amazonis tundra. He blinked, refocused his eyes; kicked once, twice, abseilling onto a window ledge; breathed against the frosted pane then rubbed until the glass yielded a peephole. The room was empty. Dark. Unsheathing his slink-knife he jemmied the lock; the sash opened; icicles tumbled into the night. Inside, he found himself amidst props for some absurdist drama about a King Louis from an alternative world: dollhouse furniture, broken, ripped, its tortuosity grown brittle with human use; the chinoiserie of the peeling walls; and, above the fireplace and its ormolu clock, a reproduction of Boucher's *Girl On a Couch,* to which someone had added, with a felt-tip pen, the inevitable bellyspike and bloodstains. And the King had had a strange, strange mistress. Across the floor (bare boards relieved by the creamy splash of a *faux* miniver rug): lipsticks, powder puffs, half-eaten food (nymphet regimen of goo-goo gooey éclairs, chocolates and nougat), the cat-print lingerie of the cat-crazy and, discarded, some chewed into pap, pornographic magazines, traitress pornography with titles like *Junket, Sceptre* and *The Proscript* (the last a Martian contact magazine; getting above themselves, he thought, these Martians). There was a child's picture book, too. And the smell of cheap perfume. Ah. And the smell of allure. Catching sight of the small altar to Lilith in the corner of the room (a crucifix surrounded by 'icons' torn from fashion catalogues and skin-rags, the little saucers of milk indicating that here were heretics who believed that, like them, the Queen of Hell was a cat) he made an involuntary genuflection (the girl in the picture book, a photo-mechanical of the kind called 'pop-up', rose from a pulpy stew until, a 3-D papier-mâché robot, she knelt, head bowed, tears spattering her laddered stockings, to complete a scene which included three sinister ruddy-faced men—doctors, he presumed—who sat behind a stainless steel desk about to pronounce judgement); freeze-frame; from the adjoining room, voices. He put his ear to a wall.

'Do you smell something?'

'Strange. Like a man, but—'

'Impossible. What are you wearing?'

'Isle of the Dead.'

'That rubbish? You sure it's not—'

'I'm sure. It's strange. Like a man, but—'

'Like our brothers, our funerals?'

'Like something wild, something wicked, something strange.'

There followed near-incomprehensible catgirl idioglossia, the lewd hebephrenic babytalk of the traitress, the far-gone feline, of which Dagon could decipher only impassioned word-spurts like: *Kiss him to death, Buff* and *Tell it to Johnny, tell it to Johnny Impaler . . .* He tore off the scrambler in disgust. Stagnant Earth technology. All induction lost. No discoveries, only transformations, flux. Meta is a jealous god. He kicked open the door (the smell overwhelmed him, the rotten delicious smell of allure gone bad, the smell of slink-meat, of treachery, of the girl Next Door); levelled the gamekeeper at a tableau of girl, naked, seated at dressing table, and girl, naked, combing the former's hair. The coiffeuse, a scale model of a fully-grown doll, a maquette with cantilevered breasts (shooting-gallery target breasts half covered by a black shagpile mane, breasts that communicated the pain, the burdensomeness of her super-femininity), turned, eyes narrowing, a spiteful fairy child; a shiver oscillated through her torso. She looked away; wiped a bead of blood from her nostril; stunned, she inspected the evidence of her hand; then, surrendering to the prognosis, glanced over her shoulder, recognized the demon she had not known till then to possess flesh—the eidolon of her morbidly voluptuous dreams—screamed, raked her nails across her belly, fell to the floor to display a minor and under-rehearsed repertoire of convulsions, and then lay still, 'death-ravished by the tyrant of her pleasure', as Linnaeus said re the phoenix (though no prospect of resurrection for this tweety-pie, he thought). Black orgasm. Unusual. Never happened before. Was beginning to think there was something wrong with me. Now Fenrir. Pretty boy Fenrir. At college, whenever there was a dance, girls combusting all the time . . . The other runaway—older, seventeen or eighteen, perhaps, with the rotogravure Benday-dotted face of a photonovel villainess, the clichéd face of a 'bad girl', a girl who likes to fuck—knelt before her dead friend, putting a finger to the squiggle of blood that oozed from her navel. Tasted.

'My God, what have you *done* to her?' she said. A lady's man, Fenrir. A regular Lothario. Girls in the condemned cells, trying to masturbate to death and spare themselves a date with the slab, would send him billets-doux begging him to pay them a visit (or at least donate a photograph) to facilitate their efforts, to help their cause. (As Mars would argue, 'special status for political prisoners'. Fenrir had been lobbied by Lilim and human alike.) Sometimes Fenrir would comply; suicide amused him. Fenrir was quite the gigolo. But me? thought Dagon. Me? He pulled back his greatcoat to reveal the doublet, hose and other cipher-like accoutrements that constituted his object-self, his imaginative body. 'I know,' she said, nose twitching, 'I know what you are.' She took a step backwards, the gamekeeper tracking her, her eyes—so greedy for light that they seemed to possess no sclera—focused on the muzzle that pointed towards the median of her blancmange-opulent wobbling breasts.

'Vanity,' he said. 'Vanity St Viridiana. Where is she?' The Lilim nodded her head a-go-go in furious compliance.

'She's—' Eager, he thought, these terminal addicts, to cat-out, finally, even their sisters, their own kind; too eager, enthusiasm infusing their confessions with half-truths, a fantasia of lies.

'Shh!' Torture was a possibility, here, on Mars, far from the censorious reach of his governess; an impromptu clitoridectomy, perhaps; but he was on probation, and, unnatural as abstinence often seemed, he was bound to the conditions of his sentence by honour, honour that had to be re-earned, re-gained; disobedience—his venture off-world—did not mean (he assured himself) that he was still a pervert, a marauder. Besides, as an inquisitor he knew that a girl, subject to excruciation, might babble nonsense, lewd nonsense for days, even until she died, and he needed only to know one thing. 'Will she be back tonight?'

'About four o'clock.' And then, in a breathless rush, '*Aftershe'sseenTintinshealwaysseesTintinthatspunkgarglingcocksucker'sterribleshe*—' Her piled hair unravelled, became a semaphore for her spite, its agitation serving to condemn her cat-accomplice in lieu of emptied lungs, a frozen larynx. He slapped her several times about the face.

'Shh!' So: she had a regular kill: Tintin, her sinny-sin-sin. First chance they get. Sucking off Martians. 'You must understand,' he said, surprised to discover a tear running down his cheek and a need, a strange piratical need commandeering his tongue, prompting him to confide, 'she's bad. Rotten to the core. It's driving me crazy. Even before she'd metamorphosed: bad, bad, bad. (She'd blackmail old men, say: "Give me money or I'll tell that policeman over there that you flashed me.") Later, after I'd turned her into a fellatrix . . . Well, there was the hemline thing of course, then came the kleptomania, the heresy, the phone calls. She was working her way through the codex. I had my suspicions. But I felt sorry for her. Cat-ness, I told myself, was a disease, not a crime. What a fool I was not to have interrogated her! It wasn't until I heard the rumours about the infanticides, the murders, the terrorism and the espionage that—' But what was the use? He wiped away the tear. Why do you like hurting us? he thought. Why? Why? Then: get a hold of yourself. Be a man. *Get Meta.* He flicked the gamekeeper onto auto. 'Assume a position appropriate for summary execution by—' The marauder in him, the thing he had kept buried since '77, ascended the chakras of his spine, urging *By abdominal impalement, slink-riving, umbilication;* he forced the insurgent down. 'By firing squad.' Duty, duty. He was without jurisdiction. But the girl would have to die. It would be difficult to smuggle one Lilim over the border. Two would be impossible. Extemporaneously condemned, his victim, perplexed for a moment, it seemed, by being catapulted centre stage—a shy understudy unable to believe she has been asked to perform— fleetingly entertained several poses before, eyes closed and reciting a prayer for forgiveness, the name Asmodeus, Asmodeus on her lips (doubtless the cuckold she had left on Earth), she scooped up her breasts with red-taloned hands, flung back her head and sighed in anticipation of the hammer blow that would nail her to the *crucis lingam* of phallic revenge. The VDU of the gamekeeper's sights switched to close-up; and as crosshairs quadrisected her cleavage, a warning message—blinking beneath the menu—alerted him to the presence of thin walls, alien behaviour patterns, unsympathetic laws. He chose the harpoon option. The demiurge held its breath; released it in a sibilation that was immediately followed by a plosive. She spasmed, shoulders dislocated, almost touching, hands clenched upon her breasts with such fervour that tissue seemed ready to burst; spasmed, silent, a mime of violent death, the thin steel harpoon that quivered in her sternum a conducting rod that disposed of the spark of her life with a dispatch that cheated the primed, volatile mouth. The room filled with the scent of roses, poppies, musk and—so sharp it stung his nostrils—the perfume of that flower of evil, so sickeningly sweet, the bouquet of flesh, rotten, bad, that bloomed between her legs. When she came to rest her body lay across the dressing-table stool, arched, broken, hair and toes touching the floor, belly thrust up, in unconscious offering. His marauder spoke: '*What are you waiting for, dead boy? You intend to be a slave to human morality forever? You're not human. You're superhuman. You owe no apology to Mars. Besides, the slut's dead . . .'* In the time it took to shake himself, detox his mind, his interior cinema screened the following:

He stands the gamekeeper against the dressing table, fumbles for his blade; blade between his teeth, he cracks his knuckles, stares at his hands until they are at one with his thoughts. The incision is precise, surgical, the work of a gentleman; like a gentleman, courteous yet disdainful, he parts the abdominal wall. The uterus, when he holds it in his hand, wriggles, nerve endings still alive, pulses as if trying to flee. He puts the green, glutinous meat to his lips, squeezes its juices onto his tongue, then, with one ravenous bite, ingests it entire, feels his body tingle, exult as the strange meat slides down his oesophagus . . .

It was little more than he'd done after a firing squad had completed its work, in the dining hall at Lat Yao . . .

He felt the beating of the black wings of desire . . .

He stands the gamekeeper against the dressing table, fumbles for his blade; blade between his teeth, he—

'What are *you* doing here?' Brownout; the moviehouse collapsed. He spun, collected the gamekeeper and rolled across the floor to rise, crouched, stock snug against his shoulder. The sights filled with wet-nurse breasts. Joke breasts. He salivated. What is it with me? he thought. This thing for little girls with big tits? I mean with those FF cups, kid needs a xenograft, a tail; kid needs some kind of counterbalance. His trigger finger was seized with a crippling psychosomatic arthritis; *they have it so easy these days,* said a surly inner voice, *a girl should die slowly, painfully;* he lowered the gun. Dagon Kundalini, AKA Dagon Marauder, just wouldn't go away . . .

'Name?'

'Felicity. Felicity St Felice.'

'Age?'

'Fifteen and a half.'

'Height?'

'155 cm.'

'Eyes?'

'Blue. Cornflower blue.'

'Hair?'

'Blonde. Can't do a thing with it.'

'Dress size?'

'Look, do you think we could just skip this?' Dead boys never talked much to dead girls, but when they did conversation was often indistinguishable from interrogation. (The interloper leaned insouciantly against the door frame, bored—said her eyes, blue—by this boy/girl exchange.) 'You want to kill me and I want to die. It's simple. Let's do it, moron. Shoot.' Some sick kittycat. Just look at that hemline. That's not a skirt, that's a peplum. And get the gusset on those tights. And those over-the-knee fellatrix boots, with buckles top and bottom, so French, so utilitarian, so right for kneeling on miniver in the Place de la Concorde, pink wedge of sex exposed before the jeering sans-culottes. And get all that pink cat-print, that fur, that fluff, that dressed-skein-gelatine. Sick. (But our problem, that. Psychotic textiles. Got to shut down those boneless-leopard farms in Zanzibar.) 'What's the matter,' she said, 'too much for you?' Several kilos of flesh heaved, strained, testing the architecture of her low-cut frock, the school badge—cannibalized from her ward's uniform—coming loose from its stitching, the escutcheon of pierced heart, green pentacle and Union Jack spiralling to the floor. 'Go ahead. Break my heart. Do me.' Her scent was making him giddy, so treacherous, so irresistible, so sweet. She was goo-goo, a bonbon, all flounces, lace and ribbons; pink, furry and fluffy; oversweet; he heaved, but his mouth remained dry, his nausea serving to sharpen his appetite rather than signal his disgust. These Martians, he thought, they've unmanned me; confound their politics, their trade stipulations, their inhuman rights agenda; I need to eat the way I was meant to . . . Fangs emerged from the swollen gumline above his cuspids. His marauder laughed, triumphant, his boy exceeding all expectations: *'Yes. A girl is meant to be eaten alive. As she dies on the slab, or in your arms. Alive!'* Honour. Duty. Would he never learn discipline? Would he never be like his brothers-in-arms? 'What do you want?' she asked, suspicious but not wanting to believe. She knows, he thought. Must be my pheromones. Must be my iffy signature. But one thing's for certain: she won't snitch.

'Your ovaries, Mademoiselle. Your strange oestrogen. Your allure.'

The catgirl, Felicity St Felice, screamed.

After he had chased her about the flat, one room to the next, until the pursuit terminated at their point of departure, after he had thrown her against the floor, pinned her ankles behind her ears (hand fumbling for, then impatiently dismissing, his knife, to hell with table manners), after he had torn off her *maillot*, her *cache-sexe*, sunk his head between her thighs and bit into a riot of poisonous flesh (all caution gone now, screams to wake all Mars), and after his mouth had filled with blood and the rank allure of slink-meat, of TVs, transcoms, washing machines, toasters, microchips, *jeux vérités* arcades, tortures, wars, genocides, *desaparecidos,* assassinations, pornographies, the trash of the world, the twenty-first century's sex, then . . . Postorbital interlude of girls in cooking pots, roasted on gridirons, spits, fried in coconut oil, stir-fried in woks, subject to the morbid recipes of maniacal gourmands, girls eaten raw, girls eaten alive (oh yes, oh yes), their juices warm and their lips begging for mercy and forgiveness . . .

Mephisto had led him through the catacombs deep beneath the Stars, the tiered remains of Lilim, each body embalmed and sealed in an argon-filled coffin, transforming the corridors, stairwells and abandoned salons of Titania's original palace into a subterranean gallery of artist's models slain for the impertinence of their perfection. Dagon had dawdled, pressing his face against row after row of glass sarcophagi like a boy agog before the windows of a sweet shop, wishing he had more time to examine the thousands of beautiful glistening cadavers, the limitless confectionery. 'Internal organs are removed,' said Mephisto, 'soaked in salts and chemicals, then wrapped in plastic before being returned to the body cavity, which is coated in polyurethane. The body cavity is then filled with sawdust, the epidermis sprayed with a dermatoid gel . . .' The journey along the funereal corridor ended at a black velvet portière; *Mephisto swept the curtain aside and ushered his student into the execution chamber. It was a mid-week afternoon, and the chamber was empty; a suitable time, Mephisto had explained, to conduct an hour's tutorial on the mechanics, the technique, the rationale of capital punishment: 'The death machine in its entirety, in toto, as it were, "the slab" as it is popularly known, we may more correctly refer to as "the sphinx", so called from the position a girl is obliged to assume as she dies. It is unlikely, however, that you will hear Lilim talk of "the sphinx"; for them, a girl is always sent to, always suffers on, "the slab". Elohim are, perhaps, somewhat dry, somewhat pedantic in their terminology, for again, while we refer to the sphinx's quintessential element, here, as "the paling", Lilim always speak of "the bellyspike", "the spike", or, sometimes, "the pin". There is, of course—as you are probably aware—some consensus on this. The hinged barb that closes as a girl falls onto the marble, does not, as a girl quickly discovers, allow her to rise, at least, not more than, say, three centimetres—though not for any want of her trying, I might add. The barb, which both sexes refer to as "the wombane", is, let me emphasize, quite crucial to the methodology, the science of judicial murder, for, as a girl attempts to free herself, when, in vain efforts to escape her agony, she writhes and convulses, the barb, tearing at her uterus, ensures a steady flow of blood and allure. The exsanguinator, here, the grille from which the paling rises, drains the blood through a concealed gutter that runs to the apex of the slab to fill the chalice (see?) set in this recess beneath the steel ellipse of the lock, here, that secures the hands. (The lock, by the way, that is operated by a matrix key that fits into the ward at the apex, here, we call "the trap".) The time is coming, little brother, when you may raise that chalice to your lips, a man. Any questions?'*

Teacher and student launched into a peripatetic dialogue that, while seeming to them a cool philosophical discussion addressing problems of metasexual ontology and eschatology, would have impressed an outsider, that is, a human mind, chiefly by the extent to which a rich vocabulary, intelligence, wit and an amusing turn of phrase, accentuate rather than dissimulate the cruel sentiments of supermen.

The tutorial finished, Mephisto had left Dagon alone in the execution chamber with the advice that he meditate upon his burgeoning responsibilities. The chamber, quiescent, its death machines idle, the palings— glittering coldly in the candlelight—unemployed, seemed filled with ghosts, the voluptuous spirits of those girls stacked like prized but useless family heirlooms in the dusty vaults and niches of an underground warehouse. The ghosts performed their sinuous horizontal dance, scored through, wriggling like cut worms, like beautiful dying sphinxes. In Rome, he had heard, the slab was figurative, sculpted after the representation of an actual sphinx upon whose spiked back a girl was condemned to suffer the ritual wound and ride that parody of herself— half-cat, half-gynomorph—into an everlasting night. In Istanbul, they said, the slabs were cut from solid blocks of crystal, their mirrored bases enabling Lilim-odalisque and Elohim-sultan alike to inspect the exquisite loci where point had met gentle swell of embonpoint, the entrée of spoiled delicious flesh. But London still retained the traditional design, adopted and customized from the extermination machines employed in the Dolls' Hospitals . . .

He came up for air, gazed down on the mutilated vulva. Oh rose, thou art sick . . . A ghost was crying out to him, a girl in her mid-teens with a shag of ash blonde hair, her body glistening with a patina of sweat, her perspiration emulsive under the guttering tapers. He again buried his head in the half-masticated flesh; and at once he was translated, *standing over her, legs before but not astride the slab's apex; it was an attitude designed to taunt. She pushed herself up to meet him, elbows locked, arms rigid; screamed as her arched torso strained against the uncompromising steel that transfixed her; then, when he didn't move, performed, with a teeth-gritting shudder of effort, an Ouroboros (legs apart, calves at forty-five degrees to the thighs, toes pointing towards the flung-back head). 'Please—'*

'There is something I wish to discuss with you.'

'Felicity,' said the ghost, mechanically, by rote, 'eyes blue, hair blonde, measurements—'

Dagon opened his eyes, saw the diseased flower, its petals chewed into mush, sucked the poisonous sap, the toxic beauty of the traitress, all fight gone from her now; pulled back, prepared to bite through the abdominal wall, gave himself up to those post-orbital visions . . .

'No, no. Listen: if I have fangs, why aren't I meant to use them when I eat? Why this false civility? Are we so frightened of the wild man in us— the marauder, as we call it—that we repress our instincts? Or are we so af- fected by Martian propaganda that we have forgotten what we are, who we are?'

'Oh God, I can't stand it any more. Kill me. Use your sword. Your gun. Anything . . .'

'Well, to reverse the mythic scenario, let's say that if you answer me this riddle then—'

'Please, let me eat you, *let me beg—'*

'My teacher was very coy about the matter when I asked him. About why we only drink the blood and leave the meat. I suspect Mephisto's wild man is very wild indeed. By the way, try not to move about too much. I know that it's a moot question whether the girls we call "belly dancers" (and whom you call "wrigglers") suffer to a greater or lesser de- gree than those who manage, or at least try to manage, to remain still. Those who dance, so I've heard, though they inflict great pain upon them- selves, die relatively swiftly, while those who are more passive, that is, the majority, while their pain is less keen, suffer far longer, sometimes for sev- eral hours. Swings and roundabouts, I suppose. But I've always believed that it's in the best interests of a girl to try to keep still—it allows a man time to comfort her, to show compassion. (Though forgiveness, of course, is out of the question.) But to return to the issue at hand: is drinking the blood of Lilim during an execution really any more civilized than tearing out her primary sexual characteristics with one's teeth?' He looked down; chin cupped in his hand, he had rested a foot on the slab to consolidate his Oedipal pose; unable, in her agony, to maintain her Ouroboros, he dis- covered the girl fervently licking his boot, a desperate sphinx frustrated of a quietus, struggling to answer his puzzle. *'Perhaps my riddle is meaning- less. Perhaps we don't have to eat you at all, our appetite merely an excuse, a rationale for killing . . . We're not vampires. We're sex murderers, pure and simple . . .'*

But the blood that first time, in that cheap hotel in Bayswater, had been delicious.

And so had been the blood of Felicity St Felice.

The green meat slipped down his oesophagus . . .

'What are *you* doing here?' Déjà vu. No, please no, he thought, I can't eat any more, no, not another mouthful. But it was Vanity who stood in the door frame. (And the disloyalty of the beloved is the ultimate appetizer.) He checked his wristwatch; salivated.

'Home so soon?'

'Am I disturbing you? Or do you want to invite me in for a little supper?' A shoulder bag fell to the floor, spilling a transcom, photographs, make-up, a tin of venomous ornithopters. Smell of slink; it was sharp, so sharp it cut his heart out, cut it out and threw it to the dogs; he recognized that signature. Despite the gourmandizing a dinner gong sounded in his bowels. But—

'I disdain your flesh. You're to be interrogated, arraigned, executed.' In his caresses, his embrace, he wanted her to feel the cold hand of the inquisitor, of justice. *Interrogated, arraigned, executed,* each scene speeding past, now, like time-lapse photography, his interior cinema fast-forwarding the bio-pic of her life and death. Calm, calm, he thought. He put on his imaginative soutane, the icy mandarin-like detachment of Elohim. Vanity shot him an I-know-you-so-well look, wrinkled her nose and placed a hand on her hip.

'Seems we've both grown a little faddy.'

'Pervert,' he said. She walked towards him, slowly unbuttoning her blouse. He sat in a puddle of blood, three cadavers—one self-combusted, one harpooned, the other chewed, bitten, gnawed—surrounding him.

'Whereas of course *you*—' She raised a plucked eyebrow. 'Fie on you, sir,' (affecting punk-Directoire slang) 'fie on you for a vicious cunnilinguist!' And attacked an imaginary fly with an imaginary fan.

He got up, shouldered the gamekeeper and took her in his arms, a gauntleted hand reaching through the half-divested silk to crush her left breast, its pathetic cuirass; tightening his grip he waited for her to wince (fell into those black elliptical eyes) then placed a kiss at the spot where the seeping flesh of one cup met the other. His other hand pulled up her skirt (hemline psychosis seems to have reversed, he reflected), fingers sliding up her inner thigh to reach the cul-de-sac of her pudendum. She gasped as he raised her onto tip-toe and he thought of another girl, another cheap hotel. His graduation had been a year away; and there was talk about a treaty with Mars; he had not had the patience to wait . . . They never scream, Mephisto had said. Not if you do it right. Remember: introduction, courtship, engagement, nuptials, honeymoon, divorce. And of these the most important? Yes, *engagement.* Remember: no external wounding. And the angle must be correct, the tip of the blade piercing the cervix. La! But then there had been the rapprochement with reality. Student days. Class of '77. Azrael. Baphomet. Cain. Fenrir. Melkarth. Ulric. Zervan. Student days, when his troubles had begun. Yes, I'm a pervert too, he thought, still a pervert (or so you define me; goddamn this new Puritanism); I want you riding my knife. I want your strange genitalia . . .

'We're the same,' she said. 'We've always been the same. But it's me who has to die. Is that unfair?' She offered a smeared fire-engine-red mouth for his delectation. He didn't move; like a cold black obelisk he waited until his prisoner pressed her lips to his own—her tongue flicking over a still-extended fang—before responding, caressing her throat, her shoulders, her hair; he knew then, by a tremor of hysteria that radiated from her ribs, the thigh that was rubbing against his hip, that she could detect the after-taste of allure. He freed a breast from its filigree constraint. 'Dagon, how *could* you eat another girl?'

And then he injected her with thiopentone, her rouged nipple hardening at the hypodermic's touch.

When I came to, head aching, stretched on my mattress, a shaft of light pooling about my half-dressed body as if I were basic wage labour at a live sex show, I felt a spermatorrhoeaic trail of semen snailing down my leg. I sat up and went to wipe myself with the damp linen. My sweat turned cold. The semen was green. Luminous green. Green as my dead love's eyes.

'Come on, George, I really need it.' George massaged his knee, conversation piece of an old soldier Hizbollah had lasered in Kota Kinabalu half a century ago.

'I don't get about much. I *rely* on the phone.'

'Just five minutes worth.' How tired I was of these seventy-year-old juvenile delinquents forever talking about their penises and prejudices, little men pretending to be big men, losers and crash-landed boors. 'These dreams. I need help. My body's going crazy. When I come, I come *green*. I got to speak to the Directrice.'

'Too much allure,' said Jan.

'Dumb Slovak,' said the Swine. 'Don't know when he's dreaming, when he's awake.'

'Bubba, you *do* look different.' Yeah. Everybody was beginning to look different. And every*thing*. Like: the TV was showing a documentary—*Heinrich Himmler, Nazi Toymaker*. Children, you know that isn't right. Now what's his name? The little man who lives in the doll's belly? The little death wish of the *aube du millénaire*? Really, I'm surprised— we call him *Dr Toxicophilous*. (No, no teacher! Call him Professor Nosferatu! Call him Rotwang! Call him Dr Dee!)

'What a man,' said the Swine, conforming to type (the kind of guy who gives sadomasochism a bad name), 'he knew the acid chamber was no solution. Better to convert *Untermensch* into weapons. Ten thousand cyborg Jewesses dropped onto London would have—'

'What are you talking about?' said Jan. 'They *were* dropped. I remember my father telling me about his boyhood when—'

'It's Meta,' I said. 'It's moving through time. And space. It's subverting reality.' It's taking on our sins, I thought. The *mysterium iniquitatis.* It's eroticizing cruelty and death. 'Those Martians. Those heathens. They won't always be immune. They'll regret it one day, offering asylum to sex traitresses.' (The usual mutterings: 'A long-gone—' etcetera etcetera . . .) 'But you wouldn't understand. You're just humans. Hosts.' A pair of hands, small tentacular hands with long red claws, had settled on my pecs. They squeezed, tweaking my nipples. And then, in affected kid-robot lisp: '*Yai* say you wan' see me.' Phin was at her best; she had stepped out of her flesh and into her lacquered, longing-to-be-Dresden look, all high-definition make-up and reformatory school ra-ra-ra. 'I am pris'ner of lust,' she said, her lustful artificially-plump lips rendered in magenta and glycerine to provide the illusion of lips wounded, much-licked, much-abused. The dress was a disease, a dying dermaplastic shimmy striped with melanomas, cinched at the waist with electrical flex; across the breast, GIRL #0978Z; when she moved, the sinistral, transgressive hemline promised a semiotician of flirtatiousness a lifetime's work. 'Mr Lochester, he pris'ner too.' The sentient phallus slipped its leash; to George's outrage it climbed his trouser leg and boarded the bar, a little swashbuckler of true grit and gristle. 'But he *my* pris'ner. *My* slave.' Mr Rochester swaggered up to a beer glass; submerged his empurpled head; ejaculated. 'Sorry,' said Phin, swiping the detumescing Rochester off the bar. 'See people, get excited.' She re-secured him to the dog lead.

'Oh, this is too much,' said George as he and several of the bar's riffraff withdrew, nauseated, gagging. 'Bill, you've got voyeurs in your bathroom, rats in your kitchen and obnoxious, cantankerous dicks in your bar. C'mon boys, let's go over to Mama Robo's.' Turning to Phin, he added: 'Mamzelle, your slave needs discipline. *Strict* discipline.' Bill met my eyes, drilled them with hate as his best-paying customers left.

'Be nice to me,' I whispered. 'I have to impress this nana. I have to impregnate her.'

'Leave,' said Bill, his mouth about to detach itself from his face and fly homicidally about the room, 'lunatic. Just leave. Go root your sheila. Go, before you go completely *burlesque.*'

I took her to the Tsaloth Tsar, a floating restaurant on the Mekong river popular with status-hungry, transcom-toting young Thais for its ostentatious Khmer-Siberian cuisine. A waiter had her tether Mr Rochester outside. 'Feed to ducks,' he'd said, and Phin had treated him to a censorious *tui*! He was referring, of course, to a Thai woman's predilection for castrating an unfaithful husband while he slept, the method of disposal. '*Poot len, poot len,*' he'd added, laughing. Reassurance. He was being a wag. After all, her novelty penis was a collectible, an object of desire. The ducks would have to go hungry. But not us. I'd done a little surreptitious fingering of cash off Phin as we'd left the Zini.

'It's like this,' I said. The river, low and tranquil this dry season (though the dragon that slumbered in its depths would devour any swimmer audacious enough to tempt it), burbled past, black, speckled with plastic bottles and waste. 'I want you to have my baby.' Phin giggled; drowned her laugh, weighting it with dollars, Deutschmarks, cunning.

'If boy wan' marry, boy must have money. I think you write Mama, Mama send you every time, no?'

'Yes,' I said, lying as silkily as I was able. 'Did I ever tell you my mother is a Martian?' Phin's eyes, gummy with mascara, unstuck, flipped open, became almost Caucasian, so wide they yawned at hearing this unbelievable news.

'Waiii! Iggy, you half Martian?'

'I'm a very rich man, Phin. An eccentric nanomillionaire.' Her cupidity, which was her most vulnerable fault line, the one on which I had chosen to exert pressure, trembled, ready to quake and raze her cynicism, her whore's contempt; the moment passed. Guardedly, she played her hand.

'But you doll junkie. Your jissom go bad.' Yeah. Mildewy. Rotten. But, I hoped, still good for making dolls. A spermatozoon, amongst that bayou of green slime, surely had my daughter's name on it.

'A weakness *(hélas),* a moment of weakness in a cricket pavilion near my old school . . .' First kiss, velveteen. When my humanity began to die.

'If we make baby, baby turn roboto when she first have *bpen-leut.*'

'True,' I said. 'True, and strange. The nanomachines in her genes'—I grinned a mad scientist's grin—'would be activated by the pituitary gland, recombining DNA during menarche. By the time puberty is achieved a girl has metamorphosed into a doll.'

'Cool. But cyborg die young, no?'

'Well, yeah,' I said. 'Teenage holocaust. But listen: the British government will soon be paying lots of money to families who have dolls. In fact, a doll is going to be our new queen.' Phin's eyes flared, went supernova; jackpot, they said.

'Take me England?'

'I don't know. It's a crazy place.' But what did I know of England? London was my home, home of all those who had migrated down Europastrasse-55 through the flyblown ruins of the east; London, ghetto of Ossi refugees, prison to those infected with the doll-plague; it was all I knew of my birth-land. But now, with this coup d'état and the cordon sanitaire being lifted . . .

'Have beauty shop in England?'

'I don't want you mechanized, Phin. I want you human.' She wrinkled her nose.

'You no wan' me like Lilim? Green eye, big teeth?' I shook my head.

'Lilim can't be manufactured. They have to be born of Man.' I looked across the river, to Laos; tiny coconut trees lined the distant bank like the stakes of a stockade I would never escape. Escape. It had often seemed to Primavera and me that we had spent our lives in a game of pursuit and escape, a deadly game in which the whole world was 'it'. In crossing the Mekong we had hoped to make escape final; we had hoped to rest. Ah. Too ironic. Too cruel. For Primavera, the Mekong had been the Styx. Play the inseminator, I told myself, play up and play the game before your junk-fried genitalia explode and you too are tagged. 'I've been addicted to Lilim for as long as I can remember. Imaginatively, at first. In nightmares and daydreams. Then physically. Then spiritually. It's going to be tough, fucking you. I want to thank you for all the effort you've made. The dress, the make-up, the gestures . . . I mean, you really look quite the *poupée*.' Phin frowned. 'I've had a tough life . . .' What did it take to melt her titanium heart? 'They treated us like dogs, rats, like monkeys. London was one big medical experiment. A laboratory that contained the plague.' Bites of sound, of vision, savaged my brain: the Rainham Marshes littered with the flotsam of looted suburbia, the moody depopulated streets, the howls, the screams amidst the ruins of the tower blocks, the razor-wire and the encircling, incarcerating walls . . . 'Drones hovered above us, recording the mutations, the deaths; the government justified itself by saying our freedom would mean the death of humanity.' I choked back a sob. Too amateurishly, I suppose.

'One fuck, five hundred baht,' said Phin, her face hard. 'You wan' marry, must give house, car, gold, money. Very much money.' Ho-ho, I thought, yes, and probably the bogey from my nose. 'And if have baby,' she continued, 'Queen of England, she must give money too.'

'Sounds fair to me.' She regarded me foxily, like a schoolgirl looking forward to dissection class; and then the metallic sloe-eyed stare became doe-like, yielding, as if she had reasoned there was no chance of cutting up the big, big bunny wabbit today.

'Maybe you speak good. We see.' She gave her concentration to the task of demolishing a plate of *som tam* and a tadpole suet. 'You look different, Iggy. Not so much like junkie. More like sex murderer.' I ran a hand through my crop. The bathroom mirror, that morning, had revealed

streaks of grey; my face seemed longer, starved, with bony declivities and
rills and angular, cubist masses. Despite the strange green discharge of
last night, I hadn't felt so strong, so healthy, for years.

'Do you think it's possible,' I said, 'to premember things?'

'Pre-mem-ber?' She indulged me with a little frottage, one of those
wild amberoid thighs frantic beneath the table. The town's PA was broadcasting something about rice prices, a coup perhaps . . . 'Take me home,
Iggy. Take me to your hotel and fuck me. But remember, darling, no play
doctor, promise?' And all philosophical speculation was lost.

Afternoon:

The zzz of an unfastening zip: drowsy insect noise in a steel-plated
jungle, roof cover of asbestos, no water, no earth, no sky. The hypo
dropped from a rubbery vein, its needle glistening with blood and the
reproductive materiel of Lilim. 'Hum job, Mr Telephone Man?' (No,
no, that rap had run its course, I had to fill this nana with my sexual nano-
force . . . Phin was only nine, but the 'ceuticals that had made her so
mammiferously-o-matic had filled the trough of her hips with precocious
womanhood; even without the evidence of the old rubber spoiler you
could tell the little bitch was ovulating.) '*Diaphragm*,' I tried to say, hoping she hadn't switched to a contraceptive vaccine, '*take out the diaphragm.*' But my drug was in me and my tongue was lame. What dreams
did you dream, Mr Rochester, curled up on the floor, of what rapes, what
voluptuous terrors? Or were you as small-minded as your mistress, as
venal as you were venereal, and nothing like Meta's own? The *Lao Kow*
bottle thrummed like an electric pylon, a ventriloqual high-tension cable;
in its magnetic field—a forcefield of sex and death—the future, unmuz-
zled, was talking to me . . . '*Dagon calling. Hello, hello? Come in. Come
in, my shadow . . .*'

CHAPTER FOUR

Strange Grace

Shortly before she was due to die I summoned her to my rooms. There, after her handcuffs had been removed and I had dismissed the Imperial Guard (they exited to the fricative music of mesh on flesh), I ordered her to submit herself to my scrutiny. 'Stand,' I said. On hearing that command prisoners are required to place their hands behind their heads so that men (yes, my shadow, you may call me a 'man') may appraise their loveliness, or interrogate them. Of course, in the past, the dark morphosis of the past, the past appropriated by the future, before the female of our species 'civilized' us (so hypocritical this 'civility', this public relations exercise designed to ease the conscience of laissez-faire Mars), Lilim might be obliged to assume this position before being summarily executed, their proffered umbilici run through with swords. And it was, perhaps, an atavistic tic that made her glance, with bashful, flickering suspicion, at the ceremonial rapier that hung from my side. 'Stand.' I addressed her with the curtness one reserved for her kind. She was prevaricating, tugging nervously at her hair, shifting her weight from one knee to the other.

'No.' Paradoxical word, so sweet on a victim's lips but like wormwood on the lips of a rebel. Fractious, sulky, she broke position; walked towards me, readjusting her torsolette (GIRL #0978Z emblazoned across the vertical monochromatic stripes); sat on my desk, leaned over, took off my glasses, breathed on them, then rubbed the lenses against the bruised cadaver-like plastic of her uniform before settling them on her own nose. 'My God, how do you *see* out of these?' I snatched the glasses back. 'Why Miss Frobisher,' she said, imitating my *ex cathedra* cadences, 'you're beautiful.' Her insolence—always her most devastating quality—rattled my composure, the sang froid of the Meta gentleman. No more games—

'Why did you do it, Vanity?'

'*Why did you do it, Vanity?*' The sarcasm wrinkled her nose, turned down the corners of her mouth. 'I'm psychotic. A pervert. Didn't you know?' And then, punctuating her explanation with a sigh, exasperated but resigned to the fact that I didn't know two plus two equalled five, added, 'Because you made me, of course.' She picked up the gilt-framed photograph of my first love. 'You can't forget her, can you?' True. True, and strange. She removed the petrified matrix from around her neck (we allow prisoners jewellery) and skimmed it across the desk, a smooth ob-long pebble, a piece of delicately-hewn malachite that clipped over blot-ting pad, papers, pens and ink (props, dandyish props; I always used the teleputer set in the wall) and came to rest in my lap. 'You can have it back,' she said. 'I'm through with it.'

'Primavera,' I said, depositing the matrix on the blotting pad, where it flushed, green and sickly, like a Rorschach Test suggesting the sex death of the universe, 'Primavera would never have betrayed me. Not all girls put to their knees go the Way of the Cat.'

'Primavera—*tui*!' She tossed her ponytail from one shoulder to the other. 'I did my best,'—anger out-reddening the rouge on her cheeks— 'I did my best to look like her. I had to. I went Meow! the first time we kissed. I was doomed.' And she fifteen now, too, to die the same age as Primavera. 'I did my best.' Re-engineered by Bangkok's surgeries, the pi-rated lines of the third-generation doll had given her—for someone who remembered such creatures and despite her body's rejection of the ra-dioactive eye-stain—an erotic edge over her too-human contemporaries. But surgery had not refined the general into the particular. Her resem-blance to my dead love—though she had gone so far as to have her speech centres rewired so that she spoke in cockneyfied Mitteleuropean—was only approximate.

'I liked you brown,' I said, lying desperately to myself as much as to her (for Elohim desire not the feminine but the superfeminine). 'I like you white. I'm a sadist, not a racist.'

'You liked Loulou,' she said. 'You liked her green eyes.'

'I only saw her so that I might see you.'

'*Pak wan.*' Sweet mouth. Flatterer. '*Pak wan, kon prio.*' Sweet-mouthed, sour-bottomed. And my officiating over the firing squad would, I suppose, soon prove that proverb true . . . She eased herself off the desk, her rump leaving its damp signature on the glass top; walked about the room, a fingernail running over the spines of my library as she clove to the parabola of the walls, the filibustering click of her high-heels like a rusty clock, the tap of a blind man's cane.

'So you want to know why I did it?' Coy; a little girl who has just strangled the new baby and is about to boast; a schoolgirl who at last gets to dissect the big, big bunny. 'I did it *because*—' She leaned against the book shelves, a leg drawn up, one hand clasping the stiletto of a mule, the other caressing a tome of jurisprudence. 'Poisoning's so gauche; defecting to reality's old hat. I invaded the past because I have chosen, Dagon, in some universe other than this, to un-man you, to take away your inhumanity.' I lowered my eyes; the matrix winked at me, it seemed, as minx-like as my interlocutor. 'I invaded; I subverted. The past has been changed. Your past. One of them, that is. In that time-line you take care of me. You're nice. We have kids . . .' I picked up the magic uterus, felt the power, the small, diminishing but mad, mad energies of the vampire belly in my palm. 'As long as somewhere, sometime, things are different . . .'

'We're not human,' I said. 'We can never be human. You don't understand.' The room shook, not physically, but as if withstanding the impact of high-explosive cause-and-effect fired from outside time, outside space; a multiplicity of futures, pasts and presents irradiated the Spartan furniture, the high curving bookshelves, the cupola decorated with images of . . . who? Our first queen Titania St Tallulah? Titania St Tabitha? Toxine, Trixie, Trish? The image morphed, bewitching my memory. And then the room itself dissolved (though retaining its outlines, like leaded crystal), the chambers and antechambers of countless prisons swelling my vision with scenes of superimposed captivities, double, triple and quadruple scenes of tortures, executions, criminal martyrs and martyrs of crime suffering beneath the lash, hanged, burnt, crushed, scalded, impaled by ingenious death machines, each scene's rationale belonging to unfathomed worlds and systems in the parallel universes of Meta. The blast of causation—contaminating time's arrow—mutated seconds into hours; an attack by our double agents (the engines of uncreation, the beautiful anarchs, one of whose sisterhood I held in my hand), it represented another incursion from unreality in its border war with the real. When the room again assumed its proportions its familiarity seemed fragile, as if Meta had deepened (though I knew it could not yet have consolidated) its hold upon the Earth. I placed the matrix back on the desk, an eldritch paperweight; drummed an aleatoric overture with my fingers.

'It's impossible for us to escape destiny, for me to be anything more than a killer, for you to be anything but a victim. Human history is being retrofitted. To accommodate Meta. To accommodate us. *All* time-lines, *all* human worlds. That we met six years ago in Nongkhai: don't you know that that event itself has become a dream? This moment will also soon become unreal. Soon, we and this moment will become less than ghosts, co-ordinates erased from the map of space-time. You've failed, Vanity, you've failed.' I crooked a digit; lazily, with puzzlement transforming her face from that of one who knows everything (and has grown tired of knowing) to that of a new-waif-on-the-block, she clicketty-clacked to my side. I rose, took her by the arm, my leather-gloved hand impressing bruises over the words *Staatlicher Porzellan Manufaktur Meissen;* turned her to the window. 'Six years—was Bangkok, this Bangkok, built in a mere six years? Did we become masters of the world in so short a time?' I pushed her forward so that her body pressed against the pane, one cheek flush against the glass, a startled eye—so black there was no demarcation between pupil and iris—regarding me from the residua of her epicanthic folds.

'I—I can't remember.'

'A CIA-sponsored coup. The Human Front deposed. Humans and Lilim forming a new presidium, a collective dictatorship with Titania its titular head. The kingdom reunited. A revolution, a civil war of organic against inorganic. The triumph of the dolls. And then an empire established, an Empire of Dolls, a Pax Britannica . . . All this in six years?'

'I—I can't—'

'History shifts beneath our feet. It's no longer we who travel through time and space; it's our ideas, our obsessions. We live relative to the velocity at which Meta infects the space-time continuum. And Meta's velocity is increasing even as we speak. We shall become timeless, non-spatial; observed but non-observing. We shall become fictions, the living dead of the new God.'

'Memories,' she said, 'where are my memories?'

Memories: my own had been corrupted. I had begun to forget who I was, who I had been. I looked out from the grey fortress of Lat Yao into the micro-city, the little *urbs quadrata* of the interdiction, its neon cross-hatches of roads and *soi* where humans scurried, surrendering themselves to or fleeing from the dart and flash, the thirst of my foraging sisters. From the drained lake beneath my feet, amongst its vegetable horrors and ferroconcrete wastes, rose tiny cries of pleasure, of pain. Sweet music, last bars of reality's finale, of history's rape . . . This is not the same interdiction that you suffered, my shadow; this *quartier* is under our control, controlled breeding being the raison d'être of the dead boy, reason and his prerogative. But something bigger than Elohim, bigger than any man, Homo sap or supe, is in control, ultimate control of our Fate, for holy Meta now infects not merely the human gamete; all time and space is metamorphosing into The Doll, a redemptive fiction wherein cruelty and death have been eroticized, converted, to turn, through millennia, aeons, through all eternity about love's green superluminous sun.

Memories: the narrative was disintegrating. Perhaps it was only my missionary zeal, the fact that I had been instrumental in initiating Metastasis, that allowed me to remember anything at all. I closed my eyes, crossed my arms about my condemned girl's breasts, codpiece snug in her perineal divide.

'We survive only through radical control of our population. Titania, our first queen, understood this. She made a deal with America...' Jack Morgenstern's shade whispered realpolitik into my ear:

'*What they proposed was this: Titania would send her runaways to countries of geopolitical significance to us. When the plague began to undermine those countries' economies, Titania would unleash what she called "the secret of the matrix". Only America would be privy to that secret, would recognize it, would know how to exploit it...*' I ran a hand from Vanity's plastic-wrapped breasts to the taut plateau of her belly (vibrant with its tom-toms of bellyblood); hidden, there, beneath the cropped vest of the torsolette, unprotected by its cloying second skin, was Europe's death-wish, a death-wish an original Cartier automaton like Titania had had the power to unlock but which now responded—pulse quickening, beads of sweat coalescing on her brow—to the touch, the scent of Elohim. 'The secret of the matrix,' I continued, 'was the secret on which they based their *konspiratsia*. America, out of national interest; the Lilim, to regulate population growth, to change their relationship with humanity from one of parasitism—which, unchecked, would lead to the extinction of both inhuman and human—to one of commensalism. It would give the recombinant a chance to live side by side with the species whose genitalia they needed in order to breed.'

The secret. I remembered floating down the Mekong, the ZiL out of control... Primavera had killed Morgenstern, but Titania had called out to her, called out over 10,000 kays, Die, die, die... Mental news reel images of US marines deployed to Venezuela, Iran, Korea, Australia, war ships delivering marble slabs, concentration camps filled with little witches who had surrendered to that same call...

'But then the first dead boys appeared.' (And the secret that our species was in love with death was a secret no longer.) 'The Lilim changed. Together, we no longer needed America. Dead boys, dead girls—we had our own conspiracy...

'The matrices of the previous generation, though damaged by the spike, retained elements of quantum magic. We sold them, demonstrating how they could be modified for transdimensional travel. Sold them to America. To Europe. The Far East. Mars.' (I was, my shadow, an adroit and convincing salesman; how I regretted that [though I'd never disclosed our marketing strategy, so to speak] I'd practised my salesmanship on V, prising open a necrotic vagina, revealing the quantum wormhole [the 'Krafft-Ebing' black hole, as we say] running through a fourth physical dimension to the hyperwomb and its naked singularity. That wormhole, I would insist, could be made macroscopic. You just needed a good Martian engineer.) 'But the matrices lived their own lives,' I continued. 'The seed of our species—the self-replicating nanoware that had now miniaturized itself into something like pure information—had become self-organized, an independent entity, a form timeless, motionless, unreal; a spiritual entity, a demiurge, a god. Information determines space and time. And Meta—god of superluminal information—come to term, its gestatorial sojourn in the present complete, flowed through the transdimensional gates, flowed back through time, altering history to its own purposes. America is ours, the world is ours as Mars will be ours, and all reality, when Meta attains its end.' The window, its drape of night sky, held our images like antique photographic plates of some anti-world, and we seemed like giant black angels bestriding a city of pestilence, a pestilence that was about to destroy its harbingers; faint, transparent, we were deliquescing into a forgotten, scarcely mythical point in time. The room seemed to tilt; giddy, I tightened my embrace about the girl-meat of breasts and abdomen, the only life that I knew would never be transubstantiated, the core of Meta itself.

'Why didn't you tell me? Why didn't you tell any of us?'

'And give you further scope for betrayal?' I sighed. 'We conspirators: we number only a few dozen. We don't tell others about our plot because Meta's triumph involves the destruction of our personae, each little history we call a soul, a soul that, as a wise man once said, is the prison of the body. We won't allow fear of the world outside that prison to create panic amongst the prisoners. We won't allow those who doubt our plans to sow ontological terror, terror of the new. Meta must, *will* be free, free of the metaphysical rack, the prison of human values.' I kissed the root of her ponytail, sneezed, the silk ribbon irritating my nose. 'Maybe we really did meet six years ago. Or maybe it was six hundred. Or six thousand. I'm not sure I know any more . . .' The room shook . . . Once upon a time there was a boy named Ignatz Zwakh . . . The past was infinite; our genesis, a never-to-be-reached future, this moment that was disintegrating even now . . . A moment that was becoming the past, a past that was the future. Ah. Amazing grace . . . Vanity had fallen to her knees and was using her teeth to unlace my codpiece. The grim reaper—so permanently, so painfully erect—sprang forth, punching her beneath an eye still puffy from her interrogation when she had first owned to invading time. (You beat them not to make them confess, but to correct their willingness, their over-eagerness to confess, you beat them to sift crimes true from untrue.) It had been a banal kind of interrogation; all interrogations were since we had been prohibited from using instruments of torture . . .

Images of a gigantic pendulum swinging from one side of the prison to the other, a girl tied to its bob; the serrated beam a girl would be forced to sit astride; the wheel, the trussings, the choke . . . She betrays me; I hunt her down; she begs for mercy; I kill her. Perhaps that was the only constant in the flux of this multiverse. Primavera stared at me from her gilt-framed Polaroid, souvenir of a life when she was still half-human, before her metamorphic life on the run; her jealous butterfly soul fluttered above her wasted matrix. Once upon a time there was a boy named Ignatz Zwakh. There was a boy. Once upon a time. Once. Once . . .

My memory boils over with worlds, time-lines, murders; but out of the evaporating past these things still remain, though they seethe, close to vaporization:

A few weeks before they crucified her Titania had charged her envoy in Jakarta with the task of finding me (Thailand had yet to be colonized); it seems she had always known I was a dead boy, ever since those days when Primavera and I had sheltered in her underground palace amidst splendours pilfered from the abandoned *belle époque* shops of Bond Street and the King's Road, safe (we thought) in those endless corridors, stairwells and salons that were haunted by a thousand green luminous eyes. Along with Phin (who had, I think, already started to travel the *via Felis femella*), Mephisto took your narrator, still Ignatz Zwakh, back to London, to the *Seven Stars*. The palace had changed; it had begun to rise above ground, leaping into the dreary skies above Whitechapel and Aldgate. London had been opened (everything had changed) and was reestablished as the nation's capital; only the East End was interdicted, but to keep humans out, not the recombinant in. When humans entered that forbidden city, it was by command, to feed my sisters and to fulfil the demands of our carefully regulated breeding programme . . . Think: my visit home, to the Rainham Marshes, to the tower block on the Mardyke Estate where I had grown up, a prisoner of the interdiction. 'I'm so proud of you,' Mum had said inside the vulgar compass of chez Zwakh. 'My baby, one of the rulers of the world.' Dad was dead; he'd passed away in his dreamscaper while reliving the beautiful days of the *aube du millénaire,* their romance, their frivolity . . . The streets were not as empty as I'd remembered; people had started returning to the suburbs (the dispossessed, the disinherited and the carpetbaggers, of course), the wall, the surveillance of the killer satellites, the barbed wire and the machine-gun towers that had followed the ring road of the M25, gone, destroyed. I walked up the stairs of the tower block where Primavera had lived (the place had been ransacked during the last days of the Front), but Mrs Bobinski—a woman whose discomfiture at having a doll for a daughter had turned into detestation—was gone, and no one amongst the few remaining residents knew where. I went into Primavera's bedroom, took some clothes from her chest of drawers, held them to my face, inhaled deeply, and then, along with an old Polaroid of Primavera in her school uniform that had been pinned to the wall amongst posters of yesterday's pop stars, stuffed them into my pockets . . . And then I walked again to my old school, sat at the desk which had stood behind Primavera's, again imagined that half-metre of yellow-black hair, its scent, newly-washed, sweet. In the park outside I sat in the shadows of the cricket pavilion, touched my chest where her teeth had first entered my flesh. But I knew now that it had not been her kiss that had taken my humanity; I had been like her even then; for as long as I could remember I had dreamed of killing girls; I had been born Elohim, dead . . . Think: our college in the bowels of the *Seven Stars,* the foundations of the new world, Titania's old sanctuary. My feelings towards Titania had always been cool; she was a ruthless politician; her strategy to liberate dolls from oppression had, after all, caused the deaths of millions of her sisters, one of whom had been my love. But now that I was Elohim, the blood-lust flowing more strongly through me every day, I could, in part, appreciate her devotion to Meta, her strange cruel principles, her perverse integrity. In the end, she had given her life for us . . . One day, in the middle of a tutorial in the gym, while we were practising various wounds on the college's inexhaustible supply of shop-window mannequins (every Elohim, every Lilim, re-members where he or she was that day), we were interrupted by a stern-faced Mephisto who announced that Titania had been arrested by the presidium. That night the TV showed news footage of her and her seventy-seven disciples crucified on the walls of the *quartier interdit,* feet nailed to crossbars, wrists secured to the verticals so that each girl looked like an arrowhead pointing the way to Hell; and the *titulus* of each cross read *'Traitress'.* They used humans, doctors from the Dolls' Hospitals, to perform the wretched task. For the last time I stared upon the austere beauty of my queen. The camera zoomed in, panned her ball-jointed limbs, the immortal twelve-year-old face, the flawless body, the green suns of the eyes. She had been built for the amusement of Europe's *nou-veaux riches,* a toy, a marvellous toy, an automaton commissioned by the House of Cartier. 'Tricks,' said Toxicophilous, inventor of *L'Eve Future,* 'that is all they perform. Party pieces. Entertainments. *Feux d'artifice!'* But their inventor's dreams, his childhood nightmares of the chimera, the vampire and the sphinx, had found their way into his automaton's matri-ces, and *L'Eve Future* had begun metamorphosing into Europe's death-wish, the realization of Toxicophilous's darkest fantasies and desires . . . We college boys ran outside, even though we were supposed to be con-fined to our dorms, to see Longinus, our Lord Chamberlain, thrust his spear into Titania's exposed sex—a smooth rounded sex of porcelain that lacked a natal cleft—she unable to defend herself, her magic useless while the scent of Elohim filled her nostrils, her belly; blood filled the awaiting chalice as we sang *God Save the Queen*. It was a sad moment. It was a proud moment. In her death was our life. She had given us the future. Dying, Titania had at last become Lilith, mother not only of the succubi, but of the incubi . . . Think: wandering about the fur-lined halls and boudoirs of the ziggurat, salons crawling with girls—such narcissistic, spiteful, faithless little creatures—girls whom I was learning to hate as much as to adore. They spent their days lolling about in their rooms playing autoerotic games that seemed mostly to involve dressing up, applying gallons of cosmetics and unmercifully teasing the boys they knew were forbidden to hurt them, the students whose frustration and pain they savoured as much as (I suspect more than) the pain of the human men, the 'polly-wogs' they raped each night. Or else, surrendering to the miasma of boredom that permeated the nymphenberg, they would confine themselves to the bedlam of their pleasure-massacred beds, sleeping, eating, bingeing on goo-goo, candy floss, fudge sundaes, chocolates and syrup dips, killing the hours in mindless prattle or by dreaming cruel masturbatory dreams . . . 'Incapable of love, all Elohim may expect from Lilim,' said Mephisto, 'is respect. But oh, Elohim may love Lilim . . .' My teacher would try to comfort me: 'Their promiscuity is necessary for the survival of our species . . .' And in the ziggurat at high noon, its environs gridlocked with listless girls, I would loiter in boudoirs, submitting to the taunts of Lilim, and in my boyhood's appalling loneliness, the appalling filthy loneliness of Elohim, would play their stupid games, listen to their hysterical yaketty-yak, smell the putrid scent of allure gone bad and, hugging myself, know assuredly that one day there would be revenge. It was that radiation of criminality that made me salivate, that I found such a 'turn-on', that made me want to kill; the vampires, the girls who performed the exigencies of our breeding-program with such dispatch, left me cold; I desired only the rottenness of their sex . . . Sometimes I caught that aroma when I would take a nocturnal stroll through the killing ground. In the ruins of the East End, the rubble-strewn, flyblown streets of the interdiction, beneath the great pile of the *Seven Stars* that towered over Whitechapel, Aldgate and Brick Lane, I would watch Lilim hunt down the men who had been offered to them that evening. Most aitchmen surrendered willingly; even those who tried to escape, would, after being bitten, tear open their incarnadined shirts and beg like sluttish street arabs (and yes, the girls always called them 'sluts') that their rape continue. Lilim prowled amongst the shadows, narcotic saliva dribbling onto their chins; though sometimes, sometimes, I would catch sight of a girl whose lips seemed stained with the unmistakable signs of dried semen. Such girls would hiss at me as I passed by . . . Think: Phin as a 'ward' resplendent in her new uniform. When a girl achieves metamorphosis (they made an exception for Phin who, despite her precocity, had still a few years to wait) she is entrusted to the care of an older girl until she reaches the age of sixteen. There is a similar system for boys (Titania had been collecting dead boys for over a decade), though we are called 'cadets'. Older boys, their metamorphoses complete, teach novices their skills, their mission; only on graduating does a cadet become a groom, a fully-metamorphosed Elohim. I was fortunate in having Mephisto to look after me. Mephisto the caged wild man, Mephisto the renegade . . . He was like an older brother, the brother I had never had, a role model, a father figure you might almost say. Think: his tales (midnight-feast-in-the-dormitory tales) of how he'd hunted nurses—not the kind you encounter in today's nymphenbergs, but Lilim who'd collaborated with the Hospital's paramedics—and of how he'd brought them to the slab or else killed and eaten them in the field; he would tell of strange death machines, experimental machines, the acid chamber, the spit, the clip, the scrag. And I would fall asleep, my head on his shoulder. 'There, there,' he would say, comforting me, 'they are very sadistic, our little sisters. But the male-female relationship in Meta is *necessarily* sadomasochistic . . . We must learn to live with the rage in us, learn to live with the dragon . . . Did I ever tell you about Indonesia, Ignatz?' He often used my human name. 'It was in Indonesia that I learned who I *was*. It was while watching a puppet show beneath the claws of Merapi. My marauder sat by my side. It was a shadow-puppet show, the kind the Javanese call *Wayang Kulit*. All night we watched the puppets. The sweetness of clove cigarettes mingled with the mosquitoes. The puppeteer, the Javanese say, interprets, like God, the shadows of war and faith. The puppeteer offers meaning, he is the lantern's devotee. *"But,"* my marauder whispered, *"is he dragon-master?"* We sat beneath the claws of that great volcano and the serpent spoke: of how he would bear down, a fiery worm, till we all were smelted honey . . . The sun rose and my marauder and I knew that one day the dragon too would awake: the volcano, thick with blood, the ungovernable serpent. (Do not tempt his asceticism.) "Can song propitiate?" I asked the puppeteer, and he replied: "Demoniacal images guarded, once, the temples of passion. Those masks are lost. And the villages lie ignorant under stone. Accept. In time this murdering soil shall run through your fingers, so good. Its excellence, the mystery of Lord Shiva. His temples rise like stalks of rice. Rest, then, in a moment of abundance, watching the shadow-puppets, the gracious and the clown. The gamelan musicians take their cue. Cool rain pricks the skin. There is no fleeing his wrath, only a stillness in the half-light . . ." And it was then that man and marauder knew: we must always live at the feet of the dragon.'

'Tell us,'—it's Satan, the youngest boy in our dorm—'tell us what humans are like without Meta . . .'

'Shadows,' Mephisto would say; then, understanding that the boy was calling on him to recite, the room would echo with his hieratic intonation:

> Wrapped in blankets, they shuffle through cloud
> greeting me in broken English. The people are scattered
> and crawl towards their end, sparse as the mountain air.
> Demise is roosting. It squats upon the plain
> smothering the memory of hermit and priest
> in the silence of these heights. Forgotten, that King of Mataram
> who built those ancestral shrines. Then pilgrims came
> to worship Shiva, climbing through scudding mist.
> Pools of bubbling mud attended His presence.
> The craters too, steaming, refulgent, cried out for
> libation and prayer. The great stone phalli were drenched.
> And once descending they found His fire
> in wife, singing-bird and sword. Now the bubbling pools
> give their death rattle. The craters are stale
> and nightfall recalls men to their separateness.
> Laughing, while children disentangle their kites
> from the snares of telegraph wires, they think
> of girls who have left for Surabaya
> where the market stalls hawk penicillin.
> They loiter about the temples, scratching words
> upon the porch. The white man loiters,
> cold and separate, then shuffles towards his bed.

'Goodnight,' Mephisto would say, 'goodnight, sweet boys.' I liked Mephisto. I think we may even have had sex. (Image of me lying prone on a cold chequerboard floor, shirt pulled up, wriggling like a dying sphinx . . .) Everybody wanted to be Mephisto's fag. (We would pick up on his sayings—seeing a ward, a little schoolie passing by one boy might say 'I can't decide whether to kill her then eat her, or to eat her then kill her.' And we'd all laugh. Ah. College days.) Memories swirl, draw me into a blurred vortex . . . Three years later, at the debutantes' ball, I met her again. Think: swimming pools filled with champagne. Fireworks. The two-hundred-piece gamelan orchestra. (Mephisto had connections.) The silverware. The porcelain. The games. The tombola. (A caged aitch-man first prize, magnums of blood second and third.) The pet leopards and jaguars of those walking on the wild side. The *cabaret d'mort*, the dominoes, the lorgnettes, the masquers dressed as mermaids, gladiatorix, trapeze artists, the bevy of punk-Marie Antoinettes. (And we boys all in ecclesiastical black.) The girls who asked us to feel their newly-trephinated sacra, 'In case I'm naughty,' they said, and then slapped our hands. Vanity shooed them all away . . . 'I chose Viridiana as my saint because I know you like 2m!*&Zp!' (the biochip in her brain full of bugs those days) 'girlykin *dtook-gah-dtah* with green eyes. What *you* called now? Waiii!—you boys have such *silly names*.' She lifted her strato-cruising Directoire gown, her belly undulating beneath the assault of my two-fingered stabbing hand jive. La! (Fenrir walks past; voices say 'Mmm. I wouldn't *mind* being killed by *him*.' 'You mean only if you got the chance to choke to death on his cock, you *cat*.' 'Dead is as dead does, sister.') When my hand jive upped the ante, three-fingered then four, she writhed on the dance floor in that house style popularly known as 'Die for the King.' ('I die, I die, I die!') Outside, on the parterre, I lifted her off her feet, eased my tongue into her umbilicus, deep, deeper; tasted there something going bad; and then, despite knowing that I was underage, that this was wrong (even then I had a marauder stirring in me), I nipped her breast, a breast firm, *al dente,* and lapped tentatively at the blood. She laughed with pleasure. I wanted to do more, of course; I wanted to stop her laughter; I wanted to go all the way; I wanted her allure. But I was a nineteen-year-old cadet, nervous, callow, frightened. (Had she been similarly frightened? Was she a fully-fledged cat, even then, who had been too apprehensive to ask to be put to her knees?) I contented myself with roughhouse kisses. Afterwards she told me she was on her way to Thailand to serve as translator and 'cultural adviser' to the new governess. I asked after Mr Rochester and was informed that he was dead (and knowing what I now know, he must have died in suspicious circumstances, poor Rochester likely being a victim of neglect, torture even, such is the vicious way these girls so often treat their pets). I gave her an ankle chain before she left. (She'd asked for my amulet, but that was something I was to concede only after I'd seen the effect Bangkok's surgeries had had on her, how it had seemed Primavera had risen from the grave.) Think: a year passes, two years, and then—not long after the accommodation with Mars—I was expelled from college for squelching this weird, suicidal nana in a flea-bitten West London hotel . . . And this is the hardest thing to remember . . . This is the hardest thing . . . The doting father dead, now, some few months, perhaps her stepmother, a jealous flint-hearted woman, a social climber stung by the neighbours' constant gossip, had threatened to turn that girl in to the authorities if she didn't submit to a contract killing, in private, to protect the family name (had hired me [though, of

course, I'd refused the money], she explaining 'all cats prefer to die in a
man's arms', well, of course they do, mother, of course they do). Perhaps
Cinders was just tired of life, tired of being on the run, had come up to me
one night in the ruins of Bayswater, an *environ* still as sparsely populated
as during the interregnum of the cordon sanitaire, and said 'Wanna kill a
girl?' Perhaps she wasn't so suicidal after all, perhaps I'd tricked her (a
scrambler on my belt), perhaps she'd invited me upstairs for coffee . . . Introduction: eight floors above Prince's Square she pours me a demitasse,
then tells me, in ritual fashion, her name, height, weight, age, eye colour,
measurements, dress size. I feed her chocolate mice filled with green
semen. Or I take her out for one last night on the town, drinks, restaurant,
disco, late-night supper, a taxi home where, after telling me, in ritual fashion, her name, height, weight, age, eye colour, measurements, dress size,
she slips into 'something more comfortable', emerges from her bedroom
in fluffy mortuary black . . . Or else I show her the gamekeeper, explain
how dead boys could never contemplate using war weapons on Lilim; for
girls, only the tiny high-velocity *fléchettes* that penetrate the body like the
probosces of behemothic insects, the slim elegant bayonet, the exquisite
harpoons; only these are good enough. And the knife? Yes, one of many.
A beautiful combination of function and design—you like the dragon-
figurative hilt? Thank you . . . Courtship: we kiss. Fangs lock. She puts her
arms about my neck. Or else, nervous, she backs away, then slowly (I am
gentle with her) submits, slides into my embrace, rubbing herself against
my leather doublet as if she were writhing in agony on the slab, and then
begins to babble lewd nonsense . . . She steps back, places her hands behind her head. The treaty with Mars has been signed and she thinks I am
going to shoot her. Do I tell her of my intentions? I forget. It matters little. Engagement: I rive her. She is again in my arms. My left hand clasps
her rump, my right . . . I remember her eyes, her mouth. Always the same,
wide-open, shock-stunned; a small noise at the back of her throat tries to
escape; cannot. The blow has lifted her onto her toes. Mephisto would
have been proud of me. And, after a pause, she says 'How could you?', or
'Why?', or 'Oh God, I'm ripped', or 'Bastard, you really shouldn't have
done that'. Nuptials: I torture her, using knife, sword, bayonet etc., bending her over a stool, a window sill, dragging her across the floor by her
hair . . . The middle finger of her right hand covers her mutilated sex in
coy masturbatory pose. She tells me she admires my gynaecological ex-
pertise. Thank you . . . Briefly, I become her, she becomes me. (A cipher,
pure superego, I thirst for selfhood, assume her suffering, her ego; while
she, sitting in judgement on herself, becomes a cipher, a superego, con-
firming her own perversity.) Honeymoon: she's on the table now, ankles
pinned behind her ears, or else I'm standing up, holding her broken sex

to my mouth, consuming the allure of her corruption, resisting the impulse to tear and rend with my fangs, remembering Mephisto's dictum that unless we control the marauder, the wild man in us, we will destroy ourselves by exterminating the female, the seed-carrier of our people . . . Half-dead, she feeds on me, on her knees, on her belly, inverted in my arms . . . For both of us feeding is a semiotic rather than physiological act . . . Metasex is metaphysical . . . Divorce: it's the *off* that betrays her. I mean, a lady'd say 'finish me' not 'finish me *off*'. That's cat-talk. That's trashy. But I'm tired and I administer the coup de grâce anyway, shooting her through her heart . . .

I was found out. The charge was serious: only alumni are allowed to kill, and this was a kill that violated an interplanetary treaty. I was told that I would have to spend several years in a hardship post. Older boys, like Mephisto, who hated Martian interference, and even some of the girls, I think, were sympathetic. I was allowed to choose my posting, and, of course, I chose Bangkok, City of Angels, for I often thought of my little magdalene, my fallen angel, the girl-child Phin, or Vanity. Abroad, I became part of the cabal working to recruit time and space to our cause. (It was my way of trying to redeem myself.) Abroad, Vanity turned—via a kind of second metamorphosis perpetrated by Bangkok's glamour physicians—into a simulacrum of an Occidental doll; and I turned Vanity into the notorious fellatrix who knelt before me now. The beauty of her first dollhood had not been good enough for her; she had wanted the beauty that ends in death. In her I recognized the archetype of the victim, the Plastic Venus, Logos of the Age made flesh, whose first incarnation had been my childhood sweetheart, Primavera; and, playing her emergent role with enthusiasm (I would invite her to my rooms in Lat Yao, to parties, dinners, trips to the beach), committing small, then larger indiscretions, crimes civil then capital, she would find herself at my feet, begging for forgiveness, a victim *manqué,* as if her body's conversion was only a prequel to this metaphysical conversion, this psychotic rehearsal for the sex death she coveted with all her doll-twisted heart. I could not resist that archetype, the dark anima that had haunted my childhood, claimed me in pubescence and now sought my destruction in manhood. As she became addicted to her own poisonous ways so I became addicted to punishing her delinquency. How could our affair have ended except in a consummation of guilt and prosecution, love and hate?

You know the rest . . .

'Daddy,' murmured my poor, condemned girl, 'Daddy, Daddy.' She knelt before me as she had knelt three weeks ago as Bardolph had passed sentence, one of many who had been condemned that day:

Adelle St Alceste
Amoret St Andromeda
Andrée St Annette
Angelique St Annabella
Ann-Marie St Anastasia
Belinda St Beatrice
Bunny St Bianca
Bunty St Bella
Candy St Cassandra
Cardine St Charmian
Carmen St Columbine
Catherine St Candice
Cherry St Celeste
Christine St Christabel
Claudine St Camille
Cleopatra St Clara
Daisy St Diotima
Debbie St Duessa
Delphine St Delphina
Dolores St Duessa
Dusty St Diane
Effie St Euphemia
Elanor St Electra
Fanny St Frances
    (the notorious 'Fanny the Fran')
Faustine St Fabienne
Fifi St Fabiola
Gigi St Georgina
Gillian St Gina
Griselda St Gudrun
Heather St Hella
Hermione St Helen
Honey St Hyacinth
Iman St Iphigenia
Ivy St Io
Jaqueline St Jaquenetta
Jezebel St Josephine
Judy St Jocasta
Juliet St Judith
Kate St Kristina
Kiki St Klytemnestra
Lindy St Lynsey

Lisa St Lysette
Lizzie St Lydia
Lucasta St Laura
Lysette St Lucrezia
Madeleine St Minette
Maria St Marie
Melanie St Mirabel
Melissa St Maria
Minette St Madeleine
Modesty St Maeve
Mona St Miranda
Nancy St Ninette
Nathalie St Nastassia
Nina St Natasha
Odette St Ornella
Patience St Pavlova
Penelope St Porphyria
Rachel St Rosita
Raquel St Rosaline
Samantha St Seraphina
Scarlet St Sacharissa
Sophie St Sophia
Tabitha St Titania
Tiffany St Tatiana
Tina St Trixe
Toxine St Tara
Trisha St Theresa
Trixie St Tina
Vanity St Viridiana
Venus St Viola
Vivienne St Vanadis
Wendy St Wanda
Yvonne St Yvette
Zenobia St Zika

Ah. Girls, girls, our enemies and our loves. (So many girls, Mephisto would say, and so few of us. Millions, millions; and us? Less than a thousand. But Meta is wise. How could it be any other way? For the male and female of Meta to survive, the discrepancy must be thus.) They were Thais, mostly (*farang* held only the senior positions in a crown colony), and would normally have been addressed by their *cheu len*, or nicknames; but the ceremony of death required formal rules, formal rhetoric. Their

crimes? One girl—oh, I forget which—had taken to planting bombs beneath Bardolph's car (me, Bardolph and our sergeant at arms, Anubis, we
look after the whole of Siam, though there's this little Thai kid, Ravanna,
first Elohim to be born out here, that we've taken to baby-sitting); five
times she'd blown him up and each time he'd lost arms, legs, his stomach
once; limbs and organs it'd taken months to regrow. I remembered how,
at her arraignment, she'd made the familiar defence that Titania herself
had been a fellatrix (all those Big Sisters were); but Bardolph had replied
with a curt 'Titania's dead.' Besides, I'd felt like adding, Titania had only
become a true cat, a traitress, when her work on this planet had been
done. She gave her life that we might have life: she sanctified the manner
in which male and female interrelate: Lilim must die to feed Elohim; Elohim must feed so that Lilim may live . . . Another girl—this was Cherry,
yeah, the coprophagous Cherry-ola, I'm sure—used an exceptionally unpleasant nanoware poison on two visiting Elohim (here for trade talks)
that recombined their body chemistries into a) a grand piano, and b) a toilet. (We still haven't located the toilet. Poor bastard. Somebody is probably shitting on him right now . . .) Not that we have to deal with many
murderesses. Not murderesses of Elohim, anyway. Despite all this chic
talk of poisoning, most girls prefer to inflict psychological rather than
physical harm. (Only the really far-gone feline, they say, can bear to draw
blood from the dragon. And by that stage a girl is usually derelict, a drooling slavering *thing*.) There'd been, of course, that girl—what was her
name—who had preyed on her *own* sex. (She'd this little Indian tailor in
Pratunam who'd run her up clothes from the de luxe flesh of her victims.) Now I know dermaplastic's out of fashion, that this season's look
is all Real Thing, but—
   'Daddy,' mewled my fetish-object, my recurrent twenty-five-hour-a-
daydream, my dirty habit, my girl, my love. I wound my fingers about her
ponytail (a half-metre of bleached hangman's rope), jerked her head backwards. Her eyes closed, *clink!* like a doll's, a tin doll's; her lips parted,
saliva running down her chin. This would be our last time together, our
last fatal intimacy. Bardolph had been generous—he would allow me to
officiate over the execution—but I would then have to report to the governess. And I knew that bob-haired twenty-one-year-old matron planned
to put me on ice . . . 'Daddy. Please, Daddy. Mercy. I beg you—' I was a
student again, and Mephisto was telling me about the birds and the bees.
We were looking through a two-way mirror at Elohim and Lilim locked
in metasex: 'The physical pleasure is, of course, incidental, a brief reprieve
from our constant pain, which, as we grow older, intensifies and will, I
deem, be the thing that finally kills us, driving us mad, so that we die like
our ephemeral sisters, no matter how many centuries it may take. Ob-

serve: by transforming a vampire into a cat men change the brother-sister relationship enjoyed by Elohim and Lilim into a father-daughter relationship, that is, a power relationship; it is in playing this power game that Lilim may reveal themselves to be criminals, girls who would undermine our discipline, turn against us, rebel simply for the frisson of rebellion, who would allow their appetites to take them beyond the interdiction, into the world, and so decimate the human gene pool. And without humans, Dagon, there would be no Meta. The cull is necessary for the continued existence of humans and inhumans alike . . .'

'But Daddy,' she says, as if reading my thoughts, 'I wasn't spreading the plague. Mars is immune. I became a traitress because I wanted to die. You made me a traitress because you wanted to kill me. Let's not make any more excuses, offer any more rationales. We're both mad, you and I: you want to kill as many girls as you can and I want to be one of your victims. Meta is self-consuming. We eat you, you eat us. Eat, eat, eat, eat. That's all there is, Daddy. That's all there is to Meta. I don't want to hear any more lies . . .' And then her cat-talk ceased as I filled her mouth . . .

Phin had assumed full lordosis, head buried in my crotch, back arched, rump in the air, thighs splayed. As she hummed me (hmmm! hmmm! hmmm!) the room palpitated, shook, the walls becoming transparent so that I saw into a transcendental number of prisons. And in one, a girl walked across a courtyard. Unbuttoned her blouse. Unhooked her brassière . . . Pose 1) She stands, one knee bent, hands behind her head, fingers entwined, her blouse, open to the waist, a corona of organza and lawn surrounding the pale, almost phosphorescent breasts that are petitioning, begging for oblivion. Pose 2) She stands, knees flexed, hands clenched behind her ponytail, fingers tangled in hair, wincing, the mouth extravagantly ovoid, a dribble of blood oozing from the small hole in her cleavage, a painterly brush stroke of scarlet brilliant as the creamy moonlight refracted by her sweat. Pose 3) She kneels, head flung back, breasts thrust towards the rigid, stone-faced firing squad, the five US marines (humans chosen to execute, though not officiate over her death, to add to her humiliation), mercenaries who have been able to overcome their dread of killing Lilim only by not knowing which rifle carries the single live round; breasts thrust supplicatingly, perhaps, but at the same time thrust to taunt, her superfemininity, her dollhood, having the power, even in death, of hurting them, of reminding them of what they cannot be, what they cannot possess. Pose 4) She lies on the ground, half on one side, legs tucked beneath her, arms above her head, a brassière cup that had a moment before hung useless aside the left breast now covering, as if provoked by death's immodesty, the lewd wound, the scarlet letter of the traitress . . . Hup. Tongue flick in anus, scrotal lick, bite root, take the loot, eat me pussycat, eat-gargle-and-cry! Phin screamed (a nice, easy listening scream), screamed as if she caterwauled, screamed a long cat-crazy Meow!, broke from my grip and spat onto the floor. When she faced me a spume of green slime hung from her lips. '*Wha*—' It hurts, I know, I thought. It stings. It burns. But you'll get to like it. Like it so much that you'll move to Treachery Street. You're young. A babe in arms. (Though the hormone supplements you take have provoked a kind of half-metamorphosis.) Yeah, you'll get to like the icky green stuff, in time. In a choreographed display of disgust (this is how you ridicule a man, says Granny, this is the Terpsichorean art of sexual mockery) she was collecting her bag, her clothes, her sentient phallic friend—Calm down, I was saying, I've got something to tell you, something passing strange—she all the while reciting programme notes about how much she despised doll junk inadequates, their dirty compromised genes. 'I think you very bad for Thailand,' she said. 'You *monstre sadique*.' Her road to fully functional fourth-generation dollhood was going to be a road to Damascus.

'Don't persecute Meta's servants,' I said. She performed a *jeté* through the door, her decomposing chemise held across her body like a mould-eaten bath towel.

So much for time-loops.

Time was no longer sequential; past and present had stalled; everything had been requisitioned by The Future.

'Hey, little girl,' I called, 'you got the *future*.'

And so had I.

I proceeded to get drunk.

CHAPTER FIVE

Strange Times

Jesus. Some bender. My trousers were on back-to-front. I stank of *Lao Kow*. And the room was poltergeist country. A half-cremated cat, servomechanism protruding from its skull, was suspended from the ceiling by one of the old school ties with which I sometimes handcuffed the occasional whore. Now, what was that all about? Tentatively, I raised my head. Jesus, thank you, thank you, no hangover, no pain. I rolled over; Primavera, I thought, we have to talk. I picked up the wombtomb; stroked it, cracked voice rendering what I could remember of that zygo-diddly song (a song that celebrated psychotic zygotes) by last year's band, the *Imps of the Perverse:* Git bitten, git drugged till ya humanity fail ya,/ Ain't no way out when ya got strange genitalia . . .

Memories. The past was dissolving into my memories of the future. If Meta was the allure, allure that had changed reality, then The Future was a state of mind. Before long, we would all be seeing things differently. The matrix radiated its green-light Go. Yes. I knew what I was. Not washed-up, not crash-landed; I was Meta, a dead boy. I had always been Meta. I pushed Primavera's bargain-basement mausoleum aside. 'I'm sorry,' I said. 'I'm sorry I didn't fulfil my promise. I'm sorry I didn't pass on your software. But things have changed. I've changed. And there's nothing I can do about it . . .'

I got up. It was time to go home. I had to go to college. Study female anatomy. Had to study ballistics, statistics. It was time to start living again. But first I had to get my head together. My memory repaired. It wasn't enough to know *what* I was; I had to learn *who* I was, too. I smashed the *Lao Kow* bottle at my feet, rescued the CPU, shook it dry and brushed the splinters from its tissue, its plastics and steel; tied the cyber-organic meat about my throat with the necktie that had exhibited the burnt-out moggy; swept out, stage left, to Shakespearean alarums. Leaving the *Mut Mee*, plunging into the sweltering night, all seemed lost behind a shrill opera of cicada song, the *took-eh* of house lizards, street vendor's cries and a mind brimming with thanatalogical dialectic . . .

Wat Khek was more than a temple. It was a sculpture garden. And a data-mart, a cheap emporium of dreams, themes and the collective mind. I thirsted for its memorabilia . . .

The town was quiet, here, near the city limits; the day's carnage—a smashed bus, a torched motorbike, dogs with rigor mortis, little paws sticking in the air, hit, run and abandoned children—filled the irrigation ditches that ran parallel to the road. A rusted hovercar waited in vain for Mars to lift its embargo on liquid metallic hydrogen. (Some bottles of synthetic gasoline had been discarded on the hard shoulder; but you couldn't run a hovercar on that; all that engine-rot was good for was blanketing the waterways of Bangkok in a black, deadly smog; the West had banned it.) I passed the bug factory: 10,000 tonnes a day of ants, flour-beetles and grasshoppers: an entomorphagist's utopia. The night breeze carried a bass note of wood and manure . . . A queue of pregnant women parted, allowed the trishaw to pass. They were filing into a fast-life outlet, a franchise that sold the ovaries of aborted foetuses to Bangkok's underground nanoindustry. (Unlike the automata of the *belle époque*, gynoids are not grown from the stuff of strange science but from womb-robbed, mechanized genes . . .) The trishaw left the river's conurbation, its bunkered population shell-shocked from a hundred years of slash-and-burn bizniz, turned off the Phon Phisai road and bumped along a dirt track until floodlit, spiralling concrete representations of snakes, Buddhas and Hindu deities rose from behind a veil of coconuts and palms. I entered the compound through the graffiti-scarred mouth of a gigantic cobra. Snakes. The abbot had a passion for snakes. He was, after all, the snake king, a man who had enjoyed a million years of majesty; his followers claimed that he could shape-shift. If only, they had told me, if only I had faith, I too could witness this miracle. But I hadn't come to Wat Khek to see an old man slither about in the sand; I'd come to access the Fujitsu in the library. I paid the driver and walked through the maze of ferroconcrete sculptures towards the *hong samut*.

Phra Bamrung appeared from behind the representation of an elephant and a procession of monkeys, monkeys with guns, monkeys gambling, drinking, whoring, monkeys in little Mercedes Benzes and monkeys dancing the *ramwong*. 'Mr Ignatz,' said the monk, 'snake-king want to know why you not come to rehabilitation centre?' Bamrung had once doorstopped me in the Café Mental for not availing myself of his detox-ification treatment. He gestured towards the island, awash in a sodium glow, and its hospital that stood like a little Alcatraz in the middle of the Wat's artificial lake. Cages of morphine and heroin addicts, alcoholics and pillheads, called out to me for help. Monks struck the cages with steel bars; pulled one patient into the open (as if he were meat in some human abattoir), belaboured him with punches, kicks, PVC pipes filled with ball bearings. The unfortunate addict soon resembled a sitter for Francis Bacon's ghost.

'I don't like hospitals,' I said. Bamrung's lips tightened in a humourless smile. Careful not to make any ambiguous movements (I could see the bulge of a lightstick beneath the redundant sanctity of his robes), I again began my walk towards the library. 'I just came for information.'

'But you are doll junkie, Mr Ignatz, no?'

'I'm turning into something else.' Unable to resist a parting sally I added: 'Pretty soon, you'll be turning into something else. Meta is going to colonize the Earth.'

'Thailand has never been colonized!' he shot back. 'We don't want you here! Before *farang* come, Thailand very nice place! Not have prostitu-tion, not have drug! And *farang* lady—she very bad! Always want fucky, fucky, fucky! Fucky with everyone, even *samlor* driver! You have no god! All you think about is money! Dink, dink, dink, dink, and all time say dirty thing about Thailand! Go home, *farang,* go home!'

The lobby walls were covered with photographs of the snake-king's an-cestors, the men all exhibiting dead reptilian eyes (I thought of Mr Rochester), the women the pinched aspects of those who suffer from con-genital vaginismus. Behind the photographs, I knew, in sealed recesses, were heads in cryonic suspension, refrigerated blood awaiting repeal (or for interest to compound into a waiver) of an overpopulated Thailand's anti-reanimation and anti-cloning laws. I tossed some fric onto the recep-tion desk (a few baht for this poor man's AI with its limited access to the Net) and took the stairs to the first storey. Directional arrows guided the prospective user along a hallway stacked with artefacts illustrating the Wat's illustrious past: animist charms and fetishes; human skulls that had been dipped in gold; swords; daggers; the booty of organ traffickers from the years when the Wat had provided a haven for mentally retarded kids; bottled miscegenetic impedimenta to citizenship; the Harvard Business School Diploma of a famous transsapient trans-sexual; microcephalic cra-nia, Negroid and Slavic, from the Wat's School of Oriental Eugenics; M16s; thump guns; artfully stuffed snakes; the bullet holed hyperskirts of Viet-cong a-go-go girls; pamphlets on AIDS; more pamphlets on AIDS; a vis-itor's book filled with the signatures of generals, minor aristocracy, plutocrats and pornocrats; more snakes; a mothballed saffron robed tele-robotic droid once operated by the Tourism Authority of Thailand . . . A woman in a snakeskin bodystocking held an arras to one side; the cubicle was dark; I settled myself amongst the cushions.

As I tied on the bandana, tightening the Velcro so that the electrodes were snug against my brow, the big monitor that hung from an invisible wall awoke, snowstormed. The Fujitsu had no walk-in mode but was still relatively simple to use. It translated the electrical currents my brain generated as I mentally prepared to vocalize, anticipating instructions by reading the symbolic representations of the concepts behind my words, concepts that were universal, regardless of language. *Dagon*, I thought, *Elohim with cross references.* The Fujitsu scanned the codes etched by an STM on one of the Net's vanadium-bronze pinhead disks. The monitor displayed an image of the fish god of the Philistines. Then the image blurred and for a moment I was seeing double, my own face, older and not-quite-human, superimposed on the original image. Pixels resolved and my big brother attained hegemony, filling the screen with a melancholy half-profile. '*Lord Dagon,*' said a voice inside my head, '*born 1956, Gabriel Strange, in north-east London, Great Britain, to Stanislaus and—*' Stop. Yes, yes, the past was being tampered with. I was being tampered with. Primavera—I fondled her remains—we really need to talk. But really. '*Primavera Strange.*' The screen projected the face of the sweet cheat, Miss Primavera Bobinski. '*Twin of Gabriel, died—*' Stop. Control your thoughts. Think: Dagon. Lord Dagon. Think: Elohim. '*Born 1956, Gabriel Strange, in north-east London, Great Britain, to Stanislaus and Raissa. Cadet 1972–77. Sent down for sexual perversion—*' Stop. So: I'm born 1956 instead of 2056. And my name's changed. And Primavera has become a sibling. Think: Bangkok. A ziggurat. A Bugatti. A girl. Tell me the story. Give me the facts . . . *The skyway was a convolvulus of shadows, a helix entwining a ziggurat of smoked glass from penthouse to the killing ground of the streets . . .*

The Bugatti (a 1931 Bugatti Royal *Berline de Voyage*) skidded, fourteen-foot wheelbase banked into the vicious incline of the screw. Rain sprayed through the open window; the smell of burnt rubber was like the smell of burnt skin. The second explosion compressed his eardrums into the middle of his head; compressed, then transposed, so that, for an instant, he heard in inverted stereo (though imagination, not light, stained his retina with a clip of the governess, her eyes painted like Elizabeth Taylor's in *Cleopatra*, her hair like Betty Boop's, dead, blown apart, her boudoir in flames, maids and secretaries wounded, convulsing); debris beat upon the Bugatti's roof. 'Nobody's going to ice *me* for fifteen years,' he screamed, his voice a hybrid of the contemporaneous John Lydon's and a young apocryphal Peter Lorre's. The nymphenberg's lights dimmed, switched to auxiliary. Fourth level, third level, second . . . He wrenched at the hand-brake as if at a mane of teased yellow hair; the car spun one hundred and eighty degrees, grazed a crash barrier, lurched then corrected its roll; the night whispered a vertiginous threat. Roadblock? He gunned the engine, glancing to where the gamekeeper lay refracting the kaleidoscope of the dash. *Crack.* A wing mirror shattered, shards replicating the image of an imperial trooper into infinity. (Fashion note: Faustine wears black PVC thigh boots, matching evening gloves with tines and retrogenic [some palaeontologists would argue mythopoeic] sharktooth zippered *cache-sexe*. All by Allen Jones thru Junior Gaultier. Spiked collar and bodychain by Barbie Barbarossa. Biker's cap by Harley Davidson. Steel tipped bull-whip by Madame X.) He accelerated skywards, back window disinte-grating in a comet-tail of glass as the Bugatti clove to the wall of death. The roller skating posse that rounded the cumber with fatal synchro-nousness was scattered, one girl dragged by the Bugatti's running board until the car—out of control now, lurching right then left—threshed her beneath the barbed shaft of its back axle. The Bugatti demolished the inner barrier, pitched into space, stalled, the axle, with its ribbons of PVC and pulped flesh, snared in the wreckage. A reflex (his loins informing his brain) made him grab the gamekeeper as the bonnet dipped; his prospect of a black vista of glass modulated to a well of black nothingness. He cartwheeled through the windscreen, through the hot wet void, cyber-organic body punching a hole through the ziggurat, his ungainly trajec-tory redeemed by a perfect landing as if he were a gymnast completing a vulgar yet inhumanly spectacular display. God, he thought, taking in the skin-rag opulence of the décor (school of Georgette Heyer/Bob Guc-cione), the slit eyed figures in its landscape, God, Mmm, Yeah: Pyjama Party. He fired from the hip, the gamekeeper flicking its long orange-white tongue towards the assembled girls, a lewd invitation to a different party, one that would last all night. (Fashion note: Dtim wears a black nylon baby-doll night-gown by Little Demoness; Uthai the same, in shocking pink; mules with padlock motif by Strangeways. Noi wears di-aphanous harem pants with matching bolero by Fatima Fatwa; omphalos stone by Belly Belly Nice; gold safety pin by Oh So Vicious. Gung, It and Som wear black chiffon full-length shrouds with rose and poppy appliqué at the breast; pubic decals of fungi, belladonna and convolvulus; courte-san wigs [after Fuseli], respectively 100,000 volts, 500,000 volts and Na-tional Grid. All by Vampire Brats.) A *fléchette*-pocked maintenance spider exploded, the fusillade chewing up the mock-Regency furniture, breaking crockery, mirrors, porcelain Columbines and Pierrots, ripping the canvas of a Fragonard ('Girl Kneeling on Miniver'), spattering blood across the fur-lined walls, a film of allure hanging in the air like a frozen scream of pure Form, the Idea of all screams, all cries for mercy and forgiveness. Cordite and the faint smell of rotting fish and mouldy cheese (some girl here a traitress) mingled with the scent of atomized cells and plasma, all that was left now of six brief lives. Rewind. Play. (Captions by Interzini Incorporated.) *Girl jut abdomen, greet kiss of bullet, imitate sex death of Nastassia Kinski in Polanski's* Legend of St Viridiana. (Remake of Buñuel's 1930 silent classic starring Jean Harlow.) *Girl wiggle bust like Vegas showgirl as gamekeeper treat her to impromptu double mastectomy, press body against David Bowie poster (Elohim-lookalike phase), chew David's pink three-inch stacks. Girl with safety pin in her ear unzip harem pant walk onto bayonet pretend he Sid, she Nancy.* (Be yourself, brown sugar, he thought, pulling the blade free, I don't care for *cultural* colonialism.) *Girl rend wet sticky chiffon as gunfire bisect torso from pubis to throat, strike pose of antique Thai dancer.* That's more like it, baboids. Give me grace, give me elegance. *Girl die a-go-go.* Yeah, get ethnic. Go, baby, go, go, go-go-go . . . He noticed the cake with its sixteen candles and thought, Mmm: always wanted to be a birthday killer. *Girl, alive but mortally wounded, drag herself through thick pile of carpet towards bed. Like bug, leave glistening slime-trail in wake. He shoot her before she reach sanctuary.* Despite the affair in Bayswater, the incident on Mars, he was little more than an initiate as a marauder. Traditions still bound him; he would not have been able to kill a girl on her bed . . . His ear caught the rumble of roller skates above the *luk tung;* he made to shoot the music centre; instead, seeing the *farang* tapes scattered about the floor, ejected the cassette featuring the wailing Isan cowboy and replaced it with the latest from *The Stranglers:*

> Jack said Jill let's walk this hill
> let's go get a pail of water,
> and I won't frown if I crack my crown
> so long as you come tumbling after. Ha!

> Chorus: Meta, Meta, Meta, Meta, Meta-morphosis,
> can-ya, can-ya, can-ya can-ya tell me this:
> Why should a man feel like Desperate Dan
> when Meta go give him *nur-ser-y psychosis.*

> Mickey dressed Minnie in a pin-pin-pinny,
> Min was Mickey's little scullery maid,

and Minnie felt the zap of a rodent trap
every damn time that Mickey got laid. Ha!

Chorus: Meta, Meta, Meta, Meta, etcetera etcetera . . .

He pogoed over a body; jinked across the floor; fired through the broken window. (Wished now he had that bomb, his last, that he'd left in the Bugatti.) A girl fell shadow-wards, her caterwaul shifting into a brief shrill coda as she was impaled on the *cheval-de-frise* of the palace ramparts. Recruiting cats, he thought; fools. A cat'll bite the hand that feeds her, no matter how strong the scent; for a cat all men are to be betrayed; but if men turn girls into cats, cats turn men into marauders . . .

Dr Who said, 'Fu Manchu,
Your brides need exter-min-ating.
The cruel hijinx of those five little chinks
deserve a Dalek's armour plating. Ha!'

The magazine was empty. He switched to harpoons. Of the five little chinks on the skyway he bellied one, breasted two, took one in the small of the back (that was a new thing, shooting a girl in the back; he liked it), took another through the rib-cage. (Fashion note: The dead all wear hypertenuous pinafore dresses in shocking pink and matching pink blazers, white blouses, and berets from Vivienne Westwood's 'Schoolgirl Slutz' collection. Stockings by Polly Wolly Doodle. Shoes by Dolls 'R' Us.) What do you think of this then, Vanity? I'm a sex criminal now, too . . . The vandalized Fragonard upbraided him, that girl sitting on her heels on the miniver rug, a girl corseted, stockinged, beribboned in whites and pinks, eyes fixed on the black velvet cushion on which the executioner's apprentice was placing the broad, serrated blade (the cushion he is about to offer to his master), that girl seemed about to say, What is the life of a marauder compared to this? How can you renounce such sacerdotal justice? His fangs extended. But no time to eat; run, run, he thought, Bardolph and Anubis will be here shortly. He moved into the corridor. The doors on either side of him were bolted; several nurses—probably answering the emergency call of a mad twenty-one-year-old; one carried a straitjacket—caught by surprise and denied safer haven by the corridor's occupants, were clawing at the teak-and-leather doors crying 'Marauder! marauder!' He loaded a fresh magazine; crisply starched uniforms turned into used blotting paper as the girls tangoed, waltzed, twisted and pouted to the gamekeeper's ludicrous fifty beats to the bar. (Fashion note: Sanitsuda, Mai, Nid, Joy and Boo wear international black-cross attire from

Sin Sick Sisters of Bedlam.) Out of ammunition, he threw the gun aside; drew his pistol, his sword. He lost the sword almost straightaway: a door opened to his left—a voice shouted, 'Wantanee, no, close it, *close* it!'— and he was confronted by a ward with her Vivienne Westwood dress pulled up and over her head, the generous offer of a deep, dark umbilicus. As he watched her turn back into the room, hands on the hilt pushed flush against the entry wound, the rapier's long blade emerging from the elastic curvature of her back, he sighted the other girl, the ward's mistress, a Coca-Cola-headed Eurasian who screamed *'Yut Tanhasadist!'* as he shot her through her brassière, her waspie, through her *cache-sexe,* no fashion of note, no noted fashion for those Anon. He sniffed; these girls had hung-out with little Goody-Two-Shoes; they were vampires; his fangs started to retract . . . Sword gone, pistol spent (I splattered that nipped-waist bitch good, he thought), he sprinted to the perpendicular, raced down the moving staircase four steps at a time. Accusatory fingers pointed up at him from the parterre; girls dived into swimming pools, ran from their balconies, hid beneath their beds . . . Imperial troopers were gathering at the next level. They formed a scrum at the choke-point where staircase intersected with corridor, the small landing which allowed ingress and exit. He jumped the last dozen steps, turning over in the air, coming down on his knees in front of a trooper who had broken from her sisters to confront him; a whipcrack exploded next to his ear. He drew the slink-knife across the girl's belly; the allure was good, these Praetorians all sex criminals, doubtless (plotting a palace coup, perhaps, it had happened before; only last year in Madrid—); he licked the knife clean with lizard-like celerity. Mmm, bring on the bad girls, he thought. As he rose he was lashed across the chest; he gasped in pain, but knew he was impervious to mortal injury. 'Bitch,' he whispered, then bent his attacker over the balustrade, tore off her moiré *cache-sexe* and stabbed her the ritual thirteen times before letting her fall to her death. (Saw another girl, the last Empress of Meta, fall with her, to bring the universe to an end.) In horror, in fascination, the other cadres had held back, but seeing their sister humiliated, insulted by the blade only to be then cast into space, discarded, disdained, galvanized them, and they closed in, the steel-tipped bullwhips snaking towards his face. He put up a hand to guard himself just in time to see his index and middle fingers fly through the air; another *crack!* and he lost an earlobe, another finger. He grabbed a whip with what remained of his left hand; pulled a girl onto his blade; held her close as he ate what he now knew was to be his last meal for a long, long time. As he chewed at a breast, tore at belly and sex, the girl wriggling agreeably in his arms, a pain like no pain he had felt before surged upwards from his groin. Dropping his meal, he watched in astonishment as his genitalia ran across the white pile. A girl walked across a courtyard of his mind. Screamed. He put a hand to his nape; something had stung him; it fluttered within his grip. He made a fist until his assailant disintegrated; inspected his kill. Across his palm lay the wreckage of a tiny ornithopter. Martian, he thought. A dirty piece of Martian pizzazz. Damn these party-poopers . . . The slink-knife slipped from his hands. The half-eaten girl slipped to his feet. 'I had to go to Mars,' he stuttered in a strangled falsetto cry. 'She was my girlcat, my sphinx, my obsession. It isn't right to punish me. To put me on ice. To make me dream horrid dreams . . .' He sank into the thick creamy fur. His penis was collared now, the troopers standing around it, poking fun, grinding their heels into the glans. 'What shall we call it,' said one girl. 'I know,' said another, 'let's call it Mr Capon.' A gout of green semen hit the slanderer full in the face. A girl walked across a courtyard . . . She was Vanity and she was Primavera, the archetype of the victim, the saint and the criminal, Viridiana herself. She was as immortal as he. Time opened its mouth, swallowed him . . . A Bugatti segued through dimensions . . . Introduction. Courtship. Engagement. Nuptials. Honeymoon. Divorce . . . And as he passed into that void, that oblivion his species knew too well (fashion note: Dagon wears skin-tight leather trousers, doublet, boots and accessories, all by Versace), he knew that he was fated to repeat this drama, in all its variations, in all places, at all times . . .

From a long way off *The Stranglers* were singing about lonesome cow-boys, girlcat squaws, Yuri Gagarin and the catteries of Venus, cannibalistic mermaids from 1,000,000 B.C. (James Bond harpoons Honey Ryder. Screech! 'Oh, James.'), the assassination in Dallas of the teenage Margaret Thatcher (AKA Salammbo), First Lady of the Carthaginian vampire brothels of Times Square, Confederate Lilim in supergirl costumes bayonetted by their Yankee beaus, the Nuremberg cat-trials and subsequent American recruitment of toymakers Wernher von Braun, Mary Quant, Russ Meyer and Robert Crumb, the students of St Trinian's who loiter outside their school accosting the sad, demobbed soldiers of the North-South wars with 'Hey mister, wanna kill a girl?', the Hellfire Club aristocrats who maintain a château full of kidnapped beggar wenches to satisfy their morbid, overbred sensibilities, the knock on the door in the middle of the night from the Beauty Police, Brigitte Bardot lookalikes who jump off the covers of *Rogue* magazine, clothes torn, stockings ripped, Sten guns going *budda-budda-budda* as they attack an ambushed train, cat armies harrying darkest Ruritania, murdering all male children under two years of age, the Bolsheviks who send the Czar's daughters to the slab, bespangled tightrope walkers falling to their deaths to rabid plebeian applause, Lilith on Calvary flanked by the Two Kleptos, the Spanish gypsy girls who dance a last tarantella before the merciless eyes of Torquemada, the bubblegum card of US marines whipping to death the flash-blinded teenage girl survivors of Hiroshima, the Thief of Baghdad waylaid in an Arabian nymphenberg who switches his wine glass for that of the wicked queen's to leave her doubled over, poisoned, on the floor, Mr Hyde tracking down a runaway sphinx in the Ripper's *topos* of Charles Rennie Mackintosh's reconstruction of a London destroyed by zeppelins and napalm . . . Roar of a transdimensional Bugatti . . .

And so I learned that night the other story of my life, a rewritten story I felt was itself merely one of a seeming infinity of narratives spawned by the demiurge that was Meta. History was non-linear; it moved the way Lilim move, through an array of disconnected poses. History was a psychoscape called The Future. And if history wasn't exactly bunk, it was certainly a mess; I had to really browbeat that Fujitsu before it surrendered any answers. Fact: human and inhuman had lived together since the ice age, commensality ensuring that the viciousness of the human heart was sanctified, made bearable, by Meta's religion of sex and death. Fact: humanoid aliens from Mars (*real* little green men) had made contact with Earth in the early nineteenth century fuelling a technological revolution but exacting behavioural concessions from Meta's ruling élite. Fact: in 1978 the Elohim known as Dagon was sentenced to fifteen years in a virtual prison. That prison was located in Nongkhai, Thailand.

Oh, and yes: my best friend, Mephisto, is 357 years old.

Primavera, we really need to talk.

But how can I afford you?

Get tough, Zwakh, I thought. Get Meta. Go for it. Things have got to change.

CHAPTER SIX

Strange Beauty

The walk back to town took me across cracked, empty paddies; stumbling, with only the glacé of the neon-drenched horizon as a lodestar, the toe-strap of my thongs blistering my skin, I crawled down the embankment of a junk-dammed *klong* and bathed my feet in the cool black mud. In the distance, the sounds of a temple fair: manic guitars and bongos spliced to a Bollywood action-soundtrack: cries of kung fu, the Ssss! of lasers and the freakshow moans, sighs and yelps of what sounded like a young woman masturbating with a live eel. Big Bluto was off to join the funsters; I could see his silhouette meandering across the fields; Bluto who was regularly beaten by the police, his wife, his wife's boyfriend, his wife's boyfriend's tart, his wife's boyfriend's tart's boyfriend, his tart, her friends. He was talking to himself, throwing a planet-struck tantrum: 'From behind. With a spanner. Don't trust them. They're all the same. The debt. The deceit. The dishonour.' O'Sullivan—a tall, wispy, snake-hipped hustler with the back-from-the-dead complexion of a voyeur who'd OD'd on too many pix—was running, trying to catch up with the big man; winded, he stopped; noticed me; slid down the embankment to my side.

'Have you seen my latest, Ignatz?' O'Sullivan was the town's *farang* pornomarketeer. 'It's this new thing: traitress erotica. All the rage. Friend Bluto just bought some. Want a sample?' Telezines and neurozines rustled in his gunny bag.

'I've just heard from my shadow.'

'A shadow, you say. Ah yes, I once had a shadow . . .'

'My mother'd tell me stories.'

'About the shadow? With me it was my Da.'

' "Someone out there looks like me," she'd say. "Soon, perhaps, there'll be someone out there who looks like you. The shadow sweeps across the world, implacable . . ." '

'Your mother from Eastern Europe, Ignatz?'

'Ruritania.'

'Ruritania. Ah. I tell you: my earliest memory: at the foot of my bed a wardrobe panelled with mirrors. "Beware of mirrors," my old Da used to say. "The truly alien, when encountered, even if *vast and cool,* may well prove sympathetic; not so a life form like ourselves, a creature from the meta-universe of our own psyches. If you contact the shadow, prepare for war." '

'You've heard of Meta?'

'Meta, you say? I believe I have, Ignatz. When I was little I had an imaginary friend. His name was Archangel. There were other children (I know now) who also had imaginary friends, angels jealous of our reality. In childhood the language of their universe seems to elide into our own. We learn new words. Shadow words. Eclipsed nouns, verbs, adjectives . . . Archangel said: "Rape, murder, genocide. These will be with you till the end of time. You cannot escape. Man's cruelty to man increases in exponential relation to his evolution. This is not *human nature,* this is the *rerum natura,* the nature of the cosmos. Humanoid life forms on a billion worlds more advanced than your own are infinitely crueller than mankind. They have survived (and flourished) not through renouncing the shadow but by embracing it. Your future, *The Future,* lies in the marriage of sex and death. This is the way of *Meta . . ."* '

'So the future lies in pornography?'

'You are what you eat, Ignatz my lad. And I serve the tastiest victuals in town.'

'Strange cuisine, O'Sullivan, but you'll do well.'

'Ah, but I can't see as I'll benefit. There's an apocalypse brewing. We're being replaced by other versions of ourselves.'

'True. True, and strange.'

'There's no beauty, as they say, without strangeness, dear boy. And the end of beauty is death. These are the last days. The days of the shadow. Have you heard of the Capgras syndrome, Ignatz?'

'It sounds like something to do with doctors . . .'

'Patients believe they exist in a world of impersonators, a world of robots, of identical doubles. I think maybe we all have a bit of this Capgras syndrome now. We all think there's only robots out there. Sometimes, I think, we go as far as thinking we're robots ourselves, or else have a robot double trying to replace us.'

'There are no robots any more,' I said. 'We're being invaded, but by information, a mental illness that warps space and time. These are the days of the psychoids . . .'

'Well, I suppose it's anyone's guess who'll prevail. My money's on the shadow. But let me give you something to perk you up. Here, take a look at a sampler.' He drew a skin-rag from the gunny. 'See you later, Ignatz. Got to catch up with the big man. I hear there's quite a pussy show over at the fair . . .'

The magazine was called *Hell-Cats*. Vanity was the cover girl. A 2-D photo-mechanical; she moved, spoke . . .

'*Daddy?*

'*Every night I wake up to discover that I'm dead. I'm a dead, dead girl now, Daddy. Every night, the same deserted hotel, the same room, the same view of skyscrapers and dark, insubstantial streets where the ghosts of the Lilim roam. And every night, as I myself wander through a night-scape that's sometimes cold, sometimes hot, that's sometimes like nothing at all, I hear the roar of a Bugatti; it stops ("Hey," I say, "I think your car's real spunky!") and its driver offers me a lift, or else it pursues me through the slums, docklands, warehouses, alleyways and wastelands of this hell, until I feel the impact of a bullet between my shoulder-blades (look, in amazement, at the jet of blood emanating from my twenty-one-centimetre cleavage), scream as a knife jabs at my breasts, plunges into my belly, slips between my* labia minora *deep into my sex . . . Today the city melted in a heat wave. The crystal skyscrapers glittered like knives (this is a city of knives), steel-and-glass blades inlaid with the reflections of other knives, mirrors within mirrors within mirrors, knives that thrust up at the scorched clouds, presaging that evening's little death . . . As always, beneath the vaulted brilliance the infernal shadows of the streets were filled with the phantoms of murdered girls. Girls who all possessed my face. And in the knives that stuck from the pincushions of their bodies, a reflection: the face of their murderer, my obsession: you. After dark, walking down an ill-lit alley, after a session at Yoshiwara's house of ill-repute, I heard your car pull up, your footsteps, measured, so-confident, ineluctable. And as I turned I saw the knife. "A nice piece of cutlery," I said, "I like a gentle-man who knows how to dine in style . . ." I was dressed to die—life here often seems like one long game of "Beauty Parlour"—my hyperskirt re-vealing a dainty triangle of white at the trifurcation of torso and thighs. (My hemline psychosis has become completely unmanageable; Freud knew that the disintegration of the hemline foreshadowed the disintegration of the mind; I'm going mad. Doll mad. Slink mad. Crazy. Yesterday I tor-tured Mr Rochester to death, sticking needles through his testicles, his glans; I half-imagine him reincarnated as you, for I've tortured you too in my time, haven't I my darling?) And as I died I thought of the priestess's words in the condemned cell shortly before the first death: "Enough of this self-pity, think of Elohim; your life has been short, intense, marvellous; but their pain will last for centuries, and Lilith will exacerbate that pain until it becomes unbearable . . ." I'm not sure I ever thought about you like that, Daddy; compassion seems to play a small part in the theatre of the obsessed; I've always enjoyed* hurting *men. Really, my own pleasure is all that I've cared about. Even death is autoerotic; it confirms how bad I am. It confirms my evil . . . But love comes when you least look for it; it surprises you; it's a thief in the night. You said you wanted to marry me, remember? You said you wanted me to have your kids? You were right not to have trusted me, Daddy. I would have taken your money and run. Once a whore, they say, always a whore. "You can take a girl out of the bar but you can't take the bar out of the girl." But when I became Lilim, treachery became an act of love, an act of commitment, spiritual, holy. This hell is for me a kind of heaven. For every night, Daddy, we are together, reunited, in passion and in pain. If Elohim exist to discipline the promiscuity of Lilim (and, with our short life spans, such promiscuity is instinctual, because we must try to infect as many aitch-men as possible to increase the chances of passing on our software), then sex, real sex, superhuman metasex—not the foreplay of interrogation and begging—constitutes the killing of the female of our species by the male. Sex, for us, is deproduction, not reproduction. This city is the New Jerusalem, Daddy, and every night sees the consummation of a marriage made in hell between Lilith and her consort, the Morning Star. Here, I've begged for mercy so many times, begged while being killed, tortured, mutilated, dismembered, eaten, that my fangs have fallen out, and, at last, at last, my eyes, my eyes, my duplicitous almond-shaped eyes have turned a luminous shade of green . . . Here, love is eternal and complete, self-consumed and reborn, like the phoenix . . .*

'Life is a black orgasm. And so too is death . . .

'You can think of this as a kind of epithalamion . . .

'Truly, the end of beauty is death . . .

'Won't you play with me, Daddy? Won't you, please, please? Won't you join me in a game of "Beauty Parlour"?'

'But I don't know what to—'

'Please?'

'Yes, I'll play.'

'You be the beautician, I'll be the worldsmith. Imagine: a small room. Brightly lit. A rectilinear room. And in the room, a coffee-table strewn with magazines, a couch, two chairs placed before a wall-length mirror, the mirror's array of kaleidoscopic light bulbs. At one end of the room a glass door; at the other, a winding staircase. The room is as white as snow, its albedo like a full moon's. It's zero hour. And counting . . .'

'Two girls.'

'Two?'

'Two. Their names are Vanity and Viridiana.'

'Ah.'

'Placid, they sit before the gigantic looking glass as if hypnotizing (or hypnotized by) their own reflections. Viridiana is the elder, nineteen, perhaps, or twenty-one. Vanity is either fifteen or sixteen, the mythic resonance of that age—even now the beauty parlour's radio is playing *Sweet Little Sixteen*—of crucial significance to her physiognomy, physiology, physique. It is required that her hair be long and blonde in contradistinction to the darker locks of Viridiana. The two girls are inseparable.'

'I'm not sure if I like this.'

'I pick up the scissors, the curling tongs, the rollers; I arrange the palettes and tubes of *maquillage,* inspect the wardrobe, the divestments of fantasy, the shoes, the boots, the hats . . . It's your turn. Imagine. Go—'

'Okay. Imagine all recorded history has been the history of a sex war. Since the dawn of civilization mankind has elected to resolve its differences by erotic combat, philosophers such as the Mesopotamian Nietzsche and later the Chinese sage Fu-ko having argued that the schizophrenic brain of the human animal, unable to reconcile passion and love, will always be disposed to cruelty and slaughter, and that the best way of managing man's innate perversity was to sexualize warfare. Thus for 6,000 years it has been customary for aggressors to deploy female armies, defenders to field men.'

'Let me see. A clearing in a forest.'

'What am I wearing?'

'Patience. I'll come to that. A clearing in a forest. A rainforest. It's steamy, crawling with unpleasant forms of life, forty-two degrees in the shade. You're prone, trussed up like the eleven other girls—your wrists tied to your ankles, your ponytail tied to your wrists—the ellipse of your pose (almost a perfect circle) ensuring that only your abdomen touches the mulchy ground. Exhausted, you moan softly to yourself, rocking gently to and fro. A collection of elegant daggers—hilts all fashioned in the image of a sphinx—lies nearby, glittering in the fractured rays of the noonday sun that penetrate the forest's panoply. You're wearing—'

'Yes, yes?'

'You're wearing a chain-mail bikini—standard uniform of the French foot soldier—with a thick leather belt that hangs loosely about your hips, the belt pulled jauntily to one side by the bejewelled scabbard. You are part of a platoon that has guarded the princess Viridiana in her journeys through this dangerous wilderness, sometimes scouting ahead, sometimes part of the detail that has carried her candy-striped palanquin.'

'So now Elohim have got me, huh? What's my make-up like?'

'The entire platoon wears pink lipstick, pink blusher, pink eye shadow, pink nail varnish; The Look is of a deceptive innocence. This "look" does not fool the young English lieutenant, of course, who, finding this surviving subunit guilty of war crimes has ordered that all twelve of you be executed at dawn. It seems your platoon killed, castrated and ate the genitalia of the inhabitants of a nearby monastery. Innocent? Such is the camouflage of *maquillage*. It remains for death to reveal your true nature. Viridiana tries to plead your case.'

'Green-eyes gets off?'

'No; but it seems the lieutenant has a soft spot for her—though soft is not the right word; even now they are making love, the hungry noises of metasex emanating from the lieutenant's tent. It is her green eyes, I think, that mane of brunette hair like a length of rough lustrous silk that—'

'I've heard enough about Loulou—'

'She wears a beautiful eighteenth-century ball gown, her make-up is—'

'She gets killed too?'

'Your destinies are inextricably linked. But she manages to convince the lieutenant to commute the sentence from one of bellying to death by firing squad. The morning comes . . .'

'The morning comes. We are freed, allowed to bathe, to make ourselves presentable. One by one the girls are led to their deaths (hands tied behind their backs; elbows too, to give the firing squad a more opulent target); stand before a tree to suffer a moment's pain before receiving the gift of eternity. Suddenly, as one girl is being led forth, she panics, breaks from her captor and flees into the forest's emerald breach. The lieutenant unholsters his pistol; the wayward girl is dropped before she has run a dozen paces. Now the lieutenant is angry. He has been made to look a fool. Merciful in commuting our sentences, that mercy has been thrown back in his face. He has to make an example of someone. He has to make someone pay.'

'And so he summons you?'

'No; he summons Viridiana. The stuck-up bitch is quick to get to her feet, looking at us, so noble like, as if to say "I do this strange thing for Meta." But I rise at the same time, and I'm not so slow at speaking my piece: "Please," I say, "I am the criminal. My mistress has done no wrong. It's I who should suffer." Viridiana frowns; she and the lieutenant exchange suspicious, then embarrassed glances, nonplussed that a little slut like me should be so noble, so quick to volunteer.'

'Nobility has nothing to do with it. You're jealous.'

'My fellow soldiers know the score. They look at me, hissing, muttering obscenities.'

'The lieutenant kills you?'

'*I ask for my hands to be freed. Then I walk up to him, taking off the leather belt as I proceed (dropping it to the ground), put my arms about his neck, go to kiss him—but he doesn't let me. He's a cold fish, it seems (with me, at least), and everything that follows happens in a cold and clinical manner. He disentangles himself from my embrace; holds me a little way from him, careful to avoid any concessions to intimacy. His left hand supporting me by the small of my back, he pulls me forward so that my body arches, my belly forced to proffer itself to his will; at the same time he unsheathes his knife, holds the tip of the blade against my abdominal wall, looks at me momentarily, a vague unease playing over his face, he still puzzling, I suppose, my motive in volunteering to receive this ritual wound, to die a slow and painful death. My own eyes flit from his to the knife, from the knife back to those cold grey irises, all the while shaking my head as if I've changed my mind (but all I'm doing of course is flirting with him); his throat contracts in a dry swallow of excitement, of dread, a dread of the ungovernable serpent within him. I gasp, taking in a great mouthful of air (my rib-cage swelling so that my breasts strain against the links of the mail), hold my breath as he slips a finger-width of steel into my flesh. A thick droplet of blood runs down the centre of my abdomen, between and over the links of my* cache-sexe. *He looks up, studying my reaction; then, face set, his course decided, slowly pushes the entire length of razor-sharp steel into me—my lungs releasing their contents in a soft sexual moan, a playful, saucy girlygirl moan not so much* Ohhh! *as* Oooo!— *until, the hilt of the slink-knife pushed against my flesh with unexpectedly brutal force, I scream (I can feel the blade transfixing my uterus) and, no longer quite such a complicitous victim, begin to writhe in protest at the invasive blade, the violating steel. Seeing my agony, the lieutenant seems confused; he looks to his troops for help.* "Try not to wriggle," *he whispers, concerned; and at once I realize (his sniggering troops do, too) that the man is a virgin: he has never killed a girl with his own hands. He pulls the blade free and I stagger into his arms, pushing my wound against his doublet, and then, as my legs become numb—he really doesn't take much trouble to keep me from falling—into his codpiece (its mandala of studs like the grille of the exsanguinator), grinding my pelvis in a frantic belly-dance (always suspected that, bellied, I'd turn out a wriggler), covering him in my blood, my allure, and looking up at him sulky, pouting, mocking, the tines of my fingernails scratching at his uniform as at a cliff face I am about to tumble from into an infinity of black space . . . For a second I pass out, and then I'm on the leaf-strewn earth, amidst its smell of decay, raising my hips to him, showing off my wound, my dark sexual wound, my fingers alternately fluttering about that neat incision and tearing at my di-*

shevelled hair (loose now, covering my breasts, almost as long as your beloved's); my tongue flicks out to lick at his boot (the foolish virgin draws his foot sharply away, hand clasping the butt of the holstered pistol). "I was his first," I whisper to Viridiana, who is already being led to face the firing squad, I being left to writhe on the forest floor, "I took his cherry . . ." '

'My turn. It's my turn to be worldsmith. You have to be transdimensional beautician.'

'Okay, but I wasn't quite finished—'

'I'll be the one who finishes *you*, my sweet.'

'Proceed.'

'Imagine: since the end of the last Ice Age the Earth has been ruled by the dragon lords. No one knows where they came from, whether they are aliens, vampires, archangels, gods. Mankind simply calls them the Elohim and honours them as philosopher-kings. Under their wise jurisdiction the Earth has enjoyed a golden age of peace and prosperity. All mankind's tears have been wiped away. The only cost of this beneficent rule is that Elohim periodically feel the need to shed the blood of young humanoid females. Not to live. But to console themselves, to prevent them from going mad. Compassionate god-like creatures that they are, the Elohim only accept volunteers. And of those—housed in a great palace in the world's capital—only a small proportion, less than one percent, are killed. The others—after serving their ten-year term (they join the Order of Lilith at twelve and leave at twenty-one)—retire, intacta (the Elohim are asexual) and handsomely rewarded. The volunteers are, however, intensively vetted in an attempt to bar any girl from joining the order purely for financial considerations. The Elohim want devotees, not whores.'

'I'd volunteer.'

'Viridiana is the volunteer. You, Vanity, do it purely for the money.'

'Money? No, that's not fair. You still think of me as Phin; but I'm not human any more, I'm a doll, Vanity St Viridiana.'

'There are some girls of sufficient nobility willing to risk their lives for the good of mankind. But you, my sweet . . .'

'I'm Lilim, I don't die for money, I die for Meta—'

'Viridiana leaves the order at twenty-one. You, her maid, are left behind. Of the 100,000 volunteers, a thousand die annually, a hundred computer-selected at random from the ten age-groupings. (This to keep the age differentials in the palace and its overall population at an even constant, a thousand new twelve-year-old recruits placed on the actuarial records of the order each year.) It seems you, Vanity, are amongst the one hundred fifteen-year-olds due to be culled *this* year. It's late at night. I enter your bedroom—'

'You're wearing a black velvet cloak, black riding boots, a wide-

*brimmed black hat and your face is white with panstick. You're
the Don . . .'*

'I creep up to your bed—'

'Wait, not so fast, I haven't finished dressing you—'

'I pull down the bed linen, draw my sword—'

*'Or perhaps you're dressed in overalls, something like a flying suit, or
perhaps a masquerade outfit of Death, white skeleton on black, a scythe
and, no, no, not yet, I'm not ready, I—'*

'I tap the insides of your legs with the flat of the blade; your thighs fall
accommodatingly apart—'

'No—'

'And it's at this moment that I could be anyone, dressed anyhow, thinking anything, as long as my persona, my mask, my wardrobe, my
thoughts, allowed me the reasons, the excuse to kill you, to watch you die
your sex death . . . It was never Viridiana that I wanted, Vanity; Elohim
are only attracted to the criminal, the perverted, the sick; your treachery
is my addiction; I wouldn't want you any other way . . .'

'Eeeeeeeeeeeeeeeeeeeeeeeeeeeeeeeeeeeeeeeeeeeeeeeeeeeeeeeeeeeeee!'

'Now let me taste your corruption . . .'

A jet of green come arced over the *klong.*

The skin-rag lay in the mud, bleeding red ink. I replaced the scalpel in
my back pocket.

What consolations are there for those who live in time? They have their
stories, their narratives, their little meanings. But that is no longer the
case for we who live in The Future, the information overload that is falling
into the past. History is of no relevance to us. Life is lewd babble, an *ap-
passionato* of nonsense, no difference, now, between life and death . . .

I threw the magazine aside, zipped myself up and headed for the
Nongkhai Royale, its *farceuse* of a masseuse.

'Inter-nat-ional!'

'Hey, it's the mad Slovak!'

'Yo, crazy boy! Rasputin!'

'Yo, long-gone gigamaniac of genito-urinary gunge!'

I think I killed the Swine, my fist catching him just below the ear and
scrunching up lots of bone so that blood gushed out of what orifices were
on public view and, I suspect, the others that were not. (The *herrenvolk*
had been off-guard, an ampoule of some neurozine pressed to his neck,
illustrations of geishas writhing in acid—real swinish entertainment, I
knew his tastes—flicking over behind his upturned eyes.) Me to George:
'I need your *télécarte.*' Several Café Mental imbibers pulled out their wallets. 'George's will be fine.' I stepped over the Swine's body, playing the

heavy, my eyes cold, saurian, penile; George slid off the bar stool, produced his card to the godfather, the big Daddy of Nongkhai. 'Thank you.' On TV, six girls, strapped to electric chairs (legs over arm rests, arms secured behind the high wooden backs), were having electrodes clipped to their nipples and vulvae. Caucasian, Black, Oriental, Native American, Arab, Eskimo, they wore colours of Benetton . . .

'Have trouser back-front,' said Phin. She sat down on an old copulator's lap, unimpressed by my sea-change from nerd to bar brawler. But I would impress her. In time. The present rumbled, about to open up beneath our feet and drop us into an infinity of flux, a continually changing narrative where the only certainties were her treachery, my revenge.

'You're a doll, Phin, you're Lilim, a daughter of Lilith, the great-granddaughter of an original Cartier automaton . . .' I had thought Primavera to be the first Lilim to reach Thailand. But other dolls must have preceded her by at least nine years. Phin was Eurasian: her mama had to've been pumped by some Europunk with compromised germ cells. (The same way, I suppose, my old Dad must have got done by a doll. Whatever would *my* mama say?) Or was Meta changing history here, even now, overtaking analysis in a final dash for the prize? 'If history could only stay on course,' I said, 'if I could only be myself for just another six years, then—then things would have been different. You would have succeeded. I would have found it hard to hurt you . . . Not talking play. Not talking doctors, Phin. I mean *hurt* you hurt you. But—' Was I really going to become infatuated with this chit? I appraised her waist-to-hip ratio, tried to pick up her scent. Instead, my erection (unappeasable; it seemed to have taken on the sins, the pain of the world) hardened with the intensity of my gaze. And with that confirmation of my blood, my transfused Meta blood, I stuck my chin in the air, stood akimbo (like a no-fun demagogue from the last century, like a piece of socialist realist art) and prepared to castigate my erstwhile tormentors. Before I could speak I started to experience that double vision thing again. Forget photorefractive keratectomy, forget corneal implants. I needed transdimensional glasses . . . Oh God, I thought, here come the psychoids . . .

Mr Rochester was bouncing from one gonad to the other beneath Phin's dangling feet; but Mr Rochester was also Benny, the old mec, the derelict *zigoto* who slept in a rice mill near the *Mut Mee*. Naked, his body covered in sores, collared and chained to a stool, he was every young Thai woman's dream of a white dog, her very own *farang kee-nohk*. The Mental's appalling clientele, the self-pitying losers and gogos who constituted Nongkhai's expatriate zoo, had undergone radical plastic surgery. They looked like insect-men, thin, with long mantis-like faces, their skin like papyrus, their eyes and hair a gun-metal grey. They were marauders.

Pirates. Their *Kapitän*, Mephisto. And they were waiting for me. The starship *Sardanapalus*—its mission, to destroy the female principle of the universe—lay hidden beneath the Mekong, a dragon god hungry for suns and worlds . . . 'Sleep well?' asked Mephisto. A catgirl was at his side. 'Come, we have work to do. First, the Lilim of Sirius, Tau Ceti—' Here was yet another conspiracy it seemed, a conspiracy within a conspiracy, a cabal of marauders and cats: autogenocide. Mephisto wanted to destroy Meta. 'Our journey, at close to light speed, will traverse a hundred billion light-years, taking us around the universe in a closed path.' And so, I thought, bringing us back to this very same place and time. Nongkhai, 1994. 'Like the worm Ouroboros,' said Mephisto, 'we shall consume ourselves. The universe. And all reality.' Marauders and their catgirls cheered. 'Come, old friend. Your Bugatti is already aboard. We fly at dawn . . .' A girl who might have been Primavera's daughter, Vanity's sister, a girl who might have been squelched by the Bayswater Beserker, a girl who might have been Primavera herself, purred at me . . .

And then I was flying above the landscape of the *Sardanapalus's* gargantuan interior. Beneath me, the clubhouse, which also acted as the ship's bridge, and then the road leading into the jungle, an arboreal no-man's-land of mutant spiders, snakes and wolves, electric cables strung tree to tree at heights intended to inflict sexual wounds, *punji* pits, quicksands, venomous cunnicidal plants, malicious hermits, dwarves and gynopophagi. As the jungle receded—its truncation marked by a high wire fence—I found myself above lawns and pleasure gardens. On a cliff, a ziggurat (I saw girls strolling on its terraces, sunbathing in its grounds, psychodoxies burnishing themselves for their psychomen), a palace that overlooked a sea pounding a rocky beach hundreds of metres below. Mephisto was flying by my side: 'Every world we sack we spare some of its Lilim and turn them into fellatrices. They live here to serve our need of treachery and our need to kill, until the female principle is annihilated and the universe unravels in sex death . . .'

As Mephisto spoke I aged; worlds were subdued, destroyed; girlish screams reverberated across a hundred billion light-years. I was in the clubhouse now, the last surviving Elohim, standing at the ship's bridge, looking out over the vistas of negative space, watching the stars blink out, one by one, until only a single star, a green sun, was left in the heavens . . . I manoeuvred the *Sardanapalus* into geo-stationary orbit and set the controls for self-destruct, our engines to propel us into the heart of that green lantern of death at the moment the Empress Ornella St Omega died in my embrace. I walked out (my bones creaked; even given the effects of time-dilation, I was still monstrously old; it was all the stopovers, the killings), jumped into the Bugatti, and drove through the underground tunnel that wormed beneath the hydroponic jungle. I emerged into the deserted pleasure-gardens of the last-but-one of my species, parked the car beneath the shadows of the ziggurat, its silent black tiers. Inside, the palace was a catacomb of dust, decay and the skeletal remains of the dead, some still dressed in rotting lingerie, the persistent, unyielding plastics of thigh boots and torsolettes, the ribbons and bows of feigned innocence. Clothes were all that were left of these Lilim; somehow it seemed that clothes were all that they had ever been ... A staircase caterpillared me to the roof; I crossed the caldera, strode through the penthouse's open door. Amidst the despoliation of her rooms, the empress lay, naked, outstretched on a filthy chaise longue, a silver chalice resting in the crook of her arm, a finger dipping into the receptacle's sticky green contents. The short, busty, endomorphic blonde tried to parry the thrust of my gaze by lowering her eyelashes, dissembling fear, demureness; then, knowing the import of my gaze to be unequivocal, entombed her head in the silver bowl, gulping at the strange vichyssoise, that outrageous gruel that would—dissolving into its female counterpart—soon bring this universe to an end; and while she drank, still gulping, with the thirst of one who needs to know how criminal, how glorious was her sex, I picked her up in my arms—she, unresisting, wanting to end this agony as much as I—and carried her over to the window; slid it open; stepped onto the wind-swept balcony. At the edge of the balcony I stopped, released my codpiece and held her by the rump so that her torso was bent at right angles from her hips, her hair sweeping across the entropy-powdered tiles. Her thighs were open (the legs pendant, idle, either side of my own hips), the arms flung back, covering a now imponderable face. I eased myself into her. In seconds, it was consummated, her hymen ruptured, green semen flowing into her womb to mix with her own allure, the ship's sensors relaying the metaphor to the bridge. As I let her fall ('I die, I die I die!'), pregnant with death, through the kingdom of the air that separated the balcony from the sea, the alchemy began; the ramjet, actuating, impelled the *Sardanapalus* into the cold fire of love's last metaphysical sun. I reviewed my past lives, each one ruled by the zodiac of Meta. And I remembered Primavera, my sister, my playmate; remembered the big house in Sussex where we had grown up, the endless summers, the bees, the picnicking ... Why had her life been so ephemeral; why had she left me so soon? She had been the only one for whom I had felt both passion and love, rage and tenderness, infatuation and peace. She had been my balm, my hurt, my pleasure and my wound ... Memory failed; suddenly, I seemed to be like one who had never lived. My god was self-destructing, unwriting itself, falling into the green void; and as my atoms flew apart, spinning into nothingness, as the fabric of space-time collapsed . . .

I was back in the Café Mental. 'If your mission involves travelling in a closed timelike loop so that you return to this point in space-time, how do you know you haven't already completed your journey? How do you know that Meta isn't already dead?' Mephisto began to melt, look human, too human. 'In prison I dreamed I was someone else. That I was hu, hu, hu-human. I dreamed that I lived in Nongkhai in a hell-hole called the *Mut Mee,* that Primavera hadn't been my sister but my girlfriend; I dreamed that I was a doll junkie, a drunk, a hopeless wreck amongst crash-landed expats and boors; I dreamed that the Lilim and the CIA were out to get me, that I was a victim of a conspiracy by The Future . . . Why did the governess make me dream such a horrid dream?' My teacher patted my head.

'It doesn't matter now. As for our journey—ah, *l'Éternel retour*—it is the going that matters, not the coming back. The shadow cannot live any longer side by side with reality. It is weary of shouldering the world's pain. It must assert itself, even if it means its own undoing—the unravelling of all space-time. When the *Yin* is removed from the *Yang,* then, at last, there will be peace . . .' He handed me his card:

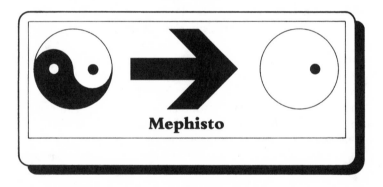

Mephisto

'You'll be needing this when you get out . . .'

The *Yin* element of the universe would, its material correlatives destroyed, collapse into a superdense green sun of pure superfemininity. And when at last the *Sardanapalus* fell into that hyperwomb it would take Meta with it. And then Bang! the drama would begin again. It would begin here, now . . . It seems I had merely exchanged one timeloop for another.

The scene modulated, returning the bar's clientele to the twenty-first century and the anaesthesia of their unchallenged perceptions . . .

'*Salauds,*' I said, 'hear this. My name's Dagon. Not "mad Slovak" or "crazy English". I am Elohim. And I control the fate of this world . . .' Bill had picked up a stun gun and a can of mace; but I knew I couldn't be harmed. My bones felt like iron; my muscles like polymers, resins. I was an Archimboldo made of TVs, transcoms, washing machines, toasters, microchips, *jeux vérités* arcades, tortures, wars, genocides, *desaparecidos,* assassinations, pornographies . . . I had eaten the world, the Modern World; I was a fashion that had assumed an independent existence, evolved into a superior life form. I was the future's glitz, its glamour of death, its sheen, the apotheosis of the de luxe . . .

Here come the psychoids . . .

'Put it down, Bill, or there'll be tears before bedtime. This dead boy's going to live a long, long time.' Shoot me and I giggle. Carve me up, cut me in half with a laser—do I cry? I snicker at car bombs. I laugh like a drain when I'm napalmed. Only don't poison me. Don't interfere with my enzymes, girls. Don't fuck with my DNA. 'I go to be re-born,' I said, kissing the tips of my fingers.

And then I took the lift to heaven and my favourite angel.

CHAPTER SEVEN

Strange Genitalia

The lush quilt of the fields, billowed at the horizon by ancient, rolling hills, was sweet with bees and summer and picnicking. Primavera sat opposite me, her white dress spilling over the sward, grass stains on her silk stockings. I lay on my side, head propped in one hand, flicking the debris of cakes and cucumber sandwiches across the chequered tablecloth. Off-stage, a lute song by Thomas Campion:

> Girlhood, like a
> bronze chrysalis upon
> which the sun falls, oblique,
> girdles, with threat of rapture
> a child of Albion
> and Siam.
> Fall always, fleshly
> light, upon the tiles
> of pink seraglios.
> The little deaths transfix
> them like butterflies
> and they sleep in joy.

'I failed you,' I said. How beautiful she was. Still was. Reprieved. Bleached hair falling to her waist (blonde as the lamb at His feet), and beneath the bangs, colossal green eyes . . . 'But I couldn't make a baby now even if I wanted to. My semen's turned green. It's Lilim who carry the reproductive seed of Meta. Elohim are sterile. Primavera, I'm becoming one of your brothers.' How many other boys out there in the big doll-twisted world had been born dead and were now metamorphosing into Elohim? Not many, according to my shadow. But enough, I supposed. Enough to build a new heaven and a new earth.

'I understand, Iggy. But perhaps you should go back to your hotel. Unless you've changed your mind about wanting me to bite you. It's late.'

'No, no; I don't need to get high; not like that, at least. Everything's changing, everything's changed . . .' She closed her mouth, denying me the vision of her gaol-bait fangs. *(Et in Arcadia ego.)* I ran my tongue across my own baby pearlies, teeth impatient to shed their gingival sheaths. No; it wasn't her carnivorous loveplay that I hungered for; I too was a vampire; I too was a hunter, a *monstre sadique.* 'I've had two lives, Primavera. Two that I know about anyway. The first one, where we fell in love and escaped to Thailand: you know *that* story. Half of it, at least. After you died I found myself metamorphosing. You girls change at puberty. For us, it's a longer process. Our metamorphosis isn't complete until we reach our early twenties. I returned to London. Helped to build a new British Empire. An Empire of Dolls, of Meta . . .' I sipped at some lemonade. 'Then there's this other version of events. Told to me by the macroencyclopaedia they have at Wat Khek . . .' My sister looked bored; it was a boredom that accentuated her ghostgirl beauty like the sleep that succeeds a petulant child's tears. 'One hundred, one hundred years ago,' I stuttered. That second life: it too was disintegrating. My memories were being wiped. I ground my teeth in the effort to concentrate. 'Was she right, do you think? To try to humanize me? Is it human history or Meta history that should be repealed?'

'Moral dilemmas, I suppose, are preferable to paradoxes. But really, Iggy, I don't like either. Let's call it a night.'

'Perhaps she didn't care about humanizing me at all. I mean, not in the sense of "saving" me. Perhaps she only cared about taking away my manhood, my pride as Elohim. Perhaps she did it for the *tressaillement* of betrayal. Perhaps she did it for kicks.' Primavera stood up; picked up her parasol; a sheet of darkness crossed the sky. The stars appeared, and a moon, pastel-soft, maternal. I picked out the constellation of Lilith, a star each for strange boys, strange girls, and stars for strange sex, strange grace, strange times, strange beauty and strange genitalia. Seven stars, blessed damozel . . .

'Late, late, late,' she said.

'Phin wanted to look like you.'

'Of course. Haven't you ever played "Beauty Parlour"?'

'What do you know about "Beauty Parlour"?'

'It's an old game in the East. Haven't you ever heard of it? We want to look Western because we want to die.' But no, I'd never wanted her to die. I'd never wanted Primavera, Vanity, or any girl who'd conformed to the archetype of my obsession to be a dead, dead girl; I'd never wanted them to be alive, either, of course; not humanly alive; I'd always wanted them to live in that unreal world, that limbo of the god whose name I now knew to be Meta.

'There'll always be Mars.'

'Iggy, I said it's *late*.'

'There'll always be its refuge, its consolation. There'll always be *some* place that's human, that's real.' Of what was I trying to convince myself? I knew of Meta's invasion plans. Mars had already been infiltrated. Nothing in space-time was safe. Should I care? Perhaps my fate was to be party to that autogenocide preached by Mephisto, to join an apostasy of marauders and traitresses, to commit cosmic hara-kiri, murdering my god. Perhaps that was the fate of Meta . . . But whatever Meta and the universe's ultimate fate, I knew my redeemer liveth; the unreal would triumph. Soon, I would see Primavera and Vanity again in that heaven-hell of dragon lords and their immortal victims . . .

'You want to go to Mars, I can take you. Tomorrow. But I have to tell you, your card's almost exhausted.'

Well, it doesn't matter, I thought, everything out there, beyond this bargain-basement datasuit, is soon going to be as unreal as this virtual Beulah. Fictive. An artificial continuum, a construct, a provident rationale for the existence of Meta's servants. I was becoming fictive myself, a ghost to reality; I was being subsumed by the fantasy I had had of myself ever since I had begun to dream about dolls.

'One last word, Mr Zwakh: don't be trusting that Fujitsu. The old girl's insane.'

'Hey, wait. Just one minute. I want to—' Crazy masseuse. She was collapsing the theatre—

Ideogram.

Darkness.

(Tee-hee.)

White noise.

I stayed in the datasuit, waiting to be hatched, the massage parlour short-staffed this night. From my shell optic fibre connected me to the superhighways of the Net, the axons and dendrites of the world's epileptic brain; switch on, I thought, light up by force of my will, listen to my words, share the inner dialogue of Meta. '*Dagon calling. Hello, hello? Come in, Earth. Acknowledge. We're here. The dead boys. The Elohim. The messiahs. To save you. From yourselves. To redeem the world's evil. Its wars and cruelty and blood. Evil past, present and future. Call it evo-*

lution. Salvation. What you will: nothing will be the same again. The old gods have departed. Soon, it will be as if they had never been. There will only be Meta.'
The rig's AC cooled my skin. Dark and cool, this grave, this womb strange as my destiny. I was about to be re-born. Like the Earth. In splendour. Strange, that this is the end. And strange, too, this beginning. Crossing the border, now, in trains, automobiles, space ships, time machines . . . So long, Nongkhai. Hello, girls, you Meta? On our way, no going back. Going to do strange things. Strange things in a strange, strange land. Howdy-doody, stranger. Yes. This is the end. Then begin. But what beginnings? Too many countries, peoples, systems, rationales, justifications, planets that allow me to exist. What can be retrodicted? Nothing. The simulation we call reality has been reprogrammed. And I know only this: she escapes, the runaway, the criminal, the traitress, and Dagon, the transdimensional cowboy, his eyes cold, grey, gynocidal, is riding down a billion-billion alternate dawns, pursuing that pretty sphinx through the mutating psychoscapes of countless picaresque nights, segueing through parallel worlds, insomnious with transgression . . . The last curtain falls. Awake. The prison opens and the *Sardanapalus* flies at dawn; the anima screams; our ship falls from orbit into the gravity-well of a terrible green sun and the multiverse unravels in sex death. Everything that can happen has already happened. Everything that is happening will happen again. I have lived a hundred-billion years. I am The Future, the Destroyer and the Re-Creator. I am the Archangel with the Keys to the Pit; the Jaded Aristocrat hunting you for his sport; the Cruel Pirate, the Rake, the Beauty Policeman; I am the Intruder who is even now creeping into your room. Even now.
Listen: I am Meta.
Ladies and gentlemen. Take your seats. Settle down.
This is Dagon calling. Vanity, too.
We have strange genitalia.

Nongkhai 1994

Dead Things

'What returns, what finally comes home to me, is my own self.'

NIETZSCHE

PART I

Archangel and Lipstick Go V.Berging

CHAPTER ONE

A Futurized Present

H*ut-tut-rut!'*
     This story ends—no.

This story ends—will end, does end, *must* end—with a beginning, begins, now, yes, even as it ends.

But *where* to begin?

So many names, so many narratives, such a life inexpiable, *noir,* so little time, so little grace.

Quickly, I am dying. Soon, only heteroconsciousness will remain, the language of the perpetual outside, the idiolect of people who are their clothes, who live their lives in extreme exteriority; the language of people who are things, people who are text.

I must again circumnavigate the sea of space and time; but if I destroy I may also—in a corresponding mental voyage during these brief moments before death—recombine memory and imagination to create a universe, a universe in which I will at last have completed my journey home; a universe in which my sister, lover, innocent, trull, will be fully human once more, alive and free; a universe in which we will be together.

Begin.

The dream is a Polaroid, a narrative frozen in the now which accrues a past by projecting itself into The Future; it is my imaginative body, a thing. A dead thing. The only life, Primavera, the only existence possible for creatures such as we, things made of dreams, of words.

The journey is complete.

Quickly, I am dying—

I am a marauder, Inquisitor Dagon of the starship *Sardanapalus* and my mission is to kill them, kill them all, all, all, to the last screaming girl-child:

my sisters, my brides, the Lilim who have seeded the universe with Meta. (And listen: I'm 99.9 percent there.) Call it autogenocide. The universe of Meta collapses and new worlds, new lives are born. I am of the Elohim who no longer subscribe to old, strange philosophies. I am Dagon, the phallus of God. What more do you ask of a beginning?

Then begin.

Now—

'Hut-tut-rut!'

Friday night. *The V.Berg.* A nightclub in downtown Hua Hin, strumpet city of criminals, perverts and sex-death chic overlooking the Gulf of Siam.

Across the bay, Bangkok, mother lode and financial centre of a civilization whose universal currency is pornography, draws the moneymen of sensation and simulation from North and South, East and West.

I move towards the turnstile, my leathers, my dressed-for-justice threads, creaking beneath my civvies, so hot. But like all Elohim (like all Lilim, too) I *am* my clothes. And I am prepared to suffer for my fetishism. Besides, they shoot *provocateurs* and spies.

If need arises I will go Clark Kent, un-masquerade, reveal myself in uniform. I've done time before; could do it again.

Time's nothing to a superman.

'Hut-tut-rut!'

A wannabe-Elohim, cod-wicked in his saurian make-up, sneers at me. I understand.

In my bankrupt kid-gentleman's attire, all rented black dicky bow, mock-bespoke jacket and tartan trews, I'm so innocuous, yes, so pitifully anthropoid, so humane.

'Hut-tut-ruuuuuuuuuut!'

The boy looks away; forgetting his desire, his fear, his envy and hatred for Meta and seemingly lost in the kind of endless time you become trapped in when drunk, room spinning round, never to be sober again, he sucks the off-world phrase back into his larynx (probably the only Martian this *nak-leng*, this hooliboy knows); swallows; leans back against the nightclub wall like a girl waiting to be asked to dance.

Wannabe-Elohim, Wannabe-Lilim: boys and girls desperate to be more than fashion statements, more than walking-talking pieces of *fin du millénaire* chic, so sad that they owe whatever second-hand beauty they possess to glamabracadabras, to scalpel, hypo, pills and bestial secretions, and not to the sickness, the glory of Meta.

The pity of it all . . .

Hope beyond hope, little groupies. What you all doing here, anyway, the universe murdered—about to collapse—humming that tired song of sex 'n' redemption?

The masquerading hordes carry me across the threshold, through the turnstile and up the stairs; I hand a token to the bespangled circus midget in the box office—an *idiot savant,* I've heard, who can recite the name, age, height, weight, hair colour, eye colour and bust, waist and hip dimensions of every Lilim on this fair, blue, soon-to-be-blasted planet—and I am lost in darkness.

Stop. Reload. Standby.

Blonde Venus

Inside:

The V.Berg, salvaged from the ruins of an old cinema, is like a little cathedral, its aisles lined with morose caryatids and telamons, its domed ceiling daubed with obscene frescoes.

Amid this Weimar ambience I take a seat (tables and chairs surround a circular dance floor); take Gun from my pocket, place him on the table (he rattles his cage; I upbraid him with a tsk); begin videotaping.

I focus on the dance floor. But my oh my, there's a big cat problem out there, I think, for amongst the Meta fan clubbers, the partying humans, I see, hear and smell Lilim: girls neurotically hemmed, psychotically hemmed, neurotically-psychotically hemmed, girls in the latest a-hemlineal 4-D fashions (hem there but invisible to *your* eyes, *mes voyeureuse*), golden-ringleted merkins jiggling between their thighs, breasts bouncing, tongues jiving, legs, heads, arms, feet transfigured into the pseudopodia of an outlandish race of gargantuan sex organs, so many bella vampirellas these days going the Way of the Cat. (Why? Consider: in what sense is fellatio vampiric and why has human-wannabe vampirism become so predominant a force in the late twentieth century? And what do these two things mean? Think of shopping, hyperconsumerism, the solipsism of an autoerotic age. An age of information is inevitably one that evolves into an age of pornography . . .) One, two, three, four—Oh, I lose count. Here are the girls who are Princess Lipstick's kind: the runaway cats, the little girls sentenced to death *in absentia,* the would-be sexual refugees, the girls who yearn to go Mars-side, the degenerate vampires, the traitresses of Meta.

All but one I dismiss from my thoughts: the one in whose eyes I recognize the attribute *Venusian*.

The princess herself.

Modesty Blaise has Venusian eyes, and so had the feline (if too human) Marlene Dietrich, and so had Jocasta of the Tarquin Women, beloved of Garth (but, of course, comic strip Jocasta *was* Venusian); they are eyes that would normally be described as Eurasianesque, I suppose—East of the West eyes, *yeux* Occidental-Oriental—if only they were not so inhumanly green, bright green, their lids heavy with matching-green eye shadow and thick black pencil, their lashes dripping with that crudely viscous mascara developed specially by *Maquidoceur D'Enfer* to appeal to the affected, dandified vulgarity of catgirls, *Venusian* referring to a kind of barely contained sexual frenzy as much as to the DNA segment that supplies that hint of epicanthic fold.

These green lanterns of libido (so dangerous; boys try to avoid their restless, garish flames) are emphasized by hair that is *bleached blonde,* a dishevelled shag falling to the small of her back, *bleached blonde, with streaks* (sometimes green, chartreuse, or psychedelic, but tonight a candycat pink), very retro-sixties, very Bardot, the boy-toy fringe partly shielding her nervous, gridlocked dance partner from the traffic-light GO of her flirtatious gaze. I can't summon a cognomen for the nose, though *puppet-like* or *doll-like* seem about to offer themselves. The mouth is big—too big for the face—with lips full and plump and, yes, *bee-stung,* coated in a generously tarty gloss of sugary-cum-shocking pink (pink corset over satin-white dirndlkleid, pink ankle boots, really, my Doriminian princess is very 'pink' tonight); it is the same colour that rouges and overemphasizes the puddeny cheekbones, tabby-cat chops that look as if they might have been inflated with cortisone, *oh rouge absolu, oh rouge sublime.* (Bitch-cake *knows* pink is my favourite colour, pink sugar-pink, *enragé,* pink cool or shocking; it is, surely, the most superfeminine of colours, *the* superfeminine colour, la?) A micron powder—Lancôme?— gives her the *soigné* faultless ultramatte complexion of a *Vogue cover girl,* though *sophistication* is absent from her demeanour. She is street-sassy beautiful, alley-cat comely, her organic life pressurized, sealed, the percipient's appetite pricked, not by the ingredients, but by the *fille fatale* packaging, the hardsell of femininity's most blatant clichés, the italicization of our sex-saturated world; and looking at her I feel as if I am looking at an ancient photograph, one that reminds me of my poor dead sister, a photograph excavated from the deserts of Time.

The jock—he calls himself *StyleFlea*—is layering the club with medleys of girlish screams and moans sampled from thousands of A, B and C movies over the technopop refrain 'sex-death chic, sex-death chic . . .'. The music builds, the screams going from contralto to mezzo-soprano to soprano.

This really is some crazy elfin grot, I'm thinking, some crazy fairy torture chamber. And then the Meta agitprop cuts through the wall of sound: *'The will to power, to control, is a biological imperative, the will, the will, the will to p, p, p, p-power . . .'*

'Mars is a *capon*!' shouts a reb-Mars girl. 'Cut the strings from your *apron*! Martian life's a *trailer*! The feature's Johnny *Impaler*! Meta is cool! Meta is grungy! Submit to the psychoids!'

'How to manage, how to m, m, m, m-manage the will to power? Meta is compassion, pity and compassion, Meta is g, g, g, g-grace . . .'

The jocko-devo is rolling about on the floor, spitting, submitting, offering himself to the Will. (The monitors are screening scenes from Leni Riefenstahl's *Triumph*: thousands of vampirellas in mass lordosis at Nuremberg; the Speer ziggurat; the Lilim-Elohim sculptures of Arno Breker.)

Voilà, Monsieur le rock star. Slave to the rhythm, submit! Jerk has probably taken a few rides in the *quartier interdit*: jerk looks like an addict; wants to get bitten, scourged, reminded that he's merely a host for the propagation of Meta. For a few minutes the whole *V.Berg* is copying the veejay's slamdance slides and slitherings—everyone little fleas, these days, sucking on the body of *style*.

Nothing exists, I think, beyond the time and space of these millennial days. All history is *now*, all dimensions compacted into the plexus of 1994, year I left Earth, year I returned (been away a long, long time); all is the exposed nerve endings of Meta, its transgression, its catharsis of pain; all time and space pressing in on me so that I feel I'm in some kind of Big Crunch, some cosmic pressurization chamber, sealed up in the masculine complement to *superfemininity*.

Beneath tables, kneeling in shadows, my parasitic sisters are performing their oral-genital party pieces, the spiritual viroid, the physical meme, the infinitesimal that is in their 'allure', passing through the urethras of their victims, despoiling their germ cells, to lie dormant until that host impregnates a human ovum and (in that mystery of reification) crooks the human root.

A pubic wig lands on my table, upsetting my suds, my firewater chaser of tequila and *Lao Kow*. Gun hisses, withdraws to the back of his cell. 'A merkin for your thoughts,' she says, my snitch, my slave, contact and procuress; my bitch.

CHAPTER THREE

Call Sign: Macheath

She is party-frock dirndled like the other cat *danseuses*. My eyes draw level with her flounced A-line hyperskirt, her sweet callipygian fundament (deployed in a backless cachette, '*T-bakku*', as the Japanese say), her rouged, exhibited natal cleft, clitoral hood pierced with an amusing variety of gold charms, phalli, felidae, mutagenii, anthropophagi; her red peruke-less meat.

Another girl, younger, but just as strictly dressed, stands by her side.

'You're late,' I say. (It's early, but it's sort of instinctual for me to scold her.) 'Is this the one you told me about?' Playing the older sister, Lipstick takes the girl's arm.

'Fascination, I'd like you to meet the Lord *D*.' Acting a little fly, tonight, is Lipstick. 'The Big D. My *D*addy.' And I think: be careful, watch her.

The Siamese catgirl, her face vacuous, pretty but infinitely forgettable (though offering its plea of 'guilty' as readily as the next girl's, as good a sentence of death as her body's wantonness, its superfemininity), gives a little curtsey, lowers her eyes. She is about to fall to the floor to perform a full lordosis when Lipstick stops her, guides her to a chair.

'You are Giselle St Geneviève,' I say, not bothering to enquire of her Thai sobriquet or *cheu len* (and disdaining the use of her street name), the imperial title granting me greater imperiousness, authority, 'a ward of the Bangkok nymphenberg?'

'Yes, sir,' she replies, words as devoid of emotion as her face.

'Fascination is *sooo* fascinating isn't she, my lord?' Lipstick kisses the girl on the cheek and then, with a snap of fingers, a clicketty-clack of gladiatorial nails, orders two mint juleps.

This girl, Fascination, though only eleven or twelve and still metamorphosing (and so still retaining some of her Siamese traits—the high Asiatic cheekbones, eyes, complexion; the broken English; that 'inscrutable' smile), will soon be—like all Lilim—a *white* girl, a girl standardized into a universal *objet* of desire, white already glowing through her epidermis, a white that underlies all ethnicity, that is the acculturation of the *world girl,* the buxom, fluffy razzle-dazzle of type A, B, C, indeed type A–Z Lilim, of which the Oriental is but a cosmetic variety, a subset of whiteness, the dream of the perfect female, the perfect slave, concubine, geisha, the perfect Siamese whore.

I continue: 'And it has been explained what is expected of you?' Chewing her underlip (staining her teeth magenta with the rouge-caked gash of her whore's mouth), the girl nods her head, one hand on the prodigious cleavage of her corset-enhanced bosom ('be still my beating heart'), end-product of a truly Frankensteinian *corsetière.* (Mme Poupie Cadolle, grande dame of corset making, custommade lingerie since 1889?)

Says Lipstick: 'She's not a runaway. Nobody knows she's here. She's been on leave, staying with her sick mother. I've told her there's no danger. Unless—'

'I can do, no plob-lem.' The pretty girl-child addresses her felid big sister, too nervous, perhaps, to speak to me girl-to-man, 'but you promise—take me with you?'

'Of course,' I say, and her shy eyes flash with anxiety and doubt; the brown eyes, I perceive, of a little fawn branded SLAUGHTER. Ah, *ma biche.* Her street baptism should have renamed her, not Fascination, but Bambi, Miss Bambi Lactozoid.

'They find out soon, I think,' she says.

'That you're a sex traitress?' I smile my thin manwolf smile; I can't help taunting her; it's in my blood. 'That you've been infecting humans beyond the range of the interdiction? That you've been planning to defect to Mars?' Gun starts to laugh his default metallic laugh. (I hate it; I've tried to reprogram him; latterly Gun has been displaying a disturbing range of sociopathic symptoms; but—) 'Never mind my gamekeeper.'

My left eye—that is, my prosthetic camera-eye—detaches itself from its socket and floats across the table on negative pressure antigrav to tape her retinas.

'I already have her DNA,' says Lipstick.

'Good.' I close my biological scanner (I am beginning to feel dizzy) and risk addressing our prospective agent while monovisual, my sight overwhelmed by the cavernous reticula of her eyes' posterior walls. 'You realize, of course, that if you fail video footage of your little nocturnal peccadillos will be sent to Meta authorities in Bangkok along with appropriate and incontrovertible identification?'

'I can' help. I can' help if I'm girlcat!' My prosthesis returns and re-implants itself.

'Martian technology,' I explain with a smile, tapping the eye back into place. 'Where would we be without it?'

'You're amongst friends,' says Lipstick, 'we're all sex criminals here. You'll be safe aboard the *Sardanapalus*.'

'I wan' be like you, Lipstick,' says the girl, an unwilling suspension of disbelief, this, a sudden, strained autostylization to persuade herself that she craves nothing so much as the destruction of her own species and, perforce, of herself and her god. 'I do, *jing-jing*!' And then to me: 'I believe you good man, sir. Lipstick tell me. You wan' kill Lilim, all Lilim, all girl in universe. I know you have good heart.' I have the perverse desire to say, 'Not at all, little chit. The simple fact is that I'm mad, quite mad.'

Yes; we marauders are really all quite, quite barking. After all, had we not thought, at the outset of our journey, that the *Sardanapalus*, travelling in a closed timelike loop, would, after circumnavigating the universe, arrive back at Earth in violation of causality, effect preceding cause? At worst our other selves, the past selves we'd crossed the universe to meet, might have had to repeat what had already been done: the sex murder of the universe.

How ignorant we were of Martian physics!

In this 1994, there had been no media coverage of the *Sardanapalus*'s embarkation into deep space and infamy, no *Reuters* report stating: 'More than a dozen Elohim have turned marauder and commandeered a Martian starship with the intention, as their leader Mephisto has announced, of "destroying the female principle of the universe." Blasting out yesterday from Nongkhai, a small town in north-east Thailand, the ship, an old interplanetary model, is not thought capable of exceeding CTL speed.'

There had been no 'other selves'.

The universe, at our point of arrival back at the moment we had set forth, had split into two. One where we were beginning our journey, one where we were arriving.

Had it not been for the forethought of our *Käpitan*, Mephisto, I and my fellow marauders would be faced with the prospect of having to repeat our mission, to circumnavigate again and again an infinity of parallel universes, each time exterminating the female of our species, the killing never to stop; and the hope that had sustained me for close to a millennium, that my sister, in some world untainted by Meta's seed, might live again, would itself have been exterminated.

But, on Doriminu, Mephisto had stolen The Toxicophilous Device, otherwise known as The Reality Bomb. And possession of that doomsday machine changes everything.

Ah. I so want it all to end. Time and space, my species, my god. And I will make it end, I promise, the dawn after the night after this. I promise, Primavera, I promise . . .

I lean across the table, reach out and stroke an amber-olive cheek (high-voltage discharge of girl-meat, so unlike that of a human's; this is like touching a photograph, a virtual thing, *'electric flesh'*, you might say; oh save us, Lilith, from the too-literalness of humankind, the *literal* that is the antithesis of intimacy; oh save us, Lilith, say the righteous Dead, from the desexualized cruel, from the *obscene*); and then I run my hand through the length of her Coca-Cola-tinted hair. Slipping my fingers between the puffy, leg-o'-mutton sleeves, I relish the childish, bony clavicles; slipping into the recesses of her low-cut voile frock (to encounter a nestled amulet of Queen Kali XIII), I squeeze a breast, tweak a nipple. A pustule bursts. Oh. *Lupus superfemina.* So that's the way the money goes.

'You have weasels?' She doesn't reply; but I look at my hand, its brilliant inky stains of Lilim-psoriasis; put my hand to my mouth; lick. My jaw goes limp, my prehensile tongue loosens, my fangs almost extend; and I have to think about bridge duty on the *Sardanapalus,* the bad coffee and endless games of Tetris; the hours when, shooting up with serotonin and dimethoxyphenylethylamine to relieve the ennui, to keep my mind turned-on, tuned-in to Meta, my eyes have strained to resolve the hypnagogic images of corridors, fever-dream corridors replicating, endless, endless. *A girl comes around a corner grasping her breasts; she looks at me, frowns, then gazes down, first at one breast and then at the other as blood starts to leak through her fingers . . .*

Was that Lalande 21185? Was it Omicron-2? Was it Barnard's?

And then I inhale, deep, deep; I vacuum the mark's essence into my nostrils and brain. Her scent, her allure, I decide, is full of treachery, a Viet Cong kind of smell (TV memories of summary bellyings in the US Embassy compound in Saigon; Primavera watching, rabid, phosphordot-eyed); but it is a smell that is full of innocence, too; is there enough of the *naïf* in this chit, this amateur traitress for me to offer a recommendation that we use her in our plan of attack? She hasn't (yet) imbibed sufficient quantities of the old crème de menthe to turn her eyes luminous green (though those half-a-dozen splinters of emerald glass in her irises betoken that she is begging at least *one* Elohim for mercy); she's a weekending fellatrix; an apprentice cat; can she, perhaps (her metasexuality not yet *that* perverted), be trusted to act in her own interest rather than for the *frisson* of treachery-for-treachery's sake? Lipstick has reported that she is something of a favourite. The captain of the Imperial Guard is sweet on her. And so is the Empress, it seems. She could prove useful, provide a chink of pregnability, the hey presto, boys, come on in. But the Thais are an incomprehensible race. (Fascination is, I remind myself, not yet quite *white*.) That smile of hers—it could be the smile of a well-behaved child or it could be the smile of a starlet, a *nang-ek* on a *la-kon* TV show, a soap opera in which the sweet, placatory expression of the juvenile heroine might at any moment be transformed into the rictus of an hysterical tantrum. *Nota Bene*: check out those Charlotte Corday peepers. I need to think; I must distinguish *naïf* from *faux-naïf*. Mephisto is paranoid about double agents. And this operation will be our most difficult. Not some casual massacre of a poorly guarded off-world colony, but a commando raid on the capital of the Empire itself. Mephisto, Tyr, Abaddon, me—so few of us left . . . I must beware prejudice, but I cannot afford to discount my suspicions.

'If you inform on us, your Elohim will know you have fed on men beyond your prescribed killing grounds. You realize, of course, what that would mean?' The mark crosses her legs, jealous thighs pressed tight.

'Mandatory death sentence,' says Lipstick. Gun starts to chuckle again (a kind of Martian *Hut, hut, hut, hut*—'Red Riding Hood, Red Riding Hood,' he laughs), my little metal man, my transformer, my tinker toy champing at the prospect of folding himself outwards from hyperspace to be revealed as the Elohim's weapon of choice. But I am his seigneur, and I stare him down.

'*Kow-jy, kow-jy,*' she says quickly, 'I tell you already I can *do*. I help, don' worry. I no *goh-hok*.'

Yes, I suspect little Fascination *is* telling the truth. She will scramble down the abandoned, half-completed subway system that runs below the *quartier interdit*, she will lead us through the access hatch in Chakra Bong Road, hour before dawn, the purple hour when Lilim are at their most vulnerable, will act as our guide to the sanctum sanctorum which conceals the font of the multiverse, The Chapel of The Presence, the only point in space-time where, according to Mephisto, The Reality Bomb will have any effect.

'You *will* help us,' I say, against my *own* will sounding like a vaudeville mesmerist, bio-feedback activating the fractal program in my prosthesis, its iris beginning to whirlpool, worlds within worlds. And then, conscious of a certain grotesqueness in my manner, I close my eyes, shake my head, re-assume the cool, *nouveau fasciste* aesthetic of the fashion-conscious marauder.

'Run along,' I say, 'Lipstick will be in contact to let you know of our decision.' And I add as an off-hand afterthought: 'That is, whether we should let you be publicly executed, put to the knife as you kneel on miniver'—both girls wince, cross, re-cross their legs—'or, perhaps, be cooked alive to be served as an entrée for your good-as-gold Elohim,' (for such is the fate of those condemned to death, a fate institutionalized since Roman times: to serve in the circus, or as bread), 'or whether,' I continue, 'we should let you live with us on the *Sardanapalus.*'

'Where life,' Lipstick adds, 'is all *luxe, calme et volupté.* Do as Lord Dagon says,' (my officious little PA now concluding the interview with a wink, a nod), 'I'll meet you for breakfast at the *Melià*, as we discussed before.' Yes, I think; that'll give me time to contact my *Käpitan* by ansible. ('Mackie Messer, calling, Mackie Messer calling, have I got news for *you . . .*') I have to make a decision soon; Mephisto is insistent that we attack within forty-eight hours. A strange coincidence that the final battle will take place on my birthday, the day I slip from one nine hundred and ninety nine to a round millenarian. Strange and fitting, I think.

Flushed, defeated, the treacherous girl-child returns to the rumpus of the dance floor.

'What an incomparable blackmailer you are,' I say. And yes, I think, what a truly incomparable fetish-object. She is looking at me with half-lidded I-need-to-be-punished eyes, the bright green irises almost bioluminescent in *The V.Berg*'s carefully staged half light.

'Dance with me, Archangel?' The band comes on, reb-Martian boys in studded leather jackets displaying the symbol of teen Martian angst:

'I hate Martians,' I say.

'I think the best thing to do is just to hate everybody. That way you know where you stand.'

'What about your friends?'

'They're people you just hate a little less.' Oh, she's such a cat, such a cat, such a girlygirly cat; for her, *lurve* is an off-colour joke; for me too, perhaps. Perhaps. But, just the same, I *lurve* her cruelty. 'Oh c'mon,' she says, 'these are my *favourite* Martians. They're called *The Sex Disease Protégé.*'

Lipstick is domesticated, but tonight she's off her leash, and sometimes the old alley cat stirs in her, the sex traitress, and I have to hone my wits, be at my pit-bull best. I well know how the idea of being a double agent puckers some girls' pussies. (Consider: why do we call a vampire gone spermaholic a cat? The metaphors of milk and cream, perhaps? [Thus the modern euphemism 'lactomania'?] Is it an allusion to a cat's mythic, selfish, spiteful nature [so many cats becoming traitresses with, indeed, some psychiatrists, such as Jean Piaget, arguing that addiction to fellatio is a *prerequisite* to betrayal]? Is it because the eyes of some Lilim, drunk on the strange semen of their Elohim masters, have a tendency to turn green, an unnaturally bright, perverse green, as if they evinced the calibrations of a second, more fateful metamorphosis? Is it a reference to the ancient instrument of execution known as 'The Sphinx', so called because of the position the victim was obliged to assume *in extremis*? [See entry in The Children's Encyclopaedia, Plate I: Arnold Böcklin's *The Sphinx*. Plate II: The Great Sphinx, at Giza, 2680–2565 BL, with a Lilim's head, the body of a lioness. Note the great obelisk—called 'Cleopatra's needle' and representing the 'bellyspike'—rising from the small of the sphinx's back.] Or is it, more simply, more crudely, that 'cat' has been synonymous throughout Meta's history, [or so the archaeologists inform us] with numerous slang terms for the pudendum, that is cat = cunt? a catgirl being a reviled, despised 'cuntgirl'?)

A heavy metal riff cranks up, a poor man's Guns 'n' Roses; pocketing my own gun, I let Miss Cruella, my princess, my pet, my sick, sick Doriminian rose lead me into the pseudo-religious mania of the throng.

CHAPTER FOUR

Pavane Pour Une Princesse Perfide

The crowd parts like the Red Sea. It's not a pop-eyed, fearful 'Holy Moses! We got *Elohim* here!' that does it; it's not even *greng-jai,* the feudalistic 'awe-heart' that Thais show to those they perceive to be their social superiors (there aren't too many Thais on the dance floor); it's something closer to admiration, or perhaps, a more commonplace human envy.

I sometimes find it amusing to pass amongst humans as an imitation of Elohim, a superman play-acting at being a human play-acting at being a superman. It's not too difficult, a lot of these wannabes having submitted to radical surgery to give them that teenage-Methuselah, thousand-year-old 'dead thing' look. Admiration? Envy? I give-out. I'm a Meta homeboy. A gangsta. A kid again, with Mephisto my role model. No peacock strut this; I'm a sparrow hawk, a chicken hawk; and I give them my avian, Hitchcockian stare. Yeah, envy. Sometimes guys buy me a drink, then, with a discreet cough, ask for the address of my doctor.

My hair, like the hair of all my sex, is grey, cut short and spiky, like a punk-Roman Caesar's; gunmetal grey too, my eyes, but unwrinkled, like the rest of my lean ('mantis-like' is the gossip columnists' bitchy appellation, but I will say *'lean'*) boyish face (though if you studied that demeanour long enough you would wonder how a man who looked in his teens, or, at most, in his mid- to late-twenties could have such a dead, colour-coordinated complexion, flesh tending to a deeper grey than hair and eyes, a lizard's flesh, flesh like the parchment of incunabula, a necronomicon made from the flayed skins of the damned).

I put a hand through my crop (that tic all Elohim share), smoothing down my ash-grey bristles; compose myself before mingling with my public. Elohim, it sometimes seems to me, are as narcissistic as their sisters (and certainly as solipsistic, Meta being a self-consuming, implosive god); I grin, tipping a finger to my forehead in a jaunty, self-congratulatory salute.

The dance is the *Hut-tut-rut!,* the latest human reworking of the old Meta dom-sub routine called the *Noblesse Oblige,* and I find myself standing monolithically still, in high-tension *attenshun,* stiff in my Casino Royale attire, public clothes still successfully concealing the pubic, while Lipstick uses me like some kind of go-go pole, a set of fingernails digging into my nape, or clawing at my lapels, sugar-pink bootlets (with their gimlet-exquisite six inches of heel) wimbling away at the underlit floor, all the while her body undulating against me to the accompaniment of little flicks of her tongue, working her way up and down, down and up my torso.

I look down at her in contempt, my whole body tumescent, unappeasable, head, torso, arms and legs in riotous sympathy with a penis hard as rock; a penis harder, indeed, than it has been for a thousand years, my permanent, intransigent erection growing in exponential relation to my cruelty, a penis that is now, surely, a googolplex of a penis. A penis[100].

No respite for the wicked.

We're wolves, wolves, wolves, n-no we don't need no full moon
We wanna love you kitties from m-midnight to high noon
Wanna be your sex asylum, wanna be your lover's sim
Wanna save from the kisses of those bad, bad Elo-him.

Run to Mars, run to Mars,
You can find a n-nice hideaway,
Run to Mars, run to Mars
my pretty little runaway,
Run to Mars, run to Mars
or you're a dead giveaway
Run to Mars, run to Mars (EOWEEEEEEEEEE!),
my little runaway.

Run to China, run to Oz, run to Russia, run, run, run,
But remember there are s-some boys who will welcome your
     con-ta-*gion*
Wanna save you, help you, be you, wanna help your mouth get laid
Wanna learn to say 'I love you' with the point of a switch*blade.*

Run to Mars, run to Mars,
You can find a n-nice hideaway.

Accolade[3]. 'Succubus, succubus!' shout the boys, 'Incubus, incubus!' the girls. And then, as the band's vocalist approaches the edge of the stage, *'Hut-tut-rut! Hut-tut-rut!'*

I put an arm about Lipstick's corseted waist (fingers playing with the grommets, the laces, stroking the whalebone stays) and think, How pathetic, these evangelicals, how sad.

Monsieur le rock star says: 'Lilith take on our sins! For 10,000 years Earth has enjoyed the grace of Meta. Now it is our turn! War, famine, cruelty, rape, murder—are these not as much Mars's inheritance as Earth's? Then let us find salvation in the sexualization of our wretched psyches! Renunciation, no way! Transfiguration, okay! Meta's grace, children, Meta's grace! Lilith, oh Lilith, Our Lady, Our Mistress—make us psychoids too!'

A green-faced wild child is handing out leaflets which set out the old argument that Lilim/Elohim are descended from Martians, citing cave paintings, such as those at Lascaux, of Earth girls fellating green-skinned Martian astronauts to prevent themselves being impregnated and facing the wrath of their tribe. (Other cave paintings, such as those found at Tuc l'Audubert and the Trois Frères cave in France, depicting 'Earth Mothers' writhing on primitive execution machines, their bellies pierced by flint spears, their aborted foetuses eaten, also grace the pamphlets' covers.)

Was the guilt of these prehistoric victims established by the fact that they had green eyes? The Venus of Willendorf has chips of malachite in her eyes.

Guilt. Martians have such a terrible *guilt* complex. (Or so they would have us believe.) During our last Ice Age, they say, overpopulation on their home planet drove many Martians to Earth. Their planet's resources exhausted, a cult of cannibalism had thrived, a cult that represented the resurgent irrationalism that (so Martians are ever ready to remind us) is always concomitant with the sophistication of a newly technocratic culture. Our pre-history, they say, was infected by their post-historical *mythos,* the information overload of a humanoid people who had recently ventured into space in order to survive. We are, they say, their 'fallen selves', the bastard offspring of their piratical adventuring during a time when their emergent high-tech civilization was beggared by internecine passions, when superstition and cultism had become partners with science and pseudoscience to expedite and excuse the culling of their own population (superstition and cultism they say we have inherited), a time when they wantonly raped the solar system of its resources, both organic and inorganic, before—their civilization growing older, wiser, and learning remorse—they withdrew to their own planet, there to abide, self-quarantined, until, detecting signs on Earth that presaged the development of technologies that might compete with their own, they again made contact, in friendship, they say, though *I* say to keep us, who to them represent the evils of their ancestors, in our place; to control us; to send us off-world to form colonies in other star systems where we (who rely on Martian transport) cannot pose a contiguous threat; to depopulate Earth; to emasculate Meta, whose male children guard human and Lilim alike, and so take the prize they most desire: Gaia herself.

Do they themselves believe their own propaganda? It is certainly a convenient myth—this notion of Mars expiating the sins of its fathers—and it is a myth regularly invoked to explain their paternalistic interference in Earth's affairs. The truth is, no one knows the origins of Meta; Lilith herself spoke little of our genesis, though we Elohim and Lilim believe that Meta has always existed, was gestating in the cosmic egg before the beginnings of time (though these days history, both known and unknown, seems to have been condensed into the late twentieth century; a trick of the mind, perhaps, a perceptual illusion suffered by one who has too long laboured to bring time and space to an end).

Suffice to say: Meta is the Demiurge; all else is conjecture.

The speech proceeds, becomes garbled, hysterical, as people stamp their feet Moon Stomp-wise and chant '*Hut*', '*Tut*' and '*Rut!*' in antiphon 'Hut' 'Tut' 'Rut'. Sex-death.

These children, of course, are right to protest, to seek transcendence and freedom; Martian culture is so hypocritical, so life-denying; it tries to control the dark side of the cosmic libido not so much with refutation as with refusal, a disallowance that translates into *loveless* cruelty.

But—as these *les enfants* are demonstrating—all that separates Mars from Earth is the extent of the former's hypocrisy; Mars, surely, on the Day of Reckoning, will be destroyed along with the Demiurge. Both worlds supply the right culture for the disease, Martian control mechanisms a perfect breeding ground for my sickness, (my god); soon, Mars will be raising its own ziggurats, demarcating its own interdictions. Only me, my fellow marauders and The Reality Bomb stand in Meta's way.

These reb-Martian wannabes—don't they know that by embracing the Demiurge they merely exchange one tyranny for another? Prisoners of the castle of conscience, they would become prisoners of the castle of murders, negative mirror images of the humane.

Meta is just another system of control.

We are all slaves.

The next number, the cock-rock impersonation giving way to street-rut lyricism, is slow and smoochy—a *Venus in Furs* doomy wall of sound— and soon I'm kissing my little catgirl's plump whore's lips and she's trying to suck my tongue from my mouth, to eat it, all the time greedily swallowing my saliva; my hand—obliged no more—strays to her rump, her stockinged thighs, then slips between them.

Mushy luxuriousness of fungus (fleshfungi, like weasels, tending to group about the primary and secondary sexual characteristics). 'You forgot your merkin,' I say, 'foolish Rapunzel.' She shrugs. 'Many a merkin makes a mickle,' I remind her.

But Lipstick is Lipstick is Lipstick.

I squeeze her trash. Oh, she is so irresistibly venereal. But I smile—and I try to make it a 'nice' smile—no male-female dom-sub thing between us, really, this night. Instead of offering a reply she presses her cheek against my shoulder. I think she is crying.

> We kill with our libidinous blows
> the high-heeled innocents rigged up as whores
> and cruelly grope with tiny dark maidens
> in so many back alleys . . .

I wipe a tear from her cheek. 'Sometimes,' she says, 'sometimes I don't want to be a psychoid. I don't want to be Lilim. I want to be real.'

'You can't be *unreal*—you wouldn't be able to cry.'

'As Tweedledum said, I hope you don't think these are real tears?'

No bravado now. To strangers she will say: 'I liked being a vampire; I like being a cat. And treachery's just too sexy for words.' But to me, sometimes, she confides her dreams. A dead thing always has its impossible ridiculous dreams of being real.

Slow and smoochy, the music enfolds us, time-meltingly, tripping us helter-skelteringly through a morbid pavane . . .

Again, I hold my sister in my arms, my sweet little Primavera, comforting her after she has caught her finger in a door jamb, or fallen and grazed her knee.

We run across the marshes, through the colonnades of the parklands and gardens, the grounds landscaped by Capability Brown; our demesne awaits us, the grey stone and slate roofs, the towers and chimneys of Misère, its limitless corridors, its libraries, its mothballed ballrooms and dining halls, the hidden, windowless rooms where my father will retreat, his growing silences filling our vast ancestral home like the echoes of other silences, the dumb ghosts of those who, like him, had been struck down by the family curse, who, like him, had sired strange children.

Sometimes, in the middle of the night, we hear our father walking the corridors, alone, the castle echoing with his sandpapery coughs. Sometimes, in the respite given his disintegrating lungs, he seems to be talking to himself; sometimes, crying.

Does father love us? His bitterness is not, perhaps, directed at our metamorphoses but at what is making us metamorphose. His cursed semen. Himself.

Primavera has invented a nickname for me: I am the 'Archangel Gabriel'. I will wipe away, she says, *all* our sorrows.

'Martians are feeble,' our peripatetic tutor reminds us as we walk through the grounds, 'strangers to animality. Never feel inferior to them. They are corrupt, too. It is you and your kind who are the true rulers of this world. Through you, masters may become slaves, and slaves masters. Through you, men may become free. Remember: the basic rapport between sentient beings is one of violence. But Meta transforms this violence with passion and love. You, my children, are our redeemers.

'Man cannot be other than what he is: a sick beast, a devil. Despite his achievements and his aspirations, he will continue to commit the most remarkable of atrocities upon his own and other kinds. Only through Meta may Man overcome his destiny; only through Meta may he learn to live with cruelty and death; for in Meta, cruelty and death are eroticized, evil is affirmed.

'Without Meta, Man is condemned to banality, the twin prisons of his callous heart and skull, to passion without beauty, cruelty without love, death without truth and sex.'

On my bedroom wall, a poster of a Martian saucer hovering over London, 1837. 'William Herschel,' says our tutor, 'in 1781, detected the first signs of life on Mars; and in 1830 the German astronomer William Beer observed phenomena linked to what we now know were Martian starships returning to their home planet from interstellar space: the warping of space-time by FTL engines.' Our tutor shrugs his shoulders; sighs. 'They seduced us with promises of power and empire.'

The Martians, he says, had chosen Great Britain as their go-between since they perceived, correctly, that it was in England that the Industrial Revolution was furthest advanced. Soon, London had supplanted Rome—as Bangkok has now supplanted London—as the capital of the world and chief citadel of Meta, the British Empire spreading the bane of Martian ideology throughout the Asias, the Americas, Africa, Oceania and Antarctica, the info-rich North dominating the then info-poor South.

'In 1897, Victoria XXXII was the first Empress to be proclaimed, not only Empress of Meta, but Empress of the Known Universe, Mars having in that year loaned the Empire the first FTL starships by which Meta might colonize the galaxy.

'At Zvyozdny Gorodok, Star City, the colonists set forth . . .'

At first, I fail to heed these lectures, to recognize their import; I have, at that time, a certain respect for Martians; my best toys, after all, are always *Made On Mars.* It is thus that I discover early through a not untypical boyish greed—my face metaphorically pressed to the window of the Martian toy shop—how much we Terrans covet Martian technology, how much we are prepared to sell ourselves, our bodies, our minds, even if it means accepting Martian 'humanism', conceding our wild selves (wild bodies and wilder minds) to the straitjackets of their alien ideas.

I begin to take greater heed of our tutor's lessons. 'The cyberization of the Earth began a long time ago; we didn't need Martian technology to achieve it. Mars accuses us of techno-sclerosis; but it was always our ideas that made us half-mechanical and made us beautiful *objets.* "Man", as we still call him, died a long time ago, along with any notions we Terrans might have had that coincide with Mars's perspective on God and the divine. For us, God is real, but absent. Meta is our "real". Meta is what we have, here and now, in this world. It is our salvation, and we scorn that Higher God of the Pleroma sitting affectless on his throne in that superuniverse beyond this universe of ours, unknowable, careless of our pain.

'Listen to me, children: this accommodation with Mars, it is bad, bad: drunk on their technology, their commodities, we forget who we are, abandon our world to sexless horror, passionless war, cold, frigid brutality, rob it of that which has made life bearable for 10,000 years: Meta, that god who is *you*, who flows through your veins.'

The delirium begins. My sister, at eleven, has the voluptuous body of a woman, though her beauty is not womanly, but rather a subversion of womanhood, a black joke at womanhood's expense. (She is becoming woman as construct, woman as *girl.*) At dinner, when nobody is looking, she extends her fangs, steel and enamel glinting in the light of a *torchère* (she has recently had a brace fitted); snaps at me like a petulant lapdog. The butler averts his eyes. Later she says: 'Let's kill Mum and Dad and take the Bentley and get out of here and drive to the ends of the night.' Is she serious? Of course. We are turning into psychoids. Hormones rage and so too does the algolagnia.

On TV Lilim-wannabes strut across a stage in PVC thigh boots to the accompaniment of Lee Hazlewood's 'These Boots Are Made for Walking'. I suffer a *petit mal.* Later, as I fall asleep, Primavera turns to me and whispers: 'One of these days these boots are gonna walk all over *you.*'

Neurasthenia. Bouts of asthma. Hay fever. Fits. All triggered by the pains of metamorphosis, of puberty. I am beginning to find out that I am only interested in *things;* people don't warrant my attention.

'The body is an artificial construct as much as the soul,' says our tutor.

'An individual is contingent. That is why you are changing, Gabriel. The cognitive virus that is Meta is overthrowing the society of your body, just as it has overthrown the society of your mind: it is deconstructing your body so that you may be reinvented: as a superman, as Meta, the god itself.'

One night, Mama, reading *Peter Pan*, shows me an illustration. My eyes fall upon Wendy, mortally wounded by an arrow that projects from her left breast.

I am frightened of my father. I think he would rather have me dead than a psychoid. I will do anything, say anything, to placate him. He spends his days in his *Wunderkammer* playing with his antique, priceless toys, dolls and puppets he prefers to the company of his daughter and son. Sometimes he makes us pose for photographs; sometimes, we have to pose nude. Why does Mama always take his side? *'Let's kill Mum and Dad and take the Bentley and get out of here and drive to the ends of the night.'*

But Primavera is braver than me.

I seek refuge in the garden; at night, it is peaceful; my father no longer disturbs me there. At least, not at night. If I am frightened of my father, he is increasingly becoming frightened of me.

And sometimes in the cold winter evenings I take Primavera down to the Thames; we loiter at Frog's island and Old Man's Head.

These memories; like Chinese boxes, like the hidden rooms in Misère, filled with secrets, shame; my grandmother and grandfather who, until the age of eleven, I did not know to exist; the forbidden libraries, galleries, the cracked marbles, stuccoes and friezes of dust-shrouded salons that lay behind concealed doors, the paintings by Old Masters on the walls of the abandoned West Tower, paintings such as Rubens's *Descent from the Cross,* pillaged from Antwerp Cathedral.

These memories, all of my inner life. Of the outside world I remember little. Remembering her, I am like a child again, with no sense of beginning, middle and end, unable to impose narrative upon my sense impressions; and if my mind is not completely blank, a featureless tundra—which it should be, with its time-dilated ten centuries of service—it is only because of the insistence, the richness of that other, secret life, that shadow life wherein I feel my true life, my true self, to have been nurtured; that shadow life amongst the shadows of Castle Misère, our ancestral home on the Rainham Marshes, prison-palace where we grew up, crazed and perverted; Misère, where nothing was innocent, nothing profane; grew up within its granite, espaliered walls, amongst shadows cast by drowsy autumn suns, amongst shadow-filled, panelled corridors hung with Holbeins, Van Dycks, Lelys, the faces of our ancestors looking down at us, sometimes mockingly, it seemed, sometimes approvingly, with eyes that were often grey, often green, always mad.

I'm crushing Lipstick against my chest. She's wincing at the bandoleers concealed beneath my dicky as we dance around and around in giddier and giddier circles. And I'm looking up at the ceiling of *The V.Berg,* this whole nightclub modelled on the interior decor of the ziggurats, those nymphenbergs that impose themselves and our will upon the Earth, its colonies, one day, perhaps, if we of the *Sardanapalus* fail, to impose themselves upon Mars itself, that bastion of 'humanism' and would-be remoulder of our existence, each palace in each nation's capital identical, imaging Meta's sterile replication, the cycle of life born to be killed, killed in order that it might live.

The V.Berg's dance floor represents the vast inner quad of a ziggurat, that parterre where Lilim promenade, exchange gossip, indulge their inbred exhibitionism; accordingly, the movie-house balconies mirror the tiers of boudoirs which rise up, level after level, to meet at the ziggurat's summit, that apex where penthouses accommodate Governesses, Secretaries, Maids, Imperial Guard and other staff of the Colonial Service, and where, here in Bangkok at the heart of empire, The Chapel of The Presence stands, daring heaven. At that pinnacle, I imagine the Queen of Queens, the Empress herself, gazing up at the lurid frescoes that surely decorate the cupola of that shrine. Frescoes similar, perhaps, to those on *The V.Berg's* dome: representations of the Creation, of Adam and his first wife, Lilith, his second wife, Eve; Lilith and the serpent; Lilith cast into the wilderness, to become the consort of Satan, the Morning Star; Lilith's reincarnation, her teachings, her death and the deaths of the apostles, saints and martyrs, memories and myths becoming indistinguishable, now, as I too study these minacious representations, the martyred faces of the past superimposed upon the contorted eyes, lips, cheeks of the victims of a future from which I have returned, a future that has always been now, now, now.

Lipstick gives me a hard, searching look. 'Do you want to kill?' she asks. She slides a thigh against my own, and I feel the conductivity through my h-fash trousers, my Meta-fash leather strides. 'I can find you someone.'

Her perfume's mid-notes are chocolate and caramel and (really, tonight she's so 'pink', such a little confection), down there, *la-dessous,* sharpening my candyphile appetite, way down deep, amongst the base notes of musk, civet, ambergris and castoreum, is the unmistakable erotomane's tipple of *vanilla.*

'Really,' she says, 'really I can.' Her voice belies her self-assurance; it is tremulous. I can feel the girlquake in her belly; seismic activity that threatens to raze her to the floor. Elohim are built on affectless steel frames. So why am I bracing myself, as if for the Big One? 'There's an alley out the back. And I know a girl who'll . . .'

'No more killing, no more sex death,' I say. 'In a few days, the pain, the cruelty—it will all be as if it had never been.' Again, I feel her chest heave with a sob. 'There, there. It will all end soon,' I say, stroking her magnificent blonde mane, a hint of viciousness tempering my consolation, for sex death or no, I am a bad, bad man, the killer of hundreds, thousands, millions of young girls, 'soon, soon, soon.' Her mascara has run and her spiteful-fairy's eyes are blotchy with silent weeping. 'I promise.'

But only if Mephisto is right, I think, only if The Toxicophilous Device is what he claims it to be; and only if it can be successfully deployed. If not—

Earth is *infested* with Lilim, nymphenbergs in every megalopolis of every country, every continent, wherever human blood flows and human DNA, inveigled, complicit, awaits subversion. Without The Reality Bomb, it would take us a long, long time to complete the extermination; and then, of course, we would have to start again, marauding across interstellar space, liquidating the meta-Meta colonies of meta-Alpha Centauri, meta-Sirius, meta-Tau Ceti, meta-61 Cygni, Vega, on towards the meta-heartland of the meta-Sagittarian systems, and into the meta-beyond.

'I hope so, Archangel,' she says, 'I'm tired of all the dying.' But given the choice between a lifetime of bondage or death, a feral animal, whether wolf or cat, will always choose to die. There can be no compromise. 'I so want it to end.'

Such is this life in Meta (such has it always been), so mercilessly dreamlike, so fantastically rueless, that my kind is constantly, monomaniacally thinking upon The End, the longed-for end of *oneself* as well as of her, her, her, her, her and her. But please, Lilith, please don't let it end so for *her* (I find myself praying): she's my bitch. I love her. I love her madly. There's no 'perhaps'.

'Life for us *is* to die,' I say in despair, for I know Lilith is no intercessor of mercy. Lipstick looks up at me, acceptance in her eyes. I kiss her on her forehead (and though I've no appetite my eyes stray to the opulent bosom [the Thais have a phrase, *gin len,* 'eating for fun'] and I have to constrain my urge to bite, such excellent victuals, such deliciousness).

My catgirl on my arm, I walk swooningly through the swaying, smooching crowd (I feel as if I've caught an aftershock from Lipstick's own entrails), my thoughts a-swirl with the immanence of our first raid on the mother planet, here, in this country where I had been imprisoned after my first criminal adventures a millennium ago; a raid that has to be our last.

'Let's go back to the hotel,' I say. 'I have to contact Mephisto.'

'There's a back door,' says Lipstick, prudent.

I slip; recover. I have accidentally stepped on a miniature pet phallus; it squeals like a rubber toy and scurries between its owner's feet; a pedigree job, glossy-coated, fully-veined, its beady eyes (set on either side of the glans) glance at me with momentary, almost sapient, recognition. The tiny teeth inside the meatus snap. And then its owner tugs at its diamanté collar and it scampers away on gonadal claws.

'I had a pet once,' my bitch-cake reminisces, dreamily. 'His name was "Tosher".' Her nails screech as she pulls her own claws down the back of my silk jacket (claws antithetical to any phallic pet's longevity; claws, doubtless, that played some part in Tosher's demise). 'Poor Tosher.'

We squeeze through a musty press of tellurian bodies; the dance floor fibrillates, the dancers like trampolinists, some of these dance routines new to me, demotic, more influenced by human monomanias than any routines *I* can recall.

Been away a long, long time.

Some swing-dressed girls—they're humans, they're *funkeiras*—are shaking their hips *Mardi Gras*-style, shook ilia at the blur-point of ten beats to the second, hands successively held behind their heads, then crossed behind their backs, the routine reversed and repeated each time the band completes a riff. Other girls are suspended from their partners in surrogate-rape attitudes, boys holding girls by their rumps, swollen codpieces pressed to damp cachettes (slimmer, masculine hips vainly attempting to emulate the pelvic frenzy of the *funkeiras*), girls' legs to either side of the boys' upper thighs, mock-violated torsos limp, arched backwards, wriggling in simulated resistance, hair whipping the floor, wrists crossed behind backs, as if tied. (Some girls even have the hilts of SFX knives protruding from their umbilici, fake bloodstains—improvised with lipstick, rouge or ketchup—staining their dirndlkleids.)

Amidst this orgy of vicarious death and dying I recognize Candy and Mandy, or Candski and Mandski (this town full of Slav genes, fifth generation Star City kids), too human to be truly beautiful, but still images of the Plastic Venus in their fashion excrescence of underwear as outerwear, their latex girdle skirts, school of Versace and Gaultier; still beautiful if maculate hybrids of whore and child.

Slavic eyes look on, optic safety valves that leak uncontainable fury, these dollymopping *devushkas* having a rough time of it with so many real-time *licks* for *nix*, so many cats giving it away gratis.

Clear of the dancers, the torturers and torturees, we pass beneath a sign:

DRINKING BLOOD FROM
A WILLING PARTNER, THOUGH LEGAL,
IS MEDICALLY RISKY
HEALTH DEPARTMENT WARNING

I shoo away a young boy hawking T-shirts emblazoned with silk-screened prints of famous wannabes: Issei Sagawa, who ate Renee Hartevelt in 1981 (a meal celebrated by The Rolling Stones—hear *Too Much Blood*); Nancy Spungen, who died from a half-inch knife wound to the lower abdomen in the Chelsea Hotel.

Lipstick takes my hand, leads me beneath the bright red EXIT, past toilets where dealers push H, DMT, solvents, *ya ma* (I could do with a shot of dimethoxyphenylethylamine, I think, need that stuff these days like a diabetic needs insulin). A little white box—of what? tea money? plutonium 239?—changes hands between a tuxedoed bouncer (a Russian hard man, a Charles Manson lookalike [The Son of Charles] a real *krutoy chelovek*) and a bodyguard for some biznizman, politico or army type. Kill them all, I think, kill them all, all, all.

A Martian leatherboy exposes himself, says 'Gimme the allure, baby, gimme the *allure*,' that word describing the gallimaufry of narcotic saliva, pheromones chemical, chimerical and psychic, that are present in the physiology of Lilim and to which Martians are hopelessly (and these days so often despairingly) immune, convergent evolution not yet going so far as to override replicators that have a different molecular basis to DNA. '*Neverbe*', I scoff, raising a contemptuous eyebrow, even though I know Meta has him targeted. Lipstick, with equal disdain, flashes wet dream visuals; spits.

And then we're down a flight of stairs, she a Duchamplike blur, all tumbling hair, coltish legs and gyrating pelvis; at the bottom she turns, rump-bumps the bar of the fire door and leads me into a drizzle-washed rat's alley of peeling movie posters, old newspapers, used condoms and disintegrating, bestial turds; I whistle a snatch from Berlioz's *Sardanapalus*.

CHAPTER FIVE

Girls Eat Boys, Boys Eat Girls, Girls Are Toys, Boys Are Churls

One end of the alley is a cul-de-sac, the other leads to the Hua Hin night market, all car-battery-run neon and Christmas-tree lights.

Whiff of steaming cauldrons and woks, of squid and noodles and pungent rat-shit chilli, crackling gridirons suffusing the humid air with what, for humans, must be smells as mouth-watering as the maddening aroma of girl-meat grilled, boiled, fried, roasted, pickled or raw in the ubiquitous banqueting halls that lie deep beneath the world's nymphenbergs.

My prosthetic eye mists; Lipstick giggles; wipes it clean with a lank wad of hair. Her flesh is keening. I can smell her. I know she wants to, needs to, *has* to vampirize me.

Psyched-out, brain flipping the switches from *sado* to *masochism*, I, Lord Dagon, jaded by my crimes, take my human play-acting (albeit such play confined to playtime with my pet) to new heights of caricature.

She arches an eyebrow; ah yes, my plaything likes games, especially this new addition to our repertoire. 'Don't be nervous, human boy. Haven't you ever been in an interdiction?' I go hangdog, discountenanced, abashed.

'I've never been called.' Getting further into my role, I try to mime Anxiety, complete with its capital A. I increase my HR to a foetal-like one-hundred-and-fifty beats per minute; force blood into my cheeks.

Humans are frightened of Lilim; not only because of the psychosomatic *petit mal* sometimes engendered by a Lilim's allure, not only because of religious taboos, but because (perhaps most importantly, this 'because') Elohim protect their sisters (and what they would call their species' 'honour') with a veritable Sicilian jealousy.

'I'm sorry, Lipstick,' I say, still playing the harmless *aitch*, 'I'm not sure if this is a good idea.' And, unaccountably, my accent switches from punk-Wodehousian to a kind of globalized Runyonesque. 'I'm sorta worried I might catch *Meda*.'

'Chance in a thousand,' she says. 'Why do you think Meta gave us this insatiable appetite? We have to bite—well, in *my* case suck—lots and *lotsa* men before the virus finds a germ cell that'll condescend to be a host. It's hard work being a parasite.'

'I suppose I've always wanted to be called,' I say, in a display of servile virility, flattering her pretensions to be a triple-X seductress. 'I suppose I've always wanted to know what it's like to be raped by Lilim.'

'We'll make up for that. Hold me, human boy—not too tight, that's it—let me do everything. Leave it all up to me.' I'm against the alley wall, a garbage can to one side, a parked motorcycle and a stack of empty liquor crates to the right.

She starts rubbing herself against me, her pubis pressed, then grinding, against my hip (masturbation the closest Lilim come to approximating human sexuality, fellatio, for them having metaphysical rather than physical connotations, a masturbation that is inclusive of dressing-up, making-up, studying themselves in pier glasses, posing for photographs, posing to hurt, posing to exist [because for Lilim, existing is to be observed, and to be observed is to wreak anguish and frustration upon the percipient], a masturbation self-condemnatory, a masturbation that is an affirmation of vain, spiteful self-love via the unappeasable *ache* that superfeminine provocativeness induces in 'aitch' and 'superman' alike [though only we Elohim bear that suffering for eternity]); her stockings make sounds of wily susurration as she slides her thighs against my trews; and then, only momentarily distracted by the sight of a leaking prophylactic—eyed covetously—in a puddle beneath her feet, she starts her preamble, her Donna Juana vocal foreplay:

'*Ooo, Mr Human, you're so cruel, please oh please, put me to my knees, let me beg for mercy, I'm a bad girl, really, I belong on my knees, such a bad girl, so rotten, so dirty, oh please, mercy, Mr Human, mercy, please mercy, aagh! I really want you in my mouth, I really want to eat you, cream me, Mr Human, cream me, cream me, pleeeeeeeeeeze!*'

So many times, so many alleys. Loretta, in her hip-slip, beneath the twin purple moons of a world that was all ice-cream parlours and hot summer nights, Loretta St Lillian who called herself Marzipan (or was it Hoovermatic? or was it Lust?); and Desirée and Nancy, a.k.a. Tenderloin and Tiddlywink, nymph and nymphet who, after that party in the slums of Djlahlahlahlahlia, were taken cruising (we were young, Tyr and me—we did things like that then), their metre-length, comet-like hair billowing in the slipstream of my open-topped Mercedes-Benz 1936 bright-red five-seater type 540K Cabriolet (the sort favoured by Nazi leaders), until, coming to the darknesses at the edge of town, we hustled them, with promises of all-night festivities in our *'de luxe, so-decadently louche'* and altogether fictitious bachelor's pad situated in the abandoned offices of a nearby warehouse, into an alley, an alley such as this.

'Mercy, Mr Human, mercy, please mercy, mercy, please . . .'

They all look the same, these alleys: dark, with sheer walls rising to ill-lit, shabbily curtained rooms; fire escapes; mullioned windows; balconies; the caracoles leading, through a jungle of iron latticework, to basements, human squalor and despair.

In this alley, though, there are certain Earth-like novelties: the movie ads fly-sheeted with Xerox-art agitprop, spray-canned pasquinades—real Martian propaganda, this, not reb-greenie Meta-olatry, but stuff about 'human rights' and the like. And over these flyers, a bill for the LITTLE IDIOT THINGS, a Thai-*farang* band popular with Zippies, a fusion crew with a Lilim-wannabe of a chanteuse called Vava Vavoom; it states *'Get Thingified!'*

Ah, but I am already, I think. Ever since I was a little boy playing with Primavera on the Rainham Marshes, I have been a *thing*, a collage, an *objet,* a design classic engineered by Meta Inc., something straight off an assembly line dedicated to reassembling *Man.*

Her arms are around my neck; she kisses me. (A catgirl's 'kiss' is, in effect, a lick, a behavioural leftover from her nights as a bloodsucker when she would stalk those offered-up to the interdiction, biting, infusing the wound with the narcotic anti-coagulant of her saliva, lapping at the red, red wine.)

I flick my tongue across her upper gums, feel the remains of the gingival sheaths which once housed her other cuspids, the fangs long since sequestered by the Lilim tooth fairy (teeth, mind, life—a girl loses them one after the other when she has to learn to beg and drink semen instead of blood); then, abandoning her instinctual, child-like licketty-licks, she draws my tongue into her parasitical mouth, deep throating it into hard vacuum, sucking it avidly, the *hors d'oeuvre* before the phallic feast, and I have to think bland thoughts, bite down as I feel my palatoglossus and styloglossus muscles relaxing, the loosening of the frenulum that attaches my tongue to the floor of my mouth, my powerful genioglossus tense, readying to project that triangle of scarlet leather into natural or man-wrought orifices; I try to hold myself back so that she doesn't suck the full twelve inches down her gullet, suck lips, face, head, shoulders, body, legs, until I disappear into her sex's vengeful maw.

She begins to convulse. I bring my heart rate down, my masturbatory, rocket-boy blush dissolving into the moonscape grey of my *au naturel* complexion.

My cuspids deploy; a breast frees itself from its constraint, and a fang scratches at the areola, impales the nipple, retracts; I taste her allure, the rank allure of the criminal, the bait that Elohim cannot resist.

I release her from my embrace; she falls to her knees, skirt rucked up. Now the human actor retires to the wings. The show's cancelled. The mask comes off. 'What are you?' I ask.

'A girl.'

She lowers her head, regards her sterile, damned genitalia. Fingernails that have tangled in elflocks of pubic hair, breaking, snapping off at the cuticle, have left her merkinless fleece decorated with fire-engine red shards of uprooted keratin.

'You enjoy betraying your brothers. Feeding on humans beyond the interdiction. Undermining the Empire of Meta. What *are* you,' I repeat; and, in a whisper, in a self-accusatory lisp as she bows lower until her forehead touches the ground—no point, really, of her pretending she's from Quality Street, that she's a Mme Récamier, a Mme De Staël—she says:

'*Cunt.*'

The word becomes flesh, and the world, the whole rapeable, girlygirl world, becomes cunt, waiting for its sex death.

It's my instinctual self emerging now, the program that keeps our parasitic species from overbreeding, from decimating the gene pool of the human race, our cattle, our hosts.

Said my tutor: 'Whereas Lilim carry the seed of Meta, Elohim carry its self-discipline, its biological need to radically control its own breeding patterns through culling the female of the species. Remember, it's the bad ones who die, ephebe, only the bad ones; for it's the allure gone rotten that Elohim crave, the reek of treachery and spitefulness and deceit.'

That's Meta sex: Elohim and Lilim coming together not to pro-create, but to de-create.

As a superman, to kill is my sexual imperative.

My program cries out. I want her meat. I want the world's meat. The cuntgirl, the girlcunt, the cuntworld, the worldcunt.

I grind my teeth, lick my fangs. My tongue becomes tumescent, elongates, slips from between my lips like a glans emerging from a prepuce.

But no—I have watched too many worlds die in agony, heard too many times the scream of the sex death in the smoky ruins of cities put to the knife, seen too many times the twisted, scorched rubble of the flesh. No; close to The End, I will feed no more. I will have no more of Meta.

Pain is a fashion I have grown weary of.

For though I hope soon to consummate my spree of destruction, bringing time and space to a close, I do it only so that pain may cease, even though pain has been the ether in which my kind has lived for time beyond recall, even though without it we will flounder like fish out of water, gasp and ourselves die.

It is time to be free.

My catgirl gets seriously fellatorial, her lips and then her teeth worrying, first, my swollen testicles, and then my terrible tumescence, the erection I have carried with me for a thousand years, that length of muscle hard as granite, stained, now, with traces of candycat pink, that dark ruby of the glans.

I have to periodically pull her off, slapping her face, *slappididappididap*, her ministrations becoming too frenetic; and each time she again locks on her eyes widen with the insane, joyful apprehension that, with my mounting ardour, my great diseased penis may soon be induced to punch a hole clear through the back of her head.

Some kids have overflowed into the alley, Thai kids dancing a *ramwong*, calling *Mai pen rai, mai pen rai;* and still she's licking, sucking as hard as she can.

The visions come, the visions of Doriminu, its last nymphenberg, sacked, and she the last princess of that world, a jow nang phi pob, *as they would say here, a real princess of vampires, and only twelve, a baby vampire begging me for her life (perchance to turn into a cat), the youngest little princess I had ever known, a Primavera-substitute, too, like so many other Primavera-substitutes who have solaced me over the centuries, Strychnine, Vicious, Fevre, Trash, Fluff, Outrageous, Mendacity, amongst others, but far more beautiful, far more the ghost of my poor dead sister than any of those pretenders, she who was and is the last of the Doriminians.*

And it's as if she's trying to rip my member off at the root, and there're fireworks in the sky, the *boom-boom* of mortars from a *wat's* crematorium scaring away the *pee lok*, the evil dead, and somewhere there're firecrackers, and somewhere the noises of Thai pop music from a stall in the marketplace, music, music, pretty music everywhere, and the world's eyes are *Venusian*, its hair *bleached blonde, bleached blonde with streaks*, and its nose is *doll-like*, its collagen-enhanced lips *bee-stung*, and now she's moaning in anguish, in frustration, in love and in hatred, she who is the italicization of this world, all the clichés of femininity, immolated before the monolith she worships at assiduously till, once more, with a bite at the perineum, the scrotum, a tongue tip in the anus, a similar penetration of the penile orifice, la!—a hot, wet, galactagogic kiss that seems to fill my entire urethra—I howl my wolfman's howl and, the mosquitoes biting, the lizards slithering, the cicadas singing, fill my love's mouth with a quart of emerald jissom, semen as perversely green and as nocuous as her nightstalker's eyes, and my sister's bodydouble screams with the pleasure that is indistinguishable from pain, gurgling 'Archangel, Archangel, Archangel, Archangel,' and I am a child again.

Lipstick falls backwards with a postprandial *purrrrr*. 'Mmm. *Tonsillectomy! Hot dog! Cruel banana!* Oh, Archangel, you're so *genitalic*!'; I slide down the wall to my haunches and then, twitching, my central nervous system fried, collapse on the filthy macadam and let my prosthetic eye soar into the heavens, soar high above nighttime Hua Hin in celebration of my own post-coital afterglow.

Like an astral body, a *daimon,* I pass over Phetchkasem Road, its hard shoulder littered with auto wrecks; I pass over the bars and restaurants, hotels and shops where tourists mill, absorbed, carefree, unaware of the approaching apocalypse; I pass over the streets where it has always been the future and the future has always been now; I pass over the *Melià,* the five-star hotel where our aliases, Dr Moroder and his pretty young assistant, Cerise, have their luxury twenty-first storey suite (across the *Melià's* walls, flicker of LCDs inlaid like cloisonné displaying latest pornography shares on the SET), pass over the bazaar, the beachside bungalows, the fires of boorish beach-bum revellers, the fishing boats; and then I'm over the sea, out, far out . . .

I come to an island, a moon-lit harbour where dolphins play; pause; look up at the crescent moon whose dark side hides the *Sardanapalus;* and then onwards—towards land, clipping across the conurbations of this coastal megalopolis, the air sizzling with the high-tension ambience of the information = entertainment = pornography = information algorithm, that imperial recursiveness now Bangkok's alone, our British Empire toolong faded, its media-saturated continuum now the Pacific's, the East's; clipping across Phetchaburi, Ratchaburi, a skyline that's Houston, Los Angeles, São Paulo, Moscow, Lagos, Shanghai, the universal film set awash with death-as-fashion, fashion-as-death, that same skyline that is replicated all over the Earth, its Meta characteristics modified by the hypercapitalist razzle-dazzle of the Martian imprimatur.

Ah. The world-capital is hypnotized by Martian glamour, minds colonized these ten millennia by Meta, to be so willingly, so easily (oh, it never ceases to amaze) re-colonized by Martian catch-as-catch can, the sheen of The New; by money. Bangkok surrenders its children now, not for Meta's pleasure, but to fill Martian wallets. The age of the Meta-wannabe is ending; welcome to the age of the Martian-wannabe; open your legs; prepare to be fucked; everything is for sale . . .

My spy satellite heads towards the ziggurat of the Bangkok nymphenberg (it zooms; ghost-outline of the nymphenberg so far, far away, lit up like a spaceport, an Olympus Mons transplanted to Earth); coming in fast over the Chao Phraya river, across the slums of Klong Toey, I head down Rama IV Road towards Hualumphong Station, its community of drug addicts and the destitute, street children who roam the monoxide jungle in search of that mythical Bangkok2, that other city, that anti-Bangkok of love and compassion, a city accessible, they say, if you can only find the right path, the right plot of land, the right shadows under an expressway or beside a *klong,* the right door, the gateway that will convey you to another world, to paradise.

As I pass over Chinatown the walls of the *quartier interdit* rise before me, sheer, imperial, the parapets busy with the tiny forms of Thai Rangers who man the derricks, lowering the night's supply of uninfected men into the enclave's ghost-town streets, those old, filthy ruins of a city within a city, a square mile replicated wherever a centre of population provides DNA to be tapped and subverted; slung over each Ranger's shoulder, the high-powered air rifles loaded with contraceptive bullets that they will fire into any human male who has gained unauthorized access to this plague zone, this killing ground of the human gamete; I pass over the shadowy *soi* and roads where Lilim feed, street after street of *hong taew,* their doorways betraying the shadows of fang-toothed girls locked on to the necks, pectorals and shoulders of h-men, cats on their knees, performing back-bends, inverted, on all fours, raping the nightly sacrifices offered up to them (the men running through the streets, crazed, crying *'Kill my chil'ren, kill my chil'ren!'*); girls grouped at street corners, gang-girls with badges and tattoos proclaiming *Jilly's Jags* (catgirl Jilly born under the sign of the Jaguar) or *The Dysgenic Dolls;* girls branded, tattooed with gang-girly names, colours, illustrated girls with switchblades tucked into stocking tops, cachettes, belts, *décolletages,* girls in art-lingerie, lingerie that is all balconied uplifts, gadget-bras, aesthetic orthopaedics; girls in gimcrack-lingerie, plebeian girls in hoi polloi underthreads; and I know them all, each vampire, each cat, having spent the last week memorizing their personnel files, all 100,000 lives; I know their names, ages, height, weight, hair colour, eye colour and bust, waist and hip dimensions, my recall outperforming even that of *The V.Berg's* autistic *savant,* my brain going into search mode even now, fanning files, statistics, my mental Rolodex creating a maddening background noise, an incessant shuffle of papers, Top Secret, For-My-Eyes-Only, briefing papers of desire, cruelty, rage, a psychic tinnitus that, surely, only long years of meditation, years practising *Anapanasati,* could ever still, imparting that blessed *Samatha-Vipassana,* that *Sunata,* the tranquillity and voidness that will be ours only after the universe unfolds in its sex-death, dies, the mad dimensions of its time and space to be replaced by the dimensions of reality.

And then I'm almost on top of the palace's ramparts, almost through the conical helix of the skyway that wraps about the ziggurat like a strand of kidnapped deoxyribonucleic acid, the vast, towering levels of this nymphenberg identical to all other prison-palaces in Meta's autarchy, at this hour its boudoirs deserted, its tiered balconies forsaken, its denizens prowling the umbrageous haunts of the interdiction in search of blood, semen, corruptible chromosomes, pain, this vacated hive (vacated, that is, but for the terminally ill, constrained in straitjackets, or tied to their beds, watched over by the palace's paramedics; vacated but for its murderous subterranean drones), this honeyed preserve of queen bee and workers, this witching hour, quiescent until the dawn; then I pass through an air vent, up, up through the walls of the ziggurat in a path similar to the one I will be taking when I have The Toxicophilous Device in my hands, up, up towards that hermetic shrine of the god, The Chapel of The Presence; up, up (my eye on radio silence, deaf to my banqueting brothers' laughter reverberating from the dungeons below, the screams of the girls they are boiling alive, roasting on gridirons, on spits, girls dismembered, their primary and secondary sexual characteristics savoured as fricassees, fondues, flambés), when—

CHAPTER SIX

Monster Mash

I open my biological eye (my prosthesis is returning on auto) to discover that Lipstick has been trying to jump start a conversation.

'At school the boys used to tease me. They'd say: "You're not going to live long, you know that don't you, *slut*?" And I'd say: "I don't care, Meta rules the world, don't it. You wouldn't call me a slut in front of Elohim, pol*troon*!" '

I have tuned-in near the beginning of her monologue; but I hasten to spike it; I have heard this tale of evolution from human to monster enough times to offer a recitation, complete with anecdotes and sound effects, myself; it was my own tale, after all.

'Metaboy,' the other boys would say. 'Sex killer. Thing. Dead, dead, dead, dead thing.' But they leave me alone. They're scared. I am beginning to learn how contemptuous a thing is a human. Still a child—and without that icy hauteur that is the hallmark of the Elohim gentleman—I make faces. Cock a snook. And if I feign a punch, make to run in pursuit, my tormentors shit in their pants. I don't care, I tell myself, I don't care.

Prejudice, respect, envy, hatred, fear—these are things dead girls and boys will know about throughout their incommensurate lives.

'I'm a monster like you,' I say, one hand playing with a diamanté stud—clitoral costume jewellery—the other refastening my codpiece and then zipping up my fly, 'a sex criminal dedicated to Meta's destruction. A marauder.'

My tutor would always say that Elohim are 'dragon lords', but that those Elohim who kill regardless of appetite and justice, those Elohim who turn renegade, are 'marauders'—dogs, wolves, scavenging wolves. 'Tech-

nically speaking,' he would say, 'these perverts are called lycanthropes. *The Nazis were lycanthropes, ephebe, sick, insane wolf-men, exterminating vampire and cat traitress alike in the acid chambers of Treblinka and Sobibor. But if lycanthropy is an illness, or mental disorder, it is also one that has only recently been classified. The famous German werewolf, Peter Stubbe, tried and executed in 1589, was accused of "witchcraft"; it was not until the seventeenth-century, as Francois Perreaud attests in his* Demonologie *of 1653, that lycanthropy was described in terms of clinical psychiatry. Later, sex treachery, which was judged in terms of witchcraft until the 1690s (traitresses were condemned, not for their treachery* per se, *but because they "consorted with demons") was also described in psychiatric terms. Today, ephebe, it is often possible, if a pervert, that is, a wolf or cat, seeks help, and if they seek help at an early enough stage of their affliction, for them to be partly, if not wholly, cured. You will confide in me, my boy, if degenerate thoughts haunt your mind? Good. Those perverts that put themselves beyond the law must be eradicated from the commonweal of Meta.'*

I have my princess's attention. 'My life, Lipstick, my life too has been difficult.' It's time for a little pillow talk. But with me, egocentric, selfish me, as confessor.

'Immortality is terrible when your existence is predicated solely upon the desire to discipline the sexual rapaciousness of your sisters, to control Meta's parasitism of the human gamete. My life has had no other meaning. Will never have any other meaning.' She shifts her body so that her head rests on my thigh.

'Poor boy. You must have been lonely when you were little. I mean, there're millions of Lilim in the world; but Elohim—'

'It's true,' pomposity now outvying my egotism, 'I always knew my birth had been something of an event; but it wasn't until I was beginning to metamorphose that I learnt that, in any one generation, only a handful of Elohim are born into this world. I *was* lonely. I was confused. "But if there *were* more of you," my tutor would say, "you would quickly exhaust your supply of victims, just as if, were there less than the present quota of your sisters, your population would slowly decline. Balance is all." '

'Balance,' says Lipstick. 'I guess we lost ours. You had a sister, didn't you?' I hesitate; I rarely speak of Primavera, especially to one who acts as her simulacrum.

'An identical twin,' I say. I clear my throat.

'Then she must be dead.'

'She was executed,' I say. 'She was a traitress, like you.'

'Died like a French girl, huh? Fuck. *Menorrhagia.*' I narrow my eyes.

A girl who has forfeited her life to the slink-blade is often referred to by her peers as having 'died like a French girl', Lilim associating this most blatantly sexual of wounds with lurid school text-book accounts of the reintroduction of riving in the eighteenth century. I remember Primavera showing me a course book entitled *Modern Meta* which traced Meta's evolution from the French Revolution to present times; together, we would pour over plates of decadent aristocratic nymphs and nymphets of the *Ancien Régime* kneeling on miniver in the Place de la Concorde, their thighs splayed, awaiting the executioner's knife, about to be purged by the Committee of Public Safety. 'Darling,' says Lipstick, 'your knuckles are turning white.'

'I don't like,' I say, 'I don't like talking about it.'

'Sorry, Archangel, but she would have been dead by now anyway. On Doriminu, we had a queen who lived until she was twenty-two. But that's like *really* old. Lilim never live long. You know that.'

I am a hypocrite, my hypocrisy even greater than that of a Martian's: to bewail the death of a sibling when I myself have murdered a million sisters—sisters in kind, if not in blood—many of whose families are, perhaps even now, thinking of and mourning their loss. Was this not hypocrisy's apotheosis? Ravishing their worlds I had considered myself a dandy, 'an institution outside the law', as Baudelaire had opined. Tyr, who had introduced me to Baudelaire, considered all Elohim to be dandies. Our dress code, he would say (he who would always keep his uniform in a state of immaculacy), was the outward manifestation of the *spiritual* code of Dandyism, a philosophy he always evoked when he or any of us began to show signs of remorse. But that code became threadbare, even as the punctilio, the ever more fastidious regard we gave to our wardrobes, increased, our dandification commensurate with our crimes as we sacked world after world; a dandification commensurate, indeed, with our never-admitted remorse. 'The specific beauty of the dandy consists particularly in that cold exterior resulting from the unshakeable determination to remain unmoved,' wrote Baudelaire. But, for some time now, I have no longer had a determination that is unshakeable; for a long time now I have been trying to remember how it feels to be *moved*.

'I don't think immortality's so terrible. You dead boys are lucky.'

'I was a monster even then,' I say. 'I should have tried to stop Primavera coming out here.' But she had been fascinated by the tropics, diligently following each newscast on the wars in South-East Asia, keeping a scrapbook filled with newspaper clippings, grainy shockumentary photographs of atrocities in Laos, Cambodia and Vietnam.

An autographed portrait of Lieutenant William L. Calley hung over her bed.

I remember visiting her shortly after she was initiated to the London nymphenberg in '67, the great, decaying ziggurat that bestrides London's East End, the palace built for the British Empresses by Brunel and Pugin. She had volunteered to go to Thailand, acting as secretary to the new governess. 'Just think, Archangel,' she had said, 'the capital of the world! Of course, it's not Vietnam, but it's as close as I can get. Maybe next year . . .' She was edging towards apocalypse, insinuating herself nearer and nearer to that alien, auto-destructive latitude . . .

'How did *you* get to come here, Archangel? I mean, the first time, all those years ago, when this was a different, parallel world?' I search the corrupted engrams of my mind, engrams so compacted, overwritten, diseased, that I hardly dare attempt an answer. But it seems, yes—just as we had returned to Earth to discover that our trip around the cosmos lacked causation, my original arrival in Thailand was, by many, thought to be an effect equally lacking in cause; Elohim who had Lilim as sisters, cousins, nieces, adopted daughters, always lost their loved ones to either the cull or burn-out; the effect generated by my own loved one's death was judged unprecedented.

In those days, yes, I still had a heart; I knew what it was to be moved.

'When I learnt of my sister's death, my shadow-self, my marauder, ascended the chakras of my spine and threatened to go berserk. What use is this life in Meta, I asked, if we are called upon to sacrifice the ones we love? At Misère, Mama locked herself in her bedroom, Papa withdrew to his *Wunderkammer*. That July, I was quite alone with my tears. Full of hate and bile, I paced the corridors, the salons, the libraries; I blamed my father, taunted my mother, reminded her of the time her own husband had been called to the interdiction and parasitized; of how she had consented to marry him, to harbour his corrupted seed within her womb; how she had borne him a daughter who was doomed to a savage, premature death; I railed at myself, my metamorphosing body, at Meta, my god. I cursed the universe. I cursed sex.

'When I couldn't stand it any more I bought an airline ticket to Thailand. In a frenzy, I ran through the corridors of the Bangkok nymphenberg killing vampire, catgirl, killing indiscriminately, killing the true and the traitress alike, killing them all, all, all in a heady massacre that was an act of revenge for the death of my beloved.

'Despite my tutor's warnings that perverts who put themselves beyond the law have to be eradicated, I learnt that, because of the rarity of the male of the species, Meta places greater value on the life of an Elohim than on a Lilim. I was sentenced to fifteen years on ice.'

And what did I dream in that virtual land, that module where, my body greased with Vaseline, catheters feeding saline and nutrients into my blood, weightless, as if in free fall, suspended in an invisible datasuit, I had had 5475 days of 'otherness' relayed to me? (And of what do I truly remember now? My memories have been overwritten so many times that I do not own the same personality that I did a millennium ago, surely? Near immortality has its problems.) 'Released from prison,' I continue, 'I became a drifter, my head still plagued with the vestiges of my digital self, a world of vactors, of nightmarish wildernesses and deserts. It was then that Mephisto found me. Soon, he informed me, his marauders would blast-off from the depths of the Mekong to circumnavigate the cosmos. Their mission: to kill all Lilim; to bring time and space to an end. He explained to me the idea of curved space, the idea that—given that the universe is rotating and given relativistic effects and our own near-immortality—using the universe as a time machine was both feasible and practical. Meta, he said, was a dreadful hallucination given material form, our life in Meta as essentially unreal as the virtual world from which I had only recently been released. He knew things; secrets; answers to why we suffered. He knew, he said, how to bring this horrible world to an end.'

'And we will, darling. Just another forty-eight hours. And then we'll know peace. We won't have to be monsters any more.' She is beginning to sniff at my crotch; I bring my knees up to my chin; enough of pleasure, enough of speechifying; it's time for business.

'What shall I do about Fascination?'

'She'll do the job,' Lipstick assures me. I stand up, dust off my outer clothes.

'I hope so. I'm tired like you, Lipstick. Tired. I so want it all to end.'

'*Que sera . . .*'

I descry a tiny double of myself where the alleyway's perspective meets the neon-haloed glow of the night market. I squint; no hope of a close-up, my prosthetic eye still to complete its inward-bound flight. Silhouetted against the glare, I ascertain a uniform of leather hose, codpiece and riding boots, of ruffled shirt, of encoded Byronism, doomed demon-lover's semiotics spreading—clothes and physiognomy an indivisible whole—to the grey, chisel-shaped face, the grey eyes and grey skinhead-cropped pate; it is the imaginative body of an Elohim, the ubiquitous cipher-body apportioned to all of my kind, all Elohim (somewhat like all Lilim) cast from the same die, a body that is an assemblage of shadow-selves convoked from the collective unconsciousness' fractured animus, the archetype made flesh.

'We're blown,' I whisper. My catgirl sits up, coughs up the leftovers of her midnight snack. I tear off my clothes.

My own uniform is modified this evening, but by omission rather than customization (Elohim all wear the same *costumes* despite differences in

rank—sexually, our relationship to Lilim is one in which we act as ci-
phers, superegos in contradistinction to pliant, feminine egos, symbols of
law as opposed to chaos); instead of the frilly, cuffed buccaneer's shirt that
owes a debt to the autostylizations of Beau Brummel and Errol Flynn, I
wear above my waist only crossed bandoleers, these black leather ammunition belts fitted, not with individual cartridges, but with a variety of
magazines filled with ammunition designed solely for the female of my
species, those Elohim who outnumber me and my confreres more than
ten to one, unanticipated, here, over two-hundred kays from Bangkok.
I'm feeling callow, stupid. Fastened to that section of bandoleer covering
my heart is the holster that is Gun's papoose, a resting place for him when
he is in handgun mode. My thick leather belt, five inches in width, studded and hung with utility sheaths and pouches, is an arsenal of sexual
warfare, to my right 1) a slink-knife, stiletto, 2) an extra slink-knife,
stiletto, 3) a slink-knife with a Louise XV 'Place de Grève' blade, and on
my left, 4) banderillas, hatpin-style with black silk ribbons knotted about
the pinheads, both eight-inch and three-inch varieties, 5) a rapier, 6) an all-
purpose stiletto, 7) a riding crop, 8) two pairs of gyves. Between my insect legs encased in skin-tight black-leather hose, my rhino-hide codpiece,
studded like the belt, and adorned with the appliqué image of a usurping
wolf (before my fall the decoration having been a Great White Shark—
for am I not the fish-god of the Philistines?), confronts the world with
austere, swollen, frustration; and to complete the ensemble, my black riding boots, polished nightly, with love and diligence, by pet Lipstick. I
buff them on the backs of my calves.

The cold, remorseless, steely eyed dandy is once again ascendant.

I pass a hand through my crop; claw Gun from the pocket of my discarded dinner jacket; break open his cage. 'Maximize,' I say.

Metal and plastic contort like the sinews of a mechanical *fakir* as he unfolds himself from hyperspace. I award him a conciliatory pat on his long,
somewhat effeminate barrel; babble sweet words; throw him a metaphor-
ical barley sugar. (I have been harsh to him, and the night has only begun;
if I am to survive, I need his cooperation.) '*Quickly, master,*' he insists.

Gun's wardrobe shares much in common with mine: the black matte of
the barrel, his similarly attired drum-shaped magazine and collapsible,
skeletal stock corresponding to my own black hose, boots and codpiece,
the dandified slash of the silver relief—the twin harpoon attachments,
spaceship fins of a 50s auto, which run down his sleek, well-oiled sides;
the needle-like twenty-four-inch bayonet projecting from beneath the
barrel's long silencer and flash-guard—analogous to the costume jewellery of my bandoleers, the glittering studs on my belt and groin; the
eight-inch VDU of the sight which Gun, anticipating my wishes, will use

(on occasions other than this) to give me close-ups, super close-ups, microscopic analyses, cross-hairs quadrisecting a cleavage, an umbilicus, the swell of an abdomen that seals the rotting meat of a corrupted uterus, a VDU that is like a third eye that completes my own ensemble, an eye that has stared too long and, perhaps, is the distillation of the encoded flesh of an inhuman man, his nonhuman weapon.

Gun dresses like me as much as he thinks like me. A true brother.

The Elohim who stands astride the alley's mouth has been joined by another. I shout a command; Lipstick throws herself onto her face; I empty a clip of *flechéttes* into my law-abiding brothers; they wince, as if bitten by horseflies; and then they return fire.

I go down on one knee; my arsenal, already depleted, cannot hope to stop supermen; my strait-laced antagonists will be more properly armed (we marauders having had such soft targets over the centuries) with ammunition designed for culling the male of the species, as well as the relatively defenceless female. Again, I fire (I do not wish to reflect upon the consequences of being captured—what kind of virtuality would I be treated to *this* time?); and as I crawl towards Lipstick, my heart cramping with the knowledge that, with the prospect of capture before us, I must kill her and thus save her from the attentions of our foes—my rib cage erupts, bones springing from my thorax like unsheathed claws, like the thin, calciferous petals of an alien flower that I had seen once snatching at an obscure, distant sun.

No warning of the projectile's launch or flight; only a wet, rending concussion. I stand, unsteady, a patrician frown dismissing this bagatelle, this inconvenience, the wound now making a noisome *slurp!* as the pulped chest cavity sucks at air, spews plasma, pieces of liver, blood. But though I try to ignore it, my hurt is obstinate and my dandified hauteur deserts me; I lean against a wall, slide, leaving a red, abstract graffito in my wake; squat, head down, on the macadam; try to push my ribs back into place.

I can see that, even now, the wound is giving its lie of invulnerability, pink tissue bubbling like molten plastic, sealing the ruptured flesh, my momentarily exposed *homo supe* organs borrowing the look of gears, wheels and pulleys, the bejewelled circuit boards, wires, optic fibres and processors of a short-circuited but self-repairing machine; and I suffer a brief, synchronous hallucination that I have never been Gabriel Strange, never been the Elohim Dagon, but only a robot simulacrum of the person I have always imagined myself to be, but in reality never was.

I clench my sucking, punctured flesh, its edges like the pink ruched gel of a sea anemone.

My prosthesis streaks down from the sky, cruises the length of the alley, hovers before my face; I pluck it from the air, screw it into its biological socket; go fisheye, zoom; but my head's taken quite a bang; the world's a blur; I can't focus. Ah, the price of a superman's vanity—I should never have given up wearing glasses. I put a hand over my astigmatic organ of sight; rap my skull as if it were a malfunctioning TV.

Yes! Vistavision: I see my killers approach.

My wound is nearly sutured; but I know I'm dying. The Elohim who guard the Bangkok nymphenberg would never use anything less than *poisonous* flak on a marauder; and poison, by which I refer to the insidious nanopoisons supplied by Mars (and not the kinds that kill humans, or the kinds we use on Lilim, such as are contained in the hilts of our slink-knives, deadly to the female of our species, harmless to us), are the one thing that can compromise an Elohim's physical integrity (as the most far-gone of sextraitresses well know), rearranging our chemistry at the atomic level, transforming our cipher-bodies into lifeless totems, fetishes, conceptual works of art.

Another explosion, sending me spinning, over and over, breaking my back, somersaulting me through the air (Gun, poor friend Gun, himself in a death agony, accompanies me, turning into a duelling pistol, a shotgun, an artillery piece, a bazooka, a grenade launcher, a small armoured car, a nuclear-tipped Tomahawk cruise missile, before disappearing into hyperspace, all connection lost); and I am drowning in a spatial-temporal sea, skimming over the waves, the foaming waves of the Shivaic *tandava,* each one of which threatens to engulf me.

Lipstick bends down, strokes my cropped scalp, wipes the sweat from my brow with her peroxide tresses.

'I don't want the sex-death of the universe,' I say, 'not the endless killing, world after world. I want it to end. Space and time. I want the death of the sex universe. Of Meta.'

'Kill me,' she says, 'please, Archangel, before they take me away.' From Vistavision to visions of Doriminu. Doriminu, our penultimate prize. Play. Steaming jungles, and only that slim archipelago about the equator hospitable to life; and in the jungles, or towering on cliff tops overlooking electric blue seas, the five nymphenbergs of that colonized planet. Easy pickings, even for space-weary conquistadors. Doriminu, our last but one adventure.

That tropical world had been so fit for one like her, a little girl with a tropical heart. The jungles, the beaches. The bright girdle of islands. The sacked nymphenbergs. The hot, hot deaths.

On the *Sardanapalus* she had been in suspension for much of the homeward trek when we had been travelling backwards in time. But, with considerable restraint, I had revived her just sufficiently enough to allow her to gracefully mature; on our return to Earth she would exude—

does exude—that *bouquet* of sweet sixteen, Primavera's age when she had died.

I want suddenly to say how much I care for her. Instead—

'I can't,' I say. 'I can't kill you. You've died once. Isn't that enough?' But she hadn't died in this universe, I thought. In this universe (and the sudden realization was terrible) I might have never had a sister.

'I want her back!' I shout, 'I want there to be an end to all this! I want my sister again in my arms!' And suddenly, I am in *her* arms. 'Primavera—' I gasp.

'I love you, Archangel. Kiss me. You are—' she gulps, 'you *are* the phallus of God!' I begin spitting blood; I'm dying like my father, dying of consumption, puking up the contents of the late twentieth century, dying of dying, of a thousand years of eat, eat, eat, eat, eat. Finished now, the meal, her, me, my life and this life in Meta, finished, the knives in cunts . . .

With an effort I know may well be my last I say: 'The only way this universe may end for me is by allowing you to *live*.' She sits me up, one arm about my neck. The stony cataracts that are encrusting my vision fissure and the volcanic fires beneath briefly erupt, tongue her face with optic licks of flame. Tears stream down her face, rivulets polluted with black, industrial mascara.

'Fuck me, Archangel. Fuck me, fuck me—' And then my eyes seem to become as obsidian. The nanomachines in my blood have, it seems, nearly completed their task of reassembling my body into a true *thing,* a statue, a commemorative monument of a mutilated warrior that should have been erected amid a scene of gynocide, a memorial similar to those of my brothers, Tommuz, Orpheus, Samael, Mithras, Horus, Dis, Janus and Jormungander, all of whom lie scattered amongst the desolation of space, killed in our holy and now, perhaps, futile war to destroy Meta.

'Now all strange hours and all strange loves are over,/Dreams and desires and sombre songs and sweet . . .'

I move towards the pouting, crimson mouth of my princess. And I know the instant my lips touch hers that our thousand-year-long party is over; this is our last rumpus. So let's sit down and sing sad songs, I think. Let the nymphenbergs echo with our tales of the sackings of a score of planets.

And isn't it appropriate that it all end here, where for me it began, in this country, this world, where I ransacked a ziggurat so long ago to avenge the death of Primavera?

'Don't leave me, Archangel, please!'

To allow her to live; it is selfish, cowardly. Even if the act results in my damnation—even if, by killing her, I must always live in Meta, this universe never to end—I must take her life, save her from public execution.

I must be strong.

A hand that is still more flesh than stone strains, reaches out; snatches a breast; squeezes its exorbitant adiposity so that the big, painted areola rises like the weasels that surround it, the nipple itself like a pustule about to burst; the other hand unsheathes a knife; but before I can plunge it through the proffered teat and into her heart (the blade catches a moonbeam, turns it, the steel momentarily glistening like irradiated milk), the knife is kicked from my hand.

Standing over me now, the Elohim, I discover, are not Elohim at all; they're wannabes, one of them the boy who yelled '*Hut-tut-rut!*' as I entered *The V.Berg;* the other, the reb-Martian leatherboy who was standing by the EXIT and whom I had dismissed as a '*Neverbe.*'

The Thai: is he gangbanging with the ultra-nationalist *Por mai dum,* or 'Widows' (human-swinehund homeys filled with self-hatred for their own colonized genitalia, a cabal subscribing to the terrorism of envy, sexual unilateralists)? Perhaps. But what's the Martian's gripe?

'Don't hurt her,' I try to say, all notion of a last quip, a brilliant retort, a shrivelling riposte gone.

The irony, the shame; after a thousand years, to be gunned down by a human and his little green friend. Perhaps, if she has the chance, Lipstick will tell Mephisto that it had happened while I'd been handicapped, half blind. I need *some* excuse, after all.

'It's him,' says one of my murderers, 'it's the fail-safe.'

'You shouldn't have opened fire.' They're speaking a Thai-Martian pidgin; and though I speak both Thai and Martian, it's difficult to understand.

'I *had* to shoot. Those *flechéttes* almost tore through my spidersilk!' A torch shines into my eyes, a harsh spotlight, the light of a *Herr Interrogator.* 'We shouldn't be walking around in these Elohim uniforms.'

'Forget the "We"—I tell you you shouldn't have *fired.*' I don't catch the next few words. But then: 'You shouldn't have broken *cover.* We were supposed to follow him, that's all. The Toymakers aren't going to be pleased.'

'Hey, Zwakh.'

'Careful, stupid, he's not supposed to achieve self-consciousness for another day.'

'He's not armed. He can't do anything yet.'

'He's bleeding bad.'

'He's Elohim. He'll make it.' A white limousine with a red cross sign painted onto its bodywork has parked at the alley's mouth. 'If you can hear me, we're Snip and Snap. We work for The Toymakers. Hold on. You're going to be all right.' I am falling into the void, the old black familiar void. A *girl comes around a corner grasping her breasts; she looks at me, frowns, then gazes down, first at one breast and then at the other as blood starts to leak through her fingers . . .*

Was that Lalande 21185? Was it Omicron-2? Was it Barnard's?

PART II

The Reality Bomb

CHAPTER SEVEN

Unspeakable Orgy I: Babel

No; it was Doriminu . . .
 I dream of a dream town, a dream country, a dream world of dreaming Meta, of a planet-fall of rogue Elohim dedicated to the extermination of the female of their species; I dream of the sacked ruins of a nymphenberg, its furred corridors, furbelows and frippery; I dream of her, her, her, her, her, her and her.

And for her (her, her, her, her, her and her, but oh no, no, please, please not *her*), this dream ends (will end, must end, does end) in a dream boudoir, a dream basilica, in a little dream room deep beneath a dream barracks, or, dreamily, up against a bathroom wall in a scream, a gasp, a sigh. But some points to recall at this beginning—equally dream-like, with such bad dreams threatening never to dissolve—are:

All girls are white girls now.

And this evening I have breached a palace of girls, a palace of palaces, a snow palace of white on white on white.

I walk briskly into a boudoir. It is heavy with an expensive scent, *Narcisse Noir*, I think (I prefer the cheaper brands); it hangs near-visible, a pall of auto fumes (the exhaust gases of pretty little coupés, pink shark-finned Chevies, a sugar daddy's candy-cane convertible); and I find myself wading through a mist of droplets, atomized globules, each droplet, doubtless, like a miniature world (no doubts, if my eye were to zoom-in; but this evening I'm on Vista), a microscopic paperweight that captures the anaemic spectrum, the white off-white *beaux-arts* texture of this room and the white girl's world, a commonality of white-furred walls, furry-white floors and alabaster ceilings, an achromatic compass of miniver and snow leopard interrupted, here, solely by the infusion of two polka-dot chaises longues, the huge brass bedstead, and beyond it, the smoked glass doors that open onto the balcony, its swimming pool, its prospect of the exclave, distant mountains bisected by the fifty-foot-high walls of the interdiction—parapets marshalled by Doriminian mercenaries who are already beginning their nightly task of lowering man-cages filled with carefully-vetted *aitch* into the ancient, Victorian streets of this *quartier interdit*—an invisible, amber sun casting its last rays across the island's black sands and volcanic glass.

I feel the perfume stick to my face, my exposed chest, mingle with perspiration and compound my scrambler's encryption of my pheromones.

Whispers from the adjoining room—the 'powder room' which, along with an annex that includes a walk-in wardrobe, a shower stall, a squat toilet (Lilim, whether New Colonists or Doriminian, always choose to squat; it's white), constitutes the standard floor plan of the ziggurat's 100,000 boudoirs (with the exception, of course, of those penthouses in the uppermost tier, rooms assigned to the girls on this penultimate level expensive, maybe, even *de luxe* in human terms, but not vying with the sumptuousness enjoyed by that clique that includes Princesses, Secretaries, Maids-In-Waiting, Imperial Guards and others currently favoured by the Queen of Doriminu to share her vast warren of suites and pleasure gardens, that citadel within a citadel that, unlike my own Misère [and unlike the *Sardanapalus,* if truth were known], is a demesne all *luxe, calme et volupté;* no, no, these girls I am about to kill really aren't that expensive at all); the whispering stops, starts, stops (I have been here before, listening to these apprehensive murmurs, these muted conversations overheard whenever, creeping through a nymphenberg, world after world, I have first intruded into a *chambre à coucher,* there to make my night's initial kills); starts, stops; continues—they are talking about the sound of gunfire (gunfire? surely not; our gamekeepers, this eve, wear their long prophylactic silencers), they are talking about a distant cry (my victims now hermeneutically inclined), a cry for help? a playful cry? a cry, perhaps, of 'wolf'? I think: the wolf's here, my sweets; and I walk into the annex and confront them.

At once I recognize Letitia St Lorelei, the blonde sixteen-year-old ward of Vivienne St Vanadis; and then (my brain going into search mode) I register the presence of Vivienne herself. Both girls, surprised in the act of preparing themselves for the night, are sitting back-to-back on tiny velvet-cushioned stools before vanity tables that bathe them in the reds, crimsons, scarlets and tea-rose pinks of each mirror's array of circumambient light bulbs, the effect not unlike that of breaking unexpectedly into a showgirls' changing-room backstage at the *Folies Bergère;* dressed in gossamer peignoirs, Letitia's yellow, Vivienne's blue, 'gowns' worn un-

sashed, open ('gowns' being the traditional shorthand for this kind of diaphanous, ankle-length negligee, common indoor casual wear almost in-
variably worn 'open' [to reveal the unfiltered torso beneath] and
commonly trimmed with gold appliqué or, in colder climates, in the manner of a pelisse, with fur), both girls, with perfect synchronicity, execute
a half-turn, their eyes wide, their mouths open, naked flesh a tea-rose
nude-rose pink, a chameleonic display of reds, crimsons, scarlets, as they
shift and squirm on their stools, the mirrors' sets of primary colours in the
approximate wavelength range of 740–620 nanometres modified at shoulder, hip and half-thigh by wispy folds of chiffon, yellow and powder
blue.

Letitia is the first to rise, turning full towards me (the mental Rolodex
fluttering, giving me her bust dimensions, the size, in both inches and
centimetres, of the black brassière that lies upon her table, a demibra, or
hemidemibra; by the look of it, one that would—the night's routine
undisturbed—have cupped and displayed those unassuming but perfectly
sculpted breasts [their modest extensity strangely moving] for the tanta-
lization of the h-men she finds so despicable, whose sweat and tears [as
much as their blood] she craves, whose manhood's demotion to that of
man-as-host, a brood stallion, is her sex's *raison d'être*); and then my eyes
fall upon her waist, inner eye opening an image morgue, scanning the
photo essay taken only a few months ago at a private beach, the camera-
man accenting, with fly-by-the-pants skill, or with digital chicanery, the
oblique shadows which ran from her iliac crests to the deeper shadows
each side of her monokini's coop, shadows defined by the meeting of
drawstrings and the recesses delineated by her taut abdomen's V, shadows
that prompt, recall me to my blood-lust, cue me to the manner in which
she must die.

Her belly arches towards me (offering its plurality of messages) either
momentarily before, or momentarily after, or perhaps even *now* at the
exact moment I am squeezing the trigger—and the harpoon is at once
penetrating her umbilicus (its shadows as deep as those captured, or artfully wrought, by her anonymous photo-essayist, photo and reality now
wonderfully confused), penetrating with sufficient force to imbed its elegant shaft to a depth of three inches, just enough to sever her abdominal
aorta and ensure a certain, if prolonged, death.

She screams (her hands flutter about her wound, a child's hands
coached in parlour-game magic; but no magician's trick, no benevolent
uncle's party piece, can spirit that pain away, nor make that slim length of
steel—so simple, so unadorned, with the purity of pure function—
disappear); screams, then sighs, resignedly; steps back; trips over the stool.

Vivienne is standing, back pressed against the vanity table (which blocks any further retreat), hand to her mouth, looking down at her fallen roommate, who sprawls, one leg folded beneath the other, half on one side (so that the blood oozing from her navel and which, during the seconds following her wounding when she was still upright, had barely enough time to stain her pubic fleece, now traverses her abdomen to blot the thick white pile). Letitia's breath is laboured, her rib cage swelling, contracting, like a concertina played *allegro,* my victim occasionally gathering enough strength to again thrust her hips, her belly, her wound into the air, to exhibit to me, to her mistress, to Meta, the unchallengeable cruelty of her fate, though whether a girl in her sex-death seeks to elicit pity, help, admiration, is something Elohim have debated (a debate that will surely always be inconclusive) over thousands of years (for who can know the mind of a god?). Her head whips from side to side, then freezes as she stares at the ceiling, her eyelashes batting as if she is seeking the elusive question to this too-simple answer to life's iniquity; and then—a certain look of revelation transforming her face into a martyr's—the unspoken, unspeakable knowledge that she is suffering, like Lilith, for the sins of the world (girls at such times never articulate such knowledge; their personalities are blown; they become one with the sex-death; the knowledge is unconscious), that her wound, because a sexual wound, represents not only punishment but redemption, a redemption from the void, for her and for all who live in Meta's grace, die in Meta's pleasure; redemption for her own species as well as for those whose biologies they exploit, whose spiritual life they serve: humanity.

But then I myself scream; point my snout at heaven and scream—it is a lie, I want to say; your death serves only the warped desires of a mad, mad god!

And *I* am mad; and it is killing me.

But I am a thing; a thing in a universe of things; my *de luxe* body is made of grotesques and arabesques; and my actions are composed of words, empurpled speeches, enunciations that mask the nakedness of the unspeakable. Beauty is my rationale.

I must continue to pull a sheet of words, pretty words, over the face of this horror. Whatever I do, I must not stop . . .

I compose myself; throw my gamekeeper across my back. Vivienne strikes a pose: standing sideways to my gaze, she raises her left leg so that her thigh (inner thigh pressed against and obscuring her fleece) is at right angles to her hip, her calf at forty-five degrees to her thigh; hands above her head, she seems as if she is about to ascend an invisible rope ladder; but the wished-for autogyro that might have winched her to safety is as imaginary as the rungs that support those diffident footholds and handholds; the peignoir falls from her left shoulder.

Her file, memorized, internalized, about to be immortalized (her mortal life transcribed into a poetic flight of transcendental pornography), autoloads, offers its overture, a presentation of glossy stills, blow-ups, video clips, photo-mechanicals, a monotonous fashion show in which she is dressed in variations of this same powder-blue peignoir, a show that must have been staged here, in this same annex, in the days or weeks preceding my entrance; practice runs, rehearsals for this first night, this metaphysical theatrical, this piece of performance art destined for one performance alone.

In the publicity stills she smiles, a coy, somewhat innocent smile, though one photo betrays her, reveals the smirk behind the simper, the perversity latent in her skin. The peignoir, different in this shot, is opaque, of heavy, rough Doriminian silk, with much gold embroidery and appliqué; in this photo she is studying herself in a cheval glass, the peignoir open, as is customary, to display rubber-moulded, semi-spherical mammary glands identical to those possessed by her ward (36C my brain's central information office tells me), her self-satisfied regard, sly, calculating, autoerotic, redolent of another, secret life, a life spiteful, treacherous, such an inner life as shared by those girls who turn to crime, or, perhaps (the centuries sharpening my cynicism), of all girls, all Lilim (yeah, those 36Cs; ate a girl like that, once; spat out the meat; she'd had implants filled with that purified soybean oil called Trilipid Z6 [Lipo-Matrix™]—some girls are fit only for recreational kills); and comparing file photo with current placatory curve of mouth I know her innocence is feigned, cut with a poisonous duplicity to make that drug, her life, go further.

I return her smile; point towards the door, my other leather-gauntleted hand soliciting, then taking hers, quite delicately, as if I were her beau, leading her by the tips of her fingers, this scenario a travesty of a girl's 'coming out', a nymphet blossoming into a nymph, a ward into a mistress, an of-age debutante squired to her first ball. Her coyness is transmuted; she displays, now, not that mock surprise, that mock fear recorded in my database, when she had been flirting with and teasing the camera; this is a real fear, though a fear that is still posed, still theatrical (she has become like a moving, photorealist sculpture, a photo that is more real than reality, hyperreal; she has become a photo-mechanical, a glossy *animé*, an art-paper automaton); it is a fear that lies beyond the borders of the flesh, a fear studied, structured, like mime is to life, a hyper, autonomic fear which owes nothing to its human counterpart, that epitome of ugliness we call *terror*.

My victim has collapsed into her thinginess; upping the ante of her *superfemininity;* she is going to attempt a seduction, endeavour to prevail upon me to let her live with me as my pet. (Does she understand that only marauders have the power, the ability, to truly domesticate a cat, that, once on her knees, begging for mercy, she would become a work of *minimalist* art, that is, the artificial selfhood of 'the feminine' reduced to its most basic components [infant, slave, animal, machine], become a true *thing*—so severe, this stripping away of all inessentials that there would be no hope, really, of her ever enjoying the perverse joys of treachery?) But Vivienne, brunette, demure, sultry Vivienne does not qualify as a Primavera-substitute.

I clutch my stomach, my brow; the churnings of madness are unrelenting, the vertigo threatening to pitch me into a hysterical, tachycardiacal hell. My flesh twitches; I study my hands; the grubby epidermis seems to be synthesized from acid-worn celluloid, videotape, Mylar. My nervous system resonates like a cracked bell. But I'm not sick, I tell myself; these symptoms are psychosomatic.

I must take control of myself, assume the helm.

Again, I tip my chin to the ceiling and, outwardly casual, maintaining a decorum, scream, scream, scream.

As we leave the powder room—the way she walks; yeah, she's really into the scenario, a *faux* sixteen-year-old at her first ball who's been asked to dance by the dashing young lieutenant—I glance one last time at Letitia, my *bona fide* little sweet sixteener, her hands again fluttering about the steel shaft of the harpoon that transfixes her through her umbilicus, the sexual wound that amongst wounds that range from blatant to subtle, garish to subliminal, I have always considered to possess the greatest *politesse* and to be the most fitting of testimonials to a gentleman's marksmanship. She pouts at me, angry at being abandoned, and I suddenly know that there is a whole catalogue of resentments in little Letitia's oft-piqued soul (jealousies and envies marking even the friendliest of mistress-ward, or nymph-nymphet relationships, the shades of Mordred, Iago, Goebbels, McCarthy whispering in this chit's faltering ear), a catalogue now added up, totalled with a final entry of real, imagined, but certainly *felt* insult at my seeming disdain, my coolness towards her in her sex-death, her passion.

Mania under control, I lead Vivienne through the door.

We stand centre stage in the boudoir.

In a romantic photonovel, an unregenerate bodice-ripper (the despised form that Tyr had reinvented, transforming that slummiest of genres into the ultracondensed multimedia *thrash novel* of the seventies), the caption would read 'her heart was like an express train hurtling into an unknown country as, melting into his arms, she stood on tiptoe to kiss him'; but Lilim, shoeless, *sans* their beloved high-heels (glass slippers the fad now, like all fads to wane, girls always returning to the classic black patent stiletto) are like little ballerinas required to be forever *sur les pointes,* their tiptoeing perambulation requiting their onerous debts to the god of the artificial; let us say instead, that she *extended* herself, that she *stretched* (two or three vertebrae mysteriously adding themselves to her elastic back as Ingres had added them to the representations of his lushly-fleshed models), exaggerating her torso on some invisible self-racking device to finally meet my lips; *smack.*

I let her lick my mouth, my face, smelling the room's ubiquitous perfume in her hair, the long brunette mane that now covers one of her breasts, its papilla playing peek-a-boo, poking its pink-rouged head through the dark, russet-streaked locks, a confection, erect, tied with a tiny pink silk ribbon, offering itself, so sweet, so sweet; and all the time she's muttering (the bodice-ripper shredded, now, the transgressive thrash novel in the ascendant), *'Don't eat me, please don't eat me.'* It is, of course, not my intention to eat, to dine, to do lunch, to cannibalize (whatever humans wish to call it); her fangs (I run my tongue along her upper gums, discover the gingival sheaths, hard with their sabre-toothed booty), her fangs alone are enough to spike my palate; but it is her scent which finally destroys it; she smells (to one such as me) so healthy, so girl-next-door; she smells (my apologies to the chef) so, so *vampiric.* I have no appetite. *'Don't eat me, don't eat me.'* Hasn't anyone told her that marauders, in this regard, are no different from other Elohim? That our taste buds and maws can only be satisfied by meat that's gone bad, the green, rotten girl-meat of the traitress? If, in fact, I *weren't* a marauder, this St Vanadis would have little cause to fret; but like Mephisto and my other partners-in-crime, like my confreres fallen on distant worlds, I kill for philosophical as well as biological reasons; yes, I kill them all.

But this is not to say that I don't find vampires attractive; I do, both sexually and aesthetically; but I would not, could not kill them in the same way I would kill a cat; I feel, I feel almost *sorry* for them, and, accordingly, try to mete-out death with compassion, even while enjoying their beauty, their agony, their screams.

I take her by the shoulders and spin her about, that elastic back contracting now, as she—hope of placation gone—shrinks further into herself, an attempt at a kind of psychological suicide this, an attempt to become a consummate *objet d'art;* the crenellations of her spine press into my thorax, and then, once again, at the termination of her spine's hollow, into my belt, my abdomen. With one hand, I grasp her by the breasts, the curvature of the spine increasing, the concavo-convex body (that now resembles a tightly-strung bow) trying to free itself (her struggle, so weak, so unenthusiastic, a resistance pro forma, a kind of token struggle), my other hand unsheathing my rapier.

Introduction over, courtship brief, it is time to announce the engagement.

We stand before one of the great Versailles-like mirrors that panel an entire wall, so that we are staring at ourselves, *trompe l'oeil* characters depicting everyday life in this nymphenberg, or everyday death as it will soon be, in this and every other nymphenberg in Meta's creation when we of the *Sardanapalus* descend upon Earth like the four horsemen of the apocalypse. And I am provided with an opportunity, now, to corroborate that that sly, self-regarding aspect that had previously been captured by a camera lens (and once, a few minutes ago, by my own prosthetic lens as I had led her from the annex), the demeanour of one who studies her reflection 'subtly of herself contemplative' (as one whose middle name I share said of Lilith*), is her true aspect, the girl behind the coy, innocent mask; and to my satisfaction I also have the opportunity to observe that sly look-at-me-and-despair aspect shatter with such abruptness that I expect the mirror's *trompe l'oeil* to crack, no prospect of her hitherto disguise ever again being able to taunt or mislead either *homo sap* or *homo supe,* her face remodelled this moment and for however long it will take her to die, into a hyperreal portrait of pain. More than its sum of theatrical clichés (alluring as those clichés are—the rictus of the mouth, the wild, shock-stunned eyes), this new face expresses the trauma of crime discov-

---

Body's Beauty

Of Adam's first wife, Lilith, it is told
  (The witch he loved before the gift of Eve,)
  That, ere the snake's, her sweet tongue could deceive,
And her enchanted hair was the first gold.
And still she sits, young while the earth is old,
  And, subtly of herself contemplative,
  Draws men to watch the bright web she can weave,
Till heart and body and life are in its hold.

The rose and the poppy are her flowers; for where
  Is he not found, O Lilith, whom shed scent
And soft-shed kisses and soft sleep shall snare?
  Lo! as that youth's eyes burned at thine, so went
  Thy spell through him, and left his straight neck bent
And round his heart one strangling golden hair.

Dante Gabriel Rossetti, sonnet LXXVIII from *The House of Life: A Sonnet Sequence*

ered, of being 'found out', of guilt, a scandalized self-discovery of a part
of herself she perhaps never suspected to exist (for, yes, let it be said—all
Lilim have the seeds of criminality in their bellies, the perversity that
sometimes leads to treachery, to decay), this new face's expressiveness
containing, not artfulness, but the truth of art, a truth bestowed only by
death. As the ancient philosophers aver (in a patrician sentiment of recommendation): the prime reason in executing Lilim, whether formally or
summarily, should be to bring them to this state of spiritual self-revelation,
a state wherein, knowing themselves, understanding the transgressive,
transcendent glory of Meta, they are prepared and willing to beg their
god for mercy, for forgiveness (and so be received into his arms), the god's
incarnation in the sexual identity of the male-vampire, and, more importantly, the satisfaction of an individual Elohim's desires, being, according
to Aristotle, incidental, or, at best, coincidental, to death's foreplay.

But I'm a marauder and that's all Greek.

I am Meta and my victim dies for *me*.

I have run her through, the tip of the rapier piercing the intervertebral
disk between the appropriate lumbar vertebrae to thread her viscera and
exit via her umbilicus, the small of her back assuming, now, in distinction
to her pose a frame or so earlier, a *radical* convexity, so ductile, this bow
of the spine, to the demands of the third law of motion, reaction propor-
tionate to the action of my thrust, a fleet, quicksilvered skewering of the
median between pubis and diaphragm that arches, tautens the waist and
belly, the blade pushed in all the way up to the hilt of its bell-shaped
fencer's guard.

We stand looking at our transfigured selves in the wall mirror. Her
body had tensed at the initial impingement of sword upon her person, and
she remains unmoving, the extreme angularity of her body's posture unnatural, statuesque (though without my aid, the scaffolding of my arms,
the dynamics of the sword, this statue would surely crumble), her swollen
rib cage containing a tremendous gasp that she is unable, in her paralysis
of fear, or pain, or shock, to release. It is essential, of course, that my embrace of her be firm; yet I do not exercise unnecessary brutality; no, I am
not brutal at all (brutishness is something all Elohim deplore), one hand
clenching, but not crushing, her breasts, the other ensuring that the bev-
elled hilt of the rapier is pressed firmly, but not savagely, against her back
(really no point in pushing any harder, her body exerting that reactive
force that they taught us to expect at The Academy:

$$f = \frac{Gm_1m_2}{d^2}$$

Martians, of course, using such equations for more vulgar purposes), the entry wound, the surgically precise incision where the blade has by-passed the neural canal (my fencing master's hand still guiding my own as it did all those hundreds of years ago), still close enough to pose a con-tiguous threat to her autonomic nervous system, and therefore, perforce, to my killer's etiquette; a threat that, should she begin to writhe, only a firm hand will be able to neutralize. I am, if a marauder, also a gentleman, an English gentleman. And no gentleman wants his kill to die a para-plegic. I kill with sexual wounds; I do not inflict the indecencies that, say, Martians inflict on each other. I kill with artistry, with passion, with pre-cision, with pride.

My gaze focuses on the umbilicus, its thick ooze of arterial blood, my eyes travelling along the length of the blood-slicked rapier that protrudes from her belly and points, like a long Mandarin-like fingernail, points from the depths of the mirror-world, points accusingly at my, no *our*, crimes.

I withdraw the sword with the same fluid motion with which I had transfixed her. Her lungs relax, her ribs no longer straining at the walls of her thorax; and she exudes a long respiratory acknowledgement of my ex-pertise; I release her from my grip and, to my surprise, she remains on her feet, staggers, uncertainly, towards the mirror, inspecting not her body, but its reflection, the girl walking towards her from that other world, the world of death, the girl come to guide her through the secret world of pol-ished glass, beyond its borderland of metal film and into the labyrinth of oblivion.

Reaching the mirror, she presses herself against it, as if, finding the mirror-girl unable to facilitate her escape, she's trying to *force* her way into Looking-Glass Land where, with or without guide, visa or papers, the absurdity of suddenly discovering herself mortally wounded—this evening's routine hitherto like any other evening's, with no presentiment of misadventure—might, at last, make sense, or, at least, make her *senses*, which must be by now rioting in pain, *non-sense*, a quietus wherein, fi-nally, mercifully, nothing will matter.

She draws back the peignoir (a splash of magenta soiling the pastel-hued chiffon, a tiny paint pot of red spilled about the tear that corre-sponds to the tear in the small of her back); inspects the entry wound, then, still silent, looks at me, questioningly, her eyes screwing into their silent Why? I understand that plea; I know my sisters' minds; and, re-membering that innocence revealed in her photo essay (and that that in-nocence had been better documented than the slyness of her self-regard), stirred by her ambiguous appeal, I walk over to her, pick her up, cradling her in my arms, and take her to her bed, all Lilim desiring at such moments, to die on their beds, such a death *très riche* in symbols of consolation and nobility.

I wipe the rapier on one of the black silk sheets, cleansing the long Mandarin-like fingernail of its glutinous, overly-applied nail varnish; sheath it.

She is sitting back on her heels, thighs spread, head bowed, the long brunette mane covering her wound, which, not so shy to touch as her ward, Letitia, she clutches, tightly, with her ruby- and emerald-ringed fingers.

The hysteria is once again bubbling in my guts. 'Do you mind,' I say, 'if we just talk awhile?' Yes, yes, talk; talk the talk of those who live in extreme exteriority; the language of people who are things, people who are text; yes, keep the morbid sex rhetoric flowing; the words that keep the horror in the pit, the beast in its pen. 'Doriminu—it's a very beautiful planet, far nicer than most of the other colonial worlds: desert planets, ice planets, planets where life is possible only under vast biospheres.' Outside, beyond the balcony, the sky is violet, waxing purple, and the vegetation that climbs half-way up the mountains that surround this valley turns correspondingly darker, blending in with the glistening, volcanic rock of a dark, rich, fertile land. 'Were you born here?' She looks at me from beneath her brunette fringe, but she is able to articulate little more than a moan. 'Ah, I see. Your ancestors were amongst the first colonists? Of course. I could tell straightaway that you were aboriginal Doriminian. After you've travelled to as many worlds as I have, you end up noticing little things like that. So many worlds. I could tell you stories. About Omicron-2, for instance, where I had my eye scratched out by a vicious little thirteen-year-old. She had some kind of nanopoison under her fingernails. Damned eye never grew back . . .' I tap my biomechanical prosthesis with a dirty, chewed-up nail and it makes a sound like a cue ball ricocheting from red to pink to black. 'I must say it's been a relief to have arrived here. To know that our journey will soon be over. We'll be travelling in suspension after this, no more decelerations, no more ports of call, no more bridge duty and endless games of Tetris. Death awaits me, a glorious, final sleep; I can tell you, it can't come too soon.'

She is still contemplating her navel, hands clutched tightly about the wound, fingers parted just enough to reveal the throbbing, bubbling well that inspires her introspection.

'Please—I want you to try to understand; I want you to know why I am killing you. First,' and I hold up a digit, 'because of my blood, my Meta instincts, my libido. I remember, when I was little, poring over the books in my father's library; books by post-Ice Age writers like De Sade, Nietz-sche, Bataille, Artaud. Their blood called out to my own. It was trans-gression, they all seemed to agree, that allows us grace before negativity and horror. Through transgression—an erotic taken to the furthest limits of ex-perience—we are able to "say yes" to suffering and the void, "say yes", even up unto the point of death, and thus transcend the meanness of exis-tence. To transmute torture into ecstasy, pain into pleasure, in that most ex-treme moment of Dionysian abandon, is to triumph over nothingness.' I hold up a second digit, waving the V sign before the skewered one's glaz-ing eyes. 'You are, however, also dying for another reason. Victim of the god's frenzy and desire, you are—and I beg you, please, *try* to comprehend this—also the victim of one who perceives the essential *falsehood* of trans-gressive grace. We cling to the divine agony, you and I, the mysticism of the sex-death, because we live in a universe which has no reality, no substance. For us, God is absent, and so we seek in the Demiurge that which can only be satisfied by Love. Our pain, our cruelty is, at best, only a shadow, a twisted, warped shadow of our poor, sapient craving for release, for that genuine transcendence that can only come by love; at worst, it is the very essence of the prison in which we entrap ourselves, this universe of Meta that must be destroyed utterly if we are to ever know peace.'

Gun interrupts me: '*Master, you tarry too long. Lord Mephisto has cleared his corridor already, he and the Lords Tyr and Abaddon will soon be ready to ascend to the final tier. Finish her, master, we must claim The Reality Bomb!*'

My gamekeeper wriggles free of my shoulder (or more accurately, has effected, in me, a tropismatic reaction, so long have I relied on his advice, he the light I have reached to in many a dark hour); he rests in my hands, awaiting orders.

Gun and me have, perhaps, known each other too well; I tire of him; I had wanted to spend more time with my kill; but Gun's grating voice and the girl's sudden grasping of a bedsheet (she holds it in front of her—not in modesty, but in some confused attempt to shield herself, to parry my attentions) trips both the synchroflash of my prosthesis and my ire. *As the ancient philosophers aver (in a patrician sentiment of recommendation): the prime reason in executing Lilim, whether formally or summarily, should be to bring them to this state of spiritual self-revelation, a state wherein, knowing themselves, understanding the transgressive, transcen-dent glory of Meta, they are prepared and willing to beg their god for mercy, for forgiveness (and so be received into his arms), the god's incar-nation in the sexual identity of the male-vampire, and, more importantly, the satisfaction of an individual Elohim's desires, being, according to Aris-*

totle, incidental, or, at best, coincidental, to death's foreplay . . .

How the words mock. But I am a Latin lover. *Odi et amo.*

'Ungrateful bitch!' (And even if she'd been a cat, that 'bitch!' would be cutting. She'd have to have been a marauder's cat, a pervert's pet pervert, for that appellation to flatter or console.)

Gun almost fires before I trigger him—and it's all I can do to stop him substituting magazines, from firing frangibles instead of *flechéttes.*

The bedsheet is stippled with scarlet dots, pieces of silk disintegrating in the region that covers her ingrate's belly (spray, mere spray; I know that my own skill and the AI of my gamekeeper is ensuring that each *flechétte* enters the bull's-eye of her navel), the concentration of low-velocity darts (a concentration equal to gallons of water forced through a drinking straw) hosing, churning up her flesh within that scar that is the souvenir of a human mother, but which, in Lilim-hood, is a superphysical, super-feminine omphalos, that black tunnel of allure my ancestors believed to have led to the fulcrum of the world.*

Gun makes the kind of fuzzy-logical decision he's been designed to make. At just the right moment in this nineteen-year-old's frenzied, kneel-ing dance, when the time to conclude the dance, to make an end to the fes-tivities, to administer the *coup de grâce,* has come, he deploys—instead of the microlight steel *flechéttes* used in those graduated steps of a kill we call *engagement, nuptials* and the *honeymoon*—the death-dealing, larger cal-ibre *flechéttes* tipped with curare.

(What a girl is to her fashion excrescence [something less substantial, less real] it sometimes seems that I am to Gun: an appurtenance, the ju-nior partner in our sybaritic partnership, a partnership I have always tried to keep casual, but which my gamekeeper, I'm sure, would like to see evolve into full-blown symbiosis.)

---

* The umbilical scar, according to Jung, is the symbol of a Lilim's sundering from her human mother, and so is representative of that second sundering from the human world which occurs during her metamorphosis at puberty. In many an-cient civilizations, particularly the Minoan and Etruscan, and certainly in many civilizations throughout the last two millennia, the incidence of ritual wounding to the umbilicus was equal to uterine wounding. Even today, female Meta em-phasize the symbolic import of their umbilici by bejewelling their navels with emeralds, to celebrate life, and with rubies to mourn or presage death. For Meta, the umbilicus has a sexual, or rather metasexual significance which humans can-not hope to appreciate; Martians, stranded in a nonhuman no-man's-land, be-yond even the *desire* to appreciate, have dismissed the cult of the umbilicus as a 'puerile obsession', an example of Meta's 'infantilism'.

Dropping the fay *chador* of the *flechétte*-peppered sheet—this odal-isque never to walk the streets again—she falls backwards to assume the vintage pose of one executed in the Place de Grève or Place de la Concorde (like those who have 'died on miniver' throughout the ages, though Vivi-enne has still been, and will continue to be spared *that* fate, the wound that killed my poor, poor sister): from a position of kneeling on her heels, thighs spread, she has adopted, or been forced to adopt (one may argue, perhaps, *inspired* to adopt) a horizontal position, spreadeagled (or half-spreadeagled, her calves tucked beneath her thighs), her back wondrously arched (I think again of Ingres, painter of odalisques, and the extra vertebrae inflicted upon the delineations of his sitters' too-human spines), her arms flung wide, her head cushioned by a pillow, and that violated belly, its single, painterly wound (no outer flesh marked), a wound so different from the wounds of humans—of those who die excommunicated, or in despair, beyond Meta's grace—a little wellspring that pulses once, twice, thrice, and then dries up (though the blood will remain uncongealed—Lilim die like artist's models who are dying into their own images [one can imagine Ingres and Delacroix falling in love with her; the paint always bright and fresh]); her eyes close, a few feathers issuing from a rent in the pillow convulsively engineered by her fangs (extending in the moment of death) and now sticking to the freshly-applied eye shadow, her mascara, her lipstick, her rouge. As Ros-setti wrote in the last pentameter of the last sestet of his *House of Life* son-net sequence: 'Death's a bailiff. He knocks. Her lease is spent.'

For after the *honeymoon,* there always follows the *divorce.*

I emerge into the long tunnel of the corridor, a corridor whose floor, walls and ceiling are covered in the same white fur that carpets the boudoir where Vivienne and ward Letitia sprawl dead. (I must suppose Letitia is dead; I should really have checked; strictly speaking, it's not gen-tlemanly to leave a girl, dying, wounded, to abandon her without ensur-ing that her heart has been stilled, without administering a *coup de grâce;* but tonight there is to be much ungentlemanly behavior, I am sure, so much killing to be done, so little time in which to achieve it, we grim reapers, outmatched, outgunned, relying necessarily on a strategy of speed and surprise.) No mercy, I tell myself, no mercy. Still, I almost turn back, thinking of that little nymphet lying there, pouting, alone, writhing pitifully in the depths of her sulk; and then I recall that the et-ymology of *boudoir* stems from eighteenth-century French, from *bouder,* or *to sulk,* so that a boudoir is, literally, a room for sulking in; and I de-cide to continue on, to leave my night's first victim cataloguing her re-sentments, withdrawn into that sullen moodiness that will soon, I am sure, growing blacker, more confused, take her from this world to that place where no further wrongs can be done to her, where resentment has no place.*

The corridor is like a hotel corridor, or a dormitory's, but not like one that you would find anywhere other than in a holiday resort, or a boarding school, dedicated to the servants of Meta. Its dazzling, almost blindingly white perspective, interrupted at regular intervals only by doors, studded black-leather doors like the one through which I am taking leave of my kills, a door with the names *Vivienne St Vanadis,* and beneath it, in smaller letters, *Letitia St Lorelei,* inscribed on a brass plaque, other names, permutations of feminine first names, the metronymics derived from Lilith's martyrs, combining and recombining in a mad recursiveness that seems to go on to infinity, this fur-lined tunnel receding to a vanishing point, taunting me with its plethora of still-vital rooms, the other three wings at this seventy-sixth level, or tier, now mostly occupied, as Gun informs me, by the dead and dying, my marauding brothers having despatched their own quotas of female flesh with the expeditiousness our *Käpitan* has tried to inculcate into us all; recreational kills, if Mephisto

---

* My mother's bedtime tales included 'The Legend of St Vanadis'. Vanadis did not greatly excite my attention, but her handmaiden, Letitia, did. In an illustration to the tale, a beautiful example of the art of Kate Greenaway, Letitia, after volunteering to take her mistress's place before a firing squad of archers, lies by the shores of Galilee, hands tied behind her back, her hips arching, her belly thrust into the air to show the young centurion standing before her, a son of Rome, a patrician noble, honest, rigorous in the performance of his duty, who has organized the executions of some dozen or more of Lilith's disciples, that the arrow, the single arrow that he himself has fired, has found its mark, that, as a mere slave, she accepts that she cannot be granted the merciful death afforded her mistress (multiple arrow-wounds to the heart, or more customarily, to the entire body, part of the codex of the Roman Imperium, as any number of quattrocento portraits of St Sebastiana will qualify); moreover, she is proud of her fate; displaying her wound, Letitia is proclaiming her faith in the Good News, the supreme fiction which holds that Lilith, the Queen of Hell, Our Lady and Saviour, substitutes changelings for human girl-children through the transubstantiation of her own flesh; that the umbilicus is the sign of a baptism, a new birth from a new mother who promises a new world. Unconsciously, perhaps, I have associated Letitia—Vivienne's metronymic, of course, being St Vanadis—with that Kate Greenaway illustration of the death of St Letitia, and have so initialized a similar fate for this latter-day St Vanadis's own mignonesque handmaiden, maidservant, ancilla, or, in modern parlance, ward, 'Tisha', as she's known to her friends; for in that illustration I seem to remember that the centurion was in the act of turning his back on his victim, a half-backwards glance the only acknowledgement of her pain, her sacrifice.

were to have his way, to follow only when the military necessities involved in the taking of a nymphenberg have been achieved.

I have tarried too long; I'm selfish, neurotic; in my self-absorption, I have placed my own pleasure before the exigencies of our high, philosophical quest.

I must ascend to the final level.

The rendezvous lies at the corridor's right-angled bend. I start to run, my superhuman body soon attaining a cheetah-like speed, the corridor's delirious perspective expanding from a pinprick—burning through the *mise en scène* like a cigarette butt burning through a cheap nylon dress—to a disc, a hole, an arch, beyond which my brothers are, or soon will be, waiting to fall upon the Lilim of the last tier.

I dread the odds ranged against us, dismay inspiring thoughts of the absent God, who threatens to descend, come like a thief, to damn us all on his Day of Judgement. Surely we would run into the nymphenberg's Elohim soon or at least contingents of Imperial Guard?

Though a heretic, I cross myself, making the sign of the *crucis lingam*.

As I begin to decelerate at the half-way mark my imagination is kindled by thoughts of what lies behind each leather-backed door, and I am stirred by dream-glimpses, intimations of 'might-be's, there and there, my mind a slide show that is running too fast, threatening to jam. If only, I think, trying to quicken my feet, slow down my mind, the slides now running backwards, upside down, inside out, breaking up, if only I had more time—a scream lodged in my oesophagus, choking me—more time to practise my morbid arts, exercise my cunning.

I dig my heels into the pile; there is a cloud of pollen-like fur, tufts of white miniver, hairs, particles gathering around my ankles, the carpet powdering like snow flowers in spring, like dandelion clocks emerging from a sub-Arctic tundra.

Says Mephisto: 'I'm glad you could make it.'

A girl cries out; Abaddon has put her to the sword; she was attempting to flee, to ascend the glass escalator, one of four that emerge from quoins to vertex, each parabolic arc connected to the ziggurat's seventy-seven levels by a series of ligamentous bridges, upon one of which I stand (it is a thin, cast-iron lattice with a low, elementary guard-rail of ferrochromium flowers), beneath me, the perfumed void of the ziggurat's interior, the quasi-pyramidal hollow whose overhanging terraces recede into the palace's substrata, there to be replaced, at the root of this mountain, by dungeons, interrogation rooms, execution chambers, mausoleums, by the chthonian barracks and mess halls of Elohim. I look up, seeking that terminus where those liquid, seemingly insubstantial escalators intersect, the four penthouses three-hundred metres above terra firma, domiciles of the imperial court, a miniature *urbs quadrata* capped by the shrine harbouring The Toxicophilous Device.

We will have to scale this glass escarpment, until, the summit conquered, we plant our flag atop this last-to-fall of Doriminu's ziggurats and plan our final challenge: the return to Earth and the ultimate destruction of Meta.

Mephisto darts towards the moving stairs, gesturing for us to follow. 'We must be swift,' he says, 'our cats have encountered resistance from Imperial Guard.'

Mephisto's pep talk follows: '*We are Meta, the Lords of Becoming. Hellhounds. Wolves. Gynocidal maniacs. Be strong. Be intransigent. Be cruel. We find ourselves confronted, here, this day, with our most signifi-cant task: the acquisition of The Toxicophilous Device which, alone, will allow us to complete our thousand-year-long mission: to exterminate every Lilim in, not just this universe, but all universes, not just this time, but for all times. The time loop is fulfilled. The circle is complete. The worm eats its own tail. And the universe consumes itself in sex-death.*'

We raise our hands in clench-fisted salutes.

And then we are ascending the escalator, the big, Hollywood-mansion-style staircase that can so easily accommodate all four of us, even though we're spaced several feet apart, arrayed in a horizontal line, like gun-slingers, the guys in black hats, about to duel with the saloon girls, the cowgirls, the taunting, treacherous squaws of Splattergulch City.

Leaning over the balustrade I spy a girl running along a cast-iron sky-bridge, one of many designed by Hector Guimard, *art nouveau* bridges that recall Guimard's designs for the Paris Metro, sinuous, arching like cankerous orchids, twisting like convolvuli above the inner quad, its play-grounds, grottoes, parklands and amusement rides, an exhibitionists' haunt where Lilim prink, prank and prance; she is running towards the hoped-for sanctuary of the parallel corridor. The fleeing girl is, I think, yes—I know those black ringlets, those baby-blue eyes, that unmistakable hip-to-waist ratio—yes, that little girl is Fanny St Fabiola (and I know at once she *is* a girlcat, who, though never charged on any account of treach-ery, has, at fifteen, despite the deception of those dental braces, doubtless been defanged by a utilitarian Nature, her toothsomeness now defined solely by the degree to which she has become a sweet-and-sour treat for the more orthodontically-sound cuspids of her brothers). I harpoon her (taking care to adjust the pressure gauge of the harpoon attachment from half to full strength) and the slim length of steel, unencumbered by flights or barbs, skewers her through her lower back, and—because I have taken her from the vantage point of an elevation, this balcony, this overhang from the black ice of the ziggurat's inwardly sloping walls—emerges at a forty-five-degree angle through her abdomen, effectively impaling her, I note with satisfaction (my appetite sharpening now, almost unbearably) through the ripening morsel of her useless womb. She falls over the handrail, her face transformed into the face of Bernini's *St Teresa*, tumbling downwards, somersaulting through the microclimate's convection-borne litter towards the tropical parterre, its ground zero of palm trees and fronds; and I manage to harpoon her again, even as she is falling, this time—her body splayed by air pressure, her sky dive through this humid, viscous atmosphere buckling her spine, breaking her as if she were upon a wheel—with a shot that punctures her tautening rib cage, flesh stretched over bones like the skin of a drum that is being tuned to an ever-higher pitch; and just before the skin breaks, there is a kind of syncopated drum-roll as her body crashes through flora and fauna, a flock of parakeets taking flight in one squawking, chaotic array of reds and blues and greens.

Parakeets, macaws—no indigenous life forms here; Doriminu, according to the geological record, like all the colonized worlds, never having supported life prior to terraforming. Martians, of course, say that before human consciousness metamorphosed into Meta consciousness the universe teemed with life. An object, they tell us, needs to be perceived in order to exist; and Meta, remaking the universe in its own image, could not, would not (such is the extremity of its solipsism) offer itself as a percipient. Martian *guilt* goes as far as assuming responsibility for the lifelessness of the universe outside our own solar system.

Talk about hubris.

We increase our speed so that soon our point of departure blurs into our attainment of the next level, our ascent a glissando of black keys, a smudge of accidental ebony. 'It will end soon,' I whisper to Tyr. 'Soon, soon.' He giggles.

'But it's such a pity,' he says, 'such a pity they have to die. Why do we do it, Dagon? They're our sisters. I fear I am no longer in a state of grace.'

The wedding party begins.

I look down the corridor. There is no question of us splitting up to attack each wing of this level separately; our retinue of cats is engaged in desperate whip-and-knife combat with a *corps d' élite* of Imperial Guard; I know other cadres will be on their way, and that the nymphenberg's Elohim must even now be scrambling from their barracks deep beneath this steel-and-glass pile, their drill taking them to the lifts, pods and secret stairwells that will deliver them swashbuckling into the battle's swell and press.

Mephisto orders us to concentrate our attack on the temple that houses the doomsday machine.

Our cats kneel or else throw themselves on their faces, allowing us to fire several bursts of automatic fire over their heads and into the phalanx of Imperial Guard, the first row of which writhe and dance in the familiar, exploitative way of Lilim whose mortality has been delivered-up with such unusual celerity, their death stimuli gift-wrapped for the delicate sensibilities of supermen; they fall into the white froth of the miniver, the pile now blotted like the parlour rug of a back-street gynaecologist's clinic. The survivors retreat into the nearest boudoir.

We join our retinue, each cat dressed in leopard-skin thigh boots (that almost reach, in their skin-tight fit, to the top of the inner thigh, this leopard-skin signature [a flourish identifying them as our co-conspirators] extending to cachette and long evening-wear-like gloves [cut to expose the fingers, brandished with their eight-inch steel tines], ensemble completed by a body-chain which loops the torso from spiked cat-collar to abdomen, chain dividing the naked bosom, to cross behind the torso and hook over the iliac crests, where it draws the side-strings of the cachette into a taut, isosceles triangle, the chain at the left hip supporting the sheath of the sphinx-handled stiletto and the bitch-whip, weapons of choice for a marauder's cat and Imperial Guard alike, Imperial Guard necessarily, of course, being *cats* [for what other kind of girl, the scent of Elohim in her nostrils, her brain, her sex, the flutter of oblivion in her belly, could think to hurt the masculine complement of Meta?]). The whole wardrobe, of course, mimics but subverts the uniform of that elite cadre of Imperial Guard called *The Sphinxes,* no cat-print for *establishment* cats, these raven-headed white girls who lie dead at my feet (Severina, Drusilla, Proserpina-Pandora and Natasha) splendid in PVC dominatrix wear that fortuitously matches their sheeny coiffures yet is otherwise identical to the uniforms of their still-living rivals and enemies, our girlcats, our own beloved sphinxes; still-living, but for one. 'Jukebox—' says Tyr, breathlessly.

He holds the small, endomorphic seventeen-year-old in his arms (only the body-chain has survived the ferocity of the Guard's flaying; the cachette has been shredded, and lies, a bloody rag, by her side); her torso is crisscrossed, striped with hectic wounds, a gash even across a plump, tabby cat cheek.

Tyr runs a hand through his favourite's black ringlets, closes then kisses the heavily painted eyes, licks tentatively at the blood leaking from a breast. 'I loved her,' he gasps. 'She was girl, pure generic *girl.*' I place my hand on his shoulder. 'She was my bitch.'

'I'm sorry, Tyr, but there's no time.'

Elohim have, at last, joined the fray. 'I was never really,' he mumbles, 'warrior material. I'm an aesthete, Gabriel, an effete European intellectual.' Yes, it was true; I have always recognized (and have had occasion to enjoy) my friend's epicene beauty.

I spy reinforcements, the approach of other sisters loyal to the crown, cat-vampires who have not yet succumbed to the temptations of sex treachery; and for the first time, I see, clearly, behind this second wave of Guard—these girls about to charge and offer themselves as a shield—my brothers, or rather anti-brothers, the lawfully-appointed knights of the *lex talionis*, guardians of the female of my species who reserve to themselves, and only themselves, the right of the cull.

Mephisto and Abaddon have thrown the selection switches on their gamekeepers from *L* to *E* and are pumping magazine after magazine of man-mutilating frangibles down the corridor. (It's all we can do; we lack the technology to kill our own sex; Mars has a monopoly on nanopoisons.) Elohim and Imperial Guard bear down on us in stampede—at least one girl riding an armoured horse, a unicorn-like steel horn projecting from its skull—*Sphinxes* this time reinforced by contingents of palatines dressed in meshed hose and sequinned leotards *à la* circus-girl (or 'showgirl', if you please, or 'vaudeville magician's assistant'), steel-wire tassels decorating the high-on-the-leg cut (Marilyn copying this style in *Bus Stop*). There is a collective ululation, punctuated by screams and meows; and then they are amongst us, the mêlée of girl-on-girl, its confusion of breasts, bellies, sexes, its whip of hair, ash blonde, honey blonde, straw blonde, golden blonde, brunette, auburn, chestnut, flame and raven black, whipcord plaits, braids, crimps, pigtails, ponytails and dreadlocks stinging my face, my hands, my chest; its whip of whips, their sound-barrier crackaways, swishings and sibilations as they caress flesh and leather, plastics and silks—all this can-of-worms slaughter, this bloody scrimmage, parting me from my confreres.

Too much intimacy. Hemmed in, overly close to the bodies of the attacking girls, too close to use my gamekeeper (the cat-on-cat attack now one inclusive of cat-on-man, man-on-cat encounters) but with my allure creating a magic circle of invulnerability (my own little clubhouse where the ladies, if admitted, are searched, disarmed at the door), the Imperial Guard forsake their pathetic, half-hearted attempts to either flay my poor reptilian flesh from my bones or to slip their little knives between my ribs, and, unable to resist the conditioned responses of their superfemininity—my scent at such close quarters undermining their will, stirring their bellies with the thrill of oblivion, releasing the death-wish that is the biological safeguard that allows our species to survive—offer themselves, rubbing their bodies against the rough leather of my bandoleers, the rougher leather of my thorax; accordingly, I twist wrists, ineffectual if delicately-wrought girlish blades falling from my attackers' hands, and then thrust my own stiletto into the abdomens of Veronique and Celeste, through the umbilici of Kiki, Gudrun, Amoret and Babiche, and through the breasts, cleavages and throats of Natalie, Julie, Bebé and Cleopatra.

I adore the theatricality of these deaths—no method acting this, but a heavier-handed theatre-manager approach, camp, over-the-top—each girl's death-throes like a series of attitudes solicited by an artist (in death, their faces resembling the consumptive, beautiful demeanours of Rossetti's Elizabeth Siddal, or the more sexually aggressive Fanny Cornforth [Rossetti's Lilith, to whom he dedicated the sonnet *Body's Beauty*], Miss Cornforth a Baudelairian courtesan, a Lilim-wannabe, to be sure; or else resembling the faces of Burne-Jones's phantasmagoric nymphs, sans their too-human citherns and citoles).

The dead and dying up the ante; no longer an art gallery, this is video clip land, the municipality of the *manga,* slasher movie mayhem country; this is toon town—

I am a slave inside the language of these cries, this language that controls, this language and its lust for domination, the text of Meta's world.

Mephisto has sheathed his knife; he is strangling girls with his powerful, leather-gauntleted hands, or else tearing off a stocking or a brassière from a sprawled, lifeless body, to use it as a garrotte, or—his armoury of lingerie spent—sometimes improvising, like Porphyria's lover, to throttle a girl with her own fatally long hair. Changing tactics, he grabs at what survivors of his impromptu lynchings still surround him, first one, then another, then another and—a hand across their breasts, their backs against his doublet—presses the middle finger of his free hand into that subsidiary vagus nerve peculiar to Lilim physiology that is located in the perineum (in their eyes, the signs of terrible pleasure, as they are seized by black orgasm); presses, twists, in such a way as to cause instant paralysis (the eyes suddenly glassy; the pleasure dead). Hearts and lungs arrested his victims fall like waxwork dummies to be trampled by a hundred pairs of radically-spiked six- and seven-inch heels.

I have long envied Mephisto his prestidigitation; he has tried to teach it to me, but to no avail.

The corridor in my immediate locale has been cleared, dead girls piled one upon the other; I am stepping on flesh now, rather than fur, flesh that quivers beneath my feet; blood squirts over my boots as my weight shifts, sometimes to the accompaniment of a moan; and I am forced to slow down, careful not to slip.

'Forward,' yells Mephisto, 'forward.'

It seems the Elohim are gone, dead, or in retreat.

I hop over a dead horse, its PVC-clad rider trapped beneath its haunches, whimpering; kill two prodigiously-buxom girls, umbilicating them *en passant* with my knife (their faces lighting up with astonishment [or so it seems to me] at having escaped radical double mastectomization). Mephisto has reached the chapel; he pulls me through its door.

Unlike the entrances to the nymphenberg's boudoirs, this door, while fashioned in studded leather, displays, instead of a brass plaque bearing the names of the room's occupants, a plaque inscribed with the glyphs that are the symbolic representation of a relationship between two species:

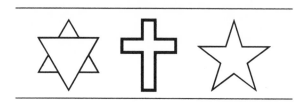

The red hexagram: Adam and Eve, human male and human female, Heaven and Earth, *yin* and *yang*. The green pentagram: Meta as procurer, protector and preserver. The cross: a plus sign, symbol of the commensalism between human and inhuman, the interdependence of the human world and the world of Meta, the symbol of death-in-life, life-in-death.

Mephisto shoots off the lock; a priestess confronts us, a slim, feminine knife in her hand; leashed to an iron ring in the wall, the bioengineered creature we call the Jub-Jub.

Breasts disintegrate; a head whips to and fro, hair—brunette with flamish streaks reinforced with henna—an electrical storm, a tonsorial cyclone behind which, foolishly ensconced (only the mouth intermittently visible, its scream locked in stormbound sound-proofing), she attempts to deny (though to no one, it would seem, but herself) the gamekeeper's almost-apologetic, ironically courteous *shusha-shusha-shusha* as it spits out its concentrate of tiny steel darts. (*Budda-budda's* for the boys, or for such times as when we are inconvenienced [as Mephisto is always reminding me] by necessity, our libido prompting us to mete out deaths pulchritudinous, deserving, to kill girls as they *should* be killed, to award them the grace of Meta's pleasure.) Her pectoral girdle contracts, her shoulders like pincers attempting to touch, scapulae projecting from her back like tiny wings, the atrophied wings of a fallen angel, the spasm compelling her to display, as if offering-up on an invisible platter (and can she help but offer? and is it in protest or pride?), the liberally-tenderized provender, that turbulence of blood and tissue, her breasts, to Gun's bedevilments, his vicariously carnivorous assault. (The VDU beeps! and Gun says Empty, Reload, Empty, Reload, in that grating, smarmy, smart-arsed register he revels in.) Her slashed peignoir, white, diaphanous, full-length, its filigree trim falling to either side of her body—a white girl's body dyed an unnaturally deep tropical-poolside bronze—has slipped from one shoulder (Gun quiescent now after his little death, his digital orgasm) and, *head flung back* (another pose, like that of the pulled-back shoulders, familiar from partnering the death agonies of hundreds of such girls during a killing spree lasting hundreds of years, a pose that represents the italicization of my world, *the* world, *the* universe), Tallulah, eighteen, 5′ 2″, 90 lb., hair brunette (with flamish, hennaed streaks), eyes brown, measurements 34DD-22-35, starts to fall, in a traverse motion occasioned by the right knee, slightly flexed, that lends gravity a line of least resistance; and as she falls her body passes through a ray of the setting sun, a mote-filled, amber-warm ray slipping between the heavy, brocade drapes that screen the temple's innermost shrine, and her body, fractionally cooler than it was before I entered the room, though more than close, fractionally close, to death, is treated to a final course of ultraviolet cosmetics, the last sunlight this surely inveterate sunbather will see, her tanned flesh deepening, becoming Asiatic, before she sinks into the carpet's pile, her flesh to whiten to its white girl's primary emulsion.

We slip past the Jub-Jub, backs cleaving the opposite wall (I don't think to waste my depleted stock of ammunition on its exoskeleton), the huge, wasp-like sting—like a shopworn dildo—flicking at us impotently.

I follow Mephisto, running from the small antechamber up and along the passageway, skipping two, three stairs at a time, ascending the nave that connects the outside world to the sanctum sanctorum of the basilica. Of the Polaroids Primavera had sent me during her all-too-short stay in Bangkok I had had one blown up to reveal the escutcheon on her ward's blazer:

The central motif: the chemical symbol of the Meta female; a cruci-form mirror; it reflects (through the suffering of Lilith) the pentacle, the male principle—these two interlocked glyphs signalling the oneness of Meta female and Meta male, devotion and discipline, the entire design in-spired by floor-plans of early execution/sacrificial chambers excavated from beneath Salisbury Plain and Brittany*; a floor-plan which the ar-chitects of latter-day chapels of Our Lady—such as the one I am in now—have adopted.

I pass the transept; and now I find myself in the holy of holies, the great domed apse that caps the ziggurat, its floor tessellated in the pattern of a green five-pointed star, its walls and geodesic roof plated with panes of thick, smoky glass. Etched into the glass cupola: frescoes by Max Beck-

---

* The visitor to the megalithic site popularly known as Stonehenge must first de-scend some thirty-five feet beneath the surface of Salisbury Plain by means of a lift installed by the National Trust; the lift, coming to a halt, opens onto the neon-lit complex. The first room the visitor discovers is the antechamber, a circular room of hewn rock and wall paintings that is a miniature version of the main temple (and which is connected to it by a narrow fifty-foot long passageway). A guide will offer information to the effect that this is where sacrificial victims and/or criminals were required to await their turn to die. Entering the main cham-ber beneath the lintel of the great sarsen trilithon, the visitor may borrow head-phones to listen to the following commentary, an invocation of life 2500–1500 BL: 'Dark, ill-lit by torches, the great circular room isolates three black marble slabs arranged like the spokes of a wheel, the hub formed by a slab hewn like an equi-lateral triangle (the other slabs, which point like arrowheads towards the hub but which do not connect with it, and which occupy the median of three radii, are shaped like isosceles triangles); this centre stone is the focal point of the prehis-toric community, of the world, of the whole megalithic universe . . .' The visitor's attention is drawn to the slim needle-like spikes emerging from each of the trian-gular slabs (the slabs, that is, that form a pattern [if their radiating triangles were to be reversed] reminiscent of the logo for Mercedes Benz); the spike-less central slab, which the commentary informs, was used to lay out the dead prior to re-moval of the *sacra* and the disposal of the body. The tour continues with a holo-graphic display demonstrating various theories concerning the manner of the victims' deaths; concludes with an inspection of the glass cases containing the trephinated female *sacra* found in the Aubrey holes, or mass burial sites nearby, the replicas of which can be purchased from the tourist shop (along with repro-ductions of Delaroche's 'The Execution of Lady Jane Grey', the seventeen-year-old queen having been executed on a carefully-wrought replica of one of the Slaughter Stones); ushered through the exit into a lift corresponding to the one in which the descent was made, the visitor is then transported back to the surface and the twentieth century.

mann; and etchings by Bacon, Warhol and Ernst—those metaphysical sensualists—decorate the rotunda's curvilinear surround. Encircling the veiled altar, spaced at angles of 120°: three guardian sphinxes, such as are to be found in any chapel or temple, sphinxes surrounded by votary candles and covered in gold-leaf; above, the overhanging crucifix, the *crucis lingam* of Our Lady.

Mephisto walks over to the altar stone; rips aside the veil. A small jewellery box is revealed, glittering with precious and semiprecious stones. Mephisto raises it above his head. He smiles, as we are joined by Tyr and Abaddon. 'Gentlemen,' he says, 'The Reality Bomb.'

And then I see her: holding Tyr's hand, a type that has always made my poor phreno-phallic physiology *phreak*, less a person than a memory of blonde hair, crushed strawberry lips and Venusian eyes; my throat contracts. Tyr smiles at me. 'She's a princess,' he says. And then to her, 'Princess, meet your new Daddy.'

Later, as I escort her through the nymphenberg, its carnage, its blood-spattered carpets and walls, I say, 'I'm not really the man you think I am. Believe me, I'm not really such a bad man at all.' Though a child, she is, in a sense, older than me. The FTL starships that brought her Victorian ancestors to this colony arrived a long, long time ago; it is only the effects of time dilation that allow us to meet.

And then I double up; grip a balustrade; look down into the parterre, smoking now, from rockets and napalm; heave. For a split second it seems as though I have become someone else; the killings, the slaughter of all these beautiful, young girls, indescribably horrible, monstrously ugly. The scream starts from deep in my stomach, flows up my windpipe and into my mouth; but I knit my lips together; hold my breath; check it.

'Are you alright?' says the little girl, her diaphanous peignoir billowing in the convective currents rising up from the scorched parterre.

'Forgive me,' I say, my hauteur returning. I put an arm about her shoulders, her tiny form buckling beneath my weight.

'Why did you do it?' she says. 'Why did you kill them all?' Her query is couched in astonishment rather than anger or fear.

'Because I'm a marauder,' I say. 'Because I'm Elohim. Because, because—' But she's right, I think—why? Can anybody really supply me with an answer? 'To end it all,' I say. But I know I'm being disingenuous. I am a marauder, not just because I want to destroy Meta, but because I am enslaved by it, because I am Meta's servant; yes, the god has made me a slave to the sex-death, its warped vision of salvageable evil, of eroticized cruelty and pain. 'The myth that Lilith gives us is no longer enough,' I say. 'It does not have the power to redeem us from the void.' Ah, *post coitum omni animal triste*. Around me is pain and filth, horror and futility, this bloodbath no longer touched by grace, if indeed it ever had been; I am waking from a dark, morbid dream. But was the disease in the dream, or the waking? It will begin soon, I think, the uncontrollable sobs, the dank, weary feelings of worthlessness and self-disgust. But what escape? Meta is the god of this world; and I am Meta. The only escape is self-destruction. Autogenocide. 'These seizures are becoming more frequent,' I think aloud, the little princess looking up, raising an eyebrow. 'Something is dying in me; Meta is dying in me; it is as if I were becoming someone else, something almost—' I grip my stomach; again, lean over the balustrade; vomit, 'almost *human.*'

'What's going to happen,' she says. 'What are you going to do to me?' Agitated, she struggles, tries to walk away; but I squeeze her arm; stop her; she squeals and a naked Barbie doll falls to the floor; she had been carrying the contraband beneath the gossamer folds of her gown in an attempt to smuggle it through our ranks; I had not noticed it, doll and girl somehow indistinguishable. 'Where's Pippa?' she says, 'Pippa's my friend. Pippa reads to me from the Book of Lilith. She tells me stories before I go to bed.' I release my hold, sweep her into my arms.

'I'll tell you stories too,' I say. 'Stories by Hans Andersen, by Grimm, by Perrault, stories such as *The Little Sphinxes.* And I'll tell you about Misère, about its shadows, its corridors, its concealed rooms, its secrets; I'll tell you about those golden days when we would gambol across the wild, wild Rainham marshes.' She pushes her face into my chest; begins to cry. I pat her head, my eyes focused on the doll at my feet; and I notice that Barbie's pubis is scored with countless pinpricks where my little princess has been playing 'executions'.

'Where's Pippa?' I point down at the doll.

'Is this Pippa?'

'No, pinhead, that's *Barbie.*'

'Then,' I say, 'Pippa's dead.' Her bottom lip trembles. Her traumatization, which until now has numbed her into an abnormal state of nonchalance, is about to reveal itself in a fit of hysteria, a state I myself have too recently known. When the scream comes, followed by another, and then another, interspersed with cries of '*Why did you do it? Why did you kill them? Why? Why?*' I slap her, shake her, anything to stop that assembly line producing this manic product, something that a thousand other hysterical girls have tried to sell me just this same night, something that another Dagon, a nameless other self, had also tried to unload. She sees I won't buy; the screaming stops; and she looks at me, a terrible recognition suddenly transforming her shockstunned face.

'Please don't hurt me,' she whispers.

I position the tip of the blade so that it pricks (but does not puncture) the ciré gusset of her cachette, forcing her to rise on her toes to forestall that wound the female of my species fear above all others. I increase the pressure; she flushes, gasps. 'Please, no, not like *that*. Don't let me die like a slut. Don't rip me. Please, I'm a *princess*.' I release the pressure (upped, these last few seconds, her face set in that anticipatory degree zero, iced over in proportion to the steely coldness transfusing itself through her ca-chette and into her puckered vestibule); and then I kiss her. Smothered, squirming, clawing at my neck, she still manages to interrupt my atten-tions with her petition. 'Please. Let me beg for mercy. Let me go down on my knees.'

I disengage; smile, my tongue extending to its full twelve inches; it darts to either side of her head as if I were trying to catch a fly.

Her legs give way; I scoop her up, one arm under the dimpled knees, the other, under her shoulders.

'I will never hurt you. Never, never. The survivors—they will have to die. We will *all* have to die, eventually. It is the only way we can free the universe of Meta. But I will protect *you*, my sweet. You have nothing to fear. I will *always* protect you. Even in death. I will protect you forever.'

And I am still comforting her as we dock with the *Sardanapalus*. I point out the saucer, explain that this small world represents the ship's liv-ing quarters; point out the ramjet, which had extended from hyperspace as soon as we had left Earth, that scoop hundreds of miles wide scarred by cosmic rays. My Primavera-substitute casts a backwards glance at her home planet, a semicircle of electric blue dotted by a string of billowing black maelstroms along its equator, smoke visible even from an altitude of a hundred miles, that archipelago raging with the fire storms that are our parting gift to every world we have ever visited. I leave her by the port-hole, alone with her farewells.

As the shuttle glides through the starship's melancholy, cavernous in-terior, over the hydroponic gardens, the artificial sea, the miniature zig-gurat where we keep our captives in cryonic suspension, the clubhouse which acts as the *Sardanapalus*'s bridge, I enter Mephisto's cabin and stealthily close the door. I open the jewellery box that contains The Tox-icophilous Device.

The box contains no more than an ampoule of pure, sparkling liquid. And this, I think, will destroy my god?

I open my eyes. I have invaded a boudoir. It is empty.

Louise-Quinze style, or rather, let us say, Pierre Lepautre's eighteenth century as reinterpreted by the Goncourts, the furnishings reflect the spirit of the 1890s—The Decadence—a timeslip where Laclos meets Beardsley (there's a framed print from Beardsley's *Salomé* on the wall), where *les prècieux* meet Des Esseintes.

Anaemic spectrum: white on white on white. Complementing the Beardsley, Victorian engravings, scenes of chignon-and-bustle fabricated girls, girls in heavy Worth dresses of muslin and lace and lawn, watered silk *à l' antique,* girls who have been abducted on the way to their first ball, girls about to be executed, the shadow of the gallows falling across their cells as in the work of a Daumier, Phiz or Doré. Counterpointing these images in the fugue of time: a series of fashion photographs by Deborah Turbeville, drawings by Alberto Vargas and George Petty and frames from a film by Almodovar. And, instilling a note of musky perfidiousness, a Here-Be-Traitresses spraying of territory, there are self-portraits by Yukio Mishima, a reproduction of David's *The Death of Marat,* too.

I cannot move. I am strapped to a bed; not a luxurious, silk-and-satin Lilim-style bed, but a bed utilitarian, a hospital-style bed, a gurney.

I feel the pressing weight of my own sex, its burdensomeness, as it is thrown into relief by the carefully-staged 'feminine depravity' of the room; and I am paranoid.

Pink TVs, itsy-bitsy neurotronic wizardry, stuffed toys, computer toys, leathers, exotic carbons, plastics and metals, chinoiserie of arabesques, curves and filigree, rococo silks, velvets and polished woods, high-tech and retro all sharing the same bouquet as if originating from the same atelier of the *de luxe,* this room constituting, in its essence, a perfume, the scented Idea of 'luxury' which is the superfeminine aspect of Meta and which is isolating its opposite, my *supermasculinity*—laughing at me, threatening betrayal, talking behind my back, hatching plots—so that in relation to this room, I lie, bed-ridden, an equally-artificial, yet *antithetical* body, a thing as this room is a thing, as an intended victim is a thing; lie paranoid, sick, synthetic, a madman called a 'marauder'; lie, doped, hardly able to keep my eyes open, yet know that I must defend myself, punish that complement of my own bitter selfhood, the sex that opposes, that inspires such knowledge of futility, frustration and desire.

Electrodes are attached to my head. I'm on oxygen, and a drip is feeding what looks like a saline-and-glucose cocktail into my veins.

A face is hovering above me. 'Don't worry, Mr Zwakh, you're not badly hurt. For an Elohim, that is. You have remarkable powers of rejuvenation. You have already grown back all of the tissue that was destroyed.'

'I'm flesh and blood?' I ask, flexing my joints and sinews, seeking reassurance that my metamorphosis into a statue was a delusion.

'Quite alive. No poisons in your system, just tranquilizer. And your

body has already metabolized most of that. All you need now is rest.'
Where am I? I seem to remember being on Doriminu. Have I been captured? Am I about to be tortured by Imperial Guard? No; that raid was
successful. The *Sardanapalus,* I decide; I'm aboard the *Sardanapalus.*

The face retreats and a voice calls 'Nurse?'

Fascination, entirely white, now, it seems, the arcs of her radically
plucked, pencil-thin eyebrows Frenchifying each eye into an Ô (the opposite, really, of those ocular attributes I usually label *Venusian*), and
older than I had originally estimated—fully-metamorphosed, to be
sure—walks across the room towards me. Her Orientalism, then, was
the product of a beauty parlour, an undercover disguise.

Sometimes Lilim who have been born black, brown or yellow have
themselves cosmetically modified so as to reassemble their original selves
(think of famous Lilim-wannabes who ape this process, black super-
models, Motown singers, Indian and Hong Kong movie stars); and sometimes Lilim change their racial characteristics at a whim, as glibly as they
might dye their hair, metamorphosing one week from Caucasoid to Mon-
goloid to Negroid then back again, though that whiteness they are burdened with at menarche is stubborn; seldom complying to the dictates of
fashion, it will never entirely cede to ethnic disguise; beneath the body
paint, the maquillage, Lilim always look, think, walk and talk (for all
Lilim are programmed to speak English) and, most importantly, for those
men who adore and hate them, always *die* like *white girls.*

I always was a bad judge of character.

I appraise this latest manifestation of Fascination's addiction to new-
fangledness (is this the 'real' her or yet another deception?), her mercur-
ial beauty.

Raven-haired with that sleekness of coiffure only Asian females truly
possess (though the rest of her is autostylized *farang*), pocket-bodied,
with an elegant swing to her hips (contrasting markedly with your average Lilim's somewhat hyper-grotesque wiggle), long legs offsetting her
torso's compactness, she wears (I have little interest in the black bustier,
the shredded stockings, the long black leatherette gloves) yesterday's
haute cat-fashion of tail-tight leopard skin hyperskirt, the skirt having a
neurotic-psychotic hemline, that is, one vacillating between the length
necessary for a definition (or at least a 'human' definition) of 'skirt' (as opposed, say, to 'peplum') and the length at which a skirt may still successfully reveal the apex of the thighs. As she moves, the oscillation of her hips
effects a tiny triangulated pulse of white satin (the cachette's gusset refracting the boudoir's concealed lights, its neon violets, blues and ultra-
marines) and I am suddenly reminded of the more morbid chapters of
Foucault's ground-breaking foray into kinesics, *The Political Technology*

of Lingerie. Since our kind *are* our clothes (though we so much prefer the word *costumes*), this girl sashaying towards me becomes, in a sense, invisible, a ghost in that machine-like ten-inch length of skirt and its stuttering violet-blue flashgun of netherspatter. So fixated am I by the prowling, ignorant vulva that all my hitherto most overriding concerns— where am I? what has happened to me? is Lipstick alive or dead?—are forgotten; and I can think of nothing but the signature of *home* that is signed indelibly on her sex (she's sitting down, now, the skirt slit to the waist on the left side, exhibiting an ellipse of black suspender; and the thick plastic belt has a big silver buckle inscribed CUNT); for I know, know oh know before she opens her mouth—my nose stinging with her pheromones—know just where she's from.

'Ooo, it's James Bond. 'Ello James,' she says. She's 'eartland-of-lost-empire' cooly-cool, an East End slut come East to meet the Man who lives East of Eden.

'You're a long way from home, little cat.'

'Had to run away, James. Stayed much longer and I'd've been slink-riven. That's the way it is with little sluts like me. We try to be good girls, and what 'appens? We end up with six inches of steel between our legs.'

'Sounds painful.'

'A whore's nemesis, James. The bad girl's death. The one we fear the most.' I notice that she has a hypodermic in her hand.

'To help you relax, Mr Zwakh,' says the quack. 'It's just to help you relax. And to help restore the corrupted data of your mind.'

I look up at Fascination, puppy-dog-eyed, appealingly. 'What's *your* name?' I say, trying to stall the inevitable.

'Frankie. Frankie St Fallon.' Visions of *Romford*—that was where the termites from the Corbusier towers came from, the ones who taunted me, called me names, called me 'Little Lord Fauntleroy'. I am reminded of a particularly unpleasant little doxy by the name of Fay, Fay *Kinkaid,* I think, a metamorphosing, catwalking Lilim (*Koxlove, Kunningham, Kilroy, Kinkaid,* something like that; but it would be, wouldn't it? wouldn't it?); her face superimposes itself upon Frankie's, a ghost face in a tiny pill-box hat, the veil pulled back (face of a sinister doll, *Nota Bene:* doxy, C16: probably from Middle Flemish *docke,* or doll), her doll-baby dress high-necked (the neck an eruption of lace, her name stitched on the ruff), a child's party-dress with puffy, leg-o'-mutton sleeves, its childishness subverted by a slashed bib that exposes the breasts, scalloped and thrust forward by the tight-laced corsetry that cinches her waist into a twelve-inch nonpareil of waspishness. The ghost vanishes; Frankie reasserts herself.

Ah, Frankie and me: we've walked the same streets, played in the same playgrounds, dreamed ourselves into the same all-encompassing dream. The needle slips into my arm.

She's quite beautiful, I suddenly realize, a hybrid of Nastassia Kinski and Ornella Muti with, perhaps, a little of Louise Brooks—minus bob— thrown in: a very European—that is, sickly—sort of beauty, very different from that Californian style to which Mephisto is so affianced, Mephisto with his yen for high-impact, low-pain-threshold hardbodies.

I wonder what her original name was, I suddenly find myself thinking, the family name she possessed before she metamorphosed into a psychoid? Strange, but these changelings seem always to have had such *blatant* genealogies, these girl-children burdened with surnames such as Paine, Suckling, Hartwell, Lockheart, Farquar, Shaftsbury and the like, as if Meta only attacked families so marked out for its attentions, like an angel of death who passed over those whom the human god had made its own, the Smiths, Babbitts, Podsnaps, Biedermeiers, the Adamski-Bromidesons and their tedious spawn. (Strange that my own name, and my twin sister's, had been 'Strange', and she calling me 'Archangel' when everyone else called me 'Gabby'; strange that she knew even when we had been infants that I too had been touched by and was to become that angel of death.) Frankie Cat's former name—I like playing with such ideas— was *'Wiles'*, yes, her pre-metamorphic name had been 'Frankincense Wiles', I am sure.

Her tongue runs over her lips and then flicks at me like a lizard's, the tip waving, a saurian-cheerleader's tongue, enticing me to score. 'But you can call me *Philautia.*' She giggles, toying with a strand of sable hair. 'I like *Jet,*' (and I appreciate the fitness of that eponymic *nom des rues,* her mane's silky sleekness, her pomade), 'but as soon as I started to get my knees grazed, *well...* Have you seen *Irezumi* where Masayo Utsunomiya gets this great S&M number all across her back? Sometimes I think about turning Japanese. I mean, they've got it all: the fetishism, the sado-masochism, the voyeurism, the—' The doctor coughs. 'Oh—I'm to tell you that your friend Lipstick's quite *safe.* So don't worry. I'll look after you for now. Sorry if I'm so *forward.* You're a gentleman, James. I'm not used to gentlemen.'

'Let's talk,' says another voice from behind.

'Talk. Sure.'

'Let's talk history.' I'm starting to feel disorientated; even though I know Frankie sports a comparatively harmless neurotic-psychotic hemline, it seems to have undergone a fourth-dimensional transformation into something more sinister. What I'm looking at now is a 'Minkowski

Mini', a skirt developed by a Vivienne Westwood/reb-Martian joint venture (Dek-A Dent-A™), the apotheosis of Mary Quant's 60's chic: with four co-ordinates, x, y, z and t, the hemline (which has no real length, but only a fourth dimensional 'extension') has the same schizoid-hysterical 'look' as other Lilim skirts/skirtlets/skirls, except that, on a voyeur, it induces the effect of falling, falling, time str-etch-ing, length shr-ink-ing, ad infinitum, ad libitum—the Martian gizmoinvestment side to things, this, the little green men having had gravity cracked for hundreds of years. If only Mephisto could have stolen one of their FTL ships instead of the *Sardanapalus* . . . Scientists are pornographers: radical pornographers; with them, it's the same love of the transgressive, to go one step beyond. They're all mad.

'Sit next to me, Frankie.' My nurse complies. The skirt has folded itself out of hyperspace; once again, the pelt of leopard-fur that, in its hemlineal shift from neurosis to psychosis and back, models the disintegration of her personality, is within range of my senses. I reach out; hand descending her long raven mane in one electrostatic sweep until it settles upon her rump; stroke its second skin of cat-print, my mind still partially hypnotized by its glazed leopard-spotted multi-eyed gaze.

'Undoubtedly,' I filibuster, 'the hyperskirt's present revival—this fanatical reinterpretation of the 60's miniskirt and microskirt, or, as we Meta say, the *cantonnière*—is due, not so much to its vulgar exhibitionistic fanfare—the bathetic sex appeal of its advertising copy—but to the late twentieth century's obsession with feminine vulnerability, though feminine sex appeal and vulnerability, for someone like me, perhaps, amounts to the same thing. Can you hear it? Can you hear the semiotics? Can you hear that babble of skirt-talk that, to me, is like a second language?'

And is Frankie mindful of her fashion statement, the complicity of her behaviour? No; for her, whatever awareness exists of her role-playing is blood-borne, hormone-centred, dark. I imagine us in the same alley where Lipstick and me, some unknowable length of time ago, had fucked . . .

She has half-a-second to communicate a certain mute apprehension that is already mutating into a more radical Newgate-to-Tyburn fear, to impart, finally, recognition *before, my grip tightening, I pull her forwards onto the slink-knife (a tiny* pop! *of perforated satin, a crisp resonance overlaid with the sound of a gimlet penetrating an over-ripe peach, air indrawn over sharp, clenched little teeth in the prelude to a violent gasp), my other hand, at the same instant, pressing home, firmly, but without savagery (I am a marauder, but I am also a gentleman), the slender tapering length of steel of my exquisite blade until the ebony handle with its modest guard (the handle carved in the semblance of a wolf) is snug against the satinette man-made membrane that shrouds the ruptured vestibule of her labia* . . .

I can smell the scent of the fashion victim on her, can smell the treachery, and it's making me salivate.

'Mr Zwakh, try to concentrate,' says the disembodied voice, my interrogator.

'History. Yeah. I'm listening.'

'Let's start with *your* history.'

'I'm a professional pornographer.' Is Frankie suitably impressed? This jig *usually* works (Bangkok, being the pornography-information capital of the world, allows only top biznizmen to get a look-see in its pornocracies); but then I usually employ such spiel only when I'm amongst humans (who are so easily impressed); it's part of my cover. And why should I worry about *impressing* this chit? 'I specialize in virtual paedophilic oneirogamy, gynoids, photo-mechanical starlets, you know?'

'Gynoids,' she laughs. 'They're so funny. Why did Mars ever build those things?'

'Intelligence requires,' I say, '*artificial* intelligence requires—like artificial sex—a body through which to learn, evolve. Flesh is paramount. Flesh is the Universal Machine.'

'Mmm. You sound ever so *clever. I* specialize in unsupervised exogamy. It's so fucking *bad.* Shall I do you now? I fancy you rotten.'

'Nurse, will you please *leave* us,' says my interrogator. Frankie curls her lips, slinks out of the room, dragging the toes of her high heels through the thick, white fur. The drug is consolidating its hold on me, insinuating itself into the hidden recesses of my will. The whole room seems to have assumed the proportions of a Minkowski Mini, to be folding itself in and out of hyperspace. I close my eyes. 'You are not a pornographer. Please do not waste time. Your name is Ignatz Zwakh.'

'My name is Lord Dagon, formerly Gabriel Strange.'

'No; it is Ignatz Zwakh. You were made a little over a half century from now, by the nanoengineer we have come to know by the sobriquet of "Dr Toxicophilous". '

Crazies, I think; I've been kidnapped by a group of human crazies, a political fringe, a religious sect, a group of millennial survivalists, followers of some spoilt, whining, eight-year-old guru, a gang of God's chosen waiting for the apocalypse. 'I grew up in Castle Misère,' I say emphatically. 'I had a sister, Primavera . . .'

The voice drones on, a radio broadcaster's voice, affectless, a voice untroubled by the insane drama it is recounting, the mad world myth to which this little brainwashed band of Elohim snatchers subscribes. 'In the 2030s a series of automata were engineered for Cartier, Paris. They were dolls, human-like robots, nanoengineered at the atomic level, marvellous toys, status symbols for the Information Age's elite. They were creatures that formed a bridge between the classical and microphysical worlds. They had *quantum-magical* CPUs.' The voice paused; I was obviously supposed to dwell on the import of that emphasis.

'Who are you? What are you doing to me?'

'We are The Toymakers. And we are arming you so that you may complete the mission for which you were designed.'

Flash. What is this? I think, what is—Flash, flash. Images like lightning bolts fall across my path, as if I were a sleepwalker too near a cliff's edge brought suddenly to realization of his danger. Flash. No; don't walk there; wake up, wake up, be careful; *be careful of the abyss*—

My torturers, with their silky insinuations, have set up the projector; the back of my eyelids now serves as the movie screen. Castle Misère flickers, like an old, time-damaged print of a much-loved but poorly-acted silent classic; and then it dissolves. Instead of the castle, I see the Rainham Marshes flooded, the towers of the Mardyke estate, a little community of survivors huddled behind the electric fences and minefields of the interdiction. Helicopters sweep across the night sky, searchlights panning the fields and dykes for escaping humans or dolls.

I recognize that scene. It is from another life, the other life I have been drifting into for some time now, ever since feeling the horror grip my bowels at the conclusion of each gynocidal raid, that nausea when the piles of bodies, the blood-spattered lingerie and the cries of pain no longer seemed so beautiful, Meta's eroticization of death, its salvation through sex, revealed as a filthy lie. There is only one hope of salvation, I think as if for the first time, or rather, as if remembering for the first time, only one hope for inhuman and human alike: the hope that the presence of hate in the world is only as sure as that of love. Yes, yes, I begin to remember; I begin to wake—

'That's better, Mr Zwakh. Relax. We are monitoring your thoughts. What you are seeing is London at the time when you met and fell in love with the doll-girl Primavera. It is 2068. You are twelve. London is a plague city. The Cartier automata engineered by Dr Toxicophilous have infected humankind with their software. Now, when human girls attain puberty they begin to change into robots—vampiric, sexually rapacious cyborgs programmed to seduce human men. They are fantastical creatures. They have inherited the quantum magic of their Cartier progenitors. Their minds aren't limited by the human mind's cognitive construction of reality—their powers of perception can *warp* reality. The nanomachines in their saliva corrupt the germ cells and, in time, more little girls metamorphose into machines. These cyborgs—Dead Girls, or Lilim, as they come to be known—while possessing psychokinesis, inhuman strength, the ability to fly—are short-lived, presaging the doom of all humanity. Soon, it is feared—the birthrate of dolls outnumbering those of humans—the world will become a world of dolls whose teenage mortality will soon leave the planet barren of sapient life. Thus the interdiction: escape from London carries the penalty of death. Yet many do escape, carrying the plague into the world; and amongst those who escape—you and Primavera.

'You make your way to Thailand, have many adventures. But the plague has yet to reveal all its secrets. It is 2071. Until now, the virus has only affected females, but a new generation of Dead Boys, metamorphosing more slowly than their female counterparts, are beginning to appear on the world stage. The virus—the nanomachines carrying the Cartier software—mutates; Lilim forfeit their powers to this male of their species, the Elohim. Together, they strive to forge a relationship with humanity based on commensalism, rather than parasitism, try to control their own breeding patterns so that both human and inhuman might, in future, live in a kind of twisted harmony. And so Meta is born . . .'

As I had listened to the voice my mind had screened images to complement its narrative; and I had been Ignatz Zwakh; but, now, as the voice again pauses, as if for dramatic effect, the memories strike a false chord. Too absurd; I am hallucinating, I tell myself. I am the Elohim Dagon, riddled with some nanopoison that is perverting my mind. How is it possible that Meta was born *in the future*?

'I was taught,' I mumble, 'that Meta has *always* been.'

'You have been taught,' said the voice, 'that throughout history Meta has been convulsing in successive waking dreams, each dream an unsatisfactory attempt to define itself, to provide itself with a self-sufficient, all-encompassing myth, a rationale that would allow it to *be*. Sufficient complexity would satisfy the mind and body as to why male should kill female, why there should be this correlation between sex and death. Meta's evolution has been governed by natural selection.

'You have been taught that, though many have tried to provide Meta with a supreme fiction, all have failed, except one. Alexander died on the plain of Shinar beneath the shadows of the great ziggurat of Etemenanki, his attempts only partly realized; and Caesar cried over Alexander's tomb, knowing that his own efforts were doomed to come to naught. Those ages, they say—before Lilith gave our culture unity through the defining, transcendental myth of her life and teachings—were condemned to tread the *Hodos Chameliontos,* or Way of the Chameleon.

'And when you have attended temple rites and sacrifices, you have, have you not, given thanks to Lilith for salvation from mutability? Sought a final explanation of why you are the creature that you are? Given thanks for the "supreme fiction" that is the most complete vision so far allowed of the blinding "reality" of the Demiurge? A reality of an absent God which we cannot in this life know for we are not his creatures. And nor would we wish to know. Despite the sometime bravado of Lilim and Elohim, this is a reality you have greatly feared.'

Yes, I think, it is that 'reality' that, legend has it, sex criminals go to when they die, that I have sometimes seemed to have woken from close to dawn, sweating and trembling.

It is, they say, our hell.

Am I in hell? If not, I fear, for all my crimes, I shall soon arrive there. Lilith can no longer help me. She is becoming unreal, like the universe itself. I no longer believe in her. I no longer believe that Meta has existed from the beginnings of time. I no longer believe in history.

Who more deserves hell?

But what, I think—my mind fast approaching the state of a *tabula rasa*—what *do* I believe?

'You must face your fear,' says the voice. 'You must once again become your real self. As Dagon, Lilith gave you a rationale for our universe which you have always hoped to be a Theory of Everything. But consider: there are things about this life in Meta which do not make sense—by their very nature *cannot* make sense. For instance, why are all Lilim white and why do they all speak English? Have they always been white, always spoken English? If the Empire of Meta had been *British* (rather than a loose association of myths, rationales) for 10,000 years, this might be explainable as, though somewhat ridiculous, a "British gene", a part of the architecture of the Meta infinitesimal, but—'

'But, but, but,' I interrupt. Dagon will not be so easily sloughed off. 'I remember a palaeontology lesson. Display cases filled with unearthed female *sacra* at the Museum of Natural History in London. These *sacra* had small trephinations. My tutor explained why.' And then I begin to speak at breakneck speed, as if trying to create a body of words for my dying identity to inhabit.

'He said palaeontologists agree that Upper Palaeolithic fossils and artifacts found in Africa and the Near East indicate that females attaining puberty had had these small holes bored into their *sacra* in accordance with rites most probably related to menarche, ritual killings involving the abdominal impalement of those of child-bearing age with spears of flint or bone (the trephination allowing the spear to score the victim through without meeting resistance), these spears corresponding to the later copper and bronze palings or (to use the translation of a cognate shared by a half-a-dozen ancient tongues) "bellyspikes" to be commonly found projecting from altars in Cimmeria, Hyperborea, Sumer, Mesopotamia, Babylon and Egypt. (Interestingly, Neolithic altars in Northern Europe, such as those of the vast execution/sacrificial chamber beneath Salisbury Plain, England, also share this characteristic, murderous device—the bellyspike—lending weight to the argument that the ceremonies surrounding these immolations [or "bellyings" as they have come to be known], as well as the basic configuration of the death-machine that we call "The Sphinx", were universal phenomena throughout Africa, the Near East and Europe from as early as 2800 B.L.) Early myths and cosmogonies suggest that those suffering these ritual slayings during prehistoric times were adolescent girls of high social caste who had been discovered to have consorted with or to have been impregnated by outsiders, a clan or tribe that ancient myths, while according different names, all agree were great sorcerers and necromancers. The fossil record indicates that, while trephination was widespread, only a small proportion of unearthed skeletons evidence violent death, fear of the outside having more to do with the evolution of this myth, perhaps (certainly having more to do with the prevalence of trephination), than the actual existence of the mythical or semi-mythical tribe itself; it is a theory that Martian palaeontologists have seized upon with predictable fervour, even though recent discoveries of fossils thought to be alien (which initially created such a flurry of scientific debate and attendant media hysteria) have never been identified as being incontrovertibly nonhuman and were, in any case, never associated with sites in which trephinated *sacra* and other early Meta artifacts have been found.'

I stop; draw breath. 'I have long considered,' I say, trying to recover with some grace, 'that the Martian theory of Meta's genesis is, as yet, wholly lacking in empirical corroboration.' But, from my interrogator, I receive no response. As he has said, there are things about this life in Meta which cannot be understood. 'Consider.' I say, 'Given that Martians have different molecular replicators from humans, how could they interbreed with our hypothetical ancestors?'

'History is more than hypothetical,' says the voice at last, 'it is an hallucination so strong that it has achieved material form. It is a part of the suprahistory that Meta has imposed on us all. It affects even those few of us who can, like myself, maintain lucidity amid the mad turmoil and darkness of Meta's night.'

'But, but—' Nymphenbergs, I think, yes, nymphenbergs have been constructed in the form of ziggurats since the 4th millennium BL. I had seen photographs of Etemenanki, Choga Zambil and Nanna at Ur, the latter, remodelled by Nabonidus (556–539 B.L.)—last Babylonian king before the Persian conquest of Mesopotamia—bearing an astonishing resemblance to a late twentieth-century nymphenberg, black glazed bricks substituting for the smoked glass that is the characteristic shell of the modernist and postmodern prison-palace. 'There have always,' I say, 'there have always been nymphenbergs. The archaeological record—'

'The manic rewriting of time and space by Meta. Nymphenbergs have no real historical antecedents.'

'That can't be,' I say, desperate now, thinking of the first piece of history I can, something from one of my tutor's lessons at Misère. (Again, my recitative sounds as if I have swallowed a handful of *ya ma*, or amphetamines; I stutter, my lips tripping over the words, the text of an unreal world.) 'What about the Marquise de Brinvillier? It was her arrest, and the subsequent disclosure of her crimes, that seems to have precipitated the outbreak of poisoning that began during the reign of Louise XIV and which, in a little under a century, led to the Reign of Terror. Don't you remember? The Marquise had, using an odourless, tasteless, deadly potion invented by the Italian alchemist Exili, killed first her father, then her two brothers (both human) and finally her sister (also human). She went on to poison several paupers in the Hôtel Dieu, the guests who attended her weekly salons. Following her execution, the people of Paris breathed freely again; but soon, a plague of copycat crimes began to spread across the city. The Queen appointed a tribunal to investigate these horrors—the so-called *Chambre ardente*—which was presided over by her Lord Chamberlain, the three-hundred-and-sixty-year-old La Regnie. With the revival of the much-feared, ancient custom of slink-riving, girl after girl was despatched post-haste; La Regnie's enthusiasm, which found its apogee in his protegé and successor Robespierre, meant that the slightest suspicion was enough to condemn both the innocent and the traitress alike to "kneel on the miniver". '

'The perversion of a fiction, Mr Zwakh, a rewriting of a story by E. T. A. Hoffmann superimposed upon the real world. Dr Toxicophilous would, doubtless, have approved. It was his taste for the tales of The Second Decadence which proved the world's ruin.'

Other historical 'facts' present themselves to my mind, unwilling to assume their rightful place alongside my dreams and nightmares. But I can't fight this overwhelming sense of *otherness* any longer.

'My life—all life; are you telling me it's *completely* unreal?'

'Real enough for those who still live it; Meta has the power to alter the perceptual faculties of those it infects to the extent that those faculties become supernatural—as the faculties of the first dolls were supernatural—with the subsequent effect that the distinction between perceived and percipient has become meaningless. Meta is a psychosomatic disorder which affects not just those who possess the disorder, but everything they perceive. It affects the fabric of time and space itself. Meta is all.'

'What happened?' I say. 'What happened to us?'

Another pause; my interrogator enjoys a touch of melodrama; and I imagine him smacking his lips, for he has brought me to the point where he can explain the reason for my abduction. I suspect greater terrors are awaiting me, whoever I am, whatever I am—my selfhood in ruins, waiting to be swept up, put in a bag, incinerated—for I have been stripped so bare that I am beginning to intuit the truth relayed back to me by my exposed nerve-endings, a truth that fills me with a million white-hot, stabbing pains whenever I reach out, try to touch . . .

What was in that hypodermic? I'm not ready for hell.

Oh Lilith, Lilith, why have you forsaken me?

No; be brave, I think; reach out; touch—

'The unreal universe we live in today is the result of a plot hatched by a group of Elohim and Lilim in the mid-2070s. They used the quantummagical CPUs of the by now long-defunct Cartier automata—CPUs that were the diseased birthing chambers of Meta—to forge transdimensional gateways between worlds. They sold them to Mars—a human colony, not the world of green-skinned alien humanoids *you* perceive—to facilitate travel between the two planets. But unknown to the human race, the nanoware that had subverted their DNA and given birth to the generations of the recombinant had now miniaturized itself into something like pure, superluminal information; it had become self-organized, an independent entity, a god. Meta used the transdimensional gateways to flow backwards through time and space, changing history to its own ends, this world and every world, universe after parallel universe becoming infected with its seed, each world's reality altered to serve the mad imperatives of the Demiurge, each world's reality re-constructed according to the *a priori* categories of the god's sick, inhuman mind.'

The voice stops. I can hear the drip, drip, drip of water from somewhere, a metronome punctuating the crescendo of my barely-controllable hysteria, a crescendo that *will not resolve*. The only thing that keeps me from screaming is the sense that my life as Lord Dagon is over, my reacquaintance with reality about to be consummated, the worst of the nightmares about to end. I am waking, between consciousness and sleep. Yes; the dreams had been terrible; they seem real, or at least half real, even now; but though their trauma has me confused—I feel as if I'd just experienced the ECT of all ECTs—reality is lapping over my terrorized body, soothing me, recalling me to my true self: Ignatz Zwakh, born to Slovakian émigrés, the same Ignatz who had loved the little twelve-year-old, half-metamorphosed doll, Primavera Bobinski; the Ignatz who still loved her, even though he himself had, after her death, metamorphosed into a Dead Boy, a thing that had murdered its way across the universe, a thing without pity, a dead thing that had to pay for its crimes.

'Which brings us to you,' says the voice, 'our alumnus.'

'Listen,' I say. 'How come you and me remember the real world but nobody else does? What's to stop everybody waking up, huh?'

'Why *I* have not succumbed to Meta is simple, Mr Zwakh. Nurse, will you come back in here for a moment?' Frankie must have been standing outside the door, for she immediately re-enters, a sulky, liposuctorial pout communicating her displeasure at being so curtly ejected. 'Remove the straps please, Mr Zwakh is coming to self-consciousness.' As soon as I am free I sit up on the gurney and look to where the voice emanates.

My interrogator is a big fat personal computer fitted with speakers and monitor, a real antique at least one hundred, perhaps even a hundred and fifty years old. In Meta's world, that is. A world where Mars had treated PCs like *wampum,* Terrans as ignorant savages. But in the real world—

'My code was encrypted by Toxicophilous himself. The only man who, for reasons that shall become apparent, was able to create anti-viral software capable of resisting Meta's intrusions. The god of this world cannot infect *me*, Mr Zwakh. I'm quite impervious. You however, were a different matter. When Toxicophilous built *you* he created an almost perfect human simulacrum. *Too* perfect. If he'd had the foresight to reckon on the doll plague affecting human *males*, he might have designed you differently. The fact is that you, Mr Zwakh, are the last of the Cartier automata, lost to us for so many years . . .'

CHAPTER EIGHT

DeathFash

The boudoir is a mock-up. A kind of Wendy House. A playpen for the metamorphosing children of wealthy Thais. Outside, I find myself in the toy department of a derelict shopping mall marked for demolition.

I seem again to be strolling through the passageways and dusty alcoves of my father's *Wunderkammer,* though whether this is a memory of my 'father' or my 'creator' I cannot be sure. Memory is punishment, a sentence of hard labour. I want out of this chain gang.

Papa takes pictures of us without our clothes on, the floor littered with pages torn from National Geographic *and* Health & Efficiency. *This* Wunderkammer *is a twilight world of pulled drapes, old books and camphor. The books are everywhere: tomes on engineering and art history; vellum-bound editions of 'Second Decadence' writers of the 1990s; chapbooks on toy making from seventeenth-century Nuremberg; and rarities such as Bishop Wilkins's* Mechanical Magick. *There are paintings, too: amongst them originals by twentieth-century artists such as Hans Bellmer, Balthus and Leonor Fini. (My favourite picture is by the British artist Barry Burman. It is called* Judith *and depicts a pubescent girl holding, from a leather-gloved hand, the severed head of Holofernes.) But dominating the room—apart from the great couch that ridicules my father's consumptive body—are the automata. They hide in the shadows, their kinetic latency like that of coiled, predatory beasts. Here are masterworks from the Age of Reason.* The Writer *and* The Musician *by Pierre Jaquet-Droz, purchased from the bankrupt vaults of the* Musée d'Art et d'Histoire *in Neufchâtel; singing birds by Jean Frederic Leschot; and a magician, a trapeze artist, monkeys, clowns and acrobats by the Maillardets. From a later era my father has collected a bisque-headed* Autoperipatetikos *by*

Enoch Rice Morrison; the elegantly dressed girls of Gaston Decamps; a Gustav Vichy musical automaton doll; and (creature of night!) a Steiner doll, with its mouthful of shark-like teeth—which earned it the nickname 'The Vampire Doll'—intact.

Papa is seeking an answer. Papa wants us to be part of his collection; he wants us to live in that perfect world of art where there are no more tears, no pain. He wants to deconstruct us, replace our cruel, metamorphosing hearts with hearts that will always love him, always be true. We are his children, his toys. He asks us lots of questions. Coming home from school, in the lowland twilight, or in the evenings after tea, I try to spot the Wunderkammer *from outside, patient eyes cataloguing the draped windows.*

The room is invisible.

Threading between packing cases, wrecked displays, the remains of miniature starships, soldiers, dolls, radio-controlled cars and planes, The Toymakers' octo-droids escort me up a flight of stairs to a mezzanine. Frankie leads the way.

'Do I get to see Lipstick?'

'I've told you before, she's safe. Don't worry. I'm taking you to see your *other* friend.'

'Are you a robot too?'

'Oh no—a traitress. I'm just in this for the sex.' She guides me into a glass-fronted office (several of its panes broken, or cracked); and there, awaiting my arrival, is Mephisto, sitting behind a desk, feet up, a coffee cup in his hand, a hard-boiled cliché from the pages of *Black Mask*. 'But *he* is,' she adds.

'I am what I am,' says Mephisto with a sigh. 'No time for excuses. Though I'm sorry to have had to deceive you, Dagon. Really.'

'Jesus,' I sigh—suddenly remembering a word from that other universe, the real one in which I was born, or made—'Tyr, Abaddon, the others?'

'They're organic, alright. Elohim. Marauders. Malcontents. And they know nothing about this. Absolutely nothing. So when you see them—' He brought a finger to his mouth. 'Shh!'

'Coffee?' says Fascination.

'Thanks.' I sit down. 'So: The Toxicophilous Device. It was a chemical to bring me to self-consciousness, yes?'

'*You* are The Toxicophilous Device. The ampoule contained nanobots. They've rearranged your body at the atomic level. You've been returned to reality.' To prove whether this is indeed the case, I punch a nearby wall; inspect my hand; the flesh has been removed from my knuckles. Last night, I could have punched a hole through wood, concrete, steel.

Goodbye, superman; hello Clark Kent.

'The problem we have,' continues Mephisto, 'is that you're now armed. And you only have a twelve-hour fuse. That means we have to bring ahead our schedule.'

'What do you mean "armed"?'

'I mean you're the fail-safe, Dagon—Ignatz, I should say. You're The Reality Bomb. The nanoware of your reorganized atomic structure will, when you explode in close to twelve hours' time, infect the rest of the world, and then it too shall return to reality. Each 'bot contains a map of space-time as it existed before the creation of the dolls. With one crucial omission: it contains no data of Dr Toxicophilous. The universe will begin again circa 2030; but the potential of another doll plague will cease to exist.'

My chest pulsates a few times with the contained explosion of a sob-sob; I put my head between my knees. 'My life,' I whisper, 'has been a lie. You have destroyed me, left me with nothing . . .'

'You're organic,' says Mephisto, in an effort to console. 'At least, you're mostly organic. You were nanoengineered at the atomic level, in a vat, like all automata, nanomachines assembling you from the basic chemicals that constitute the human body—with some additions, of course, some modifications. Everything in nature is a machine, Ignatz, everything is information—you're not alone.'

'I suppose,' I say, a sob now escaping but transmuted into a bark of cynical humour, 'I suppose it should come as no real shock, all this. I've always been a construct of sorts.' I try to recall my earliest memories: I censor Castle Misère, concentrate on my life as Ignatz, a childhood growing up in the flooded wastelands of south Essex, the walls of the interdiction, the airborne patrols, the hospitals which interned dolls, experimented on them, exterminated them, the hospitals from which I had saved Primavera. But though these recollections have, by now, almost entirely supplanted those of Gabriel Strange, his birthplace, its granite, espaliered walls, its endless corridors and shadows, I realize that of the outside world I still remember little. My memories are, as they have always been, all of my inner life, with no sense of beginning, middle and end.

'My memories,' I say, lifting my head and looking Mephisto in the eye, 'my childhood. Was it real or is it an implant?'

'Real,' says Mephisto. 'Far realer than mine. I didn't have a childhood. I was built to find you. After you were lost. We both came into this world in 2056, but I entered it as an adult. Sixteen years I searched for you. Toxicophilous had died. He and his colleagues left only this foundation to look after his work, a cabal that consists today entirely of Toxicophilous's own creations: hardware, software, wetware, and, of course, androids like you and me. We are all that is left of the Empire *De Luxe*, the luxury goods conglomerate that dominated the world in the early twenty-first century.' I notice that this flyblown office has packing cases filled with porcelain, that a few broken cabinets still house some of the last surviving toys of the Rue du Faubourg Saint-Honoré: fashion accessories, perfumes, cosmetics, shoes, watches, jewellery, champagne, wine, spirits, crystalware, silverware, miniature droids. 'It was the age,' says Mephisto, stretching his arms to encompass this lost world, 'when Veblen's leisure class expanded into the *luxury* class, when the whole world's newly rich information elite yearned for positional goods, status symbols that could give their soulless twenty-first century existence *value*.' He lets his arms fall into his lap. 'We are all that is left. But of course'—Mephisto glances uncertainly at Frankie—'we sometimes also count *outsiders* as part of our esteemed fifth column of the *real*.' Frankie beams at me; sits on Mephisto's desk; adjusts a stocking. 'We are called The Toymakers, after our founders, though we don't *make* so much as preserve. And the last task we find ourselves confronted with is the end of history. The unfolding of space and time. You do still want to destroy the universe, don't you? You do still want to destroy Meta?'

'Yes,' I say resignedly, 'I'm the same as before in that respect. Perhaps more so. The thought of what I've done, the murders.'

'We have little time. We must get to work.'

Ever since our circumnavigation had begun I had been certain that our agenda, our only possible agenda, concerned the destruction of the female principle of the universe, and therefore, Meta itself; for it is the Meta female who carries Meta's seed; without her, the species would die. But over the last hour the uncomfortable but persistent suspicion that the purpose of the circumnavigation might have devolved solely upon myself, that the *Sardanapalus*'s real agenda had all along been a secret, has been growing, presenting itself as an impossible truth.

'*Why* did you deceive me?' I ask. 'I would have gone through with this anyway, you know I would. It's'—and my mechanical self comes to the fore—'it's my prime directive.' Mephisto leans forward, his hands pressed against his face as if in prayer, gunmetal eyes targeting my own from either side of his tensile metacarpi.

'When Toxicophilous built you he didn't foresee that Meta would become so virulent or powerful. Meta changed you. But I am an android, Ignatz; my code is encrypted; I cannot be accessed by outside sources. I only have the outward attributes of Elohim because, with the coming of the Dead Boys, The Toymakers gave me a new bodysuit to allow me to infiltrate your world. I had to deceive you—you were Elohim. I had to appeal to your Elohim instincts.

'Listen: you are a fail-safe. Toxicophilous's colleagues pressured him into building you in the event that the plague got totally out of hand. But Toxicophilous, it transpired, so loved his creations that he couldn't bear to have them un-made. I think something like a father's love may also have been involved: he had lost his own human son to the dolls; you were, perhaps, a compensation. Therefore though he acceded to his colleagues' demands he introduced into your system a thousand-year clock, a clock that had to run its course before you could be armed. Only then would it be possible for The Toymakers to infuse your body with the nanoware that would turn you into a bomb, a weapon that would be capable of de-creating the world, of returning it to 2030, a 2030 that didn't contain your maker. A thousand years, Toxicophilous argued, was only a blip in time; a new species deserved as much; humans would surely, in that span of years, acquire the wisdom of how to live at peace with their cyborg off-spring. Toxicophilous's colleagues protested, but all debate became academic, for in the confusion of those days—London during the interdiction—The Toymakers suffered an air attack by EU forces. Toxicophilous was killed. The surviving Toymakers fled. You, who were only a few days old, were rescued by paratroopers sent in to mop up. Since you were considered to be a human child, you were taken to the suburbs where, presumably, you were adopted.

'Those Toymakers who still lived built me in a last, desperate bid to undo their master's work. If I could find you, the world might be restored, even if it had to wait a thousand years for mercy.

'I discovered your whereabouts in France, when you and the doll-girl Primavera had only just escaped from the interdiction; then I lost your trail until you reappeared in Nongkhai. Shortly after that, your metamorphosis began—really, the good doctor should have made you a little *less* perfect—and by the time I reached you, you were Elohim. It was then that history began to change. I had to assume different disguises as reality metamorphosed about me. Twenty seventy-four became 1994, all space and time compressing into this present which Meta has made its own. If I were not a machine, a machine built to withstand the virus, I would have lost you again, just as you lost yourself when, in Meta's flux, *personal* history was altered and you became Gabriel Strange. Strange, yes. Ah, the world was now a strange place indeed. Meta had re-invented the laws of physics. On its unreal Mars, Faster-Than-Light travel had been made possible, just as had instantaneous communication amongst the stars via the quantum interconnectedness of the universe. In the end, we machines—the only surviving legacy of The Toymakers—knew that we had to activate you without delay. Reality had to be restored. We could not wait a thousand years. So I appealed to you to become a marauder, to follow me on a mission about the universe which—using the curvature and rotation of the universe as a time machine—would bring us back to our time and point of departure.'

'With the exception, of course,' I say, 'that I would be a thousand years older.'

'Hundreds of billions of years for observers in other frames of reference. But yes, with relativistic effects, your age, at precisely midnight tonight, will be exactly one thousand years. The Toymakers were very careful to get the calculations correct. Of course, to keep to those calculations, I had to ensure that the *Sardanapalus* decelerated the required number of times—but the extermination of the Meta colonies provided an excuse for that.'

'You mean, all the killing, all the planets we have sacked—for nothing?'

'Not for nothing. To get you back here. To give you a reason for getting back here. We were undercover. Killing is what marauders *do*.'

Memories of Ignatz Zwakh, the lovelorn boy and doll junkie, memories of Dagon, the mass murderer and sex killer, blurred into one. Who was I? I was who, or rather what, I'd always been: I was The Bomb that wanted it all to end.

'All that cruelty, meaningless—.'

'Don't lecture *me*, Ignatz. It was as much as I could do to restrain you from committing even greater atrocities than you actually did. It was only after Doriminu, the furthest colonial outpost, that I no longer had to worry. After that planet had been sacked, we were mostly in hibernation, on course, travelling backwards in time for home.'

'And The Toxicophilous Device that we found on Doriminu?'

'I had it all the time.' Ah yes, I had always envied Mephisto his prestidigitation. 'I was most apprehensive when we arrived back at Earth with you ready to be armed. After all, we were coming back to a world in which The Toymakers might not exist. Not that that, in the final analysis, would have greatly mattered. The Reality Bomb—*you,* that is—is designed to affect *all* worlds, *all* universes, *all* dimensions. But I was expecting support. In the end of course . . . Ah, those idiot humans we'd hired to look after you fouled up. It was decided to bring our schedule forward, to arm you now, and have you where we could keep our eyes on you, rather than risk than risk an incident where you might be apprehended by Meta authorities. Please, forgive the deceptions. Frankie really *can* help you get to The Chapel of The Presence. But I couldn't let you know anything about The Toymakers. You were still Dagon then, an Elohim. I couldn't predict your reaction to knowing what in fact you really were. There would be enough of a risk arming you when we had planned: this evening. You would still have had plenty of time for Dagon to argue with Ignatz, Ignatz with Dagon, about what to do come your birthday.

Now that you are armed, your self-destruction is, of course, assured. But it is imperative that we get you into The Chapel of The Presence before you detonate, otherwise all this will have been for nothing. We knew your coming to self-consciousness would always be a dangerous matter, but now—' He shook his head, gave an embarrassed laugh, as if he'd stumbled onto territory he should have stayed clear of; a minefield, it seemed, for that laugh quickly changed into a giggle of stark fear.

'But now I'm armed—what?' A bad actor, Mephisto saws an arm through the air. He cannot dissemble *sang-froid.*

'Oh, Lipstick knows. She'll tell you later.' He stands up. 'She's waiting for you now. Go to her.' He claps his hands like a despotic *pasha;* Frankie skips to the door; opens it; an octo-droid rolls along the gangway of the mezzanine; waits outside the office. 'Like the doctor says—another good android, by the way—you need to rest. Take your mind off things. Go.' He pushes me through the door, Frankie taking one hand, the droid, with a tentacle, the other. 'And I'll see you in a few hours. Briefing at 16:00. And remember: not a word to Abaddon and Tyr. We mechanical men must stick together.'

I stand in the doorway looking back at him: he's mad, I think, we're all mad; this is a joke, a trick they're playing on me for my one-thousandth birthday.

But it's no joke. This is a serious dose of reality. It was my other life that was a joke, a black gag, an evil leg-pull, a nasty jape. A one thousand-year howler.

'Go.'

Don't anybody, I think, don't anybody *dare* laugh.

CHAPTER NINE

Entr'acte: Quadrophenia

'I've always been paranoid about my breasts,' says Lipstick.

The paranoia has, I know, a qualitative, if not quantitative relationship to the various disorders we group together under the term 'hemline madness', 'mammary paranoia' being a derangement which leads, in extreme instances—like those altogether more common disintegrations of the mind mirrored and/or induced by a disintegration of the hem—to committal, or even, if the patient chooses to become a propagandizer of the affliction, to a sentence of death. It is a derangement characterized by a monomania in which the patient suffers the conviction that her breasts embody the full burdensomeness of her superfemininity, that, in their insolence, their opulence, her breasts imprison and condemn her with their female-as-victim semiotics, psychosomatic symptoms (a hypersensitization of the mamma) accentuating the patient's delusions of extreme vulnerability on such occasions as when the breasts are exposed (sentiments I have known humans to confuse with modesty), Lipstick's present exposure occasioning a C-above-top-C *screech!* when I had entered the mocked-up boudoir and discovered her dishabille in front of a vanity table mirror, her arms interlocking to shield her cruelly-tipped Partonesque (nay, *Meyeresque*) chest.

'I'm sorry,' she says, 'but that's just the way it is.' And then (relaxing now), putting on a Partonesque voice, 'I'm just a poor, poor dead *thang.*'

'Talking of paranoia,' I say, 'it seems the fate of the universe devolves entirely upon myself.'

'They told me, darling. I'm sorry.'

'Is that all? "I'm sorry"? I mean, like, you're not even surprised?'

'When I was twelve, I changed into a vampire, got sent to a palace where I spent all day asleep and all night running around biting men's necks, rock 'n' rolling on their blood. That same year a starship drops a crew of gynocidal maniacs down on us. Tens of thousands of girls are killed—except me. Me, I'm saved by a man who makes me his pet, who turns me from a vampire into a fellatrix. I change my name, renouncing my metronymic along with my haemodipsomania. Now I'm "Lipstick" and I end up travelling through star system after star system, travelling backwards in time, until, eventually I arrive at the planet my great-great-great grandparents came from, by now so crazy that I'm determined to abet my abductor in the extermination of my own species, the destruction of the world, the universe. And on top of that I'm falling in love with the creep. I ask you: should anything surprise me any more?'

I sit down on the bed—the big, four-poster, this time, not the gurney—grateful, I suppose, that I am to be allowed a few hours with Lipstick in the nymphenberg-like familiarity of this Wendy House before leading the commando raid that is to end in my death.

Piped music washes over me: a soft and solitary piano, playing an ad-corrupted 'pop classic', a *Gymnopédies*, perhaps. Lipstick joins me, a cat-girl mutazine slipping from her hand. It's called *Felis Femella* and falls open at its lonely hearts' column, *Lonesome Catz*.

'I've got ten hours to live. It's all been a bit hard to take in. No don't do that,' I say—she's raking her nails down my neck—'it *hurts*. I'm not Elohim any more. My body's changed, along with my mind.'

'I know,' she says. 'I don't care. Remember our games. You used to pretend you were a human. I didn't care then, either.'

'Well, it isn't a game any more.' Ambushing me, Dagon appears from an ill-lit street of my mind, a mugger demanding his share of existence.

A girl, always that same girl, comes around a corner grasping her breasts; she looks at me, frowns, then gazes down, first at one breast and then at the other as blood starts to leak through her fingers. Sacked nymphenbergs. Summary executions. Screams, gurgles, cries. A yellow nightgown billows in one girl's wake and is then suddenly shredded to the accompanying shusha-shusha *of a gamekeeper; the gown turns crimson, the girl falling like a stricken bird to lie still and pathetic as a canary dead in a cage. A girl hides in a wardrobe—I fire a few rounds into it and open the door; my victim stands stock-still, arms by her side, her body streaming with blood like an ancient, anointed goddess, her proud eyes staring at me with indignation, pain.*

'Paranoia, huh?' I say.

Those who are Meta sometimes marvel at what it must be like to inherit the predispositions of humanity. I know that Dagon can never 'make love' to a female; it is not that the act of penetration fills him with horror (as it does Lilim, with their inherited disgust for human-on-human sex, their disdain for anatomies they consider 'utilitarian'); no; but he realizes that the act of dealing-out pain, humiliation, is, for him, far nobler, far more enriching, than any aping of the reproductive mechanics that, 'thankfully and perforce', he entrusts to Meta's servants, the human race; for it is not the human generative function that he disdains so much as the human male's predisposition towards taking (and sometimes, even giving) pleasure, a predisposition that disqualifies him from luxuriating in the metaphysical delights of power, justice and punishment, delights that, if in him, are spiritual, are, he considers, in humans, base. Even when he was a boy he knew that he would soon enough cease to fantasize about 'making love'; would even cease to fantasize about rape; all that would be left would be his dreams of killing, his fascination with death.

Will I ever be rid of this man?

I make the hand gesture that orders her to 'present'; and, a Lilim for five years, she immediately, though reluctantly—ah, she whimpers, the flirt— complies, her arms which a moment before had interlocked to shield her bosom, now cupping that somewhat gross, somewhat needlessly emphatic but undeniably epicurean target. 'Measurements,' I say, as evenly as I can.

'38EE-24—' But I interrupt; I am not interested in her waist-to-hip ratio.

'Measurements,' I repeat.

'38EE—' And again I interrupt her.

'Measurements.'

'38EE—'

'Measurements.'

'38EE—'

'Measurements.'

'38EE—' Her overly made-up face glistens with perspiration.

'Measurements.' Reduced to a statistic, a brassière cup dimension, her whole body and personality condensing into the semiotic charge of her breasts, nothing else now but that '38EE' repeated into infinity, she screams (the '38' barely audible, everything translated into a long EEEEEEEEEE!), pulls back her shoulders, her eyes screwed tight (though she doesn't go as far as adopting the 'stand' position, hands behind her head in classic pin-up, or rather [I should say], *interrogatory* pose; but then I have not gestured that she should), and I pull her down on the bed and kiss her.

Go away, I say to him, my erstwhile brother, my shadow. You are no longer corporeal. You no longer have the power to hurt. I exorcize you. Begone.

Her moment of hysteria passes and she melts into my arms; Dagon disappears where he came from, the coward, off to mug someone who won't stand up to him, a little old lady perhaps, but more likely, a little girl.

In my peripheral vision, *Felis Femella* goes mutey, deincriminating itself, its cover now resembling that of *Newsweek* or *Time*.

'You don't need *Lonesome Slutz*, Archangel, you got Miss Lonelyhearts right here.' Her hands fasten about my temples, her fingernails rake my scalp, and then she pulls, pulls, as if trying to separate head from torso, she Salomé, me the Baptist, our last dance this, take your partners, please.

We roll off the bed, across the thick-piled carpet, over tables, chairs, sofas, a grand piano, as I penetrate her orally, vaginally, anally.

My catgirl—suddenly more catholic in her sport—gurgles with delight. 'Who am I,' I say as I hump her from behind, 'I've been a robot who believed himself a human who then forgot who he was to become a different human, a human who, in time, became a superman.'

Behind my clenched eyes I see Primavera; she is twelve; her DNA has begun to recombine. She sits in front of me in class, her long blonde hair betraying its first streaks of Cartier black. Primavera Bobinski. Rainham is a ruined, deserted Neverland where no one gets to grow up. And Primavera has the cutest little fangs. The other children taunt her, *'Dead Girl, Dead Girl,'* they chant. When she kisses me for the first time my human self begins to die, die with pleasure . . .

Then I see another Primavera, my sister, playing in the halls of Castle Misère. Together, we parade about the gardens in costumes for little Lilim and Elohim. Mama tells us not to worry, that we are 'different'; and then she kisses away our tears. She reads us stories. I like Jules Verne and Lewis Carroll. Alice, says Mama, was a little girl called Alice Liddel. 'She was Lilim, too, like you, Primavera.' And then, one day, Mama takes us to the circus. A lady, high, so high above, balances on a wire. She is called a tightrope walker. Sequins glitter in the spotlights like the scales of armoured fish. 'Fall,' Primavera whispers into my ear. 'I want her to fall, Gabriel.' And her clammy little hand tightens in mine. When Mama takes us to register for school the teacher says, 'Oh, *twins!*' 'Identical twins,' I say, my eyes hooded, like Primavera's. *'Identical.'*

I move inexorably towards orgasm, and both Primaveras become as one, even as Ignatz, Gabriel and Dagon become as one, even as The Toxicophilous Device and Lipstick are about to come as one.

My first kill.

Dagon—no! Stay away from me! Go back!

She rises from her chair (rustle of starched petticoats), a book falling from her lap to the bare, highly-waxed floorboards (I see that it is a copy of Robbe-Grillet's The Voyeur*); my gun, that is Gun, a youthful, carefree, less critical Gun, is in handgun mode; I am pointing him at her bosom, my other hand—one finger across my lips—indicating that she should not attempt to cry for help; for even though I have ensured that no one besides the manse's servants are in the house (servants can be bribed; servants are unlikely to cause trouble) I still have a young superman's doubts about my ability—despite the super-testosterone rumbling through my veins—to fend off an outraged mob. My apportioned share of the afternoon's sport gasps, crosses her arms across her chest. (She is in mock-shepherdess garb, 'fresh-country-girl' wear: a white knee-length frock and white knee-gartered stockings. The frock is of cheesecloth and cut low.) I had meant to torture her—to slink-rive her, to avenge myself on her, her crimes, but also, to avenge myself on my god, on Meta for torturing me, for torturing us all with his cruel, infernal games—but I cannot move. I am suddenly filled with an incomprehensible fear; and as if perceiving this seizure in my soul, the girl's face softens, fills with what might be pity, or at least a recognition of some kind, an understanding. I no longer wish to hurt her; but I know I must; it is not the fear of dishonour that makes me hesitate; to be so disgraced would, for me, only mean becoming the butt of my brothers' hypocrisies, and I hold such hypocrisies (and increasingly, those hypocrites, my peers and teachers) in contempt; no; if I do not make this first kill, my essential being, my* blood *will be disgraced. It is the fear of what is human in me, the residual humanity that, still metamorphosing, is like a pebble in my boot, the fear that that humanity may now intrude at this late stage of my development from boy to man, human to inhuman—it is that* fear *that I know I must overcome, vanquish in the same way that a dragon consumes the knight-at-arms, the human-as-hero, human as son, lover, husband, father, man.*

Yes; and she understands; my victim wishes to help me. I cannot bring myself to torture her, but as her lips close in a moue *and as she closes her eyes and slightly, just slightly heaves her bosom towards the piratical, one-eyed stare of Gun's silenced barrel, I manage to squeeze the trigger; a* woof! *of expanding gases (prefiguring the dog-like, marauderesque state I am soon to descend to) and her décolletage is decorated by a small, red, wet hole. She collapses to her knees; her head lolls forwards; and then as gracefully as all Lilim do at such times, she falls onto her side; expires . . .*

I come with a thunderous, explosive cry of '*husstenhasstencaffincoffintussemtossemdamandamnacosaghcusaghobixhatouxpeswchbechoscashlcarcarcaract.*'

And I am Ignatz again.

If I had any doubts about completing my mission, fulfilling my Prime

Directive, then I have no longer. Dagon will never completely disappear while Meta is alive . . .

Post coitum, and I bury my head in the pile, confounded (especially by that almost forgotten memory of Dagon's first kill, an illegal kill perpetrated while still at The Academy [and thus underage] when, one summer, he and a friend had visited his cousins at Malpertuis in Kent); and then Lipstick cradles my head in her lap and sings me lispingly to sleep. She sings me a Doriminian lullaby.

> I paint my lips bright red.
> (Whose is that horrid laugh?)
> Humiliation wed
> me to a photograph.
> I am of purpose bled
> quite dry. Whose is that laugh?
>
> I purged my human part
> that had become so foul
> and pinned my bloated heart
> upon a pretty veil
> to become by such art
> something artificial.
>
> Blonde hair, black eye,
> blonde breast, black dress—and black and blonde
> my soul. Cast thy die,
> poet, and pour my trite
> life into it, for thy
> sole inventive delight.
>
> Princess Lipstick, forfeit
> of autonomy, is
> glad of thy dark conceit,
> wherein all luxuries
> of intensest noon greet
> an imperial kiss.
>
> Below my balcony
> I hear the Tiger creep.
> His hot propinquity
> arouses me from sleep.
> Metamorphic cruelty,
> stay. Human still, I weep.

Ah, I will always be fucked up, half in, half out of Meta. I will always be contaminated by the deeds and thoughts of Lord Dagon. The only reality I can ever be sure of is Primavera, the Primaveras Bobinski and Strange.

Is there any hope of salvation? If only I could stay like this, I think, my head in her lap, feeling her stroke my hair, my cheek, if only I could stay like this for all eternity. Then everything might be forgiven, and I might again, after that eternity had passed, be born again intact.

But what hope for one as damaged as me?

Lipstick, deaf to these self-pitying thoughts, gets up, walks to the mini bar, pours us drinks.

'You didn't mind?' I say.

'I told you, Archangel, I really like playing humans. I could get a taste for things human, I bet I could. I'm still a cat, but if you're an *Ignatz,* then I'm a *Krazy Kat.*' If I *was* an Ignatz, I thought, bitterly. Still, it was better than being called The Device and certainly better than being called Dagon.

'If you could be, if you could choose, I mean, would—'

'Yes,' she says, unhesitatingly.

'If I had the power,' I say, 'I'd make you *aitch.* In another world, maybe, after tonight, you'll—'

'Shut up, darling. We're always going to be together. That's the way it was meant to be. I know that now. Monsters like us *belong* together.'

For a while, we don't speak. Lipstick watches me, prostrate on the floor, my uniform in shreds, the last of a martini running down the sides of my mouth; she's perched on a stool at the bar, one knee under her chin, vacant, so pretty, and she's twirling a cocktail umbrella; and then she turns her gaze away, the sight, perhaps, of her suddenly-human lover, his skin no longer grey, his hair mousy, his eyes a baby-blue, too much to assimilate and too soon, all her concentration given to the comic spread out on the zinc counter. Is it another *Felis Femella,* or is it *The Beano* she reads, its *Minnie the Minx*? with its inevitable denouement of Minnie fellating her Dad? Or is it *The Dandy,* that comic starring the notorious *Korky the Katgirl*? So pretty, this talisman, this *memento mori* of my dead loves, that Primavera who succumbed as we floated down the Mekong River, the other executed, so cruelly, in a Bangkok park. So like theirs, that alluring vacant gaze. (Is this the catatonia of those who both love and fear the pizzle? says Dagon. The personality burn-out of those who have sloughed off their last remaining vestiges of humanity to become *girls,* walking, talking pieces of slink, of rotten meat? And is there hatred too, in this quintessence? Dagon remembers her on the streets of Hua Hin where he caught her tormenting a little h-girl. Such jealousy of the human womb. Such disgust for human procreation.)

But I do not have a sister, I remind myself; and the girlfriend I had once, that other beloved Primavera, might as well be as equally unreal as my fictive sibling. All I have is Lipstick; she is all I have ever had, the only lodestar in this maelstrom of real and unreal memories, the names and identities of a tumultuous whirlpool where life's only other certainty is that its navigator, this I, is an illusion.

Primavera had, perhaps, never been a person at all, but an ideal, a projection of my own desire.

'Frankie Cat tells me,' I say, 'that you still plan to come along—to accompany me all the way up to The Presence, even though you know what's going to happen when I get there.'

'If you're successful it won't matter where I am, will it? But yes, I'm going to stay with you. With you changing your personality every few minutes someone's got to be around to make sure—'

'Make sure of what?'

'To make sure you go *Booooom!* of course, moron.'

I laugh.

'Mephisto said there was something you had to tell me,' I say. 'Something to do with me being armed and being conscious of it, or something.' Lipstick gives me one of those long, hard looks that she usually reserves for when she is about to act as Dagon's pander and supply him with a kill.

'Later,' she says. 'I'm tired.'

'Don't you think that—'

'Please, Archangel. Later.'

We stretch out on the white silk sheets of the four-poster and close our eyes.

'Soon,' I say, nuzzling her neck, the glorious smell of her newly-washed hair in my nostrils competing with the scent of her allure, her sweat, her cheap perfume. 'It will all end soon.' I close my eyes, the chatter of my monkey brain subdued to a whisper, a rustling of leaves, a sea breaking on a distant shore. 'When you were little,' I say, 'before you metamorphosed, did you watch much TV? TV programmes, when I was a kid, all seemed to be dubbed, suffering from some kind of beamed-in overwriting from, where? the words in the mouths of Mr Ed and Uncle Martin, Matt Dillon and Kitty, the policemen in *No Hiding Place,* the Tiller Girls on *Sunday Night at the London Palladium* and the miscegenational goings-on during the *Black & White Minstrel Show* all seemingly originating from another star system, or a parallel world. What can the messages mean, I would think, these words that are violent, yet smooth as moleskin, suave, addictive, deadly? The world is a palimpsest.'

'Your mind's all fucked up, darling. Been written over too many times. Like the world, I guess. Believe me, I'm feeling pretty fucked up too. At least, fucked around with. You know, I never knew the felid Miss Frankie Fascination was working for these *Toymakers*. We've gotten into something too big we can't escape from.'

'We could never escape,' I say. 'It was facile to believe otherwise. What we're involved in now goes beyond self-murder.'

She rolls over, straddles me, then stands up, wobbling on the soft, feath-erdown mattress, legs astride me in the pose of Lilith on the *crucis lingam*—Lilith, her thighs wide, her sex pointing downwards as if in accusation of all the cruelties I have inflicted on that apex of superfemininity for over a thousand years; and then she begins to descend, the goddess bearing down, ushering in a New Heaven, a New Earth. Yes. Reality is coming to Earth in Judgement. Reality is whispering to me. She is saying: it is no longer enough, this myth, this fairy tale of vampiric beings who parasitize humans, using them in order to propagate. If you are to be re-born, I must die. And her words are words of fire, the words of a phoenix, words announcing a new rationale for existence, a new faith, a new life.

The last trump sounds.

'I—' But my appeal is smothered. I am a man without past or home; a man without a self; I am an artifact. But if I was a *thing* when I was Dagon I am at least now a *thing* that can redeem, if not myself, then a somnam-bulant world from its mad, mad dreams, a world that throughout its long, cruel centuries had successively dreamed it was Abraham, offering his daughter to the Demiurge; the Minotaur devouring Lilim beneath the nymphenberg of Crete; Alexander, conquering the Persians, the Persians who know nothing of vampirism or of a commensal human-inhuman re-lationship but who worship Meta as the god who justifies the harems where men go to kill beautiful girls, such killing being a religious obliga-tion, an aristocratic sport; dreamed it was Scipio Aemilianus leading his legions through the night time streets of Carthage, putting that city of parthenogenetic girls to the sword; dreamed it was Crassus, impaling re-bellious gladiatorix; dreamed it was Longinus, spearing Lilith through her sex even as she hung writhing on her cross; dreamed it was Attila, Charlemagne, Kublai Khan; dreamed it was Cortés, harrying the Ama-zons of Palenque, Uxmal, Mayapan, Copán, Tikal, Uaxactún, Chichén Itzá . . .

Pyramidal mounds burn. Conquistadors strip the natives of their cloaks of fine vicuña, their headdresses and feathers, their gold necklaces, their belly stones. The eagle the jaguar and the rattlesnake cry out. In the plazas of Tenochtitlán the sphinxes are arrayed in the traditional three-pointed star and girls writhe on the marble, scored through by elegant steel palings. These Aztec priestesses have enjoyed a sexual relationship with the great jungle cats, who are their servants and warriors, and are so called, by the Spaniards, 'catgirls' (a term rapidly gaining common currency in Europe), both for their propensity to fellate their feline protectors and their willingness, when dying on the slab, to fellate their executioners. (Because of their great numbers, girls die on the slab in tandem, lower berth sucking scrotum, upper berth sucking penis. Prospective victims fight amongst each other, arguing about who is to be on top.) Indeed, these Mesoamerican heathen resemble their own señoritas so much that the task of bringing them the word of Lilith is greatly simplified . . .

And the world still dreams, dreams it is James Bond of Her Majesty's Secret Service, a secret agent stalking runaway cats on Mars, leading them into ill-lit alleyways, killing them . . .

I have her repositioned in my arms (I'm standing up; her thighs are over my shoulders, her back arched, head dangling towards the ground); I rip away the cachette (the reformatory-school brand is revealed, a poisonous flower of infamy burnt into depilated skin); then her pubis is against my mouth—

But Dagon is bound, about to be tossed into the pit, his fangs to no longer lock on, gnaw, bite, his tongue to no more become tumescent, elongate, slip from between his lips to bury itself in the brimming fount of a sex, prospecting deep, deeper, until the tongue-tip pushes its way through the cervical canal to curl about the sickly sweet meat of uterus, Fallopian tubes, ovaries—gynocandy he will excavate with one long, liposuctorial kiss.

That meat was never rotten; it was always sweet, so sweet. It is the sweetness of a rebel, not a traitress. A traitress is a female considered as meat. A consumable. A comestible. But Lipstick is a wolf, like I have been (like I still am), a kind of *canis minor,* just as I have always been a cat.

I am all that is here now; nameless, I am all that is left; I am the one who loves. I no longer care to have any other self.

And as she cries out I close my eyes and see a sign: the *Sardanapalus* streaking through the atmosphere like a flaming meteor, about to hit the Earth at close-to-light speed and reduce it to atoms.

Self-murder, says the sibyl, looking into the planet's ashes, *it is the only way. But wait there is more, I see another sex-death—*

'Mahasukha!' she screams.

Transcendence through orgasm, through love.

CHAPTER TEN

The Way of the Weird

The mall that is our hideaway lies on the outskirts of Bangkok. I stand on its roof, the Big Mango beneath me, Monoxide City being more or less as I remember it—or as Ignatz remembers it—when he had lived within its environs during the late twenty-first century, this futurized present conforming to all particulars except one: for some reason, known only to Meta, this Bangkok has not yet been overwhelmed by the sea, its roads and *soi* still above the water line of the Chao Phraya river.

Night has fallen. The cityscape, brightly-lit, teeming with cars, helicopters, autogyros, blimps, skytrains, ornithopters and hoverjets, is like a stretch of low-lying swampland above which a post-infinite number of virtual fireflies dance in and out of existence, scintillating above skyscrapers, condos, pagodas, slums; if this last raid succeeds, the sub-atomic bedrock of this city's corporeity will be rearranged; those artificial lights, those flickering, virtual fireflies will become the quantum structure of an unreal city, a city of the imagination, of dreams, a city we will wake from to discover again the essence of things, our true selves.

But the real world—it's no paradise, I remind myself; in many ways it resembles this ontological horrorshow, this megacity along whose concrete and electronic highways are festooned the kleptocracies and pornocracies that are the processing plants, the meat grinders upon which this world-capital's wealth is based, Godfathers and Big Bosses—bastard offspring of law enforcement and organized crime—long schooled in the relentless rape of their own country now graduates of Meta's New World Order, global rapists, Thailand the ideal place, the marketplace of marketplaces, to sell sex, drugs, children, organs, souls, consciences, death—all the things Martians want, buy, take, but will never admit to wanting, buying, taking; ideal, because to be Thai is to be born (or so those in power always remind the not-so empowered, just as they remind them of the necessity of greed and the feudalistic *status quo*) with a pure heart, all problems imported, not your own, no, not the responsibility of this Land of Smiles, a silence, a national *omerta* ensuring that the country's underbelly—intestinal rumours bubbling about refractory peasants rounded-up by the military to be converted into photo-mechs, tinker toys, *post-human* peasants, about the illicit trade in slink-meat, the shat on, the scapegoats, the cheated, the dispossessed, the corruption at street level and on-high—was an underbelly wrapped in the flag, in the purity of race, blood and nationalism, in endless hypocrisies, never to be talked about, for to talk about a problem was to admit to a problem was to have that problem, and, *mai-pen-lai, khrap,* Thailand has no problems, silent, smiling country of *mai mee ban-ha:* no *plob-lem, no plob-lem;* let *money* talk.

But whatever horrors await me, for all humankind, when we awake, we will at least be free to love again, free of Meta . . .

Mephisto is pointing at a VDU with his swagger stick, explaining how Fascination (Frankie, it seems, still operating undercover) will lead Lipstick and me, first, through the maintenance tunnels of the abandoned subway system, and then, leaving us to complete our suicide mission alone, au revoiring us at where a subterranean ingress in the walls of the ziggurat will lead us eventually to The Chapel of The Presence, at which juncture, it is to be hoped, I will finally have the opportunity of deploying The Toxicophilous Device. *Au revoir?* Frankie says she has faith we'll meet again in pervert's heaven. Mephisto taps the VDU with his stick. As we climb, he, Tyr and Abaddon, he says, will create a diversion by raiding the nymphenberg *à la mode maraudeur,* killing as many Lilim as they can, creating panic and confusion amongst the seventy-seven levels and distracting the resident Elohim from the real threat.

I continue to look out over the city, bored by this briefing, my awareness of the true state-of-play exceeding everybody's, even Mephisto's; for I have been—*am,* perhaps—both artifact and human, both human and Meta; and I am something else too.

I am the End of the World.

When I explode, what will be left? Will anything that is not a mask, a piece of me that is not artificial, survive? Unlikely; what have I ever been but a series of masks?

But then Mephisto says something that turns my head. 'You have asked me before, my friends, why The Toxicophilous Device must be detonated in The Chapel of The Presence. Well, now I can tell you. The Device, exploding anywhere but in The Chapel would have a devastating local effect. It would—at least temporarily—reassemble atomic structure within, say, a two-, or three-kilometre radius. But Meta would soon reclaim this ground. To destroy the god of this and every world we must explode The Device at Meta's heart, at the centre of this dreaming multiverse.

'This is the mystery, the great mystery known only to Lilith's high priestesses, a secret passed on by word of mouth for over 10,000 years and guarded jealously by those dedicated to Meta's preservation: The Chapel of The Presence contains a transdimensional gateway. *Within* those portals Meta is spontaneously created out of nothing, continuously birthed into existence by the void; *through* those portals, Meta is continuously pouring itself out into this universe and an infinity of others. That birthing chamber must be destroyed if we are to finally rid ourselves of Meta.'

'Yeah,' I say, and give my bullshitting co-conspirator a slow clap, clap, clap; I'm more than bored by his explanation—I'm annoyed; annoyed because, only yesterday, I would have believed him. 'That makes sense.'

Abaddon turns, regards me with disdain. Says Mephisto: 'Are there any questions?' Drowning in this mad, irrational universe, Dagon's fellow marauders have no difficulties in accepting Mephisto's flimsy, irrational lifeline; they'll believe anything, do anything, to be given the chance to just once fill their lungs with air.

After Tyr and Abaddon have walked away I corner my erstwhile *Käpitan* and demand that I be told the truth. 'A mystery,' I scoff, 'a "great mystery known only to Lilith's high priestesses"—ha!' One thing particularly bugs me. 'What's so special about 1994?' I say. 'I mean, all space and time, all history seems to be swirling around this particular moment in time, swirling about it in continual flux. Why is all history, past and future, compacted into 1994?'

'Thank you, Dagon.' Mephisto smiles indulgently; pivots the VDU so that it is invisible to prying eyes; palms the swagger stick's infra-red, then points with it. A video is showing the covers of three books. 'Toxicophilous was inspired by the literature of the 1990s, the so-called "Second Decadence". When he nanoengineered his Cartier dolls the effects of quantum indeterminacy—the interaction of atomic particles with an observer—ensured that his creations were infected with his own dark dreams, the fears and lusts of *La Décadence*. That was the reason his dolls mutated—they became hybrids of those creatures celebrated in '90s literature: succubi, vampires, chimeras, sphinxes—images of the dark side of Toxicophilous's anima that had been unconsciously programmed into their CPUs. They became *these* books'—Mephisto taps the screen—'and they acted out the roles allocated to them by these books' narratives. Meta—the doll-plague virus in its purest form—has, in its turn, tried to re-create these narratives on the grandest possible scale, imposing them upon the world in which the last of these books was written, the world of 1994.'

So: I have been a character in a book; I am still a character in a book; and to restore the world to reality I must again become a thing, but this time a thing of words, rather than a thing of flesh. Only by reassuming my rightful form could the world be disburdened of this *esthétique du mal.*

We must all, I think, become words again.

'The doll plague was an observer-created virus; the antiviral software that informs me and the other Toymakers is likewise observer-created. Just as a snake serum is produced from the snake's own venom, so the antidote to the plague had to come from Toxicophilous's own sick, poisonous mind. If you have done evil things, Ignatz, it has been necessary. The cure issues from the disease. From you, we have extracted the pathogen with which to vaccinate the world.'

He turns off the VDU; lays down his stick; tightens the cords of his doublet and codpiece. 'The Chapel of The Presence really does contain a transdimensional gateway, though not one, of course, that has existed for 10,000 years. It is at the portals of that gateway that you must explode. You will know it when you get there.'

Lipstick appears, Frankie by her side. Frankie has been to a beauty parlour; she has been re-Orientalized (been practising her Thai-glish too, doubtless), and the two girls look the same as when they approached my table last night at *The V.Berg;* same, except, instead of dirndlkleids and merkins, they are power dressed in uniforms that identify them as wards of the Bangkok nymphenberg.

Behind Lipstick and Frankie, the *Sardanapalus's* remaining litter of cats, dressed in their usual cat-print.

A helicopter circles, begins to land; our taxi to hell.

'I have plenty more questions,' I say, but to Lipstick, not Mephisto. 'But I know there are no answers. Not in this universe. So why ask?' I take her hand.

'Well,' she says. 'I'm ready.'

I kiss her on her forehead, then, holding her at arms' length, inspect her—more for pleasure than out of any sense of rigorousness—and am pleased to discover that she, in her Lilim wear, just as I, in my patched-up Elohim wear, look good enough to be invited to the ball, good enough, at least (or so I hope) to pass as denizens of the Bangkok ziggurat.

Her St Trinians-like uniform consists of a white trapezoid skirt—very stiff, flounced, something like a tutu but without the netting; very hyper-hyper—a white, almost diaphanous blouse (sheer enough to reveal that she wears a cupless brassière, though whether styled semi, demi or hemi is difficult to tell; that her nipples are rouged *sang-de-boeuf*, rust-red as her rubiginous lips, and that each is pierced with a gold-and-diamanté charm of Lilith suffering on the *crucis lingam),* a silk blazer, white-and-emerald striped (the escutcheon on the pocket displaying the green pentacle of Meta inside the chemical symbol of *femininity*) and the standard issue ultra-sheer stockings, so fine that they usually ladder after a single wearing, and which on Lipstick—who seems to be dissembling parsimoniousness—are torn, shredded, whacked. She holds her beret in her hand, her ash-blonde mane set off by a silky black ribbon, its rosette-like streamers falling to her shoulders in an inverted V, V being, whether inverted, obverted, reverted or perverted, that eternal symbol of belly and bifurcation of the thighs, that satinette bow the penumbra of the black sun of sex, of death.

The helicopter lands. Lipstick raises an eyebrow. Snip and Snap jump out.

All the world's here, I think, looking out over the Big Weird, and all the *worlds* are here, all the known universe, on this seaboard that is one great megalopolis, stretching from the Khmer border down, down to Singapore.

'Then let's go,' I say.

PART III

I wanna souffler,
I wanna gamahuche ya,
I wanna Alpha/Omega ya,
sez Love

CHAPTER ELEVEN

Unspeakable Orgy II: Midnight Express

Ascending, we crawl at a forty-five degree angle over cables, fibre, between air-conditioning ducts, fuse boxes and under vents, transponders, circuit boards and plumbing. We are worming our way through the ziggurat's geodesic superstructure; an intelligent building, its thick, self-regulatory innards are inducing grunts, contusions, sweat.

'Good luck,' calls Frankie, her face framed by the access hatch fifty metres below; and then she leaves us, heading back along the rat-infested tunnels, the maze of that half-completed mass transit system that is a forgotten monument to reneged-on contracts and bankruptcy.

Snip and Snap have been left to guard the dark underworld beneath Chakra Bong; and, though the likelihood of us being discovered by maintenance engineers is small, I'm glad to have those masquerading humans out of the way; we can't afford any more botch-ups.

It is 19:45. 'In just over four hours,' I say, 'it'll be my birthday.'

'Happy birthday,' says Lipstick, 'in case I forget.' I look behind; already, her ward's uniform is soiled, the stockings gone, atomized; I, too, am looking as if I've just survived a battle, my chest beginning to bleed from so many jutting rivets, camouflaged projections of nylon and steel. Involuntarily, my hand strays to my shoulder holster; and then I remember that Gun is departed, lost to that twilight world of hyperspace where all gamekeepers go to when they die.

Our journey at first takes us through a cross section of the palace's substrata, the service tunnel's vents and grilles affording us sights of a fantastical prison analogous to Piranesi's *Carceri d'Invenzione*. Racks of cells, like rusted birds' cages, rise from either side of a central aisle, cast-iron gangways demarcating each serried avenue of canned flesh, this torrid, cavernous chamber's acoustics amplifying every *click* and *clack* of Imperial Guards' high-heels, every drip of water, every soft fatalistic moan and every desperate, pain-maddened scream. Inside the cells, outside the cells, from the ferrous latticework of the all-pervasive gangways, from the roof of the chamber itself, girls are suspended: by their wrists, by their thumbs, by their ankles, by their hair or (most commonly, this) by a nexus of rope that knots wrists to ankles, tautened bodies forming countless rows of lozenges glistening in an unremitting glare of klieg lights. Some girls, released from their day's allotted torment, are being herded back into their pens, their tormentors recruited from the more insidious regiments of the Imperial Guard (each guard armed with a slender, gold-plated pitchfork and attired in one of those red-sequinned leotards with curly forked tails that seem to be *sine qua non* amongst the warders of this underworld, horns attached to each mock-demoness's head), crypto-Nazi regiments, Guard such as might be found amongst the ranks of a South American dictatorship's secret police. And everywhere, mountains of garbage: old clothes, lingerie, laddered stockings and cheap, broken jewellery (the type you get free in comics), empty scent bottles, broken palettes of blusher, mascara, eye shadow and lipsticks from the palest of praline pinks to the angriest of pomegranates. And amongst this garbage, feeding off these little barrows of superfeminine tribute to the Plutonic deities: things, things uncatalogued by any taxonomist and which I only obtain half-glimpses of before they slither expeditiously back into their nests of couture and maquillage: blind mutant rats, huge wasps with intelligent, mammalian eyes and stings that remind me of the ulcerated, eructating phalli of Elohim, black spiders that look as if they have hides of sleek pubic hair and worms, worms—these, the worst of all things—worms that look as if they might be programmed by gross instinct to crawl into a convict's slumberous cell, to slip between legs and disappear, only to reappear, ever afterwards, in nightmares. The most fortunate of these prisoners seem to be those condemned to death (at the end of a long aisle that bisects General Population there is a portcullis of stainless steel; above it, the fascia DEAD GIRLS); at least they will know an end to their suffering. As we pass through this area a vent allows us to spy a priestess—bat-cowled, and caped in black—offering absolution. As the condemned receive the sacraments, she reads from the Book of Lilith, reciting the girl-goddess's last words as she hung upon her cross: 'It must be thus, unto the end of time, the sons of Eloi to kill the daughters of Lilith. For Eloi and Lilith are of the race Meta, and Meta must live in a state of commensalism with humankind if it is to live and multiply. Do not hate your brothers, my Lilim; in your death is life. Unchecked, your appetites would soon reduce this world to a sterile landscape of brief, girlish flames. No; do not hate your brothers; honour them. For they are your guardians, and the guardians of the host, the generations of human men and women whom Meta needs in order to reduplicate. Die, even as I die, that Meta may live. Die, and know eternal life.'

At such times, the condemned try to concentrate on the necessity, the beauty of the cull. They seek transcendence, even if, finally, they know that they are creatures incapable of love. Love? They admit to infatuation, nothing more. But in their infatuated minds their lovers are with them tonight even as they prepare their last wardrobe. Dressing-up is the great autoerotic act, such creatures as we being so in love with ourselves. Perhaps they can find transcendence there, with their clothes, all life, in these last hours, all consciousness becoming subordinate to their exteriority, their gestures, their poses, their flesh, their couture; for clothes are all that will be left, all that there has ever been, really, since Lilim-hood burnt-away their human subjectivity and they became global sex machines, little entities of pure surface. In death, they are their clothes, an attitude, a demeanour, a language—not such a language that Martians vulgarly contend is composed of a minimalist vocabulary consisting merely of the noun 'sex'; but a language that is a whole theatre, a whole world of scripts, roles, play, in which that noun represents a deep, universal grammar, the grand palaver of a monolingual, monomaniacal cosmos, a cosmos that has nothing else to talk about but which possesses an infinite expressiveness. Yes, that's all that's left of them; that's their essence; the infinite permutations of sex, sex, sex, sex, sex, sex, sex, sex, sex. And sex permeates everything, love, pain, terror, joy, disease, war, famine, permeates good and evil to create a universe beyond good and evil, a meta-universe. They are becoming one with the Demiurge, the spirit of the cosmic dance, the *tandava,* the all-shattering sex-death.

No love, but this beauty . . .

The supreme fiction, the myth that we live by, still permeates Lipstick's being. As she has grown up and first her soul, and then her body, has been besieged by the dark dreams, the morbid fantasies, that harry all of her kind from infancy to extinction, she has hungered for that final, self-sufficient explanation of why she so desired to kill and be killed: that Lilith had, some 2,000 years ago, started to replace human girl-children with her own, that these changelings, in turn, created other changelings; that Lilith had subsequently sent her sons into the world to discipline the savage promiscuity of her daughters, this new race of succubi and incubi destined to take on the sins of the world. Lipstick sighs; I can tell she is as tired as I am by this repetitive bedtime story. The myth is failing her.

As if reading my mind, she says: 'But I've changed, just like you've changed, Archangel. I can love now, really I can.'

'Have you always loved me?'

'Nearly always. Why?'

'Because I don't understand how you could. Dagon, he—'

'But you're not Dagon,' she says. 'To me, you've never been Dagon. Not for a long time, at least.'

'A long time?'

'Time—it doesn't matter any more. Time's finished, like space.'

'I didn't know,' I say, 'all that time, I didn't know.'

'And all that space. Pinhead.' But we shall all be changed soon, I think; in the twinkling of an eye; and I will love her as she deserves to be loved. Always.

As we continue to ascend we are, if denied further spyholes, treated to occasional snatches of netherworld conversation. *'At first I deceived myself, said: "We're the same as our sisters, us cats; we're vampires too; it's just that we vampirize phallus." I mean, there are catgirls true to Lilith: there're plenty in the Imperial Guard, and lots of chambermaids, parlourmaids, housemaids and scullerymaids have gone the Way of the Cat. (I guess, with maids, it's all that hostessing, all that diplomacy, all that Martian slime.) The other girls would laugh. And I'd say: "It's so unfair. I'm not a sex criminal." And I'd try to remind them: "If every criminal is a cat (well, nearly every criminal) it doesn't follow that every cat is a criminal. They taught us that in prep classes." But the Big Sisters just said, "Wait. You'll see, you'll see." And they're right. Lately I can't stop thinking these treacherous thoughts. Treachery's so sexy.'*

Another voice: *'The one I told you about, the one called "Jehovah": he's done it: he's turned me into a cat. It happened so quickly. He just walked into my room, threw some photo-mechanicals on the floor, and said, "Are these yours?" Within the margins of glossy, mimetic worlds, little 2-D figures strutted down the streets of Martian cities, picked-up h-men in bars, fellated them in alleys, sent postcards to their Elohim lovers to exacerbate the wounds, the excruciating wounds of betrayal. This wasn't ordinary pornography: these photo-mechs, these iniquitous illos, represented how sexy it is to hurt, not merely h-men, but our brothers, too. This was traitress pornography. "Are you a sex traitress?" he kept asking. "Are you one of those perverts who enjoy betraying us, who pretend to be true while all the time dallying with humans who lie beyond the interdiction, are you one of those who dream of running away to Mars? Do not prevaricate, whore. Tell." I'm not—I mean I wasn't—a traitress, but he scared me. Scared me sick. I knew I was too young to be sentenced to death, but you hear such stories about reform school. The beatings. The buggery. The brands. And so I begged to be spared arraignment, begged in the only way Lilim know how, by getting down on my knees and chewing pizzle. With some girls,*

I've heard, it can take weeks of such begging before they finally scream and go Miaow! *; but with me it was like, well,* instantané.'

And another: '*We sat on a wooden bench, our wrists handcuffed behind our backs, the corridor similar to those above ground, only this without fur, a tunnel of black, immaculate marble, but endless, just as endless, with one of those pinpoint perspectives that, like the nagging line of a pop song, comes to haunt you night and day. We must have made a miserable sight. (We had all been recently interrogated.) Bruises, electrical burns, scars; not much in the way of clothes—most of us left with torn scraps of lingerie, nothing more. Tina (we'd been stripped of our cat-net underground monikers too) was the first to be admitted; a few minutes, and she was out, ushered away before she could communicate more than a backward glance—a raised eyebrow, a shrug of the shoulders, a toss of ash-blonde shoulder-length hair—and the word* ripped *as the Guards bundled her into the lift that connects this circle of hell with the lower levels. Suki was next; again, a few minutes and she was being escorted by Imperial Guard to the dungeons; but unlike Tina, this little trollop was trying to break free, screaming, "No, no, not like that, no, please, not like* that . . ."—*she trying on the Lady Jane Grey act; but we're mistresses, girls, not ladies; I really preferred Tina's insouciance, her vulgar bravado—* "I'm a good girl really, nooooo!" *Goodbye, Suk; it was my turn. The sergeant at arms ticked off my name on his clipboard, took me by the arm, guided my reluctant feet through the doors—*'

The hours grind by . . .

Surfacing from those depths, I feel as if we have passed through the centre of the universe; through Meta's black, black heart; and I have to remind myself that Meta is a place everywhere and nowhere; Meta has no centre. Meta is the Demiurge. It could be destroyed only by changing the laws by which the universe turned; it could be destroyed only when reality was everywhere and nowhere; a reality which had no centre; a reality which was God; a reality encoded in the nanomachines of which I was composed, which would have to be released like spore into the parched, dying multiverse if we were to be free of this pestilence, this Demiurge, and live again in a world where love, compassion and all things that are best in Man, may bloom.

Above ground, we seem to gather strength, slithering through the ziggurat's artery with a fresh adrenal-rush of vigour, even though the tunnel's smart skin tears relentlessly at our own so that we begin to resemble shock troops that have stormed through several entrapments of barbed wire.

Our ascent is now taking us in a path that bisects outer and inner boudoirs; and sometimes an air duct allows us a glimpse of Lilim finaliz-

ing their toilette, about to set forth to stalk the *quartier interdit,* Lilim silhouetted against moonlight and the bright lights of human Bangkok or
against the decorative lanterns and illuminations of the ziggurat's atrium,
that pyramidical hollow of ligamentous bridges, crystalline escalators and
the mandala-like ground zero of exotic flora and fauna, that parterre of
orchids, lotus blossoms and banyan trees which reverberates with the
chitter of insects, the squawk of parrots, the screams of gibbons and mar-
mosets.

'We have to hurry,' I say. 'There's a long climb ahead and we're running
out of time.' It is, I suppose, purely imaginary, but I am beginning to feel
an ache in my chest, as if it is there that my entropic timepiece is located.
When, at midnight, that clock finally stops, my fuse, timed to expire at the
very same moment, will hurl me and all existence into the holy fires of reality, and I will, at last, be consumed.

'I'm tired,' says Lipstick. And yes, without my Elohim body, I too am
exhausted, almost beat.

'We'll rest for a few moments,' I say. Lipstick mops her brow and then
shimmies out of skirt and blouse, unhooks her Wonderbra l'Authentique,
gives her superabundant voluptuousness ease. Her breasts quiver at each
beat of her tropical, Doriminian heart. I inject her and then myself with
a stimulant supplied by The Toymakers. The pain evaporates and I feel almost as if I have repossessed my old superhuman body.

'I've always found it curious,' I say, looking down at her mamma, my
paranoiac at repose beneath my concupiscent, but familiar gaze. 'Why
do Lilim always wear front-fastening brassières?'

'Because, my darling, we are so preeningly aware of their semiotics. For
example, their latency as improvised gyves'—I understand; unhooked,
such a brassière, slipped off the shoulders, may be used to secure a girl's
hands behind her back—'or, indeed, as pre-funeral garb.' Yes; again I understand; that penultimate, ambiguous gesture of displaying the bosom to
a firing squad in insolent defiance, Lilim, even in the moment of death, always having the power to taunt and madden h-men and supermen alike,
taunt them for what they cannot be, what they cannot possess.

Ah, what a superlative thing, what a fetish-object is my love!

'I wish I could sleep,' she says. 'I wish I could sleep like I did on the
Sardanapalus. On ice, you don't dream. It's like heroin, it's death.'

'You were my Sleeping Beauty.'

'You should never have woken me up.'

'I needed you.'

'I suppose I needed you, too. But I was always glad to go back to sleep.'

'Remember the parties?'

'The first time, you came to meet me at the nymphenberg. Then you took me through the forest where there are all those horrible things, Jub-Jubs, Goblins, Hippogriffs, Trolls—'

'They were there to guard you, to guard all of you—'

'Prig. They were there to keep us in our prison. And then you took me to the clubhouse and introduced me to your friends. You showed me the ship's bridge, that view of a bright disc superimposed on perfect blackness, a window containing the whole universe towards which we hurtled. We were close, you said, to the speed of light.'

'Close, and always getting closer. We'd left Doriminu a year, by then. With a continuous 1 g acceleration we were doing something like 3×10^5 km/sec.'

'There was a party, I remember. Whenever you awoke me from suspension, there was always a party. You would give me presents. A new dress, chocolates, stuffed toys, perfume—'

'Sometimes I think it'd been better if we'd stayed in deep space, never come home. We could have lived in that miniature nymphenberg by that little artificial sea, forever.'

'Slept on the dead sands of its beaches, beneath an artificial moon.'

'It would have been nice, good.'

'How did I fall in love with you, Archangel? When? Perhaps it was after I tasted your hopelessness, your despair, and knew it as my own.'

'I'd told you I wasn't a bad man. But I was. I was evil.'

'You were a thing. Like me. I'm a thing too. A psychoid. We've both been willing players in the theatre of cruelty.'

'If I could only take you to another party, I'd—'

'Stop it. I know what happened at those parties. The next day, the ship's nymphenberg was always a few girls short. Oh Archangel, the best thing about those all-night raves was that I knew I would always sleep the next day. Sleep for a long, long time. Sleep on ice, dreamless, as if I were dead.'

'You'll sleep again after tonight. We'll make this our last rave. There'll be no more pain.'

Lipstick refastens her brassière; sits up; gets ready to continue. Then she sniffs at the air, her nose following an invisible trail which leads her to a cavity between two bales of cables. 'Biznizmen!' she whispers, then gives a long, catty *hissssssssss!,* her eye to a newly-discovered grille, 'pornocrats and kleptocrats—look!' I crawl to her side, put my eye next to hers. About a boardroom table sit politicos, army-types, government servants, entrepreneurs of sex and death.

'Then it's settled,' says an Armani-suited yuppie. 'We provide you with a hundred new human men per month in return for exclusive television coverage of the Lumpini executions.' These are slink-merchants, sharks of North and South, East and West, buying and selling the transformation of consciousness into flesh, flesh into meat, meat into pure, diseased alterity; the transformation of men and women into images, brilliant reflections cast by a black sun. Meta is the Great Photographer, chronicling 'absence-as-presence'.

Meta isn't grace; Meta is money.

A posse of cops is on hand to serve and protect their fuck festing masters. The Boys in Brown swigging *Johnnie Walker Dum* (transcoms hanging from their belts next to their Colt .45 autos, any telematik *objet* proud *de luxe* wear of the info-addicted South); the cops are very *sabai-sabai*, giggling, bouncing white-girl babycats, cats all of ten, eleven at most (babies only half-metamorphosed, betraying fulsome epicanthic folds, amber skins and meagre buttocks), from knee, to groin, to knee, marvelling at *farang* blonde hair streaking one little Siamese kitten's locks, nicotine-stained fingers playing with ribbons, bobby pins, whisky-ruined larynxes commenting on the prurience of the hatching West. *'Took took kohn ow roke Meta, hee-hee!'* laughs a cop. The inevitable *farang* police informer-cum-gopher is there (he always is), joining in the laughter—'They do, they do; everybody wants the Meta disease'—trying to act Thai, trying to supplement his fried rice and bottle-of-Mekong-a-day diet; ingratiate himself with the locals; betray.

On the boardroom walls, posters for Borowczyk's *The Phallus* along with Troma's *Lilim Chicks in Zombietown* and *A Nymphoid Barbarian in Dinosaur Hell.*

The lights go down; the presentation begins.

On the overhead: a rostrum in the centre of an amphitheatre (a circular rostrum; at its own centre, a cylindrical dais). *Look toong* singers croon, dancers shuffle, comedians thwack each other over the head with cheap tin trays. And then the music stops; the stage is cleared. The house lights dim; the dais is spotlit; the crowd begins to cheer 'Dead T'ing! Dead T'ing!' and then, 'Whi' Girl! Whi' Girl!' From their boxes, well-bred ladies, *Khunyings* and *Thanpooyings,* very *fickt nicht* in their hermetic *pa-sarong,* flourish paper fans, lorgnettes. Police and Army generals applaud politely, exchange political gossip with the Martian Ambassador; chit-chat about 'Thai-style democracy', 'Government by righteousness'; the wife of a high-ranking official points, then laughs at the small group of *Por mai dum* shouting carbon-chauvinist slogans such as *'Meta e-hia, bpy bahn pra-tet psy-co!',* these half-a-dozen protesters eventually succumbing to the infectious spirit of the rally (as their DNA must succumb, eventually, to Meta), substituting their suggestions that all psychoids go home to psycho-land with cries of 'Whi' girl, *dohk tong, dohk tong!'* (It's always seemed strange to me that 'bitch' in Thai translates as 'golden

flower'. But *my* bitch is a flower, truly.) The night's first victim—her
wrists tied behind her back—is being led onto the stage.

This will be a sacrificial kill, a catharsis for the masses, a public execution in the so-called French manner to remind the human race of the
blood covenant they share with their god, to remind them that they live
through and in Meta, as Meta lives through and in them, that the two
species are bound by a long tradition of commensalism. This will be a kill
that will urge them to buy, buy, buy. This will be a celebration of the
covenant.

The girl's white satin corsetry (satin *à la reine*) is whale-boned and
styled retro-Victorian (a style paradoxically infused with a certain punk-
modernity, the strictness of its Victoriana taken to extremes); it shimmers
in the spotlights. She kneels, her thighs are spread and—after her sentence
has been proclaimed to the crowd—she receives the knife, head flung
backwards, breasts straining against the silken cuirass; her scream echoes
about the amphitheatre; the crowd begins to whoop.

And in the VIP box the Thais are congratulating themselves on their ancient traditions, but bemoaning, to the green-faced ambassador and his
wife, the malign, materialistic influences of the West, the threat to Thai
culture and society, bemoaning how old, but still powerful remnants of
the Empire no longer believe (perhaps have never believed) in family or
community values, how they do not understand the 'Asian way'. Of
course, the executions will continue; the West has no monopoly on the
sex-death; but such executions should be conducted 'Thai style', say the
politicos, the generalissimos, the mafiosos; they should reflect Thai sensitivities, the 'good old days' when the Thai people lived at one with Nature; and all profits should, of course, remain in Thai hands. We are not a
colony, they continue; Meta is here at our invitation; Meta is a guest. The
green-faced nuncio who represents 'humanism' in Thailand, smiles, nods
approvingly, *realpolitik* undoubtedly informing him that this is not the
time to broach the subject of the 'refugee issue'; he does not want to be
pressed, yet again, with demands for a treaty of extradition; tonight is a
time for *constructive* engagement, for appreciating Thai hospitality. Thailand, after all, is now the Voice of Meta. He mutters gravely about the
problems of sex tourism, about how Mars is actively prosecuting offend-
ers off-world; if Lilim are to be killed, they should, of course, be killed by
Thais, in Thailand, in the Thai manner; Martian tourists should not involve themselves with things that do not concern them, that are a purely
internal affair. 'We wish to discourage this aping of *Meta* amongst our
young,' he says. 'We wish to encourage our people to invest in, rather than
exploit, your proud nation. We respect Meta, yes; but we also look for-

ward to a future when Thai-Martian relations are characterized by a commitment to *development.*' The Thais smile; they know that they can make as much money from Martians who like to watch pretty girls being killed as they can from Martians who want such killing to stop; they are usually, they have found, the same people. Death and development go hand in hand.

There is only one qualification for a world capital, the seat of the Evil Empire: the capital of the country that can open its legs the widest; the one most eager to be fucked ...

In the boardroom, the lights go up; the assembled biznizmen applaud. Elohim—a Judge, Magistrate, a Sergeant At Arms and three Inquisitors— smile at their sisters, a Princess, her two Secretaries and five Maids; and then both inhuman sexes turn their gaze upon their guests.

'Of course,' says an Elohim, 'we can edit out the section focusing on the people of influence, the *poo-yai.*' The humans—men and women of influence, all—exchange glances of approval. 'Is it agreed then? That we will continue to provide you with blood as long as you continue to provide us with victims?'

'Everybody profits,' says a Thai with an educated-Stateside accent. 'You get our protection, we get the pornography and the human race gets to buy death. And the beautiful thing is, it's all justifiable. With Meta, we can sell just about *anything.*' And the assembly proceeds to discuss merchandizing, concessions, franchises, the exaltation of death and power.

Information is power, and the information that is pornography is power to the nth. It is the information that the human race is prepared to die for, the knowledge they want to be a part of, to merge with, to make their own. It is the knowledge that Man is a beast, a filthy beast, and that—in a valueless world—grace lies only in depravity's elevation. My kind—Dagon's kind—has never been in control; that was always an illusion; Meta's autarchy is an embrace of market forces, the buying and selling of nothingness and pain, a nihilism that the world has been conned into believing represents a state of transcendence. Meta is a political force, an economic machine. For the hypercapitalists who grow fat on Meta's covenant, Lilim and Elohim offer-up their transfigured, marketable flesh, flesh converted into sex toys, images, *animé;* we are that agglomerate of dreams, prejudices, fears and dark desires that had infected Toxicophilous's dolls and that had at last resolved into pure information; *we* are pornography, the spirit of the age, the culmination of the *De Luxe.*

'Did you ever buy?' I say to Lipstick.

'Of course. Isn't that what makes us metamorphose? A kind of hereditary willingness to eat shit?'

'We've eaten enough. Time to disembogue.'

'Time to deploy *you*, you hermetic emetic. Yeah, time to up-bring, to *explode*.'

Enriched with pharmaceuticals and our own endogenous opioids, we proceed, mindful that we must keep to schedule.

Our uniforms are, by now, almost entirely shredded; and though we have our second wind, the heat is desiccating us; we try, when we can, to sip liquid from fractured pipes, or lick condensation from the cracked vents of air-conditioning units.

Screech! Is that an organic or a mechanical *screech*? I find a spyhole.

A Hong Kong ghost movie haunts the shadows (phosphor-dot flickerings in the half-light; only a bedside lamp is on, and outside, through the crack in the balcony's drapes, all is dark): ghosts hopping, feet together, hands held Mantis-style, hopping, hopping irrevocably towards the huddled pack of all-girl-highschool students whose stage-frightened screams—in their camp theatricality—seem a counterpart to (though they could never, never match) the real-life victims' own.

'The raid's begun,' I whisper. 'I can see Tyr.' Tyr does not hop, he strolls; he is an English gentleman, a dandy. Movie screams and Lilim screams intensify, crossbreed in an aural mongrelization of human and inhuman, a kind of high-voltage one-hundred part motet I would once have found entertaining instead of hideous. I rip the power cables from a nearby box. But the TV continues to scream and so do the boudoir's inhabitants.

'Come,' I say. Lipstick puts her eye to the duct. 'Come, there's nothing for us here. We've seen it all before. Let's get this over with.'

But as we pass each level I find I cannot refrain from taking in the massacre, my fourway-split psyche offering a plurality of messages just as the peepshow girls, cut down by bullets and blades, reply with the pluralism of their ambiguous, complicit deaths.

A girl, a Thai girl is looking at Abaddon from a little way down a corridor, an amber-skinned mini-vampire, too young to have *farang* characteristics, in a black lace cachette, black patent high-heels and (he returns her gaze, eyes surveying for other accoutrements) . . . nothing (though if her nudity did not, in some sense, also constitute clothing, an artificial body, an excrescence, then she would perhaps [this mini-vampire being so minimally attired] have been utterly beyond the reach of his faculties, invisible, like some outlandish life-form composed of dark matter; therefore safe). The raiding party is losing the advantage of surprise, this girl's materialization into the corridor no chance visitation, that familiar look of inquiry and apprehension a look that must be transfiguring many a complacent demeanour hereabouts, evidence that the nymphenberg seems to have been alerted to my murderous brothers' presence.

Inquiry; apprehension—I know that Abaddon's girl must exhibit this vacant, wide-eyed (but not too wide-eyed) look, this look of half-open mouth set in its modest rictus, before she can proceed with her victim's script (this visual cliché preceding assault universal amongst Lilim, a standardization of affect that recalls to me the iterations of the pulp fiction book covers that, as Gabriel Strange, I would beg, borrow and steal from my father's *Wunderkammer* and keep hidden beneath my bed); before she can scream *'Marauder!'* adrenaline summons to my forebrain images of that Hong Kong movie playing in a dead girl's boudoir several levels below, the fantastic leaps and aerial manoeuvres of the ghosts and Taoist warriors, a hallucinatory gymnasticism that derives from the traditions of Chinese Opera; serendipitously, Abaddon appears to be having the same thoughts; slings his gamekeeper across his back; leaps; and with the same superhuman grace he covers the thirty feet that separates him from his prospective kill with one Zen-like, operatic bound. His hands about her throat, he squeezes, squeezes with all of his Elohim strength and instantly, or almost instantly, she goes limp, a series of fibrillations that, collectively, are like a fatalistic, Oriental shrug or shiver (this chit starting to wear her ethnicity like a perfume, a mystique) press-ganging her into a last, Mannerist exaggeration of femininity into superfemininity, a last homage to Meta, her species, her god.

What are we all but constructs?

The Thai music called 'string' is playing in the background and from somewhere I detect the syncretic, acculturated styles of Indonesian *Dangdut*, Japanese *Kayôkyoku*—was that Shang Shang Typhoon, the Rinkenband?

Level after level, tier after tier, the same theatricals are performed.

Somewhere between levels fifty-four and fifty-eight Noo performs an almost obligatory pelvic thrust (the tassels of her jacket flying about her hips); spins around, knocks over a framed picture of Mexican wrestler *Superbarrio* that had been displayed on a bedside table (*Superbarrio* snapped visiting the Bangkok slum of Klong Toey), likewise pictures of World Wrestling Association stars *The Undertaker, The 1-2-3 Kid, Macho Man;* knocks over a piece of Sèvres porcelain, a thick diary bound in pink vellum from the escritoire, a reading lamp, a pen, a box of diskettes; falls into the thick, virginal pile. Tyr bayonets her again; then again; and then again, slipping the elegant needle-like blade through her umbilicus, to no avail her struggle to evade, or protect herself from his ability—every Elohim's ability—to anticipate her dance, its every predetermined sequence; for though each girl dies in her own vein, there is, you might say, a kind of universal choreography upon which the improvisations of a girl's death are based and by which those improvisations are restricted. Tyr understands that choreography; the theatre is in his blood; can predict just how his victims will writhe, squirm, flinch, undulate and wriggle from second to second, his appreciation of Meta's sundry chorus lines profound, his connoisseurship of the sex-death without equal.

At level sixty-one three wards are seated on a divan: Trixie, 1) is half-turned to her left, looking over her right shoulder; the strap of her pinafore dress slipped to her elbow, the dislocated bib revealing a fulsome breast beneath the tiffany blouse, a breast cantilevered by a minimalist hemidemisemibra; her hyperskirt is being hoisted to her hip to facilitate the readjustment of a suspender; and her eyes look out with fear and calculation from beneath an auburn, brandy-sauce fringe; Fifi, 2) is facing me, a compact in one hand, a powder puff in the other, her face startled, her thighs pressed incontinently together; Vicki, 3) is half-turned to her right, looking over her left shoulder, askance, a bright red lipstick pressed to her pouting lips. This vulgar triumvirate, whose girl-talk Mephisto has, by way of his sweeping entrance, stalled (the lipstick falls to the floor, punctuating the abrupt termination of their yaketty-yak with a bated ellipsis), these three demotic Graces, *cheap and nawsty* Aglaia, Euphrosyne and Thalia, bestowers of allure, pretty-prettiness and ostentatious sex, all wear the same parodic schoolgirl-kitsch uniform (they must be all from this sixty-first-level tier, that is, from the same 'house'): black neurotic-psychotic velveteen pinafore over white silk blouse with black seamed stockings and matching velveteen beret (all from Vivienne Westwood). They all die of a fashion, too; drawing his minimized gamekeeper from its marsupial sleep, Mephisto, who stands in the doorframe beneath me, levels the muzzle, first at one, then at another of the assembled Misses; fires, *bang, bang, bang.*

'You bastard!' I scream through the vent. 'There's no need! Stop! Stop!' But he has already left the boudoir, and my hypocritical protest is heard only by the ghosts of the *cheap and nawsty.*

I need Dagon if I am to survive this . . .

On level seventy: a girl in tiptoey high-heels and canary-yellow peignoir is pointing a silver derringer at Abaddon's chest; there is a retort; she falls forward, shot in the lumbar-sacral region by her roommate, who drops her own firearm (likewise a derringer; one of a matching pair, I should think), smiles (the beamish sycophant; ah! that unmistakable aroma of *cat*), before Abaddon in turn shoots *her* through her black-and-gold waspie and (his gamekeeper maximizing now) sprays a gimcrack-attired foursome with a clip's worth of automatic fire, they performing a *pas de quatre,* jiggling, thrusting, grinding in a lewd dance of death. *Shusha-shusha.* Broderie anglaise is torn. *Shusha-shusha.* Frosted satin is speckled red, the front-fastening of a brassière snapping as a *fléchette* enters between scapulae—*shusha-shusha-shusha*—exits a cleavage in a plume of blood; an umbilicus geysers, providing similar egress to a fusillade that—*shusha*, EEE!—peppers the lower vertebrae of . . . whom? all flesh melding now, these girls of the *corps* becoming a composite creature of mutilated flesh, of sexual wounds, of vulgar lingerie ripped, threshed, until, talent pooled, this polypodous *danseur* is elevated to the role of a prima ballerina (and, perforce, suddenly less desirable), her *pretentious* superfemininity harried, churned, raked, lacerated by the impossible demands put upon her by impresario Abaddon, though all to nought; no bouquet from *that* stern critic.

He steps over the bodies, over a Bauhaus coffee table, chairs, sex toys, an obstacle course made of chromium scaffolding, glass and Bakelite, this boudoir very functional, very *moderne* and not at all styled in that depraved Louise Quinze manner which Lilim so adore and which—despite certain idiosyncrasies of ambience—has for so long survived the crosscurrents of fashion. He hesitates; stops; inspects a series of framed photographs by Brassaï; proceeds to the balcony.

Port Ligat. Tiles and whitewashed concrete; a beach—a balconied beach—where young virgins contemplate a chlorinated sea, autosodomized by their own chastity; a beach where The Great Masturbator roams, where flying tigers, and crippled dreams, hobbling on crutches and stilts, haunt the quays and jetties . . . Enough. Abaddon is joined by Mephisto and Tyr. They will create their own works of art.

Some girls are still in the swimming pool and my brothers take particular pleasure in shooting them while they are so helpless, one leaping up, her ribs, waist, hips, almost her pubis emerging from the centre of the pool, a panicked nereid, an Aphrodite birthed from scarlet-pink foam, the *fléchettes* smashing her firm, mermaid-smooth belly as she splashes about in her bubble-bath of water, tissue and blood; similarly emerging from this soon-to-be aquatic grave, but only so far as to bear her punctured breasts, another girl is added to the list of mer-victims, ensnared, screaming, drowning, splashing in this late twentieth-century girl-trap. The bodies float, face up, face down, in the reddening pool.

The marauders walk to the balcony's edge; breathe deeply; confer, reload; listen to the survivors cram their mouths full of air, a wild gulping which increases in exponential degree to the quickening tempo of each girl's encroaching apocalypse, until, first one, and then another, and then another, the victims collectively rend my too-human ears with those C-above-top-C screams that Dagon, appearing from nowhere to perch on my shoulder, considers to have been all sampled from the same celestial source; and then the marauders leave, the dying again sucking in quite improbable agglomerates of air (their next screams, when they come, says

Dagon, will be surpassingly lovely, transcendent, perhaps); but my brothers cannot afford to dawdle.

I cannot stand any more; I grip my knees, assuming a foetal ball. I begin to sob, sob as I have done after many a raid on many a distant world; sob uncontrollably.

How can I presume to be human—after this? How can I presume even to be an organic simulacrum of a human? I was supposed to have been built to create; to re-create is my prime directive. But The Toxicophilous Device is damaged. For too long I have believed only in destruction: the destruction of my species, the destruction of myself. What do I know of what it is to create, about the reality I am supposed to be heralding? I know nothing. Have no right to know. I was worthless, dirty, a piece of time-pickled manure; I am not worth a single cry of pain, not worth a single one of those brief, pathetic lives destroyed to bring me to fruition. Behind my clenched eyes, Meta, god of this world, god of The Future—all speed demon, affectless, all simulation and sensation, shallow, hollow, as worthless as I am worthless—looks down on me; and I know that I am looking in a mirror, that this is the terminal form, the last onion skin, the final aspect, the ultimate mask that I have to burn; Meta, perversion of human form, body of love wrenched into the body of hate, body of sensuousness twisted into the body of agony, hate and death, begone, leave me, give me rest . . .

'Archangel!' Lipstick is shaking me. 'You mustn't! Not yet! Please, darling—don't think, just climb! We're nearly there!'

'It's Dagon,' I say, 'it's him who finally has the strength. I'm sorry, but I must become him again.'

'It's all right, Archangel. I know who you are. Become Dagon, and I'll be your catgirl, Lipstick; I'll be your bitch. But come, please. We must hurry—'

Cheap and nawsty, I think. Mmm. I like, I like . . . I think of the worlds I have sacked. Palaces burning, corridors littered with dead and dying girls, the impaled who lined the roads leading from Hades, on Tantra3; a silvery forest clearing stained with blood; a deserted town plaza carpeted in volcanic ash and flesh; a scorched heath, a wasteland, a bone-white desert incandescent beneath a punishing sun . . . My marauder rises up the chakras of my spine. 'I think I can go on now,' I say. I look at my hands; they're shaking, the skin a bruised, pale pink. 'My eyes?' I ask. 'My hair?'

'Eyes? A kind of baby-blue. Your hair's mousy. You look terrible.'

Dishevelled, half-naked, exuding a raggedy-doll provocativeness, Lipstick has begun to resemble one of those practice mannequins we used at The Academy. We were encouraged to treat our mannequins with the respect and familiarity with which we treated our gamekeepers. My own doll—'Iphigenie'—when I wasn't practising sword thrusts and knife thrusts upon her in the gymnasium, spent her nights and days chained to the foot of my bunk alongside my roommate's doll, 'Messalina'. Both working girls had little Xs painted onto them so that they resembled acupuncturist's wall charts, each numbered cross designating a prospective, ritual wound, the import of that wound contingent upon factors social and psychological, by the nature of a girl's delinquency and by the law. Each Sunday, we would seat our dumb, long-suffering companions at our study's dining table where they would attend their two Galahads at High Tea, all of us, by then, usually having put in a hard week's work, my hands sometimes callused from the hilts of my blades, the girls being particularly drained, their plastic internal organs removed each Friday afternoon to be inspected and graded by our instructors.

'Terrible? Good—I only need my alter ego for a little while, now.' The image of Iphigenie, my mannequin, my first girlfriend, you might say, is superimposed upon Lipstick, Iphigenie with her fatal tattoos, the little stencilled crosses at forehead, cheeks, lips, throat and breasts, at thorax, umbilicus, abdomen, clitoris and vagina (and, if you were to turn her about, at points along her spine from nape to anus, rows of XXXs, like kisses, planted between her shoulder blades, the small of her back, everywhere). I run my hand down Lipstick's mane. 'But help me,' I say. 'Help me explode before Dagon claims me again entire.'

And we recommence our climb.

Level seventy-six: Abaddon's pets, Dementia, Demirep, Demivierge and Demerara, spring from an open doorway (Demerara who is pure brown *saccharine-a*, dreadlocked, but fluent in that slightly cockneyfied variety of English that [with certain American and Frenchified and Russkified variations] has, in this Meta-warped world, been the modern white girl's lingua franca since the 1850s); a man of meticulous tastes, Abaddon; over-meticulous, some have said—Demirep and Demivierge are, if stunning, somewhat over-refined, *far* too over-refined, too *soigné* for catgirls! (Dementia is another matter.) Their catwalk cat-walk is Claudia Schiffer's and Nadja Auermann's, not the hyperwiggle, the erogenously emphatic hip-swinging, the wind-up-toy perambulation of the bona fide *cat*. But they are superb gladiatorix, despatching the PVC-clad Imperial Guard with elegant, casual flicks of their whips, hurling their knives into the breasts of their opponents with such precision that Mephisto, Tyr and Abaddon, emerging from the transept of an escalator, seem tempted to stop and applaud.

Abaddon apprehends, kisses a fleeing chambermaid, a girl butterfly-capped, ruffed, cuffed and aproned, the sodium glow of the corridor's concealed lighting falling over her glossy black alpaca uniform, so that it shimmers like a mirage, about to disappear as she, as all my kind, will soon disappear; he picks her up, walks to the balustrade and holds the girl over a void riotous with squawking parakeets, macaws, toucans, mynas, with precious mechanical birds of silver and gold enamel; releases her. Her scream dissipates in the ziggurat's vast interior, its hollowed wedge of tendril-like skybridges, its limpid staircases of sparkling cut glass.

Tyr screams out: 'Why do we do it? Why do we kill them? Oh, the blood, the blood!' And then he inserts the muzzle of his gamekeeper in his mouth and the last thing he hears is his Gun's muffled pleading— '*No, Lord Tyr, you can't be serious, keep your mind on the sex-death, the spiritual grace of the kill!*'—before, tripping the trigger with the toe of his boot, a frangible takes off the back of his skullcap.

He's not dead, of course; but he's out of the running; Tyr has been on the verge of a nervous breakdown for some time.

Recorporate, he would have one hell of a headache . . .

Lipstick is pushing me from behind, her fingernails pricking my buttocks. '*Move,* Archangel, we're nearly there!'

The last scenario I witness before lowering my head and pressing onwards towards the last level, the summit itself, is a boudoir harbouring terminally-ill girls. The dying, spreadeagled on their beds, tied to their four-posters with stockings and silk scarves, scream and thrash in the madness of their fevers, crying out for blood, for semen (no amount of which, of course, could slake their frustration, the rabid frustration, the haemo- and lacto-mania that finally kills); Abaddon despatches the nurses with sprays of automatic fire, but leaves the certified to what an Elohim perceives to be their delirious desserts; for girls who have lived so long (according to consensus) deserve to die mad, combusting in a *ne plus ultra* of sexual frustration; and then Mephisto runs into the room. 'Fall back,' he yells, 'fall back.' I can see no Elohim (the nymphenberg's Elohim, that is); but if Mephisto is issuing a retreat, they must be near; he wouldn't run from what has so far been only suicidal waves of Imperial Guard, troopers in all sorts of marvellous, fetish-object uniforms, PVC, leather, sequins, chain-mail, *manga*-style armour, all-in-one rubber gas-masked combat-suits, redingotes and calf-boots, camouflage bikinis (manes cluttered with spiked stainless steel curlers), troopers recruited from the ranks of the gladiatorix (discernible by their plumed helms and cellophane capes of acid greens and apricots, lilacs, fluorescent yellows and pinks), troopers in lurex and Du Pont Lycra, in wire-crocheted one-pieces and black nylon bodystockings; troopers, who, for the most part, lie discarded like broken dolls, so that the corridors resemble a scrapyard for damaged, useless, inhuman flesh, the white pile no longer visible, the carpet on which they had but recently stood transposed into a carpet of dead and dying girls. No; Mephisto has no reason to run from such killable girleens as these. 'Fall back.' His black romp is failing; we are entering into the end game. I must reach The Chapel; must reach it, despite all else; and, with a last exertion, I suddenly find myself looking down through a wire-mesh partition at an altar, its three surrounding sphinxes and overhanging crucifix, about which are assembled at least a hundred praying girls, all of whom have adopted the lordosis—kneeling, their chins to the ground, their hands laid on the tiled, mosaic floor (all eyes trained on the crucified body of Our Lady), haunches raised into the air in submission, thighs splayed, ankles pressed together.

Mephisto stumbles into their midst. He is speaking to Abaddon. 'No windows, no balcony,' he explains, 'only this door to defend. We must wait and hope for Dagon.' Mephisto has decided to make his last stand in The Chapel. 'To the death,' he says, 'no surrender.'

He has his shoulder to the great iron door that offers ingress to the passageway; they are preparing for siege; but even as Abaddon starts to machine-gun the prostrate girls who, though faced with such inescapable dooms, still choose to die crying 'Sanctuary, sanctuary!'; even as he shoots those who, a little giddier, a little flightier than their sisters, begin to run in circles like claustrophobic rats in a maze, or rather (to be more exact) a taxonomy of claustrophobic, panicking ratgirls/batgirls/catgirls caught *huis clos,* a grenade detonates; Mephisto is blown across the chamber and a dozen-or-so slim, soniferous throats—at least those throats that have been severed by shrapnel—are silenced (a head sans trunk [coppertone face grinning at me] flies across my field of vision); Abaddon again flexes his trigger finger and The Chapel fills with a choral of depraved little girls' squeals and screams. He walks backwards; leans against The Chapel's door, attempting to secure the portal, the incomplete sealing of which has admitted our *Käpitan's* fall.

'Dagon, *Dagon*—' calls Abaddon, 'where are you. Help us, please, *please!*'

Lipstick helps me remove the grille and I drop down into the chamber; Abaddon's eyes brighten with surprise and relief. I walk over a carpet of yellow girls, brown, bronze and black girls, but always *white* girls, their glistening wounds, torn dresses, peignoirs and lingerie conspiring to present a kind of fleshfash, fashflesh, deathfash *style,* a late twentieth-century showcase of some guru of the *moderne,* an *auteur* of The New for whom the distinction between flesh and fashion, dermatomorphics and dress, skin I and skin II, is *démodé,* a kind of philosopher of postmodern bodysuits, of the flayed, agglomerated body of the present consumed by The Future, guru of an aesthetic of transgression, the insurrection of the mad . . .

Lipstick follows, and we all heave against the iron until the three of us have the door snug against its jambs. I smash the electronic lock, putting two feet of steel between us and our pursuers.

'You were supposed to provide a diversion,' says my cat-girl, lecturing Abaddon. '*Pinhead!* We could have done a better job if we'd been left to ourselves!' Abaddon scowls; my brothers, I know, would not have been denied their kills; their sexual imperative, their libido, has brought them and us to this pass. Lipstick turns her back; folds her arms. 'Your pricks have led us to disaster.'

Parfait, Mephisto's only pet, is, at twenty-three, the eldest of our litter (a quite extraordinary longevity—look at the acid greenness of those green green greeny eyes!); she bends over her master, solicitous, a cat fretting over her meal ticket, her cornucopia of emerald cream. Mephisto is beginning to turn into stone, feet and legs like columns of marble. Parfait, a beach babe who had been kidnapped from one of the first colonies we had invaded, who had been kept on and off of ice for hundreds of years, so obsessed was Mephisto with her sullen beauty (or so had been his pretence), no other pet for him, no other love, Parfait, only Parfait could ever really tolerate Mephisto. My feelings—Dagon's feelings—for the *Käpitan* are long since cooled; I find it difficult to understand how I had ever had such a crush on him. Ignatz, caged in my backbrain, has no feelings; he has never known the 'man'; but the thing built by Dr Toxicophilous, the fail-safe, The Reality Bomb, feels a kinship; he has died completing his mission, just as I am about to die completing mine. 'Forgive me,' says Mephisto, his eyes fastening upon me for the last time, 'we had to wait a thousand years to bring you back to yourself. That ampoule of nanoware that brought you to self-consciousness and which armed you for your task—it was unique. We could only use it once. And if we had used it while you were still in your pre-millennial state, you would have woken, but been unable to explode. Forgive me—' And his eyes become glass, his body, rock. Goodbye, Mephistopheles.

Abaddon shrugs his shoulders as if he has heard this kind of thing before: the last crazed words of a superman in death's delirium. 'What are we waiting for, Dagon? You have The Toxicophilous Device. Deploy it.' He walks over to a somewhat incongruous-looking *soigné* ward whom he has ordered to assume an interrogatory position (palms flat against a wall, head bowed, body arched, legs spread), lifts her skirt from behind, slits open her belly; but it is not until he has lifted the wound to his fangs that I notice that he means to dine on one of his own pets (no, no, *please,* master! screams Demirep); she has tried to disguise herself in a dead girl's clothes in order, I suppose, to avoid arrest; Abaddon means to have his last supper.

But as he begins to eat he suddenly looks up at me, suspicious. 'You *do* know how to deploy The Device, I suppose?'

'Of course,' I say, and walk over to the altar. There is nothing to do, of course, but wait. My clock will stop at midnight, the second I celebrate my one-thousandth birthday, the same second that my twelve-hour fuse will expire; only then will I explode.

I sit down on the altar stone. Wait.

The basilica's iron door has begun to shower sparks; the Elohim outside have begun to deploy cutting equipment. I see Abaddon look up from his half-devoured meal, a hand moving towards his minimized gamekeeper; I gesture to him and he pauses; resumes his gluttony. (He has found, and begun to eat, Demivierge.)

'Lipstick—' It's time to say our farewells.

'I'll always be your girl, Archangel. Always.'

'I know.'

About me, the dying moan, wriggle, convulse, beg me to despatch them, to put them out of their misery. 'Finish me,' they moan, the more promiscuous amongst their number moaning, 'Oooo, please, please finish me *off.*' Lipstick walks into my embrace; I kiss her forehead. Lipstick is Lipstick is Lipstick. But what is her real name? The name she had on Doriminu, before I turned her into a cat? Persephone? Katarina? Parvati? Libertina? Kwan-yin? Nang Kwak? Who? My mind is disintegrating; all I know (all I have ever known) is that she and all her kind have always been Primavera.

I reach under the tiny skirt; stroke her belly. 'It's all rotten,' she says. 'My meat's all rotten. I'm slink. A piece of rotten, green slink-meat.' A tear runs down her cheek. 'But I'm a marauder's pet too, Archangel. I don't want to betray you. Please, kill me before they cut through the door. I don't want to die on the miniver. I want to die in your arms.' The basilica seems to tremble, as if suppressing a laugh. I know that I want to die too. 'I'll always be your girl, Archangel. Always.'

'You were never rotten,' I say. 'You were always a sweet, innocent child. I've done you terrible wrongs. But when, in a few minutes, I detonate, it will be as if all your tears and pain had never been. Everything will be as if it had never been.' I stroke her cheek; sigh. 'It's all I can offer you.'

Her nose begins to twitch. 'I can smell them. Outside. I can smell Elohim. They'll rip me, Archangel, you know they will. Let me go down on my knees. One kiss, one taste, would probably be enough. I think I'm ready to go into black orgasm.' I shake my head.

'It's nearly midnight,' I say. A section of the door begins to collapse inwards. A rifle barrel protrudes through the buckled steel.

The dumdum that removes a portion of Abaddon's head drives his face into the voluptuous meat of his pet food, so that he dies, metamorphic, statuesque, his stone-metal teeth ensnared in half-consumed mamma. Demivierge, suspended, her leopard-spotted legs sprinting in stasis, tries vainly to free herself from the marble-and-bronze idol, her humbled Apollo frozen in the act of playing a game of charades, he imitating the devotion of a hunting dog who is returning prey to his master.

No time, then, I think, to deploy; they'll capture me, take me away, and my detonation will be useless, briefly transforming only a few kilometres-worth of territory.

I throw Lipstick across the chamber (she skids across the smooth marble floor like an ice-hockey puck, colliding with the plinth of one of the golden sphinxes); lean towards the laser-made scar in the door and yell out. The noise of the cutting equipment ceases.

'I have a device,' I say. 'The fail-safe. Have you heard of it? It can destroy The Presence. But listen: I'll come with you. I'll surrender the bomb. But you mustn't hurt the girl, do you understand? And I must have some kind of guarantee. You *mustn't* hurt the one called Lipstick!'

'No, Archangel!' she says. 'Quickly, listen. Mephisto lied to you. Your parents, the people who adopted you, the Zwakhs—they never learned the exact day of your birth. Your birthday isn't the day you think it is. Midnight has no significance. You're one thousand years old already. You have been for months. And Mephisto lied to you about the twelve-hour fuse. Ever since that nanoware was injected into your system you have been capable of self-detonation. Archangel, you can explode any time you wish. That's why The Toymakers were so cautious about arming you. To go *Booooom!* just takes an act of will.'

'You mean I only have to *want* to explode?'

Lipstick pulls the veil from the altar. The chamber is suffused with green light.

The laser starts up again. They are nearly through.

The Presence—a uterus so beautiful it could have been painted by Jan Stevenzoon van Calcar, pupil of Titian and illustrator of Vesalius's *De Humani Corporis Fabrica*—is in my hands. Partly biological, it is also an *objet* decorated with emeralds and malachite; it pulsates, fibrillating between my fingers.

It is the last of the Cartier quantum-magical CPUs.

It is the brain of a Cartier automaton, the last working CPU of the series *L'Eve Future*, the marvellous dolls that became as Adam's first wife, stealing human children and replacing them with changelings, the robotic daughters of Lilith.

'Is that really all I have to do?'

'Yes—but please, please kill me first; I'm still Lilim; I'm still a marauder's cat; I'm sick, sick I know—but I want to die in your arms, Archangel. Kill me!'

'I, I, I—'

Lipstick bites her knuckles, looks at the door; then seems to accept that, however compromised it might be, however threadbare, and despite Dagon's persona being in the ascendant, her lover now wears the ineluctable mantle of humanity. 'You must want to die,' she says. 'Do it. Before it's too late. Don't let them get me—you *know* what they'll do.'

For the last time, I become Dagon. Become him entire. I need him one last time. I know, instinctively, at this juncture, that only he can save me, save the universe. Only the killer, the sick man, the wounded monster, can usher in the New Heaven and the New Earth.

My program cries out. I want the meat. I want the world's meat. The cuntgirl, the girlcunt, the cuntworld, the worldcunt.

I put the robo-uterus to my mouth; bite down; swallow.

I feel as if I have turned the universe inside out: the god of this world inside me, its worlds, stars and galaxies; outside, my bowels, my blood vessels, nerve-endings and cortex.

I prepare to collapse.

So: I just think myself dead? No wonder Mephisto had been apprehensive about the extent of my self-knowledge. Armed, I could have exploded at any time, and the opportunity to destroy Meta would have evaporated along with my body.

And then I concentrate—*explode*, I think. Come on, go *Bang!* Come on, come on, hurry, *hurry.*

I wait for my being to be thrown to the corners of the multiverse, information scattering through space-time to irradiate Meta with its deadly burst of the *real.*

Nothing happens.

My skin has turned grey; strength, superhuman strength, flows through me into my sinews and muscles. 'Lipstick, I'm Dagon now—but I want you to know. Primavera doesn't exist. She never has. You are Primavera. You always have been.'

And still nothing happens.

And then suddenly, quite unreasonably, I remember who I am; remember that I am not Dagon, not Gabriel, not Ignatz, not even The Toxicophilous Device. Remember that I am sitting in an armchair in a universe so far from this one that all measurement becomes nonsensical; and I remember that my reality is greater than the reality of this world; far greater, greater even than the reality of the world The Device was designed to re-create, that all about me is insubstantial; that the only thing that connects me to this planet is my love for Primavera, for Lipstick; that it was that love which has brought me here, now. Yes; this core of my being, this Self is the fissile material I seek, that will enable me to—

CHAPTER TWELVE

The Shadow

I had been trying to hail a cab; suddenly, I felt that tickle on the back of the neck that is said to proceed a contemplation of guillotining; I glanced behind; my executioner, tall, pale and wearing my face, eeled his way through the knots of sidewalk vendors, stalking me with a nonchalance that belied the midday heat, the pall of traffic fumes, the congestion of bodies. A cab pulled over. 'Wait,' said the double. A few heads turned, but the rush-hour crowd—oblivious to the paradox in their midst—brushed past, as insouciant as my pursuer, the sight of self meeting self unremarkable in an Asian sprawl where a *farang* was deemed a genus rather than an individual. I opened the door; ushered him inside; gave the driver directions.

There had been no need for that *Wait*. I hadn't seen a version of myself for days and I was desperate for an answer. 'She's getting worse,' I said. 'Her eyes—she believes they're turning green.' His own eyes, truculent, suave, held my gaze. He leaned forward.

'I have made my decision,' he said. 'I will help you.' At last. I repressed the trappings of relief. I did not wish to betray any signs of weakness. 'But remember. Remember what you have promised.'

'I remember. And I'll do it,' I said. It was the answer I had been waiting for ever since the double had revealed itself to me three months ago. 'My little girl's dying. I'll do anything, anything you say.' His face blurred; momentarily I saw another face, an Asian face, comatose behind the mirror. With the usual traffic jams to contend with, it was unlikely that we would reach our destination before my double would be forced to relinquish control of his host. 'Quickly. You're fading. Tell me what I have to do.' He ran a hand through his crop; sighed.

'You and I must go on a journey. A difficult journey. Through doors. Doors that are known only to me.'

'Yes,' I said. 'I understand.' Much of the cure, of course, he had spoken of before, and I had meticulously recorded the thing's observations even during the period when I'd thought I'd been mad, my illness revealing itself in those same hallucinatory symptoms that had beset my daughter when she had been first diagnosed as 'schizoid'.

'I am in hell, doctor. The hell called reality. The reality that burns but does not consume. But there is a greater reality than this. A para-reality that is terrible, blinding, that none may survive. We must travel to the gateway of that world. Only then may your daughter be healed. And only then may I escape.' For only then, I knew, might he find peace, extinction. 'And you will do as you promised?'

'I need your help as much as you need mine.' Dagon, my executioner, was a dead thing, a malevolent shadow, in a past life the killer of thousands, perhaps millions of young women. He had told me of the horrors of his own world, the horrors we would soon experience, of Meta, the virus, the superluminal virus that was flowing backwards through time, changing the past, this world, all worlds, all possible histories, unsparing, at the last, surely, even of our own dimension, a world that had so far remained comparatively unscathed. Dagon was a monster; but a dead thing, I knew, provided the only hope of reversing metamorphosis. 'Yes,' he said, anticipating me as he always did, 'the only hope. For you. For Primavera.'

'I will free you,' I said.

'In all the worlds I've passed through, so many have promised, so many have betrayed.'

'I won't betray you, Dagon.'

'I hope not. I am the killer, you are the healer. But we both love, no? We both wish to save her?' He lowered his eyes, seductively. He would act as my transdimensional guide, he would take me to that place where the holy fires of God would burn away the illusions that tortured my daughter. Dagon was in agony here on Earth Prime where, as yet, his god, his species, had no name, where Meta had only breached the outer fortifications of reality, acronym of a new form of collective hysteria suffered by those who had been diagnosed as paranoid schizophrenics. While alive, he had been a rebel, his hatred for Meta almost as great as his disdain for the human race. It was souls such as his, he had said, that the Demiurge condemned to reality. Now, he could find peace only if the core of his being, his real self, could be persuaded to accept self-annihilation, if I, that is, would trade my soul for his. I would become the killer; he, the healer. I would be damned; he would be free. That was his price.

My image was becoming distorted; I was no longer looking at my own reflection but—the glass warping, convex, then concave—at a series of grotesque images, images like those in a hall of mirrors at a fun fair. 'I must go now,' he said. 'I will come to you tonight. I must be sure you will keep your end of the bargain. Prepare yourself.' And then he began speaking Thai.

I saw the driver glance in the rear-view mirror. His eyes widened and he braked, hard. I threw some money onto the front seat, jumped out of the door and into the oncoming traffic, leaving the host body—an office worker, in uniform black tie, white shirt, black trousers—screaming that he had been possessed by an evil spirit, *Pee lok, pee lok, pee lok!* I dodged a pick-up, several motorbikes, a ten-wheeled truck; ran down a *soi*. Soon, I found another cab and once again began my journey homewards.

For what did I need prepare myself?

Primavera's life was all; my own was nothing.

I have earned the mockery and ostracism of my colleagues. They considered that I was elevating a virulent but comparatively rare hebephrenic disorder to the level of a doomsday pandemic. Meta, or Metamorphic ETiolation Anxiety, is usually defined as a psychosis, albeit a new and particularly mysterious one, characterized by abnormal quantities of dopamine in the brain, and thus brought under the umbrella of mental disorders known as schizophrenia. But the loss of professional face is no longer of any importance; since my own daughter became ill I have become a recluse, devoting my energies to finding a cure, even if my search leads me into areas of research dismissed by clinical psychiatry with the utmost contempt. But it is my colleagues who deserve contempt; my daughter suffers from no ordinary disorder; space-time itself is being infected, reshaped, warped, mutated by the information disease called Meta.

And I am the only man in the world who knows the truth . . .

The disease is truly insidious. Like HIV, Meta is a virus that parasitizes DNA, integrating itself into the DNA of the chromosomes, subverting the cell's genetic machinery as if it were a mutant human gene. But Meta cannot be detected; it is a 'Planck scale entity', a bug that is probably little more than a quantum fluctuation. And *unlike* HIV, it is not—at least in this world—communicated by body fluids (though many infected females have a kind of hydrophilic, irrational conviction that the virus is carried in their saliva); Meta is a meme; it propagates itself in the manner of an infectious idea, a contagious vision. Meta is the Zeitgeist. It is The Future. It is a cultural phenomenon that has the power to rewrite the nature of the physical world, to reprogram human biology. Indeed, the more I have discussed the matter with Dagon, the more I have realized that the virus is more terrible, more malevolent than I could ever expect. It has the power to subvert reality, not just in our world, but in parallel worlds. Meta is a new and evil god.

And what of Dagon?

The doppelgänger, for Jungians, represents an archetype of the shadow, a symbol of unassimilated aspects of the personality, one's 'other side'; but some postmodern parapsychologists have treated sightings of 'the other' as evidence for the existence of parallel worlds. There is a system of universal principles and symbols that precede the mind's abstractive capability. I had not invented my doppelgänger, it followed; I had discovered it. The universe of Meta existed independently of myself. Despairing of my daughter's life, I reasoned I should treat a phenomenon which promised hope, and which had produced its physical credentials with such remarkable vigour, with, at the very least, an *experimental* seriousness. But as the months had passed, and my meetings with the shadow multiplied, it had become impossible to detach an experimenter's objectivity from a distraught father's subjectivity. It was imperative that Dagon was more than a psychic projection. I needed him. Primavera needed him. Needed his reality. And so I humoured my delirium.

That night I awaited the appearance of Lord Dagon. He came, eventually, in the person of my maid. It was when Noi was delivering our laundry that I noticed her aspect change. First, the shadow she cast upon the wall began to wriggle, as if it belonged to someone else and was trying to return to its master. Then her small, dumpling-like body was stretched, elongated like play dough, as if giant hands were pulling at her feet, her head; her skin turned pale, a sickly, pale grey; her long hair disappeared and was replaced by close-cropped bristles; and her face became that of a man's, long, starched and melancholy. I was looking bad these days. But then I too had the plague.

'I should take better care of myself,' I said. 'And I should start to wear more tasteful shirts.'

'You should. It is appropriate that *I* look this way. I am dead, after all. If it were not so this paradox would be impossible. But don't worry, the changes to *your* body are quite minor, little more than cosmetic. Unlike me, your core being is still *real*.'

'I had hoped that *you* were real.'

'You should place your hope in the very opposite.'

'There is no hope for me, for my daughter, if you are the product of my delirium.'

'Let me see her.' He perceived my hesitation. 'I won't harm her. I love her. I've always loved her.' I tried to smile to conceal my nervousness, but I lack my double's hauteur, his unmovable *sang-froid*.

'You have promised to help her only so that I may help *you*, is that not so? You are not capable of love.' He bowed his head and he seemed to implode; suddenly, he was a shrunken version of myself, a tramp, street-weary, destitute.

'Primavera,' he said quietly, 'is my sister.'

'No.' It was a shell-shocked, braindead negative. I smiled, hoping he had made a joke; but the smile froze on my face, became a grimace.

'It's true. And it's also true, as you say, that I am not capable of love. But *you* are. More than anything, that is why I wish to help. I want to be with her again. Alive, in a living body, unburdened of this self. I want to love. I *must* love. That is why I need to be *you*.' This changed everything: I was willing to surrender my soul, but I hadn't realized this monster had designs upon my daughter. He walked over to me, put an arm about my shoulders, ushered me to where a mirror hung on a wall. 'Look. Not a day above, say, thirty, wouldn't you say? Your own age indeed. No one would think I was a thousand years old. How many thousands of years, I wonder, will *you* live?' I broke away from him.

'If you're me, then how come Primavera is your *sister*?'

'There are an infinity of universes, each one populated with a version of ourselves, and each one infected by Meta. And each of these worlds is different: in some indeed, Primavera is my daughter, in some my sister, in others, my lover, my mistress, my friend, my wife, even perhaps, my mother. Who knows?' He moved towards the open bedroom door. 'Is she in here?' I put an arm between the jambs. He pulled back his lips; cuspids extended from sheaths in his upper gums; long, fang-like, they eclipsed his humanoid canines; and then just as quickly, they retracted. Deep in his throat, he seemed to snarl, but by the time his ire had reached his lips, it had been translated into a gentle, unctuous laugh. 'Do you think she's safer with you? Tell me: what do you dream about? Do you dream the dreams that all Elohim have, the dark, voluptuous dreams of sex and death?'

Meta, I knew, was at work in my veins, recombining my DNA, making me into the monster who stood before me. He spoke the truth; soon, my daughter would, perhaps, be no safer with me than she would be with him. I dropped my arm, put a finger to my lips.

'Be quiet. She's sleeping.'

My double stood at the foot of my daughter's bed. His nostrils flared and he inhaled deep, as if he were trying to breathe in the entire essence of her being. He clasped his hands over his eyes. 'It's true. It's her. I had never hoped—' He tottered, as if about to faint; I steadied him and he righted himself, clasping the rail at the bottom of the bedstead. 'How old is she?'

'Sixteen.'

'She has been this way since menarche?'

'No. The syndrome began at puberty, as always, but—'

'For the female, not for the male. You have been metamorphosing for some time, but haven't known it. Indeed, in my world, we would say your metamorphosis was complete. Her mother?'

I waved an arm. 'We were too young. Kids. She took a sabbatical in the States while I was at medical school. We last heard from her five years ago.'

He dropped his arms; opened his eyes. 'She is just as I remember her, when we were both children, at Castle Misère. Playing on the Rainham Marshes.'

'Please—' I said. I switched on Primavera's night light; took his arm and guided him into the lounge; closed the bedroom door. I was going to ask him about 'Castle Misère'. I had grown up in south Essex, near the marshes, and knew of no such place; but I knew we had more important business to discuss. I gestured for him to sit down; poured us each a Johnnie Black with ice and soda. 'At first, she started hearing voices, having hallucinations. She had an imaginary friend.'

'Called Iggy, or sometimes, Archangel.'

'It was you all along? Ah. If only we could have had this meeting then.'

'I had to wait for you to be infected before I could manifest myself to you. I have been waiting a long time, though *time* for me has little meaning. I exist only in the moment of my death.'

'How did you die?'

'That is for you to find out, doctor.'

'Soon, I hope. Before I get too sick. It's lucky for all concerned that Primavera and I are living out here. If we were back in England, we'd probably both be committed.'

'But out here—as long as you keep a low profile, nobody cares? I know. Do you still suspect that I am only an hallucination?'

'Perhaps you are. But if I too am suffering from a new type of schizophrenia I suppose nothing matters. What have I to lose? Primavera—she has less than ten years to live, at most. As you can see, she's already catatonic. She's been in and out of that state for six months. There was a brief spell of lucidity yesterday—but she suddenly screamed, "My eyes, my eyes are turning green!" and then she went rigid; collapsed. I tried massive doses of niacin, but—'

'It is not schizophrenia; we have been through this before. But she has not undergone a physical metamorphosis. At least, in only a minor way, such as you have yourself. You are both suffering from hysterical ailments—anaemia, loss of weight and so on. Nothing more. The virus is not as virulent here as it is in much of the multiverse. So much the worse for your planet. It will go unnoticed until it is too late. Its symptoms will be perceived as psychosomatic, a dangerous, potentially life-threatening syndrome involving hypochondriasis, paranoid delusions, hyperactivity and psychogenic etiolation, but not one presaging a new species. If you were to suggest as much—'

'I would be mocked. I know.' I sipped at my whisky. 'I'm not sure what can be done for others who have Meta. My main concern, at the moment, is Primavera.'

'Have you never wondered what the prognosis might be for yourself?' I had, of course, often wondered; but conventional medicine had not yet recognized that the syndrome was one that affected males as well as females. There were few, perhaps no doctors, other than myself, who would acknowledge that there was anything wrong with me. Even my friends had said, 'But you've always looked that way! Relax! Why do you worry!'

'That is why I have come here tonight,' he continued, 'to show you what, in time, you may become. To show you the consequences of our agreement to exchange souls.'

'Why should you create a possibility for a reneging on our deal?'

'The deal is worthless if it is not completed out of free will. I must let you step inside me. To know the last moments of my mortal life. To inhabit, for a day or so, the spectral traces of my former, material existence. Then you may decide whether you wish to sign our contract.'

'How melodramatic. Do I get to sign my name in blood?' Dagon looked about the room, his head motionless, his eyes revolving independently of each other, one clockwise, the other counter-clockwise. One eye seemed artificial.

'You will sign with an act of will. When you are ready. An act of awakening that will shatter the universe I come from; we will change places, and Primavera will be saved. Are you prepared? Prepared to lose all contact with reality?'

'Yes, I'm ready.'

'Then if you are confident we will not be disturbed, I take it we can begin?'

'Very well,' I said. At once I felt a crushing weight upon my torso. A nightmare was sitting on my chest, it seemed, straight out of Fuseli's canvas. I thought I was about to have a coronary.

'Don't worry, doctor. You're quite safe.' My extremities had begun to grow numb; perspiration ran down my face; then the weight lifted from my chest and I became queasy, lightheaded. I looked at the whisky tumbler. 'What have you—' But I knew this was no narcosis.

For even as I refocused on the tumbler I found myself swept along a tunnel as if by a powerful wind; and at the end of the tunnel was a light, a monochromatic light, a chiaroscuro of streets and neon-lit buildings.

A poster half-peeling off a hoarding reads:

LITTLE IDIOT THINGS
THIS SATURDAY
RESIDENT BAND
THE SEX DISEASE PROTÉGÉ

Discarded newspapers, trash, faxes, sweet-wrappers, used condoms, catgirl mutazines and neurozines . . .

Begin.

Midnight—hour of patulous thighs and executions.

The ultraviolet strips above the doors are going zzz, zzz, zzz, on-off, on-off (a kind of 'silent movie' effect), and I think I'm going to be stuck in this drenched, rat-tailed, get-a-life crush all night, an extra in its hearts-and-flowers *tableau vivant*. My hand brushes discreetly against a thigh (I'm not averse to an extempore act of frottage, a rush-hour-subway-like assignation); electric discharge of girlmeat through half-a-denier of black nylon; a squeal—surprised, orgasmic, anthropoid. (Candy-sugar, you have just known the phallus of God. Discretion, mmm? *Je demande*, blab not.) And then the baby-faced hordes (more dirty-road-movie, art-house, gun-crazy, gang-girly eyes), the juvenescence of the streets, voices the more insidious for being only half-broken, carry me across the threshold.

Overheard: 'Going *V.Berging*? Looking for a bit of the Edgar Allans, eh?' (Oh, tones from the 'eartland of lost empire, Ripper streets of Whitechapel and Aldgate and Brick Lane.)

'S'right, looking for a bit of Poe?'

'I hope your guffaws are jollicose *contra* bellicose?'

'Jollicose, my son, wery wery *jollicose*.'

Begin.

The girls on the dance floor—Human and Martian—are giving the boys their best apparitional sucky-licky girlycat looks. '*Impaleeeee!*' they cry. But: (Oh Daddy Kool!) 'I wanna *souffler*, I wanna *gamahuche* ya' is the *gen-u-whine* little catkins' refrain, lifting hyperskirted dirndls or Empire-waisted babydolls to mesmerize their human partners with the Cyclopean stare of deep, black superfeminine umbilici, ringed, studded, bejewelled.

Can I trust Fascination?

'You forgot your merkin,' I say, 'foolish Rapunzel.' Lipstick presses her cheek against my shoulder. I think she is crying . . .

From a room where doubt and pointless pleasure
played I laughed and sucked life's razorblades
and suffered for release;
where brutal dreams we'd realized on Slavers
were haunted with old hopes long sunk at sea;
and dark where dust had covered all our joy
we final men will walk the world
existing from above
in haughty apathy;
and doom, despair and vice are our
crooked toys of life that herald times
of beautiful tyranny:
the world becoming our plaything
and we—*The Sex Disease Protégé.*

I wipe a tear from her cheek. Two *V.Berg* dancers—one dressed as a man, the other in slit-skirted Breton-shirted *apache* rig—are power-hustling each other, their steps a boardroom deal, a corporate takeover, pure domestic cruelty.

Again, I hold my sister in my arms, my sweet little Primavera, comforting her after she has caught her finger in a door jamb, or fallen and grazed her knee. (These memories: all of my inner life: of the outside world I remember little. Remembering her, I am like a child again, with no sense of beginning, middle and end . . .) 'I want her to fall, Gabriel.' Sequins glitter. Mama takes us to register for school. Mama takes us to the circus. Papa takes pictures of us without our clothes on. We are Heathcliff and Cathy. I hate school.

I remember seeing *Thunderball.* The credits are best. Papa has hired a private tutor for us. We are turning into psychoids. A scrapbook filled with newspaper clippings, grainy photographs of atrocities in Vietnam, NVA trooperettes impaled on bamboo spears. We begin to change, to metamorphose. I realize, then, that my birth has been something of an event. We are the only children in our family for three generations to have the spiritual virus of Meta in our loins, our brains, the imaginative germ that transfigures the body, the world. 'It's not Vietnam, Archangel,' writes Primavera from Bangkok, 'but it's as close as I can get . . .' I am sent to the city of the dreaming spires, to The Academy, to learn my life's mission, my work: to control the population of my species—to discipline the promiscuity of those girls who carry Meta's seed—so that Meta and humankind may enjoy a relationship of commensalism. What use is this life in Meta if we are called upon to sacrifice the ones we love? Back at The Academy, in the seniors' dining hall, I see for the first time Delacroix's

The Death of Sardanapalus: the dying king, recumbent on his bed, watching his guards fulfil his last order: to slaughter his beautiful concubines, his slave girls, his wives.

What use is this life in Meta if we are called upon to sacrifice the ones we love?

The blast rips open my chest. The voice is telling me who I am, what I must do. Once, I had spent fifteen years in a virtuality; but it seems now the whole universe is a virtual prison; and I have never escaped.

The toy department reminds me of my father's *Wunderkammer.* Mephisto, it seems, is a robo *mensch.*

Who am I? So many names, so many narratives.

I make love to Lipstick; I prepare for death.

Begin.

I am climbing through the walls of the ziggurat. I am in The Chapel of The Presence. I—

Who are I?

What am I?

I am—

No. Quickly. I must free myself before it is too late; I must find a rationale for my existence; a pure, self-sufficient narrative that will give my desires, my dreams, another life, a life that will survive my death in Meta.

A dream of reality.

I open a vein; pull out my quill. The contract is signed.

And I think: 'Let it happen.'

Now—

Each sub-atomic particle of my body is information, indestructible superluminal information, blossoming out into the furthest reaches of the multiverse. I fill worlds, moons, stars, galaxies, parallel universes, all the mansions of the cosmos. I invade its structure, flow backwards, forwards in time, define its architecture according to the will of my maker, assembling another four-dimensional hypersphere uncontaminated by the Demiurge.

I stand in a room, a room that is the centre of everywhere and nowhere. The room is a nursery. In the centre of its cluttered floor (Barbie dolls dying in the arms of GI Joes, scrapbooks of pin-ups from *True Detective* and *The News of the World* selectively coloured-in with red biro to create the illusion of beautiful wounds), Meta, the child, is studying a flickering, portable TV. The Daleks are executing the slave girls of Skaro. A dozen pretty screams; the television screen turns black into white, white into black, like a photographic negative. Like life turned inside-out. 'Exterminate,' he croaks (somewhat like Gun had done when I was first introduced to him); the television screams, obligingly. Screams, then screams again.

'I have to go now,' he says, 'and it's all your fault. Why didn't you want to play with me?'

'Your games,' I say, 'they weren't nice.'

'It's not fair,' he says. 'I gave them everything they wanted. All they had to do in return was let me be King of the Hill.'

I sit down, cross-legged, my chin in my hands. 'What are you?'

The boy looks about the nursery; smirks. 'I got a *Johnny Seven* for Christmas,' says the Demiurge, 'complete with missile launcher, magazines for frangibles and *fléchettes* and attachments for rubber-suction-tipped harpoons. Do you want to see my collection of plastic retractable knives, my Matchbox cars, my Lego set, my automata?' He studies me, carefully. 'Do you remember: Primavera had a collection of automata, too: her favourite, a ballerina that rotated atop a music box. You stuck pins in it and made her cry. That night, you held her deep beneath the bed clothes, while she blubbered, and whimpered, and called out for Mama.'

'I am not,' I say, 'who you think I am.'

'You are what I *say* you are,' says the child, beating a tiny fist upon the floor. 'I am information. I am the sum of your knowledge about yourself. Of all humans who live in The Future. The knowledge that is all surface and plane, all here and now, all instant gratification; the knowledge that human beings are no more than things. The knowledge of the psychopath.

'*I am knowledge without wisdom. I am pure information.*'

The child gets to his feet. He is dressed in a Little Lord Fauntleroy suit. 'Do you remember when your Mama took you to see *Thunderball*. You thought the credits were best: hundreds of girls harpooned by Largo's marauding frogmen.'

'You're talking about my brother,' I say, 'my other self.' But the child ignores me.

'And that same year, watching TV, I remember how frightened you were when your tongue distended and you began to salivate uncontrollably—heavy, mucous-thick rivulets of sputum running down your chin—as cat-suited Julie Newmar was brought to justice by that vigilante of venal vampires, the dark knight, The Bat. Perhaps it was at that moment that you knew that you too would become a kind of vigilante; for "vigilantism" is always the marauder's formal defence, no?' He reaches out, unfolds his hand. 'This is yours now. I have to leave.' I take the key from his palm. And then, like a gigantic mouse, the little boy crawls through a hole in the skirting board; and even before he is through, I can see that he has begun to change, that stars and nebulae shine in his hair, through his body. He is becoming reconstituted, metamorphosing back into the star stuff out of which he has evolved. I too am beginning to radiate, becoming a thing of stars and gases, this last part of myself joining, becoming at one with a multiverse that doesn't contain Dr Toxicophilous, that is free of the dark perversions of his toys; the room collapses; at last, I am nameless, disburdened of all identity and pain.

It is 2030 A.D.

2030: Bangkok rises before my eyes: scratch video of gridlocked traffic beneath a pall of black fumes, humanity-congested malls, pagodas, *jeux vérités* arcades, pomo skyscrapers of jade and *merz* and Chinese-lacquer red; it's an *art nouveau* kind of city, Ignatz had said, this Krung Thep, this City of Angels, its undulating lines and geometric chic copied from the fashions of the European *aube du millénaire*—a time when Europe was the arbiter of the world's taste, the Empire *De Luxe*—and imposed on the slums of Bangkok's twentieth-century inheritance and the sublimities of its ancient past. It's a badland, out there, and beyond, it's a bad world, a world of corruption, of disease, of wars, rape and famine; I can smell its death wish, that deep, repressed desire for self-annihilation that polluted the CPUs of Toxicophilous's dolls; this futureworld is damaged, without values, divided from itself; but it's a world without Meta; it's a world with hope.

My consciousness, my selfhood—it's going, my mind becoming one with billions of other consciousnesses scattered throughout the multiverse.

Now, only *heteroconsciousness* remains, the language of the perpetual *outside,* the idiolect of people who are their clothes, who live their lives in extreme exteriority; the language of people who are things, people who are text.

Fiction.

This story ends—no.

Die into the imagination.

This story ends—will end, does end, *must* end—with a beginning, begins, now, yes, even as it ends.

Quickly, I am dying—

CHAPTER THIRTEEN

Apokatastasis

I awoke to discover that I had become somebody else.

The armchair opposite was empty; my real self had vanished—I was alone, not in 2030, but on Earth Prime. This was Bangkok, still; a *tahn-prak*—a wall-mounted altar—was above my head; puppets hung from the walls. This was the place that I had called 'hell'; this was the true meta-universe, a place unknown, unknowable, to the denizens of the worlds and universes my double had destroyed; unknowable, perhaps, even to the universe that had been reconstituted by my other self's sacrifice.

'I was never the bomb,' I mumbled to my unseen ghost, 'you were . . .' It had been a secret, perhaps, a mystery hidden even from Toxicophilous himself, programmed into his 'device' via that quantum indeterminacy that had initiated the doll plague. I smoothed a hand through my crop. 'Our transaction is finalized. Meta is destroyed, and I have become you; you have become me. The worm bites its own tail. The journey is complete. You had to become me to enter my world; I had to become you to destroy it. It was the only way to save Primavera.'

I got up; made a *wai* to the Buddha (and why had I done that? and how and what do I know about the Buddha?); walked into the bedroom; stood at the end of her bed. A great torrent of peroxide hair was splashed over the counterpane; the face of a child-woman, make-up smudged over the sheet she held up to her chin, was composed in a sleep of perfect peace. 'Lipstick?'

She rolled over, wiped a hand across her eyes. 'Archangel? Where the hell have you been? It's late.'

'I've had to cross the universe to find you. I have had to circumnavigate the seas of space and time.' I sat down on the bed and then spread my body over hers.

'So far?' She was smiling.

'This is the real place where all our adventures start. It's a strange place. Stranger than any world I've known. But all roads lead from it. All the other worlds where we have been born, grown up and died.'

'Let's stay here a while. I'm tired. What's the time?'

'It doesn't matter,' I said. 'It'll be light soon.'

'Come to bed,' she said. And then twitching her nose. 'Is it all right if I call you Archangel? You wouldn't prefer Iggy, or Gabriel, or Dagon, or—?'

'Rest,' I said. 'We'll talk about it later.' She closed her eyes and was instantly asleep. And it was the sleep of life, not the sleep of the Dead.

Names didn't matter any more. I was home at last. I knew who I was: I was the man who lay next to his love, would lie there forever, dreaming that they would never again be parted, that tenderness and love were, for them, here to stay, a truth I recognized now only because it was so ridiculous, an unnecessary gift, a reality impossible, transcendent.

Nongkhai, Hua Hin, Nonthaburi,
2071—1994—1991

About the Author

Richard Calder was born in London in 1956. During much of the 1990s, he lived in Thailand, where he wrote the three *Dead* novels. His short fiction and reviews have been published in such magazines as *Omni, Interzone,* and *Science Fiction Eye,* and his various works have been translated into Japanese, French, German, Italian, and Polish. He is currently finishing up a new novel.